Banished From Memory

Mary Sheeran

Aquafire Sulis

Published in the United States and the United Kingdom by Aquafire Sulis, NY, NY.

www.aquafiresulis.com

Cover Design and Illustration by Melissa Williams Design

Publisher's Cataloging-in-Publication Data

Names: Sheeran, Mary, author.
Title: Banished from memory / Mary Sheeran.
Description: New York, NY: Aquafire Sulis, 2019.
Identifiers: ISBN 978-0-9826321-4-7 (Hardcover) | 978-0-9826321-3-0 (pbk.) | 978-0-9826321-5-4 (ebook)
Subjects: LCSH Hollywood (Los Angeles, Calif.)--History--20th century--Fiction. | Motion picture actors and actresses--Fiction. | Man-woman relationships--Fiction. | Blacklisting of entertainers--Fiction. | BISAC FICTION / General | FICTION / Historical / General
Classification: LCC PS3619.H4513 B36 2019 | DDC 813.6--dc23

First edition 2019
Printed in the United States of America

1 2 3 4 5 6 7 8 9 10

However, in some instances, the names of who starred in what movie and who won what Academy Award have been changed for purposes of the story and its characters or as an affectionate critique.

It can be fun to play with "what if" about movie casting, for some things are on record as *almost* happening or they very well *could* have happened if someone had turned left and not right on Hollywood Boulevard one day. And let's face it, not all casting decisions were or are on the mark.

But this approach is not new. As you may know, Hollywood was substituting names and faces and banishing others with regularity for well over a decade before 1960, when the events of this novel take place.

The Thirty-Second Academy Awards

1

With all the changes that happen at sixteen, is losing your talent one of them?

It seemed so to Dianna Fletcher. One day, she had been able to let another person into her body whom she would become, but the next day, she was left alone, floundering and confused. One day, she'd been able to speak a line and, no matter how stupid the words, give them fresh meaning. The next day, she'd stammer through the same words.

How had this happened?

Standing on a set that represented a cozy parlor at the turn of the century, Dianna muttered a line as someone tugged at her dress, another at her hair, another at her lips.

"Dianna, we scheduled a photo shoot for tomorrow afternoon. On set and candid photos on the lot, in costume."

"Okay." She heard the studio's publicist and didn't hear. Her uncle's office would take care of all that, anyway.

"Number two up two, and number five up one," a tech yelled from the catwalk. "Dianna, stay right there."

The lights grew stronger. She adjusted her eyes, instinctively.

"Better!" called the director.

"You look gorgeous, honey," said the cameraman.

"Thanks to you!"

Thanks to a lot of things. Dianna had her mother's long, sleek black hair, long legs, high cheekbones, and wide blue eyes that had fascinated audiences for two decades. She had also inherited her father's dramatic presence, an intensity that simmered behind those blue eyes looking for a place to land.

Dianna's mother, musical and dramatic star Anne Foster, enjoyed a vintage past of performing families that stretched back through vaudeville and theaters on the wild frontier. Dianna's father, the renowned John Fletcher, a Shakespearean actor turned movie star, traced his family, all actors, back to Shakespeare's Globe. He considered acting to be sacred, more so than any religion. So of course all the Fletchers acted, and they were all stars. Dianna's older brother, Nick, had soared to teen rebel star and was now rebelling against that. Her younger brother, Chas, possessed a natural charm that spilled all over screens all over the world.

As a child, Dianna had believed that everyone got up in the morning and went to studios to pretend they were someone else. She'd been astonished to find that most people went to theaters to watch others do that. She came to believe her talent was for serving those other people and helping them escape, and improve, their lives trapped in reality. And because the Fletchers were famous, and possessed the power that went with fame, the kids were protected, breezing in and out of sets as if they owned them.

She moved off her mark and down to her chair in the dim light among the crew hurrying, shouting, pushing equipment, and setting lights. What she was doing here? And why did she even question what she was doing here?

Movie sets had always been her second home.

Dianna knew how to find her mark without thinking and how to handle props so that the coverage would match up with the master shots. She knew how to not blink or move during close-ups, how to look at an actor who fed her lines from the camera, and how to deal with an actor stealing her light.

Most importantly, for master shots, close-ups, take after take, movie after movie, Dianna always had been able to keep her character's life in her skin. Until now.

"Ready for that medium shot, honey?" said the director. "Just you."

She found her mark and looked at the camera with some panic. Why did she feel this frightened? This had been going on for several weeks now, and it was growing worse. She'd never felt this way, never, not even in the beginning –

"Smile for us, Dianna!" the bald director called out through his megaphone. She didn't need to be told. The clown handed her a gleaming ball, and she held it, smiled, and laughed at him, her high giggles sending him into high leaps for her. She didn't know it was her neighbor, Jimmy Stewart. She found that out later, and she was delighted at the surprise.

She'd been five years old then, and her father had volunteered her as an extra kid on Cecil B. De Mille's *The Greatest Show on Earth*. De Mille loved her little wordless scene with Stewart so much that he gave her another scene, this time with one line, "Can I really have the puppy?" Her face was so radiant that she upstaged her father (whose character lay dying) and Stewart (whose character was being arrested for murder), so DeMille had to reshoot the scene from another angle. Stewart still ribbed her about it.

In her next part, she played her parents' little daughter in *Showboat*. Everyone marveled that she didn't act like the usual kid actor, shouting out her lines and smiling smugly. She was tender and natural, and once again, she stole every scene she was in with "her vibrant smile and wide, tender eyes," wrote *New York Times* critic Bosley Crowther.

Dianna next did a few television plays – young Cathy in *Wuthering*

Heights with her father and *Miracle on 34th Street* with her mother. She studied dance and read plays with family and friends at home. She watched movies in the family screening room. She sang along with their housekeeper, Hilda, who belted jazz with the best of them. She learned to do the dance routines her mother performed with Fred Astaire and Gene Kelly.

Then, one afternoon, at a party on their Beverly Hills lawn, Dianna slid into home plate and insisted, vehemently, to David Niven's son that she was safe, leaping on him to pommel home the idea.

Producer Daryl Zanuck said to John, "That's her."

Zanuck meant she had the difficult part of the little girl, Lark, in *Larksong*, an epic feature starring her father, who played a controversial judge whom she died protecting. The part won her an Oscar nomination for supporting actress (she was asleep in bed when she lost to Donna Reed). Walt Disney then signed her and her two brothers to a nonexclusive contract (all the Fletchers had nonexclusive contracts, a rare thing in those days of studio contracts). John and Anne loved Walt Disney and were thrilled at forming a relationship with him. John called Disney the genius of their time, and Disney valued Anne, who had been the voice and inspiration for his great breakthrough, the animated Snow White.

Disney gave Dianna the beloved title role in *Pollyanna*, timed for the opening of his Disneyland park in Anaheim. He'd been searching for a little girl to play that part for a long time, and he had thought he'd have to put the project aside for several years. He promoted the film at the opening of Disneyland in 1955, at which the Fletchers all made an appearance. During the live broadcast, Dianna sang *America the Beautiful* while jet planes roared overhead, a moment that burned itself in the memories of the massive television audience.

After producing a remake of *National Velvet* for her, Disney next launched a series of live action movies featuring young teens. Dianna became the perky girl next door with thousands of fan clubs, regular appearances at Disneyland, and a new career of making records for the new preteen and teen market. Disney also kept Nick and Chas busy. The whole family acted by day and talked acting at home.

Now, suddenly, Dianna could not act anymore.

"Let's go, people!" called the assistant director.

"Let's go, this is a take. Quiet!"

Dianna forced a smile.

Janice Myer, the actress playing her mother, took her place next to the camera.

It felt like one big joke, all those lights on her, all those technicians and craftsmen looking at her, and that camera staring at her. She wanted to yell, "Stop!" and "What are we doing?" She wouldn't. Professionalism was too deeply ingrained in her.

So she stood there with her baloney curls, preparing to spit out the words of *Beautiful Beulah* with cute gumption. But those words! They attacked her en masse, some with mocking laughter, some with anger, then joy, then despair. She couldn't grab at one choice until, finally, as the director called, "Action!" she blurted out some mocking, desperate, jokey thing.

"But Mother, we never entertain!"

Yes, it was a stupid line, but she'd always enjoyed these movies. They weren't the only ones she'd done. There had been *A Tree Grows in Brooklyn*, *The Diary of Anne Frank*, and *Romeo and Juliet*. The first two hadn't made money, and the last had still to be released two years after being made. The light Disney comedies, however, were big hits and lured Disney away from expensive animation. *Shaggy Dog* and *Get the Parents* were still playing, pulling in more money than the year's biggest picture (starring her father), *Ben Hur*. *Detective Dog*, her previous film, was just about to release and getting a big buildup. These types of movies certainly weren't like *Tree* or *Diary*, but they made lots of money. The kids all lined up for her Disney pictures and bought her pop records. *Diary* couldn't turn a profit; it was a critically praised failure.

"All right, my girl!" The director, with whom she'd worked on her last movie before and on the movie before that, came up from behind and lifted her up from her chair. He kissed her on the back of her neck, gave her a squeeze hug and a pat on her behind, and then as his arms folded around her, the fingers of one hand lightly swept across her chest.

He turned her around to face him and gave her another kiss on her cheek.

Ordinarily, this sort of over affectionate behavior would be frowned on at Disney, but the affection was more of an affectation, the director being a man who loved men. Even Dianna's social worker didn't bat an eye at this behavior. Dianna considered it meaningless except that he poured it on when he needed something better from her.

He was really pouring it on.

"Just one more take before lunch. A bit more wistful, darling."

Wistful?

Her flown-away talent wasn't all that worried her. Even if she could act, there was almost nothing to act in. She'd expected that there would always be something and that acting would just go on and on. Her parents had bounced from Twentieth Century Fox to MGM for twenty years, doing picture after picture.

There was always a next picture in those days.

No more. The once imperious movie studios were losing power as television took hold and litigation destroyed their distribution practices. People moved to the suburbs and did not go to movie theaters every night as they used to. Movie attendance dropped by more than half.

To stay alive, the studios sold off back lots, tossed out contract players, adjusted their budgets, made fewer movies, and tried to seduce people back with wide screens, lush color, location shooting, and sexier plots.

Independent companies rose up and moved in. The studios concentrated more on distribution for those independents and less on creating movies. They also rented space to television shows. Making movies became a risky business, especially for the once generous bankers, who liked sure-thing deals.

Even if she found her talent again, Dianna would not have the same career as her mother's. People even talked about movies dying. Maybe her talent had heard those rumors and thought getting out of town was the best idea.

"Let's go, Dianna," called the director. "We have to finish this shot if we can't work too long tomorrow. What are you doing again?"

"I'm sorry," said Dianna. "It's the Oscar nominations broadcast at the Cocoanut Grove."

Another awful thing to look forward to.

"Right. They'd want your whole family on TV, but we're still going to have to fit in your three hours of school."

Sally from Wardrobe smoothed Dianna's blue gingham dress.

"Your parents are bound to be nominated. Do you have a date?"

All the boys Dianna had invited had said no thanks. Larry, her first kiss in the tunnel beneath Disney's animation building, had emphatically refused her invitation.

"They'll have me all over the fan magazines!" he'd protested. "I want to be Tuesday Weld's boyfriend. You're too sweet and wholesome."

Sweet and wholesome had been fine a few years ago, but these days, both were out. Kooky and sexy were in.

The crew yelled for quiet, Sally adjusted some lace, and the makeup people backed away. The director called for action, and the same thing happened, so Dianna just flung out the silly words.

"Cut, that's a print! Thank you, Dianna! Beautiful!"

She was losing her talent, and no one would tell her.

Now she had to go to that dinner at the Cocoanut Grove and watch her parents be nominated for Academy Awards. Even Nick had a chance. She, however, would be raising her glass of ginger ale to the end of her career. She'd have to go to regular school. She could not do this.

The last time she'd been at "regular school," some boys had dragged her into a locker room, pushed her on the floor, and lifted her dress. The football coach came in and freed her, but he'd said to her, "That's what you get for being an actress." She had been so shocked by that but also angered, so she'd kicked him in the shins, which landed her in detention. The girls had been little better, fighting each other just to be her friend and then proclaim "Dianna's secrets" all around the school. Everyone claimed to be her best friend and crowded around her no matter where she went.

Going back to school would be a horror and an admission of defeat. She had to keep acting.

But if she had no work, she'd have to go to school. The laws were against her. She'd had offers, but her father and Uncle George had turned her down for everything coming down the pike – *Lolita, Babes in Toyland, Night of the Iguana, The Light in the Piazza, The Chalk Garden,* and some silly movies that took place on the beach.

No one had approached her for *West Side Story*. She couldn't understand that. Every other young actress in town was testing for it. Dianna sang jazz and standards at Disneyland, had two records in the top ten, and her dancing was outstanding, but no one asked for her, and Uncle George didn't put her name in. She called the movie's director and producer Robert Wise. Could she test for Maria?

"I'm sorry, Dianna," said Wise. "We need someone who can carry a general audience, and you can't do that."

Right between the eyes.

But on reflection she realized that wasn't true. They were testing almost every young actress, most of whom certainly couldn't carry a general audience into a movie theater. Word must have gotten out that she was no longer any good, and although George Stevens had since publicly apologized for his earlier complaints about her, that she'd been "trouble" on the *Anne Frank* set probably still lingered in the minds of directors and producers.

The miserable day on *Beulah* over, Dianna took a quick shower, had a quicker sandwich at the commissary as she paged through the *Hollywood Reporter*, and then hurried over to the red trailer for her school lessons.

Not too long ago, for a couple of years, all the desks had been filled with kids from *The Mickey Mouse Club*, and they'd whispered and passed notes and she'd made eyes at Larry. But now they were all gone and only Chas sat there, paging aimlessly through a history book.

As her nerves had tightened about her acting, she found herself taking refuge in geometry, in the reign of Louis XIV, and in a series of essays the teacher, Mrs. Marriner, had assigned her about current events. Her grades improved, and success bred more interest.

Now, as Dianna sat reading, the air raid siren sounded.

"Take cover!" called Mrs. Marriner, and Dianna and Chas huddled beneath their light wooden desks that would protect them from radiation. Dianna wondered if the Russians would save her acting woes by attacking, but today wasn't the day they would do it, for another siren blew signaling all was clear.

She got back up to her seat, and Mrs. Marriner handed out a sheet of mimeographed paper to read, "How to Fight Communism." She would later learn how inaccurate it was, but now, she was familiar with all it said.

Socialism is spreading. Human regimentation is spreading over the earth, but we can beat it. The standard of living in the United States is twice that of the European countries that have adopted socialism, where the government controls everything. It is the next step to the tyrannical Communism of Russia, and our standard of living is five times greater than that in Russia. The Communists want to destroy our great American spirit and the great principle of private ownership and replace it with government ownership. Russia wants to conquer this blessed United States of America. This is wrong. Why? Because we are individual people, and that is how God made human beings. Private ownership makes you the master of your lives. The profit motive spurs us to develop new products and to compete to provide better goods at lower prices. Individualism made the Renaissance great.

You can generally tell a Communist because he is godless. He doesn't go to church. So long as people go to church and worship God in the way they want, the country will be strong.

This worried Dianna. The Fletchers didn't go to church often, maybe to Catholic mass once a month. A priest came to say mass in their chapel once a week for Anne, and sometimes Dianna attended, although she preferred her father's idea that God resided in everyone and that acting showed you the way to God's compassion and creativity.

Godless Communism is like the devil trying to take over the world on a relentless path toward world conquest. Like the devil, it is sneaky. Thousands of loyal Americans have been fooled into helping the Communists because they do not look carefully before joining some high sounding venture. Communists know that Americans like to help others, that we are a generous and compassionate people, and they use that to trick us. Be careful.

> This is a fight between good and evil. Good has to win at all costs.
>
> So long as you remember these things, go to church, and do well in school, you will be helping your country to stay strong against the Communists. Good luck.

None of this dismal business felt real in Disneyland, where all seemed safe. No harm could come to anyone in this magic kingdom, guarded with enchanted beings, fairy godmothers, protective dwarves, Davey Crockett, and Zorro.

And Dianna had read it all before. She turned back to the essay she had been reading by a woman named Mary McCarthy.

> Class barriers tend to disappear or become porous; the factory worker is an economic aristocrat in comparison to the middle-class clerk. The America of vast inequalities and dramatic contrasts is rapidly ceasing to exist.

The country had solved its social problems and now it was time to explore higher themes, said the author. What, a question in her book asked, should those themes be? Dianna opened her notebook and started thinking but didn't get very far as Mrs. Marriner rang the bell on her desk and said, "That's it, class. Clear your desks, and I'll see you tomorrow. Dianna, Mr. Disney is waiting for you outside." On their way out, Mrs. Marriner handed them leaflets on "How Not to Be a Dupe for the Communists."

Mr. Disney was waiting outside, and he waved to Mrs. Marriner. He put his arm around Dianna. He was smiling, but she knew that didn't mean anything.

"Dianna, just a few minutes. Chas, you go on to your car. Your sister will be right with you."

This didn't feel good. He must have seen the footage of *Beautiful Beulah*.

Dianna couldn't help but love the man, despite him assigning her pretty skunky parts of late. He was such a kid at heart. His brown hair was now flecked with gray, but he could still walk with the bounce of youth.

"You are a very talented young lady," he said.

No, he was going to give her unpleasant news.

"Lillian and I cried all the way through *Diary*. I wish I could make movies like that about young people and serious issues. The time doesn't seem to come up for that sort of thing. The last good film I made in that line was getting in on *National Velvet*. You were splendid in that, too. But things change."

"Is there anything new on the park?" she asked. It was his favorite subject, and it might ease whatever awful thing he was going to say.

"Pageant of the Presidents," he announced grandly, rubbing his hands together. "The story of America through the presidents. You push a button and it starts – no actors. All full-size audio-animatronic figures."

"You're doing away with actors?"

"Just for this," he said quickly, with a dash of eye twinkle. "Actors would be too expensive." He laughed at her frown. "It's going to be the darndest thing. You'll walk down what we'll call Liberty Street into Liberty Square, and there they'll be, all thirty-four presidents. Lincoln will deliver the Gettysburg Address. Some of the others will speak. I'll even have hecklers in the audience. Just in time for elections!"

If anyone could do it, he could.

"And the monorail and the Matterhorn," he said, "as you know."

Of course she knew. In her public appearances, she always rode on one of these new attractions.

He turned serious.

"As you must know, we've pretty much come to the end of your contract. You've done seven of the eight movies for us, but the thing is I don't have another one for you now or in the near future. You're getting a little too old for the movies I do have. I have a new girl, John Mills' daughter Hayley. She's at the right age now."

What a kind excuse. No movies. Wrong age. Thank you, sorry. She knew the Mills family. Hayley was pretty, gawky, and awkward.

"I was toying with giving you *The Road to Oz*, because that script needs the huge push that you could give it, but I should really toss it. There's also *Babes in Toyland*, which is going to be ready to go in some months, but I talked to your uncle about that, and we decided you were too young. It ends with her getting married, and Annette's the better age."

Wrong age, again. "I'm done here?"

School full time. The boys' laughing faces. The teacher's insult.

"There is something I'm working on for you. It'll take several years for it to happen, if it happens. But in the meantime, we have to keep you in the public eye. I agreed with your uncle that we can fill out your contract by you performing more in the park and doing public appearances."

She already sang twice a month in Tomorrowland and on the Mark Twain, mostly jazz and promotions of her Disney records aimed at teens. She enjoyed the park, but it took a lot of work. Would she have to give up all her weekends?

"People love the park. It's not just a place to bring the kids. It's a place to be. They love it with almost religious fervor. They love to hear you, Dianna."

Disneyland was where every child wanted to go TO. Like a sacred journey that ended with meeting Mickey Mouse. Where everyone, child and adult, could pretend. When Dianna sang in the park, she could feel that belief in magic and dreams. If you were a child, this was THE place to be. And it was safe. The only person who couldn't get in was Khrushchev.

"Yes, sing more in the park. *Detective Dog* will come out in the spring and *Beautiful Beulah* in the fall. Your records are doing well, and there are more to come, so we should use some time to keep you in the public eye. If something comes up for you, we can work around it."

No acting. Was that on purpose?

He scratched at his salt and pepper mustache, and he started coughing, waves of hacking and heaving that sounded deep and scary. Dianna winced because the coughing sounded like death. But in a moment, he was able to talk as if nothing had happened.

"I love working with the Fletchers. You are the most gifted people. I was hoping to put Chas in *Prince and the Pauper*," he said, abruptly changing the subject, "but that won't work out. I was thinking of you, too, but the girl's part is too small."

Her stomach muscles grew tighter, why, she was not sure.

There followed a long silence before Disney spoke again.

"I had to let Chas out of his contract."

"Why? He's done so well with *Pigskin Pete*." Immediately, she defended her brother. They were cutting him off just like that? After he'd done so much?

She remembered how abruptly he'd cut off the Mouseketeers. Dianna's friend Mary Jane (MJ) Adams had bawled for almost an hour in Dianna's dressing room, then dramatically cried, "I'll get even! One day, I'll own this studio!" Annette Funicello had come weeping, too, for she alone had been kept on, and Dianna was the only kid she could talk to about it. Both girls felt as if a golden age had come to an end.

But Dianna knew, as Disney talked about Chas, what he was not saying, what no one would say except her parents behind closed doors. What he did say was, "We've come to the end of the road with Pete. I have nothing else for Chas."

"All he's done is Pete. Something else would be good for him. He's a good actor."

Disney always had parts for young boys. Chas was thirteen, the right age. This was not right.

"He loves Pete. He's a box office draw."

"We all hope for the best," Disney said, and he took her hand and kissed her on the cheek. "Your father said Chas might do something at Pinehurst."

Why had her father said that? She'd thought Chas would be staying with her. Was he going to Europe with the rest of the family to make a movie, too? Was she being left behind? Why?

"Have a good night now."

"Thank you, Uncle Walt," she said as he strolled away.

She headed for the car in the parking lot but decided to get some candy at the little store just before the gate.

"Be right there!" she called to Reggie, the chauffeur. Chas was immersed in one of his comic books and didn't seem to hear.

"Beautiful work today!" one of the electricians called to her as he went to his car.

"Brilliant stuff!" called his pal.

Did they really believe that?

She stopped to sign autographs for a few thrilled people heading to meet Mr. Disney, and she smiled and waved them off.

Inside the store, the cover of *Screen Stars* popped out on the newsstand – she was one of its headlines: "Dianna Fletcher Talks About the Boys in Her Life!" She wondered what she'd said and who the boys were, but as she flipped through the magazine to find out, she stopped at the picture of a vaguely familiar and quite handsome man. William Royce.

She remembered him from *The Philadelphian*, a silly, sudsy story about high society people starring Paul Newman. Royce had played a supporting role, but his was the best part: a suave playboy who became a haunted drunk. He'd started as a sophisticate with self-deprecating humor, and when this sophisticate hit bottom, Newman visited him in the jail cell. Seeing his successful old friend, Royce had turned away so swiftly and with such painful shame that Dianna had gasped. The moment was human and excruciatingly raw, a man at the very bottom of an abyss with no way out, a genuine moment in an otherwise forgettable movie.

She'd identified with that moment. She could have been that man.

The playboy part probably didn't require much acting, judging from the story and the picture of Royce with Star Worthington, *Playboy's* nude January centerfold. Obviously, his career was on the upswing.

The article said that Royce had made his way from stunt man and extra, even while working his way through college, and that he'd started his career at sixteen. What a coincidence. She would be ending her career at sixteen. She, too, could turn away from observers in gasp-inducing shame.

The Fletcher who could not act.

2

Tables jammed the Cocoanut Grove, shimmering with bright linen, silver, and glassware. As the crews set up lights and cameras around the floor, stars, starlets, producers, more producers, directors, more directors, cigarette girls, writers, waiters, editors, reporters, photographers, singers, and more stars crowded through the narrow aisles between the tables to greet, eyeball, complain, bitch, and search with eyes trained like klieg lights for directors in order to lobby for jobs, yet somehow bumping into the palm trees that sprang up every few tables.

These were *television* cameras, and they were there, frighteningly enough, because the movie producers felt the breath of that little monster on the backs of their necks. Some producers wouldn't let a television set in their movies, and if a script called for one, the script would be sure to mock it. How could people prefer a little black box with black-and-white pictures to immense (and growing) screens with Technicolor and great stars?

Tonight, the studio moguls were taking a gamble and allowing television cameras to record the announcement of the Oscar nominations. They'd set it up to look like a glamorous Hollywood occasion, at the Grove, with stars as oblivious as the rest of the nation to the outcome, although what suspense there could be in the year of the epic *Ben Hur* was a question. As many stars and power brokers as possible who had made the year's top movies had been invited to ensure potential nominees would be present.

An invitation to this event meant you were at the top of the heap.

"Here we go, darling," said Fred Astaire, taking Dianna's arm. They followed Nick and Sherry Glennon, one of MGM's last starlets under contract, who followed John and Anne. Astaire, a family friend and a widower, had volunteered to escort Dianna.

Dianna appreciated the gesture, but it was depressing.

As the band played jazzy excerpts from *Anatomy of a Murder*'s soundtrack, the Fletchers pushed through the crowd to the checkroom, John and Anne smiling and waving at everyone in sight.

Handing over her stole, Dianna came face to face with Marilyn Monroe, who had pushed her way forward.

"You are so sweet," Marilyn breathed, taking Dianna's hands. "May I kiss you?"

She leaned over and pressed a kiss on Dianna's cheek, while photographers snapped wildly and suggested poses.

Someone said, "Shut up. She's with the kid."

"I cried and cried during your movie," Marilyn said.

Dianna was tempted to ask, "*The Shaggy Dog*?" but Marilyn sounded so sincere that she didn't have the heart.

"Thank you." She smiled at Marilyn's husband, Arthur Miller.

"You did a wonderful job," the playwright said, kissing her cheek. "Anne Frank lives because of you. The first movie about the Holocaust. Good for you."

That was nice of them.

"Hang on," Astaire said as he took her hand and led her through the mob toward their table at the front of the dance floor. The whole room was a kaleidoscopic hubbub. Dianna could make out several simultaneous conversations blurring into each other.

"Monroe took 54 takes for one scene. She couldn't get past six words. There we were, killing ourselves, standing around for hours in those high heels –"

"Troy Donahue was at Chasen's and I heard –"

"They wouldn't let Paar say 'water closet' – although why he wanted to say 'water closet' on television escapes me."

"He wanted to walk off. He's sick of that grind."

"Why are you watching television? And so late? I thought you were working on something new."

"Did you see that ad for *Scent of Mystery*? First they moved, then they talked, and now…"

"Now they smell!"

"Darling!" called a familiar voice.

"Bobby!" Dianna shouted.

Bobby Darin hugged her. "Gosh, you're beautiful. You know DeeDee?"

Sandra Dee. Who had played a sexy role in *Imitation of Life*. And was just a little older. Dianna fumed. Why couldn't *she* get parts like that?

The Fletchers had just about reached their table when that awful Sam Spiegel and his wife Betty came for kissing. "Ah, Annie," he shouted, as the old fashioned grimy producer he was, "if you'd had this part, you wouldn't have played the nun." He'd given "this part" in *Suddenly, Last Summer* to Elizabeth Taylor, which had stunned Anne into aging panic, and who, said Anne, trashed the movie with her heartless vamp of Marilyn Monroe. Anne always complained about Marilyn Monroe.

Doris Day and her producer-husband Marty Melcher joined them. Dianna heard John say, "*Pillow Talk* could well win best picture."

Was he crazy?

"I don't think so," said Marty. "*Ben Hur* will run over everything."

"Nah, too late for that," said someone within earshot. It was Tony Franciosa, who had joined the group but after his pronouncement turned away quickly with a smug smile. Coward, thought Dianna. Had her father heard? Maybe he did, maybe he didn't, but he showed no sign as he continued talking with Doris and Marty.

Doris smiled at John's compliments. Some people were saying she deserved a nomination. Anne Foster did not say so.

Day moved on, but Rock Hudson, who had joined them, said, "She is great. I was scared to death to do a comedy, and she made it easy."

Anne kissed Hudson. "I hope she gets nominated." She pinched his cheek. "And that's as far as I'll go."

"Do you mean it, Mom?" Dianna muttered as Hudson moved away.

"Are you kidding?"

Her mother really wanted the award, perhaps symbolic of her continued importance while studio kingdoms crashed around her. You'd think someone who had won three Oscars (and a truckload of nominations) wouldn't want another, but Anne did.

"Marlon Brando is going to play Lawrence of Arabia," David Niven shouted to John.

"There goes the budget," John called back. "And my salary!"

Anne grabbed Ava Gardner. "Watch out. Frank's on the loose."

"But darling, Frank's all caught up with his movie, so he won't notice me." But he would, thought Dianna, notice the Spanish gentleman standing next to Ava. Word was the man was a bullfighter.

Debbie Reynolds flung herself into Anne's arms, and, as usual, did some high kicks like the Rockettes.

"There's nothing out there," said Anne. "We're going to have to get up a script ourselves if we want to work together."

"Two actresses in search of a script," said Debbie. "Maybe that's it. But when? All I have is next week free."

Reynolds' escort, a white haired businessman, led her away without saying a word.

"She could have anyone after her fiasco with Eddie," Anne said to Dianna as Reynolds moved on. "But she's looking for a sugar daddy so she can pretend he's the one bringing home the bacon. Don't you ever think that way. Marry *with* money."

"You didn't," Dianna said.

"I must have forgotten."

Sammy Davis, Jr. (*Porgy and Bess*) hopped up to Dianna. "My God, what happened? You are beautiful!"

"What happened?" she retorted, but she was laughing. She loved Sammy.

"Hey, she's my date, man," said Astaire.

Hey, I meant you, man!" said Sammy.

As Lana Turner approached, Anne muttered, "Oh, fuck, Dianna, what's her new guy's name?"

"May," said Dianna. "The store. Not like the store. He is the store."

"Christ, everyone's slumming into retail. Lana, my sweet, how are you?"

Finally, they made it to their table. *Ben Hur* and *Anatomy of a Murder* casts and "important" personnel had tables near each other up front, as these pictures were sure to secure several nominations, or so went the conventional wisdom.

Astaire pulled out a chair for Dianna. Nick sauntered up next to Sherry, apparently not caring that his back was to the dance floor from which the nominations would be announced, and from where, even now, a lone microphone was taking up a great deal of importance.

Columnist Sheilah Graham stood nearby, describing Anne's gown into a hand microphone while plenty of photographers whirled around and popped lights. A camera dollied up to get closer to Anne's green velvet (that would look pale gray on black-and-white television) snuggling close to the actress-dancer's curves, the straps low enough on her shoulders to give it the appearance of being strapless, her shoulder length hair hidden beneath an Italian-style blunt-cut wig. Sheilah Graham said, "Dianna looks so sweet."

Dianna, the only one privileged to see her own cleavage, smiled for a camera, and as it dollied away, she glanced down at her white lace dress. All around the room, it was obvious that women had balls of their own. But she was so sweet.

"Don't you want to go with Nick?" Dianna asked Sherry, watching her brother kissing women under the palms.

"I just want him to get all this business out of his system," said Sherry.

"That's not going to happen."

"Sure it will."

Dianna didn't argue any further. Nick attracted women without trying, and he loved it.

John ordered wine and champagne, and he and Anne headed back into the crowd.

Astaire had wandered off, too. Dianna saw him exchanging happiness with Janet Leigh and Tony Curtis.

If only someone would cross the floor, grab her, and kiss her. Instead, she guided Sherry through the menu, pretending for the camera that they were having a serious discussion. Sherry played along. It would have been worse tagging along with her parents, though.

John and Anne returned, holding hands and smiling for the photographers. John held out Anne's seat and smiled at more photographers. The television cameras moved in.

At thirty-eight, Anne still (and in 1960, the word "still" would have been added) qualified as one of the most beautiful women in the world. But it was her eyes that had brought in the money for the last twenty years, large dark pools of blue that swept up any observer, whether physically present or in movie theaters. Those eyes fascinated, haunted, and exasperated. You could sink into them and never find what lay in their depths, but you never wanted to stop searching, although their owner proved singularly unknowable.

John Fletcher was a quiet man in private who became larger than life in public and larger yet on the screen. A member of a family that had been emoting to the British balconies for generations, he came to MGM in 1938 to recreate his West End success as Romeo, where his late brother Paul (shot down over Germany in World War II) had worked for a few years. John was six foot three, with broad shoulders, steady brown eyes, and black hair that at age forty-three refused to go gray or retreat. His most alluring characteristic was his gentle, cello-like voice that could, when needed, thunder forth thrillingly in any accent. It thundered now as he called out people's names and waved them over. The camera just kept its focus on the Fletcher table as everyone in the room climbed over others to get within camera range. Dianna smiled, trying to look interested in the forced conversations. These people wanted to be seen with her parents, not her, and her parents, used to it, appeared patient and charming.

The lights flickered. The band gave out a fanfare and started to play the hit theme from *A Summer Place*, signaling that the show was about to begin. Cries of "Good luck!" filled the air.

"Fix that damn light!" called a voice.

"Five minutes!" another voice called.

"Look at you, you mad charioteer, you!" Jimmy Stewart called to John as he came over to the table.

John called back, "All your movie did was lower the standards of polite language."

"Uh huh," said Jimmy. "All your movie did was prove you shouldn't wear dresses!"

"But his legs are sexy," said Anne.

Tony Curtis and Janet Leigh hurried over for some air kissing. Dianna tried to catch Tony's eye, but he never looked at her.

Anne said, "You have to tell me about Marilyn. I've heard snatches all through the room. How many takes?"

Curtis clapped his hands together. "Fifty, and we're in those heels. One went to sixty-five."

"How is that possible?" asked Anne.

Curtis said, "Sixty-five takes. Wilder goes up to her and says, 'That's all right, don't worry, Marilyn.' And she says, 'Worry about what?'"

Anne guffawed. "Oh, please."

Frank Sinatra came over. "Come on, people sit down, sit down. Hi, John! Hi, Nick, hello Annie, hello darling child!"

Anne and Sinatra had known each other since their New York days when Anne was a Broadway star and he was a singing waiter. Some said they'd become more than friends but that he had lost out to the charisma of John Fletcher and the power of the Fletcher family.

"The sooner we start, the sooner we're done," said Sinatra.

"Our schoolmaster," Anne mocked.

"How are things going?" John asked.

"I'm getting a lot of pressure, but I'm standing by Maltz. Christ, he wrote *Pride of the Marines*. If Preminger and Kirk can say they'll credit Dalton Trumbo, I'm going to be public and clear about hiring and crediting Albert Maltz. No matter how much Wayne and his pals cry. The industry will take scripts from blacklisted writers if they use fronts and charge less. It's utter hypocrisy. We have to stop it. I will do my part."

"None of this is going to break the blacklist," said Anne. "Giving Trumbo credit that everyone knows about doesn't do anything."

"Come on, Annie," said Sinatra. "If everyone knows it, what's the point of hiding it? We have to fight this crap."

Anne swatted his arm with her program. "The FBI loves to find subversives, and they'd be thrilled at catching you."

"Me? Subversive?" Sinatra cracked a grin. "Oh, honey, they wouldn't dare."

"Your film topic," said John, "does not help things. The only American shot for desertion. But Maltz is a great writer. He was one of the writers on *The Robe*, too."

Sinatra was startled. "I didn't know that. See? Nobody knows the truth. Like that French guy who miraculously wrote *The Bridge Over the River Kwai* in English."

"It's the wrong project to bring him back," said John.

"You won't help him, Frank," said Anne. "Give it up. Don't you have a show to do?"

"Maltz wants to do it." Sinatra ignored her hint. "I'm changing the subject. What are you up to now that you've found Jesus, Mr. Hur?"

"Off to Greece and England – Annie, too, and Nick and Chas."

Sinatra pretended shock. "Are you leaving your little princess alone in the castle?"

"Not exactly alone," said John, grimly, perhaps sorry that he had called that to Sinatra's attention. "She will have the staff with her. Nick and I are doing *Guns of Navarone* and then I am due to start *Lawrence of Arabia* with some shooting for *Judgment at Nuremberg*. Annie is heading off to Greece to do *Exodus* with Preminger and, we hope, *Anna Karenina* in London. After this next rush, I am going to start producing on my own."

Sinatra rolled his eyes as if he'd heard that all before, which he had.

Dianna wanted to pummel him. Larry had told her that her father's production company was a town joke. Not that anyone would say that to her father's face.

Sinatra pointed at Dianna and yelled, "You! Sing better stuff!"

Dianna threw her napkin at him.

"Those pop records!" he went on. "Awful!"

She stuck out her tongue.

"Cameras, cameras," said John.

"You have two in the top ten," Sherry murmured.

"That only matters to kids," said Dianna.

"Kids have money," said Sherry.

George Stevens shook hands with John, kissed Anne, and came over to Dianna.

"We made a good film, didn't we?"

"Yes." Not that it mattered.

Nick returned to the table, a wiry copy of his father except he had his mother's eyes. Dianna realized that he had been in a "kid" movie that adults liked. She laughed with some bitterness as he made one final visual sweep of the room.

"Holy cow. Who's that?"

A tall, broad shouldered young man with luxurious brown hair and a broad smile was making his way through the tables halfway across the room. He followed a luscious redhead with one luscious figure. Perhaps the most luscious in the room. Which was saying something.

John said, "William Royce, the drunk in Newman's movie, *The Philadelphian*."

"But who's the dame with him?" Nick stood on a chair to look.

"You never stop," said Dianna.

"He has good taste," said Sherry.

She wasn't stupid.

"Wow," said Nick. "That's Miss February from *Playboy*."

"So it is," said his father. "Royce is moving on. He was with Miss January at Musso and Frank's last month."

"Men are stupid," said Dianna.

"You have to love the little dears," said Anne, echoing her line in *The Philadelphia Story*. "He was good. I don't remember much about the movie except for him."

"Someone took out a lot of ads reminding us he was good," said John.

Astaire slid into the chair next to hers as the lights finally dimmed for good.

"I'm a lousy date. How are you doing?"

"Lonely for you."

"I'm sure you were surrounded by swarms of guys."

"And action!" someone yelled. "In five, four, three, two..."

The band played something resembling a flourish. Frank Sinatra walked on the stage and sang "High Hopes" from his movie *A Hole in the Head*. He then became the most important man in the room, and oh, he knew it, pulling an envelope from his breast pocket with a warm, smug smile.

From endless chatter and shrieks of pretended joy, now the room fell totally silent.

"Here are the Academy Award nominations just in," said Sinatra. "I haven't looked. See? A sealed envelope."

"Fuck you haven't," Anne whispered, as John lit her cigarette.

Dianna played with her lobster. It had been a long and long-suffering day, and none of this would involve her. Sinatra's voice went on and on, interrupted by applause.

She thought of how most child stars never made it out of adolescence, how most of her friends had given up and gone back to school, and how she couldn't. Nor could she play dumb teens or girls in bikinis or the victim of a teenage werewolf. She was done.

She came to attention as Charlton Heston replaced Sinatra, who immediately headed to a table near Ava Gardner's.

"Much good it will do him," said Anne.

"For black-and-white costume design," Heston began, "the nominees are Edith Head for *Career*, Hal Wallis, Paramount; Charles LeMaire and Mary Wills for *The Diary of Anne Frank*, Twentieth Century Fox; Helen Rose, *The Gazebo*, MGM; Orry-Kelly, *Some Like It Hot*, United Artists; and Howard Shoup, *The Philadelphian*, Warner Brothers."

Career had starred Tony Franciosa playing an actor with big dreams. Its storyline involved the blacklist, which Dianna found difficult to understand. She had no sympathy for people who loved Russia and didn't understand the gift of freedom in the United States. How could any artist prefer Communism? And how could Sinatra want to hire a Communist writer? Her father seemed to think the man was talented, and that bothered her, too.

She had mixed feelings about *Some Like It Hot*, about two men dressing as women to evade the mob. She'd been uncomfortable with the use of Marilyn's body for comic effect – the train's steam aiming at her rear end, the camera's fascination with her legs, the need for Marilyn to jiggle chest and rear end and use a silly voice. Sex is a game, said the movie, and we're all tricking each other. The two men playing women kept being annoyed by being pinched. It wouldn't occur to them that women would be annoyed by the very same behavior. On the contrary, the movie seemed to say, women should be honored by any attention from men. Stupid.

Heston kept going.

"For costume design, in color, the nominees are Elizabeth Haffenden for *Ben Hur*, Metro-Goldwyn-Mayer; Adele Palmer for *The Best of Everything*, Twentieth Century Fox; Renie for *The Big Fisherman*, Buena Vista; Edith Head for *The Five Pennies*, Paramount; and Irene Sharaff for *Porgy and Bess*, Columbia."

The Best of Everything's advertising hyperbole was over the top about "the ambitions and emotions of the girls who invade the glamorous world of the big city seeking success, love, money, and the best of everything – and who often settle for much less."

Were these women being punished for their ambition?

"For film editing," Heston said, "Louis R. Loeffler for *Anatomy of a Murder*, Columbia; Ralph E. Winters and John D. Dunning for *Ben Hur*, MGM; George Tomasini for *North by Northwest*, MGM; Walter Thompson for *The Nun's Story*, Warner Brothers; and Frederic Knudtson for *On the Beach*, United Artists."

Anatomy of a Murder! Dianna had had to wear a red wig to go see it so as not to be recognized going to a movie featuring rape and words like *spermatogenesis, contraceptive, completion of a sex act* – or not, *sexual climax*, and the ludicrous repetition of the word "*panties*." Why couldn't they say "underpants" or "underwear"? Why did it take a consultation in court to decide? Why did people laugh? Dianna also hadn't like the dingy homes and offices, the sloppy men, the frayed curtains, and the grayness all underscored with sultry (misused, she thought) jazz. Lee Remick, a knockout figure in slacks but obviously a jerk, had breasts that seemed to grow more pointed, and oh, the men kept looking at her. Dianna liked Eve Arden, an old friend of her mother's, who lent a touch of reality and "real woman" to the business. But who would want to be her?

Movies seemed to be running in the direction of calling independent women cold and frozen or considering women who worked not to be women at all.

At least the characters *she* played were rewarded for having gumption. But if they grew older, she fretted, they would disappear or be humiliated. The men just kept going on as they had been, still chasing after young women and even underage girls. No wonder her mother was getting touchy about her career. No wonder she wanted an Oscar. Good, meaty parts for women were disappearing.

Except for Hitchcock, of all people. Dianna usually loathed his movies. But *North by Northwest*! For of all the parts that year Dianna thought she'd love to do, other than most of the parts her mother played, Eva Marie Saint's part topped the list. Cool, direct, working for her country (as it turned out), noble, yet free. John had tossed off the movie before taking on *Ben Hur*, showing everyone that he'd held on to that snide swashbuckler everyone thought he'd left behind. (He and Cary Grant had exchanged parts during a poker game, Grant getting *On the Beach*, for which he'd earned many accolades.)

"*Suburban Rebel*'s not getting anything," Nick moaned into his wine glass.

The room grew dramatically quiet, the small talk ceasing as if on cue.

Heston was about to announce the major nominations. A camera dollied up to their table. They all smiled at Heston. Anne leaned against John, and he put his arm around her.

Dianna crossed her fingers. Of course, her parents would be nominated. They had to be. Her father had worked almost nonstop for eight months, and her mother had suffered on location in the Congo.

Heston began. "Best performance by an actress in a supporting role. Hermione Baddeley in *Room at the Top*; Susan Kohner in *Imitation of Life*; Juanita Moore in *Imitation of Life*; Thelma Ritter in *Pillow Talk*; and Shelley Winters for *The Diary of Anne Frank*."

Room at the Top. Another guy with an eye for girls, just spiraling down, hurting them. As for *Pillow Talk*, everyone loved it, though Dianna couldn't understand why. Doris Day played characters who resembled her own perky kids but somehow was always in the wrong for being intelligent, creative, and strong. In *Pillow Talk*, a woman enjoyed her career, and a sleazy man insulted her for doing just that. Day's sense of herself and her job was considered a joke. Why was this considered an Oscar contender? Everyone loved it, though. Dianna couldn't understand it.

Dianna had initially liked *Imitation of Life* – in fact, she'd wanted to be in it – except for the part where Lana Turner just flew up the ladder to success. Not laughable was John Gavin's distinct unhappiness when Turner landed her dream job. *You can't do that! Because I love you!* She's in the wrong by doing what she wants to do? That, it seemed, was the entire message of the movie: Turner getting punished for succeeding at accomplishing her dreams.

After the announcement of this category, there was some appreciative buzz. Juanita Moore was one of the few Negroes ever to be nominated for an Oscar; Heston let that buzz continue for a bit. Dianna looked for Shelley Winters and waved at the woman and jumped up and down to show her excitement. Winters was crazy and brilliant, and Dianna had loved working with her.

Anne muttered, "If Lana Turner gets nominated, I'll become a fucking accountant."

One of the cameras swung back her way. Anne smiled, her teeth gleaming.

Heston continued. "For best performance by an actor in a supporting role, Hugh Griffith in *Ben Hur*; Arthur O'Connell in *Anatomy of a Murder*; George C. Scott for *Anatomy of a Murder*; William Royce in *The Philadelphian*; and Ed Wynn in *The Diary of Anne Frank*."

"I'm so glad," said Dianna, meaning for Ed Wynn. She stood and blew him a kiss. She was pleased to see one of the cameras caught her, and the operator gave her a thumbs up.

She saw that William Royce was up on his feet, dancing a little turn with Miss February and shaking hands with Paul Newman. He had an easy grace. He really was handsome.

Heston snapped her back to attention. "For best performance by an actor in a leading role."

Anne murmured, "I thought it was ladies first. Shit."

Heston began the Best Actor nominations with, "John Fletcher in *Ben Hur*."

Anne hugged John. The photographers crowded the table, and the television camera zoomed right in as John kissed Anne. Over this, Heston went on, "Nick Fletcher in *Suburban Rebel*."

Dianna and Sherry shrieked, "Nick!"

John stood up, aiming a butter knife at his son. "Et tu, Oedipus!" he yelled, then he dashed around the table, hugged Nick, and kissed him on both cheeks to enthusiastic applause as the cameras captured the first ever father/son nomination for Best Actor. Anne leaned over and kissed Nick. Dianna grabbed an orchid from the centerpiece and tossed it at him. She was envious, even though he certainly deserved the honor, and she had to do something for the camera.

Nick said, "Hell, I'm going to lose. They didn't have to do that."

Stewart yelled, "Mr. Heston. Are there any more nominees?"

John jumped up to kiss Stewart on the cheek.

"Yes, there are," said Heston, glowering at John, and he continued. "Jack Lemmon in *Some Like It Hot*."

Tony Curtis made his way through the room to presumably shake Lemmon's hand.

Dianna was incensed. She loved Tony Curtis. He could do anything. Even if she'd hated his movie, she loved him.

Heston continued. "Paul Muni in *The Last Angry Man* and James Stewart in *Anatomy of a Murder*."

John and Jimmy both stood up, glasses in hand, tossed the contents at each other (both missed), then solemnly sat down. Anne and Gloria blew kisses.

"Come on, Chuck," Anne muttered. "Move it. God, I need another cigarette."

Heston did move it. "For the best performance by an actress in a leading role."

Dianna caught her mother's eye and put her hands together in a championship grip.

Heston said, "Doris Day in *Pillow Talk*."

"Oh, shit," Anne whispered.

Then Heston said, "Dianna Fletcher in *The Diary of Anne Frank*."

"Whoa!" said Nick.

"Dianna!" called John.

"Hey, scrapper!" yelled Stewart.

A photographer snapped Dianna with her jaw down.

Heston then said, "Anne Foster in *The Nun's Story*."

The room exploded with gasps and shrieks. John spread out his arms, grabbed his wife and gave her one huge, long kiss. The cameras went mad, not sure which Fletcher to close in on. John lifted Dianna into a hug. As he set her down, she saw George Stevens, best director nominee, standing. He put his hand over his heart. She nodded to him, and what else could she do, blew him a kiss.

Nick kissed her. Sherry kissed her. Dianna turned to kiss her mother and as she did, she saw cold eyes and a frozen smile. As the photographers snapped away, Dianna sat down slowly, her smile growing more forced as her mother's reaction sank in.

Others had jumped out of their seats to hug and shake hands with the (undoubtedly) first family to have so many nominations at the same time if at all. Dianna sat in a daze, scarcely hearing the congratulations around her.

Someone handed Heston a bell, which he rang like a school principal. "Other nominees, everyone!"

The hall went quiet.

Dianna tried to catch her mother's eye but couldn't.

Heston said, "Thank you," as the crowd quieted down. "Katharine Hepburn in *Suddenly, Last Summer* and Simone Signoret in *Room at the Top.*"

The crowd started murmuring again and moving toward the major nominees so as to be in camera range. Heston wrapped up with the Best Picture nominees, which were no surprise at all: *Anatomy of a Murder, Ben Hur, The Diary of Anne Frank, The Nun's Story*, and *Room at the Top.*

"Good night and good luck!" called Heston over the noise. "See you at the Awards on April fourth!"

The band started up with the charioteer music from *Ben Hur*, a challenge for the one lone trumpeter. Dianna hopped up and waltzed by herself, trying to feel happy, until Fred Astaire took her hand and said, "I'm going to be the first. Congratulations, darling," and waltzed along with her. He kissed her cheek.

"But you're not the first," she said.

"Oh, dear," he said. "Don't tell your dad."

John cut in. "Don't tell me what?"

"I'm emotional," said Astaire. "It's like a graduation, watching the kids moving up."

Dianna's eyes blurred with all the flashbulbs going off. She saw Astaire steal her mother away from Sinatra. Anne looked happy enough.

Dianna began to relax.

"We are so proud," said John.

Jimmy Stewart cut in. "Let a real man dance with her!" He stooped down to dance cheek to cheek.

Was that a stag line forming for *her*? Yes! And all because she'd been nominated for an Oscar! (Say it again!) She'd been nominated for an Oscar! Did this mean she could go on and be in real movies again? Have a romance on screen that had nothing to do with a dog? She'd been nominated for an Oscar!

Would her talent come back now?

She spun from partner to partner, was offered a little wine here and a little champagne there. Paul Newman and George C. Scott and Tony Curtis and Ernest Lehman and her *Diary* dad, Joseph Schildkraut, and her *Diary* love, Dick Beymer (they jitterbugged to wild applause as the CBS cameras rolled right in), and Rock Hudson and Cary Grant and Danny Kaye danced with her. Dianna started asking other men who were happy to oblige – Charlton Heston,

Jack Lemmon, Sam Spiegel, Bobby Darin, Pat Boone, even Ed Wynn, who offered her a sip of his champagne. As she backed away from the table, she bumped into a couple. Turning, she saw William Royce dancing with Tuesday Weld. She had to dance with him!

"Hi," she said. "Congratulations!"

He seemed startled.

"May I cut in?" she asked.

She was about to tell him how much she had admired his performance but the look in his eyes stopped her. For his smile faded, his eyes narrowed, and Dianna thought for a weird moment that he was going to hit her.

He stopped dancing and released Weld who waved at Dianna and moved on to find another man.

Dianna smiled. She must have read him wrong.

Royce looked down at her. "Do you think you're a real nominee?"

"I beg your pardon?"

"Well, it's pretty well known that Disney and your family paid for your nomination," he said succinctly, barely moving a facial muscle, his voice low with a gravelly sensation Dianna found compelling. Except that it made what he said far worse. As it sank in, she felt it between her eyes and in her gut.

Now he gestured with his head as if to say, scram kid, and he walked away to Sandra Dee.

"Your loss," she muttered to his back, and she hurried through the crowd.

Someone said, in her earshot, "Now the Fletchers can only go down."

She stared at the man, a producer at the flailing Twentieth Century Fox. Seeing her, the producer blew a kiss. The hypocrisy of that kiss blew into the room, widening its lens until all the congratulations and the excitement appeared as bitterness or power grabbing. She could not stand to look at it, for this was the world she loved betraying her even as it congratulated her, even as her nomination had been paid for to prove the superiority of the Fletcher family. And how much else was paid for?

After all, *Diary* was losing money. *Romeo and Juliet* had not been released yet. Two years in postproduction and not one word about it. Her parents, when she asked, referred vaguely to some "glitch." Now she knew. She was the glitch.

She hurried to the ladies' room, flung herself into a stall, and beat a fist against the locked door. Her despair turned entirely on herself. She had not been nominated for any other award. Why an Oscar? It made sense. *Disney and your family paid for your nomination.* If this Royce fellow knew about it, most people would, too. Why would Royce lie? She'd never met him, never seen any other movie of his, no one in her family had worked with him. What he said had to be true. Of all the people in the room, he was the most honest.

She flushed the toilet so that it would be understood that she had business there, wiped her eyes, and left the stall.

Miss February stood at the mirror. Her long light red hair streamed down her back, shining and straight. She wore a clinging black gown that showed all the curves that qualified her for her title. Now she was examining herself critically as she capped her lipstick.

"Congratulations," she said. "You must be very happy."

"Thank you," Dianna murmured. "Your fellow must be happy."

"He could use a good break. He's had some bad luck."

Good, Dianna thought. Get some more.

Going back into the room, she was swept up by George Stevens.

She was too shaken to do anything but accept his kiss. They smiled for the cameras.

Jack Lemmon did a little bow. "When can we do a picture together?"

Sol Siegel said, "You're turning into your mother."

Willy Wyler said, "I'll want to work with you in a few years, Dianna, when you're out of school."

"That's what everyone wants," said Dianna, pretending flippancy. "Me out of school. Including me!"

She couldn't believe a word, but even if she did, she knew she'd get no good parts for years. And would they be good parts or just women playing second fiddle to men who didn't want them to do anything?

People were heading for the exits. Work started early the next morning for almost everyone in the room. Dianna followed her parents, William Royce's words growing stronger in her thoughts. Her father turned, and his strong arm took hold of her shoulders.

"I could not be more proud of you," he said.

She tried to smile as the photographers snapped the sweet father-daughter picture.

In the lobby, there was confusion over claiming coats and stoles. Dianna handed over her mother's mink stole, but her mother turned away to kiss Sinatra on the cheek. Her father and Willy Wyler were kissing each other's cheeks, Nick was shaking hands with Ernest Lehman and looking surprisingly normal, and Dianna felt adrift as the crowd started heading out the door.

Charlton Heston pushed his way through the diminishing mob and came right up to John.

"Congratulations," he said. "To all of you."

"Thank you," said John.

"I never got to tell you, John, what a fine job you did as Ben Hur."

John, who was one of the few actors tall enough to look Heston in the eye, said, "Thanks. It was damn hard work."

"Congratulations to you all," Heston's voice was warm and sincere. "You're quite a gang. John, I wonder if you'd like to help with something."

"If I can, of course."

Anne took her husband's arm. "Our car's here, Chuck. Can you call us?"

"I'm heading to Oklahoma City next week," said Heston, ignoring Anne, "to show support for the lunch counter sit-ins. It would be really fine if you, any of you, all of you, came along. Brando's doing it, too. You'd be a fantastic presence."

"It's a great cause, Chuck," said John. "Those kids down there are damn brave."

"Yeah," said Heston. "Why not bring your kids?"

Lunch counter sit-ins? Dianna thought that sounded silly. What else did you do at lunch counters but sit?

Anne said, "It could be dangerous."

"I don't know about that," said Heston. "John, you'll want to come, won't you?"

John hesitated before answering.

"Chuck, I do not think it is right to participate in other people's politics because I am famous. I do not think it helps anyone change their mind. Making movies to criticize prejudice is one thing, but saying I support this and I am famous so you should pay attention – that is another. Besides, I would be a foreigner telling people what to do. That would not be right."

"It is right," said Heston. "It'll grab the nation's attention, make people think."

"No," said John. "You will not convince anyone, and the people who disagree will be angry. I love this country, but I do not think John Fletcher is going to change any minds marching for Negro rights."

"Sure, I get it," said Heston. "I thought I'd ask."

"You do not get it," said John, smiling.

"I'd like to go."

That was Bill Royce, who stepped into the lobby with Miss February.

"Great," said Heston. "Give me a number to call."

"I'm not famous," said Royce, scribbling his phone number in Heston's little notebook, "but I want to support those kids."

"Me, too," said Miss February.

Dianna was angry. Were they trying to show her father up?

"Great! Thank you!" After writing down Royce's phone number, Heston went hurrying after others.

For a moment, Royce and John looked at each other.

And for a moment, Dianna felt that Royce would hit her father. It was the same look he'd given her.

John held out his hand.

"What a fine performance you gave," he said. "I am very glad to meet you."

After a long pause, Royce shook John Fletcher's hand.

Later in the limo, John said, "Heston's a fool. We are actors. We should keep our real selves private. Otherwise the public gets confused. It will all come back to bite him. He will be swept up in an avalanche of activities."

"Over which he'll have no control," said Anne. "By the way, what's with that Royce fellow? He seemed strange."

"He is coming out of obscurity. Probably nervous, choosing to do something like this with Heston. He will learn."

"Actors should not get involved in politics," said Anne. "Unless you want to kill your career."

"The politics of the Oscars should be enough, right?" John patted her hand. He looked over at his daughter. "Why so glum, princess? My two ladies are winners tonight."

"Of course they would nominate Dianna," said Anne. "It was a prestige picture."

Well, that hurt.

John said, "She deserved it."

Anne said, "They're not going to give an Oscar to a kid."

Dianna kept her silence. She was afraid to ask the question because she already knew the answer. She understood why Bill Royce had flicked her aside. She hadn't really been nominated, and he had been working since he was sixteen. But why was he angry at her father?

3

Evenly spaced palm trees waved the way down Beverly Hills' broad North Roxbury Drive. Past Jack Benny's, Lucille Ball's, and Jimmy Stewart's houses, a gateway opened to another avenue that wound up a canyon to Anne Foster's magnificent house, mostly hidden from view by palm, pine, and oak trees and gigantic hedges.

It *was* Anne's house. Louis B. Mayer, MGM's legendary mogul, had gifted her with this baronial mansion back in 1941 as a gift both of gratitude for her talent and to honor the birth of her first born, Nicholas. Mayer had, quite characteristically, deducted the mortgage payments from her MGM salary. When the house's final mortgage payment was deducted in October 1957, Louis B. Mayer died.

"If I'd known that would have killed old weasel face, I would have paid that mortgage off long ago," Anne told her friends.

What John thought about why Mayer would "give" Anne the house when he was away fighting the Germans is not on record. To be sure, he did balance the record when he returned: he built an annex across the courtyard that housed a dance studio/ballroom, a screening room, a gym, Jacuzzi, and a massage room. He also landscaped the lawns and created several adjoining rose gardens, which Anne loved to tend between pictures. Eventually, everyone called the place "The Manse," and it was written up and photographed and shared across the country with pictures of the Fletchers behaving just like ordinary Americans – barbecuing, swimming in the pool, playing baseball, Nick washing his dog, Dianna sharing hamburgers and sodas with her friends, the kids all playing whiffle ball in the big yard. Yes, they were the all-American family.

Dianna's bedroom suite housed a parlor, a bedroom, a dressing room, and a mammoth bathroom with a round marble bathtub set on a pedestal, a shower stall, a dressing table, and that most southern Californian of bathroom luxuries, a working fireplace. Outside, along the whole of her parlor and bedroom, a balcony framed with Spanish grillwork provided a place where she could look over the spacious grounds, Anne's rose gardens, the canyon's walls dense with sage and brush, and the lights of Beverly Hills and Los Angeles.

Several cabinets held her international doll collection and gifts from officials from all over the world. Stuffed bears, lions, bunnies, and tigers ruled from her chairs. On her walls hung pictures of her with celebrities and ambassadors and Walt Disney, letters of thanks, certificates of appreciation along with drafts of drawings from *The Sleeping Beauty,* for which she'd provided the princess's voice. Another cabinet was crammed with awards from educational institutions, topped off with the miniature Oscar that the Academy presented to her in 1955.

On her bedside table stood a small black-and-white photograph of a lively, vivacious woman holding a baby in her arms, a beautiful young woman smiling down on them. The young woman was Dianna's mother, Anne Foster. The baby was Dianna. The woman holding Dianna was Anne's mother, Alice, who in 1947 was killed in a hit-and-run accident.

This was the most personal of Dianna's pictures in the room, and a vase of fresh flowers always stood beside it. Alice Marrs had worked hard to get Anne a career in Hollywood, and she had been victorious beyond anyone's imagining. Dianna loved the stories of her grandmother, who practically willed herself across the country during the Depression while toting her daughter Anne, finally making it to Hollywood, where she became the most renowned dance teacher, so good that studios sent their dancers to her. Anne, still a kid, lied about her age and found work in nightclubs and in movie chorus lines. Lucille Ball spotted Anne in a nightclub and recommended her to RKO, and the two remained friends even after Anne's career in movies eclipsed Ball's.

Alice Marrs and Anne Foster – hard work and guts.

A few nights after the nominations dinner, Uncle George, John's uncle and agent/manager to the Fletchers, arrived with his entourage to discuss the family's potential work. It was all Dianna could think of as she fretted in her room, her grandmother's picture taunting her.

She had to break in. Go right through the library doors. Demand great parts. She had to keep working. Her talent would simply have to come back.

But as she burst into the room, she realized she was too late. Uncle George, tweedy Aunt Dot (his mistress, but no one said so out loud), and the secretary were packing up.

"Are you going?" Dianna demanded. "I want to talk to you."

Anne, stretched out on the sofa, and John, in his wing chair, looked startled.

"What's the matter?" John asked.

"What parts do I have? Did the nomination do anything?" she practically shouted.

"Ha!" Anne shouted back. "I'm up for *Breakfast at Tiffany's* against Monroe and Audrey. The entire range of actresses in this town! Not that I want to play that whore."

Dianna laughed. "Audrey Hepburn couldn't do that part. Are they crazy?"

She had to side with her mother. Then her mother would side with her.

"She could not," said Anne. "She'd turn her into a classy model. But Capote wants Marilyn. No, the nomination did nothing. George, you work up *Tiffany's* for me. And *Anna Karenina* at Pinehurst."

Anne already had Otto Preminger's epic, *Exodus*, lined up. Dianna had been considered for a part in that, but Preminger and her parents decided that one movie playing a Jewish girl who died was enough.

So she had nothing?

"What about me?"

Uncle George gestured to his two assistants to sit back down while he sat behind John's desk, a big smile on his face. Although one of the most influential men in the entertainment industry on both sides of the Atlantic, with the Bennett bankers of London behind him (into which family the Fletchers had married), George Bennett looked positively goofy when he smiled. Slim except for a pot belly, and balding, his grin, with his bucked teeth, charmed and disarmed the unwary. He was sixty-five years old and looked forty. (John said he'd always looked forty.)

"Did you hear?" said John, obviously wanting to insert some levity into the room. Dianna guessed he'd gotten what he'd wanted. "Anne's most fervent admirer called today to congratulate her."

"Did he now? What did he say?" asked Dot.

"He said, 'congratulations,'" said Anne.

"He said a lot more," said John.

"It's not fair," Anne said, "to make fun of the Vice President of the United States. A man who will probably be President."

"But he does not want to be President," said John.

"Crap," said Aunt Dot. "I read that he will want every citizen to take a loyalty oath and that anyone who does not will be considered an alien. John, a dual citizen will have to make a choice. You know Nixon. Everyone who disagrees is a Communist agent."

"No," said Anne. "It turns out he does not want to be President."

"Could have fooled me," said George.

"He wants to be Pope," said Anne.

George and Dot laughed. The secretary scribbled on.

"Then we'd know he was truly infallible?" asked George.

"He went on and on about it," said Anne. "But there's a catch or two. He's a Quaker. And he's married."

"So they say," said George. "I somehow can't picture it. Does he still have a picture of you in his bedroom? That came up in one of those friendly interviews in *McCall's*."

"He was joking," said Dot.

"He was serious," said John. "Imagine my anxiety."

"Shut up," said Anne.

"Does he still have the picture?" asked George.

"I don't ask," said Anne. "The man's not stupid. He was way ahead of things where Castro was concerned. He never believed the man when everyone else was singing the guy's praises. He told me that Cuba won't be a problem before long, so I'll bet there's going to be some kind of action before the election, and the Communists will be gone. And so he will win." She reached for her martini, then her pitcher. Silence fell over the room.

If they were going to talk about politics – Dianna broke in. "Mr. Disney has nothing except six months of public appearances. I was just nominated for an Academy Award. Doesn't that change anything?"

"Didn't change much for me," said Anne.

"We'll get you something, Anne," said George. "Away from the musicals, you know. Think about *The Children's Hour*."

"God, no," said Anne. "I don't want *Gypsy* or *Roman Spring* or God help me, *Return to Peyton Place*."

"It's just a change," said John. "The parts will come."

"If it comes to it, I'll go back to Broadway. That got me somewhere before." Indeed it had.

Anne Foster, a multiple Academy Award winner (her first one at eighteen), could be anything – wholesome, bitchy, sexy, smart, vulnerable, and Fred Astaire's favorite partner. But she'd fought to get where she was and to keep her talent alive.

In 1938, just when she'd been signed to a contract at MGM and begun to move out of the chorus — and sung the role of Snow White — a powerful man in the studio (she never said who) raped her, leaving her pregnant and unable to face her mother.

Contract or no, Anne fled California, knowing she angered the powerful Louis B. Mayer. Changing her name, she crouched in the cheap seats of passenger trains crossing the country. Upon reaching New York, one of Alice's friends helped her obtain an abortion. Via Western Union, this woman notified Alice, who promptly came to New York to join her daughter. Alice convinced her daughter that they were all going to fight back for her.

Bolstered by this support, Anne auditioned for Broadway shows but was rejected time and again until one day, after singing a beautiful ballad, she made a flying leap across the rehearsal floor while holding a high B flat. The thrilled producers combined the leading acting part with the dance lead, and on opening night, under the name Alice Frances, she leaped out onto the stage singing, landing in her leading man's arms. That brought the Broadway audience to its feet to offer her ten minutes of applause. Even now, more than twenty years later, people talked about that moment.

Naturally, Mayer recognized Anne in the publicity, showed up at the theater, handed her a bouquet, and apologized. More publicity resulted – the missing contract player breaking free! The voice of Snow White herself! Anne became national news, nationally beloved.

John Fletcher, a British matinee idol with a powerful family of agents and lawyers behind him, fell in love with the voice of Snow White and then with its owner. When she turned eighteen years old and went back to being Anne Foster of the movies, she married him. Both embarked on long, prominent careers that were still going strong, although Dianna knew Anne was concerned about the younger actresses nipping at her heels.

"Walt has parts for you, Dianna," said John. "Just not right now."

"There are other producers in town! Other people my age are working! Tuesday Weld, Sandra Dee, Deborah Walley –"

"They're a little older," said George, "and those months or years make a difference. There aren't that many parts for a girl your age, and until you're eighteen, you have to go to school."

"Not in summer, and that's almost three months!"

"Dianna and I could both do *Lolita*," said Anne.

"Annie, please," said John.

"You could do what's his name, Humper."

"Humbert," said John. "No."

Dianna said, "Why did you turn me down for *Blue Denim*?"

"You hated working with Kazan," said George. "Dianna, you're at a strange age, and there's a lot of teenage garbage out there because of the growing teen market. None of it is for you. It's all beaches or nervous breakdowns or girls being held prisoner or being whiny daughters. *The Explosive Generation, Gidget Goes Hawaiian*. These are not your movies."

"I do not want," said John, "to see you part of a bunch of noisy, rowdy kids just trying to win a boy's attention."

George continued, "And *Splendor in the Grass*, again with Kazan, but the script is just focused on sex."

"What movie doesn't?" Dianna shot back.

"Nothing you've been in," said Anne. "No one thinks of you and sex."

"Do people have to think of me and sex?"

"They want to sell movies," said Anne.

"You're at an in-between age," said John. "No one would be comfortable."

"You wouldn't," said Anne.

"*Romeo and Juliet*," said Dianna.

"No one's seen that yet," said Anne.

"And why not?"

"There's a glitch. But that's not adult sex. That's different."

"Your fans are not ready," said John. "I am not ready."

The conversation was getting stupid. Dianna needed to ignore what they were saying and force it back on track.

"There's *West Side Story*."

"Yes, there is," said George. "I'm afraid not."

"Why not?" she pounced, not admitting that Wise had already turned her down.

"You have played girls other girls can relate to," said Uncle George. "Don't underestimate Walt's movies. He has the popular touch, and his movies are popular. *The Diary of Anne Frank* was not. Critically acclaimed, yes. People read the reviews and went to see other pictures. *West Side Story* isn't going to make much of a splash except in New York. We need to get you in a major movie the whole country will want to see. Right now, you are a leading force in the kid market."

"You gave a beautiful performance as Anne," said John. "Not many parts come up like that in any lifetime, honey. You have had several."

"I have done enough of these silly, perky girls whose only problem in life is *nothing*. I used to have good parts. Why can't I play Lolita?"

"It would rattle the nation," said George.

"Be serious," said Dianna. "It's a beautifully written novel."

"Let it stay a beautifully written novel," said Anne. "Once it's a movie, it's all about men taking over. Whoever plays that part will be forgotten in ten minutes. Women have to be careful, especially with the Production Code getting so weak. You could laugh at what it had us do, but it also protected women because in the end, the camera is a man."

"Have you read *Lolita*?" asked Dot.

"Sure," said Dianna, still digesting the camera's gender.

"Don't tell anyone."

George said, "Dear, you are still Disney's chief star until after *Beautiful Beulah* releases. We can't shake that tree too much now. You have five thousand, *five thousand*, active fan clubs in the United States. Disney organizes them. They are set up to organize premiere parties for your movies, coast to coast, and to buy your records. They are loyal."

"*West Side Story*," she countered. Uncle George could get her that film, no matter what Wise thought.

"Not possible," said George.

"You should sing more jazz on the Mark Twain," said Anne.

"*West Side Story*," said Dianna. "You haven't said why not."

"You're too young," said Dot.

"I'll be seventeen when they're filming."

Everyone laughed. "Old lady!" said John.

"Dianna, think a moment and you will know I am right," said George. "*West Side Story* will have an intense schedule. Bob Wise can't lose time with Maria going to school three hours a day. They're going to start in the summer in New York and by the time the school year is in, they will be shooting at Goldwyn, and I am sure they will be behind schedule. Big musicals always run tight on the schedule and are hard on the studio's budget. Age is irrelevant. They tested Carol Lawrence, who played Maria on Broadway. She's in her late twenties."

"I'm Maria's age," insisted Dianna. "And we did *Anne Frank* in two months. Why shouldn't I play her?"

Playing Maria would bring her talent back. She was sure of it.

"*Anne Frank* wasn't a musical," said George, "and that was summer, and you didn't have school. They're hiring kids who are nineteen or in their twenties. They look like teenagers, but they're not, and there's no school problem. You wouldn't look like those teenagers who aren't, you'd stick out. Dianna, besides, there's every reason to keep your image where it is for a year or two."

"You are all dancing around the real reason," said Dot.

"Shut up," said Anne.

"What real reason?" asked Dianna.

"This is a business," said Dot. "*Diary* didn't make money. *Sleeping Beauty* was a loss."

"That wasn't my fault," said Dianna. "I was the voice, that's all."

"They were released one after the other," said Dot.

George said, "Outside of Disney Studios, the industry thinks you cannot carry a movie for general audiences. Your parents can, alone or together. Nick can. You can't. Even with the nomination, there's nothing. Everyone is talking about how wonderful you'll be two years from now, and even then there's nothing to ensure you can bring in money."

"How can I bring in money if no one lets me into a picture that can bring in money?" she cried, exasperated.

"And," said Dot, "Robert Wise and Jerry Robbins can't cast you as Maria. *West Side Story* is an ensemble production with a lot of young dancers the public will not recognize. Tony will probably be played by some young up and comer from Broadway. Nick was up for it, but he wasn't interested. They need a bankable star at the top to play Maria who will pull in audiences of all ages. This is a sophisticated musical and they need someone to bring in the bucks. That star is not Dianna Fletcher right now. I'm sorry, Dianna, that's the fact."

"My nomination, hit records, don't they add up?"

There was a silence.

Now she had to ask.

"Did someone pay for my nomination?"

There was a silence. Then John laughed. As if, Dianna decided, they had been caught.

"What?" asked Anne.

"Like Uncle Walt or – someone –" She couldn't bring herself to point a finger. "I didn't get any other nominations."

"You got a Foreign Critics special award," said Anne.

"And the Screen Actors Guild citation for best performance by a juvenile," said George.

"And a host of others," said Dot.

John said, "You cannot buy an Oscar nomination. This was a nomination by your peers, by other actors. You earned this. You can up your press to try to influence people, but everybody votes. You gave a good performance in a good movie. That is not the reason there is precious little out there for you. What we have to do now is figure a way to ease you into work that will enlarge your audience so you will be in a better position later. Do you understand?"

"You have great earning power now, in your own corner of the market," said Aunt Dot. "Your Disney movie will bring in big profits."

A kid movie.

So William Royce had been lying? She remembered the look he'd given her father. There was genuine hatred there. Why? She still half believed what he'd said. Nobody was going to offer her anything. Nobody believed in her.

And they were, she felt, right.

The only other explanation was that her nomination, perhaps not paid for, was simply an honorary one for the movie. They were really nominating Anne Frank. She wouldn't win. It was a gesture, having nothing to do with her acting.

"I should play Maria," said Dianna, stubbornly, although she believed it less than before. "I played Juliet," she said, pulling her last iron out of the fire. "What happened to *Romeo and Juliet*? What's the glitch that's holding it up?"

"Something to do with the color," John said.

"Can they fix it?"

"They're trying," said Anne.

"It could be black and white."

"Not these days. They will fix it," said John. "Dianna, Uncle George does have something for you."

"Why didn't you say so?" Dianna shouted.

"It's just a television movie," said George. "Mark Dante wants to do *Picnic*. He called me up and asked me if you were available. He's starting it pretty soon. He hired Michael Angelini, who did *Suburban Rebel*, to direct it. And he's trying to get some stars for the thing. Mark called about your playing Millie."

Anne said, "Inge is all about sex. They're putting it on television?"

"Repressed sex," said George. "That's why Dante wants a cast that won't necessarily scream sex, except maybe the two leads."

"Is it really about sex?" asked Dianna.

"It's about men being the supreme beings of the universe," said Anne. "Except Millie wants to go to New York and be a writer. She's fourteen or fifteen or sixteen. I forget."

Like Anne Frank. Did Millie have talent like Anne or was it just dumb show?

"It's just television," said George, "but it will be a special event. Dante is rounding up an impressive cast."

"Who's playing Hal?" asked Anne.

"William Royce. The drunk in *The Philadelphian*. He's on the verge of a very interesting career."

The one prospect she had! Maybe school would be better.

"And he got Arthur O'Connell, who was in the movie," George added.

"Who is playing Madge?" asked Anne.

"Miss January."

"Who?" asked Dianna.

"The playmate, Star Worthington." George actually looked embarrassed. "Hal without his shirt and America undressing Miss January with their eyes, it should be quite a show. In color, no less. They're trying to get Lucille Ball to play the teacher. Annie, maybe you could give her a nudge. It will do her good."

"Right," said Anne, "appearing as a spinster schoolteacher begging a man to marry her while she's going through a painful divorce. That should cheer her up."

"You know what I mean. Work. Different from *Lucy*. Challenging."

"Uh huh," said Anne. "She was over today, wailing away. She loved the guy. He was a louse. What can she do?"

"Work would help."

"I could play that part," said Anne.

"Ha," said George. "You who were married when you were barely older than Dianna."

"I don't know the play," Dianna said.

"The script is here somewhere," said John, leaning over from his chair and peering through books on the shelves. "When are they doing it?"

"April. May. We must sign fast in case SAG strikes. Angelini and Dante want to meet with you, Dianna, but I think that's just a formality. I mean, if you want it."

"It would fill out the school year," she said. If it was the only thing, it would have to do. "But then what?"

"Well," said George. "There is another opportunity."

"What?" Dianna tried not to scream.

"George, for God's sake," said John. "Are you holding back on us?"

George cleared his throat.

"I don't think it's a possibility. It's a western."

Dianna imagined herself galloping on a horse, chasing bad guys into a gully. "Would I ride horses?"

She and her father used to go riding every weekend until *Ben Hur*.

"Plenty of horses," said George. "It's a family. A father, two sons, a daughter your age, a tomboy growing into a young lady. The father was the first governor of California and now he's returning to legal work and his ranch. He is determined to eradicate corruption. He champions the poor and the underdogs. The girl is his daughter, and she's pretty feisty."

"That sounds like fun."

"Yes," said George. "It's a television series."

She felt she'd been punched in the stomach. Television series! Had she fallen so low?

"No, no, no series," said John. "There is no arc, no character development. And no time to do any good work. She won't be able to get back into movies."

George looked offended. "Jack Goodman is producing. He wrote B western movies, and NBC called him in to do a series, for an hour, in color. NBC is owned by RCA. RCA wants to push its color television sets. They want a glorious series on television, an hour, with great scripts, a family drama, and great scenery. The show will be set at Lake Tahoe. Not only will NBC get behind this show, but RCA."

They wanted her to sell television sets? Rather like being Benedict Arnold.

"You cannot do an hour long, color show, motion picture quality, every week on television," said John.

"Goodman says you can. RCA is pouring money into this thing. Chevrolet is sponsoring. Marty O'Miles will play the lawyer."

"I thought Marty retired after all that mess," said Anne.

"What mess?" asked Dianna.

"It's over," said Anne. "It was politics."

The only reason someone got involved in a political mess was if he'd been a Communist. But they wouldn't let a Communist star in a prestigious television series.

"Mary Everett was supposed to play his wife," said George.

"She agreed to do a TV show?" cried Anne.

"And then had a heart attack," said George.

"I'm sure," said Anne.

"Goodman has her in reserve in case she wants to come back," said George. "In the meantime, he decided to hire a daughter for Marty rather than replace the wife, and he thought of Dianna right away. He's suggesting a leading role in eight of the shows, a featured part in several others, and a few lines or no lines in still others. Dianna, you could be free to do other things if they came up, but you would be under contract for nearly forty weeks and wouldn't have to go to school full time."

It sounded great except it was television. It was admitting defeat.

"Dianna can't prove herself a bankable movie star by being in a television series," said Anne.

"I'd rather you not do it, honey," said John. "You never get out of the little box once you get in. A few can make it out, if they start there, but it's the land of no return."

"I won't," said Dianna. But that was all to be had?

"All right," said George. "I'll keep looking. I'll get you the reading for *Picnic* if you want to do it."

Dianna got up and walked to the door. "Okay," she muttered.

"Going to give me a goodbye kiss?" asked John.

He was going to the Cannes festival to represent *Ben Hur*. She went back but didn't respond to his strong hug.

"Honey, one more thing," said Anne. "Mr. Disney is canceling Chas's contract."

"He told me. Why?"

"He is thirteen, getting too old for Pete," said John.

"There are other parts for him to play," said Dianna. "Uncle Walt is setting up a unit in England to do *The Prince and the Pauper*. Chas could do that."

"We don't think so," said Anne.

John puffed on his pipe. "Chas needs to take a break from acting."

"Why?"

George riffled through papers.

John said, "He will come with Nick and me to Greece and London. I will arrange some training for him."

She had almost forgotten they were all going away. An ordinary teenager might think that was a wonderful thing, but Dianna loved the stimulation of her family around, all of them working on movies and parts together. Except that she wouldn't be working.

"They lifted the restrictions on how much money we can take out of England," said George. "Tally ho!"

"You won't miss us at all," said Anne. "You'll move to Malibu. You love that place. We'll find a good school for you. A girls' school."

"Okay," said Dianna. Her acting was dead, but she was not going to any full-time school.

John handed her a book. "Here is the script for *Picnic*. See how you feel about playing Millie."

"Okay," she said, backing out the door. "But I won't go to full time school."

"There may be no choice," said Anne. "When you're older, you can pick up your career. The business may be more settled then."

Dianna hurried up the front stairs and stopped at Nick's rooms. He was sitting on the floor, hanging up the phone.

"Long face, little sis."

She leaned against the door frame. "It seems that I'm not a bankable movie star like you."

"That won't last. Teenage rebel – just a fad. So when I'm in London, I'm going to work at the Royal Academy."

He had a plan for himself. But she couldn't imagine herself going to silly acting classes. They'd all find out she had no talent.

"I'm thinking movies will be past tense," he said. "When the studios give up the last of their movie theaters, that will be it. They'll try to bring in audiences by shocking them without regard to plot or character. I have to get out of here, sis. You do, too."

"I like movies," she said. Even if she didn't like the ones she was in. She loved the art, the community of people doing things together, the piecing together of well-planned pieces to make a whole picture. How could they end?

"Uncle George still thinks a two-studio nonexclusive contract is visionary," said Nick.

"Someone wants me to do a western television series."

"Do it. If it's a part that gets you away from those perky bitches. Keep your name out there by doing something different."

"You can't be a movie star and head down to television. But there's a play by Inge they're doing for television. *Picnic*. Your Angelini is directing. That won't be as bad."

"Oh, him," Nick looked worried there, but he shrugged. "At least, he won't try to score with you."

"Huh?"

He laughed. "Although you could use a sex scandal. That would put your career in high gear. Have an affair with Sinatra."

"That's stupid," said Dianna.

"Okay, why don't you play a killer? I am."

"There are no parts like that. And I beat you to it. In *The Bad Seed*."

"Just don't go up in flames like every other child star."

"Shut up."

"No one remembers that movie. Disney grabbed you. You need a sex scandal. Look at Liz Taylor."

"Everyone hates her!"

"Nope. Next year, they'll be sorry, and she'll win an Oscar."

"Are you out of your mind? The people loathe her."

"The people tire of their stories and want new ones. The press is happy to oblige. She's going to win an Oscar next year. I'll bet you fifty bucks."

The phone rang. Nick picked up the receiver.

"Hello, Nat! You gorgeous babe. I'll be right over."

He shoved his arm into a leather jacket, "You are going to be passé, little Disney princess, if you don't do something about it. When the studios fall, they will make such a noise."

"The studios can't fall. There will always be movies."

He put his hands on her shoulders and looked at her earnestly, the look that launched a thousand fan clubs overnight. "Dianna, sweetie, they *have* fallen. They're renting space to television. Might as well put up the white flag. Agents are coming in with package deals. Actors are going to have to fend for themselves, and they're not trained to do that."

Dianna turned fast around and sprinted into Chas's suite.

He was lying on the floor, playing with an old fire truck.

"I'm trying to get this old truck to work again," he said, without looking up.

She sat next to him on the carpet. He wasn't really fixing it. He was saying "zoom, zoom" and rolling the truck on the carpet. There wasn't anything to fix. There wasn't a motor or anything. It was just a little toy truck.

"What's wrong with it?"

"It keeps stalling," he said. "A fire truck can't stall. All the people would die."

"Yeah," she said. "Hey, I thought you might want to get the bikes out."

He looked up at her with the wide, wistful eyes that had made all the Fletcher kids famous.

"No. I'd better sit with this guy. He needs me."

"Sorry about Pigskin Pete."

He looked at her, confused. At first, she thought he didn't know. Then he shrugged. "Oh, that. No loss." He bent over his truck. "Zoom, zoom."

4

The Screen Actors Guild struck. Work halted on major studio productions, throwing a layer of uncertainty over the city. Uncertainty brought layoffs. Layoffs meant less money flying around. Less money meant more fear.

Independent productions could proceed if they went along with the SAG requirements. Mark Dante, the producer of *Picnic*, had arranged for office and studio space at Desilu, which was not included in the strike, and which is where Dianna and Aunt Dot went to meet with Dante and the director, Michael Angelini. The meeting was held in Desi Arnaz's office, which, Dianna thought, was sad. She hated that Lucy and Desi had broken up. She had known that their marriage had never been the happy, joke-filled relationship they'd convinced the public they'd had. Still, it was sad, the ending of all that laughter.

She tried to shrug off the mood and think of Millie, her only way out of going back to school this spring.

Mark Dante, a stocky, hearty man who didn't seem able to stop smiling, shook Dianna's and Aunt Dot's hands vigorously. "I'm so glad you could make it. Do you know Mike Angelini?" And he waved his arm at the director with a grand gesture.

"We've met," said Aunt Dot.

"We have." Angelini resembled an Italian choir boy, with long thick black hair, sulky lips, and a lithe, skinny body. He seemed to be sulking right then; his handshake was not what one would call hearty, and he did not smile at either Dianna or Dot.

They sat. Dianna clutched her script.

"What do you think of Millie?" Dante asked.

Angelini sat back, appearing bored.

"She is pretty, but she doesn't want to be," Dianna said. "Madge is the one going around saying that, but she goes with men who are attracted to her *because* she's pretty. Then she enters that beauty contest. Madge doesn't mind that Hal thinks she's pretty. And she seduces him with that dance! Madge doesn't mean what she says, but Millie *really* means it, and it's tough because being pretty seems to matter to everyone. So Millie rebels and doesn't care about how she looks. Her mother always nags her and pays more attention to Madge, always complimenting her, boosting her. If Millie could get rid of Madge, she'd get more of her mother's attention and love and she wouldn't always be compared to Madge."

"Interesting," said Dante. "What do you think, Mike?"

Mike shrugged. "You don't have to make up gobbled gook. It's all in the script. She's not pretty like her sister Madge. She's jealous. Just go with the script. And her mother says she favors Millie more."

"But she doesn't."

Dianna felt Aunt Dot's restraining hand on hers. Tough. She was going to talk.

"Susan Strasberg wasn't ugly in the movie, although people kept saying she was."

"And that didn't work. No one's going to believe Dianna either when she says Madge is the pretty one, implying that Millie is ugly," said Dante.

"I'm not doing the movie. The script uses material from the play and the movie. Makeup and hair will help," said Mike. "If she's an actress, she can do the rest. I'm doing an entirely new approach."

"Of course," said Aunt Dot, giving Dianna a warning look.

"Everyone knows what Dianna Fletcher looks like," said Dante. Dianna could already see he had a weakness for wanting everyone to be happy. "It would be interesting to see if we can make you look plain. Your mother did it for *The Heiress*."

Her mother had done it for *The Heiress*, but Catherine Sloper was a *real* character.

Anyway, she realized she was arguing herself out of a part that could keep her out of school. She had to give in.

"If Millie is supposed to be plain, she'll be plain."

She didn't mean it. She just didn't want to go to school.

Aunt Dot and Dante smiled at her.

Angelini didn't surrender to victory. "I'm looking for someone who can convince me she's Millie. Read."

Dianna looked at the script. She couldn't decide on a reading – too many voices in her head – but she mustered up frustration, which wasn't hard. "Madge is the pretty one! That's all I ever hear!" she piped out.

Angelini said, "That's not the flavor I'm looking for."

Aunt Dot said, "Dianna is an Academy Award nominee and has won special awards for her performances. I think you could listen to a full reading."

Dante said, "The name William Royce does not bring in an audience. Great actor, great guy. He's up for an Oscar, too. You'll enjoy working with him. Not many people know him the way they know you, though. You'll help bring in an audience, along with the rest of the cast."

She was supposed to help bring in an audience to help that fink? She almost threw the script down. But she couldn't.

"I have Lucille Ball," said Angelini.

"That's not enough," said Dante. "Dianna is a movie star with a big following among the kids. Her name ensures a good project."

"This isn't a story for kids," said Angelini.

"We're packing in the names. Dianna's an important one, and people will know it's an important show to watch. And it will be in color."

"Not many people own color sets."

Dianna looked back at the script during this infuriating conversation. When Angelini stopped to take a breath, she quickly charged into Millie's next line.

"When I go to New York and become a writer, I'm not going to ever get married."

Even as she read it, she thought it was a stupid line and that she'd read it stupidly. Inge had given Millie a love of books and words and art and hadn't connected that love to Millie's actions. He kept driving back to Hal and Madge and their explosive romance. Poor Millie was a muddle left behind, and Dianna couldn't find her. Angelini wouldn't be fooled. She was ruining this reading.

"I think she'll be a hard sell, Mark," Angelini said.

"Could I please do more than one line at a time?" Dianna asked.

Dante said, "Mike has a vision. Don't you worry."

"You'd better have one, too," Angelini said to Dianna. "Okay, if I must, I must. You handle the rest." He walked out, the stupid spurs on his cowboy boots clanking.

Dante said, "He's young. He has ideas. He was like this in *Suburban Rebel*, but the cast loved him. Nick must have said so."

"Not to me," said Dianna. "But it doesn't matter. I'll hit my marks."

"You'll do more than that," said Dante. "You'll be fantastic. We agreed on seventy-five hundred?"

"Ten thousand," said Aunt Dot. "You said Dianna will draw people to watch. So will some of the others, but not your stars."

"I did, didn't I," Dante muttered. "That George. I'll have it all drawn up and sent to your office."

Picnic was not going to be a picnic. But Dianna had the part, and she wouldn't have to go to real school for the rest of the year. She'd gotten it because she had a "name." How long would that last?

Once home, feeling temporary relief, Dianna headed to the kitchen for a Coke, and found Aunt Kathy, that is, Katharine Hepburn, taking everything out of the refrigerator. Dianna wasn't surprised. The last time Aunt Kathy had visited, she had re-organized Anne's shoe closet.

"It's a mess in here," Hepburn was saying, dumping bottles and packages on the counter.

Joanne stood aghast, holding a knife, and looking as if she might use it.

"What's wrong?" Dianna asked, peering into the refrigerator. "Did the power go off?"

"It's organized all wrong," said Hepburn. "I told your mother she should pay attention to what's going on in her kitchen. The meat should go here and the condiments there. Help me out, Di honey."

Amused, Dianna handed Hepburn what was ordered, rather like a nurse helping a surgeon.

"There, that's right now," said Hepburn, and to Joanne she said, "That's exactly how it should be."

"Of course," said Joanne, gripping the knife.

Dianna smiled at the cook.

Hepburn helped herself to a pitcher of iced tea.

"The lemons look awful. How old is this tea?"

"Get her out of here," Joanne muttered.

Hepburn didn't hear or didn't react as if she had. "Doesn't anyone drink lemonade around here? Hey, congratulations on your nomination," Hepburn poured the iced tea and gave a salute.

"Same to you," said Dianna.

"Oh, that thing." Hepburn waved her hand and laughed. "That's a loser. They're not going to give any Oscar to a movie about cannibalism. What an awful thing that turned out to be."

"Yes," said Dianna.

"You tactless child. Where are we drinking these?"

"Mom's getting a massage."

"I thought I'd drop by. I haven't been in ages. I heard you were done with Disney."

"Except for appearances."

"Thank God."

They went out onto the patio and sat at the glass table in the midst of the heavily scented flowers bursting in oranges, reds, and yellows.

"I don't think I can bring myself to see *Detective Dog*. You have to take charge of your career. What's next?"

"Not much. Mom and Dad said no to *Lolita*."

"I would think they should. It'll get a lot of publicity, but it won't go any further."

"And Mr. Wise said no to *West Side Story*."

"You don't want to do that. Great story, but she's just another soubrette. I heard you're being considered for *Picnic*. Lousy part."

"I got it. But I can't figure her. And Maria is more than a soubrette."

"No, she's not. Forget her. Just get through *Picnic*. Play her like yourself. Think of an image, like Sean Huston told me to think of Eleanor Roosevelt when I was floundering in *The African Queen*. Worked like a charm."

"I don't have Huston as a director."

"Going on the stage would be good for you. Everyone but you and Chas has done it."

"I may go on television," said Dianna. "Uncle George put me in for a western series."

"Oh, God! Do that and I'll disown you!"

"Raymond Burr, Donna Reed, Fred MacMurray, Carol Warner…" Dianna began.

Hepburn waved her hands as if to erase Dianna's words. "I don't know why Fred did it, except he's getting stuck in the Disney swamp, too. The others are second tier. Good second tier. You don't need a job. And you don't want to be so accessible every week for free. No, no."

"Mrs. Fletcher says come up or get out," was the charming message from Lynne, the maid Anne and Dianna shared.

"Let's go." Hepburn tossed her iced tea into the flower bed. Inside the door, she picked up a flat box.

"What's in that?" asked Dianna.

"I picked up a dress on the way over."

"You bought a dress?"

"The world is just changing so fast, isn't it," said Hepburn, running across the lawn to the annex.

They found Anne in the room next to the gym wearing only a sheet and moaning in ecstasy as a sturdy Germanic woman pummeled her.

"Quiet, dear, you'll shock your daughter," Hepburn said, striding in without knocking. "What are you doing inside on such a glorious afternoon? Why aren't you playing tennis?"

"Dianna had a reading, and I'm resting my weary bones," said Anne. "For me, that makes it a glorious afternoon. You'll forgive me if I don't get up."

"I'd forgive you if you did."

"Dianna, don't you have songs to learn?" Anne asked.

"I don't feel like it."

"God, I hope not." Hepburn settled on a stool. "You've done so many miserable songs already. They keep blasting over the radio no matter what station you dial."

"Glad you noticed." Dianna settled cross legged on a sofa.

"Annie, I've come to talk about Dianna."

"Shouldn't we get Hedda Hopper in here or something? We have three Oscar nominees in the room."

"Precisely," said Hepburn. "A new generation's in town. We have to plan the attack."

"Don't you have anything to do? Ow!" Annie burst out, as the masseur pulled and pushed some back flesh.

"I don't want work right now," said Hepburn. "I'm doing *Long Day's Journey Into Night* later on. That's work enough to prepare for. You need to do the American classics, Annie."

"I'm not that old yet. Why are you here? Our cat reunion isn't until next week."

"And I cannot wait. Just to see Ginger's smiling wrinkles."

Anne laughed. The "cat" reunion was a gathering of actresses who had played in the film *Stage Door*, Anne's big break after being a chorus girl.

"Why don't you drop it?" asked Hepburn. "Ginger, Eve, Lucille, Gail, Andrea —"

"Oh, you want to come," said Anne, as the masseur draped an oversized towel around her. She sat up, swinging her multi-million dollar insured legs. "It's like a class reunion. Lucy needs the encouragement."

"Uh huh," said Hepburn. "How's Gail's television series doing? What's it again?"

"*Perry Mason*," said Dianna. "It's a big hit, Aunt Kathy."

"I hear you're thinking of letting Dianna go on television," said Hepburn.

"No, but she wants to act," said Anne, wrapping herself in a blanket.

"It's selling cars," said Hepburn. "The trouble is that she looks like Disney when people see her. Sweet little thing."

"Stop!" Dianna cried.

"Yes. Shut up," said Anne.

"Did you see what Sinatra's doing?" Hepburn obligingly changed subjects.

"I did," said Anne. "I called him up and chewed him out. He comes right out and says he is going to produce and direct *The Execution of Private Slovik*. Do you know what it's about?"

"I do."

"By God, they're going to have his prick. And he hires Albert Maltz, another Hollywood Ten Communist who went to jail. Trumbo's going to get credit for his work. Now Maltz. All that work Congress did to protect us from these guys."

"Will Communists be writing movies?" Dianna asked.

No one answered her, but Hepburn rolled her eyes.

"Sinatra's such a jerk," said Anne. "He's in with the Kennedys, and everyone will see this as – Jack Kennedy loves the Communists."

"Oh, he does not. And why should you care?" asked Hepburn.

"Because I love Frank, the old jerk, and he's asking for one ton of trouble."

"Let's change the subject."

"All right. Why are you doing that horrible play? What has gotten into you? Shakespeare, O'Neill."

"You should try some of that, Mrs. Ben Hur. I'm playing Cleopatra this summer at Stratford. I'd like to see you try that."

"I'd like to see *you* try that! And I was not married to Ben Hur. I was married to Christ."

"My God."

"Exactly," said Anne. "I've *been* on the stage. I came up in vaudeville, like Mickey Rooney, and look how we turned out."

Hepburn waved her hand. "My point is the stage."

"I know, la de da, you're such an actress now, Miss Hepburn."

"Dianna, you should try the classics. Something like *A Winter's Tale*."

"Or *Romeo and Juliet*," said Dianna, pointedly, but Anne did not take the bait.

"It's tough work," Anne said. "John and I did *J.B.* a couple of years ago, and I was crucified, but you know, I'd like to do it again. But John had all the good lines. Let *him* play Sarah."

"You should go on the stage, Dianna," said Hepburn. "We should think of something."

"Why all this interest in Dianna and not yourself?" Anne said. "It's completely out of character."

"It is not. I am here to make an announcement."

"Are you coming to the Oscars?" asked Dianna.

"God, no. I have a telegram from Vivien."

Anne was instantly alert. "How is she?"

"Sad," said Hepburn. "I can't believe that marriage is over, and neither can she. I was a witness at their wedding, you know. What a night that was! Both of them fighting like storm troopers. She writes me, please be my understudy godmother for Dianna and keep her out of television."

"Wow," said Dianna.

"And I thought, what do godmothers do?"

"Turn mice into coachmen," said Dianna.

"And then," said Hepburn grandly, "they send their charges to the ball in a beautiful gown."

"Is that in the box?" asked Dianna.

"For the Oscars," said Hepburn. She glared at Annie. "I knew you wouldn't have the nerve. This girl has to strip Disney off her back."

"Dianna has a dress for the Oscars," said Anne. "From Bonwit's. A princess style blue gown."

"Annie, the girl's sixteen, not twelve. She's got a good figure. Open the box, Dianna."

Dianna tore it open, unruffled the tissue, and unfolded a dress of pale blue satin and tulle that seemed to go on forever.

Dianna held it up against herself and whirled. "Look at it, Mom!"

"It's strapless," said Anne.

"Look how the satin flies up on half the skirt to show the tulle. How gorgeous! I love you, Aunt Kathy!"

"There's a satin stole," said Hepburn, laughing.

Dianna burrowed back into the box and pulled out another waft of tissue, which, when undone, became the satin stole.

"You could get cold in that old theater."

"Of all people," said Anne. "You wouldn't be caught dead wearing anything like this."

"Of course not. Anyone who saw me would turn to stone. Everyone knows I'm a woman. It's high time they learned Dianna was one."

"Did Viv set you up to this?"

"I just needed a hint. Don't do Disney, she said."

John poked his head in.

"Annie, are you done?"

"Daddy, look at what Aunt Kathy brought me!" Dianna whirled around with the gown.

"Which Aunt Kathy will return," said Anne.

"No!" Dianna stomped her foot.

"Go on, try it on," said Hepburn. "Take your bra off, don't forget."

"Hi, Kath," said John, as Dianna disappeared behind the door he'd opened. "Have you come to see my wife naked?"

Dianna rustled the tulle so they'd remember she was right there.

Hepburn tugged at his ear lobe. "You darling boy. You'll never know my secret."

"Which one?"

"She brought Dianna a strapless gown, and she's still a girl, and you know these people," said Anne.

"These men, you mean," said John.

"They'll be all over her," said Hepburn. "That means they'll think of casting her. Anne, stop being jealous. John, how was Cannes?"

"Boring, mostly."

"I know what they'll do," said Anne. "Right when we're leaving the country. We have to put bars on the windows."

Dianna appeared, her shoulders bare, some cleavage actually showing.

John's jaw dropped. "My God, Anne, look what we did!"

"Do me up, someone?" asked Dianna. Hepburn, looking smug, hurried to help.

"Christopher Columbus! I never dreamed you'd look like this."

"Look at her, Annie," said John, who seemed quite pleased.

"The sneakers help," said Hepburn.

Dianna giggled, kicked off her Keds, and twirled around.

"Drop the pony tail," John said.

She shook her hair out over her shoulders.

"Oh, my God," said John. "How'd all that happen?"

"She'll make a sensation," said Hepburn.

"No one's going to see it but the people in the audience," said Anne.

"Unless she wins," said John.

Dianna laughed.

"Everyone in the industry will see her," said Hepburn. "They'll want to-"

Anne threw her hands up in the air. Hepburn hopped up next to her and put an arm around her shoulders.

"*Hire* her."

"Maybe," said Anne.

"You think so?" Dianna asked.

Hepburn said softly, to Anne, "You're thinking this is the same old time. It's not. Dianna's not you."

Dianna stopped whirling. "What are you talking about?"

"Nothing that bears repeating," said Anne.

But Dianna knew. Once, when having too much to drink, and telling Dianna to get an IUD, Anne had blurted out the whole ugly tale of having to get an abortion and why she had fled to New York. But Dianna hadn't gotten the IUD, and Anne seemed to have forgotten the whole conversation.

"Is she old enough for this dress?" asked John.

Hepburn said, "If it stays up, she's old enough."

John laughed. "Let me see you run down the aisle for your Oscar."

"Oh, Daddy," said Dianna. "You and Mom are winning. All the papers say so." She ran to the door. "I'm going to look in the *All About Eve* mirror."

She scurried out but then hung back to hear if they would blurt out big secrets with her gone.

"I didn't want her to stay in the business," Anne muttered. "I did once. Not now. I'm hoping she'll get disgusted. She still might."

"What the hell? Teach her to be tough," said Hepburn. "The kid's talented."

"To fight like I did? To have to put up with fools – why would I want my daughter to be in this business?"

"Because she has a gift."

"I should have insisted she play Karen, despite Preminger. Then we'd be working together."

"Dianna's a good actress," said John. "I hope she doesn't mind losing."

Dianna backed a few steps away, holding the tulle still.

"She was nominated for *Teacher*," said Anne.

"You want it, don't you," said Hepburn. "You selfish thing."

Anne said, "I've got Marilyn and Taylor on my heels and now that Shirley MacLaine."

Hepburn said, "Simone's getting it."

Anne said, "I thought I did a good job."

"You did a smashing job. But darling, you have three. Simone will win. Dianna was nominated because it was a fine, brave movie that George did, and she was its star. She should go looking like a young woman. Once they see her, they'll jump on her. Metaphorically. You shouldn't be jealous. It will help her career."

"It's either Doris or me," said Anne.

"No," said Hepburn.

John said, "*Diary* did not do all that well, although it was a great work, and I do not think they would give it to a youngster. It is going to be either Doris or Anne. Forgive me, Kath."

Hepburn said, "Well, I sure won't win. Doris won't win. Comic actors rarely win, and *Pillow Talk* is a silly comedy. You already have three statues, Annie. Guess who that leaves. Simone's getting it."

"I don't want them jumping on her literally or metaphorically, Kath," said Anne. "Who knew she'd grow up?"

"She's going to grow up whether you like it or not. Start liking it. You and John have enough power to keep the wolves off. You were all ready at sixteen for big parts and so's she. This is how to get them for her."

Anne leaned back. "All right, Kath, she can wear the damn dress."

Dianna hurried to the mirror. Maybe it was better that she didn't win. An Oscar at sixteen? No one had ever done that. It would curse her. She just wanted to be accepted for more adult parts. In this dress, she could earn more than a statue! (Maybe, maybe Nick was right.) Losers were often the best winners. People saying so and so should win, then didn't, and suddenly, so and so was getting great parts.

She went back toward the room to get the box but held her skirts still so she could listen in. She'd always been aware of some secret that her mother and Hepburn had, but she'd never been able to figure what it was. And her mother certainly wasn't going to say anything.

"I am heading out to tennis with Greg after a meeting," said John. "He should be here now. Have fun, ladies."

Dianna hid behind the door as her father strode out.

"I'll play with you, Kath," said Anne.

"Watch it. I may do something about that."

"So you have always said. And never done nothing."

Did they mean, Dianna wondered, what she thought they meant?

Hepburn laughed. "So you have always thought. I see your boyfriend won the New Hampshire primary. What's it like, knowing he will be the next president of the United States?"

"I know you can hardly stand it," said Anne.

"There was a time you could hardly stand it. Richard Nixon as president will be a terrible calamity, you said. That was years ago, but I remember."

"He is an experienced world leader," said Anne.

"Talk to Ginger, she's in love with him, too."

"I'm not in love."

Hepburn laughed. "Good, I got you mad."

"You always do, pal."

5

Oscar parties began. Dianna joined her parents for a few of the banquets and charity balls, all crowded, for nominees went to these events to keep their faces in front of the voters, and others went to be seen with nominees.

Nick scorned all the "Hollywood stuff," but Dianna understood it was business and was proud to be part of it at last.

But maybe Nick had a point.

The first event was a dinner sponsored by the Press Club, where, to Dianna's dismay, William Wyler spoke about the blacklist while they ate ice cream cake.

"Has anyone ever identified a picture or a scene or a word that is Communist propaganda? Ian McLellan Hunter was blacklisted, and called a Communist. But Hunter wrote the original story for *Roman Holiday*. *Roman Holiday*! Trumbo wrote the script. If anything, that was a royalist fairy tale popular everywhere, including of all places, the Soviet Union. Royalists everywhere loved it."

"He didn't have to talk about that. He just focuses a light on it," Anne said on the ride home.

Dianna silently agreed.

"He could talk about anything he wanted," said John. "Thousands of people were put out of work for just being compassionate."

"Compassionate! You mean weak. Now the thing is being pushed by people wanting to make a stupid point. That line in *Ben Hur* – that argument between Messala and Ben Hur – Messala wants Ben Hur to give names. And *Spartacus*! Cassius has a list of names. It was so blatant. Let's just move on. People forget. Move on, that's the best way."

"Honey, this kind of thing happens all over history," said John. His tone had changed to one of disinterest.

"Then why talk about it?"

"He wants to fight it."

"It's *stupid*! You can't say it didn't do some good. We found spies. The Rosenbergs. We can't help the people who want to destroy us. We have to root them out."

"Yes," said John.

"Oh, you're no fun to fight with."

"I do not want to fight. Wyler spoke to the choir. Everyone agrees with him now."

"Not everyone. I may give a speech myself."

"What would that do?" John asked, raising his voice as the car pulled in front of the house. "It is not necessary to scream out loud what you and I know you do not believe."

What did her father mean about that? Her mother seemed pretty certain of what she'd said.

Mick opened the car door.

"I certainly do believe in being loyal to my country, and so do you."

"I have got two."

"Why don't you drop your British citizenship?"

"How many times do I tell you? I may be king one day. What was Willy talking to you about after?"

Dianna laughed. The king thing was a standard joke.

"King! A million people will have to die before you can be king. He wants me to do *Those Three* again. It's going to be about real lesbians."

"I cannot picture you as a real lesbian."

"I told him, fine, but don't ask me. Ask Marilyn Monroe."

John laughed as he took her elbow and led her into the door.

Anne laughed, too.

They laughed all the way upstairs.

Dianna relaxed. When they laughed that way, and they usually did, things were going just fine.

Nick did join them, at John's insistence, to a charity costume ball. Dianna went as Cinderella, and Nick, as Prince Valiant, was charged to watch over her. John and Anne donned priest and nun garb – he was the nun and she was the priest.

Nick made a valiant try to stick with Dianna. For a while, they chatted with astronauts and monsters and several Mae Wests. The band started the twist, and Dianna and Nick got everyone laughing going round and round and up and down. She jitterbugged with Dean Martin, who turned it into a comic act and pretended to be thrilled by her beauty. At least she thought he was pretending, but he really did seem to try to kiss her.

An Indian princess cut in.

"I beg your pardon," she said, and then realized it was Frank Sinatra. She had a hard time not to laugh at his face paint, his braids, and "those knees" and he said, "If I didn't know you better, I'd think you were a maid who sat in the ashes all day." He held her close, rubbed his hand across her back and then across her backside.

"Come on, please." She pulled away.

"Ah, honey, don't be uptight. You have to learn to get along with the guys."

What, did they own her body? She could have waved across the room to her father, but there was a better way.

"I get along fine with the guys who didn't date my mother."

That annoyed him, but he couldn't much deny it. "I guess that's something that will always be between us."

"Darn tooting," she said. "But I cannot deny your excellent taste."

"Yeah," he said, grabbing her close and waltzing around with her. He didn't touch her in that queasy way again, though.

John Wayne was next in line.

"You're a cowboy," said Sinatra. "How clever. I don't know if I want to hand her over to you. What you did to my people and all."

Wayne looked befuddled, but then he attempted a smile.

"I would like to dance with this pretty lady," he said.

Dianna said, "Hi," and tried to move around Sinatra, who said, "Oh, no, you don't."

He was deadly serious. So Wayne got deadly serious. Wayne was wearing a gun, and he settled his hand over it. Was it a prop?

"You and your kind, defining patriotism in your way and anyone who moves from it is a Commie," declared the Indian princess.

"It takes one to know one," said the cowboy. "You're always defending the pinks."

"I defend the Bill of Rights."

"And open the door for the Commies to take it away."

Dianna could see her father's head across the hall, turning at the raised voices.

"Uncle Frank," she said, "I'd like to dance with Mr. Wayne."

Her voice was drowned out by the quarrel and the growing buzz. It resonated like the epic encounter between the Indian princess and the Indian-hating cowboy from *The Searchers* in that it didn't seem as if this scene would end with Wayne sparing the Indian girl but rather killing her. She tried to back away, but the crowd was pressing in.

"What the hell are you working with Maltz for?" Wayne demanded. "That guy is a Commie through and through. Why are you giving him a break? And what the hell are you doing the Slovik story for? What kind of an American are you?"

"The kind who's not afraid to question my country," Sinatra shot back. "That's what being free is. That's a citizen's responsibility. I don't sit back and say, yay for freedom but only freedom for guys in power, yeah, you big boys do whatever you want. That's what the Commies do. Which side are *you* on?"

Wayne took a swing. Someone pulled Dianna back. It was Gregory Peck, eyeing the fight with something like joy.

Compared to Wayne, Sinatra was a toothpick. But he struck back fast. So did Wayne.

She heard a loud voice arguing. "Sinatra should be able to do the movie he wants with whom he wants. That's freedom. If people don't like it, they won't go. That's freedom."

She looked over some heads. That was William Royce arguing

His was, she thought, a stupid argument. The real argument was that Communists – traitors – shouldn't make any profit in a country that loved freedom.

The fight caught her attention again, Wayne having grabbed Sinatra.

"I could pick you up with one hand."

Anne appeared, pushed the men apart, and no one could tell whether it was Anne or her priestly garb that stopped them.

Wayne looked down at her and smiled. "I am sorry," he said. "But Sinatra, you are one damn fool, especially if you think you're a patriot."

Sinatra stomped off to a corner.

After that, her parents said she didn't have to go to any more Oscar parties. They threw a party, though, turning their mirrored ballroom/gym into a formal dining room. Nick went back to his spurning and headed out to the Sunset Strip, but Dianna had always wanted to be part of her parents' parties.

She sat next to a too quiet Ernest Lehman and listened through the oysters and prime rib to conversation ranging from whither the musical to whither the world if Communist China decided to send over a bomb. After the dinner came more entertainment. Everyone had to get up and do something – Lena Horne, Frank Sinatra, Danny Kaye, Sammy Davis, Ella Fitzgerald, Dean Martin, Orson Welles – who could barely carry a note, and Anne, who could carry all of them. Dianna got up to sing, too, letting go for "Summertime," her lush voice crying out its anguish of a world coming to an end.

"Holy Hell," said Sinatra. "Where'd she learn to do that?"

"From you guys," said Anne. "And our Hilda, who sings all the time in the house. You should head over to Disneyland. Dianna sings jazz on the Mark Twain. Best kept secret in town."

"And you're singing that pop crap!" cried Sinatra.

"The kids eat it up," said John.

"And nobody remembers she sang through Disney's *Sleeping Beauty*," said Orson Welles, as substantially as only he could.

Dianna went over and got her father's hug and stayed while he regaled a small group with the story about Sessue Hayakawa during filming *The Bridge Over the River Kwai.*

"He only read the script pages with his dialog and tossed out the rest," John told the the Kayes, Douglases, and Nivens with relish. "I see something suspicious there below the bridge and I'm heading down, with Hayakawa after me. Lean says to him, keep going. You follow him and you die. Hayakawa stops in his tracks. 'I die?' he yelps." John waited for the laughter, and said, softly, "You'd never know by looking at the movie. So what do you have to know to act in movies?"

Niven said, "Miss Garbo, just have a blank look. The audience will fill it in for you."

"Maybe we should be handing out Oscars to the audience," said Welles.

"How they can tell the truth from movies," John said. *"Bridge* was total fiction. If anyone had collaborated with the enemy, his men would have killed him. So is war insane or just movies about war?"

"I hate it when John tries to make us think," said Kaye, giving John's arm a punch.

"Do you think we've cracked the blacklist?" asked Douglas, referring to his film. "Now they can't use fronts and fake names."

Anne got up, looked at Douglas. "You've got guts, but where will it lead? They'll call us all Communists. It'll break us."

"It will be fine," said John. "The country is tired of all this. But there are so many writers and actors who were put out of work. That's still the blacklist going on, and they are already broken."

Anne waved her hand to dismiss that thought and went over to the bar. Sensing something wrong, Dianna went with her.

"What is it, Mom?"

Anne smoothed her daughter's hair. "Absolutely nothing, dear."

"Will they call us Communists?" The idea seemed absurd.

"They think the danger's over," said Anne. "It has not even begun."

6

Beautiful Beulah ended and with it, the security of working at Disney Studios. Much as Dianna had come to see working there as a strait jacket, it was still familiar, a place where she had respect and honor. And it had been fun when the Mouseketeers were around.

Walt Disney threw a party for her at a nearby restaurant, and he cried when he handed her a gold plaque. Not that she was out of his world. She still had her weekends at Disneyland. Even though that was work, she still had fun.

The night of the Golden Globes, she wandered about aimlessly. Nick had gone with his parents – those three had been nominated. She hunted up Chas.

There had been one disturbing thing – Chas. When he wasn't with his own tutor, he kept to his room or was outside pretending to be a motor car.

Lynne, standing at a door, gestured.

"He's out there."

It was almost dark, but there he was on the great lawn, pitching an imaginary game of baseball. Dianna ran over, grabbed a bat, and hurried back to the imaginary home plate.

"Okay, Chas, I'm ready!"

He stared at her for a moment, then he turned away, making home plate something else. He didn't even have a ball.

"Chas?" she called.

"Girls aren't allowed," he shouted.

She stepped aside, watching him snag some players, all imaginary. Oh, she recognized the names – Snappy, Jimmy, Dave, Ray. All from *Pigskin Pete*. She ran back into the house where Lynne had been watching.

"What's with him?"

Lynne said, "He's getting Pete out of his system. I'm supposed to watch him. Reggie will bring him in when it gets too dark."

"Mom and Dad told you to watch him?"

A door opened on unspoken fears.

Then it closed as John and Anne returned, both carrying Golden Globes. Dianna listened while her mother undressed. Anne was in a jovial mood. Once again, she was the actress of the year, and her husband marched right beside her.

"The joke of the evening," said Anne, slipping into the terrycloth robe Lynne held out for her and sitting at her dressing room table, "was a joint award they gave to Louella and Hedda." Her fingers plunged into a jar of cold cream, which she spread thickly over her face. "We all clapped because we thought, God please, is it the end of an era? Those damn gossips have been blackmailing us for generations. Louella reported I was pregnant before I knew! Oh, and Nick was one of the most promising newcomers. I don't understand. He's been a star since '49."

"He just now got to be promising," said Dianna, relieved that her mother seemed to be her witty self.

"Doris Day and Rock Hudson won best film favorites. Why John and I can't win that – I guess we have to do a sex comedy. Bing got the Cecil B. DeMille Award. For meanness, you know." Anne slipped off her jewels, which Lynne put into a box and straight into a safe. "You'll be happy to know *Diary* won for promoting international understanding, beating out my nun. And that William Royce won for best supporting actor."

Good for him, thought Dianna. Let him be a flash in the pan.

"And of all things, Marilyn Monroe won the musical/comedy award. Rosalind Russell won it last year and before her, me! Marilyn Monroe, the new standard! I could throw up."

Anne started to sing, shook her bust, hips, and bottom.

Dianna laughed. "You might make it!"

"Speaking of serious acting," said Anne, "after I kiss Paul Newman in *Exodus* and try to divorce Ralph Richardson in *Anna Karenina*, I'm going to Broadway to play Nora in *A Doll's House*. With your father as Torvald. George settled that today. We'll do that for a couple of months. So there, Kathy Hepburn."

"When?" Dianna tried not to show her dismay.

"Probably late fall. We'll come for the opening of *Spartacus*, and be here a few weeks. We'll close up here and you can be at Malibu. Unless," and she sat down next to her daughter on the sofa, "unless you want to go on the stage, too, in *The Chalk Garden*. That's come up."

"The pyromaniac?"

"It's a switch," said Anne. "It might be good for you to try Broadway."

Memorizing a whole play, playing it through, projecting to the back of a house, audiences judging her, critics tearing her apart? Critics in New York were dreadful. They'd criticized her mother in *J.B.* so much so that she had cried, but audiences had loved her. At least, Anne could act.

"It's a strange play." She hid her fear behind the criticism.

"If you want to, it's yours," said Anne. "*Silver Sierra* is still haggling over you. Your father's going to call and turn them down."

It didn't even occur to Dianna that it was quite odd that a Broadway lead would be offered to her when she had no stage experience except singing at Disneyland. Anne didn't even seem worried about that. But Dianna knew she wouldn't be able to handle it. She made a decision.

"I want to do *Silver Sierra*."

Anne stopped staring in her mirror and stared at Dianna. "It's television."

"It's what there is," said Dianna. "I can't go back to school. The kids are jerks. The teachers are dumb. I don't like the kids, they don't understand. You know."

Anne tossed some jewels around on her dressing table. "Yeah, okay. I suppose times are changing. If that's what you want."

She didn't approve, but she didn't care much either. Dianna pushed to justify her awful choice.

"It's riding horses. And Elmer Bernstein doing the music. And color. It might be fun."

"Your father wants you to come with us to England."

"I don't want to do a play. I'd have to go to school there, too."

"You could study acting."

Well, there it was. She was not going to be marked as the Fletcher who could not act.

"Would you be embarrassed if I did television?"

She might make a go of it at that, especially without her parents around. The thought startled her. She'd never wanted her parents out of the way before. She didn't want to fail in front of them either.

"Hell! If you want to ride horses on a small screen, all right. But we're going to have them make a tight deal so that you can get out of it in case something happens. That's the only way your father will okay it."

"Nothing's happening. And there's nothing at Disney for anyone."

"All right, if that's what you want," said Anne, obviously unhappy about it. "I guess teenagers don't want to be with parents. But the staff will be here, so it's not as if you'll be free." Then her phone rang, and she was all gaiety into the receiver.

Dianna had wanted to say she would miss them, and she wanted to talk about Chas, but it looked like a long and self-absorbed conversation with Eve Arden. She retreated to her room to study her *Picnic* script, dodging Chas, who was cartwheeling in the hall, a lifelong habit. So maybe she'd just been imagining things were wrong and that all he needed was his family. She needed them, too.

She sank back onto her bed, and the picture of her grandmother, her mother, and her baby self looked back at her, and what they saw, she was sure, were her ineptness, her inability to convince directors she was capable, and that the Oscar nomination was almost an insult. Yes, the reviews had been good, but she had been Anne Frank. Now she was this stupid perky kid with stupid perky records.

"I'm sorry, I'm wrecking all that you did," she said softly to her grandmother.

She opened the *Picnic* script. She had better be good in what she had left to do if she wanted to stay in this shrinking business in a shrinking screen. And what a story. A good looking guy with no prospects came to town and obviously, the good looking girl had to go with him. Every other plot line, including her own, especially her own, had no meaning. With William Royce lording it over all.

A hand touched her shoulder.

She smiled up at her little brother. "Hi, Chas."

"Wanna go fishing?" he asked.

A line straight out of *Pollyanna*.

"Where?"

"Out in the fountain."

Hand in hand, they walked down the back drive among the gardens and the fountains. Although it was night, the fountains were still lit. They stopped at the last one, took off their shoes, and hopped up and wiggled their feet in the water. It seemed supremely right to be fishing at night with pretend poles in a place where there were no fish at all. She wasn't sure why Chas had suggested it. It was almost as if he were reliving their work together in *Pollyanna*. She knew that when he spoke again.

"I think fishing's the best thing in the whole world."

"Me too," said Dianna.

She hugged her little brother, sensing he was in a world that made sense to him. She wished she could join him in it.

7

When Dianna arrived at Desilu's rehearsal studio, she was nervous. She was never nervous on a first day, so she was nervous about that, too. A familiar face at the long table with plates of donuts caught her eye. She'd worked with character actress Reta Shaw on several films.

"Congratulations on the nomination, honey. Look at how you've grown!"

Dianna took the chair next to Shaw, slipped her gloves into her purse, and smoothed her fluffy skirt.

"It's the heels," she said, showing off her new pumps. "How nice to see you again."

"I did this on Broadway. But I've never played Mrs. Potts."

Dianna reached for a glazed donut and nodded to the assistant director pouring juice and not coffee. Her hand, to her surprise, shook as she reached for the glass.

Several people were settling into chairs behind those that circled the table — the assistant directors, publicity people, associate producers, and anyone not the producer, director, or an actor.

Mira, Dianna's social worker, gave her a short wave. Dianna didn't wave back. The social worker's presence meant she was still a kid. Mira was in her early twenties, serious, and always studying for something. Dianna liked her because she never seemed to be paying any attention.

"Congratulations!" Dianna called to Arthur O'Connell.

"Aw," he said. "You'll want Ed, right?" — meaning Ed Wynn.

"Sorry!"

Angelini, who had been ignoring everyone and scribbling in his script, suddenly leaped up and sprinted over to welcome Bill Royce, who was just striding in.

Reta Shaw grabbed Dianna's arm. "I get to tell *him* to take his shirt off!"

Looking quite natty in a blue shirt, black jacket, and black trousers, and no tie, Bill Royce strode over to shake hands with Mark Dante and sat down next to the producer. Other than a few soft words to Angelini who took his other side, Bill spoke not a word but went straight to his work, pulling out a script and a pencil. An AD handed him a coffee cup, which he acknowledged with a polite thank you but then ignored.

Shaw spoke up right away. "How do you do, I'm Reta Shaw."

Royce looked up, smiled.

"My first friend."

"That's right," said Dante. "And Dianna Fletcher."

"Miss Fletcher," Royce said, with a curt nod in her direction before looking back down at his script.

Nice to see you, too, Dianna thought. The knots in her stomach tightened. Would he humiliate her if she was less than perfect?

"Hi, everyone!" called a high pitched, raspy voice.

"There she is!" called Angelini, hurrying toward Lucille Ball, who walked in with brisk steps. Ball, seeing Dianna, shook Angelini's hand quickly and hurried to take the seat on Dianna's other side. Someone poured Lucille's coffee. Someone else got Lucille a donut. She did, after all, run the studio.

To Dianna, Lucille muttered, "My God, he is one hunk, isn't he?"

Dianna shrugged.

"Hey, honey, I'm terrible at first readings. Help me, huh?"

"That doesn't matter," said Dianna.

Last was Star Worthington, one extraordinary, amazing, curvaceous blonde woman, who looked even better than her Miss January pictures.

Dianna was amazed at the effect Worthington had on every man around that table, their eyes wide, their chests still. Royce was the first to move, striding forward and taking her hand.

"Hi," he said, with the best smile he'd delivered so far. "Welcome to *Picnic*."

"Bill, I'm so glad we'll be working together at last," Star breathed, obviously imitating Monroe. Her clinging blue dress matched her eyes, and her gold chain matched her upswept hair.

What was it like, Dianna wondered, to know that every man in the room had studied your naked pictures in *Playboy*? And Bill Royce probably knew every curve and crevice on her. Men were a joke.

Royce escorted Star to the seat next to his.

Dante welcomed them. "This is one remarkable, extraordinary cast, and we will have one remarkable, extraordinary production. In color. Two hours. A special Sunday night that will launch NBC's premiere week. We're doing the play, with a few scenes that open it up — specially written by Inge — a scene at the swimming pool showing off Hal's and Dianna's form —"

"Dianna can do great dives," said Ball.

"Her form looks good already," said O'Connell. "We'll have to strike my lines that say Millie isn't pretty."

"Not one line is cut," said Angelini, sounding crabby.

Dante continued.

"Look around the table. We have three Academy Award nominees: Dianna Fletcher, Art O'Connell, and," he paused for effect, "Bill Royce." The cast applauded. "We have with us a most honored woman of television and movies, winner of three Emmy awards and I forget how many nominations, and lest I forget, the owner of this studio, Lucille Ball. I cannot tell you how happy your presence makes us, Miss Ball," he added.

"Lucille." The veteran's fingers shook as she reached for a glass of water.

"I'm going to put you in the hands of one of the most exciting directors of our time, Mike Angelini."

Angelini stood up. Dianna wondered if they should, too.

"First, we'll read. No stopping. Then, until one o'clock, we'll do some improvisations. After lunch, we'll get on the set and work some scenes, not all of them, just ones I think are crucial."

Dianna raised her hand.

Angelini nodded. "Yeah, yeah, I know. You have to leave us after lunch to go to school. It doesn't matter. I'm going to work on the crucial scenes with Hal, Madge, Rosemary, and Howard."

At least he was talking to her, even to tell her any scene she was in wasn't crucial.

"So let's start," said Angelini, settling down. "You show me what this play is about."

"Sex, isn't it?" Lucille muttered. "What was I thinking?"

Shaw began with authority and motherly goodness. Then, right off the bat, Royce showed Hal's dimensions subtly yet clearly by indicating nervousness, even some shyness. Dianna had to admit that he was instantly making Hal complex and believable.

She charged in but realized that she was reading with her obnoxious Anne Frank voice and overdoing it, too.

The actor playing Bomber, mocked her. "Who wants to look at you?"

"It's going to take some doing to make that line work," said Lucille.

"Don't stop," said Angelini, oblivious to Lucille's power.

Dianna's exchange with Royce was coming up. She kept her eyes on her script.

"You workin' for Mrs. Potts?" she asked. A little too stiff.

"Doing a few jobs in the yard," he said, with some hesitation, showing Hal's unhappiness at admitting to be a vagrant.

Even down to the smallest detail, he was good. Damn him.

At the break, she approached Angelini.

"How do you see Millie? She's smart, reads books, and she talks like a longshoreman. I don't know why."

"You're supposed to tell me. Didn't you prepare? You play the part. I'll let you know if I'm happy or not."

Her words just flew out. "Cushy job."

He laughed and pointed at her nose. "And there won't be any of those fights you had with Stevens."

"I don't want to fight."

But her fights with director George Stevens had yielded a fine result. They had argued into a mutual agreement. This man would not understand.

"I just thought I'd ask what your perspective was. I see you don't have one."

And she walked away.

That was rude, but she was used to respectful answers to her questions.

She heard Angelini say, "Now it starts."

She whirled around.

He was talking to Bill Royce.

"She was forced on me because she's a draw," Angelini said.

"And I'm not," said Royce, punching his arm.

As the reading continued, Dianna could hear the others begin to shape their characters while she kept hearing herself overacting and being shrill. Even Lucille, her voice shaking until about the third act, found her Rosemary. She slowed her speech, she found the humor, she found the soul. Royce worked from a center, and even seated, involved his whole body, capturing Hal's braggadocio, desperation, and the sudden calmness when he fell in love with Madge. He wasn't Method, he wasn't stagey, he simply had a way of being real, the kind of real that took intelligent preparation and thought and that would resonate on screen. Even Star had a rhythm, a one-dimensional one, but it worked. She used a petulant, breathy voice that gave the character a personality. Shaw and O'Connell knew their characters inside out.

After the reading, Angelini, without comment, started the improvs.

Dianna thought improvs were silly. Acting was working with a writer's words. But they were a fad, and, to her disgust, people believed in them.

Angelini gave Royce and Star the first improv. Star looked nervous, but Royce was at ease, and he used her nervousness to the scene's benefit. He also managed to give her a good kiss.

Angelini called out, "Now – Madge, Millie, and Flo. Let's see some of the tension in that family."

Angelini had them sit down to dinner, telling Millie to object to everything Madge said and protest everything her mother said. Dianna found it tough to go after poor Star. She couldn't find the way through. Wouldn't Millie feel sullen and isolated rather than go at everyone like a bull dog all the time? It would get tiresome.

"I see you don't have Millie yet," said Angelini.

She wanted to punch him.

When a nervous Lucille Ball went up, it was with O'Connell.

"I'm sorry," she said, after her first try. "I've never done anything like this before."

But Angelini praised her. "That was good. Nothing of Lucille Ricardo at all in that."

He tried other combinations, none of them including Dianna, and then it was time for lunch.

Angelini went around congratulating and kissing everyone but Dianna.

In the classroom, she couldn't concentrate. She could only think that she was missing something with Millie and that Angelini wasn't going to help her. He was going to let her fall flat on her face in front of the world, proving that she had lost her talent and that he had been right not to want to hire her.

The next day, she found that something had happened to her costume. It had originally been dumb enough, a flannel shirt, jeans, and baseball cap, but the jeans and shirt were too big now. Dianna thought she didn't look ugly, just stupid. Glasses completed the horror.

This wasn't Millie. This was a fool.

"He thought this was better," the wardrobe woman said. "Your stand-in did the test."

Her stand-in was an eighteen-year-old boy.

She decided she'd better not risk a quarrel. Perhaps she could work on Angelini by asking for help.

After working through a scene, she asked him, "Am I getting shrill?" and he said, "You tell me," and he didn't give her a word of direction except where to move.

She had a small exchange with Royce. After each setup — for the two of them and Royce's close-ups — he walked away without a word to her. She could sense his resentment, and she still simmered over what he'd said about her nomination. She was proving him right with every take.

The cast naturally caught Angelini's and Royce's dismissal of her, and between setups, they gathered in little circles that did not include her. She knew how that worked. She was a pariah, a bad actor, and no one wanted to catch that disease.

Once, however, Lucille — a longtime friend of the Fletchers — plopped next to Dianna during a break and practically gurgled her joy, in a nonstop emotional binge. "I know it's hard for the public to understand our divorce, but as soon as the camera stopped, we stopped. It was damn awful. I had to work. It's who I am. Your mother can do it. My God, your mother. She stood by me all the times, like when Walter Winchell was calling me a Communist. An awful thing. It almost killed the Lucy show right at the start."

"You a Communist?" Dianna thought that was funny.

"Hell, no," said Lucille. "My grandpa was one. I registered to vote Commie to please him." Now she lowered her voice. "Stupid but not illegal. I went to some meetings way back when it was just starting. Everybody did. Annie did that, too. She stood up for me when things got bad. She was brave. It could have hurt her career, but she outsmarted the committee."

"What committee?"

"The Un-American Committee. You know, in Congress. Oh, here we go again."

Dianna knew that loyal Americans testified before Congress, but why should her mother need to outsmart a committee? And why had Lucille bothered to fulfill her promise to her grandfather? It didn't make sense.

"We're ready!" called the AD.

Lucille punched her arm. "You'd better get on the ball says this Ball."

As if life wasn't already complicated, Dianna had to fit in time for costume fittings for *Silver Sierra*. Her role as daughter to character actor and once retired Marty O'Miles hadn't been announced yet, but the contracts had been signed (for two years, "but I will take care of that if we need to," said Uncle George, when she shrieked in his ear. "Just one season and on our terms. They want you."), and pre-production was moving forward.

Fortunately, Paramount, where the series would be filmed, was right next door to Desilu. Dianna drove a golf cart down the avenue of soundstages to Wardrobe and ended up on what felt like another planet. The *Silver Sierra* crew loved her, pampered her, and her costumes were stunning. Everyone called her beautiful, what a lovely figure, what great legs. She didn't want to leave.

When she came out of the studio, her cart was gone.

She dashed across the lots, scooted up to the *Picnic* soundstage, and flung open the door, ten minutes late.

"Nice of you to stop by," said Angelini. "We've been waiting for half an hour."

Lucille glared at her. Dianna had seen her direct that look toward Desi.

She went over to Royce, with whom she was to practice dancing awkwardly as Millie.

"There you are," he said lightly, but he was not smiling.

"Let's work," she said.

He took a deep breath, did a half turn, and came back as Hal, snapping his fingers.

How did he do that?

The choreographer reviewed the directions. Dianna had tried to practice them the night before but had given up, trusting that she simply had to be stiff and awkward. Royce was to move sensuously, and Millie was going to try to follow. Royce was surprisingly good. But although she was a natural and trained dancer, Dianna found that she couldn't be awkward. Neither could she lead as a partner, but it was the only kind of dancing Millie knew.

"You have to lead so I can say it's the man who leads," Royce snapped, changing from Hal's grin-happiness to simple grimness. "Mike, this isn't right at all."

She should have kicked him.

"It sure isn't. Come on, Millie. Let's get with it."

She tried. But every move she made, despite her efforts, proved too graceful.

"Stop trying to be pretty!" Angelini yelled. "Damn it, girl, you slow us down any chance you can get and then try to get it so we'll shoot the scene your fucking way. I won't be cowed, do you hear?"

'Mr. Angelini," came Mira's soft voice.

"Shut up. I know the rules," was his harsh response. "She's a damn Disney princess. Well, she's driving me to drink. Do it again."

Dianna glanced at Mira, who had stepped out of the shadows but now sat down. The swearing wasn't the problem. Angelini's growing fury was.

The dance started again. This time, Dianna still could not clap off the beat.

"Sorry, Bill," said Angelini. "We'll fake it with angles. You clap. She claps. We'll make it look bad."

"We should do it in one take," Royce said. "All those cuts will be lousy."

Dianna said, "I can get it."

"No time," said Angelini. "You should have worked on this."

Royce said, "I guess that's the price we pay for casting a name for Millie."

Don't punch him. They'll say you're difficult. When they'd finished, Angelini clapped Royce on the back, saying, "I'm sorry, but there's no getting around that manipulative little bitch. She's gotta be the star."

Dianna was beyond anger. She fled so they didn't see her tears.

Thank God the week was over. Monday would be the Oscars, and she'd feel even more like a loser, but at least she wouldn't have to be back on that set until Wednesday. She fell into the limousine and closed her eyes, hearing the crew call out "Good luck!" to Bill as he headed for his car. No one wished her luck.

On the way home, she paged through the *Hollywood Reporter*. Robert Wise was making more tests for *West Side Story*, including Barbara Luna and Rita Moreno for Anita, Troy Donahue, Dick Beymer, and Robert Blake for Tony, and Anita Sands, Susan Kohner, and Margaret O'Brien for Maria. Margaret O'Brien! Dianna slammed the newspaper down and stomped on it.

8

As the Fletcher limousine approached Hollywood Boulevard, traffic slowed to a crawl, and the sounds of people cheering and blurred voices coming from the speakers surrounded them as if coming from the skies. Although it wasn't yet dark, the piercing strobes of white search lights roamed the town in an attempt to imitate the old days and assure the nervous populace that Hollywood was just as good as it ever was.

The voice that predominated blurred through the air, but every so often a name stood out, with an enthusiasm that meant to impress the hearers with their eternal importance.

Arlene Dahl!

Debra Paget!

John Lund!

David Wayne!

"Everyone have your speeches ready?" John called over the din.

"I owe it all to Mother and Father," said Nick.

Dianna said, "I'd like to thank my wonderful parents who went through a night of love so that I might stand before you tonight."

"I remember that night," said John.

"So do I," said Anne. "You bastard."

They smooched, John considerately avoiding her lips.

Outside, the screaming grew louder. Hundreds of fans had been cordoned off in the bleachers on either side of the entrance to the Pantages Theater and were overflowing into the street. A phalanx of security guards protected the limousines as they pulled up.

Finally, their car was second in line. Art Linkletter's voice sounded clear.

"Mr. and Mrs. Eddie Fisher!"

That generated plenty of boos.

"Were we behind *them*?" Anne yelped.

"The bad, then the beautiful," said John.

Their car pulled forward and stopped, their door lining up precisely with the blood red carpet.

"Here you are," said Mick. "Good luck, everyone."

Someone opened the car door.

Chas bounded out.

Art Linkletter cried, "It's the Fletchers!"

The cheers and applause grew wilder.

"Take that, Liz," said Anne.

"And the first one out the door is Chas, Pigskin Pete!"

"Pete! Pete! Over here! Chas! We love you, Chas!"

Chas extended a stiff arm at the car's back door. Anne gathered her skirt, put on her glittering smile, and placed one gorgeous leg out on the street.

"That leg," said Art, "can only belong to the beautiful, brilliant Anne Foster! Nominated for Best Actress tonight for *The Nun's Story*. The prettiest nun with the prettiest legs, Anne Foster!"

Whistles and applause greeted Anne as, helped by John boosting from behind, she gracefully left the car, holding Chas's hand.

"We love you, Annie!"

"Annie, you're great!"

"You'll win, Annie!"

Nick got out. He waved at the joyfully shrieking fans, bestowing on them all a charming grin. It was all just one silly thing to him, Dianna realized.

"Nick! Nick!" screamed the fans, drowning out Linkletter's introduction.

"I may throw up," said Dianna, attempting to joke, as her brother helped Sherry out of the car.

"Mr. Fletcher?" someone called from the curbside.

John pushed himself out. Dianna got up carefully, hunching over, clutching her stole, hoping she wouldn't fall out of her dress, hoping she would not throw up, hoping no one would boo.

"There's John Fletcher! Nominated for Best Actor!" called Linkletter, who was sounding hoarse. "What a family, those Fletchers!"

It was like a beast roaring, that mob.

Dianna gathered up her tulle and satin skirts and stayed bent over. The sidewalk blurred. Her father moved down the blockade, shaking the hands of "the people." Did he have to do that now? Her back hurt from waiting. Finally, John came back to the car and reached his hand to her.

Linkletter called out, "And he's turning to help out — well, it's got to be—"

"Dianna!" screamed the mob. "Dianna!"

Dianna grabbed John's hand.

"Smile and wave," he said.

"Dianna! We love you, Dianna!" screamed the mob.

She smiled and waved and went over to sign autograph books at the end of grasping hands desperate for her signature, who knew why. She just knew she had to smile and say polite things.

"You're beautiful!" people called out to her.

"You've grown up so!" a woman shouted.

Dianna smiled and waved and, as she turned back to her father, gripped her stole around her. She felt she needed some defense, and she wasn't to bare her shoulders just yet. And it was chilly

"What an exciting evening for you all," Linkletter said, as they gathered around him. "Annie, you look glorious, and Dianna, you are *beautiful*, all grown up. Isn't she beautiful?"

A masculine roar went up. Dianna was so startled that she wobbled on her heels.

"You're a top recording star now, Dianna. How do you take all this in, that and the nomination?"

"It's been so much fun," said Dianna, "and the nomination is a great honor."

"Who did you vote for?" Linkletter asked, sticking the microphone in her face. "Your mother? Yourself? Doris Day? Your father? Your brother? Who? Come on, you can tell me."

"I always vote for my parents," said Dianna, realizing that sounded silly.

"And Nick," said Linkletter. "Here he is with the lovely Miss Sherry Glennon."

"We're going to have a good time no matter what," said Nick.

"Yes," said Linkletter, obviously not knowing what to say.

Dianna nudged her brother.

Linkletter moved on. "John, you must be very proud tonight."

"Yes, I am. I have my beautiful family with me, and I'm proud of every single one of them. I'm also proud to be representing an extraordinary film, *Ben Hur*."

Dianna muttered to Nick. "I forgot to mention *Detective Dog*."

"How could you," he muttered back.

"Look who's coming up now, your next door neighbors, Mr. and Mrs. James Stewart!"

The Stewarts and the Fletchers hugged. John took Anne's arm and waved his family inside.

Frank Sinatra, Joseph Schildkraut, Willy Wyler, and Peter Lawford surrounded Dianna right away, all trying to kiss her. She had no idea what to do, so she laughed and tried to dodge them all.

Lawford pinched her bottom. She resisted the urge to slap him as he said, "Hey, you're turning into some tomato. Frank, she should come on the yacht next time?"

"A fabulous idea," said Sinatra

Anne had told her, "You don't go on Sinatra's yacht without at least two parents along."

Dianna smiled. "I love boats."

Surrounded by the elite of the industry, watching her parents interact easily and gaily with them, made Dianna feel more inadequate. She just tried not to sound too stupid or to protest when some hands grew too curious. Her career was sliding, after all.

Nick appeared.

"Hey, off my sister!"

"We weren't on her," said Sinatra, chucking her on the chin.

Charlton Heston approached with the now dulling refrain, "Aren't you gorgeous!"

"Yes," said Dianna. "People keep asking me, so I might as well tell them."

Why didn't someone come up and say, "Aren't you brilliant!" or "Aren't you clever?"

Nick took her hand and led her back to their parents. Photographers posed, re-posed, and re-re-posed them. Dianna was sure her teeth had gone out of whack.

"My feet, John," Anne muttered, so John obligingly took her arm, and they started down the aisle to their seats, sixth row in the center, the *Ben Hur* section. The old vaudeville theater, gloriously red and gleaming gold, filled Dianna with a sense of history and some pride at being part of it. But that didn't last long.

Paul Newman rushed through the crowded aisle up to Anne, his next co-star, took her arm, and marched her right down the aisle.

"Hey, that's my wife," John called.

"How about a good luck kiss?" Paul asked, stopping by his row, where his wife, Joanne Woodward, was sitting.

"It's mine," called Woodward. "I gave it to him for you."

"How sweet," said Anne. "Thank you, darlings."

"Hi, Dianna!" called Joanne. "You're beautiful!"

"God, yes," said Paul. "I'm kissing you, too."

Blue eyes, lips pressed hard. Wow. She should have taken that part in *Exodus*. And *Exodus* would certainly be better than working with those vultures on *Picnic*.

Speaking of which.

Bill Royce was with his gorgeous Miss February. Her red hair was wrapped up in a coil on top of her head, a stunning effect. Dianna could only see a part of her dress, a quilted gown of black and gold. Royce, admittedly too handsome in his tuxedo, stood up and moved out into the aisle as if to greet her. What pretension! Taking Chas's arm, she walked right by without acknowledging him.

Arriving at their row, John Fletcher directed who should sit where. Chas sat in the center, near the Wylers. He put his head down, like an old man ready to nap. Nick and Sherry sat next to him, then Dianna, then Anne and John on the aisle.

Dianna turned to gab with Doris Day and Marty Melcher in the row behind her. She tossed her curls back, and tried to look sophisticated, gripping her satin stole, and feeling that she had dressed in her mother's clothes.

The air seemed taken over by italics and exclamation points. Everyone from Darryl Zanuck on down came by to talk to John and Anne, and Dianna had to be ready to meet smile with smile. Zanuck was still trying to persuade John to get behind his beloved project, *The Longest Day*. He was with his wife, Virginia, but everyone knew what a farce that marriage was.

Anne muttered, "All parts for you, John. Where are mine?"

He patted her hand.

The lights dimmed.

Photographers, like shadows, hovered everywhere. A television camera in one corner panned the audience in the front rows while another hung from the ceiling. Wouldn't it be fun if it fell, Dianna thought.

Up from the pit rose the orchestra with André Previn conducting a medley of music by Harold Arlen.

On the stage, a thin curtain held the legend in big black letters, "32nd Annual Academy Awards" and a mammoth statue of Oscar.

John and Anne simply talked to each other now, faking for the camera. Dianna widened her eyes and adopted a look of smiling wonder.

The camera kept panning. Dianna followed its path — Jimmy Stewart, chin in hand as he sat scanning the crowd, William Wyler looking calm, Tony Curtis and Janet Leigh laughing, Elizabeth Taylor and Eddie Fisher smiling and waving, but no one stopping to visit with them.

"Here we go," Anne said, as an elderly bald man, the President of the Motion Picture Arts and Sciences, B.B. Kahane, told them that the awards were important because they represented the judgment of peers. Then a bald Price Waterhouse representative introduced the emcee, Bob Hope, as Previn launched into Hope's theme, "Thanks for the Memories." The comedian, in white tie, strolled down the ramp past the way larger than life Oscar statue.

"Good evening!" he called, as the applause settled down. "I'm Bob Hope, known by the trade as Better Luck Next Year." He looked out at them, with mock solemnity, ready to milk the joke that he'd never won an Oscar for his acting. He was rewarded with mild laughter. Undaunted, he continued, referring to the president of SAG, "I never thought I'd live to see the day when Ronald Reagan was the only actor working."

That got a big laugh.

"It's a wonderful country, isn't it?" Hope continued. "Where else can a man walk off a job and refuse to get out of his swimming pool unless they improve working conditions?"

"That's not what it's about," Dianna heard Willy Wyler murmur.

"How about those pictures this year?" Hope asked. "Sex, persecution, idolatry, cannibalism. We'll get those kids away from those TV sets yet!"

They weren't his jokes, Dianna thought, he was the sum of his writers, but his predictable delivery bathed them in comfort.

She heard Nick groan.

Hope waited for the laughter to subside. "We know these awards are absolutely honest and above board because in thirty-two years neither Price nor Waterhouse has ever won an Oscar. And I can vouch for their honesty. Believe me, if they'd ever take a bribe, I'd be the first to know. But enough of bitterness. Let's get on to open hatred."

"Thank God," said Anne.

"To present the first Oscar, a talented young lady I've known since she was a child star back in the good old days when agents would be barred from the studios they now own. The lovely Miss Mitzi Gaynor right here." He waved to his right as the orchestra started up the song, "I Enjoy Being a Girl."

John reached into his inside pocket and brought out a small notebook and pencil.

"Is he going to keep track?" Dianna whispered to Anne.

"Nerves," said Anne.

The *Some Like It Hot* costume won the award; the one that spotlighted Monroe's breasts and gave the appearance of nudity. Orry-Kelly dashed up the aisle to get his award while the orchestra played "Running Wild" from the film.

"Wouldn't you know that would win? Is she here?" Dianna asked.

"I hope not," said Anne.

Hope returned.

"As the tension begins to mount, we come to the first award for acting. All the way from her home in France, a city that has seen some of the world's greatest performances: Sarah Bernhardt, Eleanore Duse, Nikita Khrushchev. Here is the talented winner of two Academy Awards, Miss Olivia de Havilland."

"Shit," said Anne.

The crowd gave a roar and stood up. John, Dianna, Sherry, Nick, and Chas stood. Anne stood too, slowly.

"All the way from Paris to get a standing ovation. God, I hate that bitch," said Anne, as they all sat down.

"She hates you," said Dianna. "For stealing her parts."

"They're only yours if you play them."

"She's not working anymore, Mom."

"She'll be back."

De Havilland looked right and left, gesturing grandly, stretching her vowels, and sounding not a whit like shy Melanie Hamilton.

"She belongs to the old Delsarte, grand actress days," Anne muttered.

"Okay," said John. "Ease up."

"You're awfully bitchy tonight," Dianna whispered.

"It's that or snoring," Anne muttered.

Dianna knew this was all an act. Her mother cared every bit about what was going on.

De Havilland was still stretching her vowels. "For the best performance by an actor in a supporting role, the nominees are Hugh Griffith for *Ben Hur*; Arthur O'Connell for *Anatomy of a Murder*; William Royce for *The Philadelphian*; George C. Scott for *Anatomy of a Murder*; and Ed Wynn for *The Diary of Anne Frank*. May we reveal the winner, please?"

"May we reveal the winner, please," Anne mocked.

Dianna crossed her fingers for Ed Wynn.

"The winner," said De Havilland, "is William Royce for *The Philadelphian*."

"Damn," said Dianna, perhaps too loudly.

She heard the cheer from *The Philadelphian* section and turned around. Bill Royce was shaking Newman's hand, and some other man's — probably the director's — and walking slowly down the theater's aisle.

"He looks as if he could cry," Sherry said.

He did look deeply moved. He paused, breathing deeply. Then he smiled, looking confident as he strode to the stage, taking the steps two at a time.

"That's one handsome man," said Anne.

Royce kissed De Havilland, stood the statue on the podium, looked out at them, and paused. He caressed the statue, looking at it as if he didn't believe he held it.

"Talk, dammit," said Anne.

As if he'd heard her, Bill Royce said, "That —" and he hesitated for several seconds, seeming to catch something in his throat. "That is quite a fine group of actors with whom to be associated. I'd like to thank Jim Gunn and Vince Sherman for a wonderful opportunity. And a fine cast, especially my pal and colleague, Mr. Paul Newman, and not, of course, forgetting the beautiful and magnificent Miss Billie Burke." He paused again, looked out at them with something — was it anger? What was he going to say, Dianna wondered, for she knew that harsh look — and then he smiled. "I'd like," he said, "to dedicate this to my parents, who were both actors and who are both gone now. Thank you for this honor to their son."

"That's sweet," said Anne.

"Very nice," said John. "Good voice. Good actor. He could use the boost. Even if my movie lost the first one."

"His parents were actors," said Anne. "Did we know them?"

"Royce?" John shook his head. "Nope. Probably regional actors. Pity they couldn't see this. How's he doing on *Picnic*?"

"Fine," said Dianna.

She wondered how Bill Royce would behave now that he had an Oscar. He had been oh so humble accepting the award. But she knew the truth.

"There's a new wave in Hollywood today, ladies and gentlemen," Hope said, picking up the show, "a wave of youth and freshness and talent. To present the sound award, Miss Natalie Wood and Mr. Robert Wagner."

The orchestra played, "Love and Marriage." Dianna choked back a laugh at that irony and glanced at Nick, whose face never changed expression, although he'd been after Wood for weeks. Unlike most of the women, she wore a short, tight dress that went with her short, tight hair style.

Hope lingered for some inane dialog, Wagner read the nominees with no flair whatsoever, and *Ben Hur* landed one.

Edmund O'Brien came next. "Ladies and gentlemen, I've been asked to present the award for the best performance by an actress in a supporting role, or to put it more succinctly, the best picture stealer. The nominees are: Hermione Baddeley in *Room at the Top*, Susan Kohner in *Imitation of Life*, Juanita Moore in *Imitation of Life*, Thelma Ritter in *Pillow Talk*, and Shelley Winters in *The Diary of Anne Frank*. And the winner is," he said, gazing at the card in his hand, "Shelley Winters."

"Whoopee!" cried Dianna, jumping up and clapping. Winters, in a dark blue gown, came running down the aisle, and as she reached over to take Dianna's hand, she started crying, and then kept going while the orchestra played the theme music from the movie.

Every time Dianna heard Alfred Newman's gentle music, Anne Frank seemed to return to her body and her soul. She closed her eyes and bent her head, hoping a little of Anne Frank would stay. It had been some time since she'd felt a character breathing inside her.

Shelley thanked everyone, especially that lovely little girl, "oh, and that other lovely little girl, Dianna Fletcher."

That was nice of her.

Fred Astaire walked out on stage.

Astaire said, "Mr. Yves Montand."

"Fred's introducing *him*?" Anne shook her head in disgust. "To dance? Are they insane?"

Indeed, Astaire disappeared, and Montand started dancing.

A buzzing grew in the audience, for people were not interested in Montand's dancing, although they were interested in the fact that Montand had had an affair with his co-star, Marilyn Monroe, during the making of *Let's Make Love.*

"Promoting the damn film. Stupid Academy," said Anne.

Dianna put her mother's mood up to nerves and loyalty to Astaire.

Danny Kaye ran over, and he spoke loudly, as if he were competing with the dancing on stage.

"I have a ticket here that says I just won a kiss with Anne Foster."

Around them, people started laughing.

John got up. "Oh, yeah?" He reached into his pocket.

Anne grasped his arm. "No, John! I'm not worth it! Don't throw your life away for me!"

Dianna jumped up, too, joining the game. "Daddy, no!"

Everyone around them laughed and applauded.

"It's too late now to beg for mercy!" Kaye yelled.

Montand kept dancing, but you could tell he knew he was losing the fight. The orchestra played louder. The television cameras had to stay with Montand, for they could only move to the audience when someone was coming to claim an award, so the television audience saw only Montand and heard strange applause and laughter.

John held up his finger and said, "Bam, bam."

Anne pushed past John and fell weeping over Kaye's body.

"Mom! Not here!" Nick called.

Anne sat up. "Look! He has a strawberry mark on his cummerbund! He must be my long lost co-star!"

The audience roared.

Kaye sat up and cried, "My sister!"

John said, "So you certainly can't kiss her now!"

"My brother!" cried Kaye, springing to his feet. "I'll kiss you!"

And they did. Passionately.

The hall rocked with laughter.

Montand did a little turn and bow.

"They're my parents," Dianna said to an amazed Sherry, as they all settled back down.

The applause for Montand proved surprisingly strong. Anyone watching television wouldn't know it wasn't for Montand.

Dianna settled back, reclaiming her nerves. The show lifted and sagged, and she wished it would hurry up.

Bob Hope came back.

"To present the award for film editing is one of the best edited girls I know, cut to exactly the right length and I defy any critic to say she doesn't have a beginning, a middle, and an end."

Anne groaned. "I despise that man."

The show kept moving on.

"The winner is *Ben Hur*."

"The winner is *The Diary of Anne Frank*."

Ben Hur would take the awards for films in color while *The Diary of Anne Frank* took most of the black and white film awards. Dianna roused herself out of her own torpor to feel proud of her movie.

Sammy Davis, Jr. sang "High Hopes."

Gogi Grant sang, "Strange Are the Ways of Love."

"Strange indeed," said Hope, "are the ways of Hollywood. For the first time in the history of the Oscar, a young woman is up for an award for putting her head on a pillow. Miss Doris Day."

Day, walking up to him, to him, recalled, "You gave me my first lines on stage."

"Yeah," said Bob. "Mother Nature helped a little bit, too."

"Television or not, I'm going to sock him," said Anne.

Making jokes about women's bodies did seem to be the rule of the ceremony. But everyone seemed to be going along with it.

Day announced the song winner, which of course, was "High Hopes." Jimmy Van Heusen made his thanks quick.

"Mr. Walt Disney," snapped Hope.

Dianna snapped awake. "Is he here?"

"Shh," said Anne, looking tense. She took her husband's hand.

Disney said, "I ask you to praise, along with me, a young man who has been performing in several of my motion pictures, always giving his best, inspiring young and old alike to be better people, and to have a good time – with sports, with each other – these were motion pictures that honor the people who make this country great and the children whose future we live for."

"Mom?" Dianna whispered.

Anne waved her to be quiet.

Disney continued. "This young man has a natural ability as an actor. I am certain that everyone in this theater tonight and watching at home has seen at least one *Pigskin Pete* picture."

At the name of the movie, people began to applaud.

"Oh, Mom," said Dianna. She was thrilled. She looked over at Chas, who was playing with his program.

Disney continued. "In honor of his contribution to these films all families can enjoy, and to his great contribution to the image of youth of this country, the Academy is proud to present Charles Fletcher — well, we all call him Chas," he added, with his trademark twinkle you could see at the back of the auditorium, "with this award for very special achievement."

"Oh, Chas!" Dianna cried, leaping up, clapping her gloved hands.

Nick pushed his brother up and pushed him toward the aisle.

Looking both confused and happy, the boy clambered over the others, taking hugs from Sherry, Dianna, and his mother. His father shook his hand, and Dianna thought it might be the greatest moment in Chas's life, so radiant was his face as he looked up at his father. John gave him a playful shove toward the stage, the applause still loud. Dianna was startled to see Anne was crying. John's smile turned tense.

Dianna said, "Mom, he said Chas could act."

"I hope he does tonight," said Anne.

"Maybe he'll give him a part."

"Oh, no," Anne whispered.

Chas made it to the stage and shook hands with Disney.

Facing them all, holding the Oscar, he looked young and scared.

"Thank you." His trembling voice sounded sweet, and it silenced the applause. "This is very special and important to me. I enjoyed playing Pete a lot, and I think we taught each other something. Thank you, Mr. Disney, for giving me the pleasure of playing him. I thank you all for this honor." He hesitated, and then he sang the first two lines of a famous, sweet song from *Pigskin Pete*, "*Look at the stars, far away shining, they are but us by and by, remember, and always see.*"

As he walked off the stage, an usher steered him down the steps to a door that did not lead toward the press room. Dianna wondered if they did not trust Chas with the press.

Anne said, softly, "Nice. Did you coach him?"

"All but the song, do you believe that? Otherwise, it was like pulling teeth," John muttered under the applause. "It was better than him saying something odd. But," and he laughed. "How could anyone distinguish something odd from anything else here?"

Was something wrong with Chas? He seemed his normal self as he made his way to his seat. Dianna glanced at her parents, but they simply smiled for the cameras.

"Nice going, fella," Nick said. "At least one of us will go home with that statue."

Chas sat down. He held onto the Oscar. Firmly.

Gene Kelly was introduced, Marilyn Monroe was insulted again, and *Ben Hur* won for best scoring. *Room at the Top* stole a writing award from *Ben Hur*.

"Here comes Daddy's award," Dianna said.

"Don't jinx it," said John.

Deborah Kerr, looking glorious in green, came onstage.

"Next life," said Anne, "I want to be her."

"The nominees for Best Actor," said Kerr crisply, "are John Fletcher for *Ben Hur*, Nick Fletcher for *Suburban Rebel*, Jack Lemmon for *Some Like It Hot*, Paul Muni for *The Last Angry Man*, and James Stewart for *Anatomy of a Murder*."

"May I have the envelope, please?" Kerr asked. She opened it slowly.

She arched her eyebrows. "Oh, my."

John shook his head and looked down.

Kerr smiled sweetly.

"The winner is John Fletcher for *Ben Hur*."

"Yay, Daddy!" Dianna cried.

As the camera came forward and the photographers flashed, John kissed Anne, then leaned over to shake hands with Nick, chuck Dianna on the chin, then fasten his jacket before heading down the aisle, the theme music blasting, the applause strong, cheers in the air. This being his third Oscar, he had tied with Anne.

Doris Day, leaning forward, put her hand on Anne's shoulder, and Anne patted it absently. Dianna recognized it as a surrender to the inevitable. Now who could deny that her parents had made two of the great movies of the year?

On stage, John said, "*Ben Hur* was one huge effort from many people and while it was one of the most gratifying experiences of my life, I won't kid you. It was hard work. I could not have gone through it without Willy Wyler's hand at my throat" (he waited for the laugh) "and the hardest working cast, nor without my family's support, certainly not without my wife Anne, and my children. We have had a little fun with this nomination and there have been some friendly wagers, and now I am looking forward to Stewart trimming my hedges." That brought a roar of laughter. "I thank my colleagues on *Ben Hur* for a masterful result, and I thank you for this award, which I shall particularly cherish."

"Are you ready?" Dianna asked Anne, who was straightening the orchid that decorated one shoulder.

The photographers were gathering like vultures, stooping in the aisle, ready to catch mother, daughter, and Doris Day.

Anne took Dianna's hand and smiled prettily.

On stage, David Niven was saying, "I have the great pleasure to name the lovely and brilliant nominees for best performance by an actress in a leading role. These ladies are Doris Day for *Pillow Talk,* Dianna Fletcher for *The Diary of Anne Frank,* Anne Foster for *The Nun's Story,* Katharine Hepburn for *Suddenly, Last Summer,* and Simone Signoret for *Room at the Top.*"

Niven opened the envelope. He looked at it for a moment, and he smiled a slow smile.

"Read it you so and so," Anne muttered.

He did.

"The winner," he said, and he smiled out at them, "is Dianna Fletcher —"

Dianna thought, why didn't he say Anne Foster, but then realized he had said *Dianna Fletcher.*

"Oh, my baby," said Anne, hugging her daughter. Dianna looked at her distractedly.

"He said me?"

"Yes, my darling," said Anne, as the cameras went swirling mad. Anne stroked Dianna's hair and slipped off the protective stole. Dianna stood, suddenly aware of lights on her bare shoulders. Anne stepped into the aisle to make way for her. A motherly kiss, a check of the long tulle and satin skirt, and a gentle push, all recorded by the cameras. The applause kept going strong. As Dianna walked toward the stage, she thought this was not right.

She didn't hear the gasps and whispers of surprised admiration at her lovely young figure, at her bare shoulders and hint of full breasts, of her hair framing her face in curls.

"Boy, has she grown up," she heard someone say. And "youngest winner ever."

The applause was still strong as she tried to see her way up the stairs through her tears. Someone gave her a hand. The movie's theme music swept over her, and there was Anne Frank inside her again. Seeing her father in the wings stopped Dianna, but he shooed her toward the podium. Beside him, Shelley Winters looked thrilled. Bill Royce stepped forward, hands clapping. Dianna ignored him and moved toward Niven. That old friend of her family's, last year's Best Actor, caught her arm and kissed her hand. She could not speak.

They were still applauding!

"Dianna, you look lovely," Niven said, with his charming clipped accent, his merry eyes even merrier than usual.

The applause died down. Say something and get off.

She took a deep breath. She took the statue.

Heavy.

She set it on the podium and looked out at the audience. Niven had slipped her his handkerchief with the winning card, and she dabbed at her eyes. It gave her an opening to help her think as a camera zoomed toward her.

"Mom," she began, so that would be the first word out. "You were right." She hesitated, timing the line. "I did wear too much mascara."

Their laughter helped her relax.

The joke wasn't true, but it fit the occasion, and it might be true. And it directed attention to her mother, who ought to have won.

Talk, for heaven's sake. Say thank you and get off. But she couldn't. Anne Frank was in the music.

Anne Frank should have been here. That thought stung. Because this was her night. Her movie had won many awards.

"It is a lovely honor to have been nominated along with Miss Hepburn and with the wonderful Doris Day and Miss Signoret, and especially in the company of my mother."

She paused for applause, and it came, long and warm. She let it go on. She couldn't look directly at the audience, though, only at the camera. She wanted to speak right to it.

"And such an honor to speak as Anne Frank, to let her live in me a little bit so she could live in you, to have met Mr. Otto Frank, to work with such a splendid, wise cast, and to learn from a most splendid director, Mr. George Stevens." Again, the audience applauded warmly.

She thought André Previn would be starting the music, but he was standing there, baton at his side, looking at her as if he expected her to say something else. So she did.

"When I went to the Anne Frank House with my class from school — being there, in that tiny hiding place is an extraordinary feeling. Anne had all these pictures of movie stars on her wall in her room. I like to think they helped her. Some of you were on her wall. Ginger Rogers, Fred Astaire, Clark Gable, Judy Garland, Merle Oberon, Ray Milland. But. Anne had *three* pictures of my parents on her wall, from *Zorro*." The memory came back fresh, and her voice quivered as she said, "I realized Anne loved my parents before I could."

The auditorium grew completely, chillingly silent. In the front row, Jack Warner stared up at her. She returned her gaze to the camera. André Previn had still not made a move.

"Anne Frank loved movies. She wrote about acting and writing. If she had lived, perhaps she'd be here tonight. I don't think I'll ever understand why she's not," she added passionately. "We can't give her a happy ending. But we who make movies could help her keep her courage, for without her courage there would be no diary. I am honored by this award, and I am grateful to have grown up among you in this art that sometimes, perhaps more than we know, does wonderful things. Thank you so much."

She did not expect the strong applause that followed, accompanied by bravas. She was overcome by the thought that her mother should have won and embarrassed that she might have spoken too long. She flung herself in John's arms, weeping, as photographers circled them.

9

"Dianna," said David Niven, "why don't you sit on my lap anymore?"

"Because she's going to sit on mine," said Hope, who took her hand and said something she didn't catch. John waved him away. Hope grinned like a guilty kid, and hurried over to one of the starlets buzzing around backstage.

John Wayne said, "I want a hug."

Shelley said, "I do, too!"

Bill Royce stepped forward. He was smiling at her.

Dianna turned her back on him.

"What's happening?" she asked. All she could think of was her mother sitting there, with empty seats on both sides of her.

"Best director," said John.

"Him?" Dianna gestured to Wayne, at the podium to present the award.

"He just directed his first picture."

"Oh," she said. "How could I forget *The Alamo*?"

Wayne said, "And the winner is William Wyler for *Ben Hur*."

"Yes, sir!" John shouted.

Ben Hur's chariot wheels had run over just about everyone, including George Stevens, who hadn't directed a chariot race or thousands of extras but had created a claustrophobic atmosphere for a wide screen.

Gary Cooper walked past them onto the stage to present the best picture award. At the mike, he said, "I would just like to say that the real winners tonight are the two people who raised that lovely young lady."

"Did he say that?" John asked, through the warm applause. "The bastard. Now I am going to have to be nice to him."

He put his hand out to Royce.

"Good job. You deserved it."

Royce did not immediately lift his arm.

"I am sure your parents are proud," John added.

Slowly, Bill Royce reached out and took John Fletcher's hand.

"Thank you." His voice sounded hoarse. Dianna glared at him and turned back to see the stage.

Royce retreated back into the shadows, looking not at all like he'd just won an Oscar.

Meanwhile, Cooper was saying, "The nominees for Best Picture of 1959 are *Anatomy of a Murder*, Otto Preminger; *Ben Hur*, Sam Zimbalist;

The Diary of Anne Frank, George Stevens; *The Nun's Story*, Henry Blanke, and *Room at the Top*, John and James Wolfe. And the winner is…"

Coop took his time opening the envelope.

"He is a bastard," said John. "And now I've got to be nice to him."

"Daddy."

Cooper opened up the envelope and took out the card. He looked, looked again, and smiled.

"The winner," said Cooper, "is *The Diary of Anne Frank.*"

"What?" Dianna cried, clasping her gloved hands to her open mouth and nearly knocking herself out with her Oscar.

"My God," breathed John.

It was a complete upset. Voters had actually decided not to give *Ben Hur* the ultimate honor.

"Oh, Daddy," said Dianna, through Shelley Winters' squeals of joy.

He gave her a hug and whispered, "This says good things about us."

The applause nearly drowned out the music as George Stevens approached the microphone. He took the statue slowly, cautiously, and stood before the podium for a moment before speaking.

"It is not an accident," he said slowly, "that two of the leading pictures this year had to do with struggles of the Jewish people. For my part, having fought in the war and seen what insane hate can do, I felt this must be shown in ways that people can understand. I had a wonderful ally in Anne Frank, with her young voice pitched against the hoarse shoutings of Hitler. I am deeply grateful to Spyros Skouros, to Otto Frank, to everyone who worked on the picture, and a cast sent from heaven, including a brilliant young actress playing Anne Frank, Dianna Fletcher, daughter of two of our finest actors, who made it her business to show us what we lost in Anne Frank – her energy, her humor, her sensitivity to life. I can only hope that Dianna's generation will do better for peace than we have done. Thank you very much."

Back in the wings, Stevens embraced Dianna, shook hands with John, and gave Shelley a kiss.

"What a surprise," he said to Wyler.

Wyler said, "They got it right. You could win for producer and director, and I could win for the chariot race. Both pictures point to hope."

Stevens took Dianna into his big bearlike arms. "You're the reason," he said. "Don't lose your nerve."

Was that what it was? Her nerve? Did she have to fight all the time to keep her talent like the White Queen in *Through the Looking Glass*, running as hard as she could to stay in the same place?

Bob Hope strode back onto the stage.

"Well, ladies and gentlemen, that about knocks it. It's all over but the sniveling. Before we go out to the press tent to see the winners, I must remind you our program tonight was sponsored by the motion picture industry, distributors of such quality products as Marilyn Monroe, Jayne Mansfield, and Gina Lollabrigida."

After the dignity of what had gone before, that seemed tactless and tasteless.

Hope kept on going. "Tonight you've seen Hollywood bare its heart. That's all we're allowed to show on television… For the winners, there will be a great victory celebration at the Grand Ballroom at the Hilton Hotel. The rest of us will gather in the monoxide room at the Price Waterhouse Garage. You've been a wonderful audience – intelligent, generous, and enthusiastic. Where were you during *Alias Jesse James*? And thank you, Miss Dianna Fletcher for proving Maurice Chevalier right, again, thank heaven for little girls. Goodnight!"

John said, "Just smile."

"Oh, Daddy. He's so old."

Wayne, Cooper, Hope, Niven, and other men she vaguely recognized surrounded her, all exclaiming over her lovely speech and proclaiming her Hollywood's princess.

John took her arm. "See you all later," he said, as he escorted Dianna toward the press tent.

"I'm sorry *Ben Hur* didn't win," she said.

"We won enough. We were both part of great movies."

Inside, the tent seemed all lights. A red jacketed usher directed them onto the stage. A crush of men and women shook pens at them and shouted questions.

"What's it like to beat your mother?" shouted a chorus.

Dianna flinched. In time, she remembered Aunt Dot's press dodge. Pretend to misunderstand the question. She said, "My mother is my favorite actress, and her performance was brilliant. It was an honor to be nominated with such great actresses."

"Are you going to tease Nick?"

"That's my job."

"Are Nick and Sherry serious?"

"Ask them."

"Do you have a boyfriend?"

Good grief. To answer no was depressing and to answer yes would only lead to trouble.

"Not this week," said John.

Dianna gripped her statue, letting her father do the talking. The four acting winners then stood in a row on the stage for a formal picture. Royce's arm stole around her waist. Flashbulbs popped. Dianna pulled away from that arm but kept smiling at the photographers. She posed with Stevens, who kept kissing her cheek.

"Thank you for making my picture glow," he said, and the reporters scribbled it all down.

Someone mentioned *Picnic*.

"We're both working in that right now," said Royce, his smile still engaging. "We're having a wonderful time." He smiled through the wince as Dianna moved away, stepping on his foot as hard as she could.

"I don't see Mom or Nick or Chas," Dianna said, as she and John made their way back to the auditorium, clutching their newly engraved statues in their hands.

"Chas is going home," said John. "The others will be in the car."

During the ride to the Hilton, Anne was quiet, looking out the window, holding John's hand. Dianna didn't know what to say.

At the hotel, Anne kissed Dianna and smiled for the photographers, then walked away.

Pushing through first — Hedda Hopper and her hat.

"What a beautiful speech, Dianna. We are all very proud of you. You and I will have to have a little talk soon."

The band started a waltz, Anne groaned.

"It's the fucking Second Waltz."

The Shostakovich piece was John's favorite, a well-known fact around town.

"Mom, are you okay?" Dianna asked.

"I am not okay in the least," said Anne, smiling. "But you enjoy yourself."

Some concierge or high poobah of the dance floor came to direct John and Dianna to waltz, after which John surrendered Dianna to Bill Royce.

"You're a good dancer," Royce said, after an awkward moment.

She wasn't going to look at him. "Yes."

"You don't dance that well on the set."

She didn't see his smile.

"Not with you," she said, humorlessly. "Hello, Uncle Ed. Please cut in."

Ed Wynn said to Royce, "She may have sat on David Niven's lap, but I slept with her," referring to the fact that their characters had been roommates.

She danced with Robert Wise, who said, "Don't worry. We've got two years to wait. We'll build a great big movie around you."

Two years! In fact, all the producers who came by to praise her (and pinch her and pat her bottom and stare at her chest) said they'd have to look out for something for her. One producer said he'd love to work with her and suggested she join a workshop so he could see her progress. As men fondled and made promises, she wasn't sure if she should call out for her father or if this were just all harmless flattery. Still, she remembered those boys in the locker room.

She couldn't help feeling both flattered that she'd impressed powerful men and nervous about how to behave when they tried to impress her. Was a firm buttock all she needed in an artistic enterprise?

What she did understand was that there wasn't any work for her now. When you're older, they kept saying – and sighing. Come on, girl, grow up. The industry probably considered her award as a one-trick wonder, a gesture toward a fine performance in a movie that deserved honors, a gesture toward the past and not the future. Anne Frank had won the Oscar, but Dianna was still the wrong age. There weren't many parts like Anne Frank around. You couldn't turn Anne Frank into a beach bunny, and the teen movies were all about beaches and bikinis or discovering sex with tragic endings.

The news of her award would fade out soon enough, especially when everyone found out she was going to do a television series.

10

Dianna put the statue on her book case and put a vase in front of it. If only her mother had won.

After a perfunctory "I'm proud of you" in front of reporters, Anne refused to speak of the Oscars or of her daughter's winning one. The press didn't help with the handing down to the next generation jazz and a picture in the *New York Times* calling Dianna Hollywood's Princess.

Dianna said, "You should have won."

Anne said, "Shut up."

After the party, the photographs, the news articles celebrating the father/daughter win, the compliments on "what a beauty she is becoming," the flowers, and the congratulatory phone calls, two things brought Dianna back to reality.

The first thing was that her family was leaving the country.

For years, the family had gone off to work during the day, returning home to discuss and work together by night, a life of purpose and intense creativity. Now, thanks to the studios' need to film on location to seduce more people back into theaters, that life was coming to an end. And the assumption was that shooting on location would be cheaper.

Two mornings after the Oscars, the day of departures, Dianna dressed slowly, not wanting to start it. Lynne came rushing in, saying, "Hurry up! Joanne's made cinnamon rolls."

Cinnamon rolls came with special occasions, but Dianna didn't feel like celebrating. She finished tying a bow around her pony tail, fluffed her skirt and its starchy petticoat, and sat down on her bed to tie her ballet-and-tap-trained feet into saddle shoes. She took one more look at her Oscar, which now felt like a load on her back and glanced at the photograph.

"I'm sorry you weren't there, Nana," she whispered.

All through breakfast, she held back tears.

A few of the grips on the *Picnic* set congratulated her as she came from makeup and headed to her dressing room. She heard cheers. She turned around to see the cast surrounding Bill Royce.

Royce strode toward her, but she pretended not to see him and kept walking.

"I need you in ten minutes," Angelini said to her. "Don't stop to make a speech. We know you can do that." As she opened her dressing room door, she heard him say, "They *had* to vote for her. They wouldn't go for Hepburn's movie, her mother has won way too many, they wouldn't give it to a foreigner, and they weren't going to give it to Doris Day. Who was left? Anne Frank, the chatterbox."

"Now, Joe," said Royce.

"Not all Oscars are equal," said Angelini, with an insistent tone that refused correction. "Yours was well deserved. You beat out *Ben Hur*'s Griffith! But sometimes the choice is the lesser of five evils."

Dianna shut her door. She put on the stupid jeans and the too big flannel shirt. She put on the socks and sneakers and wiped her eyes.

Well, Millie felt everyone was against her, and that was how *she* felt. Enemies all over and her family leaving her. She'd use it. She was an actress, no matter how they would try to devalue her Oscar.

On the set, she grabbed her prop cigarettes.

"Do you have a light?" she asked an electrician.

"Sure, honey," he said, and she practiced puffing away.

She hardly moved in this shot; she would simply rock on her heels and survey the newcomer Hal with admiration and suspicion. She could do the suspicion part.

"This is a take!" yelled the AD. "First team!"

Dianna took her place, stooped, puffed, rocked, and delivered her line to Hal.

"Print that," called Angelini.

"Could we do it again?" she asked. "I don't think I had it."

"It was fine," said Angelini.

"I could do it better."

"Okay," said Royce. "Let's do it."

"There's no time," said Angelini. "Let's set up for you and Madge."

"I just think it would be better," said Dianna.

"I doubt it," said Angelini.

She snapped, "You don't know much."

She walked away.

"Snippy kid," she heard Angelini say.

As the day continued, the pit in her stomach grew. She felt less able to act, the cast's dismissal of her Oscar convincing her that she had not deserved it, Angelini's ignoring her fueling anger and despair, and the sense of aloneness and apartness that hung over her. She paid no attention during her classes, and told the teacher that nothing was wrong.

"You're recovering from the Oscars, of course," said the woman.

Right.

At home, in the middle of the big parlor, her parents were giving instructions to the staff. Chas sat on a trunk reading a comic book. Nick was on the phone saying, "It won't be long. Promise. I'll write you."

He hung up, called someone else, and said the same thing.

Anne put on her wide brimmed hat. "So unsuitable for the plane, but who cares? There you are at last, Dianna."

John hugged her, and there were tears in his eyes. "You can reach Uncle George and Aunt Dot by phone while they are in New York. You have our numbers, George has our numbers, and if you need us, wire, call, and we will call. Use Tony and MaryAnn at the office for anything you need. When you are done with *Picnic*, the staff will move you to Malibu, and they will close this place up." He yelled, "Nick! Time to go!"

Nick smooched into the receiver and hung up.

Anne took Chas's hand. "Let's go, darling. Bring your book."

"I wanted to take my truck with me," he said, as he hugged Dianna. Really tight.

"It'll be safe here," she managed to say. "I'll polish it."

"I'm never going to be Pete again. They killed him."

"You can be someone else." She looked up at Anne, whose face was tense as she regarded her youngest.

"No," Chas said. "Goodbye."

His lost look scared her, but Anne's worried eyes quickly brightened, her face transforming into her bright dancing with Astaire smile.

"Let's go, Chas," Anne said.

Nick gave Dianna a firm and long hug. "You call me if anyone gives you any trouble."

"Sure," she said, her voice catching.

She waved them off down the drive. Her chest hurt as the two cars disappeared, one loaded with luggage, the other loaded with her family. She watched until they disappeared down the canyon road.

She had made this decision to stay. She wished she hadn't.

The house resonated with emptiness, even with the maids dusting about and the chatter in the kitchen. Dianna hurried to her suite, but the echoes of her family and of happy times that would probably not come again followed her.

She sat on her bed, looking at the picture of her grandmother holding her.

Her empty feelings were compounded by her confusion at publicity surrounding the Oscars. Already Twentieth Century Fox, Disney, and *Silver Sierra* were working overdrive at her victory, and yet no one had mentioned any current or upcoming project. So all that was left was television. Her pictures would get smaller, and she'd fade away.

The next day began with an early morning appearance downtown at the May store, arranged by Disney's publicity people for her to sign records. It was supposed to last half an hour. It ended up as a crushing experience as kids on their way to school along with their mothers crowded into the store. So she was late to Desilu. On Friday, cutting the ribbon at a puppy store to publicize *Detective Dog* caused another delay when her car got stuck in traffic. So she was late again. She tried to explain, but Angelini waved her off. He continued to ignore her whenever she said anything. While waiting for set-ups, no one sat down with her. They did sit around Angelini or Royce and laugh their heads off.

After a few days of this, she decided she'd better do something and headed over to the bungalow where Angelini had his office.

She walked right in, ignoring his secretary, and going right up to his desk. He hung up the phone with, "I'll have to call you back. There's a brat in my office."

She wanted to pitch his Golden Globe at him.

"I need to tell you – to explain that it wasn't my fault I've been late."

"I don't care if it was your fault, Santa's fault, or God's fault. You show up on time."

Dianna protested. "I have ideas about Millie, and you don't want to hear. And you don't give me any close-ups."

"I want Millie to be what I'm getting from you. Or trying to get from you. As for close-ups, they take time, and you are stealing that time. We don't need them. The story is Hal and Madge."

"You let everyone else have ideas but me. I know you didn't want me in the cast, but we are stuck with each other."

"I am certainly stuck with you," he said, coming toward her. "You are the one false note in the whole cast."

"If that's so," she retorted, wishing she could hit him, "it's only because you don't give me any good direction."

"Everyone else benefits from collaboration. You don't want to listen. You demonstrate to me and everyone, cast and crew, that you don't care about your work or ours and that you are pretty lousy."

"That's not true!"

"You browbeat poor Stevens into doing what you wanted. I couldn't believe his Oscar speech."

She slammed back. "He had a reason for his ideas, and I had a reason for mine. He respected mine."

"What could he do? Your old man and he go back. You and your family and your mother and your brother who won't do as he's told either."

"What'd he do? Turn you down for a dance?"

Angelini hit her, hard, on her face. She staggered back and grabbed at the wall. She fought back her tears. She looked at the door and at him standing between her and it.

"You little bitch," he said. "And your lying bastard brother. Your whole family is sick. That fake marriage. Those fake goodie smiles. Cavorting with Disney."

She hurried to the door. He caught her arm.

"This is how much Nicky lied," he said, and he pushed her against the wall, pressed his lips on hers and his tongue in her mouth. She kicked at him, finally groining him with her knee, spitting out at him, and running for the door.

"And that's why you're a lousy actress!" he shouted. "You're a cold fish."

She ran out of the bungalow and toward the administration building. Mick stood by the car, but she didn't stop. Once inside the building, she found Dante's office, burst in, and sputtered out her story, this time not holding back her tears.

Dante patted her shoulder. "I'm sure he didn't mean it. He's under lot of pressure."

"You don't believe me."

"Creative people have differences, often seeming to be violent, and you're a pretty girl. Tomorrow, it will be like this never happened. If you were a little older, I'd be tempted myself. Just brush it off." He smoothed his hands around her breasts and said, "You seem older than you look, you know."

She ran out of the office, pushing past some people in the hall, and dove into her car.

"You okay?" asked Mick.

"I'm tired. Sorry I kept you waiting."

The locker room, all over again. What gave them the right? Something did. She loved this business, but the business hated her. No, that couldn't be. She had fans. Her parents were two of the most respected people in Hollywood — in the country.

Telling would just make trouble. She could report it all to Mira, but that would hurt the show, and that would get her a reputation as a troublemaker, if she didn't already have one.

She'd have to finish *Picnic*. She'd have to do as good a job as she could and avoid Angelini as much as possible.

The next day, on time on Stage 9, she roamed the parlor set as the crew adjusted lights. She fingered props, bounced in the chairs, and clumped around as Millie would. When the AD yelled for places, Royce sat next to her on the sofa.

"Big western star, huh?" he asked.

The Hollywood Reporter had broken the news about *Silver Sierra*, calling her "a special guest star," an arrangement Uncle George had made to ease the sting.

"Let's go!" called Angelini.

At the sound of his voice, she tensed up.

Bells rang, buzzers sounded, the AD yelled for quiet, then, "Action."

Royce, as Hal, said, "You folks should've seen Millie this morning. She did a fine jackknife off the high diving board!"

A long pause followed.

Royce said, "What's the matter, kid? Think I'm snowing you under?"

"Cut!" yelled Angelini. "Thanks, Bill, but it doesn't mean much without her line. Miss Fletcher!"

"Can I have a minute?" she asked.

Why couldn't she think of her line?

"No," said Angelini. "Let's get this done."

"Do you need the line?" called Babs, the script girl.

"Cut it out," said Dianna, which was the line.

"So let's try again," said Angelini. "Can you be here, please, Miss Best Actress?"

Buzzers, quiet, clap, action.

Royce spoke his line.

Again Dianna could not think of hers.

"Cut!" called Angelini.

"I'm sorry," said Dianna.

What was wrong with her?

"We have nothing to do especially," said Lucille.

Dianna remembered how Ball went around firing people for the least bit of incompetence.

"Boy trouble, I'll bet," said O'Connell.

"Take it from Alan's line," said Angelini.

"Is something wrong?"

That was Mira's voice, coming from the shadows of the studio. Dianna barely recognized it.

"I'm fine." She took a deep breath. "Okay."

This time she delivered the line. A little flat, but the words were there. She didn't dare ask for another take.

Everyone was mad at her again. Royce wouldn't even look at her.

A "C" on a history test further unnerved her. The teacher proved sympathetic and told her she could try again. Dianna almost confided in her, but that would bring trouble, too.

In the following days, Dianna huddled into her dressing room with her school books. She read the trades, and in them she read that Diane Baker, who had played Margot in *The Diary of Anne Frank* (which, incidentally, was making some more money and had broken even at last) had tested for Maria in *West Side Story*.

Her only respite was lunch. She would find a corner table to munch and study. At the end of the week, Royce leaned against her table.

"Excuse me, ma'am, but no one's using this salad. May I take it?"

"It's my lunch."

"Doing homework?"

"Yes. If you don't mind."

"You're giving me a hint. I can tell. I just wanted to tell you—"

"I don't care. I'm trying to work."

"Just thought I'd be friendly," he said, walking away.

How dare he make her feel guilty? Or make her the butt of his jokes or whatever he was doing? There he went, strolling over to Lucille and Reta and Star, and they just had eyes only for him, laughing when he laughed, and he basked in it, yes, he did.

Thank God for safe, magical Disneyland. There, she and the people were one — all ready to have fun, like old friends who understood her. She could get them clapping and dancing. She could sing, "When You Wish Upon a Star" and help them believe. She could even make Walt Disney cry. During the fireworks, she could point out Tinkerbell in the sky by the Matterhorn. The look on the adults' faces, forget the kids, was worth the work. They believed.

11

Dianna was surprised to find that the first *Silver Sierra* scripts were excellent. Betsy Drury was one no holds barred girl with serious thoughts about serious things. She had compassion. She could fire a gun. She loved horses, rode well, and would even have a romance or two with real men, not boys. The writers, Michael Edwards, L.A. Franklin, and Patrick Wagner understood Betsy amid the dynamics of the men in the Drury family. Mr. Franklin in particular wrote a character who stood up for herself and for others. If only this were a movie! This was not a teenager interested only in dates, dances, clothes, and boys, like MJ's character.

MJ was working on *The Carol Warner Show* in the sound stage across from *Silver Sierra's*, and the two had to pose walking along the studio street and laughing or talking or meeting up with the boys from *My Three Sons*.

MJ told Dianna and *Photoplay*, "I'm playing a typical teenager. I'm either on the phone or worried about which boy is taking me to a dance."

"I chase bad guys and shoot them," said Dianna, who hadn't started acting on the show as yet. It was just a fun line to say.

Her *Silver Sierra* costume fittings, makeup, and hair tests were held at six thirty in the morning at Paramount, meaning she had to get up earlier and stand for hours before heading to *Picnic*, but it was worth it. Swirling in skirts and petticoats, with everyone telling her how beautiful she looked, Dianna could feel Betsy coming to life in her as Millie would not.

It was almost worth that pleasure to arrive late or almost late to the nearby *Picnic* set. She ignored the glares and grumbles of the cast and crew. *Picnic* became an almost incidental occurrence on her schedule, for in some overscheduling blunder, perhaps due to his absence, Uncle George's office worked her as hard as Disney's: A post-Oscar interview with the *Los Angeles Times* for their Sunday edition. An interview about Anne Frank with the *Hollywood Reporter*. A luncheon with the cast of *Silver Sierra* for a *TV Guide* interview – so they hardly got to talk to each other. Then there were the Disney interviews about *Detective Dog*. And the work. A rehearsal of jazz numbers with the Disney pianist on the MGM lot after school. More costume fittings for Betsy. Photo sessions for every national magazine. A book signing at the Scribner store in the morning for her advice book about makeup, clothes, boys, dating, and poise. (She couldn't wait to read it.) On Saturday evening, she sang jazz on the Mark Twain at Disneyland.

"It's too much!" Dianna yelled into the phone.

"It's all been worked out and signed and sealed," said Tony, George's right hand man. "It's to capitalize on your Oscar. Don't worry, we check your call sheets."

"Check Disney's!" she shouted.

She couldn't prepare properly; she had no time to think. But one Friday evening, someone made a mistake. She had nothing to do.

She put on her shorts, got on her bike, and pedaled around Beverly Hills. On North Bedford, Jim Barry was hosing down a red Thunderbird. Jim was the son of Howard Barry, a vice president at Paramount, and he was, she guessed, a senior in high school. She'd known him in elementary school, when she was still going to such places. Even then he had been gorgeous and fair haired, as he was now, only now, he was wearing shorts and no shirt.

"Wow," she called.

He looked her way, shut off the hose, and came over.

His first glance went to her legs.

"Congratulations on the Oscar. You were great."

"Thanks. That's quite a car."

"Dad's graduation present. Of course, I haven't graduated yet. What are you up to now? New movies?"

"I'm in a TV movie of *Picnic*."

"Oh, yeah. With Lucille Ball. And that Royce whatshisname. Didn't I hear you were going to be on a television series? Dad says NBC's getting a whole publicity campaign on it. I was surprised. You just won an Oscar."

She shrugged off his implication. "It could be fun. It's going to be in color. I have gorgeous costumes. I'll ride horses."

"Maybe you're right." He twirled his hose around. "Dad says NBC is excited to get you, and it's not a cheap project. It's quality all the way."

He was looking at her legs again. So she looked at his.

He hung onto her handlebars. "Next Saturday, I'm having people over to the beach house. Burgers and all that, volleyball. We have a pool, too. Can you come?"

This was sudden. Although she suspected it was "bring a star to your party."

"Saturday?" Dianna fought to remember. "I have an appearance in the morning, and later in the day, I'm in the Disney parade and singing at Tomorrowland."

Boy, did that sound stupid. But Jim didn't laugh. He just grinned, a wide, broad, Beverly Hills kid grin.

"It starts at two. It'll go on forever. Come for a little while."

She had to do something normal.

"Okay."

The promise of a party helped her suffer through the week. She puzzled over which bathing suit, which colorful robe, which sandals, which shorts to wear. She even had Lynne wax her legs for the first time. She had to take two aspirins after, but her legs looked great.

Saturday came and after a dull morning in a record store of "Thank you, I hope you enjoy it" to several hundred girls who desperately loved her, she arrived early.

Howard Barry, a big, bluff man with salt and pepper hair, was prepping the fire for the barbecue. "How's it going, honey? You're pretty busy, huh?"

"Awfully."

"*Picnic*'s a weird play," he said. "Good cast. Don't know if people will last two hours for it. *Silver Sierra* will be good. Already, we've had several meetings about promoting it. You'll be busy."

"It keeps me out of school."

"The studio has to follow the laws."

"Two more years."

"Not necessarily."

Jim appeared, with a volleyball and a net.

"You're early!"

"I didn't want to miss any fun since I have to leave early."

"Great," said Jim, and he hustled down the beach after casting an admiring glance at her shining legs.

"What do you mean, not necessarily?" she asked Mr. Barry.

He said, "What are your grades? I heard you were weak in math and history."

"That's old news. I have A's and B's, A's in history and B-plus in math. You can look it up."

Mr. Barry seemed surprised. "If that's true, you could take a test to get out of the last two years and get legal eighteen status. You wouldn't have to go to school anymore."

"Legal eighteen?"

"You can get an equivalent degree, and the labor board respects that. Legal eighteen means you can work eight hours, only eight hours, until you're eighteen. The studio will be thrilled."

"Do you mean," Dianna asked, stupefied, "that I could get out of high school now?"

Why hadn't Uncle George told her about this?

Because keeping her in school kept her in her perky teen roles that made money, that's why. Did her parents approve that?

"It's April so it's probably too late. The test is given in June and January, and your teacher at the studio would have to recommend you. This won't work if you want to go to college."

"I want to act."

She was going to take those tests this year. She could get better parts if she were legal eighteen.

"Great," he said. "Talk to your teacher. I make calls on my end. It would sure help the show." He added, "Times are changing in the business. There's going to be a lot more freedom. You kids are going to benefit."

She plunged into the fun, knowing there was a way out of her trap and maybe even a way into something as good as or better than *West Side Story*. She took part wholeheartedly in the diving contests, relay races with the girls standing on boys' shoulders, volleyball, grilling burgers, and racing into the surf. Mr. Howard hired a photographer, and everyone would get an album of the party, so they posed as many silly ways as they could. It was all so normal. No one tried to get on her good side. Everyone just had fun. And Jim stuck with her rather than floating off to other girls. He even kissed her while they waited for Reggie to pick her up.

She could imagine them running the studio in twenty years.

12

B ack at *Picnic*, however, her confidence left her. She grew more unsure and more anxious that her talent was all used up. Bill Royce went back to ignoring her, and although she resented him, she still admired his work. He brought an anger, a wild humor, and a sheer desperation to Hal. This was what actors did and she couldn't. Consequently, she avoided him; his mere presence reminded her of her inadequacy. She dreaded the scenes she had with him that were coming up.

On the other hand, she continued to enjoy her costume fittings and tests for *Silver Sierra* – the crew was amiable, hardworking, and talented. She hoped she wouldn't let them down, but everything about the scripts excited her. Naturally, she lingered with them, then had to race to a golf cart, zoom it to the other side of the Desilu lot, and run into the awful world of *Picnic*. Always late.

"Dianna's here!" the AD would yell.

The cry echoed over the catwalks and the walls.

"Dianna's here!"

"Dianna's here!"

"Dianna's here!"

"I'm sorry," she gasped. "I was needed at Paramount."

Angelini shouted, "You are needed here! This is your first responsibility!"

Afraid he would hit her again, she hurried to her dressing room, followed closely by the wardrobe mistress and the makeup entourage.

Once she made it to the set, Bill Royce gave her a deliberate, long, deadly look. She understood. It was his big scene, and she had held it up. She should apologize to him, but she couldn't. He'd just insult her.

"Deep breaths everyone," Angelini said. He circled Bill and Lucille, spoke some quiet words to them, backed a few inches to the camera, then called for action.

Dianna sat and sulked for Millie. Royce was chilling in his desperation and revulsion. Lucille Ball, too, was powerful in her own desperation, grabbing at Bill and tearing his clothes. At the end of one take, everyone applauded them. Dianna tried to join in, but she was envious. Millie. Stay Millie. She was supposed to be mad at Hal and Madge.

Finally, her line came. She clutched he stomach and moaned, "I'm sick!" Thank God she delivered that brilliant line on cue.

Angelini said, "All right, everyone. That's all the time we've got for this shot because Dianna has to go to school. Try to come in on time next time?"

"I said I was sorry," said Dianna.

Royce looked at her intently, then walked away. As if she wasn't worth talking to.

Lucille Ball said, "I should kick you off the lot."

"Go right ahead," said Dianna.

The cameraman, standing and stretching, said, "Don't mind them, honey. You look great in my camera. I'll wait forever."

Was he being sarcastic?

She signed records on Friday night and worked at Disneyland all of Saturday. She slept all day on Sunday.

On Monday, she had to rehearse one of her songs to include in her Disney act at Tomorrowland. Of course, the music department was at the other side of the lot from Stage 9.

"It's the late Miss Fletcher!" the AD called when she arrived back, gasping.

Royce descended on her as did the hordes from hair and makeup.

"What the hell are you doing that is so damned important?"

He was livid, righteously so, but how dare they all judge her? Couldn't they figure out it wasn't her own doing?

"Nothing you'd understand."

"I can't work like this," Royce protested to Angelini. "I'm not a faucet that can turn on and off just when she decides to show up."

Angelini said, "I'll have to hire someone to drag her over here by the hair."

Jim called every evening. She would stay on the phone with him a little too late. He was cheerful and positive and full of news about kids in his class she didn't know and didn't mind that she didn't. There was a world out there.

On Saturday, the two of them went to see *The Unforgiven*. Dianna couldn't make heads or tails out of it. Audrey Hepburn was as believable here as she'd been in *War and Peace*. Which meant not much.

"She can't act," Jim agreed, when they settled in at the Brown Derby for grapefruit cake. "She's incredibly photogenic and lovely to work with. It's a good thing your mom beat her out for *The Nun's Story*. There wouldn't have been any heat in that thing."

"She's so waiflike," said Dianna, "and Mom's a *woman*, and yet Mom finds Hepburn haunting her at every turn. Hepburn's first on the list for *Breakfast at Tiff's*. Why? She couldn't possibly do it unless they made it into a fashion show, like *Funny Face*."

"Box office," said Jim.

That started a quarrel. "My mother is one of the top ten box office stars," she hurled at him.

"She's been around for years," said Jim.

"Do women have a shelf life?"

"Most do."

She would have slugged him, but a photographer appeared. They smiled brightly.

They both sulked on the ride home, but she let him kiss her. He made a nervous joke, so she forgave him.

On Monday, as soon as she walked out of her dressing room, the crew applauded and whistled.

Angelini called out, "If it isn't the star of *Picnic*."

"What?" she asked.

Someone from up on the catwalk tossed a magazine at her feet. *Life*. There she was, in the center, a full-page picture of her climbing out of Jim's pool. Across the spread were more pictures from Jim's pool party, and all those pictures featured DIANNA FLETCHER in her bathing suit. More pictures - on the beach, by the pool, playing with a beach ball. Dianna picked it up and read,

> We offer evidence that Miss Fletcher is growing up quite nicely, with some pictures of her enjoying a day off with the gang including Jim Barry (son of Paramount's senior vice president of production, Howard Barry), who threw a party for his friends. Dianna and Jim have been pals since kindergarten. Lucky boy. Just look at her now - a pretty girl having a grand time with friends and obviously a delight to be with and to behold.

There were more pictures, all focused on her, in poses emphasizing her legs or breasts, even delving down into her suit. At first, Dianna was appalled. They were good pictures, she had to admit, but in black and white, the suit looked almost like her skin. If that's what excited the masses...But looking up at the grinning crew, she blushed.

"Hon, you should be flattered," one of them called down to her. "Be proud of your body!"

"Are you proud of yours?" she called back.

That caused some hilarity on the catwalk.

Lucille Ball grabbed the magazine from her and read, "Miss Fletcher is currently *starring* in a television version of *Picnic* for NBC." She shook the magazine at Dianna. "And that's all you say about *Picnic*. Thank you very much."

"I didn't say anything," Dianna protested. "There was a guy taking pictures."

She was the cover, too – perched on the diving board with Jim, swinging her legs, drinking a Coke.

"Nice publicity for you, thanks," said Royce.

"Like I go around with your name just rolling off my tongue," she retorted.
She called Uncle George's office at lunchtime.

"Everyone wants you, baby!" Tony yelled into her ear. "*Life* is doing another printing because of you! The front cover was going to be that big trampoline in Palm Springs, but now it's you, baby! Great publicity!"

"Uncle George wouldn't like it."

"I think we need to go in this direction. Just to show people you're a real babe."

After school, she called Jim.

"I didn't know. Honest! Dad said it'll knock the socks off of everyone who thinks you are still a little girl. It's for *Silver Sierra*. You're supposed to be older in that. Eighteen, I think."

All right then. It was fiction, made up stuff, the usual. She should shrug it off, except she couldn't quite.

Jim asked her to go to the prom at Beverly Hills High. She decided to go.

It was a mistake. As soon as they entered the Cocoanut Grove, where it was held, she was surrounded by autograph seekers while Jim danced with other girls all the night long. Dianna never got to dance with anyone. Toward ten, she went in search of Jim and a dance. She found him smoking in the parking lot with several other boys.

"You brought Dianna Fletcher."

"Yeah," Jim said.

"You score with her?"

"What do you think?" And Jim laughed.

"She gave it?"

"To me," said Jim.

Dianna walked out and Jim grinned. "Hi, Dianna!"

The boys called, "Hi, Dianna!"

She thought of the locker room and almost turned and ran. But she didn't. She marched up to Jim and slapped his face. He grinned and shrugged and said, "Ah, Di, come on."

"Come on, Di," the boys all said.

She hurried back into the gym. She found a woman, the math teacher, by the punch bowl.

"I need to go home. Could you call me a cab?"

The teacher said, "Oh, let me take you home," and she did, prattling on about Dianna's movies and how much she loved each one.

"It must be beautiful in there," she said, as Dianna got out of the car.

"It's gorgeous," said Dianna. "You can't imagine. Ever." And she slammed the door.

She couldn't help crying that night. The prom. Something normal all kids did. Jim called several times, but she refused to talk to him.

The next week went slowly and miserably, the cast not even bothering to talk to her. On Friday, she had to do a difficult scene with Royce, where Inge's added dialogue meandered almost incomprehensibly. Although she had given up asking Angelini anything, this time, she had to. They ran it once, and she asked. Again, he was no help.

"Follow Bill. Just say the lines."

"But doesn't there have to be some through line somewhere?"

"It was fine," said Royce.

"I think so, too," said Angelini. "We have to stop. It's almost time for the Alert. We'll finish on Monday."

"It doesn't feel right," said Dianna.

"I'm not surprised," Royce said, walking away.

Why didn't he want to make their scene better? He spent time working on scenes with everyone else in the cast but her.

At two o'clock, sirens sounded over Los Angeles and in cities around the country. People stopped what they were doing, cursed the Russians for encroaching on free enterprise, and flocked to the nearest bomb shelter while radio and television broadcasting ceased.

Down in the shelter, Dianna simmered, half wishing a bomb would land. After it was over, she emerged into the twilight and found her waiting car. On the way home, she heard on the news that a U-2 spy plane had been shot down inside Soviet territory.

So here came the war. So much for her career. All those years of work. All those years of her mother working, her father in the war, the slog across the country by Nana, her own incompetence. Boom. It would be gone in a minute.

Why didn't she have her grandmother's spirit, her stamina, her perseverance, never stopping to doubt and going on with the damn dream anyway?

Dianna felt that she was getting lost, getting cowardly. She needed to get her feet back on the ground.

She needed her grandmother's nerve.

The Ride

13

On previous Mother's Days, the kids would burst into Anne's suite with breakfast for their parents. While Anne ate and John nibbled, Nick, Dianna, and Chas would perform a mock version of Anne's most recent movie. Last year, they'd performed *I Want to Eat!*, a parody of *I Want to Live!*. After breakfast, they would engage in a more solemn journey, going to the cemetery to pay homage to Anne's mother, and then head to Chasen's for several helpings of chili and banana shortcake, incongruous favorites of Anne's.

This Mother's Day was different. Lynne arranged for Dianna to send flowers to Anne in Greece, and Dianna wrote a few words and signed her name.

Dianna felt she should visit Nana's memorial, as they'd always done. Honor to Nana. Maybe it would inspire her.

But how was she to get to the cemetery? She didn't want either chauffeur to take her; she couldn't tolerate the idea of them standing around. They weren't family. Her father had always driven them. She felt shy of her decision, too. She'd do it by herself. But how to get there? She couldn't drive; she'd been too busy to learn.

Didn't Los Angeles have a department of transportation? She smuggled the phone book up from the secretary's desk to her room and sat cross-legged on her bed, trying to untangle the weird labyrinth of colored lines indicating the city's bus routes.

Finding Glendale and the cemetery, she traced a line back to Beverly Hills. The lines kept crossing, but after some time, she figured out which bus stopped on Sunset Boulevard near North Roxbury. She even figured that she would have to change buses on Hollywood Boulevard and Highland.

How hard could it be? People traveled on buses every day.

She walked down to North Roxbury and Sunset Boulevard and found the bus stop. She found information posted at the stop, but she didn't understand it, and it didn't say how much the fare was.

It was warm, a perfect blue sky, not yet noon. The palm trees provided shade along with some fig trees. She sat down to wait and adjusted her sunglasses and scarf.

Hearing a bus, she looked up. It was a double decker tourist bus.

The guide's voice came over the loudspeaker.

"We're about to go down North Roxbury Drive. I'll point out Jack Benny's house. Next door is Lucille Ball's house, a troubled house now. That

Tudor house is Jimmy Stewart's. The road next to his property leads up the canyon to the home of the Fletcher family. You saw Dianna and John win Oscars this year."

A woman's voice yelled, "Can we go up there?"

"Sorry," said the guide. "But you can see the top of the house over the trees."

A bee floated around Dianna's nose. She waved it away. It landed on her purse, and she jumped up to shake it off.

Her sunglasses dropped to the sidewalk with a clatter.

A girl yelled, "That's Dianna Fletcher *right there*!"

"Oh, my God, it is her!"

"It is! It is!"

"Hi, Dianna!"

"Stop the bus!"

"Dianna! Dianna!"

"Open the door!"

"Let's talk to her!"

Some kids were crowding around the driver.

A few hopped off at the open rear entrance. And someone must have grabbed the lever that opened the doors.

"Stay on the bus!" yelled the driver.

People piled out of the second level. Dianna panicked as they ran toward her but reverted to her usual behavior for fans, smiling and waving. With terror added.

A thin woman with a very pinched look yelled, "It's her!" She ran up to Dianna and said, "Did you change your hair?"

She actually pulled Dianna's scarf off.

Dianna yanked it back.

"Excuse me." She'd been schooled never to be rude to fans, but fans had never come up and pulled anything off her.

"It's her!" the woman yelled. She rustled into her purse and produced an autograph book. "You are so funny in *Detective Dog*. Sign this! And say where we are! I can't believe this! I'd love to get a picture of you with me! Can someone take our picture?"

Weren't there enough pictures?

As women and girls surrounded her, pressing in, Dianna thought of Orpheus and the furies who tore the singer to pieces for whatever reason. She tried to push away.

"Get back on the bus!" the driver yelled.

Dianna tried to keep smiling and waving as she struggled away.

"Why are you hiding your beautiful hair?" the very pinched face woman screeched.

"This is my daughter!" shouted a woman, dragging a toddler behind her. "I named her after you! Somebody take our picture!"

"Are you going to marry Jim Barry?"

Several autograph books pummeled Dianna's bosom as the people tripped and pushed toward her. She could see a real bus coming, but just then she realized she was on the wrong side of the street. She needed a bus going the other way, and there it was, coming fast. She struggled away from the mob.

"Please sign my book! Please!" a little girl cried.

There must have been more than twenty people now, all shouting, "Dianna, we love you!" Questions were fired at her, the words all jumbled drowning out the bus driver who had pulled the bus to the curb and was yelling at the fans as more people hurried off the bus.

They would kill her.

"I have to go, bye!" she called, smiling as best she could and pushing her way out of the crowd.

Oh, but they followed.

She remembered the scene in *Suddenly, Last Summer*, when the boys chased Sebastian Venable, caught him, killed him, and ate him. She walked faster, pushing through the people who relentlessly surrounded her as they pleaded for her autograph. The driver was still yelling.

"Sign my book, please!" cried the little girl.

"I can't believe it's her! Aren't we lucky? Why is she walking away? Dianna, come back! Don't be rude! Sign our books!"

"Hey! You wouldn't be a star if it wasn't for us!"

She despised that line.

She turned around, ready to finally say it, "Is your life so uninteresting that you have to hound me?"

A snappy red car, with jazzy chrome and rocket fins, windows down, pulled up to the curb. The driver, whom she couldn't see thanks to the mob, leaned over and opened the door on the curb side.

"Dianna! Let's get going!"

People turned to look, and Dianna grabbed the opportunity to push out of the mob to the car.

The driver was Bill Royce.

"Sorry, folks, we have work to do!" Royce called.

Beggars, Dianna thought, cannot be choosers.

She hopped into the car and slammed the door shut. At least no one followed her in.

Bill waved to the people, all gaping at them as he hit the gas pedal.

Dianna fell back. As she put her scarf, bag, and glasses down on the seat, her hands trembled.

"Who's he?" someone yelled.

"He's too old for you, Dianna!" someone else screamed.

Now that it was over, she realized she'd really been scared. Royce glanced at her, and at her knees, which her leap had exposed. She straightened and fluffed her skirt.

Royce eased up on the gas pedal.

"That was some mob. Are you okay?"

She didn't want to talk to him or look at him.

"Where can I drop you off?"

Okay, she had to talk now.

"The next bus stop." She pointed in the other direction. "That way. I was on the wrong side of the street. Just drop me off here and I'll walk back."

"I'll turn," he said. "But I'm not sure how long it will take that poor driver to herd all those cats back on the bus."

She might have giggled or even smiled, but she would not laugh at any joke of Mr. Royce's.

His car smelled new. He drove with one hand on the wheel and one elbow out the window. She planted her left hand firmly on the seat next to her, a forbidding border between them.

"The bus? Why?"

This was her day and her time. He did not belong in it.

"Don't you have a chauffeur?"

"He's off," she lied.

He was wearing a blue shirt and brown trousers, and a denim jacket lay over the seat back between them. He was always wearing blue, no doubt because it matched his eyes. His light brown hair trembled in the breeze as the car sped along, just at the speed limit.

"I'll drop you off," he said.

"You're going the wrong way."

He laughed. "Women are always telling me that."

"I have to go *that* way." She pointed back.

"Sure thing." He made a wild U-turn at the break in the road's divider. She grabbed her seat. He sped right past the tourist bus, the people still mobbed on the sidewalk. And past the bus stop.

"If you don't let me off, I'm going to yell for a policeman, and then you'll go to jail for kidnapping."

"Can't you be nice? It's a gorgeous day, I have a new car, and a pretty girl sitting next to me. Where can I take you?"

"Just pull *over*."

"Ah, you're going to a lover's rendezvous!"

They had passed two bus stops and nothing but green lights. He was taunting her, and she wanted to get out.

"Please stop."

"You'll be miserable on the bus. My new car is much nicer. Where to, Dianna?"

"I don't call you Bill."

"Not yet," he said, his voice cutting. "Where am I taking you, Miss Fletcher?"

She wiped her eyes. Hands grabbing at her. Reaching out, insisting that she was their property. Okay, the bus ride would be miserable.

Nana had probably had to make do with unpleasant people to get where she wanted to go. Why not use him? Even if he did make a joke of it later.

"Glendale," she muttered.

"That is a bit far."

"So if you'll just let me off."

"No, I'll take you. Ease up, babe."

"Don't call me that."

"You are fussy."

He turned onto Hollywood Boulevard.

"I'm going to Forest Lawn," she said. "You don't want to go there. You were going somewhere else."

"Just to get these back to the UCLA library." He gestured toward a few books in the back seat. "I can do that anytime. You're lucky I happened along, Miss Fletcher."

"That's one opinion, Mr. Royce." She glanced at the back seat and saw a couple of thick books. The title of the one on top read, *Challenges to the First Amendment*.

Pretty heavy stuff for a lightweight leading man type. Maybe he put them in his car to impress his girlfriends.

She looked out her window, determined to ignore him.

He drove quietly for a while, then he turned the radio on. And wouldn't you know, there she was, singing "Davey, Go Away."

"Must we listen to that?" she asked.

He twisted the dial. "Why do you sing that stuff? How about some good jazz?"

She almost said she sang jazz, but she was not interested in impressing him. As he dialed through the stations, she said, "That's the Italian Symphony."

He stopped the dial. "You know Mendelssohn?"

"I've *sung* Mendelssohn," she said and was instantly sorry she had.

"Must have missed that."

"Probably. It was in a church."

She put her elbow on the side of the car and gazed at palm trees, sky, and houses. Everything looked so calm and Sunday quiet. They passed a few movie theaters – *Ben Hur* with a long line around the block, *The Nun's Story* with a long line around the block, *Suburban Rebel* with a line stretching two blocks, *Detective Dog* with a long line around the block, *Pigskin Pete* with a line going down the whole boulevard, and *The Diary of Anne Frank* with a few people walking up to get tickets. At least people were going in.

When she heard him punch in the lighter, she almost protested his smoking, but why say anything? All the windows were open, and it was his car.

When the Mendelssohn piece ended, he said, "I've never been to Forest Lawn. Are there signs?"

"I guess. Dad always drives."

"A weekly family outing?"

Damn him.

There was, in fact, a sign, next to a big billboard advertising *Detective Dog*, and there she was, three times human size, hugging the stupid canine.

"Look at that," Royce said. "Is it a romance?"

"He's my dog."

"Doesn't he turn into a boy?"

"That was the other movie. This one tracks down Russian spies."

"I see."

She really should slug him.

Royce turned into the wide drive. Dianna leaned over and called, "Hi, Mr. Floyd!"

The portly man beamed. "Hello, Dianna. Come to see your grandma? Where's the tribe?"

"They're all in Europe. It's just me today." She deliberately did not mention Bill Royce.

"Okay," said Floyd. "It's Sunday and Mother's Day, so there are a lot of people around and lots of tourists. I'll get someone to cordon off the area and keep people away."

"Thank you!" She liked how he separated the people from the tourists.

"I wish I'd known you were coming. Your dad usually calls. I would have gotten more guards. We can't hold 'em back too long, but we'll do our best."

"Is the flower shop open?"

"Sure, but send your driver in. Lots of people and lots of tourists."

"Thank you! Okay," she ordered Royce. "Drive inside."

Royce kept his face expressionless at her curt direction.

"There's the shop."

He found a parking space not quite near the store.

"Thank you," she said. "You can go on now. I'll get a taxi back."

"No," he said. "I'll go in. They won't know me. So far, I've been called Who's That and Your Driver. Tell me what you want to get."

He was right, damn him. "Okay," she said, except now he was intruding too much on her private event. "A dozen yellow marigolds, and I'll need a sprinkler thing for the water and a trowel." She took her purse. "I'll give you some money."

He opened the door and got out. "No, thank you." He looked and sounded irritated.

Proud bastard.

Dianna dug up the high school tests she'd jammed into her bag to read on the bus. They would hide her face.

An essay question to compare Emily Dickinson with Wordsworth was a piece of cake. She had started to review the math questions when Royce leaned in and handed her a box of brilliant, fresh marigolds.

"They're lovely! Thank you!" she cried, startled at her delight.

He peered at the pamphlet she had put on the seat.

"Math test?"

"Yes," she said, closing up like a door on a spring.

"Where now, Miss Fletcher?" he asked, pulling out of the lot.

"By the Wee Kirk, that way."

She couldn't walk by herself with all this stuff.

He drove slowly down the road to the little Scottish church.

"I thought all your people were at Westminster Abbey." When she didn't answer he looked over at her. She was looking down at the marigolds.

"It's my mother's mother."

"Oh, the wrong side of the family."

Now she really wanted to slug him.

He got out, went over to her side. She had hoped to avoid his helping her out, but she needed help with the flowers and tools. *Nana, he's not my friend, really.* He followed her down a small path to a grove of pines, surrounded by a metal barricade with a security guard standing nearby. She stopped at a gold and silver plaque on the ground that read,

Alice Leigh Marrs, Loving and Determined Mother

April 18, 1900-November 2, 1947

She put the box down on the bench next to the plaque and handed the sprinkler to Royce. "Get some water."

She took the trowel and got down on the ground to dig up the aging marigolds.

"She wasn't that old," Royce said, when he returned.

She took the can, sprinkled the water over the flowers, and didn't answer.

"Was she sick?"

She emptied the canister and got up – Royce leaned down to help her, which she did not appreciate.

She sat down on the bench.

He sat next to her. Well, there wasn't any place else, but why couldn't he respect her privacy and go wander around looking for movie stars' graves?

"No," she said, finally answering his question. "She was hit by a car outside her dance studio."

"Dance studio?"

"Alice Marrs was a great dance teacher. She had her own studio, and she taught a lot of the dancers in the movies. We come here several times a year. Today, it's just me."

"You were pretty young when she died."

Dianna wanted her family. Anne always retold the story when they visited the grave. She should do the same, no matter what he thought. A tribute to Nana.

"She was in vaudeville. Her husband died, so she took Mom, who was just a toddler, and went from Chicago to California. She'd run out of money in a town and she'd teach dance or try to start a dance studio. It took her years. Mom was twelve when they finally got here. The line is that Mom was discovered at MGM, but Nana taught her, pushed her, made her great. They read plays every night they were traveling. That was Mom's education. Theater in her ears."

"Quite a story. Quite a woman."

That was nice of him to say, but she didn't want to think he was nice. She didn't want him here at all.

Behind them, a woman shouted, "There she is!"

Dianna moaned. "There they are."

She stood up and looked directly at the dozens of people holding cameras and autograph books hung over a metal barricade.

"Whose grave is that?" a woman called out.

"Who's that man with her?" another shouted.

"What the hell," said Royce. "You'd think they'd leave you alone out here."

"They can't have lives of their own. They might as well be dead. This is their natural habitat."

Despite the guard and the barricade, it was easy to see that the people would be pushing forward any minute. Royce grabbed her hand and ran with her to the car, opened her door fast, then zipped around to get in just as the people were starting to crowd around them. He started the motor.

"Should I run over them?"

"Bad publicity."

"Right."

He pulled slowly out of the lot, for the people were running in front of the car and along the side, waving autograph books. Dianna just smiled and waved at them, then she turned away as Royce pulled away fast.

"Sorry," he said.

"What can you do." She was thinking of how strong his hand had felt. Silly. Of course his hand felt strong. Don't make a stupid thing out of it.

They drove through the gate, Floyd waving them off.

"I left the box there, oh well, so what." She leaned back and closed her eyes. "I hope they don't trample my flowers."

"That's quite a place, but the screaming tourists are more ghoulish than the graves."

"It can be a lovely place. It's not always so bad. I should have called ahead. When we all go, there's a lot more preparation. People aren't always so awful, but this was a bad lot today. Isn't making movies enough for them?"

He turned on the radio. Beethoven's *Fidelio*.

When that station started sputtering. Royce fiddled with the knob. He found a clear station playing the theme from *The Apartment*. That movie hadn't been released yet, but Dianna had already heard this arrangement by Ferrante and Teicher several times. She listened to its grandiose choir and too grand piano spanning arpeggios and looked out at the polite lawns and greenery.

Her trip was a failure. She hadn't made it out to the cemetery by herself. The tourists had driven her out. What a coward she was, and here was Bill Royce, reminding her of her failings and tormenting her with his politeness and his presence.

The music reached a tremendous peak of noise and arpeggios and choir. It gave her some bravado to ask a hard question.

"Why do you hate me?"

He glanced at her, then looked back at the road to stop for a red light.

"Where did you get that idea?"

"Don't give me that. You make fun of me, you're mean to me, you ignore me, you insult me. And not just on *Picnic*. You meet me for the first time – for the first time! - and you tell me out of the clear blue sky that my family and Mr. Disney paid for my nomination. No one else has even hinted that. Without knowing me, you hated me. You insulted me and were cold to my father, who happens to think you're a good actor. I want to know why you don't like him and go out of your way to insult me."

He was slowing the car. The car behind them honked several times.

He didn't look so confident now. Good.

The music, a Mantovani romance, provided interesting irony.

Finally, Royce said, "You remembered that?"

"Of course I did. You said it right in front of a bunch of people. And then it seemed that you wanted to hit my father when you told Charlton Heston you'd go with him about the sit-ins. You looked so mad – but you'd just *met* him. Are you one of those people who gets mad at us because my parents are famous stars with some power and that I don't deserve any award because I didn't suffer and struggle for all those years the way you did, you poor thing?"

"I did struggle all those years. Anyway, why would you pay attention to me? You're Dianna Fletcher. A star since she was seven."

"You didn't know me, and you said that awful thing with all those people around. Why?"

The next thing she knew, they were turning into an empty drive-in parking lot advertising *The Blob* starring Steven McQueen.

"Why are you going here? It's not open yet."

He didn't answer.

She put her hand on the door handle, ready to jump out as soon as the car stopped.

14

"Why are you pulling in here?" What was he going to do? She remembered her fight with Angelini. If she would scream, would anyone hear her?

"Because I can't drive and apologize at the same time."

"Don't give me that. You meant what you said." She would fight to the finish.

He turned off the ignition. "It was a stupid thing to say. Why did you let it stick with you?"

All that hurt he'd caused, and all he could say was that? She tried not to slug him. Being somewhat nice might get them back on the road.

"You're a good actor. When a good actor says something like that to you, it sticks."

He smiled. "That's the hardest compliment I've ever had."

"Let's just go, please. I don't want to be in a car with you."

He turned toward her, one knee up on the seat, his eyes down. "Just a minute, please. I'm sorry I said that. And to answer your question, I don't hate you, but it's frustrating to work with you. Hal is a very important part for me. It could lead to a lot of things."

"Okay! I'm sorry! Let's go!"

He ignored her. "I've been in this business almost ten years, and up until lately, I hadn't had a break. Even if *Picnic* is television, it's going to be big news. You don't seem to appreciate how important this work is to everyone else. Coming in late, not knowing your lines, not being prepared. It ruins things for the rest of us. I expected better of you."

Not knowing her lines? She'd just frozen up a few times.

"The whole cast feels that way."

"Some apology that is! For your information, I am sixteen."

"That's old enough to tell time."

"But not old enough to sign my contracts. Other people make decisions for me. I get in a car. I get driven someplace, a public appearance, a fitting, wherever because if I don't, it's a breach of some agreement. I still have to go to school for three hours every day. I do know my lines, I just freeze up – for a lot of reasons and with all the negativity around me and Angelini yelling at me all the time –"

This was sounding pathetic.

"I have these obligations. Performing at Disneyland is in my contract.

Recording and dancing and rehearsing and school are all set in stone. I jump from here to there."

Oh, so pathetic.

"I can't believe you can't control that," he said. "Even so, you haven't been up to par, and I guess all that is partly why, but you're still a pain to work with."

She half agreed with him. Still, it hurt. "You don't like me. You don't like my father – whom you never met until after you didn't like him."

"It's nothing to do with you."

"He's *my father*. You hate my father, so you insult me."

"Let's keep this about you."

"But you insulted me because you don't like him. He didn't know you. If he killed your father or something, that would be a reason to hate him."

He threw up his hands in a violent gesture. She drew back, reaching behind her to open the door.

"Sure, most of us think you're a little princess. At age six, you slide into home base in front of Darryl Zanuck, and the next thing you know, you're starring with your father in one of the year's biggest movies. It galls some people who've worked at pounding the pavements every day of their lives."

"That will be the day when I get everything I want. I can't even get to Forest Lawn the way I want."

"You know what I mean."

"You would have been a lousy seven-year-old tomboy."

He took a deep breath. "Yeah. Anyway," he said, his voice calmer, "I had no right to say what I did because I hadn't seen *Anne Frank* yet. Sandi, my girlfriend, insisted I should see the movie before I voted. I didn't. I voted for Simone Signoret."

"Oh, for heaven's sake. I don't care. I want to go home."

"Not until I go through a humiliating ritual of penance and tell you that George Bennett and Walt Disney didn't need to pay for you. And of course, they didn't. I just said that to hurt you – your father's daughter, the star of *Larksong*."

What did *Larksong* have to do with anything?

Then he said, his pure blue eyes looking straight at her, "Dianna Fletcher, you deserved that Oscar."

Was he mocking her?

"I was floored. Just before the Oscars, I went to see *Diary*. There you were, Anne Frank, full of piss and vinegar when everyone else is sitting around waiting for the Nazis. You had emotions flying across your face, and every one of them meant something. You had a zillion things going on at once, and you knew what you were doing with every one of them. I was so flabbergasted, I stayed to see it again to see if I could figure out how you did it."

He saw it twice? He really meant what he said because obviously, it was painful for him to tell her.

"Everything about Anne was alive and real. I know you fought to play her that way and that got you a reputation for being difficult, which I confess I believed. And what do you know, that was the best subtextual acting I have ever seen. How did you do it?

"The best what?"

He smiled. "How do you like that? Not one acting lesson in your life. I mean finding what's beneath the words."

"You do that," she said, out of a feeling of obligation that she should return some compliment. "I saw *The Philadelphian*, and that's what you were doing."

"Thank you," he said. "But I've never seen it done better than you in *Anne Frank*, and you were on the screen almost all the time. How did you do that?"

How had she done that? She tried to remember.

"I read her diary a zillion times. I wanted to show the difference between the Anne of the diary and the Anne the people around her saw and put both of those together in one person. I thought it was an obvious way to go, but Mr. Stevens didn't see it at first."

"My acting teacher, Jeff Corey, is always trying to get us to work on several levels like that. He'll give us a situation and then give us an improvisation that has nothing to do with it, like we're waiting for a bus." He grinned, but she didn't catch his joke.

"You saw *Anne Frank* twice?" It was hard enough to get people to watch it once.

"I couldn't believe it the first time. The second time, I saw how what you did was so generous to everybody else. I saw the play on Broadway. I thought it was a big problem to have Anne so saintly and everyone else come off like fools. The script was that way, and I didn't think the movie would be any different. But you weren't saintly. You were obnoxious."

She had to laugh.

"That meant the other characters weren't such caricatures. That brought richness to the movie the play did not have and richness to Anne Frank's character. And that took guts to do. But you haven't brought that same gutsy quality to working with Millie. You've brought nothing."

Damn him.

"Sorry," she muttered.

"From what you say, you probably haven't had a chance to work on the part. Isn't anyone supervising you?"

She looked out the window. How could anyone work on Millie? She was all over the place. It was too late now, anyway.

"I have a thought," he said.

"Kill Angelini?"

"He's a damn fine director. You should treat him better."

"I should treat *him*-! He's insane and mean."

"If I were directing you, I'd be insane and mean."

"Oh, so you're directing?"

"Don't do any of that other stuff. Just do Millie."

"But I have to do all that stuff. There are contracts signed and *Silver Sierra* is starting, and people wait hours for me."

"What could happen? Your uncle can't fire you. *Silver Sierra's* not going to let you go. You're a draw at Disney."

"But it's not professional. People wait for me."

"Your job is Millie. Who's going to be mad at you for doing your job? Forget everything else, and your uncle will get blamed. Keep up what you're doing now, and you'll get a bad reputation if you don't already have it. These things get around fast. Of course, those pictures in *Life* should help," he added, with a grin. "They're probably in every high school boy's locker now."

She wasn't going to think about that. "I went to a party. Some guy took pictures. They end up in *Life*. I didn't say anything. All of that was Howard Barry. But you all come down on me."

"We weren't that bad."

They had so been bad. But she wasn't going to say some corny line like, you're all against me.

"Those pictures made me think twice about Millie," he said. "Got to thinking I was going with the wrong girl."

"You are. Madge is a jerk. *She's* not the greatest actress."

"She's on time and she tries hard."

"Yeah," she said, slamming her back against the seat. "Poor thing. Got the job because she took off her clothes. When was the last time you got a job that way?"

He laughed. "Girls without their clothes on are way more valuable than boys."

"What a stupid thing to say!"

"That's the market," he said, chuckling. "Get rid of that extra stuff, and you'll be more valuable with your clothes on."

"Thank you for your advice, Mr. Royce."

"Right." He started up the car. "But those pictures of you were something."

"Go away."

They rode for a while in silence. Dianna watched the palm trees along the road and the stores and houses. She didn't want to think about him ogling her pictures in that article and despising her at the same time. Still, he had liked her acting. She felt she should broach the subject that was most bothering her, but she didn't want him to lose respect for her now that he had maybe just a little.

Have some guts, Fletcher.

"Mr. Royce?"

He kept following the road, and it didn't seem as if he'd heard her.

"Can you really study acting? Isn't it something that's just – natural if you have talent?"

"Of course you can study it. And teach it. I've studied plenty."

"When?"

He checked both ways before turning. "Majored in theater in college, kept it up in my grad years, and taught it somewhere in there, but I can't keep that up. I still go to class when I can."

"All that Method stuff is stupid."

"Have you studied it?"

Smart aleck.

"I see these actors who are so dependent on their teachers. They ask them why they should cross the street."

"Sure, there are people who abuse it. That happens with any discipline. There are other approaches."

"Aren't Method actors like Communists? It came from Russia."

"So did Rachmaninoff, Stravinsky, and Balanchine."

"Okay. That was dumb."

"As dumb as Congress. Do you know Rachmaninoff, Stravinsky, and Balanchine?"

"I've worked with Balanchine. I played Marie in *The Nutcracker* for two nights in New York. Mom was in one of his choruses when he worked for Sam Goldwyn. When we're in New York, we try to take class with him."

"I might have known," he retorted. "You have to practice dance, right? You study acting for the same reason. To keep your imaginative muscles flexible. It's not easy to be an actor in a business that demands stereotypes. As for the Method, it brought us new understandings, especially about film acting. Don't you have a way to get into character? Like what you did with Anne?"

"I study the lines and make them part of me, and then I hop onto the set, and she comes."

Or used to.

"Come on. You didn't just hop into Anne. You worked on her."

"I read her diary before I had the part and after, and I studied it to be able to live her. I didn't look at how kids in Amsterdam in the forties would do anything. That seems silly, and all this seeking for motivation and not being able to close a door without wondering why. You close the door to close the door."

"Acting may be second nature to you. You still need to work at it."

Well, it had been second nature when she was younger.

He turned on the radio, and there was the song that wouldn't die or leave the number one spot so she could get it, Percy Faith's "Theme From a Summer Place."

Royce drove quietly while Dianna simmered. He studied acting. He was a wonderful actor. He was nice, at least today. He thought she was good. Should she ruin that? Still, if she phrased it just the right way, perhaps he could give her an answer without her having to say too much.

"Can you just stop being able to act?" she asked.

He kept on driving for the whole of Percy Faith. Then he turned the radio off.

"We all worry about that. It goes with the territory. It's just nerves."

"That's not what I mean. Is it possible to just stop being able to do it?"

"No."

Just no?

How could she explain and not expose her despair for him to mock?

"A lot of my friends – who acted for years – all of a sudden, they're just bad. Most of them can't get jobs. It's as if they lost their talent in a minute. Does something happen when you're fifteen or sixteen? Does some switch turn off?"

She looked at the palm trees and well-watered lawns and the loud flowers.

He wasn't saying anything.

She decided she'd look at the palm trees, tell the truth, and just hope for the best.

"And I can't," she said, defiance in her voice. "I can't find Millie. I couldn't find the stupid character in the stupid movie I just finished for Disney. I freeze up. I think of a million ways to read a line, and I freeze. I used to hop on a set and give the line, now nothing happens, and I have to force it. I don't understand."

He still didn't say anything. But then he put on his signal light and they were turning into another parking lot.

15

She tried a stab at humor to hide her nervousness. "You're not apologizing again?"

"No," he said. "We should talk about this."

"We don't have to, really. I've taken up so much of your time."

"It's important."

He had pulled into a roadside stand. Dianna put on her sunglasses as the waitress came over.

"Want a Coke?"

She shook her head.

He said, "Two Cokes, two hot dogs. Mustard, onions. Plenty of napkins. This is a new car."

"It's lovely," said the waitress. "Okay."

"I don't want a Coke or a hot dog."

"Sure you do. Now, Miss Fletcher, have you talked about this business to your parents?"

"They'd disown me," she said, as a joke. Or was it a joke.

"What's this about your friends not able to act? You make it sound like a virus going round."

She didn't answer. He drummed his fingers to the rhythm of the music, and they didn't say anything else until the waitress returned and hooked the tray on the car door.

Dianna wasn't fast enough with her sunglasses.

"Oh, my God!" The waitress nearly dropped the tray. "It's Dianna Fletcher! I'm in your 305 fan club!"

"Hi," said Dianna.

"Okay," said Royce. "Let's keep it quiet, huh?" He reached into his pocket, pulled out his wallet, and handed the waitress a twenty.

"Okay, shhh," said the waitress. "Can you sign my pad?" She passed it over, and Dianna signed it. Royce took it and passed it back to the waitress.

Dianna was embarrassed. Her fan clubs. Kid stuff.

Royce said, "You've cost me twenty-eight dollars so far, not counting gas. And the cost to my ego. It's obvious everyone went to the bathroom when I won my Oscar."

Her giggle came before she could stop it.

He got serious again. "I don't think you're losing your talent. On the other hand, I don't think you're using it."

"Oh, what the heck. Maybe all I have to do is put on my bathing suit."

He shot her a grin as he handed her napkins and a hotdog and placed the Coke in a special holder he flipped open. "Watch out for my car."

"I didn't want a hot dog." Let him think what he liked.

"I'll eat it."

She bit into it.

"You're corrupting me. I'm not supposed to eat hot dogs." She took another bite.

"Why do you think you can't act?"

Hard to distract this man.

"I played Anne two years ago, and okay, I was good and involved, and I loved it, but after that, lately, I've stopped feeling the characters in me. Anne was the best acting I've done, and that was two years ago."

"It's not the part," he said. "You have to take risks and find ways to take them. You haven't been doing that."

How nice of him to say.

"It's hard to take risks when everyone's mad at me and the part is lousy."

"Don't tell me that."

He was just mean. She stared out the window for another long silence. He broke it. Damn him.

"You said you can think of lots of ways to read a line."

She would not answer him.

But he kept talking anyway.

"If you're finding different ways to read lines, that's a mature talent able to imagine. You have to select. In our business, you have to learn to choose pretty fast. You need to be in the moment and seize the right reading fast."

"I guess you can do it."

"Yes," he said, with no pause for modesty. "I can. That comes with study and practice and just sheer grabbing the moment. Our job is not just memorizing lines. You have to listen. Acting is hard work, sweetheart."

He took a final gulp from his hot dog, rolled up the napkin, tossed it into a paper bag, and took a long sip from his Coke.

Sometimes it didn't come. Listening didn't always work. But he didn't know that, this superior, brilliant, smug man.

"I wonder," he said, looking at her seriously, and with a look of care that put her on edge about what he was about to say. "You remind me that child actors usually don't make the transition to adult roles."

"Thank you," she said, trying to keep her voice steady.

"It's like Shirley Temple."

"I am not like Shirley Temple."

"What I mean is that you can't see her as anything else but the kid with the curls on the Good Ship Lollipop. When she got older, she made no sense, because she wasn't an actress, and she wasn't all that good. Still isn't. Adult roles are more complex. If you're a kid, they love you if you are able to come on the set and work quickly and aren't intimidated by all the stuff that goes on six inches away from you, and if you can learn lines fast. Their characters aren't usually that complicated, even if it's Lark."

"Lark was complicated."

"To someone watching you, yes. It's when you get older that the parts become more complex because people accumulate all this baggage, and that's what makes for drama. That requires real skills, real talent. People who are experienced and trained become your competition and your betters if you don't keep up. An adult audience looks for different things in adult actors, a reflection of some sort of life they understand, or that you bring them to understand."

In other words, you *could* lose your talent.

"When you were younger, you probably made your choices naturally, because there weren't that many."

"Are you telling me to quit?"

He looked amused. "You give up easy."

"I don't want to give up."

"It's good that you imagine a lot of different ways to read a line. It means your imagination is working. Your problem is just that you're growing up. Which is probably the annoying diagnosis everyone gives you for everything."

"I've done complex parts." She was still resisting. "Anne – Velvet – Lark."

She didn't mention Juliet.

"Now don't go talking yourself out of the profession."

"Maybe my friends have lost their talent."

"You're just not using yours. You're letting it go to waste."

She wondered what it must be like to be Miss February, going out with him, sleeping with him. She was sure they slept together, made love. The touch of his hand —

Good grief.

"You have to work hard to get to the next level," he was saying.

"I can't understand Millie. I thought I had an idea, but Angelini said no, and he's been no help, but I don't get either of the sisters and even the point of the whole play."

"It isn't clear where Millie fits into the whole or how she fits in. Inge isn't clear with any of his characters."

"Right."

"An actor has to be able to handle that. Your job is to create a character to believe in. I don't understand what you said about Angelini because that's his whole way of working. Letting the actor be free to find the way."

"He hates me. I got dumped on him. He didn't want me. And he won't give me a close-up."

Royce waved his hand in disagreement. "You aren't working hard enough."

"No. He has this whole idea that Millie has to be ugly. I told him I don't think so, and he just waved me away."

"Did you show him?"

"I asked him. He said no. And I have all these stupid costumes."

"If you show him first, and he believes it, you can deal with him. He forces you to work to your best."

This view of Angelini was from a distant planet. And infuriating.

"If I'd been his choice, things might have been different. Mr. Dante pushed me at him, and it was as if he was being told he needed me in order to get the play produced. You resent me for the same reason, right? Don't think I haven't known that all along."

He shook his head, but he smiled at her. Disarming guy. "Okay, I'm sorry, but no excuses. Angelini is the director. Our work is a collaboration."

"He doesn't listen to me." She almost said that he hit her and forced a kiss on her, but she decided she'd better not. He wouldn't believe her, and it would cause trouble.

"Why should he listen to you? You slow down production."

Miss February could have him.

"It's not my fault."

"Whether it's your fault or not, you are the cause of slowing things down. I've had to reschedule my start date on *Comancheros*. It's not pretty to annoy John Wayne. I'm sure others on the cast have problems, too. Why should Angelini respect you? You don't seem to care. He lets you roam free, but you have to be able to handle that."

"Okay, it's all my fault."

"You need a better sense of technique."

"Pile it on!"

"You might think about studying in a class."

After winning an Oscar and working for ten years? It would seem like an admission of failure.

"You've got to show you care. Forget Angelini's attitude. Get imaginative."

"I do care. I am imaginative. That scene we started on Friday. I had an idea, but he brushed me off."

"He has a schedule."

"Okay, keep defending him. She stared out the window. "You two stick together. I'm sure it'll help your career."

The waitress arrived to unhook the tray and take the garbage. "You two fighting?"

"No," said Royce.

"Yes," said Dianna.

"Okay," she said, lingering. Royce dug into his pocket and handed her ten dollars.

"Thanks!" The waitress pocketed the bill and sauntered off.

"You are one expensive date."

"I am not a date. I will reimburse you."

"I never take money from women. What's your idea about that scene?"

"It felt wrong."

"That's not an idea."

"Wait a minute and *listen*. I can't play Millie as ugly. Why should she be? Madge goes around being gorgeous and saying she doesn't want to be seen that way, but Millie is sincere about it. She doesn't want what goes with pretty. This scene, when she's with Hal, is all in pieces. Millie said earlier that she doesn't know what to say to boys, and Hal is not a boy. He's a grown man. She has to talk to him and doesn't know how." She was surprised at these ideas, they'd been suppressed for so long.

She remembered something Hilda had once said. *When no one wants to hear you, you stop singing.*

Bill looked down at his brown shoe with its scuffed leather. "That's not a problem you have."

"*Listen!* He doesn't know how to talk without bragging because he's insecure around everyone, and she broods about everything. It must be something Inge wanted to show because he added lines, even if they don't seem to make sense. Because she is pretty on the picnic. Inge makes a point of that."

He played with his steering wheel, toying with one finger.

Finally, he said, "I was thinking that Hal would just be responding to whatever she said, keeping things cool, enjoying a sense of belonging. But that's not enough, is it? He wants to seem to be what he's not, like an adolescent. Millie doesn't want to be what she is, either."

"This conversation is important. As Hal keeps going, no matter how she tries, it stops and starts, and during that, she sees he can't be for her. Even if he is trying to respond to her. Men don't like smart women."

"Come on. Hal just can't follow all of her goings on about art and Shakespeare."

"That's too simple. She feels more alone as their conversation goes on. She can't reach him and she wants to, and she keeps trying different subjects. Art, Shakespeare, books. It all goes to what she says before about not knowing how to talk to men. *That's* the through line. The way we did it on Friday, it made no sense. Just non sequiturs. Just words."

So she had been thinking about Millie in some part of her brain. Or Millie had been thinking.

"With her talking about all that Shakespeare stuff," Royce said, "he may think she doesn't want him to catch up."

"Lots of things could be going on, and they're digesting everything *slowly*. What if they react to not the line that's *said*, but the line that's said *before*? You know how sometimes people take time to react to what's been said, and they react to something said before?"

"It'd have to be done fast. How'd you think of that?"

"It's a natural thing," she said. "For instance, you have those books you were going to return, and I see they're on the First Amendment. I wanted to ask about it, but I haven't said a word yet."

"The top one is," he said. "The others are on the fifth."

"You want to express yourself but you can't incriminate yourself."

He laughed. "All right, let's try it."

"Now?"

"I'll start. Give me a minute."

He was ready long before she could think and looking at the steering wheel with a changed demeanor before she could gather her brains together. How did he do that?

"I sure do admire people who can draw," he said, in a forced tone with Hal's twang.

Dianna geared herself to think slowly but speak fast. It was a challenge. "No, I'm not really any good. I just like to draw."

As they spoke haltingly through the scene, Millie and Hal took a definite shape — a conversation of frustration and mutual desire that the other could not satisfy.

"Damn, that was interesting," said Royce, hopping out of character. "It makes it more clear how he'd turn to Madge out of frustration. Can we do that again? We've got to get it going faster."

It went better this time as they stumbled toward and away from the other in the conversation.

After the fourth time, Dianna felt an intense loneliness. That, she thought, must be Millie.

Royce said, "Wow. You can't do that all the time, but it really works for that scene." He started up the car.

Someone in the parking lot yelled, "Hey! That's Dianna Fletcher! With a man!"

Dianna groaned and slid down in the seat.

Bill practically put the pedal to the floor to get out of there.

The waitress was yelling, "It's Dianna Fletcher!"

"I've been thinking," said Dianna, "I might be a good horror movie. IT'S DIANNA FLETCHER! Except that people start running at me and not away."

She was excited, though, about her discovery of something of Millie in her. Maybe she hadn't lost all her talent.

Royce turned the radio back on. A voice announced, "Senator Hubert Humphrey, despite being, for all intents and purposes, out of the Presidential race now that Senator John Kennedy won the Wisconsin primary, insists he is going to keep going after Kennedy in West Virginia."

A hoarse sounding voice shouted into the car, "It is a travesty of politics that the money machine supporting Kennedy could drive him straight to the White House."

The announcer's voice continued. "Kennedy had been leading Humphrey in the West Virginia polls, but his support seems to be slipping, perhaps because the news coverage in Wisconsin alerted West Virginians that Senator Kennedy is a Catholic."

"Damn fools," shouted Royce, his vehemence startling her. "They're setting it up so he loses because he's Catholic and that Nixon wins because he's against everyone. Stupid tactic."

"Nixon?" Dianna asked. "The Vice President?"

"That's the one," said Royce.

The report switched to Kennedy, who was holding a news conference.

One reporter asked, "Can a Catholic be president? Wouldn't he be answerable to a foreign power, that is, the Pope?"

Kennedy replied with a salty Massachusetts twang. "I was at a dinner with Bishop Spellman the other night, and I asked him how I should address the issue of the infallibility of the Pope, and the Bishop said, 'I don't know. Every time I see him, he calls me Spillman.'"

Royce laughed. "I love this guy. Not because he's entertaining, but because he's smart."

"Nixon has been Vice President for eight years. Wouldn't he know all about the Russians who would bomb us if they could?"

"What about the rights of people here at home?" Royce countered. "The freedom of speech and believing what your conscience tells you to believe?"

What did that have to do with anything?

"But of course we're free." All those performances at Disneyland – she always ended by singing "America, the Beautiful," and people sang along, weeping, at the gratitude of being part of a free nation. "Nixon can't change that."

It was as if she'd lit a fuse under him.

"Nixon," said Royce, "already has. He supported Joseph McCarthy in his attempt to smear people as Communists. Just yelling out names and accusations without proof or with flimsy proof. McCarthy never caught a Communist. He made a lot of accusations and a lot of noise and participated in a larger witch hunt that ruined lives and killed people and drove some to suicide. A lot of senators remained quiet, but they didn't outright champion him and try to emulate the guy."

Where did this all come from? She *knew* Nixon – he was a friend of her mother's.

She couldn't let what he said rest.

"There were Communists here. Still are. Should we be so free they destroy us? Isn't that the point of keeping them out of dangerous positions?"

"Like movies? Ha. And how do you know someone's a Communist? Or plotting to overthrow the government? You get evidence that they're doing wrong."

"Communists want to convert everyone to their cause. You could do that writing movies. By the time anyone found out, it could be too late. They want to hurt us from within. We should get them before they do any damage."

"The studios wouldn't let that happen."

"The studios aren't that smart."

"So what should we do? You're saying just because it's in a movie we should believe it."

He was being pretty intense.

"You keep Communists out of places where they could do harm."

"You're talking about blacklisting," said Royce, slamming his hand on the steering wheel. "You would prevent a person from earning a living at what they're good at because of what you think they believed? And who determines what's the right thing to believe? What does it mean to be free if you cannot believe something different? Is there a limit to freedom of expression? The answer is - not in the Constitution."

"All those writers who went to jail were Communists. They shouldn't be writing movies."

"How do you know they were Communists?"

"I hear people talk. Those ten writers who went before Congress went to jail. A lot of other actors and writers pleaded the Fifth Amendment. They didn't want to incriminate themselves or go to jail. They were guilty. There *have* been Communists working in movies trying to hurt us."

"It sounds like you didn't get hurt. And is that what taking the Fifth means?"

"People take the Fifth when they're guilty. I see it all the time on *Perry Mason*."

He signaled. Once again, they were veering into another parking lot.

"Am I ever getting home?"

He turned off the ignition and looked so intense when he turned toward her that she was alarmed and again backed against the door.

Had she made him mad?

Was Bill Royce a Communist?

16

"In the first place," he said, "The Hollywood Ten didn't go to jail because they were Communists but because they were held in contempt of Congress for not discussing their political beliefs. In the second place, no one should have to testify about their political beliefs or testify against themselves. Remember the Constitution was written in the eighteenth century. Not so long before it was written, people were tortured to make confessions."

"Anne Boleyn's lovers."

"Well, yeah." He shook his head, amused. "Okay. That's not so far removed from living in the eighteenth century. The people who wrote the Constitution had been rebels, remember? Even if they won the war, they'd been considered traitors in England. If they had lost, they could have been hung or imprisoned and tortured. They were thinking like *rebels*. By definition, the founders were traitors."

"They were patriots!"

"They were traitors against England. That was their government! They wanted to overthrow the British government here, and in the end, it was a violent overthrow. The Declaration of Independence was an act of treason of people violently overthrowing the government."

Dianna had never heard the American Revolution described in such an unpatriotic way.

"Imagine if someone here took up arms against this government. Well, they did, in the South, and that was treason. It would always be treason. If we had been living here in the 1770s, you might have been loyal to the King and I might have been a rebel and a traitor. Rebels could have been tortured, put in prison, forced to testify against themselves. Our system – including the Fifth Amendment – protects people from that kind of government."

"The Communist spies in America *do* want to overthrow the government," she said. "And take away our freedoms. They show us movies in class that say so. Movie writers have a responsibility to the country and shouldn't be Communists or fall for Communist propaganda."

"And what exactly is that? Now those movie writers – and a lot of other people who were caught up in McCarthy's and the Un-American Activities scare – were being attacked for their *beliefs*. Think about that. For what they believed, not for what they did. Many of them denied that Congress had the right to ask them what they believed. The Ten pled the First Amendment, but the Supreme Court didn't agree, and they went to prison for contempt of Congress."

"They were *guilty*."

"Guilty of what? Just because the Supreme Court doesn't agree with what's in the Constitution doesn't mean anything. That's not heresy. The Supreme Court is political and human. So is the Congress. So is the President. *Democracy* is only human. That's why people need the protections in the Constitution. That's why people need to speak their minds and be informed, not sit back and go, oh well, whatever you say. That's overthrowing the government. The Supreme Court can make asinine decisions. Like the Dred Scott case. Have your three hours of school a day covered that?"

But that was a long time ago, she thought. It seemed safer that a very wrong Supreme Court ruled in the past and to think that *now* the Court was wiser. What he was saying was that just because the Supreme Court or Congress or even the President said something didn't make it true or even right. It was a pretty awful thought.

It seemed treasonous.

She found herself saying, to change the subject to something lighter, "Nixon fantasizes about being pope."

Royce had been about to go further into his harangue, but this certainly stopped him. "What?"

"He calls the house every so often. He's friends with my parents. I think he has a crush on my mother. And he said he wants to be pope."

He laughed. "That makes sense."

"If you repeat it and it gets back to him, he'll know where it came from."

"And you're afraid of that?"

She wasn't sure.

"The reason people take the Fifth is because the institutions of government are flawed. No one is the ultimate authority. The government works for us. You can't take the Fifth in totalitarian states like the Soviet Union. But you can here because the all three branches are flawed, and the Constitution recognizes that. No one branch of government can have too much power. What Congress was doing when it said it was investigating was political, Republicans using Hollywood to get headlines and accusing others not in their party of being disloyal, even treasonous. But they had no solid evidence. It was a publicity stunt."

"Oh, please."

"A committee on un-American activities. Who is to say what un-American is? They never defined it. Who's to say what subversive means?"

"Overthrowing the government."

"So there should be a little evidence, right? There never was. Just words they wrote out of context, organizations people joined at one time for peace, and they were accused of a crime that could not be defined except by association. If these people they dragged in to testify took the Fifth, they wouldn't go to jail, but they lost their jobs. The madness spread throughout the country. People suspected people for the slightest of reasons. The FBI even followed Eleanor Roosevelt around, thinking she was in cahoots with the Communists. Freedom to follow your beliefs becomes a crime. Isn't that un-American? Isn't that subversive?"

"Shouldn't Congress investigate Communists?"

"Sure. So should the FBI. But Congress investigates to make laws. They didn't make any laws about this. They didn't turn up anything. They demanded names, but the FBI already knew who the Communists were. Or rather held the lists of suspected Communists, and that's a whole other thing. But Congress already knew the names they were asking for. If you knew the FBI knew all that, and you were questioning former Communists or Communists, what would you ask?"

"What their plans were," she said.

He grinned. "You just thought about it for a second. That's not what Congress wanted to know. For an investigative committee, they were a great used car lot. They just wanted publicity, headlines, Hollywood names. Most people who worked with the Communist Party here did so because the party was the most organized in dealing with Negro rights and workers' rights. The studios fought anyone trying to form unions with hoses and police. That struggle is why you get to go to school on the set and have a social worker to look after your rights. It wasn't always like that, Pollyanna. These people were fighting Hitler before anyone else was, and they get blamed for that. They were Americans working to make America and the world better."

Did he have to call her Pollyanna?

"Are you a Communist?"

Would he tell her if he was?

He laughed. "Oh, no, honey. I believe in the capitalist way of life – see my new car? – but every system has flaws, and we should work to fix them so that people can live a dignified life in the richest country in the world. I don't like it when my country abuses its power over its citizens."

"Can I go home now?"

"Yeah," he said. He seemed to relax. "I'm sorry. I'm writing my PhD thesis about all this."

"You're going to college?"

"Sad, huh? I've gotten so busy that I'm going very slowly now. I love to talk about politics. You probably don't follow along much."

"Why did you pick the blacklist to write about?"

His laughter had a hollow ring. She wondered at that.

"A cloak of fear wrapped around this town and the country affected how we behaved and what movies we made and saw. And it was *pointless*. Congress criticized movies that your parents were in, like *The Best Years of Our Lives*. And *It's a Wonderful Life*. Ludicrous. The way the studios were run, no one could plant propaganda into a script, but Congress accused any script criticizing bankers or politicians or the blue sky. Bankers have been villains before Shakespeare. Defending freedom of speech could get you into trouble. There were stars who were caught up and slunk away, like Humphrey Bogart, who ended up having to say he was a sap – for defending the First Amendment."

Congress didn't like her parents' most wonderful movies?

"But," he said, "it's probably coming to an end. The Academy has said that blacklisted people can receive Oscars, and Otto Preminger and Kirk Douglas are giving Dalton Trumbo screen credit. That means the people who deserve credit will get it. But you can't give back the years so many people lost. Most can't get back in. Movies change, and they haven't been working. The blacklist did enormous damage in the land of the free."

This rang a bell with Dianna. "Frank Sinatra is working with Albert Maltz. He was blacklisted, wasn't he?"

"Yes."

"Daddy talked to Uncle Frank at the nominations banquet. I heard him say we had to put the blacklisted period behind us."

He shrugged. "I hope so, but this country has a bad record of tolerating difference."

"No, it doesn't," she said. "I'm tolerating you."

He chuckled and seemed to ease up as he steered onto North Roxbury. When he got to her corner, she said, "I'll get out here."

"Oh, no, I see ladies to the door. I've always wanted to see your house anyway."

She waved them past the stone guardhouse where Kito, the guard, was watering the hedge, and they drove past the gardens, which were getting watered with what seemed to be an endless number of sprinklers.

"Gorgeous!" said Royce.

"The roses come out when they feel like it," said Dianna. "Some are out now. Why do you hate my father?"

"My business with your father is my business."

"Well, tell him then."

"Right." But he seemed annoyed at the thought.

Once up the circular drive, he pulled up at the door.

"Wait," he said. "You're here by yourself?"

"With a staff."

"But who takes care of you?"

"It's a whole house of people," she said, annoyed. Did he think she was an infant?

"*Paid* to take care of you. Okay, none of my business."

"Do you want to come in and meet some of them and make sure they pass your standards?"

He laughed. "No, sorry. I should get to the library, thanks."

He had hurried out of the car and before she could move, he had opened her door, taken her hand, and helped her out.

"Thank you again," she said. "It was really nice of you, Mr. Royce."

"What was that name again?"

She smiled and looked down at his shoes. "Bill."

"Okay, Dianna," he said. "Sorry I got a little intense."

"It was a nice afternoon. You were nice to drive me. My father is a nice man, too."

He took her arms, leaned over, and kissed her lightly on the forehead.

She reached into her bag, pulled out a piece of paper.

"Could I have your autograph?"

It was a charm-filled gesture, earning her Hal's adorable, rather shy grin. He signed his sprawl. "Yours sincerely, Who's He."

"Thank you."

Who knew how many women he'd slept with.

"I'll see you tomorrow," he said. "It will be a good day." Heading back to the car, he called, "We'll slay Angelini."

"Could we, really?" she called.

He laughed.

The door behind Dianna opened. "Where were you?" Lynne was calling. "I called MJ, the Barrys. Where were you? Who's he?"

Dianna watched the red car disappear behind the trees, feeling strangely bereft. Condescending blowhard, but he had been nice, and he was a great actor.

She hoped he wasn't a Communist.

17

"How is *Silver Sierra?*" Lynne asked, refilling the water pitcher as Dianna read by the pool.

"It's sure better than *Picnic.* This writer, L.A. Franklin, writes good scripts."

Lynne handed her the *L.A. Times* and pointed to an article.

Blake Edwards was going to direct *Breakfast at Tiffany's,* and he had chosen Audrey Hepburn for the part of Holly Golightly.

"Maybe Mom won't care. With a lightweight like Edwards directing a lightweight like Audrey, it'll come to nothing."

"Capote is already complaining," said Lynne. "I didn't mean to interrupt you. Keep working. Do you want to go over your lines for tomorrow?"

"No, thanks."

Lynne had had a career herself in New York, mostly at the American Negro Theater, in their productions of *You Can't Take It With You, Juno and the Paycock,* and *The Peacemaker.* She had made a few movies, mostly playing maids, and she still acted on occasion, but not professionally. As Anne's and Dianna's maid, she often helped with lines and, occasionally, criticism. She was more like an overseer than a maid, and whenever John held his readings, she and Hilda always participated. Lynne could be critical, and Dianna didn't want to exhibit her awfulness.

Instead, she put her script on the table and said, "Watch my jackknife, please?" and headed for the diving board. She did a few jackknives, then a somersault into the water.

"Don't kill yourself!" called Lynne. "That was more than good."

"I'm ready," said Dianna, splashing onto the deck. "It's Millie's time to shine."

She made sure to show up earlier at Desilu on Monday. This time, Millie could wear a dress and comb her hair, making Angelini's insistence on an ugly Millie blatantly inconsistent. She retrieved her sketch pad from the prop man and sat on the bench around which Bill had been pacing for some time. He didn't glance her way. She had another idea for their scene but she decided she'd better not interrupt him.

"Everyone ready?" called the AD. "This will be a take."

Bill sat next to her. "Hi, kid," he said, more Hal than Bill.

To her relief, he recreated the scene the way they had done it in the car. Dianna took a chance and threw in a wrench, responding immediately to one of Hal's lines. Bill caught on and even tried the same thing a few lines later. This intensified their listening and mutual desperation as they connected and disconnected with greater intensity. It was fun.

Angelini called for a print. "Damn, that was good! I'm not even sure why. Bill, you added some new touches, right?"

"Aren't you glad I added some new touches?" Bill asked her.

She laughed. She'd even felt a bit of Millie, maybe, she wasn't sure.

"That was good, kid."

Bill walked toward the door, pulling out a pack of cigarettes.

"See? You can do fine if you put your mind to it," Angelini said to her.

Of all the nerve.

Angelini wanted to go in for close-ups, that is, for Bill. Dianna sat by the camera, feeding cues. She wondered how the scene would play if the camera kept cutting to Bill, but Bill wasn't complaining, and Angelini didn't give her one close-up.

On her way to lunch, she saw Bill by his car, kissing Miss February, who looked smart in a double breasted navy blue suit.

Miss February waved her over.

Bill looked irritated at being interrupted, but he was polite. "This is Sandi. She's helping me furnish my new house."

"Can I have your autograph?" asked Sandi. "You were wonderful in *Anne Frank*."

"Thank you. Where is your house?" Dianna asked, scribbling her name on a blank notebook page. "Finally, you're dating smart women."

Sandi laughed.

"Malibu," said Bill, looking more out of sorts. "I'm going on location soon, and Sandi's going to help furnish it."

"Where in Malibu?"

"Ocean Cliff Road. Always wanted to live by the beach."

Ocean Cliff Road was a long stretch along the Pacific, and a part of it was gated off. Bill had probably bought one of the ramshackle houses in the ungated area near the beach, whereas the Fletcher house, gleaming with glass and marble, stood on a hill, hidden by tall hedges, its front drive lined with palm trees and barred by an electronic gate. She didn't know if that was a good thing or a bad thing that they might be neighbors for the summer.

Riding home, she heard that John Kennedy had won the West Virginia primary in a landslide. Bill's candidate seemed like a sure thing.

The next morning at Paramount to pose for *Silver Sierra* publicity pictures, she relaxed in her makeup chair as a woman who had done her mother's makeup in the forties and fifties examined her face and smiled. Michael Shin, the gossipy fellow who put waves in her hair, sang from musicals, and she sang along.

Marty O'Miles came in, sat down in the chair next to her, and opened up his paper.

Michael yelled, "Bald Harry!"

Bald, fat Harry arrived with a box Dianna knew contained a toupee, and as he reached for the glue, he said, "Did you hear that Sinatra backed out of the Slovik thing?"

"Coward," said Marty. "He was bowing to the will of Joe Kennedy."

O'Miles gave Dianna a brief nod as she got out of her chair. She wondered how Sinatra felt at what must have been a devastating defeat, no matter why it happened. But why would John Kennedy's father care?

As she headed for the western street, she held her long skirt carefully. She'd played cowboys and Indians on those streets back when she was a kid. She couldn't wait to play on them for real. But now, just pictures.

She patted a horse, hugged a snout, and smiled at the photographer. She saw Marty O'Miles, standing across the corral, watching.

"Why not one with Mr, O'Miles?"

"Oh, we'll get him," said the publicity man. "Just a few with you."

The show would use two sound stages, one being the home ranch, which is where she posed with the family, the men who would play her two big brothers and O'Miles, who would play her father. Chris Hill was just off Broadway and new to camera work, and both he and O'Miles were quiet. Mike North, just off his own half hour western, acted like he owned the ranch, and he was enthusiastic about the series, but she heard him say to Hill that he hoped they weren't making "Miss Fletcher" the star of the show. Still, she was treated with such respect that she loathed having to go back to *Picnic* the next day, except that the next scene would be one she was totally prepared for. They wouldn't be filming on lousy Stage 9 but over at MGM, at the huge sound stage with the tank used for Esther Williams' films.

Dianna had been practicing her jackknife for days so that Millie would shine. Even Angelini would be impressed. It was a long car ride to Culver City, but it would be worth it.

The grips were yelling at each other as soon as she walked onto the set.

"Ike's been lying to us," one of the grips called. "We have been spying on the Russians. Khrushchev wasn't lying to us but Ike was."

"What's the President going to say, yeah, we're spying on the Russians?"

"The Russians know about it. So what good is it?"

Dianna went into her dressing room and stopped, aghast. Hanging off the closet was not the previously agreed upon pink and white striped suit but a pink suit so big that when she put it on, it hung almost to her knees. And it came with one ugly bathing cap. She twisted it onto her head and kicked at the mirror, tossed on a robe, and hurried out.

As she took her place at the pool, the number of gorgeous women not wearing bathing caps and sitting around seemed to multiply. Dianna knew they were giggling at her when she handed her robe to the wardrobe mistress.

The whole country would be laughing at her.

Don't think about that. The important thing was the dive. Just give Millie her due. She knelt by the pool, splashed water on herself, and cursed the loose suit for flapping down.

Bill stood behind her, arms akimbo, obviously enjoying the attention he was getting from cast and crew, especially the models. He teased them as they surrounded him and as the photographer snapped several pictures.

The first thing they had to do was dive in the water and race. Hal was supposed to win but she decided he wouldn't.

The crew finished setting the lights.

"Let's go!" Angelini called.

Bill tossed off his robe.

What a chest.

The models gaped, to Dianna's disgust.

"Action," called Angelini from the camera by the poolside.

Bill strutted up like Hal and called something out to Dianna, which she assumed was his line. She sprang up to race him, hoping she wouldn't hit the water so hard her loose suit would fall off.

Bill yelled, "Ready, set, go!"

Just as she prepared to jump off, she felt a kick on her behind that made her shriek and plummet into the water. Bill dove in, splashing her to kingdom come while she flailed up to the sound of laughter all around. Someone yelled cut. Dianna scraped both feet on the cement floor as she struggled to stand. Bill shook the water out of his hair to great applause. He bowed.

Dianna plowed her way past him and looked up at the camera and at Angelini.

"Say print because that's all you're getting!" she shouted.

Bill caught her hand. "Hey, what's the matter?"

She wrested her hand away. "I could slug you!"

"What's the matter now?" yelled Angelini.

"We were supposed to race!" she shouted. "Both of us dive in and race. What's with the kick?"

"Take it easy," said Bill. She pushed him on his gorgeous chest.

"It's funny," said Angelini. "Let's do it again."

"Funny? Millie is at her strength! Why insult her?"

Angelini yelled to the crew, "One more take and we'll move on."

"What about my jackknife?"

"We're clearing out by noon," Angelini called. "Come on, we have to get this thing done."

"We're jumping in at the same time and do a real race. Then I'm doing my jackknife. Millie's jackknife. It's in the script!"

"Hey," said Bill. "Ease up. You're not the star of this thing." He climbed out of the pool and started toweling dry.

So much for their truce.

"You have to look awkward and gangly," said Angelini.

"The script says Millie does a jackknife."

"Inge added that. It's not in the original script."

"We've been doing lots of things not in the original," she protested. "The jackknife is important. We've mentioned it."

"I say what's important," said Angelini. "I have to think of the budget. We're all set up for one more take."

Her fury grew. Angelini was out to humiliate Millie in whatever way he could. She couldn't have that.

Bill said, "Mike, you cleared my kick with her, didn't you?"

Wanting to get out of the pool, she grabbed at a rope near her hand. This knocked over a generator, which hit the water along with its cable, shooting off sparks that traveled down the water right at her.

She didn't freeze but pushed her way to the ladder. One of the crew reached for her, yelling, "Here!" and pulled her to safety. Electricians ripped the plug out of the generator and dragged it out of the water.

A woman ran over, wrapping Dianna in a robe and towels.

Gripping the warmth of the robe around her, Dianna stalked over to Angelini.

"What about the jackknife?"

"We don't need that. We need to show Hal's playfulness."

"What did you do? Sleep with him?" she taunted Bill.

What a jerk she'd been to think they could be friends. All he cared about was his damn career and that waitresses at drive-ins would recognize him.

"How dare you make fun of Millie like that? She *dives*!" she shouted at Angelini.

"It's just a mention in the script," said Angelini. "Hal tells everyone, and that's all we need. Spending time on Millie throws the script off center. You're not the star, Miss Fletcher."

She tore off her bathing cap and tossed it at the director, hitting him in the nose. People had to see that Millie was no fool.

"I am done here," she said, dramatically. "I will not work with you again."

"None of that," said Angelini. "You stay right here."

"I am not working for you one more minute," said Dianna.

Angelini slapped her. The crew gasped. Bill grabbed Angelini's arm.

As if out of nowhere, Mira appeared. "Mr. Angelini, I have to report all this."

He stared at her as if not sure who she was.

"You do that," said Dianna. "I'm done here." She turned on Bill. "So you like kicking?" she taunted him, and she danced around and gave him a good one.

His behind was really firm.

He grabbed her arm. "I know you've just had a scare, but grow up!"

Feeling incredibly betrayed, she pounded his arm. "You can finish this stupid thing without me! I'm through!"

She walked quickly to her dressing room. She could hear Mira pulling all her professional stops.

"It doesn't matter what a minor calls you, or how she behaves, you don't hit her. You endangered her by first having her do a stunt she had no knowledge..." Her voice faded as Dianna closed her door. For the last time. When she came out, they were still going at it.

"Hell," shouted Angelini. "Boys are kicking girls into the water all the time."

"Not on soundstages with electric cables all around," said Mira.

Thank God it was all over. No more *Picnic*. Let them sue. She'd scream her protests in the press. They didn't need Millie.

When she came out of her dressing room, Angelini was yelling, and Bill was patting his arm.

"I called a cab," Mira said to her. "You'll be home soon."

"I'm done with this thing," said Dianna.

"That's for you to work out. They might sue you."

"I'm not going to school today, either."

"Okay," said Mira. "I'll get you a pass on that. I'll see what I can do. I'll bring a lawyer to your house later. We should have a calm talk with Dante."

Dianna grabbed her bag. "Thank you. But it won't make any difference."

"We'll make some," said Mira.

Dianna waved Mark Dante away. "Goodbye," she called and, seeing the cab pull up, hurried toward it.

She was free of Millie! It was Bill's show. Let him have it.

What good was a career, anyway, if she couldn't protect her characters?

18

Dianna tried to concentrate on a *Silver Sierra* script by L.A. Franklin, in which Betsy took interest in a bad guy and almost got kissed. Plus she got to gallop down a hill after a wild stallion. It was pretty fascinating stuff.

Lynne's voice called out, "You have company."

Here they were. What would Betsy do with lawyers and producers?

Mark Dante approached the pool, followed by a man in gray, a color that extended to his hair. Beside this gray man walked Angelini.

Dianna called out, "I don't want them in my house!"

Dante said, "This is our production company's lawyer, Mr. Sawyer."

That, Dianna thought, was too good to be true.

"We've come to settle this unfortunate event."

"I'm not coming back," said Dianna. "Sue me."

"It's all right, Dianna," said Angelini, with a smile. "We both just had a bad day, didn't we, honey?"

Wasn't he nice.

"Have a seat, gentlemen, and I'll bring some water," said Lynne. "Lemonade? Mr. Pepper is coming from Mr. Bennett's office, and here is Mira Ortiz."

Mira had changed to a soft rose suit that complemented her coloring. She walked briskly in on heels, taking only a moment to look around her at the pool, the nearby tennis court, the flowers and trees, with a distant look as if trying not to see it all. She smiled at Dianna, who felt both cowed and glad Mira was there for her. Tony Pepper, a thin, gangly, middle-aged man, wandered in as if he owned the place.

Everyone sat at a round glass table. Lynne poured ice water and lemonade. Manny took up a post by the door.

Dante said, "If you quit, Dianna, we will have to stop production. We'd have to sue. Come on, honey."

Sawyer said, "You cannot abandon production. Our company will sue you for breach of contract."

"There's a good start," Pepper countered. "Here is a young girl who nearly was killed, naturally terrified about going to work."

"She was causing problems long before that happened," said Sawyer. "Her temperamental behavior put the production in jeopardy."

"Now, now," said Angelini. "Let's not hash out a past that may or may not have happened. Dianna had a scare today. Of course she's upset. We need to finish the play. Come on, Dianna. Let's be professionals."

Dianna resisted the urge to punch him.

Lynne escorted Bill Royce onto the patio. Bill took a seat between Dante and Pepper. He looked grim.

"Why are you here?" Dianna asked.

"I am here for the cast. We need to finish the show and let Angelini finish his job. You need to be professional."

She felt a blast of hurt.

"When he hit me? I'm not going back. Sue me."

"You may not understand," said Sawyer. "If you don't come back, that's hundreds of thousands of dollars lost. You will have ruined everyone's chances to be seen in a wonderful production. You will deal your career a death blow."

"It's just another week or so," said Angelini. He chuckled. "We can put up with each other that long, can't we?"

"No," said Dianna.

Angelini shrugged. "You see what I had to deal with."

"You have been nothing but trouble on this set," said Sawyer.

"Dianna," said Bill, "Your parents can deal with any suit against you and turn the story into your favor. It's not right to the cast and the crew. This is kid stuff."

What an ass kisser. Well, he needed the work for his house and his car.

"It is not kid stuff," said Mira, taking a notebook from her briefcase and paging through it. "I witnessed several occasions when Mr. Angelini created a hostile environment for Miss Fletcher. I would arrive half an hour before she was due, and Mr. Angelini would discuss her with the cast in negative, insulting terms, calling her temperamental, a prima donna, that sort of thing, poisoning other cast members against her."

"He did?" Dianna cried.

"I was joking," said Angelini.

"He wasn't the only one criticizing her," said Bill. "She held up shooting."

He was too far away to kick.

"Miss Fletcher was consistently late," said Sawyer.

"The set was so unpleasant." Mira's tone was harsh. "Naturally, she wouldn't hurry. She *is* still a kid. She had other commitments. You could have worked around them with her. I asked you to, and you kept putting me off. I filed my papers with the welfare department."

Dianna realized she didn't have to talk.

"None of this is relevant," said Sawyer.

"He struck her," said Mira.

"He lost his temper," said Sawyer. "She was not hurt."

"These things happen," said Dante. "It's unfortunate, but we have to finish this teleplay."

"Did Mr. Angelini promote a hostile environment?" asked Sawyer.

"Not until today," said Bill.

"How can you say that?" Dianna cried.

"Your lateness and temperament got to him is all." To the others, he said, "The cast loved him, but Dianna was almost always late. I think he lost his mind today. The fire was an accident. No one was hurt. We should all go back to work."

"Just a thing? He hit me."

Pepper said, "Dianna is a minor. Her life was endangered by negligence. This sets social services in action. And, yes, Angelini struck her. You need to make assurances that this will not happen again."

"Of course not," said Angelini.

"To hell with assurances. It wasn't the first time he hit me," said Dianna.

Everyone looked at her. She pointed at Dante. "*He* knows. Mr. Angelini hit me, pushed me to the wall, to kiss me, you know, sticking his tongue in my mouth. I kicked him and ran away and told Mr. Dante."

Dante looked stunned.

Bill looked at her intensely. He probably thought she was lying.

"Directors, actors," Dante mumbled.

"I know it's Hollywood," said Pepper, "and lots of things go on, but not with minors."

"Oh, threats," said Angelini.

"Is this true?" asked Mira.

"Yes," said Dianna.

"Prove it," said Sawyer.

"Mr. Dante?" asked Mira.

Dante looked into his lemonade, probably wishing he could jump in.

"Mr. Dante," Mira repeated. "I will have to file this, and it will have to be investigated. The Fletchers pay me to be diligent."

"I thought the state paid you," said Sawyer.

Mira smiled. "Both."

"Cripes," said Sawyer.

"Mr. Dante?"

"Yes," the producer finally said. "She did tell me, and I dismissed it because I didn't want to hear it, but my secretary saw her run into my office crying. I'm sorry, Dianna. I just wanted us all to work together in peace, and I didn't think it would happen again."

"She kicked me!" said Angelini.

"Where you deserved it," said Dianna.

Pepper laughed.

"Well," said Mira, "with that experience, of course she would feel threatened on the set. We will bring charges. Mr. Dante, you have a problem."

"Yes, you do," said Pepper.

"I guess so," said Sawyer.

"The problem is that this little prima donna walked off the show," said Angelini.

"Why did you assault her?" Sawyer asked.

Angelini yelled, "She called me a faggot."

"I don't know that word," said Dianna.

Bill said, "This is ridiculous. Let's just forget all this and finish up."

"You play my part, then," said Dianna. "You can do all things, right? He hit me, and yes, I told him what Nick told me, that Mr. Angelini had made a pass at him. He was proving his manhood."

Lynne walked quickly to the table and put her hand on Dianna's shoulder. "I will speak to the Fletchers tonight. They will agree Dianna should not return to the set until it is clear this will not happen again."

Lynne's strong presence and her mentioning "the Fletchers" impressed the others.

Sawyer said, "Dante, what about it?"

Dante couldn't speak.

"I have a contract," said Angelini.

"You can't fire him now," said Bill. But he looked uncertain. "Dianna, you should have told me. We could have worked something out."

"You wouldn't have believed me," she said.

Bill looked up to the heavens and took a deep breath.

"The welfare department will bring charges against your company," said Mira. "If you dismiss him, perhaps reduce those charges and only make them against Angelini."

"It's just her word," said Angelini.

"Yes," said Dianna. "My word. And Mr. Dante's. And Mira's. Mr. Royce doesn't seem to want to be included."

"It's a matter of practicality," Bill protested. "You can't change directors or stop production just before it's all over. Are you going to keep his name off the credits, too? That's blacklisting."

"He hurt me," said Dianna.

"She hurt me!" said Angelini.

Everyone looked at Dante, who only wanted everybody to be happy. He looked at Mira, at Lynne, at Pepper.

"All right then. I'm sorry, Mike. You're off the production."

"He's done great work," said Bill. "So he's a jerk. Apologize and get on with it."

"I don't matter? How he treats me doesn't matter?"

"That's not what I mean."

"Never mind," said Angelini. "I can see who runs Hollywood." He grabbed his hat, got up. "Good afternoon, Miss Fletcher. The spoiled kid gets the worm." And he walked away, Manny rushing to see him out.

Even though she'd won, his words hurt worse than the slap.

Bill sat back and stared up at the sky.

Dianna felt she needed to add more proof. "Today was just the capper. He changed my costume so it would be ugly and funny. Mr. Royce and I were supposed to dive in and race, but Mr. Angelini told Mr. Royce to kick me, for which I wasn't prepared, and it hurt when I hit the water."

"I'm sorry," said Bill, still looking at the sky. "I assumed he had told you. He probably forgot. It's just one of those things."

"I don't care if Angelini said it was fine, go ahead, do it," said Dianna, knowing she was in the right and going in for the kill. "You should have asked me first. You were a stuntman. You're just defending him because he makes you look good, and this is your big part. But I hit the water hard. That's why it took me so long to get back up for air, but you were so pleased with yourself."

"I *was* acting," said Bill.

"But that was Millie's time to shine, it was in the script, and what did she get? A stupid suit that was too loose, a cap to hide her hair and make her look dumb, and then you kick her when what she wanted to do was show you what she could do. This is what Mr. Angelini *always* did! Any time Millie could show something of who she was, he'd cut it out. There's so little script left to film that there's no way that's going to change."

Dante sat back. "You're protecting Millie," he said, with a more relaxed tone.

"That day, she wanted to attract Hal. Even if it was scary."

"That might be what Angelini did not like," said Mira, with a rueful smile.

"That's trash," said Bill. "Hal's just having fun. Millie's a kid."

"Going onto that set was hell," said Dianna. "They all stayed in their little corners and talked about me and criticized me."

"You were late and unprepared," said Bill.

"I told you why. Tony overscheduled me."

"That's true," said Pepper. "Disney didn't coordinate with us. We've adjusted all that. Someone should have contacted my office and not taken it out on Dianna."

"Sounds like the tone of the set was bad," said Dante.

"It was not," said Bill.

Why was he defending what happened?

"Don't worry," said Dante. "I know a good man who can finish this up."

Dianna said, "The jackknife dive goes in. That was Millie's time to show she wasn't a loser. That her sister didn't mean what she said."

"That's not even in the script," said Bill.

Dante said, "I'm not sure that is possible."

Lynne said, "Show them your dive, Dianna."

Dianna stood and tossed off the robe, kicked off her sandals, and twisted her hair into a ponytail.

Sawyer muttered, "Damn shit."

She tread carefully on the deck and stepped onto the diving board, ran and jumped up high, then bent down straight so that her fingers touched her toes. Her curvy rear end topped the picture for but a second. She straightened out and dove cleanly into the pool, a shadowy figure until her head bopped up. She swam straight for the ladder and climbed up, dripping on the cement.

Manny stepped forward with a huge terrycloth robe. She wrapped herself in it and padded toward them.

Bill said, "Sure, it looks great, but Angelini thought it took too much time away from the story. We have a schedule. We have to finish up."

"It didn't take a minute," said Dianna. "That's the dive Millie was *supposed* to do. Hal talks about it in the script. Inge added it in this version. I practiced that dive all week because I thought I was going to do it. I'm sure Mr. Angelini just wanted to make me look stupid so Bill here could look good."

Bill grumbled. "He mentions it. That's enough. Doing it is distraction."

"It's in the script!"

Dante said, "I think you're more upset that you weren't able to show the dive than that you almost died today."

"It was Millie's moment. Angelini wasn't going to give it to her. No one cares about Millie. He," and she pointed at Bill, "has to go work with John Wayne."

She plopped down onto a chaise lounge. Manny handed her another towel so she could dry her ponytail.

"That's right," said Bill. "I was supposed to be in Arizona next Wednesday. I had to push it back to the next Monday. That's not much time to do anything but finish up what we have to finish up."

Was he looking at her legs? She stuck them out more. Why did she do that? He was arguing against Millie. She tucked them back under her.

"Angelini's gone," said Dante. "I'm sure a new director will want to look at what's in the can."

"I'm working on *Silver Sierra this* week," Dianna said. "And next week."

"We'll make time," said Dante. "We'll get your dive in."

"You'd want to do the pool scene over?" Bill asked, incredulous. "That's a whole day."

"I want to look at the footage tomorrow," Dante said. "With my new man, Tom Damrosch. Good television director from New York. He's in town."

"You say it now," said Dianna, "but if it's left for last, you'll find a way not to do it."

"I mean it. We'll need to get MGM's pool stage back."

Bill protested, "I can't hang around."

"I'll deal with Wayne," said Dante to Bill.

"I've held them up enough," said Bill. "This is all because she's a Fletcher."

"You just have to kick us, don't you?" said Dianna.

"Now, now," said Dante. "Let me figure out what we can do. Dianna, please keep an open mind."

"I don't know if I can go back. And I wouldn't want to make John Wayne mad."

"Leave that to me," said Dante.

She'd already made Bill mad. He got up and walked toward the drive. Dianna ran after him, wrapping her robe around her.

"Why are you so cold? Why don't you care about what he did?"

"You're smearing Angelini. What were you doing in his office?"

She couldn't believe he'd said that, but she found her tongue. "Talking about my work."

"Were you?"

What did he mean, that she'd been flirting with Angelini?

"PhD! You're stupid! I was in his office. But you don't have to be anywhere! I was just walking to the door when four boys pulled me into their locker room and pushed me on the floor."

"What are you talking about?"

Why had she told him that?

"You're scared of John Wayne."

"All right you two," said Dante, coming out with the others.

"And what do you think your precious Star's been doing with Angelini?"

She only suspected that. She just wanted to make him mad.

Bill stared her down. "Sweet Dianna. John's daughter."

"You'll never be the actor he is!"

Bill walked away. Damn him. So long as he was driving, he was fine.

Pepper took her arm. "I'm glad we solved this. It would have been rough if people thought you were a quitter. We wouldn't be able to get work for you again."

"Yeah," said Dianna. "I'm just supposed to lay down and die for the profits."

"Yeah," said Pepper, pinching her cheek. "You're a good kid."

So she was back on *Picnic* for a little longer. The cast would be meaner than ever. But at least Millie would have a chance to show her stuff.

"We can turn this into a real story," said Pepper. "Douse some of that gossip that you're difficult."

"It's going to be okay, Dianna," said Mira.

She didn't feel okay.

19

Mike Connolly of *The Hollywood Reporter* scooped the news that Michael Angelini had nearly killed Dianna Fletcher on the *Picnic* set.

Orson Welles stalked Angelini to the Desilu commissary, when Angelini still had the nerve to show up, and, with Kane's sweet smile, dropped several burning cigar ashes into the director's soup.

Frank Sinatra called. "Baby, if you ever get in a mess like that again, you call me, and I'll take care of it."

Dianna assured him she was okay.

"I'm sailing off to Catalina this weekend with Janet and Tony and some others. Why don't you come? "

She loved sailing, but she remembered her mother's warning. Also, she had to study for that test.

Sinatra said, "I'm looking after you, kid." Apparently.

Katharine Hepburn called from New York. "All that 'I give my actors freedom' crap. He should be thrown under a truck."

Walt Disney said, "Why didn't you tell me? I've got some muscle in this town."

George Stevens went on record to defend her and profess outrage. "This Angelini bullies a sixteen-year-old girl. He's dead in this city."

Henry Fonda called to say, "Just call and let me know when to punch someone out."

Jimmy Stewart ranted about the new, know-it-all directors.

Dianna appreciated the noise. They meant well, but everyone was busy. Not too busy to speak their indignation to the press, though. Uncle George made sure of that.

She heard from her mother, on a terrible connection. Anne sounded tired, so Dianna made light of everything.

"We cabled Dante with some curse words," said Anne. "Preminger's a prick. Newman's playing the star. My character is bland as hell, so I'm trying to spice her up. Your father is working on three movies at the same time. I can't get ahold of him," and here the phone crackled.

"What?" Dianna shouted.

"It's getting to be too much."

"How's Chas?"

"I am not having an affair with Newman. God help me. Thank God for the AD. Assistant directors are God's gift to actors."

What affair with Newman?

When John called, he was quiet, logical, with a touch of anger, like his *Guns* character. "I will straighten your schedule out with George. As for Angelini, we found him a job directing a cheap Hercules picture in Italy. You go to work on time and know your lines. I miss you, princess."

"How is Chas?"

He'd hung up.

She heard from the new director, Tom Damrosch, who wanted to reshoot a few scenes and add a few more. A few days were added to the schedule.

Good luck, Bill.

Jack Goodman called. "All this is great publicity, darling. Finish *Picnic*. We'll shoot around you."

The cast refused to comment except for Bill who said, "Angelini is a brilliant director. He'll be back. This was all a misunderstanding."

Go figure. She'd walked off the set and was the darling of Hollywood. Pictures of her holding the Oscar, at Jim's party, and as little Lark filled the papers and magazines. Her perky, determined image ruled, fighting to make the show the best it could be. Her fan clubs sent out bulletins. *The New York Times* wanted an interview. The fan magazines prepared stories about her feistiness for several issues.

Maybe none of it mattered. Khrushchev blasted that if the United States sent over any other spy planes, there would be atom bombs flying in the first few minutes.

When Dianna returned to that pool set, the crew applauded her. Lucille Ball, who wasn't scheduled that day, sat next to her in makeup. "Kid, I'm sorry. I didn't catch any of what was going on. I have been so wrought up. I should have kicked that man in the balls."

Dianna was not emotionally immature, but she was sixteen, and while she knew that Ball was fighting off her devastating divorce and had cozied up to Angelini for understandable reasons, she still felt betrayed. So she only said, "Thank you," and hurried off to her dressing room where she was relieved to find the pretty peppermint striped suit.

A few of the models posed on the pool deck, as before. Dianna, her hair tied behind her head, slipped into the pool to take a lap and get used to the water. When Bill hopped in, she swam to the ladder and climbed out.

The AD called places. She and Bill lined up at the side of the pool.

They didn't speak.

They dove in, ready set go, no kick, this time. They dove in a couple of times so that the camera would come on them bobbing back up, laughing. A polite and efficient Damrosch even shot a close-up on a wistful Millie, her first ever on *Picnic*.

Then the jackknife. Photographers appeared. Even Mark Dante walked in.

"All right, Dianna," called the AD, when the camera was set. Millie's moment to shine had arrived. She walked to the diving board, dropped the towel she had wrapped around her, and sprang into the dive.

As she climbed out to applause and accepted a huge towel, Damrosch said, "Could you do it again?"

She did.

Bill had stayed, but he hadn't said anything to her, just walked away in the company of one of the models, both laughing.

He really was a jerk.

At home, she turned on the television to relax in her triumph, but that was not to be. There were young people carrying signs: "America needs no thought controllers," "Sweep out the witch hunters," "Protect our teachers from intimidation," "Un-American Activities Committee is anti-American," "Get Out of Vietnam."

What universe was this?

The newscaster said this was happening in San Francisco. The demonstrators had been kept out of a Congressional committee room during an open hearing. Denied admittance, the students sat down on the courthouse steps and sang a song, "We shall not be moved," while hundreds of police massed and turned fire hoses on them, sending them screaming and falling on the pavement.

"What in God's name," said Hilda, who had come behind Dianna's chair to watch.

"They didn't do anything," said Dianna. "They were just sitting there or marching in a circle. Why are the police so awful?"

A policeman said, "One of them spit on me."

Another said, "One of them knocked me down."

"Poor things," said Hilda.

"Those young people are Communist dupes," another woman said to a reporter. "They're brainwashed Commies."

Another shouted, "We are finding out who is serving the enemy!"

"How can going to a Congressional meeting be serving the enemy?" Dianna asked.

"You'd be surprised," said Hilda.

"They are stomping out freedom of speech in the schools!" shouted a woman.

Police continued to go at the demonstrators with clubs and dragged them down steps, young men and women alike. The women's dresses ran up their legs, exposing their underwear.

Someone ran up to a policeman who was dragging a girl down the sidewalk and yelled, "Stop that!" The policeman clubbed the young man on the head.

Right on camera.

"Lord Jesus, have mercy," cried Hilda. "Never thought I'd see them treat white people like that."

A student, his head bleeding, spoke to the camera. "We were exercising our rights to demonstrate peacefully. Back in the days of the Revolution the British made it against the law for large groups to gather. Large groups gathering is how our Revolution began. This is our freedom. What do they do? Turn hoses on us. Treat us like rabid dogs."

Between takes on the *Silver Sierra* set the next day, all was outrage about the San Francisco students. The chairman of the Congressional committee, the House Un-American Activities Committee, a man named Wheeler, had admitted he gave passes to people who would behave decently, as he put it. He wanted to "keep the Commies from stacking an open meeting."

Marty, whose quiet on-set demeanor had been suddenly roused, explained the reason for the demonstration. "Last year, HUAC subpoenaed more than one hundred public school teachers they suspected of engaging in Communist activity. But Congress condemned its own Committee for doing that! But the Committee ignored that and sent the teachers' files to school officials where the teachers were employed and subsequently put on probation. And who knows what was in those files. Unproven allegations? That someone turned left at a corner? God help me, what is this country coming to, when representatives in Congress do not believe in due process of law?"

Paul Drury was particularly fiery that day.

Coming out of the set at lunch, Dianna took a walk. In one of the phone booths, Bill Royce's voice was loud and agitated. He hung up, then put his head against the phone.

She tapped at the door of the booth.

He looked up, opened the booth door, and frowned at her.

"What are you doing over here?" she asked.

"Sandi was in San Francisco."

"Did she see that demonstration mess?"

"She was in that demonstration mess."

"What?"

"She got dragged on the pavement, hosed down, and ended up in jail. Her brother, who's a student there, bailed her out, but the fool, she went back."

"Students? Not Communists?"

"What are they washing your brain with over at Disney?"

"I beg your pardon. I asked a question."

"It's a peaceful demonstration no matter who it is, kid. The police damaged city property just to torture them and show their power. And guess what, now thousands are back protesting. I wish I'd been able to go."

"But who are they?"

"Sandi's in a student organization of the American Civil Liberties Union," said Bill. "Some other political groups were there, including the Socialist League."

"Communists?"

"Oh, for Christ's sake," he shouted. "What the hell do you know about it, you in your precious palace on the hill? Socialism isn't Communism, got that? It's not tyranny."

Always judging her. And defending Socialism!

"And I've got this damn *Picnic* that's taking forever," he said.

"I guess that's my fault!"

"Angelini is a great talent, and you made him a pariah here. Talk about blacklisting."

"He hit me. And hit on me."

"Sure," said Bill. "Let him apologize and get on with it. No, he has to get fired and exiled to a Hercules picture in Italy. Which your dad got for him. You must have goaded Angelini beyond tolerance."

"I did not goad him! You're stupid! For a man writing a dissertation, you have a small mind. And your girlfriend shouldn't have gone. What good will it do? If they're right, the President should do something."

"How would he know about it unless people protest? And if he protests it, he's accused of being a Commie."

"They wouldn't accuse the President of being a Communist."

"They accused Eisenhower and Truman."

"How can they do that?"

"Divide and conquer us. Accuse people of treason for anything you don't like."

"Maybe Congress heard there were violent people in that crowd."

"Damn girls who know everything." He looked at his watch. "I have to get back. Big scenes with Alan. When do I have the joy of seeing you again?"

"Tomorrow. Millie's dance."

"No lines for you to forget, huh?"

"Why don't you go? You don't want to be late and push the schedule back even more, do you?"

"Sarcasm is a gift of the ignorant," he said, and he strode away, a script under his arm.

She wondered why he'd come over to Paramount just to make a phone call.

Back on *Picnic* the next day, she danced for Millie. She leaped up, swayed, threw out her arms, seeming to embrace the air. Although the camera did not cut to him, she reacted as if she saw Hal standing behind his trash barrel, bare chested. She immediately got clumsy and made faces before Millie gave up entirely.

Damrosch said, "Do it again, just that way. It describes Millie's whole character."

She did it again. When she left the set, Bill was laughing with Star and didn't say a word about her scene. She went right up to him but was interrupted by a messenger delivering a script to him.

"Fine," he said, riffling through it. "More revisions to *Comancheros*."

"Is it a good part?" asked Star.

"Second billing. I even get the girl this time."

"Who's your leading lady?"

"Ina Balin. One of those exotic fiery types. She's up for Maria in *West Side Story*."

Except for herself, thought Dianna, who wasn't up for *West Side Story*? All these old people in their mid-twenties were.

That night, leafing through *Look*, she found a two-page article about him. Up and coming, brilliant, hard worker, liked by everyone, loves the ladies, they love him back. She read praise from his *Picnic* co-stars: "He is so easy to work with," said Lucille Ball. Reta Shaw said, "He makes a point to get to know everyone and talk to them, make it an easy and relaxing set where you can do your best." "He's a great guy," said O'Connell. "I'm glad he won that Oscar."

What production of *Picnic* had they been working on? She must have missed a great experience. She went out on her balcony and, to her annoyance, cried.

Thank God she only had one more day.

The last scenes would be shot on MGM's back lot, a large, rolling green swath of ground dressed up to be a small town park.

Dianna kept company with Lucille Ball, with whom she felt most comfortable.

"What are you doing next?" Dianna asked.

"I'm going to Broadway. I'm doing a musical!"

She had nerve.

"I've got to make this studio work, too," said Ball. "I don't just want to rent the space. It's all westerns, family shows, westerns. All predictable."

"Good westerns in color," said Dianna, pointedly.

"Yeah," said Lucille. She even laughed. "When we bought the studio, I thought, let's do something to bring the country together or show a better world. I don't think that's remotely possible now. Everyone's so divided."

The AD called Dianna for another picnic game that turned out to be a treacherous stunt.

"You have got to be joking," she said, when it was described to her.

"It's easy. We'll all be here," said the stuntman.

Bill said, "Sure, I can do this."

"*Your* feet will be on the ground," she protested.

He only smiled.

"Ready?" asked the captain.

"No," she said.

"Come on," said Bill, and the captain lifted her up. Bill grabbed her with two hands, then, as the captain kept her secure, he clutched her waist with one hand and dropped the other.

"Okay, Dianna?" called the captain. "He's got you."

She clutched her knees to keep her skirts down. His hand hurt, but she clenched her teeth and smiled.

"Laugh!" called Damrosch.

Holding her aloft with one arm, Bill strode a few paces. And dropped her but quickly broke her fall with his other arm. The stunt captain arrived a second too late.

"You okay?" said Bill.

"Let's do it right," she said.

The second time proved more successful although her waist throbbed from the strength of Bill's hand.

"And that's a print," said Damrosch. "Thank you."

"That's it for me," she announced. Thank God.

"Are you coming to the wrap party?" Bill asked.

"No."

"Don't be like that."

"Like what? I can't go to a studio party with liquor. And I don't think I'd have any fun. You'd be too busy putting everyone else at their ease so they can do their best." She smiled sweetly. "Good luck with *Comancheros.*" She walked away. Goodbye, good riddance. Damn handsome Communist.

When she took her shower, she saw an ugly purple and black bruise where his hand had been.

It would fade.

20

"Dianna! My love!"

"Hi, Larry."

Finally, her old boyfriend had called. She kept on filing her nails, holding the phone to her ear with her shoulder.

"I'm in *West Side Story*!"

She stopped filing.

"Robbins called me in. He and Wise hired me on the spot."

"For Tony?"

She had recommended him to Wise, but that he would get something and she wouldn't – it hurt.

"Nah, Tamblyn's got a shot at that. I'm Riff!"

"Oh. Wow."

"They're still testing Marias," Larry said. "I hear Natalie Wood went to see Wise."

"Everybody knows that."

He was so happy he invited her on two dates. They went to movies – the superb *Jazz on a Summer's Day* and to a drive-in to see *The Blob*. They laughed so hard through *The Blob* that they stayed for the second showing and did a little necking. That made her feel good. But he didn't call again. He was busy in movies, and she was a loser on television.

Still, Betsy Drury was fun to play. She wasn't a perky teen (they had aged Betsy to be eighteen!) but a thoughtful, competent young woman with guts. The work was hard – more than ten pages a day to memorize, lots of discussions between shots (two of the actors competing against each other and her), and everything took twice as fast. She didn't have time to suffer.

Marty kept to himself, but Mike North and Chris Hill, playing her brothers, competed for the role of breakout male hunk. Both of them dealt with her politely and she made a point of agreeing with them. She loved their competitive discussions because they played fair. Even so, she realized that all "her" episodes were being filmed together (an arrangement Uncle George insisted on so she would be available for other opportunities) caused bad feeling, and she made a point of being deferential, but not at Betsy's expense. The set was easier than *Picnic*'s, even though the work was more frenetic. This was a relief, and she stayed for the wrap parties.

Her episodes were thrilling. Betsy was trapped underground after an earthquake, in love with a baddie, kidnapped and kept in a mad house, trapped in the house with rawhiders and an injured Chris, held prisoner when trying on dresses, in love with two bad guys – no, three, including a con man posing as a minister, and helping a widow save a newspaper. She was not forgotten in the "other" episodes, and if she had a strong role in them – arguing with her family, using her wits to solve a problem, or corralling wealthy men to give to her charity – she was a solid presence in that family, not wilting or caring only for getting married or – as MJ suffered – going to the prom.

Once, returning from lunch at the studio, a silver haired man with a considerable paunch walking toward her, stopped and watched her hurrying to the set, lifting the skirts of her costume to reveal her sneakers as she ran.

"Dianna Fletcher," he said, and she stopped, but all he did was look at her, then look at the pavement and move on. Probably a tourist who'd gotten off the tour.

This episode they were working on featured a scene where, even after her new beau was proved to be a murderer, she stood against her family — a great scene, rich and wonderful to play. Her problem of too many line choices vanished, or Betsy snatched them up fast, and Wray Mackay, a thirty-year movie veteran who directed the opening episodes, encouraged her ideas. Even so, it didn't take Dianna long to realize that Betsy was simply a more mature character than the one she'd been playing the last couple of years, except for L.A. Franklin's incisive and thoughtful scripts.

This episode was not so lucky, but it was fun. Mackay, a soft-spoken and yet persistent director, spent time on her big scene, filming several angles. She did have to cry at the end. A close-up required several takes because Mackay could not finalize how he wanted to see it, and Dianna, to her surprise, wept each time.

Finally, she was dismissed and found Bill Royce standing up in the back, where he'd been sitting in the shadows.

"What are you doing here?" she asked, wiping her eyes with a handkerchief, trying to ease the sting of dripping mascara.

Chris Hill yelled, "Hey, Bill! Is that you?"

"What's that fight about?" asked Bill.

"Her boyfriend's a murderer," said Chris, jogging over.

"Picky," said Bill.

"Dianna, you know Bill? We were in Stella Adler's class in New York."

Bill said, "Good God, Millie, what have you done to yourself?"

His intense eyes roamed over her in her pale blue, low cut gown, her hair tumbling down in shining waves.

She backed away from his intense look. "Why are you here?"

"I just read for your producer."

"For this little show? I thought you were too busy in the movies."

"A good guest shot is good advertising for my movies. This show's getting some good press already. Good writers and production values."

"Always thinking," said Chris "This guy never takes a day off. What part?"

"I read from four scripts, all different, and I have to say all pretty good."

"You'll be in all four?" asked Dianna, thinking she had better get out of those.

"Maybe not any of 'em," Bill laughed. "Just one. It depends on the producer. And my schedule."

"What are you up to?" asked Chris.

"I'm heading off to Arizona to do *Comancheros* with the Duke."

"I thought you'd left already," said Dianna.

"They got held up by weather. It turns out I'm not so late after all. I just read for another picture, something quick but meaty that I can do after I'm back. The director is someone who was blacklisted and getting back in the game."

Someone yelled for Chris.

Dianna started to leave.

"Wait."

"For what?"

"The other reason I'm here," said Bill, "is to give you your going away gift from *Picnic*, since you missed the wrap party. Everyone missed you."

"The cast sent me flowers."

"They did?"

"I guess you didn't chip in. I didn't get you anything."

"I'm sure." He smiled with all that charm he used on all the girls. She didn't care. That he wanted to make up with her didn't matter. He hated her father, he was smug and superior, and she wanted to move on.

"I didn't get anyone anything. I sent Lucille the flowers."

"Okay."

He shrugged and seemed to be frozen about which line to pick in his head. She knew that feeling, but she didn't sympathize.

He reached into his inside jacket pocket, took out a flat box, and held it out.

"Look, Dianna. The whole cast felt awful. And I realized —" He looked almost bashful. Oh, he could act! "I told myself when I was a young, anonymous actor that if I ever got to where I was head of a cast, I'd try to make things easier for the other actors. Make it a good set for work. You were the kid, the most vulnerable, and I sure messed up. Star told me a few things about Angelini, and I — I just didn't see it. This doesn't make up for it, but I did want to give you something to say how sorry I am."

What a charmer.

She opened the box. It was a garnet necklace. Her birthstone. It reminded her how nice he had been to her – taking her to Forest Lawn, telling her how much he had appreciated her acting, oh but then turning around and criticizing her and being condescending. And whatever was it about her father that he hated?

She closed the box. "No. Thank you."

"Don't be that way."

"Don't make it my fault! I just want to forget the whole thing."

He didn't take it, so she put the box on a generator.

"You don't like my father for some reason."

"That doesn't have anything to do with you."

"Yeah, he's just my father. Give this to Miss January or February or March or whoever you're with now."

He seized the box, put it back in his pocket, and walked toward the door.

He would become a brilliant movie and stage actor.

She'd be a television star.

But what misery. Although she told herself she liked it all, she was constantly reciting lines to herself all day. Different directors for different episodes made it worse. Some knew exactly what they wanted. Some argued for crazy camera angles that took hours to light. Dianna brought her *Monopoly* game, and that helped ease tensions. But her father had been right. There was no arc to the story or the characters. Every episode began from square one again, as if the past episodes hadn't happened. She grew more frustrated but tried not to show it. She couldn't keep being unpleasant to work with. And she liked Betsy and her place in that family of supportive men. She felt safe, even if she was acting.

She was busy, but it wouldn't last. Her featured episodes would end, and she'd have small parts in the remaining episodes. She would have to find something else. Not television. Another movie. But there was only silence from that front. If nothing happened, she would have to do another season. She had no studio contract. No one was going to hand her anything. What was she to do?

But they had horses! One or two days a week, they'd go on location and she'd be riding almost all that time. She loved it and refused a double even for touchy gallops down hills and across streams. That made up for a lot. But the horses wouldn't solve her problem.

"Get me a movie or ten," she told MaryAnn, the plump middle-aged woman who had taken over in Uncle George's office since Pepper moved to the agency's New York office. Dianna even called some casting agents herself, to no avail.

Elia Kazan called her to read for *Splendor in the Grass*.

"Have you had sex?" he asked.

She almost spilled the Coke he handed her.

"Healthy sex, that's what the young want. Kids not knowing what to do with their strong feelings."

After she read, he gushed, "You are growing up beautifully. I find myself attracted to you. That's important."

"Not doing that one," Dianna said to MaryAnn. "He gives me the creeps."

No one else called her.

At least there was Disneyland.

Walt Disney sauntered by the Tomorrowland stage and said, "You're my girl. You'll sing here forever if you want. You make everyone happy."

An old crone singing about Davey. She couldn't wait.

Finally, one of the casting agents she'd contacted called back to ask if she'd like to read for a director she'd never heard of, Fred Sybuck. The girl in the script seemed a few years older and quite mysterious, but the point was that she was beautiful and mesmerizing.

When she arrived for the reading, the man who greeted her was the same man who'd stopped for her at Paramount.

"I can't afford you," he said. "But I would love to hear you read this part."

So she read, playing the part perhaps too vivaciously and energetically.

But Sybuck said, "You are Lily. I knew that right away because those pictures of you – that big story in *Life*, and you at the Oscars – make you look like a dream. This girl is a dream, a dream very much alive. I gave your name to the casting agent, and she laughed. But after reading that article, I thought, why not try. I asked Goodman about you, and he invited me to some dailies. You're beautiful. It is a pleasure just hearing you. But I am not sure I can afford you."

Was he for real? His film was low budget, black and white, but an intelligent and beautifully written script. A young man, struggling with a poor job, killed his wife and went on the run. The character Dianna read for, Lily, was a dream girl the murderer fell in love with — and because of her, he became a different person. Lily reformed him and loved him, but she also turned him in. He was found guilty and went to death row, and Lily *still* loved him! In the final scene, he forgives her, and she still loves him. It could have been silly, but the script was so beautifully written that it was remarkably moving.

Sybuck's secretary told her that Steve McQueen, the *Blob* star, had come by to read that day. Working with him might be fun, Dianna thought. This little movie could be just the thing. She couldn't hint that she'd play it for nothing, but she asked the casting director what the situation was. He warned her that Sybuck had precious little money for distribution. What he didn't say, and what she understood, was that her name could help with funding.

She went home to Malibu now. Lynne, Reggie, Joanne, and Mick remained with her, and the rest went – she didn't know where.

Ramshackle bungalows crowded close together, perched on what looked like stilts on the beach. But then came a long stretch of sand and some soft hills where there were large homes, which you could reach by a gated road. On top of the first hill sat the Fletcher beach house, fronted by a gated drive shaded by palm trees.

Dianna loved this house, with its sweeping view of the ocean. Four bedrooms, all with a view of the water, comprised the lower floor with offices, gym, and screening room. The second floor had a living room with a fireplace and glass wall overlooking the sea, a big bright kitchen, and a sun room that doubled as a dining room if it rained. From the deck, where the pool was surrounded by lush vegetation, steps led down to a security fence winding around the house behind a tall hedge and beyond that, the beach and the sea.

When the whole family was there, they were on top of each other, making for a glorious rambunctious feel. Without them, the house felt big.

As soon as Dianna settled in, she took the test to get out of high school — one whole day of sitting at a desk with mostly middle-aged people staring at her.

She heard from Sybuck. "I would like to offer you the part of Lily," he said, rather formally. "I hope you will accept."

"Of course," said Dianna, barely believing she had gotten her own part in a movie without help from her agents or her parents.

MaryAnn called her almost at once. "Why didn't you ask me? *Every Time* is a small package for United Artists, black and white. No one will want to see it, and it's not for your fans. You know how they avoided *Anne Frank*. This new production company can't afford to pay a star's salary, just scale, so they won't get a name for the man. They're paying you a pittance. Five thousand. Not worth getting a percentage. But it's yours."

"I want to do it," Dianna said. She really wasn't that sure, but it was a movie, it wasn't Disney, and she would be a dream.

"I'll have to work it out with Goodman."

"They said that I'd be free after twelve episodes."

"He's going to ask for more. Their tests are through the roof for you."

That scared her. She might have to do two seasons.

"That's not my problem."

"Natalie Wood got *Splendor*."

"Sure, she's had sex."

"I did hear of another small movie. A beautiful, smart girl struggling with how boys treat her. Nothing drastic happens, but she has a nervous breakdown."

She remembered the boys at the prom. "I want it!"

"Your father turned it down for you, so I shouldn't say anything. It's a good director, though, from New York television. Stupid title. *Now is Forever* or *Forever is Now*. It's into next year."

"Send me the script!"

"Tell your father you beat it out of me."

It certainly wasn't her mother's career, and she was afraid that she would fail even in these little movies. She *had* to challenge herself. Betsy was an easy character, but Dianna could not forget that she never found Millie. She would have to prove herself again and again and show that the Oscar hadn't been just for being in the right movie.

21

"We made tuna casserole for you," said Reggie, after she hung up with MaryAnn. "We're all going to go see Hilda's show and then go out for dinner. Just hit the security lock when you go to bed."

Hilda had an engagement at a jazz club on the Sunset Strip for one of her last nights before going to Europe to sing with a quartet and then join Anne. Dianna had asked if she could go with them, but they told her it was a tough club. She knew they just didn't want her going to a Negro club. It might bring along too much publicity that could go wrong.

The world was stupid.

She picked up *The Hollywood Reporter* and, seeing her name in bold type, read Cindy Cartwright's column.

> Dianna Fletcher went right to television instead of movie roles. George Bennett has been turning down parts for her by the dozen — he doesn't want her in movies with social problems, beach bunnies, even *Bye Bye Birdie*, a natural for her. So now she'll be a cowgirl on television in just another western. So much for a promising career.

Dianna finished her supper, put her dishes in the dishwasher, and headed downstairs to the recreation room. The hard liquor was locked up, as was the wine cellar, but she knew where that key was. She took out a bottle of cabernet and turned on the television.

Another western, black and white poor thing. *Her* western would be in full color! This show starred a nice looking man (who looked familiar, but she couldn't place him) galloping on horseback, shooting wildly at a stagecoach. She watched for a while, but she really wasn't interested, so she turned the set off.

She had drunk almost the full bottle of cabernet.

Anne Frank, it's good you're dead. We love you because you are dead. That's why we could make a movie about you. We took the actress who played you and put her into The Shaggy Dog *and* Detective Dog *and* Beautiful Beulah *while meanwhile her Juliet lies beneath the waves with rosemary on her breast for remembrance. The studios are all going away, piece by piece, and soon I will be the only one left to tell the tale, but they would have killed me.*

She picked up the bottle, leaned on the bannister as she went upstairs, took another few long sips of the wine, and sat primly on the couch where the phone sat. She dialed "O." At least, "O" would talk to her.

"Hello? I am Dianna Fletcher, and I think you should come to my house and watch me kill myself. I live at the end of Ocean Cliff Road. Thank you. Goodbye."

After all, she was killing herself. And whatever talent she had.

She took another sip of wine and stared at the ceiling. She drank some more. She heard sirens, saw red lights.

The Russians were attacking!

She heard pounding on the door.

Someone yelled, "Open up! Police!"

They really did say that!

She skipped over to the door and opened it.

"Hello, boys!"

She'd heard that line in some movie.

"Are the Russians coming?"

Two uniformed officers took her arms. Behind them were two men in white and one woman, also in white.

It was like the ending of *A Streetcar Named Desire*.

"Come on in," she said, shaking off the arms and skipping into the room.

The woman in white stepped forward. "Miss Fletcher?"

"Are you here for me?" Dianna asked. "I didn't think you'd come. You didn't have to."

"Of course we would come," said the woman. "You called us."

"Is anyone else here?" asked one of the officers.

"Everyone's gone." Dianna flopped down on the sofa. A part of her brain said, this is serious; what do they want? Another part of her brain said, finally, "Want to play *Monopoly*?"

Another officer picked up the empty wine bottle from the floor.

"Did you drink all this?"

"I'll get coffee," said the nurse.

The officer said, "You said you were going to kill yourself."

"I was joking."

"Were you?"

"We'll take her to the hospital," said the other policeman.

Dianna was getting sober fast. "It was a joke. I'm okay."

"It'll have to be reported. Do we want to take her in? She'll make the papers. It could be nasty with her parents."

"We can't leave her here alone," said the medic. "We don't know if she was pretending."

"Then we take her to the hospital."

"No!" Dianna cried.

She hated hospitals. She'd gone there to "cheer up" young kids, who were seriously sick, burned, helpless, and hopeless.

The doorbell rang. One of the officers went to answer it. A familiar voice said, "We live down the street. Is there something we can do?"

"Go home," said the officer.

"Who is that?" Dianna called.

"Bill Royce. And Sandi."

"Go away!"

He'd come to gloat.

Bill and Sandi pushed their way past the officer.

"Just a minute!"

"Go away!" The last thing she needed was Bill Royce and his superiority. Sandi bent over Dianna.

"We saw flashing lights and heard sirens. We wanted to help."

"She called saying she wanted to kill herself," said one of the officers.

"Shit," said Bill.

"It's a lie!" Dianna cried.

"You're drunk," said Bill, noticing the bottle.

"She drank a whole bottle of wine," said the nurse, coming in with coffee.

Bill said, "Where's the damn staff?"

He hunched down by her.

"Get out," she said.

"Shut up."

She was about to say, "I can take care of myself," but instead she turned sharply away, and, it occurred to her, she'd turned away just as he had done in *The Philadelphian*.

"It's okay, sweetie."

At least, she thought he'd said that.

"Aren't you in Arizona?" she asked, her back to him.

"I came back yesterday."

"We have to take her to the hospital for observation," said the nurse. "Do you know where her parents are?"

"No," said Dianna.

"You made a threat to kill yourself," said the nurse.

"It was a joke," Dianna shouted, sitting up. "Are you stupid? Just a joke!".

Bill stood up. "She did a kid thing."

"Are you a doctor?"

"Bill Royce," said Sandi, hugging Dianna. "He's a friend. They've worked together."

"Not a friend," Dianna muttered.

The nurse said, "Mr. Royce, we don't know who you are."

"We'll take her home," said Sandi, standing up. "We live down the road. She can spend the night with us."

"I don't know," said an officer. "Are you two married?"

"Yes," said Sandi.

"No," said Bill.

Dianna laughed.

"Nobody's going to want this publicity," said Bill. "She needs friends around her more than observation in a hospital room."

"You're not my friends," Dianna said.

Sandi gave Dianna a squeeze. "Honey, we were having a party to celebrate Bill coming home, but almost everyone has gone. We would have asked you if we'd known you were here by yourself."

"I don't want to go to a party."

"It's pretty much over. Just a few good friends left. You don't have to see anyone if you don't want to. We have a cozy bedroom upstairs."

"Will you be responsible for her?" asked one of the doctors.

"Sure," said Bill.

"We'll call tomorrow morning," said an officer. "Give us the number."

"Wait, who are you?" said the other officer. "What's your name again?"

"Bill Royce. I worked with Dianna. Call the studio – MGM – they'll know me. I'm doing a picture with John Wayne."

That impressed them.

"It would keep this out of the papers," said the nurse. "The Fletchers wouldn't want publicity. We could get in trouble."

Bill scratched something on a prescription pad.

Sandi said, "Come on, Dianna. Let's pack a few things. We'll leave a note for your staff."

Upstairs in her room, Dianna had second thoughts.

"I should stay here."

"No, you don't," said Sandi. "It's either us or the loony bin, although I have to say there's not much difference."

Dianna didn't want to go to either place.

She was startled to find three police cars outside with lights going, a fire department car, a black car with tinted glass, and an ambulance. Except for the black car, every other vehicle boasted flashing red lights, which had attracted quite a crowd. She recognized the street's security guards. The photographers gathered in a threatening huddle made her stop.

"Go away!"

"Come on," said Bill, taking her arm.

The security guards were holding off the neighbors and with the help of extra policemen, keeping the reporters at bay. People flung questions at her.

"Are you all right?

"What happened?"

"Was there a fire? I don't smell smoke."

Bill stopped to speak to one of the policemen. Sandi put her arm around Dianna and hurried her across the lawn to Bill's car.

Someone with a bull horn called out, "Miss Fletcher is fine. She was cooking, and there was an electrical fire. She called for help right away. Everything is all right. Everyone go home."

Dianna wanted to get out of the car, but Sandi kept her arms around her in the back seat.

"Crowd's breaking up," Bill said, as he got into the car. "Electrical fires aren't that exciting." Still, he had to drive slowly through the dispersing crowd, and they peered into the car windows. Dianna hid her face against Sandi.

"You'll be okay," said Sandi. "You just need people around you."

"Who left you alone, anyway?" Bill asked.

Dianna kicked at the back of his seat but her foot barely grazed it.

Bill's house was a pale adobe set apart from the row of beach houses and next to the stretch of beach leading to the Fletcher house, so technically, he was her next door neighbor, even if he lived a quarter of a mile away. Dianna liked the house — the logs, the beams, the stone fireplace with the massive sofa. A glass door led to a large deck, and that was all she saw before Sandi hurried her up the stairs past the few guests remaining from their party.

Dianna heard Bill saying, "An electric fire. She saw sparks and called the fire department and she being Dianna Fletcher, everyone came. They have to fix some things, so we brought her here for the night."

"Do you know her?" a woman asked.

"She played Millie in *Picnic*."

"Yeah, the director tried to kill her," a man said.

"He did not," said Bill.

"He did so!" Dianna yelled.

Someone laughed.

Upstairs, Sandi flicked a light switch.

Dianna liked the pretty blue and brown room overlooking the Pacific with its own balcony, dressing area, closet, and full bathroom.

"We have this room for guests or just in case we need a servant in the morning, which never happens, or if we have a fight, which does," said Sandi. "This house is drenched in political warfare."

Sandi was living here? Unmarried? She'd never heard of anyone who did that. The reason kids were getting married young was to live together and, of course, have sex. What was the point of just living together? Someone, she thought, wasn't in love.

"I should go home."

"You can't go home tonight. The police called your staff and I guess whoever's in charge of you and told them to stay away until something like four in the morning because there's a big mob of reporters there. I don't know what they think they'll find out. Peter – our houseboy – put fresh sheets on the bed. We weren't sure if a guest would get drunk and need to stay."

"I got drunk."

"You should have something to eat. Freshen up and come downstairs. There's plenty of food."

"Oh, no," said Dianna. The last thing she wanted to do was meet people.

"They're all good friends. They won't tell anyone about you. We have enough on them just in case."

Dianna felt terrible that she had done this stupid thing. No matter what anyone would say or do to contradict it, the rumor that she had tried to kill herself would get out there, and she'd be Judy Garland. On top of everything else.

She heard laughter and assumed it was about her. She washed her face, looked into her eyes wondering who was lurking there, felt homesick for old times, felt homesick for her old self and her family being together, brushed her hair, and changed to her polka dot sundress with a halter. It was the sexiest outfit she could put her hands on. Why did she want to be sexy? What was she looking for? Was she that pathetic? She slipped on her sandals and went down the stairs, and all the talking stopped as soon as they heard her.

Every man in the room jumped up. Bill, at the bar mixing drinks, was already standing, but he probably wouldn't have.

"Come on in," said Sandi.

Dianna walked into the circle by the sofa and fireplace, which was lit, the night being cool. She loved a crackling fire and sank right onto the floor in front of it.

A very tall man with blond hair and big teeth said, "Wow, you are everything and more."

Dianna could only say, "Is that possible?"

"Jim Coburn," said Bill. "He's full of metaphysical statements."

"Does Walt Disney know how pretty you are?" asked the metaphysical Jim.

Bill came round, handing out drinks. "That's Jim's long suffering wife,

Beverly. Steve and Neile McQueen," he continued. Neile was quite cute, with great legs and a pixie haircut. Steve had a pixie face over a muscular body and a long, slow, easy smile. She recognized his name and his face, but she couldn't remember from where.

"Those three over at that end of the couch are Andy and Pam Story, and that lone fellow with the guitar is Bruce Johnson. The other couple is Susan Weitz and her husband Harry Fisher. What kind of Coke can I get you, Dianna? I think Sandi's getting you a hamburger."

"Ginger ale. With a cherry."

"A Shirley Temple?"

"Shirley doesn't drink them anymore," said Dianna.

Beverly said, "Did they get the fire out?"

"Yes," said Dianna.

"They sent the whole battalion," said Steve. "Is that normal?"

"She's Dianna Fletcher," said Neile. "Can't have her burn up."

Dianna pointed at Steve. "The blob!"

"His greatest role!" Bill yelled from the bar.

"I wasn't the blob!" Steve yelled. "I destroyed it!"

"I saw it at a drive-in."

"You go to drive-ins?" asked Jim. "With boys? Does Walt know this?"

"With *a* boy," she corrected, to the group's amusement. She was feeling her wit coming through and she felt a tremendous urge to shock. She looked at Steve. "I just saw you tonight. On television."

"No wonder the place exploded," said Jim.

"I didn't see the whole thing. You were shooting at a stagecoach."

Sandi drew up a little glass table and put a plate before her with a hamburger, pickles, and onions. And a fork.

"Eat."

"The blob was in it," said Jim. "He's still chasing it."

"Shut up," said Steve.

"What's it called?" Dianna asked. "Is there ketchup?"

"*Wanted: Dead or Alive*," he said. "Your show is going to change the western, I hear. Thanks a lot."

She shrugged. "I'm too busy to know." She poured on the ketchup Sandi handed her and took a bite of the burger. It was good to eat something. She felt better already and stretched out her legs beneath the little table. Steve looked at them and smiled at them and then at her.

Bill placed her ginger ale on a coaster by her plate. Dianna looked away. She didn't like that he had more to criticize.

"I saw you on *Perry Mason*," she said to Jim. "You were mean, awful."

"Typecasting," said Bill, sitting next to Sandi on the sofa and swinging his arm around her.

"You deserved to be murdered," said Dianna. "Did you work together?"

Steve said, "We've all been friends since our first struggling days in this business when we were eating ketchup soup and living in a shoebox."

"Sue Weitz and Harry Fisher are professors of mine," said Bill. "And those guys over there are my Kennedy allies at UCLA."

Kennedy allies?

"They're a folk group. They're good. They've opened for Pete Seeger."

She didn't know who that was. "Have you all ever worked together?"

"I should say so," said Jim. "Steve, Bill, and I just got off of a major motion picture. *The Magnificent Three.*"

"Is that the one with Yul Brynner?"

"Already she knows how to break hearts," Steve said to Neile.

Neile said, "You would not believe the testosterone on that set."

"Easy, she's under eighteen," said Bill. "Steve, you could cope. You drove Brynner nuts fiddling with your hat, taking it off, putting it on."

"*He* couldn't do that," said Steve. "Never took his hat off in any scene. You were the rascal. You got Sturges to write you another scene. And he cut mine! Damn you!"

"Had to. They had to believe I was a gunslinger before I showed them I was a coward."

"Yeah, yeah, the good of the show."

"Brynner brought along a huge trailer and an entourage. I think he had someone to put salt on his eggs," said Jim.

"He's a wonderful man," said Dianna. "But he can't get over being the king. He's great without hair. Why wouldn't he take his hat off?"

"I just saw you on *The Greatest Show on Earth*," said the young man with the guitar. Bruce.

"Was *that* on television? My debut! I was on for five minutes. I hope you watched the whole thing."

"I've seen it twice," said Neile, "and every time, I have to shut my eyes. I hate the circus. When Jimmy Stewart hands you that – whatever it was – sooo sweet."

"Wasn't I?"

The others laughed.

"So you are doing a western series?" asked Sue Weitz. "Is there anything special about your character?"

"She's smart," said Dianna.

"That's progress," said Weitz.

"My friend Mary Jane Adams is on *The Carol Warner Show*, and she says that all she does is talk on the phone and talk about dances and boys. I've been caught in a mine explosion and killed a man."

"Why did you agree to do the western show?" asked Neile. "Horses?"

"There wasn't much work coming round. I didn't want to go to school full time, so I decided to do it. But now movie offers are coming in." She hoped that sounded like a flood of offers.

"What offers?" asked Beverly.

"For a small production company. I'm going to be romantic and lovely. I'm in love with a murderer. It's called *Every Time We Say Goodbye*." She looked at Steve. "Aren't you up for the lead?"

"Alas," said Steve.

"That would be me," said Bill. "Just signed the contract today. They gave you that part? A romantic idyll?"

Jim said, "That's not very gallant."

"I would have loved working with you," said Steve. "I'm a nice guy."

"It needed an actor," said Bill, and Jim and Steve roared their displeasure, but it was all in fun. It was obvious they were good friends as well as rivals. But Dianna didn't want to let him win that one.

"They probably need my name to bring people in. It's been done before."

"Ho, ho!" cried Steve. "Take him down a peg or five."

Her first love story since *Romeo and Juliet* — with smug, know-it-all Bill? Whose talent would overshadow anything she did? Why hadn't someone told her?

"And I'm playing a con artist — a preacher — on *Silver Sierra* in late July," said Bill. "So you'd better start liking me."

"Six million actors in the city," said Dianna, "and I can't get away from him."

"You might learn something," Bill said.

"Shut up, Bill," said Sandi.

"Don't you like Bill?" asked Steve. "All the girls like him. You must be smart."

"I don't," said Dianna, and everyone laughed. Bill just smiled. "He's such a know-it-all."

"He is," said Jim.

"I'm glad you're getting away from Disney pictures," said Susan Weitz. "I loved what you said when you got your Oscar about being at the Anne Frank house. What was it like?"

"Terrifying. Narrow and dark."

"How did you get to be there?" Susan asked.

"I went with Daddy and Mom to Rome when they were working at Cinecittà. They wanted to put me in a school there because my grades weren't good enough, and the welfare department said I had to go to school full time or I couldn't act until my grades were better. So Mom and Daddy put me in a special school in Rome. It was good. My class went to Paris once and to the Anne Frank House."

"What happened to the girl playing Anne?"

Dianna thought Steve's eyes had a malicious glint as he asked. He must have heard those rumors about her demanding the part and, being the spoiled daughter of John Fletcher, getting what she wanted. She'd tell him a thing or two. All of them.

"Yes," said Dianna. "When I heard there was going to be a movie, I sent a cable to Mr. Stevens, and he said I wasn't right for the part. I disagreed. He said, sorry. They cast that model. I really wanted to play Anne. I felt her."

"We all lose parts we think we can do," said Bill.

Well, aren't we all saints.

"I," she said, "am not that noble. I think you should fight for what you want."

"Oohhh," said Steve. "Knuckles up."

"Shut up," said Bill.

"She loved your parents," said Susan. "That impressed you."

"I threw in the towel because Mr. Stevens complained about all my cables to him. Daddy knew I was disappointed so he asked friends of his, who were going to make a movie of *Romeo and Juliet* at Cinecittà, to consider casting me as Juliet."

"Nice of Daddy," said Bill. "What *Romeo and Juliet*?"

"Shakespeare's," said Sandi. "Shut up."

"They didn't just give it to me! I had to read for it. It's not as if I never acted before, and we're always reading Shakespeare at home. Back here, Mr. Skorous at Fox didn't like the *Diary* footage. I heard about it. I sent him a wire. So I got to play Anne."

"Pretty shrewd," said Sandi.

"Was I wrong to take advantage of this actress — so called — I saw some of the footage — flat and awful. Anne is full of life. I wanted to play Anne Frank, do her justice."

"You were wonderful," said Sandi.

"You had problems with Stevens," said Bill.

"He wanted a saintly adolescent. I wanted a real girl. We had it out, and he decided I was right. Anne had her diary side and her obnoxious side. I loved playing her."

"What about *Romeo and Juliet*?" one of the folk singers asked. Pam.

"It hasn't been released. Something about a technical glitch."

Bruce said, "That was two years ago. What's the glitch?"

"Was it Italian?" asked Steve.

"No, it was an American director working in England, Anthony Marks, and the adaptation was by an American living in Rome, Edward Grey. It was fantastic — gorgeous costumes and scenery."

"Marks and Grey?" Bill looked over at Bruce.

"Wow," said Bruce.

"There's your glitch," Bill said.

"What do you mean?" asked Dianna.

"They're both blacklisted," Bill said. "Can't have their names on anything in this country. Has it been released somewhere else?"

"No," said Dianna. "That couldn't be it." Her parents would not work with or let her work with suspected Communists.

"They both had to leave the country for work," said Bill. "There might be some sort of technicality that the movie has to be released in the States before it can go anywhere else, but nothing's going to come in with their name on it as long as the blacklist is in effect. They probably refused to use fronts and are insisting either they use their names or it can't go anywhere else, since Trumbo is now being credited. Gutsy."

"That's crazy," said Dianna. "It's not as if they could put Communist propaganda into it. It's Shakespeare."

"Communism goes back to the ancient Greeks. Congress said so," said Susan.

"Huh?" said Dianna.

"A distinguished man from Congress mentioned that Communism started way before Shakespeare's time. No one is free of suspicion, you see."

Dianna was incredulous. "That's dopey."

"Dopey was probably a Communist, too," said Steve.

"And he didn't name names," said Bill. "Did your father know these guys were blacklisted?"

"No," she said, vehemently, instantly defensive of any implied accusation against her father.

"Never read anything about it, did you, Bruce?"

"Nope, but I'm going to check."

"Bruce is president of the film society at UCLA," said Bill. "He brings in movies, excuse me, *films*, from Europe."

Dianna repeated, "It's Shakespeare! It has to be another problem. You are just obsessed with this blacklist thing."

"The American Legion has sent out warnings to all its posts to protest *Spartacus* because it was written by a Communist," said Susan. "Aren't both your parents in it?"

She was offended. "The movie is about freedom."

"It's a free country only if you're against freedom and justice for your political enemies," said Pam.

"Even if it's Shakespeare," said Susan, "they had to write a screenplay for it, and nothing with their names on it can be released here. What a shame. I'd love to see it. Harry, it's getting really late. Bill, are you going to get a rest?"

"Some," said Bill. "We have some scenes in *Commancheros* to do here, but then I'm free until after the convention."

"Are you going to the convention?" asked Jim.

Sandi groaned again. "Bill's a vote getter for UCLA."

"I register voters," said Bill. "You like voters." And he kissed her hand.

"For Kennedy."

"Kennedy's so handsome," said Neile.

"Shut up," said Steve. "They give women the vote, and look what happens."

"No one gave women the vote," said Susan. "They fought like soldiers."

"Kennedy's smarter than he looks," said Bill.

"Like Bill," said Sandi. She leaned her head on his shoulder. He put his arm around her.

"What convention?" asked Dianna, wondering how Sandi could stand being around Bill all the time. They had to be engaged. Which was surprising since Bill was such a man about ladies.

"You don't know?" Bill accused.

"Oh, for such innocence," said Steve.

"Shut up, you smartass," said Neile. "The Democratic Convention is meeting in our fair city, Dianna. Alert your chauffeur. There will be traffic jams galore. The members of this household are going to be there every single day."

"Stevenson's going to get the nomination," said Sandi.

"Can't you give that up?" Bill argued. "He didn't run in the primaries. He's acting like an ass sitting there assuming he'll be drafted. Kennedy campaigned and won primaries. The people's voice!"

"The convention decides for the party," said Sandi, evenly. "The world's in a fragile state, and Stevenson is the only one who can navigate it better than Kennedy or Nixon or Humphrey or whoever else is out there. It's the party's convention, and they'll nominate Stevenson."

"Hello?" called Jim. "Where's the knob to change the channel? We've seen this show before."

"You're not being realistic," Bill said.

"Me not realistic?" Sandi retorted. "You actor. And that's all Kennedy is, an actor with Daddy's money behind him. How can you possibly prefer him over an intelligent and experienced man like Stevenson?"

"Adlai lost. Twice. Jack Kennedy is a fighter. We need someone who will beat Nixon."

"With the mob behind him."

"That's a lie," Bill shouted. "Damn it, that's a lie. Why do you keep repeating this lie?"

"Time to go," said Neile.

"But I never see how it ends," said Steve. "Dianna, you take notes."

"You don't want to know," said Jim.

"Can I help?" Dianna asked as Bill, collecting some good humor and delivering apologies, herded the guests out while Sandi started clearing up paper plates.

"No, no, you head upstairs."

"I could go home."

"No, you can't." Sandi seemed impatient. "Go on up. Wake up whenever you want. I have to go to a meeting in the morning, but Bill's here all day, and he loves to make waffles."

Upstairs, sinking into the bed, the persona of humor she'd worn for a few hours wore off, and her melancholy seeped back in. She heard Bill and Sandi still arguing and turned the light back on.

"What is it about your fascination with this guy? He slept out the McCarthy censure, never said a word about blacklisting. Come on, Bill."

"He was sick." "

"Did you hear about his having Addison's disease?"

"That's a lie from Nixon's camp."

"McCarthy dated his sister, for God's sake, Bill. He wasn't going to censure him. And as for dates, Jack's got several a night, I hear, women waltzing in and out of wherever he goes. Is that what you like? He gets away with it?"

"Damn you! That's all gossip! Nixon spreads that stuff."

"He's a rich playboy who leaves his wife home, and he has a great vocabulary and good writers who write his books for him. Why in God's name do you like him?"

"Because he's damn brilliant!"

"Or he has everything you want? A rich daddy? Women all over the place?"

Dianna heard something crash.

"Quiet, dammit," she heard Bill say, and then the voices were hushed and intense. Dianna tried to listen, but she couldn't make out the words except for Adlai and Kennedy and even a fuck you from Sandi. Dianna hoped Sandi won. Kennedy — the little she'd heard about him — was charming, but if he wasn't qualified, didn't know anything, that was something else again. How could Bill be for him?

There was a desk in the alcove with books stacked on it. She got up and opened a folder on the desk. Inside were typed pages, with some written corrections, asterisks for footnotes, and reference citations written in the margin. She slipped back into bed and began to read.

In order to prove that there was a threat at all, HUAC should have demonstrated that films contained propaganda. They never showed that a danger existed. Therefore, it was disingenuous of the Committee to claim that, having exposed certain writers and actors as Communists (without proof or a court trial), that they had somehow saved the American public from being victimized by Communist propaganda when they could not prove such propaganda even existed. The Hollywood hearings were nothing but a hoax, meant to prey upon the fears of citizens. Promoting fear and division is the fascist's way of getting loyalty because he cannot earn it.

How could the hearings be a hoax? It was Congress! Wasn't being a Communist a crime? Why was Bill writing against Congress, which was trying to defend the people from Communists in the country?

HUAC charged people in a public forum in which the persons had no legal standing or defense, as they would have had in a courtroom. When the appeals of the Hollywood Ten writers finally made it into court rooms, juries exonerated them, but judges, politically influenced, overturned those jury verdicts.

Could judges do that? Was that true? But the juries thought those Communist writers were innocent? Were they dupes?

Even more damning is that persons brought before the Committee who had left the Communist party were never questioned about the details of their involvement; only "friendly" witnesses were. "Unfriendly" witnesses were reluctant to "snitch" — i.e., name names, which is what HUAC demanded of them. They were willing to talk about their own experiences in Communist meetings but unwilling to give the Committee names of others. HUAC never let them get that far. They insisted on names. But the names were already in the files of the Federal Bureau of Investigation. At times, anti-Semitism leaked through HUAC's intent. Many on the committee believed that the Jews were part of a Communist conspiracy to overthrow the

United States government. No one came up with any proof of such a conspiracy, but that did not stop HUAC.

Well, that seemed like nonsense. She flipped through the pages but stopped at the name "MARTIN O'MILES." Martin O'Miles who played her father?

His demeanor in this transcript, however, bore little relationship to the quiet actor. On the contrary, this man sounded like Betsy's outspoken father, Paul Drury.

MARTIN O'MILES: "You are using your office in Congress to intimidate people and have violated the Constitution. Every single person who has appeared here who has invoked their Constitutional privilege in the Bill of Rights has been placed by you in contempt of Congress, and some have gone to prison. Many have pleaded the Fifth, and so have been discriminated against and barred from working at their chosen profession. This has inflamed the nation's fears and more blacklisting results, usually of innocent people who are then driven to desperation to save their careers and their families. Don't tell me that you are against blacklisting.

REPRESENTATIVE: The witness is in contempt.

MARTIN O'MILES: I certainly am. You have hounded me, you have tapped my phone, you have intimidated my wife and children, all to have me come here and not to tell you about my own experience but to give you names of people who may be innocent, names of people you already have. You merely want to use this industry as a toy to prove that you big boys are fighting the Commies without actually doing anything. You are perpetrating a fraud on the American people.

REPRESENTATIVE: The Committee will do everything it can to protect the American people from the menace of Communism.

MARTIN O'MILES: By doing exactly what you criticize the Communists as doing. Controlling thought.

REPRESENTATIVE: This session is ended. The witness is in contempt.

Here was Martin O'Miles — sounding just like Paul Drury — Betsy's father — defiant, intelligent. Was he blacklisted for being Paul Drury? That couldn't be true.

She heard a step outside the door and shoved the folder under the covers. As the door opened, she closed her eyes, but through her lashes, she saw Bill come into the room. What if he wanted his folder? No, he picked up a book.

He was coming over to the bed. She heard a click and realized he'd turned off the lamp. Cost conscious Bill. She felt his hand smoothing her hair. It felt so sweet, so relaxing that she almost sighed aloud.

She heard him move back, flip off the main light switch, and close the door.

The sound of the surf coaxed her spinning mind to rest. In her imagination she reached out an arm and imagined herself stroking his hair.

The wine took effect, finally. She slept.

22

Bill was talking on the phone when she came down to breakfast. He didn't glance at her as he said, "She just came down. I'll bring her home after she eats."

She grabbed the phone. "I'm fine. I'll walk home when I'm going to walk home."

She read Bill's face as a reprimand and was all ready for it, but what he said was purely utilitarian.

"Waffles? Sorry we're in here. It looks like rain. There's the paper if you want it and fruit cocktail and juice in the fridge."

She got the food out, sat down, and picked up the paper. She must have dreamed he smoothed her hair; he was so abrupt. "Where are the comics?"

"This is *The New York Times*, sweetie. The fun is in the articles."

She picked up the front page. "Your Kennedy is scolding the president about our spy plane the Russians caught?"

"Yup."

"Kind of rude."

The phone rang.

As soon as Bill answered it, he grew more energetic.

"Yeah. Damn cagey fucking bastard. Oh, Sorry. No, not you, there's a girl here. Shut up. She's just a nice kid."

She tossed a piece of toast at his nose. He caught it and tossed it back without even looking at her.

He went on, energetically, to whoever was on the other end. "Here's what you do. Argue the primaries. Johnson would be better in the Senate, supporting Kennedy. He can't come into the convention and say, hey, I want in – when people all over the country have cast votes for Kennedy or Humphrey. You can't say, oh, they *would* have voted for me. What a jackass. Yeah, I know that nobody put any importance on the primaries before now, but that was then. No more back room stuff for president. I'll be there Thursday unless I'm held up on the set. Duke's okay, so long as I don't beat him in chess. See you." He hung up. "Sorry, I'll get your waffles on."

"Only one, please. Are you running the Kennedy campaign?"

"Just the one on the main lawn at UCLA."

"Don't you have enough to do?"

"This is important."

"Is Sandi supporting Adlai Stevenson?"

He took a bowl out of the refrigerator and opened the waffle iron.

"At this very moment, she and a bunch of tragic idealists are planning a massive demonstration to convince delegates to vote for Stevenson, who has lost two elections, so who wants him. She'll come on board when Kennedy gets the nomination. Above all, Richard Nixon cannot be president."

"Why not? He has experience dealing with the Russians."

Bill poured batter into the waffle iron.

"He's been Vice President."

"So what? They lost a spy plane."

"There are bad people out there. Nixon knows more about them."

"That's a pretty un-democratic idea, that only people in power can handle the country. Besides, Nixon is bad people."

"No, he's not."

"Yes, he is. There's something in him that thinks he has to destroy people in order to win. When he came to Congress, he grabbed on to the brass ring of anti-Communism because it was Congress's hobby, and he went at it full thrust because he has a weakness for approval and for wanting to look like a big man. Didn't make the football team or something. Some big man. He destroyed Helen Gahagan Douglas with smears. Just tossed out that she was a Communist with no proof. He plays the Quaker and tries to be the all-American hero, and for that, he looks miscast. But as you say, he was Ike's vice president, and we love Ike. And he's your mother's friend."

"No, he isn't. He has a crush on her, but she makes fun of him." His lecture disturbed her. She hadn't known any of that about Nixon. Why did her mother dangle her friendship in front of him?

Bill handed her a plate topped with one gargantuan waffle, and she put on butter and syrup while he cleaned out the iron. It was odd, seeing Bill so domestic. She wondered how long he'd done his own cooking. The waffle was excellent.

A long silence followed except for shrieking gulls, a loud surf, and the rhythmic patter of a weak rain on the porch. She looked around the kitchen, assuming that the rest of the floor had a bedroom and a bathroom. The porch outside looked solid, but she could see the waves coming in below, approaching the house.

Bill picked up a section of the *Times*. "I'll see you home when you're done."

"You're busy."

"All I have to do today is work on a scene."

"For an audition?"

"Class."

"You have all these acting jobs and an Oscar and run Kennedy's campaign from your kitchen and you still go to acting class?"

"You should, too."

"Do you pretend you're an apple or something?"

"It just so happens, Miss Fletcher, that I am working on the last scene in *The Heiress*."

"Mom loved playing Catherine."

"She was great. Clift had no edge, though."

The phone rang again, and Bill launched into more political talk.

Dianna skimmed over an article headlined, "Hollywood's New Look: Major Studios Losing Grip to Stars, Agencies, Independent Producers."

That song again. Except for some reason, her father couldn't get his production company going.

She went out on the porch. It had stopped raining. The pillars holding up the house looked sturdy even at the threat of the ocean that flowed alarmingly close. Dianna watched the water and listened to its sighing and the pitiful cries of the gulls as they sang through a cloudy sky. She felt like all that.

"Ready?" called Bill.

She hurried upstairs for her bag, straightened out the bed, and when she came back down, Bill was yelling into the phone.

"They won't even hear me? How about screening the damn show? Yeah, Lemmon's a name. So what? I won the Emmy for that part. I did *Sound and Fury* and *Home from the Hill*, and Hitchcock's latest and *Magnificent Seven*, and I just costarred with Duke Wayne and I'm about to star in my own damn picture. Not to mention an Academy Award in there. If you can't get me *Wine and Roses*, what can you get?"

He threw the phone across the floor.

"Are you mad or something?" she asked.

He glared at her. "You. A star at seven."

"You think you know everything."

"If I did, I could get a part I played on television in the movie."

"Life is so unfair."

Mean of her, but she didn't like his blaming her stardom for everything.

He ignored her sarcasm. "Want to drive or walk?"

"Walk on the beach. It stopped raining. You don't have to see me home."

"Yes, I do."

He picked her bag up and led the way through the kitchen down the steps to the beach. They paced along in the wet sand, the water hissing, a few small boats on the horizon.

"I'm afraid I spoiled your Sunday," she said.

He didn't answer. What a moody person. She did, however, want to ask about what she'd read the night before. And it might make him less moody. He worried her.

"I hope you don't mind. I read some of your papers up there when I couldn't sleep. I found what Marty O'Miles said to Congress. What happened to him?"

"I haven't looked at that stuff in over a year. Too busy. Did it put you to sleep?"

"Pretty much. What happened to Marty?"

"Congress and the FBI took the juice out of him. All because he worked with people who advocated voting rights for the Negro, and Communists were *part* of the group. He worked for a strong actors' union. A union. *That's* a Commie thing, according to some people. Goes against freedom of private enterprise to set market wages and exploit the working man. Marty was starring in a television series, and someone publicized his interests, and people wrote letters saying, get him off the air. It spun into mail campaigns against him. The television networks did not want controversy. Guilty or innocent, he was out."

"He got to act again, though."

"Yeah, now, years later, and I guess your producer hopes people have forgotten or realized he gave in. In the meantime, he couldn't get a job, his wife got very sick, he needed money. So he surrendered. He gave the committee names of people he'd worked with in those groups. The committee promised that he could testify privately, but they broke their word and brought in the press. He should have held out. Lots of people did. If everyone had, Congress would have been stopped." He paused. "I picked a *Silver Sierra* script he was barely in where I have to say only one line to him. That's all I could stand to do. I despise men who can't stand up for their beliefs. Now he's rehabilitated. Jack Goodman's a weakling to take pity on him."

"So you have your own blacklist."

He kicked the sand. "It's my right to complain. I'm not making a thing out of it."

"Why are you so interested in all this?"

"Someone has to keep the story alive. We're all so quiet about it, pretending it's not happening. No one in the industry says there's a blacklist. Because a blacklist is illegal. But all the studios gave in, wouldn't defend their own people. It's far from over. It's not enough that Dalton Trumbo and Albert Maltz get breaks. People say, oh that broke the blacklist. Hell. Thousands of people were driven out of work or couldn't use their own names. Even Bill Shakespeare can't break in."

"Albert Maltz didn't get his break."

"That's right. Almost."

"Because of Joe Kennedy, I heard."

"Yeah, maybe."

He looked disgusted. She changed the subject.

"I can't believe that about *Romeo and Juliet*. I'll ask Daddy when he calls next."

"Does he call a lot?"

"When he can."

"When's that?"

None of his business.

A door above them opened. "Dianna!" Lynne called.

"Coming!" she cried. "I guess I'll see you sometime?" she asked.

"After the convention, I'll be riding into your town."

She dialed a security code on the gate, opened it, and took her bag.

He took her arm gently, looking into her eyes with an intensity she could feel. A stronger Hal who had come back for Millie.

What a silly thought.

"If you ever feel like that again, you call me up." He took a card from his pocket and tucked it into the flap of her bag. "Everybody feels blue sometimes. Don't call the operator or the police. I'm going out of town again, but my service will pick up, or you can get Sandi. It'll be like having a brother and sister on call. It's easier than calling Europe."

"Where are you going?" She couldn't imagine talking to him about how she felt. She had, once, but he'd also turned his back on her in favor of Angelini.

"More location. This time with Kirk Douglas."

"Another western?"

"Yeah, and I don't get the girl again," he joked. "Sandi won't be at the house," he added. "She'll be at UCLA mostly."

"What does she do? Study law?"

"She does court work and a bunch of stuff I don't approve of. Women."

"Thank you."

She hurried up the steps. When she got to the door, she turned, and he was walking away. Kicking sand. Moody guy.

Lynne shouted, "What happened? The police were here."

Dianna went to her room without answering.

On her desk was a stack of fan mail and right next to it, wouldn't you know it, a *Photoplay* with Bill's face on the cover. His press agent was hard at work. "William Royce – Hollywood's Dark, Brooding New Leading Man." The article, which she immediately turned to, showed him at Chasen's with Sandi, dancing with her at a nightclub, and walking with her along the same beach she and Bill had just walked on. The article said they were engaged.

"What's going on?" Lynne demanded, closing the door.

"Look," said Dianna, "you get paid to do whatever it is you do. But you really don't care, do you?"

"Don't care?" Lynne cried. "What's he saying to you? Listen, Dorothy Kilgallen has been calling about why there was an ambulance here last night. She says you tried to commit suicide."

"Oh, her."

"She's not buying the electrical fire story. I think she talked to a doctor or a nurse. And if she's not buying it, I won't."

"She's lying. She can talk to Jim Coburn or Steve McQueen. Go away. I have work."

"Your fan mail," said Lynne, and she shut the door hard.

Each week, Dianna personally answered ten selected fan letters. Disney Studios and Uncle George's office handled the rest, although the publicity said that she answered every letter. She couldn't possibly, as that would have meant answering some six thousand letters a week.

Photoplay's biography of Bill pointed out that he kept missing his chances. He'd played Bo in *Bus Stop* on Broadway in '56, also Buck in *A Hatful of Rain*. Don Murray and Tony Franciosa got those movies. A hard working actor, the article said, he put his career on hold to take care of his dying mother and lost plenty of good breaks. "Now he is rising to the top, and he can think about marrying the woman he loves, and it looks as if Miss February has the beauty and intelligence to be that woman."

She tossed the *Photoplay* in the waste basket.

Some hours later, her phone rang.

"Dianna, what is going on there?"

"Daddy, it was a joke."

"Some joke. Your mother is a wreck. Dorothy Kilgallen called her and said you tried to commit suicide."

"Kilgallen's an idiot." No time like the present. "Daddy, were Anthony Marks and Edward Grey blacklisted, and is that why they can't get into the country or why *Romeo and Juliet* can't be shown?"

That created quite a pause over an expensive phone line.

"Yes," he said, finally, the end inflection going up.

"Was that my technical glitch?"

"We did not think you would understand."

"I don't! I did great work! No one saw it!"

"We thought it would all be resolved before now."

"You let me work with Communists?"

She could hear his exasperated sound clear across the ocean. "It was Shakespeare, above politics, as we should bloody well be."

What could she say over an ocean?

"How's Chas?"

"Dianna, Vivien will be out later this month. So will Larry. Try to see Viv. Larry will call you, probably to take you to dinner."

"Why do they have to get a divorce?"

"He has stood by Viv for years. It has drained him."

"How's Chas?"

"No more jokes like that, Dianna."

She tried calling Nick's flat to see if he knew anything about Chas. The long distance operator never called back.

She looked up Kilgallen's column as soon as it came out the next day.

"Dianna Fletcher's family are all in Europe and, left to her own devices, the teenager has thrown a wild party or two, gotten her director fired, and just the other night raided the family liquor cabinet and attempted suicide. Or threatened it. Sources at Saint Luke's Hospital say that an Operator called with the information that Miss Fletcher had threatened to end it all. It is not clear if she was admitted to the hospital for observation or if a boyfriend is the root of all this trouble. Anne Foster, preparing to exit *Exodus* and head to London, says the whole story is ridiculous, but she's not there. First the trouble on the *Picnic* set and now this. The kid is practically screaming that she needs her parents."

Furious, Dianna called MaryAnn, who said, "We're on it. You didn't do anything of the kind, I know. It was an electrical fire."

The Disney publicist called. "Walt is really disturbed by this."

"It was an electrical fire. She's blowing it all up from nothing. Uncle George is on it."

"Kilgallen is one good reporter."

"Says who?"

She would not be the next Judy Garland. Damn Kilgallen.

Dianna knew that Uncle George's press machine was thorough, but Kilgallen had a powerful voice, even if hers was a lone one. She could sink her teeth in a story and not let go, and she wasn't afraid of her family.

Dianna called competing reporter Mike Connolly – something she was forbidden to do – and said, "If you can find anyone who came to my wild parties, please let me know."

Connolly loved it and printed it. Dianna wondered why MaryAnn hadn't thought of that.

She looked out of a window overlooking the street.

Bill's car was gone.

23

"Is this Dianna Fletcher?" a boy asked, haltingly. She couldn't place the voice. Not a columnist, please.

"Who is this?"

"It's Bruce Johnson. I was at Bill's party. Do you remember? Andy? Pam? Me? Bill gave me your number."

Oh, did he?

"I'm president of the film society. I have two tickets to the opening of *Psycho* on Friday. Would you like to go?"

She hardly knew him. But she never got to go to a non-Disney or non-family premiere.

"Thank you. I'd love to go."

"I don't have a car. I'll come in a cab."

She really wanted this date to work.

Bruce didn't talk much during the cab ride, and he didn't talk much either when, in the theater, Janet Leigh and Tony Curtis spoke to Dianna for several minutes. People came by to say, "It's good to see you looking so happy."

"Kilgallen's nuts," said Dianna to every person.

"But wasn't I at one of your parties?" asked Tony Curtis. "That hot tub by the pool?"

"You didn't invite me?" asked Leigh.

Dianna giggled.

Bruce, confused by the exchange, didn't say anything until they sat down, and then he apologized for their side seating.

"I can see fine," she assured him.

Who started off this movie but Bill Royce, bare chested, lying in bed in a seedy hotel room while Janet Leigh, wearing only a bra and a half slip, wandered around. It was a wonder to behold, thought Dianna. Leigh had been married to her father in *Touch of Evil*. Now she was having a passionate affair with Bill, who certainly got around. Why should he be mad at his agent?

It did not take long for her to guess that Hitchcock had cast Bill only for his looks. Even so, beneath some rather not very profound lines, Bill managed to seethe. Hitch was getting more for his money.

Hadn't Janet learned from *Touch of Evil* not to stop at lonely motels? Was she going to get spooky Perkins involved in the whole thing? Or would he hold her prisoner, intending to stuff her, like his birds?

The knife flashed and flashed again and again, the blood spurted out, the audience screamed, and Dianna looked over at Bruce, who sat transfixed.

Hitch had changed something. Now it would be okay to kill a naked woman, *shockingly* kill her on screen. Naked and bloody and stabbed to death probably by some nut of a mother. Hitch and women. Her parents argued about Hitchcock. Anne didn't like him. John thought he was a genius. This scene made her feel exposed and scared to death. Perhaps it was supposed to.

"That was ugly," she said to Bruce. "And the ending was stupid."

He looked stunned. He, she realized, thought it was brilliant.

"All those cuts in that scene," he said. "It made it seem more horrific."

Whatever cuts he was talking about.

"All because he hated his mother? That was dumb."

And there was Hitch, waiting for her.

He bowed, took her hand, and said, "Please give my regards to Mr. Disney when you see him next."

She wanted to slap him.

"I so envy him. Cartoon people are the best actors. When it's all over, you can just rip them to pieces."

Janet Leigh's face went numb.

Dianna turned her back on Hitchcock and gave her a hug.

"We have to plot his death."

"Didn't you like it?"

"How could you agree to do that?"

"I haven't taken a shower in weeks," Leigh admitted.

Dorothy Kilgallen was making her way straight to her. Everyone cleared the path and watched.

"You had better take back what you wrote about me," Dianna said, totally hoping people heard.

"Dianna," said Kilgallen, with the crispness of her authority. "I had sources."

"People you paid," Dianna shot back. "What you do to get attention."

She had no idea, but Kilgallen flinched and stepped back, obviously not having expected such a response.

Hitch was watching them. Great. He'd probably make a movie of two women cutting each other up.

In the cab, Bruce talked incessantly about how brilliant the picture was.

"I think that was the first time I've seen a toilet flush in the movies."

"And that," said Dianna, "is why we will remember it! Not for the people. For the tricks and the toilet. Is that what they teach you at UCLA?"

The cab stopped at her door. Dianna waited but Bruce stayed in the cab. She opened the door.

"Goodnight," she said.

Not a spark of romance in that boy. Or sense.

Disneyland seemed more real. She sang with the old timers on the Mark Twain, men who'd played for nothing on Bourbon Street. Great old men of jazz.

Sinatra wandered in, startling the audience. What a sneak. Now she had to pay attention to her scatting. She worked through "Blue Skies," snapping her fingers, keeping time no matter what her voice did, letting it soar up and down her wide soprano range.

When she'd finished her set, Sinatra and his guys surrounded her. Sinatra only said, "We're going to have to do something with this talent of yours," and then he and his buddies disappeared.

The last thing she needed was Sinatra's help. That would only cause trouble. Kilgallen would grab at that brass ring.

Back on *Silver Sierra*, she waited for Marty to come out of makeup. "I wanted to ask you about the blacklist."

"Why don't you ask your parents?"

She hadn't expected that.

"What would they know?"

O'Miles laughed, confusing her.

He closed the door of his dressing room, with him inside.

Ask her parents? They hadn't been blacklisted, but then she remembered what Lucille Ball had said and her father's evasiveness about Marks and Grey and Bill's dissertation and his hatred of her father. It all pointed toward something. Of course, her parents were innocent, but then why was it all a secret.

How could she find out? She could barely communicate with them on the phone. And she was so busy.

Laurence Olivier, after his magnificent performance of *Becket*, took her to dinner at Romanoff's. He was quiet and obviously tired, having just been murdered by King Henry's soldiers, and his divorce was a painful subject. She asked questions about Henry II and Normans and Saxons and how he had worked out his character. She didn't have the heart to talk about anything else.

When he left her, though, he said, "When you see Vivien, you might find it difficult. Give her as much love as you can."

But Vivien Leigh, appearing in *Duel of Angels*, did not want to see Dianna and kept her dressing room door closed. Finally, when she opened the door, she screamed at Dianna and called her a whore. Hurt, Dianna tried calling Sandi, but the woman answering the phone said, "I'm sorry. She's left the city, no forwarding information."

Silver Sierra didn't need her for a week. She could sit despondently by the pool half wishing Sinatra would invite her to his forbidden yacht.

The phone rang at her elbow. Lynne called, "It's Mr. Sinatra."

Wow.

"Baby, listen," he said, and he sounded panicked. "You gotta help me out of a jam."

"Where are all those tough guys who hang out with you?"

"They can't sing like you."

This was no yacht invitation

"They can't sing like you, either."

"You're the best singer in town next to Garland."

"I thought that was you. And a few other people. Dinah Shore, Ella Fitzgerald. I'm sure you went down the list. What are you talking about?"

"The thing. The fundraiser. Before the convention. This is one great idea."

"What convention?"

He had to laugh. "The Democratic National Convention, baby. Garland was going to sing for a fundraising dinner before it starts."

"She's still sick. And she's going to England."

"The times and schedules got mixed up. We had another fundraiser this week, and she can't carry a tune, and she's leaving town and it's half a week away. I had a great, brilliant idea."

"No!"

"I want you to do the show. You'll be swell! You'll be great!"

"And they'll have all of me on a plate. No, no, no!"

"Baby, you'll surprise everyone. This party is all about youth this year. Who's more youthy than you?"

"They're all forty or fifty years old."

"Some are thirty." And he laughed. "Baby, you're brilliant in front of an audience. I've seen you."

"Prepare yourself for a shock, Uncle Frank. I'm not Judy Garland."

"Judy Garland ain't Judy Garland anymore. Anyway, she can't do it and I'm stuck. You have an incredible effect on an audience."

"They love *everybody* in Disneyland. It's the fairy dust."

"I've got Harry Brown on piano. He plays at Disneyland, too. Look, honey, you need to work. Is what Kilgallen wrote true?"

"She's an idiot."

"We all feel bad sometimes. This will make you feel good."

How dare he.

"They paid for *Judy Garland*. You want to talk suicide? I'll be ready for it!"

"It's Sunday. At the Biltmore. I'll send a car. I'll send a list of songs tonight and you can run through them with Riddle tomorrow."

"I have my own songs!"

"Okay, sure, you can bring in your own songs. Baby, you gotta do it. I'll make it all up to you."

"Everyone else turned you down, right?"

"Everyone else did the fundraiser the other night. Judy, too. It killed her. I can't get 'em to do a whole new show, and you've got the material. Baby, I need you."

"I'm pooped. I've been working hard."

"You're sixteen. You'll be fine tomorrow."

She hung up. "Damn, I'll have to practice all week."

The phone rang. A woman, slurring her words. Judy. "I pass my fucking torch down to you." Then she hung up.

"You'd better go see her," said Lynne, when Dianna told her about the call. "You still haven't given her your mother's gift."

She found Judy in bed, fading from color to black and white, like a brittle broomstick that had been stuck in a closet for years, wincing at the sunlight. Looking at the dispirited, pale little woman who had lost so much weight so fast, Dianna wasn't sure Judy Garland would last five months.

"Hey, kid, you won the Oscar."

Dianna opened the box she had brought and lifted up a silk robe with pink and yellow flowers. Judy smoothed her thin fingers over it. Dianna tried not to touch her again, but Judy grabbed her hand with surprising power.

"I cried when you did your speech. I said to Annie, our daughters are going to be the making of us. Just steer clear of L.B., and you'll be all right."

"He's dead," said Dianna.

"Keep away from him."

"There are more robes in the box," Dianna tried to draw away carefully, for Judy might break, or her fate might be contagious, but Judy held on tight. "Mom thought you might want a pretty robe for every day of the week."

"I love your mother. I'd call, please come over, no matter what time of night, and she came. Then someone at MGM would call her and say don't go over, you have to work tomorrow, but she came. They were listening on our phones. Everyone's listening. Watching. You don't have to be in Russia. We worked in that awful movie. *Ziegfeld Girls*. Lana Turner, Eve Arden, me, and your mom so pretty. She gave up songs for me. You know what lasts longer than movies? Friendship. That's important." She grabbed at

Dianna's other hand. "Honey, stay out of this business. It can tear friendship to shreds. Only your mother — she forgave me."

"Forgave you for what?" asked Dianna. She'd heard the rumors about her father and Judy having an affair when they were making *A Star Is Born*. That never made sense because Judy's husband, Sid Luft, had produced the picture and because her parents, at the end of the day, always had great affection and respect for each other. Still, the rumors persisted, and here was Judy asking for forgiveness.

"She forgave me. L.B. made me marry Vincente. I was a dope when I married Luft. L.B. made me do everything. So glad they are falling to pieces."

"I should go," said Dianna.

Judy still held on tight. "There's time for living and a time for dying and a time to give it all up."

I'm not going to be like that, Dianna decided. And as the not wanting to be like Judy grew in her, she felt a desire to sing in her place. She would be swell. She would be great.

24

Elmer Gantry, starring her parents and controversial before it premiered, earned magnificent reviews when it opened in New York and Los Angeles, but Uncle George said she couldn't be seen going to the first showings. *Beautiful Beulah*, opening the next day in New York and other cities, was hailed as "a harmless piece of corn…a silly little tale that should attract young girls."

At least, it was her last such Disney epic. But she didn't have time to think about what to plan next or even to rest. Instead, she had to go to MGM to work in the Alice Marrs studio to be worked to death by Kay Thompson for the fundraiser.

A duet with Sinatra came first, ostensibly to help her relax and warm up a disappointed audience. That didn't worry her. But when Riddle handed her some of Judy's arrangements, Dianna handed them right back. She would sing her own material. For some reason, that made Sinatra look smug.

By the time she went to bed on Saturday, though, she had lost her confidence, even if she was singing her own material. Her brain skipped from one song to another, always landing on the terrified certainty that as soon as she came on stage, the audience, having paid a hundred dollars or more to hear Judy, would start pitching knives at her.

Already the city was turning upside down for the convention, with traffic snarls and more tourists than usual out on the loose with the expectation that the city owed them a good time. When Dianna finally reached the Biltmore's service entrance, someone handed her a program whose cover loudly proclaimed, TONIGHT MISS JUDY GARLAND.

"No, no, no, no, no!" she yelled, turning right around. Kay Thompson pushed her to the backstage corridors.

"I can't wait to see Miss Judy," the bellboy said, as he opened the door to Dianna's suite.

"Don't open a window!" Dianna yelled to Kay. "I may jump."

"They'll love you!" Kay yelled back. "She was so awful last week. I'm sure they'll be relieved that you're the one they'll be hearing."

Right.

Her dress was good, anyway – bright red with a thin halter, its skirts flaring over crinolines. If they couldn't get Garland, they could at least get a pair of good legs.

She met Sinatra in the hallway.

"I hate you."

"Wait till it's over. You'll be wanting to marry me."

"Death would soon part us."

"I love it when beautiful dames hate me." He gave her a smooth kiss on both cheeks and did a cha cha up the hallway. She slowly followed him to the stage and stood in the wings while he went out to talk to the crowd, which was jabbering like mad. They gave him a wild ovation.

"Good evening, ladies and gentlemen!" Did he sound a bit cautious? "As you know, we were to have the great Miss Judy Garland here with us tonight."

What a way to start!

Disappointed exclamations resounded throughout the hall, even some angry shouts. Dianna's mouth tasted like sawdust. She was going to die. At the very least, she was going to register Republican if these Democrats let her live to be twenty-one.

Sinatra looked startled at the reaction. "Miss Garland is indisposed and she extends her apologies to you. However," and he held up his hand as if to ward off food or knives, "she recommended another singer, a young lady I have known since she was in the cradle."

The crowd quieted down.

"You know her, too, but not as the versatile artist she is, I'll bet. She can sing just about anything. Right now, she's known for her pop records, four of them in the top twenty, which is more than I've ever had at one time."

Sinatra's voice grew hoarse as the crowd's murmur grew louder. "Hers was the lovely voice you heard in Walt Disney's *The Sleeping Beauty*. And if you visit Disneyland, you can hear her sing some of the best jazz in town. An Academy Award winner this year, and nominated twice before that, just sixteen years old, the princess of Hollywood, Miss Dianna Fletcher."

"Tell me he's kidding," someone said.

"I wouldn't mind her mom, but the kid?"

"I'll bet he's sleeping with her," someone else said. Dianna almost ran out to protest that one, but an arm touched hers. The electrician handed her a glass that looked like water. She drank it down. It was not water. It burned her throat, and it felt good.

"Thanks," she said.

He winked at her.

"Break his leg. I will, if you want."

She walked out, smiling to faint applause. The audience, seated at tables close together on the ballroom floor, seemed to stretch for a mile. She could barely see any people, just dark outlines, but she could hear their resentment loud and clear. These Democrats were not a subtle bunch.

"I paid five hundred dollars!"

"We paid for Judy!"

"We want Judy!" several called out.

"This ain't Disneyland!"

She assumed they were drunk for she heard people hushing in different directions. But they couldn't hush the acrimony.

Nelson Riddle, conducting the band upstage, tried to drown the shouters out. All Dianna saw was his back, and she wouldn't even see that when she sang, but there was the great Harry Brown at the piano, and he looked grim at the horror and anger the cheated audience obviously felt.

Sinatra greeted her, gave her a light kiss, and said, "Have fun, honey."

What about their duet?

People in the back were standing up and forming little groups of loud complainers.

She backed toward the piano, smiled at Harry, and gripped the mike in her sweaty hand, feeling a little dizzy.

"When I Fall in Love," she sang. Her voice shook. She couldn't let them throw her, but people were talking away in back, probably doing their crooked politics in this smoke-filled room. People still at the tables were talking, gesturing with their hands. She was furious. Harry Brown was a great jazz artist, and they should respect him. They should respect her! This was one of her best jazz arrangements. No one cared. They were still trading votes in groups or whatever they were doing.

She sang "I, Yi Yi, Yi, Y," a peppy, old standard. She twisted her hips. No one cared.

Let Nixon be pope.

She edged back to the piano to check her song list as Brown bowed off. Nelson plunged ahead, into "Alone." She certainly was. She was the tree falling in the empty forest.

Alone on this night that we two could share, alone with your kiss that could make me care.

They talked right through it.

She put the mike back in the stand and was about to walk off, but Riddle started her intricate jazz version of "You Are My Lucky Star." This was one of her best arrangements, worthy of Garland or even Ella.

No one cared.

Who was she kidding. Still, she kept going. Her next song was a ballad that Riddle and Kay Thompson had turned into a rock-styled number. She thought it had too startling a beat, especially for mink coated Democrats, and pretended she was yelling at them. Oddly, the room seemed to shift a few degrees. She could feel it with her feet. She circled so that her skirt swirled and more of her legs showed.

She leaned back into the curve of the piano, once again with Harry, and sang another haunting lyric of loss. Halfway through, she thought, God, are they listening? The clattering of plates and glasses had stopped.

The clumps dispersed. People were sitting back down at their tables.

She sang one of her top ten tunes with Riddle's new, rousing arrangement. The audience started clapping and some even got up to dance.

The room wasn't quite hers, but at least they didn't hate her anymore. She sang "Colors of My World," then another oldie, "Fascinating Rhythm" with her jazzy arrangement.

More of them were dancing or clapping along.

When she sang "Skylark," she could feel the quiet. Good quiet. Why had they started listening? Who the hell knew what they liked?

She started another ballad, "The Best Things in Life are Free," but when the audience started laughing, she turned around. Sinatra, the heel, was doing pirouettes behind her.

Sure, let me warm them up and you come on when it's safe.

He floated back around again and sang a few words. "That's enough," she said, and the crowd laughed so hard they nearly drowned out the rest of the song. Sinatra landed a big kiss on her cheek.

He came back with two stools.

"Have a seat, kid. You've been working hard."

He held a cigarette in one hand and put his arm around her, his face close to hers. She pretended to enjoy singing with him, giggling like a kid a few times, when she wanted to slit his throat. He just gave her a saucy grin.

No wonder her mother didn't marry him.

Sinatra skipped off. She took the mike and sang "Sweet Violets," a ballad that seemed naughty but just as she would arrive at what the naughty rhyme would be, the lyric would shift into something unexpected and mundane. The audience laughed their way through.

Dianna had never seen or felt anything like that intense, wondering quiet at the end of her set. Then came the applause, cheers, people climbing on chairs and waving their arms. Dianna did not bow; she stood, looking straight at them all. The candidate, a handsome man, stood. He'd been right there in the front row all the time. She acknowledged John Kennedy with a curt, almost stern nod, took a deep breath, raised her arms, and bowed.

When she looked up again, they were still cheering. She walked off stage into Sinatra's ecstatic arms and stamped on his foot.

Even after several minutes of an ovation, they were roaring and clapping.

They were apologizing.

She came out, took an encore ("Mr. Paganini"), which she'd learned from Hilda. She leaned against Harry Brown's piano, and it came out pretty good. As they cheered, she ignored them, bowed to Harry, and walked off the stage.

Backstage, her legs buckled. Little beads of light swirled in front of her eyes. She sank into a folding chair, limp and drained. Someone put a glass in her hand. Just water, but she drank it all.

Leonard Bernstein was the first one in the crowded hallway to grab her up to a limp standing position. His eyes were filled with tears. "I had no idea you could sing like that. I wish your mother had seen it. I was telling the people to sit down and listen. You are incredible."

"She stole Annie's legs, look at her," said Sammy Davis. "Honey, you were something else out there. I listened to the whole thing. I'm coming to Disneyland."

Other actors crowded around her – Gregory Peck with his lovely wife Veronique, Ralph Bellamy with his wife Alice, Lloyd and Dorothy Bridges, Shirley MacLaine, Mercedes McCambridge and her husband Fletcher Markle, Lee and Betty Marvin, and Jane and Edward G. Robinson, all surrounding her, praising her, hugging her. Where the heck had they been?

And then there were others, people she didn't know, clapping for her, asking for her autograph.

Some skinny strip of a man with glasses pointed at her. "She has to sing at the convention. She's young. She's everything we want to represent us."

Someone lifted her up in the air.

"Look at you!" the man shouted.

Back on the ground, she cried, "Bill! Why are you here?"

"I gave money like everyone else. Were you something!" He turned around. "I thought Joy was right behind me."

Joy who?

Sinatra pushed through and introduced the glassy eyed fellow. "This is Bobby Kennedy."

"You have to come up to our suite," said Bobby. "Jack wants to congratulate you."

"Who?"

Bill said, "The next president, sweetie."

"No, not tonight," said Sinatra, and it seemed that he forced a grin. "You should go home. Where's your chauffeur?"

"I sent him home," said Peter Lawford. "We'll take care of her."

"Jack wants to see her," said Bobby.

"I'm pretty beat," Dianna said.

"The kid's been working nonstop," said Sinatra. "I'll take you home, honey."

He took her arm. She looked into his eyes. He had loved her mother and lost. Just as she thought, what a ridiculous idea, he wrenched his arm away.

"You're too gorgeous, just like her."

The way he said that worried her. She had better get out of there.

Bobby looked frustrated. "I don't see why a few minutes with my brother would keep her from getting her sleep."

She was getting the drift of things. But was Sinatra trying to save her from Kennedy or was Kennedy trying to save her from Sinatra?

Bill said, "I'll take her home. She practically lives next door."

"Yeah?" asked Sinatra. "Who are you?"

"He's Bill Royce, he won an Oscar for best supporting actor, too, so that means I can trust him, right, dear Uncle Frank?" Sinatra was proud of his Oscar.

Not that she could trust any of them, but Bill had a girl with him.

"First, come up to the suite," said Bobby.

When she moved away from the wall, she went limp again. Sinatra caught her.

"I'll get you home, baby."

Lawford said, "Really, you should come up for just a minute."

Odd, this insistence.

"When he's president," she said. "I'm going home with Bill. Extend my apologies."

Bill and his blonde girlfriend –Joy?– went with Dianna out to the parking lot. She almost staggered at the fresh air and flopped down in Bill's backseat.

"I curse you all. It was like moving Mount Everest."

Bill started the car. "You brought them around. Took guts."

"Them? You were in that gang."

"Sorry. I did want to hear Garland."

"And watch her ruin herself right onstage," said the blonde.

"Yeah," said Bill, "a poor metaphor for the Democrats, I give you. But they raised the money on her name and got — " He broke off.

"Me. Good old Uncle Frank was supposed to sing with me in the beginning, but he left me in the lurch. I thought you were in Arizona."

"I'm back for the convention. And for *Silver Sierra*."

"Right."

Through a fuzziness in her ears, she heard them mention that Marilyn Monroe and Arthur Miller, in Nevada filming *The Misfits* along with Clark Gable, were not talking to each other. Bill referred to Miller's testimony in front of HUAC.

"They were going to let him go," said Bill, "if Monroe would pose for a picture with them."

When he helped her out of the car, she woke up. "Why were Marks and Grey blacklisted?"

That was out of the blue, and he looked startled.

"I'd have to look it up."

"Call me. Paper? Pencil?"

He pulled out — of all things — a little black book. She gave him her number.

"I could sell this to Kennedy."

When she looked disgusted, he said, "I'm sorry." He took her hand. "You really were good. I'm not just saying that."

She didn't know whether to squeeze his hand or not. She knew she wanted to, but she pulled back.

"Thank you. Call me when you know. I have to find out."

"You had one killer instinct up there."

"You weren't paying any attention to me. You were all gabbing through my first half. Who's the girl? Miss March?"

"Not even Louisa May Alcott. She's Miss April."

"You are awful."

"Thank you. And you should go on the stage. You've got some power there. It'll help your camera work."

"What an awful thing to say to me."

From her window, she watched him park his car in his driveway. Both he and Joy got out. What a rat.

25

She was gorging on scrambled eggs and bacon when MaryAnn called. "Whatever you did, it's exploding on my desk in the form of cables, all congratulating you. I have some bad news, though."

For some reason, Dianna thought, Chas.

"You know that Fox bought out your mother's contract. They're losing money by the barrel with *Cleopatra*. Now I'm getting feelers that MGM will do the same."

This was an earthquake. But only her mother's contracts?

Lynne pointed to a newspaper headline: DIANNA FLETCHER BRINGS DEMS TO THEIR FEET.

"Someone might think I made them flee."

"I wish I could have seen you," said Lynne. "You have earned a rest."

She would take one. She changed into a bathing suit and a silk robe and took herself down to the beach, shut her eyes, listened to the surf, and, well, worried. She didn't want to be a singer. She wanted to act. Why couldn't the acting come as naturally as the singing? Oh, for the days of studio contracts and studios building up their stars. It was all becoming scramble and push, looking for money and not talent.

She jumped into the surf, swam a bit, then wandered back to her chaise lounge and drifted off again.

She heard the padding of sandals and looked up over her sunglasses.

He was wearing black trunks and tee shirt and looking down at her with a grin, his muscles pumping up his shirt. Did he have to be so damn good looking and damn difficult to know?

"Can I sit with you?"

She pointed. "Chairs and lounges in that gazebo there."

Lynne was at attention and brought another glass and another pitcher, but she didn't smile at Bill.

Joanne brought out the phone.

"It's the Vice President," she said, plugging it into the socket in the table that was hooked to a generator in the gazebo.

"Of NBC?" asked Dianna.

"Of the United States," said Joanne.

"My dear," said Bill.

Dianna was startled. "Hello?"

"Who put you up to it?"

"Up to what, sir?"

"Was it Sinatra?"

"He was in a spot. Miss Garland wasn't ready."

"I'll bet she wasn't. You stay away from him."

"I think I was fifth choice."

"You are a symbol of the nation. You shouldn't be appearing with the Democrats."

This was weird.

"Aren't they of the nation?"

He sounded so earnest. "Dianna, you do not understand. They do not represent the values you represent. A lot of them lean so far toward Communism that they've fallen in."

"Mr. Vice President, they are a political party in this country. How could they be joining with the enemy? I don't see what the big deal is."

Why was she defending them?

Bill was watching, obviously intrigued.

"We were hoping to have you at our convention."

She sighed. This was just awful.

"You aren't having a convention in Los Angeles. Goodbye."

Bill's obvious delight annoyed her.

"Did you just hang up on Nixon?"

"He's mad at me for singing for the Democrats. He said I'm a symbol of the nation."

"Was he drunk?"

"I couldn't tell. He said the Democrats were Communists."

"Kennedy a Communist?" hooted Bill.

Uh oh. He was starting up.

"The Democrats are not Communists."

"Okay," she said, hoping to ward him off. It didn't work.

"When the Depression hit, FDR set up the New Deal, Social Security, and health insurance for old people and the poor. There's welfare if you lose your job. The underlying idea is that everyone is entitled to dignity. The Republicans think that doing all this affects the human initiative. They think we shouldn't be putting up safety nets because people will depend on them and not go out and get a job, forgetting about people who work all their lives for pittance and can't save enough. Or places where corporate losses decree pulling out all industry from a city, and so there aren't any jobs. Oddly enough, the same people do like the government paying for war and their trips around the globe. A strong middle class makes for prosperity. Without a strong middle class, there could be trouble."

"*Is* it Communism?" asked Dianna. "I mean, the government helping people."

"Does it matter if it helps people?" Bill asked. "No one's going to start a revolution if they're happy. A strong middle class is the safeguard of any nation."

She waved her hand as if to erase it all. It was just words.

Bill obligingly changed the subject.

"Did you hear what Jack Kennedy said? That the way you took over and faced us down on short notice, that maybe you should be Vice President. Did you see the papers?"

"I'm glad it turned out all right, but I thought you were all going to kill me."

Bill reached over and took her hand. Again with the hand. "You did something only a great performer could do. Not only did you lasso us and rope us into your corral, you did it with a mob of resentful, arrogant people and some of the greatest show biz names. Leonard Bernstein kept saying, I never knew she could do that over and over. That was terrific jazz singing."

"It took a lot out of me. I don't know how singers do it." She enjoyed his fingers lightly touching hers, but what did it mean? Should she ask?

"You don't always have to stand in for Judy Garland."

She withdrew her hand, sipped from her glass, and listened to the surf.

"There was all this tension last night about me staying at the hotel and going to see Senator Kennedy."

Bill didn't say anything.

"Right?"

"He's a brilliant guy, but he's a dope when it comes to women."

"That's what I hear about you."

He laughed. "I'm not in his class."

"I'm sixteen. He's not going to try anything with me."

Bill didn't answer. That only made her wonder.

"He's going to be president maybe. That requires a certain dignity," she said.

"That just makes a woman more willing. Women love power."

"Oh, and men don't. He wanted to sleep with me?" She tried looking innocent and shocked.

"Sleep is one word for it."

She lay back down. "Wow." For a few moments, she wallowed in the fantasy. Having an affair with the president of the United States! Losing her virginity to the candidate who would beat Pope Nixon! Then she remembered. He had a wife and a baby on the way and a little girl.

"What a jerk. I'm for Stevenson."

"He's got the same problem. Women flock to power."

"Women can't be president so they have to get power in other ways."

She leaned back, closed her eyes. When she opened them, he was staring at her.

"How's Bruce?"

She waved her hand. "We had a disagreement about *Psycho*. Nice try, by the way."

Bill laughed. "I'll talk to him. I have some news for you about Marks and Grey."

"You've been sitting here all this time and you didn't tell me?"

"Grey was a member of the Communist Party here from 1935 until 1941. He quit. The typical reason people quit is that they get fed up having to follow the party line. Americans are too independent. He went to fight in the war, came back, never rejoined the party. He was called before HUAC in 1951, admitted his background, but he refused to give names of anyone else. He'd been busy writing four screenplays that year, but Fox fired him. None of the studios would take him on or put his name up. He packed himself and his family and they went to England. From there, he wrote some movies that came here under another name, but I don't know which ones. It's not an uncommon story. Carl Foreman, who wrote *High Noon*, had the same thing happen to him. His name was taken off *The Robe*, *High Noon*, *Bridge on the River Kwai*."

"Daddy's movies." Was that a clue, she wondered.

"As for *Romeo and Juliet*, it's not being released anywhere. It has to come here first. Grey doesn't want his name removed from it. He can't come into the country without risking arrest. His passport was revoked, and his family is in England, so his screenplays can't get in. He wants this movie to have his name on it, and he has the legal right to insist on it. What with Dalton Trumbo getting his name on two movies, Marks and Grey are looking to ram the door down."

"What about Marks?"

"He testified at HUAC, same time, and he skedaddled off to Italy, where he's been ever since. That's what I know. Tough enough to find this out, but the guy who sells me shoes is a blacklisted writer, and he knew all this."

"The guy who sells you shoes?"

"Has four Oscar nominations for writing. His father took him into his business."

The world was insane.

"Do you think Daddy was helping them and it didn't work?" One or both of her parents had to be involved in the blacklist business, according to Jack Goodman and Marty.

"I couldn't say anything about your father," said Bill, standing. She heard the slight irritation in his tone. "I've got to get back home. I have to study that script for *Silver Sierra* because I'm not going to have much chance this week what with working on the convention floor."

"Doing what?"

"Getting people to vote for Kennedy. Lawford wants me to help him with Jack's speaking, but I don't think there'll be time for that. The ol' Harvard boy will just have to figure out how to speak on his own."

"Why does he need votes? I thought he won the primaries."

"That doesn't give him enough delegates."

"Why is it so complicated?"

"It adds to the drama. Have you read the *Silver Sierra* script?"

"When would I have the time? If Kennedy loses, I don't have to sing?"

"Now don't start maneuvering delegates behind my back. The Democratic Committee and Sinatra want you. No matter who wins, you get to sing. I think you're replacing Fabian. For which the nation should be grateful. So you haven't read the script?"

"No. Is it a good part for you? Do you get to die?"

"In a manner of speaking," he said. "We kiss."

"You're joking!" Bill was going to be one of Betsy's romances? It was beginning to be silly. As for Bill, should she laugh or get worried?

"Too late to complain now. It's a great part. Brother Luke gets to preach fire and brimstone."

She slipped her robe off and got up.

"I need to go in," she said. "I'm feeling groggy, especially after that news."

She followed his eyes from her breasts to her legs. As if inspecting for approval. Jerk.

He pointed at a blackish purple circle above her waist.

"Did you fall off a horse?"

"That's where you held me at *Picnic*," she said. "It's faded a lot."

"It was worse?"

"It wasn't your fault. You kept me from falling."

"Damn," he said. "I'm sorry." She had the feeling that he wanted to touch the bruise. She stepped back.

"You haven't forgotten what I told you," Bill said. "About calling me."

"I did try to call Sandi once. I didn't get her."

"You all right?"

"I guess so. What happened with Sandi?"

"Adlai Stevenson came between us."

"You broke up because she supports another candidate?"

"It's like a religion with her."

"Not like with you."

He just smiled.

"I liked her. I'm sure it was your fault."

She started for the water. As soon as she waded in, she looked back. He was standing there, looking at her.

She plunged into the surf and swam over a wave into calmer water. When she stood up and adjusted her top, she could see Bill jogging home. He had put the chair back in the gazebo. For some reason, that detail charmed her.

26

"**P**romise me you won't scream," said MaryAnn over the phone the next morning. "Robert Wise wants you to test for Maria."

Dianna screamed.

"You're not needed on *Sierra* until Wednesday. Wise is sending you a scene or two, and it's tomorrow."

Finally! Last in line but what did it matter!

"I have no idea if they're seriously interested in you or this is just a let's try her out. Word is that Natalie Wood has a lock on it. No costumes, a little makeup. Do what you can. This is your shot."

The script came an hour later. It was the balcony scene and the scene in the dress shop, the pretend wedding. Dianna worked on the scenes all night, picked the simplest white dress she had, and borrowed a cross from Anne's jewelry box.

The small soundstage at Goldwyn Studios was set up simply with a makeshift fire escape that looked more like a wooden fence. But what the heck. It was a test.

Then she saw him.

In the midst of the crew putting the lights up and stringing the cords, Elvis Presley was standing up for her.

"Hi," she said, disguising her shock. "Welcome back to America. Your record just shot past mine."

That made him smile. "I just love you, Dianna Fletcher. I always wanted to work with you. The Colonel arranged it so we could. Maybe you would want to be in one of my pictures?"

He looked shy, which made her feel better. But was that the point of his doing this? To get her in one of his pictures?

Bob Wise positioned them, standing close, facing each other. "Tony, Maria," was all he said.

She looked into Elvis' eyes and saw wonder.

They held hands. They touched each other's faces. They smiled. The scene ended in a quick, sweet kiss.

"Print it," said Wise.

They could make this movie explode.

"I was listening to you this morning," she said. "'Are you lonesome tonight.' Your voice is so rich."

"Thank you." He smiled right into her eyes. "May I call you Dianna?"

"Of course." That he could be Tony. It was a dynamite idea.

"You're just so sweet."

"Some days."

The camera dollied very close. The boom mike came down over their heads.

"Trust the material," said Wise. "Don't worry about accents or being tough. Just go."

"Starting note?" Dianna called.

The pianist pounded it out.

She reached out with her hands and, as Elvis balanced on the rail, he took them.

The camera edged up closer.

They waited for "action."

Elvis took on that look of wonder as she smiled at him. She touched his cheek. He touched hers, his hand gentle, his fingertips delicate. He sang with his scooping style yet there was a richness, a longing, and a passion in his voice that was exciting, and it helped her sing with the same sort of great discovery and thrill of love. He was Tony. He put his arm around her and kissed her on the forehead, then on the lips, shyly. They ended looking at each other intensely, outside of any world or galaxy. She felt deeply, sincerely in love.

"Cut," said Wise. "Print that. Thank you both."

"That's all?" Dianna asked. She felt it was the best work she'd done in years.

"That's all I need. Thank you."

"Thank you," said Elvis to Dianna. "It was a real pleasure."

"Buenas tardes," she said.

"Thank you, Dianna," said Wise. "We'll be talking." He walked away fast.

The phone call came the next day after she was back from some dull scenes on *Silver Sierra*. She realized she was tiring of the series, and it annoyed her. What suspense could there be if the family always came out the same?

"Dianna, honey?"

Elvis. That was quick.

"How are you?" she asked.

"I wanted to call you."

"That's so nice."

"Before you heard it from someone else."

So that was that.

"The Colonel thinks that it's wrong for me now. He knows best."

He meant his manager, Colonel Parker. She sat up. "Did they offer it to you?"

"Yeah. With you as Maria. I would love to work with you, honey. But I don't think I could do that."

They'd offered him West Side Story *with her as Maria!*

"Yes, you could!" she cried into the phone.

"The Colonel knows best. I was just a poor slob a few years ago. Now I'm on the phone talking to Dianna Fletcher."

She had to say this right.

"You have a great talent. You were Tony! I wish you'd think about this again."

"Thank you, honey, but the Colonel's never steered me wrong. I still want to work with you. We'll get you a part."

One of Elvis's girls. That would at least put her on the B list. Why couldn't he push himself to do Tony?

MaryAnn called an hour later. "I think if it was just to get you in with Elvis because he asked for you and when he said no, there went the package."

And at that fortuitous moment, *Beautiful Beulah* decided to open in Los Angeles.

MaryAnn told her, "You're going with Tommy, Bobby, and a Miss Boylan. You'll have a good time."

Dianna did not have a good time. She liked Tommy, they were good pals from Disney days, but the romantic stories that poured out of fan magazines about them both had no bearing on any reality. Neither did the movie. It would make a lot of money over the summer, everyone was sure, "and you're so funny!" everyone told her. All she could think of was losing Maria.

Afterwards, when they went to the Pirate's Cove, she heard that "everyone knew that Natalie Wood was going to play Maria in *West Side Story*."

She went back to reading scripts for *Silver Sierra*. At the top of the stack was the episode Bill would appear in.

"Brother Luke" was a con man, charismatic and truly duplicitous, a juicy combination, and certainly a juicy part for Bill, who got to preach hell and damnation, declaim from the Bible, warm up to people in a smarmy way, win a fistfight with two baddies, preach to sinners, hire shills, and struggle against his will about a romance with Betsy. It was a lot for one episode to carry, but L.A. Franklin had crafted a concise drama that did just that. And Bill would upstage them all.

Goodman called with a revised shooting schedule. "You've got Paul Henreid for a director."

"*Casablanca*?"

"That's him," said Goodman. "He does a lot of television directing."

"Why did he stop acting?"

"Here's a man who was born in Austria and had to flee the fascists. He came here and became a star, but when Joe McCarthy started bellowing about Communists and when the hearings in Congress about Hollywood started up, Paul spoke up against them."

This stuff again.

"Why?"

"Because it was blatant falsehood. McCarthy kept saying he had the names of Communists, but he never produced one. The press, of course, blew it all up, so it sounded as if he had all this information when he had squat. He created suspicion and fear, and the press went along with it. So did Congress. Henreid objected to all that."

"He was blacklisted? Like Mr. O'Miles?"

"Criticizing McCarthy or his tactics could railroad your career," said Goodman. "Didn't your mother tell you about this?"

"Why would my mother know?"

Why wouldn't anyone tell her?

"Both she and your father were called to testify before Congress."

"They weren't Communists!" Dianna was amazed at how vehement she sounded.

"Of course not," said Goodman. "Dianna, a huge injustice was done to many people in our industry in the name of patriotism. I think Franklin is a front for a blacklisted writer, but I can't be sure. He's quite good. I want to help these people. I consider them real Americans."

"That's good, so long as they weren't real Communists."

"Dianna, I put the words Communist and Paul Henreid in a sentence, even to say he wasn't one, and you're already suspicious. Why is that?"

She didn't have an answer.

Goodman did. "It's the way you've been taught. Just four legs good, two legs bad, over and over."

She recognized the quotation from Orwell's *Animal Farm* and resented his implication.

"When you point a finger of accusation at a man, you'd better have the evidence to back it up. That's what Paul Drury does, right?" asked Goodman.

"Yes."

"Playing Paul Drury is important to Marty."

"Didn't he accuse other people?"

"People are still saying that? He almost had no choice. His wife took to drink, they divorced – this because of the people who don't want government to interfere with our lives. Marty doesn't like to talk about it, but he brings it out as Paul."

"I did try to talk to him."

"Some things are too close to a man. Talk to your parents."

Why would her parents know?

Why would they have testified before the House Committee on Un-American Activities?

Could she ask this on those long-distance calls? She couldn't even find out how Chas was when she asked. But these other things — she couldn't help wondering if those might lie behind Bill's dislike of her father. Still, she had never heard her parents talk about blacklisting except for that one time after the press dinner.

Bruce invited her to his film club to see *Keeper of the Flame*, a movie from 1943. Spencer Tracy played a journalist wanting to write the life story of a great American who had died in an auto accident. He persisted in questioning his widow, a reluctant Katharine Hepburn, finally realizing that she had caused the accident that killed her husband to stop him from taking over the country. And how? Hepburn explained it:

> ...I had to destroy the man to save the image ... I found the key to Robert Forrest's fascist organization. Of course, they didn't call it fascism. They painted it red, white, and blue and called it Americanism...This was the essence of their plan. Here are articles ready for release to stir up all the little hatreds of the whole nation against each other. This was an article...attacking the Jews...Here's one attacking the Catholics. Anti-Negro, anti-labor, anti-trade union. An appeal to the Ku Klux Klan...Each of these groups was simply to be used until its usefulness was exhausted. Hates were to be placed against hates."

After that, Dianna needed to screen *Mr. Smith Goes to Washington*, with her favorite neighbor Jimmy Stewart, even if it was about graft in Congress. There was Jimmy, intent on writing his bill with Jean Arthur's help, saying:

> That's what's got to be in it, the Capitol dome...I want to make that come alive for every boy in the land. Yes, and all lighted up like that, too. You see, boys forget what this country means by just reading 'the land of the free' in history books. When they get to be men, they forget even more. Liberty's too precious a thing to be buried in books, Miss Saunders. Men should hold it up in front of them every single day of their lives and say, 'I'm free – to think and to speak. My ancestors couldn't...I can. And my children will.' Boys ought to grow up remembering that.

> Girls, too.

She warmed a little to Bruce and asked her to be her escort when she represented her family at the premiere of *Inherit the Wind.* As she watched that film, she realized she had a lot to live up to.

If only *Romeo and Juliet* could be released! How could the country be damaged by Shakespeare's lovely play?

She called MaryAnn. Couldn't they do something?

"I don't know what," said MaryAnn. "The blacklist stuff is pretty chancy. You don't want to be connected to it."

Nobody did. And in the silence, it was as if it had never happened. She would probably never have thought about it were it not for Bill.

She ignored Sinatra's calls about the convention. Let him sweat for once.

MJ called her to invite her to go shopping on Rodeo Drive. Fan magazines exploited the friendship between Di and MJ, but it was true, and they often met for lunch at the studio commissary where Dianna listened to MJ's life story. Her friend had just signed for the *Bye, Bye Birdie* film, had dumped her assistant director, and was now engaged to a high society guy, Barry Richards, who had met her at a network party. MJ was doing well in her series and had made two hit records. "I want to help people," she said. "Kids. And Dick likes that. I want to get out of the business, have real money, a real purpose, a real house, real sex, real kids."

When Dianna told her about Sinatra inviting her on his boat, half giggling, MJ said, "God, why don't you go? It's just sex, and men will do anything for it."

Dianna waved that away. "Why? There are so many men around."

She couldn't think of it as "just sex," Her parents were devoted to each other, and that made what they did in private so meaningful. She dismissed any idea of affairs for either one. Just gossip.

"No, there aren't. Haven't you been reading *Time* and *Newsweek*? There's a man shortage. You've got to get in there early and get the best pickings."

"MJ, it's a life commitment. Don't you love this man?"

"Oh, sure. And I like shocking everyone, I have to say. When I got engaged, the producer hit the roof. So did Carol. They can't have Miss Normal Teenager getting married or having sex on the sly. But I don't have any big ambition like you. It's a rat race, unless it's in your family and in your blood. No, I'm just saying. I want to marry, have kids, be normal. But I have to say," she continued, "I just envy you. You can be an adult on your show. I'm this normal kid. You can have love affairs and shoot people" She laughed. "Maybe that's enough, huh?"

Dianna laughed but wondered what MJ meant. Still, her friend's lack of judgment and easygoing acceptance made her a good friend. Dianna would miss her being in the business.

"Hey, let's go in here. Bonwit's has some great hats," said MJ.

They tried on hats for half an hour, giddily laughing at themselves in mirrors and collecting a crowd, which they didn't mind at all. They took a few hats each to the counter, patiently waiting in line and signing autographs. When they reached the cashier, they recognized their friend, Terry Paganos, from *The Mickey Mouse Club*.

MJ muttered, "We shouldn't notice her."

Dianna couldn't understand that.

"What are you doing here?" she asked.

Terry took Dianna's charge card, wrapped the bill around it, and shipped it up to accounting via the pneumatic tube. As if she'd been doing it for a while.

"I'm in between dance jobs," Terry said, her eyes on her work. "I want to keep up my cash flow."

"You're so good," said Dianna. "You could have done *West Side Story*. Did you try out?"

There was an awkward silence until the charge came back approved. The girls signed several autographs before grabbing their packages, waving at people, and hurrying out the door.

"They really are friends," a woman said.

"It's too bad," said MJ, as they headed toward MJ's car. "She's Puerto Rican. Hard to get work. Well, maybe in black and white."

Dianna had never noticed. Terry was just Terry and a fabulous dancer with a lovely voice. "She would be a lovely Maria."

"They'd never cast her," said MJ. "No one knows who she is for one thing, and for another, she's Puerto Rican. Not box office."

A Puerto Rican couldn't play a Puerto Rican? Certainly, the people in power thought Yvette Mimieux could.

And it hit her, obviously too late, that this was why Lynne and Joanne, Reggie, and Hilda had taken jobs as servants.

It was like a blacklist. The thought unsettled her. She thought of all those essays she'd read in class, about how everything was perfect in the United States. Then she tried to think of black and white and brown people mixing in movies, and she couldn't. But that couldn't be right, either. She wondered how she thought the way she thought.

Box office was the thing. It was the reason Dianna couldn't move ahead. Was that the reason for Terry and Hilda and the others?

At home, she watched a little of the "national civics lesson," as Huntley and Brinkley called it. It seemed like more of a party lesson. A mob entered the convention hall with signs, singing songs and waving banners for Adlai

Stevenson. They marched around and sang for a long time. Silly stuff. Big hats and signs. How could that make anyone vote for a presidential candidate?

She wondered how Bill felt, knowing that Sandi was one of the people who had planned that demonstration and was probably in it.

The delegates started voting. Dianna watched, fascinated by the horse race aspect. Kennedy pulled ahead, Wyoming proudly put him over, and up went another demonstration of funny hats and music.

And she was going to sing to that crowd. Maybe Nixon had a point.

27

The convention's final night was held at the Memorial Coliseum. All around the entrances, people marched back and forth, yelling, and carrying placards that proclaimed "Peace on earth! Ban the Bomb! Peace or Perish!"

Dianna asked, "Is Kennedy for nuclear war?"

"They're kids," said Reggie. "It's what kids do. Believe the world can get better."

Odd thing to say.

Already things were grim. Four unsmiling men stood at the curb. Dianna thought she saw holster packs.

One opened the car door.

"Miss Fletcher? Follow us, please."

"We'd better," Dianna said to Lynne. "They have guns."

While they hurried through tunnels, a man's speech echoed through the halls. Beyond that, Dianna heard a nightmarish sound of thousands of voices on voices. Familiar Johnny Greene greeted them in the wings, which improved her mood, and a woman introducing herself as a Kennedy secretary led Dianna and her helpers to a room off the stage. Reggie stood guard while Lynne helped Dianna into her blue gown and dressed her hair.

"I can't do this," said Dianna. "Listen to that mob."

"You don't have to give a speech saying you're going to run the country," said Lynne. "You're singing a song you've sung before, lots of times."

"I think I'd rather give the speech. He's going to have the words right there in front him. If I mess up on patriotic songs, America will hate me."

A knock at the door.

"Miss Fletcher, Mrs. Roosevelt wants to see you."

Dianna stood up. The former first lady was as plain as people said, but she radiated a regal air — and humor.

"I so wanted to see you," said Mrs. Roosevelt. "I haven't seen your mother in ages and miss her. I go to the movies, but it's not quite the same."

"She's in England," said Dianna. "Playing Anna Karenina."

"You are so much like her. I am glad you are involved, even if things aren't as I would like them. Your mother and your grandmother and I had a wonderful time working together, riding in a car around California and plugging away for migrant workers and fruit pickers."

Dianna was puzzled. "Who were you with?"

"Annie and Alice."

"My grandmother Alice?" Why would her mother and grandmother

218

be riding around California with FDR's wife? Her mother frequently complained about Franklin Roosevelt and the terrible things he had done to the country.

"She wrote several of my speeches. She had power. Your mother must have told you."

Someone knocked on the door.

It was Bill. "Hi, Dianna, would —" a surprised pause — "Mrs. Roosevelt!"

"You're one of Kennedy's boys," she said, her tone imperious.

"I'm afraid I am."

Dianna couldn't tell if his abashed look was simply good acting.

"I'm one of your husband's boys, too, and one of yours. I heard you had left the convention. I am glad you stayed for tonight."

Mrs. Roosevelt did not smile. "I was going to leave until I realized I had to see this girl. You don't know what you're doing, do you, Dianna?"

"Singing," said Dianna, hoping she wasn't going to fight Mrs. Roosevelt.

"Singing for the Democrats," said the former first lady. "A cowardly party. But I shouldn't be bitter, should I, if the man I wanted just didn't have the drive."

"A good man," said Bill.

Mrs. Roosevelt ignored him. "We had such fun, we three, and we did a lot of good. I will write you. Some things are more important than winning."

Bill gave her a simple bow as she left, and, bewildered, he said to Dianna, "You two are pals?"

"I seem to be full of surprises," she said, eyeing his dark suit. "You look lovely."

"I've got nothing on you."

He didn't. Her pale blue tulle gown flowed around her in a Greek style, and with the help of a fall, her hair flowed down her back.

"I hope that counts when I forget the verses. Do I have to wait for him to talk?"

"You close the convention. There's an extra seat where I am. Do you want to watch him give the speech?"

Dianna wondered who that extra seat had been for. Sandi, probably. Or maybe Joy. Or even Star. Or…

Lynne handed her a white mink stole, for the gown was sleeveless and the arena was cold.

"Did you know about my grandmother?" Dianna asked Lynne.

Lynne said, "I wasn't hired until after she died. But it was a long time ago, and memories change. You should get out there."

"Did she work with Mrs. Roosevelt?"

"I don't know anything about it," said Lynne.

"You think she'd have said something," said Dianna.

Bill led her onto the VIP platform. Her seat was between Bill and Tony Curtis who of course sat next to Janet Leigh who sat next to Frank Sinatra. The television cameras and lights prevented Dianna from sticking her tongue out at him.

Bill pointed out who was up near the podium: Hubert Humphrey, Adlai Stevenson, Harry Truman.

Lyndon Johnson came onto the platform with his wife and daughters.

"What's he doing there?" Dianna asked.

"He's going to be vice president," said Bill.

"Wasn't he insulting Kennedy all the time?"

"Isn't politics inspiring? All this forgiveness!"

When Kennedy came out, everyone stood, cheering and applauding. Dianna thought it exciting, and he looked darn handsome. The thought that he'd been attracted to her both excited and appalled her.

Finally, as the noise of thousands of people settling down in the stands quieted, Kennedy began the speech.

As he recited the failures of the Republican presidency, Dianna felt she'd landed on a different planet.

Families forced from farms.

Unemployed miners and textile workers.

Old people without medical care.

Families without a decent home.

Children without a decent school.

Hungry families.

Starving children.

In the United States? She thought all that had been taken care of.

Kennedy kept piling it on. One-third of the world was free, one-third under oppression, and the last third suffered poverty and disease. Communism had spread from Asia to the Middle East, and now to ninety miles off the coast of Florida. Meanwhile, he said, we had the power to exterminate our species several times over.

"We are not here to curse the darkness. We are here to light a candle," Kennedy said.

But everything he said sounded dark! And he spoke way too fast.

We stand today on the edge of a new frontier of the 1960s, of the unknown opportunities and perils of unfilled hopes…the new frontier is a set of challenges… I am asking each of you to be …pioneers for the new frontier…We must prove…this nation, conceived as it is with its freedom of choice…can compete with the Communist system. Can a nation governed such as ours endure?

The delegates were standing, applauding, cheering.

"What are they applauding?" Dianna asked Bill.

"Kind of grim, wasn't it?"

Her bodyguards approached. Her stomach lurched. The nation was waiting for her.

She followed the men backstage, gave her stole to Lynne, who said, "You will be wonderful."

Dianna waited, muttering her lyrics.

A disembodied voice said, much too loudly, "Ladies and gentlemen, to close our convention, to sing 'America the Beautiful,' Miss Dianna Fletcher."

She found her big X mark for where she should stand and peered out to find Johnny. She felt the lights. The camera moved in.

The orchestra played the opening phrase. She started to sing, concentrating on the words. Out of the corner of her eye, she could detect Johnny's baton going up and down.

The lights darkened – someone had messed up the lighting. *America, America, God shed his grace on thee*. They'd fought their hearts out for their candidate, and now, as messy as it was, they had one. Concentrate on the verses. *God mend thine every flaw*. When she got to the heroes, her voice trembled. Johnny launched into the modulation, and she headed toward the last verse, soaring into a high cadenza, soothing and triumphant. *And crown thy good with brotherhood from sea to shining sea*. She watched Johnny's arms and held the last note for the cutoff. And made it. Then, quietly, she burped.

The applause was so powerful, Dianna thought at first that cannons were firing. She made a little bow and smiled at Johnny, who gave her a thumbs up and readied the orchestra for the national anthem.

As she plucked a note out of thin air, she heard a frightening, loud noise she couldn't place. Then she realized it was the crowd standing. The orchestra joined her. Thank God, she'd picked the right note, and she sailed through the anthem with a happy smile and a bit of a bounce. Once she let go of "the brave," she turned to leave the stage.

Someone took her hand and led her to the nominee.

Jack Kennedy said, "Thank you, Dianna. Thank you very much."

He had an engaging grin and he bent down to kiss her cheek.

"You are incredibly beautiful."

Confused, she said, "Senator, is it all as bad as that?"

He winced. Then he grinned and said, "Yes, but we're going to make it better. How about it? Slower, right?" asked Kennedy, and he reached out to shake Bill's hand.

Bill, right behind her, had gotten there fast.

Ethel Kennedy was blunt. "The place was down in the dumps until she started singing."

Eleanor Roosevelt hugged Dianna and walked off the platform, not stopping to shake Kennedy's outstretched hand.

Kennedy said to Dianna, "You will sing at the Inaugural gala. Bring the family! Where's Sinatra? Francis! The Fletchers for the gala!"

"Anne's a Republican."

"I don't care."

"Don't you have to win first?" Dianna asked.

Kennedy laughed so hard he wept. Lyndon Johnson kissed her in an almost painful bear hug.

"And we're gonna win, honey!" he shouted in her ear.

Bill took her arm and pulled her away from the Texan.

Bobby said, "Bill, we'll set up some sessions. He's going to work hard on the Inaugural."

"Not to mention the campaign," said Bill.

Kennedy said, "Dianna, we're having a party. You have to come."

She didn't even think about the power. "No, thank you. I have to work."

Kennedy looked at Bill as he took Dianna's arm. He grinned.

"Oh," he said. "Someone beat me to it."

"Sometimes," said Bill, "silence is best."

Kennedy laughed again and turned to shake hands with a multitude.

Bill kept his arm on Dianna's as they headed down to the tunnels where Lynne and Reggie were waiting. He wasn't saying anything, and Dianna was feeling that power again, which even shocked her.

"Your guy got it," she said. "Are you glad?"

A voice broke in, preventing him from answering.

"It was one of those moments," she was hearing a news announcer say, and she recognized John Daly's prep school accent, "that captured the hope of the country in its future, in its youth, in its longing for peace. Just a lovely ending to a lively convention from Miss Dianna Fletcher."

It was indeed, Daly, that charming news man and host of the game show *What's My Line*. She stopped to greet him, and he asked, "What did you think of the convention?"

Newspaper reporters gathered like birds for a few crumbs.

Dianna said, "It was exciting to be part of history." As she looked at the reporters, anxious to hear what she thought, an idea pushed right up front.

"What did you think of Kennedy's speech?" someone called.

"Challenging." Her heart pounded as she realized she really could say what she wanted.

"Do you support Senator Kennedy for President?"

"He is quite intelligent."

"And handsome?"

"You know, I can't vote."

"Who's the fellow with you?"

Bill pressed her arm.

"I'm Bill Royce," he said. "Dianna, I see your chauffeur just up there."

Another questioner yelled, "Vice President Nixon is a friend of your family's. Do you feel disloyal?"

"We can all be friends while we disagree with each other. This is what Americans do."

"What do you think is the country's most urgent problem?"

Why were they asking her that? The country's most urgent problem was stupid reporters.

"Dianna," said Bill.

But she had gotten her nerve up, annoyed that they weren't asking her about her work. "Who would I vote for? Urgent problems? Vice President Nixon participated in a process that has gotten out of hand. That of turning against citizens and saying they are dangerous when they are not."

You'd think Bill would like her talking about that, but instead he was tugging at her arm. She kept talking.

"For instance, when I was in Rome, I played Juliet in a film version of *Romeo and Juliet*, written for the screen by Mr. Edward Grey, a wonderful screenwriter. Because Mr. Grey is suspected of something, something unproven, that movie is sitting in a vault somewhere. Mr. Grey and his producer Mr. Anthony Marks did not do anything but their work and this movie cannot be seen by people because of this suspicion. This is simply unfair. The only dangerous message in *Romeo and Juliet* is that grownups can be stupid."

The pressure of Bill's hand on her arm grew.

"Thank you," she said to the astounded John Daly, "See you soon!"

The reporters ran after them.

"No comment," Bill yelled.

Dianna smiled and waved as Bill pulled her out of the tunnel.

"I had to say it," she said.

"No, you didn't."

Security guards met them at the entrance, as did Reggie and Lynne. Bill walked with them out to the parking lot. He was silent, but he held her hand.

When they got to the car, Bill said, "I hope you don't take headlines away from Jack."

"Geez, Bill! His speech was depressing! And how could I do that? Anyway, I want that movie released. It's the same story as *West Side Story*."

"They should give me *Days of Wine and Roses*, but I'm not putting it in the party platform."

"I didn't do that. It's something I had an opinion on, and they wanted my opinion, even though I don't vote. And is it as bad as all that? The farmers, the people in the cities, the Negroes?"

"Yeah," said Bill.

"In school, they told us that people don't starve here. That there are no poor."

"They're invisible. Or their skin color isn't white."

Reggie opened the car door for Dianna and glared at Bill.

Bill said, "I'll see you on Monday. Get rested up."

She had felt powerful, talking to those reporters. Someone would write about what she said.

Someone did.

There she was on the front page, beneath the fold and right beneath Kennedy. "What Happened to Dianna Fletcher's Juliet?" said the headline, with a lovely picture of her singing.

You're getting closer, Juliet, she thought. But not in time for *West Side Story*.

Maybe for something else.

Brother Luke

28

When she got to the ranch location Monday, everyone congratulated her for her singing and hoped that *Romeo and Juliet* would be released soon. Everyone thought that it was stupid that it hadn't been. Mike North, who had been polite and restrained toward her, expressed fury in no uncertain terms.

"This could give kids a really good exposure to Shakespeare!" he ranted. And he cursed out the government.

Chris, too, expressed his support, and Goodman offered to help through his contacts.

Marty, however, stayed in his trailer until it was time to work.

And where was Bill? She didn't see him in the makeup trailer and she couldn't tell if he was in his dressing room.

Made up and dressed in gingham, she slung her shawl over her arm and took her leather gloves from the prop man. The assistant AD ran over to her and pointed toward the wranglers surrounding a wagon.

"Charley needs you."

She hurried over to the wagon to pat the horses.

"We need a couple yards with them galloping," said Charley. "Is Kat dressed?" Kat, a young guy, was Dianna's stunt double.

"I'll drive," Dianna said.

"Oh, God," said Charley. "You and our guest star with death wishes."

Where was that guest star?

"Will we squeeze the little picnic scene in today?" she asked.

"It'll be ruinous to try to match it in the studio, but it's going to rain the rest of the week. So I'm telling you. Please be brilliant in one take."

It was just past sunrise, but the lights made it seem like a shadowy, rainy day as she made her way through the cables to the food table. She needed a donut to be brilliant.

There he was. Bill, all in black, was arguing with Paul Henreid.

"I can do this," he was saying. "I have done it!"

Brother Luke was supposed to ride up to the galloping horses, pull up on their reins, mount one horse, and pull the team to a stop, thus saving Betsy.

Count on Bill to want to do it all.

"We can't lose you this early on in the episode," said Henreid, with his charming accent. "And I'm not going to have you limping or on crutches when you're claiming to heal people."

"Good morning," said Dianna, munching her glazed donut and ruining her lipstick. "I could have told you he was trouble."

"We usually save the stunts for last," said Henreid, "but the weather is against us. I'm sorry."

"Can't I at least ride along and grab the reins?" asked Bill.

"We don't have the time," said Henreid. "The second team is finishing up now. We are racing the weather."

Bill went back to his trailer, script in hand. He hadn't even said hello.

Henreid stood watching the second unit, a morass of horses, wagon, lights, camera tracks, camera, crew, wranglers, and stunt men. The scene was short and simple, but it had to be done several times, the wagon racing along, the rider in black stopping the horse and leaping onto it.

Dianna said to Henreid. "I don't think Betsy should be completely swooning over him."

"Don't you see the good in him?"

"It's a tricky balance."

"How would you show that?"

"Amusement? Maybe some confusion after the revival meeting."

"Good. Good. I like it."

How wonderful to have a director listen to her.

The second unit done, Bill came out of his trailer and headed to a wooded area where the camera filmed him taking aim and firing a rifle.

After that, Bill again took refuge in his trailer.

Finally, it was her turn to get in the wagon and pretend to be at first calmly driving it, then desperately, with the wranglers bouncing on the back to make the wagon look as if it were being dragged by runaway horses.

"People, let's go," called Charley. "We're losing the light!"

The camera and lights focused on her. Dianna put her hands on the buggy's handle, and thanked the camera for rescuing her while Bill, standing by the camera, fed her cues. His smile was generous, honest as the day is long, a true con artist preacher. After the take, they had to wait for the crew to re-set the lights and equipment to focus on Bill, who waited apart from everyone until they were ready.

After that shot, the clouds fully blocked out the sun. The crew hustled to pack up before the rain started.

"We'll do the other scene tomorrow in the studio, dammit," said Charley. "Already we're behind."

Bill didn't say goodbye — he still hadn't said hello — but as he headed for his trailer, walking right past her, he stopped to say a few words to Henreid.

As if she were a total stranger.

"Good morning!" she yelled.

No response.

The next morning, Bill said a simple, "How are you?" before walking past her toward the set, where he began pacing around what was supposed to be a simple outdoor scene that would take hours to shoot. Dianna responded to the con man reverend with a simple charm. Bill seemed tentative, however, his words stumbling over each other, uncertainty in his eyes as he looked at her. What could have been a rather dull expository exchange took on extra dimension. Dianna marveled that he had found all of this in the script.

Bill was taking charge of the episode. Betsy was just a little cipher next to him.

"That was good," she said to him, as she headed to her dressing room.

"Yeah," he replied. "See you tomorrow."

Had he even looked at her?

She had to sit with Chris for a publicity interview with *TV Guide*, which wanted some comments about Marty for a profile. When that was done, and they were heading out to their cars, Dianna raised the subject that troubled her.

"He's not talking."

"Who?"

"Bill Royce."

Chris shot her a shrewd look. "Not you, Betsy."

"He just goes into his dressing room and shuts the door. Was he like that when you knew him?"

Chris paused at his '57 Ford. "He used to piss me off because Stella Adler always asked him to escort her to plays. An old lady wanting a handsome guy, I thought, but he didn't care. Acting is his mission. He sure can be a loner, yeah, there's something there he keeps close, but when you need a pal, he's a pal, and when you want a guy to hang out with, he's the one. I don't get his woman business. I don't think he does, but that's his business." And he added as he got into his car, "Betsy was smart not to get too involved with him. She could say goodbye."

"She always says goodbye after an hour," said Dianna.

The next morning, he was at the studio when she got there, pacing around, muttering lines on the set made up for the revival and dodging the crew, some of whom were trying to spray fake sweat on him.

Charley directed the extras to sit and called for places.

Dianna found herself sitting next to Kristen Virginia, her favorite aunt on the *Larksong* set so long ago. Kristen looked just the same, radiating bonhomie in a matronly way.

"What have you been doing?"

"I had some time off."

"Traveling?"

Kristen laughed. "Like your Marks and Grey, I couldn't get a job. I've been cleared, but I still have trouble getting work. Jack Goodman helps when he can. He's one of the good guys. Mr. Henreid had his own problems."

Gentle Kristen suspected of wanting to overthrow the government?

"A bunch of us are in the same boat." Kristen waved a hand over the extras. "We used to have careers, but at least this is scale pay. And it might lead to jobs. Still, I'm ten years older."

The lights set for a night revival, Bill took his place on a wagon platform, bowed over the Bible he gripped, and nodded as he listened to Henreid's soft instruction. The director took a seat by the camera that moved up over their heads. As someone yelled for quiet, Bill gripped the podium and gazed down at them with fierce eyes.

"I'm saved," Chris, next to her, muttered.

As soon as Bill started preaching, Dianna jolted back at the force of his energy. Delivering words with a powerful voice, he scolded them, pounded the Bible, paced in a small circle, gestured with powerful arms, and poured down fiery invective. Then he did it all again, for different angles and close-ups.

After her initial amazement at Bill's power, Dianna focused on her own part, for she did have a few close-ups. She decided Betsy would be startled, engrossed, then confused. He was calling her a sinner! How should she take that?

Bill preached hell and damnation all day and healed three men, too. While the scene was relit and reshot for different angles, he stayed in character and kept the energy. When the work was over, cast and crew stood and applauded him.

She started toward her dressing room, but Bill said, "Wait."

She prepared for his criticism.

"You don't have to ride up with your driver and wait for him every day. I'll pick you up in the morning and drive you back."

Well, hello to you.

"I have to be in earlier," she said. "My hair."

"Doesn't matter." He glanced at the call sheet the second AD handed him. "I can run through these lines while the guys set up. Five-thirty okay?"

"Sure."

"We don't have to talk. Or we can run lines."

"Your lines. I'm unconscious except for 'I can't see.'" The thought of that scene made her feel shy, for he would be holding her and praying over her.

At home, Lynne wasn't for it. "You see him too much as it is. He's got a bad reputation."

"He'll be driving a car!"

"I'll be telling your parents."

"It's just for a few days Geez." What could Bill do at five-thirty? He was a professional. And so was she.

She was at the door and ready when Bill pulled up.

After a soft greeting, he was quiet, letting the classical music station do any entertaining. She sat back and closed her eyes, but sometimes she would open them and look at his hands on the wheel and watch him rub his forehead with one and move his lips, reviewing another big speech.

When he parked, she jumped out, hurrying under the drizzle to get her hair washed, dried, and waved, and when she came onto the set, Bill was heading to makeup and ignoring her.

She had to practice a tricky bit with the three "healed" men, at Brother Luke's camp that involved a gun accidentally going off. The gun was loaded with blanks, of course, but blanks could still be dangerous. The cement floor was cushioned at a precise spot, so she had to be sure to fall in the right place. They rehearsed a few times until the timing was precise. Then they practiced it with the gun shooting off.

"You're not supposed to be around guns firing," said Mira. "There's a ten-yard rule."

"Guns aren't firing," said Henreid. "It's not a crossfire. Let's do the master. Where's the Reverend?"

"Right here," said Bill, off to the side where he would make his entrance.

"It's okay," Dianna said to Mira.

They took their places, and Henreid called for action.

She spoke harshly and punched at the man with the gun, which went off as his foot slipped on the fake grass and sand. He accidentally struck Dianna in the jaw, and she fell back on the wrong place — the cement floor — and braced herself. Bill rushed forward and caught her head, beating the stunt captain by a few valuable seconds.

"Shit!" yelled the stunt captain.

"Cut!" yelled Henreid. "Are you okay?"

"I'm fine," she said, as Bill helped her up. "Thanks."

"I'm sorry," said the poor actor who had socked her.

"Is she bruised?" called several people, and the makeup herd and the nurse examined her. She had suffered just a small black and blue spot.

"It wasn't the gun," she called to Mira, who was scribbling.

"I have to write it up," said Mira.

"Damn Spic," said the stunt captain.

"Hey!" Dianna shouted.

Mira shrugged to Dianna and sat down in the shadows, scribbling notes.

Bill stepped up to the stunt captain, glaring at him.

"I'm sorry," said the captain, stepping away from Bill.

Mira kept on scribbling.

"Come on, people," said Charley.

Dianna fought and fell. Bill ran on, fought, and then he was over her, his hands caressing her face, whispering anguished words. Again and again from different angles, he implored God to heal her. As he laid her down on the wagon bed, his hand slid down her side, lingering over the spot of her faded *Picnic* bruise.

Or did she imagine that?

At the final cut and print, the crew applauded Bill. Paul Henreid embraced him.

Dianna felt jealous and thrilled. And tired. Bill certainly must be more so. He had given his all, a brilliant job.

The ride home was not as quiet as the ride to work had been. Bill was happy, the way actors are happy when their hardest work is done and it was good. He praised how wonderful the part was written, with holes and questions that he had to answer.

"The heroes are getting badder," he said. As if he liked that.

"And women either badder or dumber. The studios are losing their grip, tossing out my mother for Gina Lollabrigida. And she was up for *Tiffany's* against Hepburn and Monroe. Yuck."

"Did you hear? I'm playing Paul," said Bill. "Right after *Every Time*."

Movie after movie without a break. Such ambition.

"Aren't you too young?"

"Doesn't matter for Paul. Who's going to look at him? Audrey liked me and threw Peppard out. That means a lot in this business."

"Especially to Peppard."

She watched his hands on the wheel and liked that even as he talked, he was alert to stupid drivers on the road who didn't signal. Once he had to brake fast, and his arm shot out to keep her from crashing into the windshield. She crashed into his firm arm instead and scolded herself for enjoying it.

"What about your dissertation?" she asked.

"I'm in the let's pretend I'm working on it mode. My friend at the Library of Congress keeps digging stuff up and sending it to me, but I haven't done too much."

"A lot of the extras on this episode were blacklisted."

Bill cast her a startled look. "No kidding?"

"Mr. Goodman told me that both my parents testified before HUAC. Did you know that?"

"When?" he asked, obviously startled. "Were your parents involved with the Committee for the First Amendment? No, they couldn't have been. They're rock solid Republicans."

"What committee?"

"A group of movie actors flew to Washington to protest the hearings when the Hollywood Ten were subpoenaed. That was when this all just started. Wyler was one of the founders. Lucille Ball, Bogart and Bacall, Henry Fonda, Judy Garland, Katharine Hepburn, Lena Horne, Danny Kaye, Gene Kelly, Sinatra, Kay Thompson, Jane Wyatt, and our director, Paul Henreid were part of it, protesting that writers were being called on the carpet for their ideas."

"I don't think my parents went." But she wasn't sure. Those were a lot of her parents' friends.

"The people who went on that flight suffered a backlash when several of the Ten proved to be actual Communists, and the writer John Howard Lawson behaved like a jerk when he testified. One of the investigators followed him to describe how many Communist front organizations Lawson had been part of. So there was tremendous backlash. Bogart was pressured to sign an article for *Photoplay* confessing he'd been duped. Lucille Ball got in trouble later. And that was before the climate of fear really kicked in."

"What happened"

"Business executives published lists of people and if they happened to hear someone, usually an actor or writer, had belonged to some organization the FBI had on its list, you'd end up on *that* list. Whether it was true or not. All hearsay. Even if true, people could have signed up so innocently. But to most people, being on that list meant someone suspected you had done a bad thing. Columnists would write that you were red through and through, without any evidence. Television sponsors were extremely sensitive to this, after all, they come into people's homes. They can't have scandals! So, you lost your living. Ah, but for a fee, the same people who put you on the list would clear you. There was no facing your accuser. It was all gossip, true or untrue, usually not close to true. It spread to Broadway. People picketed plays if there was so much of a breath of controversy about someone because they gave a dollar to some world peace fund or worked with Paul Robeson."

"Who?"

Bill groaned. "Please, no."

"I don't know him."

He pulled into her driveway.

"I can't start now."

"I'm sorry I'm stupid," she said, annoyed that he usually made her feel that way.

"I don't know if I knew who he was when I was your age. Same time tomorrow? You were good today. You got out of my way."

She stuck her tongue out.

When I was your age! He must think of her as a kid sister.

"Oh, that reminds me," he said, leaning an elbow over the seat, "Have you been kissed before?"

Damn that grin.

"Oh, sure." She tossed her head.

"Good. I'd hate this to be your first kiss."

"I've been kissed a lot. When I was Anne Frank and when I was Juliet."

"What about for real?"

"Is that any of your business?"

"How's Bruce doing?"

She didn't answer.

"I'll have to talk to him."

"Don't you dare!"

"Don't you want him to kiss you?"

"Mr. Royce, this is none of your business. How many women have you kissed?"

He laughed, backing the car out of the driveway. "Can't count that high."

29

Dianna couldn't remember the gown they'd tested but it wasn't the one she found in her dressing room — a sumptuous blue satin with silver embroidery and lace trim. It took half an hour with help getting into the stockings, petticoats, and having the skirt fitted round her. The boned bodice made her appear even slimmer and gave her breasts a boost. It must have killed the show's budget.

Charley kept knocking, asking when she'd be ready.

"Wow," said Bill, in his plain Brother Luke black suit when she finally came out. "Is that you under all that?"

Dianna looked at Henreid, gesturing her puzzlement.

"I was not happy with the other gown," the director explained. "I felt you needed a blue gown to go with your eyes, and I remembered this one. Why waste color? We did the lighting tests with your stand-in, and wardrobe broke union rules adjusting it. I think I was right."

"Thank you," she said, embarrassed by all the stares. "I'm not sure I can dance in this." She whirled slowly. Bill came up, waltzed her in a circle, his smile wide. He looked at her as if she were a different person. Maybe he was acting, who knew. She wished he wasn't. She wished she didn't wish he wasn't.

Things were getting complicated without her even trying.

"I'm sorry to hold things up," she said to Charley.

"Time well worth it," he said, and he kissed her cheek. The crew kept whistling as she walked by.

Marty, who appeared only in this scene, came over to extend a hand to Bill, who gave him an abrupt greeting.

"Rude," she muttered, sweeping past him.

"Yeah," he called after her.

Rehearsal started. Dianna joined the actors dancing to a simple waltz count, no music, just someone counting from the side. Bill, as Brother Luke, entered, exchanged a line with Marty and a few with Chris and Mike, and then worked his way over to her for a dance.

"I don't dance on Sundays," Brother Luke said, "but I do not object to it otherwise."

He pulled her in close so she had to bend her neck to look up at him. His eyes pierced right through her, his strong hand was on her back, and his smile filled with a certainty of victory that both thrilled and alarmed her. That feeling lasted through several takes at several angles.

"I was hoping to talk to you," said Brother Luke. "But in this crowd, I don't stand a chance."

"We have doors, Brother Luke," Betsy said.

Off they went, swirling through the doors, onto the veranda, the camera following them. Slowly, slowly, they arrived at their marks, someone counting one, two, three on the side.

He's Brother Luke, she kept telling herself. His face was so close, and she could read sadness, anger, confusion, humor.

"What did you want to say?" Betsy asked.

Brother Luke just gazed at her.

Had he forgotten his line? Should she say something? She really didn't know how to feel under his gaze. How would Betsy?

Finally he said, "That you are the most extraordinary —"

His hands framed her face, while she just looked up at him with wide eyes. One hand stole behind her head, stroking her hair — which would have been nicer had it not been sticky with spray — his eyes were deep into hers, and his lips were on hers. She could hear Henreid's breathing as he leaned in close alongside the camera. The camera and lights were smoking hot. She put her hands up on Bill's chest and pushed.

"Cut. That does not look right," said Henreid. "Maybe take a step back. You want to be polite about refusing him."

"Do I?"

"Yeah," said Bill.

"Bill, count to five during the kiss," said Henreid. "That seemed too long."

"Count?" Bill asked, and the crew laughed.

"I'll count," said Dianna, feeling confused, as her hair was fixed and her lips moistened.

Bill's arm around her was unyielding, his lips as well. She counted to five and held on to seven before stepping back.

"I'm sorry," he said.

"It's all right," Betsy said.

"No." He shook his head and then, looking deeply sad, he walked away.

"Good," said Henreid.

They did it again and again. Kiss. Talk. Walk. His head coming close to hers. His arms around her. It's Brother Luke. His hand so strong, and her body settling into his arms. It's Brother Luke. She didn't care if he was a con man.

Finally, the close-ups done, Dianna asked, "Can I take this thing off now?" and Charley said, "Right here if you want."

She held out her arms and the wardrobe ladies removed her skirt and bodice.

Bill whistled.

"On second thought," he called, and he ran back and swept her back up for a kiss that took longer than seven counts. The crew cheered. Dianna stepped back, blushing, smiling, wondering what that meant.

Mira called, "Easy, everyone."

Bill laughed and trotted into his dressing room. But first he wheeled around and said to her, "You're doing awfully well."

Dianna showered and lunched in her trailer before being made up again. They were filming the last scene in the script, where Luke went his own way, this time a real preacher.

Bill was cheerful, and lighter, as if relieved of some burden. They laughed throughout the scene, celebrated with ginger ale and cookies at the "wrap," but when it was over, Bill seemed to go dark. He waited for her by the car, but it seemed obligatory on his part, his voice curt and polite in an automatic way.

She didn't press him on it. This was Bill, dark, dark, dark. Brother Luke had been more fun. It was hard not to forget Brother Luke holding and kissing her since he was sitting right there.

"See you in the movies, kid," was all he said as he let her off. So it was over and she was not worth the time. He had just been acting.

He would go off into the movie sunset, playing leading roles brilliantly, while she would be left watching him ride off into the sunset, still in television until she wasn't. The end.

30

Bruce called and invited her to see a movie called *Salt of the Earth*. He told her that the movie had been made by blacklisted artists, all of them stars and leaders in the industry, and some, like Michael Wilson, were now working in Europe.

"Won't it be loaded with propaganda?"

"Like *Romeo and Juliet*?"

Touche.

"*The Bridge on the River Kwai*," said Bruce. "He and Carl Foreman wrote that script. Not the French novelist. But both of them were blacklisted, so their names could not appear on the credits. I heard a rumor, too, that Wilson was working on the *Lawrence of Arabia* script. They try to keep these secrets, but I hear things."

Dianna remembered her father's annoyance about the novelist taking credit for that *Kwai*. It would seem he worked on many movies that were written by these blacklisted people, good movies, too.

Bruce told her that Wilson had written *Salt of the Earth*, Paul Jarrico had produced it, and Herbert Biberman had directed it. Biberman was Gale Sondergaard's husband. She was an Oscar winner who had been in *Zorro* with Dianna's parents. All of these artists had been blacklisted and had made the movie outside the studio system – outside any system.

Dianna agreed to go. To her, it seemed a monumental decision.

At first, she was disappointed. The black and white movie looked and sounded cheap. The music was not well coordinated, and the sound sometimes went off.

But soon, Dianna grew engrossed in the story set in the poverty, discrimination, and struggle of people in New Mexico. Union members protested dangerous mine conditions and, frustrated after an accident, they called a strike. Their wives asked them to add better sanitation and plumbing to their demands, but the men dismissed their concerns.

The story wove it all together skillfully — a shy, nervous woman who struggled with her husband's dismissal of her feelings but who loved him regardless and supported his and the miners' action.

The mining company brought an injunction against the strikers and ordered them to stop picketing. This seeming impassable order produced a most extraordinary moment — a woman in the union meeting got up and said, the women are not miners. *We* will picket. At first, the men resisted her idea, but in the end, the women's tactic won with most men's support.

Dianna started to cry. She applauded the women picketing, standing up to the sheriff's men and their own men. She cried, too, at the loving humor that the script allowed for and the humor when the men started to do the women's chores while the women picketed. As a result, the men started demanding plumbing and better sanitation! Yes, it was an excellent script, beautifully directed with subtlety even while pushing home important points.

She loved the lead character, who grew from the shy, quiet woman to the strong woman standing up for her people's rights.

If I could have played Maria, that's who I'd be, Dianna thought.

The students in the crowded auditorium gave the movie a standing ovation, and Bruce went down to talk about it to the audience.

Dianna was stunned when he explained that the film had been denounced by the House of Representatives for its Communist leanings. Vigilantes had fired shots at the set, the leading actress had been deported, the FBI investigated everyone involved, the American Legion called for a boycott, and the projectionists' union ordered members not to show the movie, which had to be edited in secret. Only a dozen theaters had run it, briefly. Because it was a Communist film.

About people wanting plumbing and safety? At insisting that their lives were worth as much if not more than a company's profits?

Bruce didn't say much on the way home, but he gave her a quick peck at the door. It seemed so awkward but also sweet.

"Thanks for the movie," she said. "You did something important."

"Sure," he said, but he got back in the car fast.

Why didn't Bruce act like Bill or Brother Luke? Why did she want him to?

The next evening, she went with a bunch of former Mouseketeers to see *The Time Machine* starring Rod Taylor. Dianna enjoyed it until it was obvious that Taylor was falling for the idiot Yvette Mimieux. When the blonde actress asked, "How do women of your time do their hair?" Dianna had a fit of giggles. Then she remembered that Mimieux had tested for Maria. After that, she didn't care for the movie and wished that the Morlocks had eaten silly Yvette.

Afterwards, they had hamburgers at the Brown Derby and made a lot of silly noise. Dianna felt it was like old times, and it made her sadder in between noisemaking. Several kids had gone back to school, not even sure they'd try acting again. They were all going to be teachers, they said. Dianna wondered what she could teach, and she listened to their plans, not wanting to join in and feeling awkward that she was still acting, well, sort of. Out of insecurity, she paid the concierge fifteen dollars if he would bring a phone to her at the table and make an announcement over the address system that she had a phone call. When she got the phone, she felt awful, seeing her friends turning away and not paying her any attention. It had been a cruel move. She said, "Not now," into the speaker and hung up.

"You made that up, didn't you," Tommy said to her as he drove her home.

"Yeah."

"We all know you're doing well."

"I'm sorry."

"We had a good time until you did that."

She didn't let him drive through the gates. She just got out, slammed the door, said, "I'm sorry then!" And she walked up the hill to the house.

In a foul mood, she went to sit by the pool. She heard the phone ring and went to dangle her feet and kick some water. Lynne hurried out and plugged a phone into a jack.

"I'm not home," said Dianna.

"Yes, you are," said Lynne.

"Is it Mom and Dad?" Dianna asked, taking the phone. "Hello?"

Robert Wise's voice said, "Dianna, Dianna, Dianna."

She hardly felt a thing.

"I'm sorry it's taken so long. I spoke to Jerry Robbins and some people in New York, and this morning, I had an expensive conversation with George Bennett and the Mirisch people and United Artists. George told me to call you. He'll contact you later."

"Okay." She could barely get that word out.

"Lenny Bernstein called me up to chew me out after the Democratic fundraiser. Why didn't we think of you? Geez. Well, why hadn't *he*? Who knew how good you were? I sent Jerry that Elvis test. I looked at *Diary* again. Talked to Stevens. He said you're the reason they won best picture. I don't think he's just being nice, that's not George. And all this *Romeo and Juliet* business — I wangled some footage from Pinehurst on it. You're luminous!"

Luminous! Her heart pounded, but what if he didn't say what she thought he was going to say?

"You're doing a movie with my old friend Sybuck, who showed me your test. Geez. What a wonderful thing. He's great, I promise. I even saw some footage of you on *Silver Sierra*. Goodman didn't want to show it, but we go back a long way. Anyway, Dianna, Dianna, Dianna. I agree with Lenny. Jerry agrees. We all agree. You're on the cusp of something, honey. We thought we knew what we were doing, but my God."

Would you just say IT.

"We're offering you the part of Maria."

Dianna closed her eyes. Her brain seemed completely empty.

"I wanted to call you, rather than you hearing it from George or reading about it. If you want it, it's yours."

Tonight, tonight, won't be just any night.

Wise said, "Are you there?"

"Yes," she said, quietly. She was thinking of Terry, and of Esperanza, the woman in *Salt of the Earth*. They were Maria, too. Not soubrettes, but real people. Young, going through fire, emerging strong.

"Do you think I can carry the movie now?"

He didn't answer at first. Then, "To be honest? At this moment? Probably not. But in about twenty minutes, you will be one of the most important young stars out there, and frankly, I want that. Look, our picture is artistic, we've got no stars. It's all Jerry's creation and Lenny's music, and that's going to be hard enough to sell. It's a musical that ends tragically and makes people think. It's a Broadway hit, yes, but that's New York and not the nation. The nation likes happy musicals. Yeah, we were thinking of a big name star to help out, but no one came close to that test you did with Elvis."

"I'm sorry he didn't want to do it."

"I'm not. He would have been a great Tony, but he would have made too many demands to change the part around. This is not going to be an easy movie to make. We've got a strong supporting cast, and we need leads who will be leads."

She realized what he was saying, and she started getting nervous. She grew more so when she heard what he said next.

"You will be the star of this movie. No one's name will be the same size as yours, no one's name beside or just below yours. With the campaign we run, and with *Every Time* coming out, and all this *Romeo and Juliet* noise, when the movie opens, you will bring in the audiences. And to make certain, we're going to try to push *Romeo and Juliet* along. I called Fred and said we'd help out with advertising *Every Time*. We don't really have the money, but it's a great script and we'd be silly not to help."

They were taking a risk that she would be a major star when the movie was released. This was humbling. Then she remembered another problem, one that neither one could overcome. She hated to mention it, but she had better.

"What about school?"

"You can work eight hours now."

"What?"

He couldn't be serious.

"I called the Board of Education before I called George. You passed that test."

She'd almost forgotten about it.

"I passed?"

He laughed. "I guess they haven't mailed the results yet. I had to check. I couldn't have made this offer if you couldn't work eight hours. So, honey, thank you for taking that test. And passing it!"

She was an adult! She was "legal eighteen!" This was better than an Oscar!

"That footage with Elvis was wonderful. Lenny cried."

"He cries at everything."

Maybe Natalie had been too expensive. No, no, they would have not blinked at that for this film. But now they trusted her, over Natalie, to carry it. Her! She started to feel anxious. And thinking of Teresa, she felt humble.

"I hear you'll be in New York next month. You can go see Jerry, who's anxious to work with you. We've sent the contracts by air mail to your father, and he'll sign, and then you. I cabled him today." He laughed. "George is making us pay for our stalling."

She'd better call.

"Your filming starts in November. They're doing the street work in New York now. George said you're doing that television series and another movie in September and October, but that works with what we'll need. We'll record the songs first. September. We'll let you know in plenty of time."

Poor *Silver Sierra*.

"Thank you, Mr. Wise. I'm feeling pretty humble right now."

"Keep it up!" he joked. "And we have our Tony. We decided on Russ Tamblyn for a mix of poetry and muscles. You two know each other, right?"

"Oh, yes," said Dianna. Russ was an old friend of Nick's and had been to the house lots of times. He had made a name for himself as a dancer and actor, but he was no box office star either.

"There'll be costume and makeup work, you need to work on your accent all before you start recording. We'll set up a schedule."

"I'm very excited."

Actually, right now, she was numb.

"We all are. Thank you, Dianna. You'll be the Maria of our dreams"

It took a moment to register after she hung up. She was going to play Maria! They'd tested a million actresses, and she'd won out!

She let out a yelp, grabbed Lynne, and they danced around, and then Dianna took a leap into the pool, yelling, "Maria! Maria!"

Anne called.

"I got Maria!" Dianna shrieked.

But Anne wanted to talk about all the *Romeo and Juliet* publicity.

"These people were blacklisted, rightly or wrongly. You needed something to do because you were so disappointed not to play Anne Frank. Rightly or wrongly, we can't ignore they were Communists. So stop harping on it. We thought they'd let it into the country, but Marks is holding firm. Marks is the glitch."

"I met Eleanor Roosevelt at the Convention. She said Nana wrote speeches for her. Mr. Goodman says you and Daddy testified before Congress."

Anne didn't say anything.

"Mom?"

"They were not speeches, just a few lines she rewrote for Mrs. Roosevelt. Honey, I hope you're not telling anyone that."

"Not yet."

"Don't. Don't talk about Nana. Don't talk about any of this stuff. You don't know anything. Lots of people testified before Congress then. It didn't mean anything. Don't talk about it in New York, okay? We have to put all that behind us."

"You weren't Communists."

"Of course not. But it's all better left in the past. You don't understand it, Dianna."

No, she didn't. But she moved on.

"How's Chas?"

"Honey, I'm being called back to the set. Did you hear? Kerr married that writer, Peter Viertel. Very intellectual of her."

Jim called. This time, she took it. His father, after all, was big at Paramount. Still, she kept her voice cool. He didn't.

"Dad's tearing what's left of his hair out. Paramount has the movie rights to *Romeo and Juliet*. He thinks you just stumbled on this, but now he has to figure out how to bypass all the stuff surrounding the movie. They're getting letters and telegrams. They're going to have to bring it out. Bob Wise is putting pressure on, too. *West Side Story* and all. It's a great angle. But what a mess. They know they'll make money, but there's this blacklist thing still going, even after Trumbo. Even because of Trumbo."

"It's Shakespeare, for heaven's sake."

"Maybe you shouldn't have talked about it."

"It's Shakespeare!" she yelled at him. "There's not a Marxist word in it, you dope! Rich people are fighting!"

"Okay," he said. "Want to go dancing?"

She hung up on him. Why were these people so afraid of the Communists that they couldn't let *Romeo and Juliet* in? Why did they think *Salt of the Earth* was Communist propaganda? Wasn't the country strong enough for a movie? Wasn't it the Communist countries that kept people from seeing "disturbing" movies?

Under fire, Howard Barry put out a statement that Paramount would release *Romeo and Juliet* as a roadshow in December. Edward Grey and Anthony Marks were given due credit without comment. Kirk Douglas called her to cheer her for one more hole in the blacklist wall.

How could something so simple be considered so important?

"Come on over for dinner," said Douglas. "We'll talk. It's another breakthrough! You can help us bring the young people in."

"It's Shakespeare!" she declared.

She wanted so much to tell Bill. But Bill's house was empty. He'd gone to Massachusetts to help Kennedy learn to talk slower.

She was going away, too. To work. She wished she could just stop, savor, and think about Maria. But she couldn't yet.

31

Dianna liked two things about a trip to New York: going and coming. She loved the Super Chief and the Twentieth Century Limited. She loved watching the country roll by and being able to stretch out and read magazines and fun novels like the *Angelique* series by Sergeanne Golon.

On the train, she had no responsibilities. Once in New York (in August, worse luck), she'd be bouncing from the quiz show *What's My Line*, to the *Ed Sullivan Show*, to a dinner with NBC executives, to Broadway shows, and worst of all, to *Bandstand* in Philadelphia. She wouldn't have any time to go to the top of the Empire State Building, ride a horse in Central Park, or window shop on Fifth Avenue.

"Why *What's My Line*?" she'd asked "Aunt" Dot who traveled with her. "Kilgallen's there."

"It's George's master plan. She's going to be surprised when you appear, and she won't be able to be anything but charming. It will nullify anything snide she would write because the television audience will see her as being pleasant to you."

"Who would believe anything snide about me?"

Bill, still in Massachusetts, had his houseboy Peter deliver a package before she left. "Reading for the train," said the note. "It's the proposal for my dissertation. Enjoy New York, Bill." How nice of him to share his work with her after his *Silver Sierra* moodiness.

She pulled out a bound sheaf of papers with the title page: "Blank Screen: The Threat to Constitutional Ideals by the Blacklisting of Writers by William Royce/PhD Thesis Proposal, University of California/Political Science/Film and Theater."

She flipped through it, impressed by his notes and the handwriting in the margins that were mostly to himself, such as "See Hutchins on Constitutional Ignorance in by Those Who Swear to Protect It (Congress)." As she paged through, the name "John Fletcher" caught her eye, and in the margin, written in pen, the handwritten note, "HYPOCRITE!"

This word was next to a quote from

"John Fletcher, who noted, 'I choose to raise my family here. I want to share with my children the unique heritage of Great Britain and the United States, a heritage of rights fought for and won at heroic expense and liberty for which we must be ever vigilant.'"

She slammed the folder shut. How dare Bill send that to her? She shoved the bound papers into the envelope and packed it at the bottom of her suitcase.

Just enjoy the Super Chief, she thought, a train brilliantly decorated with bright colors and American Indian designs. She and her "aunt" each had a large drawing room next to each other, with couches that became beds, a table and chairs, and bathrooms with showers. The train, made up entirely of first class arrangements, was usually peopled with movie people going back and forth across country, although some were beginning to travel by plane. Dianna preferred the long journey apart from her work schedule. This trip, however, she was so busy that she only was able to walk through the train once, as she and Aunt Dot went to dinner the first day and shared a table with Danny Kaye and his wife Sylvia Fine. They had a lively conversation about their work, and Kaye hoped that she could perform in a benefit for UNICEF. When she boasted that she could sing his song, "Stanislavsky," he made her do it on the spot. Which entertained the entire dining car, which included the LeRoys, MacMurrays, and Pasternaks. Aunt Dot wasn't thrilled. "It's not your business to be sophisticated," were her pointed words back in Dianna's car.

"Aunt Dot, I'm having a good time, whatever you intend to call it."

She felt rebellious, she felt angry, she felt confined, and she felt more so as she needed to work and would have to live, eat, and study in her car for the trip. Aunt Dot had even ordered a keyboard.

To her satisfaction, the newspapers carried a headline on the lead arts pages announcing, "Dianna Fletcher Signed as Star of *West Side Story*." Now, she hoped, she would be able to drop the *Silver Sierras* and *Bandstands*.

She still had doubts about her acting: Betsy was easy to play, after all. The work came easy; it was an outgrowth of her perkiness except she could ride, shoot, argue with her men folk, and kiss.

She examined the magazines on her table. Wouldn't you know it, there was *Photoplay* with Bill's picture on the cover, right under Marilyn Monroe's breasts. He had some press agent. Dianna flipped to the story. Nice pictures – Bill in a tux, Bill in cowboy dress on the set of *Comancheros*, in a dandy gunfighter's outfit on *The Magnificent Seven*, Bill bare to the waist on *Picnic*.

"A ladies' man, Bill has escorted *Playboy* calendar girls and other young lovelies. Women are drawn to his debonair façade, old fashioned manners, and that sly look that betrays a sense of fun. Deep down, however, Bill is really looking for his lady love."

So much for Sandi.

The little story about herself, for there was one, said she was dating several boys, not one special one. "Deep down, Dianna is really looking for her true love."

So much for fiction. Bill's envelope taunted her from the bottom of her bag. She should see if there was anything more about her father. She was almost afraid to look.

"Before the young United States created its Bill of Rights, the states individually had developed such documents. These bills were written during wartime because it is during war that individual rights are more likely to be curtailed due to the government's claims of "national security." It is easy, during wartime, to suspect someone as being an enemy who argues a point that is not in the majority opinion and may even be offensive, perhaps dangerous. The idea of independence from England offended many people in power.

Dianna looked out into the night, seeing spots of light from houses and towns in the darkness, wondering how the whole country had managed to stay as one with all its upheavals in the past.

The government, Bill wrote, could remove natural rights. The people were in charge of the government, however. The people were the authority. We, the people, as it said in the Declaration of Independence.

It sounded dangerous, certainly messy.

Perhaps, Bill continued, the government would take away the people's power in the name of the people, to protect them, but that would be against the Constitution. Even in wartime – Bill underlined that. Perhaps in wartime, people would acquiesce that perhaps a right lost here and a right lost there would keep the country safe for the time being, but in the heart of the Constitution, that was not possible.

What if people forgot that, and what if the government took charge of the people's freedom? It could lead, wrote Bill, to perpetual war that the government could proclaim was for our freedom and that would set one group in the country against another in disagreement about what our freedoms should and should not be, one group siding with the coercive government and the other with the theory of natural rights of the people.

Dianna was getting nervous. She'd been so well educated that the United States was a great and benevolent power, land of the free and defender of freedom around the world, that even though she knew about the blacklist and about slavery and those awful things, it still did not shake her belief in the fundamental goodness of her government and her country. It was the Magic Kingdom! Although she struggled to understand Bill's writing, she realized that he was not saying that the country was fundamentally wrong. As she understood it, he was emphasizing that the people were what made the country and the government good.

If perpetual war, or the perception of perpetual war would convince people to give up their rights and to regard the government as the true power, then the people would give their rights to the government, and the government would keep them.

Did atomic peril constitute such a continuous war?

She looked up at the country now, dark, invisible. The great mass of the nation and its diversity impressed and scared her. How could it be conquered or destroyed? She loved it fiercely. She realized just then how strong her feelings were; before, her love was something she simply took for granted.

According to Bill, however, the people had let Congress and McCarthy and those other groups go right on damaging lives, forgetting the precious gift of freedom, as Jimmy Stewart called it.

Why had Bill called her father a hypocrite?

Why had he given her this to read?

She flipped through the pages, the typed paragraph blocks, the marginal notes in pen, and found, suddenly, her name. She flipped back to it.

DIANNA. The apple of his eye. It was a description of the Fletchers. *This* phrase was circled and arrows pointed at it. This note occurred on the page after her father's quote, next to nothing in particular, as if he'd turned the page and was still festering over something.

The idea came to her that Bill might want to go through her to hurt her father. Because for some reason, Bill hated her father.

Why?

She shoved the papers back into her suitcase and picked up *Angelique*, immersing herself in Louis XIV's France. Tried to.

Was she his pawn?

Get away from him.

She tried to forget it all in the hubbub when they reached Grand Central. Photographers took her picture getting off the train (that would look exactly like the ones of her getting on) and as she and the other stars were led through a roped off area in under the grand ceilings of the main waiting area, she smiled and waved. The crowd in the station was almost terrifying and she wondered how people managed to stay sane while in the midst of it.

Outside, the limousines were waiting. Dianna never tired of looking at New York with its tall, gleaming buildings heading for the sky. She didn't mind the traffic; she loved looking at the stores and all the people cramming into them. When they turned onto Central Park West, she could have cried. People were walking about, sitting on benches, enjoying that beautiful place, and she wouldn't be able to.

At the Plaza, they were hurried to the private elevator and finally to their suite (across from Cary Grant's – he wasn't in). Dianna roamed through the parlor, kitchen, the study with the piano, and the other bedrooms, which made her lonely for her family. The parlor held fruit baskets and flowers from the hotel, Jerry Robbins and Bob Wise, the cast of Broadway's *West Side Story*, Mayor Wagner, the Chamber of Commerce, and the Dianna Fletcher Fan Club. She perched on her window seat, watching the traffic below and in the park.

There wasn't much time to rest. After dinner, she and her aunt got into a limo (smiling and waving at the people in the lobby), and she was soon ushered into a dressing room at CBS while Aunt Dot hurried into the audience in case one of the panelists recognized her. John Daly, the show's host, came by to tell Dianna "just have fun" and check on how she would disguise her voice.

She practiced as the panelists tried to guess the occupations of a girdle salesman and a woman wrestler. Dorothy Kilgallen was definitely on this show.

Finally, it was time for her segment.

"Panel," she heard Daly say as she waited offstage, "are your blindfolds in place? Mystery guest, will you come in and sign in please?"

Dianna walked out into a blaze of light and a camera aimed at the blackboard. She picked up the chalk as the audience applauded and cheered throughout her signing her name, and were those wolf whistles?

She sat next to Daly and looked across the floor, where all four panelists wore blindfolds.

"We'll begin our questioning with … Mr. David Niven," said Daly.

She managed to fool him with her French accent, and that was something, since he was her father's good friend. She kept switching accents and languages, to Italian, German, English, then back to French, keeping the other panelists, Bennett Cerf, Arlene Francis, and Kilgallen in stitches and confusion.

Niven asked, "Do you sing in your pictures?"

Dianna went to her deep chest voice. "Sometimes."

Kilgallen muttered, "She sings, she can be dramatic or comic, she has a picture…I'd think it was Anne Foster – she does all that – but I don't think she is in town…"

Daly gestured to hush the audience from reacting.

Kilgallen looked confused. "*Are* you Anne Foster?"

"Non, non, non, mais je vous remercie beaucoup pour l'honneur," said Dianna.

"I have it," said the publisher Bennett Cerf. "Are you Debbie Reynolds?"

Throughout the next minutes, neither Bennett Cerf, nor Arlene Francis, nor Niven, nor Kilgallen could figure out just who she was. Dianna forgot the camera and just enjoyed the game.

Finally, Niven asked, "Have you ever won an Academy Award?"

Dianna, wondering if he'd guessed, said very slowly, "Oui."

"Miss Kilgallen?" said Daly.

"Are you Audrey Hepburn?"

"Non, merci beaucoup," said Dianna.

"Panel, you've got about a minute," said Daly.

Francis asked, "Do you have more than one Oscar?"

Dianna looked to Daly.

"Small conference," said Daly, putting his head near hers.

Dianna whispered, "I have a juvenile Oscar."

"Don't you know?" asked Francis.

"She lost count," said Niven.

"She's Walt Disney," said Bennett Cerf.

"Maybe it was a special Oscar," said Kilgallen.

Daly said quickly, "The question was, does she have more than one Oscar, and the answer is yes."

"It couldn't be Bette Davis. And it's not Anne Foster," said Niven, and then he clapped his hand to his forehead and yelled, "Oh! Ich bin ein dumkopf!"

"Now you're doing languages!" said Arlene Francis.

"Have you ever sat on my lap?" asked Niven.

"What?" cried the other panelists.

Dianna burst out laughing. "Oui, si, ja, many times!"

"Are you the darling, delightful, Dianna Fletcher?" asked Niven.

"She is indeed!" called out Daly, while the audience applauded. Dianna waved at Niven as the he and the other panelists removed their blindfolds.

Arlene cried, "You're Annie's daughter! Why didn't I guess?"

Kilgallen said, "I don't recall seeing that you were in town."

"She's just off the train from Los Angeles," said Daly.

"Just today," said Dianna. "I haven't unpacked yet. It's lovely to see you all. Hello, Miss Kilgallen."

The reporter, realizing she'd been played, leaned back her head and laughed.

"You!" shouted Daly to Niven. "You handed her the Oscar last April."

"Let's get this straight. You sat on David's lap?" asked Bennett Cerf.

"Many times," said Dianna.

"When she was a wee thing," said David. "She'd crawl up on my lap. She'd sit on anybody's lap."

She shook hands with them all, and when she got to Kilgallen, the columnist said, "All right. You win this round. Give your mother my love."

"Lovely seeing you," said Dianna.

The next morning, she climbed two flights to a dinky, dark rehearsal studio on Seventy-second Street off Broadway and spent several rigorous hours practicing. After a shower, she was off to the Ed Sullivan Theater to tape her performance that would be played as "live" the next month.

A few hours later, she appeared at a reception by NBC hosted by David Sarnoff to promote *Silver Sierra* and to be pawed a lot. Men's hands patted and pinched her rear end. She kept moving away and smiling. What could she do, punch them out?

Aunt Dot retrieved her for a conference. Robert Kimtner and Sarnoff wanted her to do a live telecast of *Cinderella*, like the one Julie Andrews had done a few years before. Dianna hedged. Andrews was a stage performer. Dianna only knew movies. But Aunt Dot thought it was a marvelous idea and made the deal right there.

Would she never stop working? On the other hand, the musical might help but it was such a sweet musical. She hoped she could get out of it. She had to start preparing for *West Side Story*, plus she had *Every Time* to get through.

"It will boost *Silver Sierra*," Kimtner said, of Cinderella. Then he pulled her into a corner, and she wondered what he was going to say. But he said, "Please hold off on saying anything about the Communist angle of *Romeo and Juliet*. You're right to be angry about it, but we would prefer there not be any controversy. You understand. That angle shouldn't take over appreciation of the movie or any of your other projects."

"It's the greatest love story ever written," she said immediately.

"That's the ticket!"

And he patted her rear end.

The next morning, she and Dot took a limo uptown to the rough neighborhood where the *West Side Story* cast was filming under intense heat and Jerry Robbins' and Robert Wise's powerful thumbs. Robbins greeted them hurriedly, Wise kissed her hand, Larry ran up to greet her, and photographers took her picture while she sat and chatted (drinking ice water) with him while Robbins started barking mean words that made her jump.

The dancers leaped and fought, their feet and sweat hitting the hot streets. Dianna expected to see the pavement sizzle.

Robbins' pace was unrelenting as was his perfectionism. Wise occasionally stopped the action to ask a question or to ask for a different emphasis. These interruptions irritated Robbins, and Dianna could see that his politeness to Wise barely masked anger at anyone questioning his work. Robbins had been in on *West Side Story* from the very beginning. It was his show.

The dynamic between the two directors suddenly struck her with doubt about the whole project.

Larry hurried over when she got up to go. "I'm glad you liked it," he said. "Because I am going to die making this picture. Did you know that there are gangs in this neighborhood and they've beaten some of us up? Because we're dancers, fags, you know. It's cost us some days."

"Were you beaten up?" He was certainly no fag.

"They tried. I was fighting for the guys."

"Be careful."

"I may die making this, but Jerry's someone to die for."

She slept during the car ride to Philadelphia the next morning and woke up hearing the screams of fans lining the street. Two burly men escorted her and Aunt Dot into the studio.

Dick Clark, bouncing around like a kid, had agreed to give her live musicians at the last minute. Which meant she couldn't forget any words.

She changed. Yellow shirtwaist, petticoats. Cute hair band, page boy, sprayed to stiffness.

Screams and cheers nearly drowned out her first song, the old Davey song, her first big hit. During the commercial break, as instructed, she sat with the kids and asked questions. What year of school were they in, what did they want to do, who was going to college, who was going to do what. All the girls wanted to get married and have families as soon as they were out of high school.

"Being young is the best time to have children and raise a family," said one girl. "Will you get married soon?"

"To Davey?" several kids asked.

"To me?" one boy asked, and Dianna just smiled.

She sang a few more songs. She accepted flowers from the boy who proposed and embarrassed him with a kiss on the cheek. She waved at them and hurried backstage.

"You're did just fine," said Aunt Dot.

"Okay. But can't I have a little fun of my own? Does every minute have to be work? I can't breathe."

"I would hope you were having fun doing this."

"All I do is work! Now I'm doing *Cinderella* live and in living color. I have movies and a TV series. I would like a little life, too, Aunt Dot. It's not like I need the money."

"We'll handle it."

It was as if someone had taken off her lid. "You're making a lot of commissions out of me! You make me sick. Ever since Mom and Dad left."

Dot looked offended. "I have been working night and day to do what's best for you."

"When we get back to New York, you can pay for your own room."

"Dianna, for God's sake."

"Shut up," Dianna said, surprising herself. Why was she so mad? She hated everyone, didn't know who she could trust, Bill's notes still flashing in her mind, and she could still feel the men's hands on her rear end. Responsibilities tumbled on her, and here she'd wasted time singing those silly songs, and those kids loving it when boys were being beaten up while dancing for a genius in New York.

A security guard walked in.

"Ready?" he asked.

"I am," said Dianna.

"Lots of kids out there," said the guard.

"I'm not signing autographs.

"Dianna," said Aunt Dot. "You should—"

"I'm not signing autographs! I've done what I came for." It really felt great to be angry.

"Okay," said the guard. "We'll just hurry you to the car."

When he opened the door, the blast of enthusiasm nearly knocked her down. There were hundreds of them, screaming her name, cheering her, waving autograph books. The kids pushed forward as she hurried toward the car, Aunt Dot behind her.

When did it happen, the wooden barricades falling, the kids in front tumbling, and the kids behind them racing toward her? Hundreds of them surging at her!

Aunt Dot yelled, "Get her back inside!"

She felt Aunt Dot's hand pulling her back, but it was too late. The kids surrounded them, screaming their love, unable to stop. Under the pressure of the mob, Dianna sank to the pavement. Aunt Dot fell on her, covering Dianna's head as kids tumbled on them, screaming now in fear. Dianna vaguely heard Dick Clark yelling for more guards, and then she felt incredible pain when she took a breath, and everything went dark.

32

Dianna's eyes focused on bright light and people in white.
A nurse said, "You're in Saint Olaf's hospital, Miss Fletcher. You had a concussion, and you have a cracked rib and some bruises,"

All those kids falling on her. She still felt their weight.

"Where's Aunt Dot?"

She cringed at her hoarseness. Had she lost her singing voice?

The nurse said, "Down the hall."

"She was on top of me."

"She's not conscious yet," said the doctor. "She had several internal injuries. We're taking good care of her."

Dianna's head started hurting. Her ribs burned.

When she opened her eyes again, she was surrounded by flowers and overpowered by sweet scents. Also stiffness and pain.

A nurse popped up from a chair and said, with an enthusiasm that hurt as much as when she bumped into the bed, "Hi, Dianna! Look at your blue eyes! I am such a fan of yours. Look here. You've gotten all these flowers and cards. These are from Dick Clark and these are from Walt Disney, and these are from all your friends at NBC, and these are from the kids at *Bandstand*, and these are from the *Silver Sierra* gang, and these are from Frank Sinatra, and these are from Orson Welles, these from Gene Kelly, these from the Danny Kayes, these from Fred Astaire, these from the *West Side Story* cast and from Robert Wise and Jerry Robbins and these from the Jimmy Stewarts, and these are from the *What's My Line* panel. And these by your bed were ordered by your parents."

She heard the word "parents" clearly.

"Are they coming?" she asked, her voice still hoarse.

"I don't know," said the nurse.

"Have they called? Did you call them?"

"I don't know."

"Idiot," croaked Dianna, afraid to talk too much. "Aunt Dot?"

The nurse looked hurt, poor thing, but she made an effort.

"She's in a coma. We're doing everything we can."

Dianna sat up, but pain shot through her, and she sank back down. This was all those kids' fault.

"The drugs have worn off," said the nurse.

"More?" Dianna tried to say.

"We'll meet on this in an hour."

"Why?"

"You're under age, and there's no one to give permission."

"Get out."

"It's my job to stay with you."

"Go away. If you can't help."

"You need to learn how to treat people, Miss Fletcher," said the nurse. "Just because you're a star doesn't mean you can treat people like dirt. I used to be a fan. No more."

Good. One less.

Dianna closed her eyes, heard the nurse walk to the door, and the door shut.

She heard, through the door, "I don't have to put up with that."

"She's a sick kid, Warner. You're the nurse."

"Not to that. And I went to everything she did."

The voices faded.

The door opened.

"Hi, Dianna," said a boisterous voice. She opened her eyes. It was Dick Clark.

"Go away." She closed her eyes again.

"I'm bringing best wishes from all the kids at *Bandstand*."

"Get out."

For a moment, there was just silence, and then she heard his steps going away and the door opening and closing.

"She's not in the best of moods," said Dick Clark through the door.

"She shouldn't blame you," said someone. "I'm so sorry."

Her side throbbed. She reached for the buzzer.

A different nurse came in.

"I hurt. Please give me something."

"Not until the doctor comes. Even then, he'll insist on permission."

"Mean," growled Dianna.

"No, we're not," said the nurse. "We have rules to protect you."

The door shut.

Dianna tried to be still, to close her eyes, but she still saw those kids falling all over her, screaming, grabbing.

She started to cry. That made the pain worse around her ribs. She closed her eyes. If she could just sleep.

Someone had come in, not Dick Clark again, please. A strong hand smoothed her hair. She knew that hand. But it couldn't be him.

She opened her eyes.

"Hi, sweetie."

He was peering down at her. Now why would she dream of him?

"What's wrong?"

"Bill?" she cried, trying to sit up and gasping and falling back.

His hand slipped under the covers and took her hand. "I'm so sorry."

What a nice thing for someone to say.

He looked somewhat rumpled, and he was carrying a little stuffed dog.

"Why are you here?" Her voice had no strength. Would it never come back? Had she lost Maria?

"I was up the road," Bill said, sitting down.

"Where?" Where was she if movies were being filmed up the road?

"Hyannis Port. In Massachusetts."

"Where?" That didn't make sense.

"Helping Jack Kennedy rehearse his speeches and his inaugural address. He wants me to say how sorry he is about what happened. And he let me use his plane to come down here."

"Did I miss the election?"

Bill laughed. "No, he's thinking positive."

"You came to see me?" she struggled to say. She hated her voice.

"I thought you'd like to see a familiar face even if it's mine. Do you want some water?"

She started up again, but the pain in her ribs struck, and she fell back.

"What's the matter?"

"It hurts," she murmured, "and they won't stop it."

"Why not?" He sounded indignant. "I'll talk to them. You hold on to this little critter."

He must think she was a baby.

"Wait — Aunt Dot — and my parents — are they coming?" She tried to look angry.

"Okay," said Bill.

She had to remember she was mad at him. He'd called her father a hypocrite. He was maybe trying to hurt her father through her. She couldn't let that happen, but he'd come to see her, and she loved his hands. She heard more loud voices out there. Bill's voice. What was he yelling? Something about lots of reporters out there to talk to.

She heard him yell, "You wouldn't treat a dog like this!" What a great line.

Soon he was back, taking her hand.

"The doctor's coming," he said. "The trouble is that you're under age and there's no one to sign for you, but I convinced them they should do something. I threatened to tell the reporters camped outside that they weren't doing anything for you."

"I heard," she croaked.

"Your Aunt Dot is still in a coma, but they have hope she's coming out of it. Your parents called twice. Your father is coming as fast as he can. You're going to be fine in a couple of days, and then you'll fly home in Frank Sinatra's plane. Everybody wants to help."

"Except the nurses."

"They think you're temperamental."

"Bitches."

"It'll be all right. That was a terrible thing you went through."

How nice for someone to say that. Even if it was Bill.

"I was so mean to her. She jumped on top of me to help when those kids —"

The door opened. A doctor and nurse walked in.

Bill got up to go.

"Come back," she said, knowing she sounded pathetic.

"I'm just going to get a paper. You know I can't live without the news."

The doctor gave her an injection. When she opened her eyes, Bill was there, sitting by her, reading his newspaper.

"You came back," she said. Her voice was better, thank God.

"Of course."

"I thought you were a dream."

"That's what all the girls say."

"Those stupid kids. I hate them."

"It was an accident. The police weren't prepared for that kind of crowd."

"Don't defend them. They're sick. They have to claw at me to feel human."

"Lots of kids got hurt, you know. Some people think seeing you is a thrill."

"I don't care."

A nurse came in.

"Are there kids in the hospital who got hurt?" asked Dianna.

"Yes," said the nurse.

"They can have my flowers," said Dianna. "Not my parents'. Leave those."

She was having a hard time keeping her eyes open.

When she woke up, he was still there, and all the vases were gone but one. She asked, "Did they recast me for *Every Time*?"

"Not on your life," said Bill. "You'll be all right. They did shuffle a few of the scheduled scenes. After all," he said, grinning, "I'm the star. I have more scenes."

"I'll steal them."

"That's great about *West Side Story*. I think you're just the girl for it. Sybuck was delighted when he heard, by the way, and you've brought nothing but publicity to anything you do."

"Like this?"

"You didn't have to go this far."

The phone rang. Bill picked it up, rolled his eyes, and handed the receiver to Dianna.

"If you care about your health," crackled the voice, "you'll get out of there."

"Hi, Aunt Kath! I'm fine. I mean I'm lonely, I'm angry, and my ribs hurt."

"Wonderful. Don't rest too much. Get back to work."

"Yes, ma'am."

"Stupid fans. When I was on Broadway, they surrounded me when I left the theater. I'd push through, get in the car, roll down the window, and I'd yell, 'Run 'em down! We'll clean up the blood later!'"

Dianna choked on a giggle.

"I didn't send flowers. I sent you a notebook and a pen. You take the time to write down what you're thinking. It'll be good for you."

"Thank you."

She hung up.

Bill said, "Aunt Kath. Geez."

"She's my alternate godmother."

"Who's your real one?"

"The Oliviers."

"Well," he said, "that was some christening."

The nurse came in. Yet another nurse.

"Your father is flying out of Athens."

"How's Aunt Dot?"

"No change."

"Can I see her?"

"No," said the nurse. "I'm sorry, but you can't be up and about yet."

She took Dianna's pulse, checked the bandage, and left with a curious look at Bill.

"When are you leaving?" Dianna asked.

"Tired of me?"

"I'm glad to see you. It's a little bit of home."

"Tomorrow around noon. I have to get back for costumes and stuff. You know, that movie. Want to watch television? When do they feed you around here?"

"I'm not hungry."

Bill examined the television remote, a newfangled device, and managed to turn the set on. After some tries, he figured how to change the channel. He stopped when a dinosaur appeared in one black and white film. "Do you want to sit up?"

He pressed a button and the head of the bed rose.

"What's this?"

"*The Cyclops.*"

"That's Lon Chaney. Is he the monster?"

"No. This woman needs to find her fiancé who flew into some South American place to do research, and she refuses to believe he's dead. She hires these guys to go with her. I think one was a friend."

"You remember all this?"

"This is a great movie."

The Cyclops appeared, an Empire State Building of a man with a face looking like a grilled cheese sandwich, one eye totally gone. Except for a loincloth, he was naked.

"Yuck," said Dianna.

"They had to do most of this with projections," said Bill. "Give them some credit."

The island's atmosphere made creatures grow, so the people would become giants, too, if they stuck around longer than the movie would last.

"That monster is the pilot? Her husband? Where did he get the loincloth?"

The monster looked at the woman as if he were trying to remember her. But they killed him in the end, throwing a lit stick through his good eye, just as Homer had killed his Cyclops.

"Was that necessary? The poor guy, probably missing his fiancé all that time, and there she is, and they blind him."

At the end, the woman put her head on the shoulder of the man who destroyed her fiancé. That was the end.

"You liked that movie?"

"I confess it looked better when I saw it at a drive-in."

"You liked your date. What were her eyes like?"

He flipped some more channels and stopped at an episode of *Superman.* Clark Kent dashed into an alley and, having removed his business suit and his glasses, leaped into the air as Superman, caught up with the bad guys and walked toward them as they drew their guns and fired. The bullets ricocheted off Superman's chest. But when one bad guy tossed a gun at Superman, he ducked, and both Bill and Dianna laughed.

Dianna thought, laughing didn't hurt as much.

They watched another movie, one with John Garfield on the run with Priscilla Lane. Bill uttered a surprised sound, when an actor playing an owner of a diner appeared on the screen.

Dianna said, "Do you know him?"

But all Bill said was, "He's a good character actor. He's in a lot of movies."

"He doesn't even seem to be acting. John Garfield was awfully good, isn't he?"

"He got caught up in the blacklist, you know."

"Didn't everybody."

"Congress went after him. They hounded him, and he died of a heart attack. His production companies put out movies like this. Great actor."

"He was in *Gentleman's Agreement*. He was one of the founders of the Hollywood Canteen. My mother liked him. She never said anything about his being blacklisted."

"I don't suppose she would," said Bill.

She wanted to ask him about that, and about the hypocrite thing, but she also didn't want to get mad at the only person around who seemed to care about her.

"Bruce took me to *Salt of the Earth*."

"What'd you think?"

"I loved it. I don't understand."

Over dinner, Bill entertained her with talk about the Kennedy compound but then he got serious. "Kennedy was profoundly moved by the poverty he saw in West Virginia. He's going to do something about it. Naturally, they voted for him in huge numbers there, defying the experts, so he's grateful to that state and wants to help them."

"Can't they get work?"

"No jobs," said Bill. "They would if they could. The big industry is coal, and fewer people are using coal for heat. There aren't jobs for just anyone who wants jobs."

That seemed a strange idea. "Why not?"

The nurse came in, another nurse.

Dianna said, "I want to see Aunt Dot."

"Tomorrow you can walk," said the nurse.

"Now," said Dianna.

"No," said the nurse. "You might hurt yourself."

"I'll go see her," said Bill.

"Okay," said the nurse.

When he got back, he said, "She's in a coma and not responding."

She couldn't stand it. She pounded the mattress.

They watched Steve McQueen in *Wanted: Dead or Alive*, Bill making fun of him the whole time. They watched *My Sister Eileen* and then the game show *I've Got a Secret*.

They talked movie gossip. He told her that Gene Kelly had married Jeanne Coyne, once Stanley Donen's wife. Dianna knew the gossip that her mother and Kelly had had an affair in the early 1950s, when they were making a lot of musicals together. She felt sorry for Betsy Blair and said so.

"She was blacklisted, too," said Bill.

"All right, all right."

"You're getting tired."

"Aren't you?"

"Want me to go?"

"No. But you'd better."

He was so nice to her. She must have imagined that comment in the margin.

In the morning, she finally went to see Aunt Dot. The woman looked colorless, like a dead person must look. Dianna held onto the woman's hand. "I'm so sorry."

Aunt Dot began to jerk, first her hand, then her whole body. Dianna dropped her hand and yelled for help.

The doctor tried to assure her that she had not caused the woman's stroke. "We thought this might happen."

Bill arrived with a Scrabble game. She didn't want to play, but he set it up, and no wonder. He was winning when the door opened, and Dianna tossed up the board and the markers and called out, "Daddy!"

Bill stood slowly as a tired and disheveled looking John Fletcher walked into the room.

"Careful, Mr. Fletcher, she's healing there," said Bill, much too sharply, as Fletcher tried to hug his daughter.

John Fletcher didn't even pause to acknowledge Bill.

"I can kiss you, right?" he asked, giving her a fierce kiss on each cheek.

Bill knelt to pick up the Scrabble pieces.

"Aunt Dot will be all right," John Fletcher was saying in his soft British way. "She will be here a little longer. Uncle George is flying in from London. He will take her to New York, then a little later, to London. You and I, my darling, will be flying home tomorrow, and I can stay with you a few days before going back."

"I'm so happy to see you!"

"Anne would have come," he said, finally pulling up a chair and sitting down. "She is starting *Anna Karenina*, and she appears in almost every scene."

"Daddy, it was awful."

"I am sure," he said. "George wants to sue *Bandstand*, but I said, why not the city of Philadelphia?"

"I'd better be going," said Bill.

John Fletcher looked up. "My goodness, dear boy, I am so sorry," and he stood up. "You are William Royce, correct?"

"Daddy, he came to help me out, and he really did, and kept me company. Although he made me watch a horrid movie."

"She watches too many good ones," said John, reaching out to Bill with his hand. "Thank you, my boy. You and my little girl will be in a movie, right?"

"In a few weeks," said Bill.

Bill did not immediately take Fletcher's hand.

Dianna noticed. She said, "Your package is in my bag. They brought it from New York."

"I don't think I should go through your bag," Bill said. "You can give it to me later."

"I will look," said John, and he produced the manila envelope. "This?"

"Yes," said Dianna.

John handed the package to Bill.

"Page thirty seven," said Dianna.

Bill looked puzzled, but he pulled out the manuscript and turned to the page. He took a deep breath and looked at her.

"I forgot about that. I'm sorry."

He seemed to mean it. But he was a good actor.

"Is this a new script?" asked John.

"Yes," said Bill.

"Just pointing out a problem, Daddy."

Bill said, "I'm glad you're here, sir. She's been worried about you." He hesitated. "It would have been good for her mother or father to be here to take care of her. Isn't that your job?"

"Indeed," said John. "And not yours."

"Dianna, I'll see you in the movies," said Bill, and he grabbed his tie and hurried off.

Bill had closed the door before she could thank him.

"You can take a nap," she said to her father.

"I think I will just sit here," he said, quietly, holding her hand. "This Royce fellow, is it serious with him?"

"Oh, Daddy, he's so old. He dates all these models."

"Did he come all the way from California to see you?"

"He was helping Kennedy with his speech in Massachusetts."

"Ah, political fellow. Well, none of that. It's just trouble. I think he may be too much for you."

"I think so, too." He was dark and moody at unpredictable times. He'd been her friend, and he hated her father. He was charming, and he had wonderful hands. Too much indeed.

Bruce was easier, and he was coming along.

Sinatra's plane was at least bearable, and her father was there, reading scripts and telling her stories about Nick's first days at the Academy.

Chas, he said, was doing well at his private school.

That's all he said about Chas.

Reporters met them when the plane landed, but John said, "I just want to get my girl home," and led her into a waiting limo.

John made a lot of phone calls, but he usually sat with her on the patio, both of them quiet. He left a few days later, just as she was getting her energy back. But they did have one serious conversation.

"Were you mad at me about *Romeo and Juliet*?"

"No. It will be resolved. Congress thought it was protecting the country."

"Protecting us from Shakespeare."

"Everyone was doing what they thought was right. It was both right to protect the country and right to question it. Things get out of hand sometimes. It goes with being overcautious. The world goes round. What about this Bruce boy? Is it serious with you two?"

John refused to take a stand. Everything was hunky dory. Except in his pictures, where he fought like mad.

Once, she had understood them.

Was it serious? No, no.

"I can't date enough to get serious. I have all this work coming at me."

"My master plan," said John, with a chuckle. "How did Mr. Royce know about *Romeo and Juliet*?"

"I mentioned it to him."

"We have to be above politics."

"I didn't know it was political when I mentioned I had played Juliet. Sometimes it seems if I say 'three little pigs,' people think it's political."

"Actually, that was. All this will work out in the grand plan."

"I don't have much faith in the grand plan. The country is stupid."

"No, it is not, Dianna. It all works out."

He made more phone calls, read *Merchant of Venice* with her, watched

The Band Wagon with her in the screening room, swam nude in the pool and sat nude in the Jacuzzi, and then he was gone again.

Needing to please him, making sure he knew she was all right, had taken up energy, and when he left, she felt guilty about Aunt Dot all over again and bewildered by the secrets that surrounded her parents except when they were with her, when she wanted all to be normal.

Bill called her.

"Can you come over?"

"You waited for Daddy to leave."

"I did."

"If you have something to say to him, you should say it."

"This wasn't the time."

"When is the time?"

"I'll talk to him," he said, sounding impatient. "I'm just gathering information."

"You have to gather information about what my father did to hurt you?"

"Are you able to walk over?"

"Why can't you come over here?"

"I don't want your staff to hear what I have to tell you. And I don't want to take this material out of the house. If you want, I'll pick you up."

Good God, what was he going to tell her? What did he know?

"I'm not supposed to walk more than a mile."

"I'm sorry to make you do that. I'll meet you."

She slipped on her sandals and set out to hear what Bill had been storing up about her family.

What had her father done to make Bill hate him? Would she start to hate him, too?

She slipped on the sand, as if the world trembled beneath her feet.

Alice

33

He met her halfway to help her through the sand. She was familiar with his hand's touch now. No matter what, she liked his hand touching hers.

Once inside his house, she sat next to him, gripping the sofa's arm.

He opened a cardboard box on the side table, pulled out a steno pad, and flipped it open.

"Is that a foreign language?"

"It's shorthand. There is considerable testimony given before the Un-American Committee that they didn't want released or just didn't get around to transcribing from sessions closed to the public. I've been transcribing these. If the acting thing flops, I can be a secretary." She didn't smile but watched him flip through the pages, and when he stopped, she recognized the words, "Mrs. Fletcher."

"Mom?" she asked Bill. "The Un-American Activities Committee?"

"I was looking for your father's testimony, which someone alluded to in another transcript, but I found something else."

Mr. Goodman and Marty had been right. Her parents had testified about Communism to Congress. Why?

Bill opened a folder and handed her some typed sheets:

OCTOBER 20, 1947 TESTIMONY OF ANNE FOSTER FLETCHER.

"Can I read it?"

"I feel I should make you a strong drink, but I did the best I could." He indicated an iced Coke. "That's real Coke syrup."

She was just a kid to him. She leaned back and read.

Chairman: The record will show that a Subcommittee is sitting, consisting of Mr. McDowell, Mr. Nixon, Mr. Vail, and Mr. Thomas.

Staff members present: Mr. Robert Stripling, Chief Investigator; Messrs. Louis J. Ruscal and Robert B. Gaston, Investigators; and Mr. Benjamin Mandell, Director of Research.

Mr. Stripling: Good morning, Mrs. Fletcher. Are you represented by counsel?

Mr. Duggan: I am Samuel Duggan. I am representing Mrs. Fletcher.

Mr. Stripling: Mrs. Fletcher, I believe you have a statement.

Mrs. Fletcher: I have come here only to answer your questions.

Mr. Duggan: Mr. Stripling, Mr. Chairman, my client does have a statement.

Mrs. Fletcher: I have decided not to give a statement.

Mr. Duggan: Allow me to consult with my client.

Mrs. Fletcher: I do not need to consult with counsel. Thank you, Mr. Duggan. I have observed that during these hearings that statements do not make much difference. The members of this committee do not listen too well and wander in and out. I wish to answer your questions and to keep your attention.

"Mr. Nixon: Mrs. Fletcher, we take every word seriously. If you have a statement, you should have no fear of making it.

"Vice President Nixon," said Dianna.

"Not yet," said Bill.

Mrs. Fletcher: I respectfully disagree. Several of my friends have tried to speak their piece, and they were ignored. When they protested, they were cited for contempt.

Mr. Nixon: We disregarded statements only from those who were obviously interested in speaking Communist propaganda. Some we know were your friends.

Mrs. Fletcher: With all due respect, Mr. Nixon, what they were doing was criticizing the actions of this committee, which was their right to do as citizens of a free country where the people rule and Congress serves the people. This committee labeled such statements as Communist propaganda without any evidence at all that it was. Besides, and this may surprise you, Mr. Nixon, but I do not require my friends to hold particular beliefs.

"This can't be my mother," said Dianna. "She's anti-Communist all the way. Although," she added, "she has friends she disagrees with."

Mr. Nixon: That could be dangerous in some cases.

Mrs. Fletcher: Only if one is insecure in one's own beliefs, Mr. Nixon.

Mr. Duggan: I do not think it is fair, Mr. Chairman, to imply that my client should be considered guilty because of her professional and personal associations.

Mr. Stripling: Excuse me, Mr. Fletcher. Is something wrong?

Mr. Duggan: Mr. John Fletcher has asked me to ask the Committee that, when interviewing his wife, you look at her face and not at her legs.

Dianna grimaced and slapped a hand to her forehead.

"I know where you are," said Bill.

"Men," she said, "are stupid."

"I plead the Fifth."

Mr. Thomas: We apologize, Mr. Fletcher, but you must understand that your wife's legs are famous, and we are only men.

Mrs. Fletcher: I was at a party when I had just joined MGM. I heard Mr. Mayer say, "those legs, that stamina, that beautiful hair, and the talent. I'm so proud of her and glad she's on our team." I went up and said, "Thank you, Mr. Mayer." And he laughed himself silly. "I was talking about my horse."

Mr. Thomas: Order! Order! Mrs. Fletcher, you are not in a cocktail party. You are in Congress.

Mrs. Fletcher: A government of only men, I take it, and not of laws.

"And they didn't cite her for contempt?" Dianna breathed. This was the tough broad, not the frightened wife or the dancing beauty, Anne's other film personas.

"Just wait." Bill lit a cigarette. "Sometimes the committee was more careful with a woman. It might explain why Lillian Hellman got away without being cited for contempt. But she's also charming them."

Mr. Duggan: If I might consult with my client —

Mrs. Fletcher: I wish to answer your questions.

Mr. Stripling: Would you tell us where and when you were born and state your occupation. We do not insist on the ladies giving the year of their birth.

Mrs. Fletcher: I was born on April 1, 1922, in Chicago, Illinois, and I am a film actress, singer, and dancer.

Mr. Stripling: I beg your pardon, Mrs. Fletcher, but that is not the birthdate I have here, which is April 1, 1920, in Pasadena, California.

Chairman: Quiet, please. We must remind you that you are under oath. We understand an actress's professional need to appear younger than she is, but since you have given a year, we must corroborate the record.

Mrs. Fletcher: I understand.

Chairman: We have biographies of you from MGM's publicity department, payroll documents, and other records from Twentieth Century Fox and RKO, all of them give your birth date as April 1, 1920. We apologize that we must press this point.

Mrs. Fletcher: I apologize for the confusion. I thought there might be some, so I have had Photostat copies made of my passport and my birth certificate. These may be confirmed easily by Chicago's birth records. I was baptized on April 15, 1922, at Saint Peter's Roman Catholic Church in Chicago. The church would have my age on record.

"Ah, the birthday trick," said Dianna.

Mr. Nixon: Why would the studio falsify your records so that you would seem older?

Mrs. Fletcher: I was only fourteen when I began working in pictures. I claimed to be sixteen. Many performers do this. I was in the chorus and could dance well. Nobody wanted to know any differently, and the labor laws were different. Or not enforced.

Chairman: Thank you for clarifying. We will hold onto these copies if that is all right.

Mrs. Fletcher: I brought them for the Committee.

Chairman: Thank you. Mr. Stripling, continue.

Mr. Stripling: Well, Mrs. Foster —

Chairman: Mr. Fletcher is right here. I do not see a Mr. Foster.

Mr. Stripling: I beg your pardon.

Mrs. Fletcher: It's a common mistake.

Mr. Stripling: We on this committee prefer to be accurate.

Mrs. Fletcher: I am glad to hear that.

Mr. Nixon: Mr. Chairman, I must protest the fawning over this witness. We have records of her attending Communist party meetings and those of the Popular Front.

Dianna waved away Bill's smoke. She had come to the core of what she feared, and she didn't want smoke to distract her.

"Sorry." Bill put the cigarette out.

Mrs. Fletcher: I appreciate Mr. Nixon's concern.

Mr. Nixon: For some reason, you wanted to obscure the facts of your birth. Why do your studio biographies all say that you were born in Pasadena when these records indicate Chicago?

Mrs. Fletcher: You would have to ask the publicity people about that. They obscured my background to make it more amenable to whatever personality they wanted to give me. It may have been a way to add a certain class to my story by naming Pasadena as my birthplace. I was born in Chicago. When I was twelve, my mother and I moved to West Hollywood. She taught in a dance studio. I helped her.

Mr. Stripling: Just a minute, Mrs. Fletcher. These documents do not record Anne Foster's birth, but that of Anne Marrs.

Mrs. Fletcher: That is correct. I was born Anne Marie Marrs.

Mr. Stripling: And your father?

Mrs. Fletcher: My father, Frank Foster, was a vaudeville performer and a projectionist in movie theaters. He left my mother soon after I was born. I have never heard from him since. Foster is my legal name, but when I was born, they gave me my mother's last name.

Dianna had never given her grandfather a thought. She'd assumed he was dead, and no one had ever spoken of him. What had happened to him, the louse.

Mrs. Fletcher: My mother had been a dancer and performer in vaudeville. After my father left, we went on the road. She got jobs dancing and performing. I did that, too, when I was older, and she also taught in dancing schools. She was aiming at Hollywood. I am not sure why since there was no music in movies then. She wanted to act or write. She was always reading plays to me, and we went to the movies. She used to make plays up to entertain me. When talkies started, she started to write plays and stories and send them in, although nothing happened. We reached California when I was ten. That's how long it took. It got tough after the depression, but my mother could reel in students. For about a year, we lived in a small town in California. The price was right. There were a lot of Quakers in town, not many dance students, but Mom raked in several. She had that charm.

Mr. Stripling: Where was this?

Mrs. Fletcher: Whittier, California.

Mr. Nixon: I beg your pardon?

Mr. Stripling: That's your home town, Mr. Nixon.

Mr. Nixon: Yes.

Mrs. Fletcher: My mother rented a building after a few months and turned it into a dance studio.

Mr. Nixon: The Marrs Dancing School? Alice Marrs? I didn't make the connection.

"Mr. Vice President Nixon studied tap dancing with my grandmother?" Bill said, "You'll see."

Mrs. Fletcher: Good morning, Mr. Nixon. Do you remember me?

Chairman: Mr. Nixon?

Mr. Nixon: I don't believe it.

Chairman: Mrs. Fletcher, do you know Mr. Nixon?

Mrs. Fletcher: Mr. Nixon often played the piano for our dance classes. And very beautifully, too.

"Oh, my God."

"I know where you are," said Bill.

Chairman: Order! Order!

Mr. Nixon: Are you Annie Marrs?

Mrs. Fletcher: It has been a long time, Mr. Nixon. I was never able to thank you for what you did.

Mr. Stripling: Mrs. Fletcher, are you saying that Congressman Richard Nixon played the piano for your dancing school?

(Laughter)

Chairman: Order, please!

Mrs. Fletcher; Yes, he was quite sensitive to playing the kind of music we needed. Sometimes, he made the music up. He played beautiful waltzes. I thought he would become a musician.

(Laughter)

Mrs. Fletcher: He did a lot of things to earn money for school. He mostly worked in his father's store. He was very kind to us. It was hard going for a dancing school there. People sometimes didn't pay for a while. Our money ran out many times. One day, when we went to Nixon's Market, we had so little money that my mother took some fruit and put it in her bag. Mrs. Nixon saw my mother take the fruit, and she made a big deal out of it. Mr. Nixon told his mother that my mother had paid for everything, but that he had made a mistake in the bill. He gave me a lollipop. I thought he was very handsome, very wonderful. I had a crush on you, Mr. Nixon. I am glad you turned out so well. I hope you still play the piano?

(Applause and laughter)

"A crush!" Dianna cried. "My mother and Nixon! I thought he had the crush on her. Are you making this up?"

Bill waved the notes. "As God is my witness. I couldn't have cooked that up."

"Is this why they didn't transcribe this part?"

"I've been wondering if your uncle and Duggan didn't stage the whole thing to bring out this silly story and distract everyone from labeling your mother a Communist or a sympathizer."

She stared at him for a moment, then went back to read.

Chairman: Mr. Nixon, do you still play the piano?

Mr. Nixon: Not as often as I should.

Chairman: Please restrain yourselves, ladies and gentlemen. We will try, too. Let us proceed.

Mr. Stripling: We need to move on to your involvement in Communist meetings in Hollywood from 1935 to 1938. We have had testimony from several witnesses that you were present at such meetings, that you sang and danced at them. According to this testimony, you sang to encourage people to donate money to the Communist party. Is that true?

Mrs. Fletcher: It is true that I sang and danced at parties. They were fundraisers for particular causes.

Mr. Stripling: Are you now, or have you ever been, a member of the Communist party?

Mr. Duggan: My client does not have to answer that.

Mrs. Fletcher: But I will answer that.

Mr. Stripling: Thank you, Mrs. Fletcher.

Mrs. Fletcher: I was never an official member, no. But I was very much involved.

"Mom?" Dianna cried.

Chairman: Order!

Mrs. Fletcher: These groups were quite social, filled with witty people. My mother and I enjoyed them. Many of the groups we performed for were Communist organizations or fronts, as I later found out. There was a purpose to these meetings and parties, to help people who needed help both here and abroad, and I am not ashamed of saying that I participated in that. I sang. I danced. I was thirteen years old in 1935. I started working in movies a little bit in '35, mostly in '36.

Mr. Stripling: Was your mother active in these organizations? We have had a witness here who testified that an Alice Marrs and her daughter Anne, who some people affirm was yourself, came to meetings, and did not just sing and dance. That your mother was active in meetings.

Mrs. Fletcher: As I said, it was about helping people. And it is, I'm ashamed to say, true that my mother thought that going to these meetings would help our careers. All the best writers, she said, went to these meetings.

"What career for Nana?" Dianna murmured.

Mr. Stripling: To your knowledge, was your mother a Communist?

Chairman: We can bring in your mother, Mrs. Foster, to answer that.

Mrs. Fletcher: As I said, it was a way of getting ahead and of helping people. Many people worked with the party, or perhaps the party was working with many people, as the nation pushed out of the depression. The whole economy had failed, and as I recall, there was a lot of economic talk. I attended these things less and less from 1940 on, as my career became busy, and especially after I was married and raising money for war bonds. My mother continued until after the war.

Mr. Stripling: So your mother participated in Communist meetings until 1945 or 1946?

Mrs. Fletcher: Oh, I don't think you should call them Communist meetings. They were fundraisers that brought in people from different persuasions.

Mr. Nixon: If I may.

Mr. Stripling: Mr. Nixon.

Mr. Nixon: I remember your mother. She was a dancer. A great teacher. She loved books and plays. I remember talking to her about plays. She admired O'Neill and Shaw. I thought her a most impressive woman.

Mrs. Fletcher: Yes.

Mr. Nixon: To be in a meeting with these Hollywood writers and movie actors must have been thrilling for her. Did she want to write, Mrs. Fletcher?

Mrs. Fletcher: My mother taught dance. In Hollywood, she ran the most important dance studio, which she eventually owned.

Mr. Nixon: We have had private testimony about a Frances Faulkner, who was a screenwriter for MGM and other studios, and one witness believed, but was not sure, that Faulkner was actually someone named Mrs. Marrs, and a Mrs. A. Marrs has been named as a member of the Communist party. Our records led to you and your mother. I did not make the connection, I am afraid, since it was a long time ago that I played the piano in Whittier, and Marrs is not an uncommon name.

Mrs. Fletcher: And you no longer play the piano.

Chairman: Did your mother write scripts under the name of Frances Faulkner?

Mrs. Fletcher: I don't know a Frances Faulkner.

Chairman: Did your mother, Alice Marrs, now or in the past, write scripts under the name of Frances Faulkner?

Mrs. Fletcher: May I take a moment to consult with counsel?

Chairman: He should do some work today.

Mrs. Fletcher: My mother tried to bring me to the attention of people in the business. She was successful. She had no time for political theory.

Mr. Nixon: Is she a writer for the movies?

Mrs. Fletcher: Yes.

"Oh, my gosh," said Dianna, remembering Mrs. Roosevelt. And her mother's reaction.

Mr. Nixon: Did she use the name Frances Faulkner?

Mrs. Fletcher: I don't remember. She used different names for different studios. Perhaps as a game. Publicly, she was a dance teacher and coach. She wanted to keep it that way.

Mr. Nixon: Did you know that she used the name Frances Faulkner?

Mrs. Fletcher: Frances is her middle name. She liked William Faulkner. That's all I can say.

Mr. Nixon: So it was a secret that she wrote?

Mrs. Fletcher: She submitted scripts and they were accepted. She is excellent at both writing and dancing, but she did not want to overlap with my career. Or the studios did not. I don't know. For many years, we were on the road, and we would read plays from Marlowe to Miller —

Chairman: Who is this Marlowe? We have had to deal with Mr. Miller.

Mrs. Fletcher: Christopher Marlowe.

Chairman: Is he a Communist?

Mrs. Fletcher: Christopher Marlowe was the greatest playwright in England before William Shakespeare.

Chairman: I see. Well, it is my understanding that all this goes back to the Greek playwrights.

Mrs. Fletcher: They poked fun at the rulers of the time.

Chairman: Mr. Nixon, proceed.

"They haven't figured out Christopher Marlowe yet," said Dianna.

Mr. Nixon: Your mother kept her writing a secret. Why?

Mrs. Fletcher: The studios wanted to do that.

Mr. Nixon: Because of her Communist ties?

Mrs. Fletcher: The only time it almost came out was when she won the Oscar for her part in writing *Anna and the King*. In which I played Anna. It was quite a coincidence. Mr. Mayer asked her not to accept the award perhaps because it might look bad. He was concerned about her political leanings and he liked writers to be men. I accepted for her, without mentioning she was my mother.

Mr. Nixon: And her name on the script?

Mrs. Fletcher: I don't remember.

Mr. Nixon: It will be easy to check.

"She won an Oscar?" Dianna breathed. "Why would she want to keep it a secret?"

"Your mother fell into a trap. They didn't want to know about her but about Frances Faulkner. Mayer probably didn't want them caught up in any Communist controversy."

"Why don't I know any of this?"

"Should you?"

Mr. Vail: Did you go to a lot of Communist meetings? When were these? Did your mother participate?

Mrs. Fletcher: I sang at parties, fundraisers, dinners. It is all a blur.

Mr. Vail: What did your mother do at these gatherings?

Mrs. Fletcher: I don't remember.

Mr. Nixon: Why did you take the name of Anne Foster?

Mrs. Fletcher: I've told you. It was my legal name. I was Annie Marrs at first at RKO, and it was as Annie Marrs that I was billed in *Stage Door*. Foster was my legal name. My second contract at MGM was as Anne Foster.

Mr. Vail: It had nothing to do with the Communist Party head, William Z. Foster?

Mrs. Fletcher: It certainly did not.

Mr. Vail: Who went to these meetings? Other than you and your mother.

Mrs. Fletcher: I do not remember the actual meetings. I was so young. I went to New York in 1939 to be in a play, and I became very busy, and I married.

Mr. Nixon: When?

Mrs. Fletcher: I married John Fletcher on Valentine's Day, 1940. It was in all the papers, Mr. Nixon.

Mr. Nixon: When did you stop being involved with the Communist party?

Mrs. Fletcher: I was never involved. I sang at meetings and fundraisers until about 1937 or 1938. I was paid. I was very busy. My husband went to the war. His salary was suspended, and I had to work hard. I did committee work for the war effort and worked at the Hollywood Canteen. My son was born.

Mr. Nixon: You worked with an organization for peace. That was a Communist front, as stipulated by the Attorney General. The Communists want our people to not want war.

Mrs. Fletcher: I wanted peace. I wanted my husband home.

Mr. Nixon: Your committee work included working for the migrants. What did that have to do with the war?

Mrs. Fletcher: We were fighting for freedom, weren't we? I worked with Mrs. Roosevelt. The migrants were earning paltry money and being abused. It didn't matter that it was wartime. Their need was just as great.

Mr. Nixon: That particular group was a Communist front, Mrs. Fletcher.

Mrs. Fletcher: I do not think that trying to help the unfortunate comes under the label of Communist, even if Communists are part of the organization.

Chairman: But you are no longer engaged in such activity.

Mrs. Fletcher: I am not now.

Chairman: You were obviously too young to participate in those Communist meetings. But you have provided us with useful details about Alice Marrs, Frances Faulkner. Frances Faulkner was a member of the Screen Writers Guild and a member of several committees, known Communist front organizations, all on the Attorney General's list. We should thank you and Mr. Fletcher for your service in the war and the cause of freedom in the world. Does anyone else have any questions?

Mr. Vail: Do you respect this committee's authority?

Mrs. Fletcher: Why wouldn't I?

Mr. Vail: Thank you, Mrs. Fletcher.

Mr. Nixon: Would you and Mr. Fletcher come to my office? It would be a pleasure to talk over old times.

Mrs. Fletcher: Of course.

Chairman: Thank you, Mrs. Fletcher.

Dianna put the papers down.

Bill handed her the shorthand notes. She could tell enough that they were related to the typed sheets. She could see the name "Frances Faulkner" and "Anna and the King" and other phrases spelled out in English alongside the scribbles. The writing was faded, the paper ragged.

"Why," she asked, "don't I know any of this?"

"You will have to ask them."

"But why didn't she tell us about Nana?"

Bill said, "While you were healing in Philadelphia, I looked her up. I'm sure Frances Faulkner worked on many more scripts, but," and he consulted a legal pad, "her name is listed in connection with *Alice Adams, Stella Dallas, You Can't Take It With You, Marie Antoinette, Ziegfeld Girl, Meet John Doe, Anchors Aweigh, National Velvet*— the Elizabeth Taylor one, *The Picture of Dorian Gray, It's a Wonderful Life, Anna and the King, The Snake Pit, The Best Years of Our Lives, Gentleman's Agreement, The Ghost and Mrs., Muir, Joan of Arc*. Lots more."

He put a book on the table, turned to the index, and she could see "Faulkner, Frances."

She couldn't speak.

"And these were the movies that were nominated for Oscars. There must have been many more. She must have been a valuable writer for MGM and Fox."

"Why is it a secret?" she asked, not expecting an answer. "Why in the world wouldn't they tell us? And why does Mom say she's a die-hard Republican and a friend of that horrid Nixon when she was gallivanting around with Mrs. Roosevelt?"

"There is another thing."

"What?"

"Your mother named her own mother as a Communist. Not something she'd want to share."

She looked at him as if he were crazy until she realized he was right.

"She successfully diverted attention from herself, but the Committee trapped her into pointing a finger at Alice or Frances. Given how close they had been all their lives, this may have simply been too painful for her. Hollywood has a short memory. Frances Faulkner has been banished from memory like all the other blacklisted writers. The world spins on. The Committee unveiled the truth about Frances Faulkner in a private session never made public. Once your grandmother died, it was easier to keep up the story that all she'd been was a marvelous dance coach and strip it all of the Communist taint. Of course, I'm just guessing. I don't know, but I'm sure the studios wanted to protect their investment in your mother. And your father. And later, in your family."

"Did the Committee subpoena Nana?"

"Yes."

"You have her testimony."

"And it's a humdinger."

He pulled out some more typed sheets of paper clipped to shorthand notes.

"Buried in a sea of documents. As if on purpose."

34

TESTIMONY OF ALICE MARRS FOSTER OCTOBER 31, 1947

Mr. Stripling: Please give us your occupation.

Mrs. Foster: I'll begin with what you want to hear. I have been a member of the Communist Party. I am not now. My membership began in 1934 and I left the party in 1946, as I could no longer support it in any way.

Mr. Stripling: Then you did agree with the party when you joined it?

Mrs. Foster: One joins a political party not because one agrees with everything but because those ideas that are dear to one are likely to have a hearing. I joined in the midst of a Depression that destroyed people's lives, and there seemed to be no way out except to change many things about the economic system.

Mr. Stripling: This government was working on helping the people. Couldn't you trust your government?

Mrs. Foster: They did a great deal. It was a Democratic government, I might remind you. I supported those changes, but there were not enough. This country was in trouble, and the trouble was systemic.

Mr. Stripling: So you joined the Communist Party. You agreed with them more. But eventually, you realized they were not the holders of truth, in fact, the opposite. That is to be commended. Now Mrs. Foster, we wonder if you would be so kind as to provide us with the names of those—

Mrs. Foster: I am sure that not everyone who joins the Democratic or Republican parties agrees with everything that party maintains. I did not agree with everything the Communist Party professed, but they were efficient workers. That efficiency might be a suggestion to the major parties in this Congress. I confess a passion for freedom for all, dignity for all, for women's rights, for the equal rights of all people, for the Negro race, for all races, for improving the opportunities for the poor, and for a balance of power between management and workers.

Mr. Nixon: Sounds like a Democrat to me.

Mrs. Foster: It is good to see you again, Richard. And you are not for those things?

Mr. Nixon: Mrs. Foster, we meet again. We are for different ways of accomplishing those things.

Mrs. Foster: Yes, hand out the goodies to the rich people first, and let the poor people get the crumbs if there's any left, and tax them if there is not. It's socialism for the wealthy on the backs of those who are not. It also keeps your donors happy.

Mr. Stripling: Order!

Mrs. Foster: I do not think that the bankers and Wall Street have the right to destroy the living of a nation of workers. For a while, I believed the Communist Party was the best and most effective place to express those beliefs, which I believe are truly American. I am a loyal American. I am proud to be an American.

Mr. Nixon: But putting all that power into one central government - one organization leads to tyranny.

Mrs. Foster: I would agree. This government centralizes power for the wealthy, and it is often tyrannical.

Mr. Stripling: We simply asked for your occupation, not a statement.

Mrs. Foster: I am a dancer and dance teacher. I also have a statement.

Mr. Stripling: Are you a writer for the screen?

Mrs. Foster: I have written for the screen.

Mr. Stripling: We asked you here because we had reason to believe that among the movie writers believed to be Communists, there was a Frances Faulkner, a woman. We ascertained that you, Alice Marrs Foster, was also Frances Faulkner, and your daughter, Anne Foster, confirmed that.

Mrs. Foster: If you knew that before she came to testify, why did you make her testify against her own mother?

Mr. Stripling: Why do you say against? She told the truth.

Mrs. Foster: I do not understand this committee with regard to its relationship and understanding of the treasured ideal of freedom.

Mr. Stripling: We ask you to come and freely tell us the truth. And if you are truly outside of the Communist party now, you would not be averse to telling us the names of those with whom you associated.

Mrs. Foster: But you have the names. The FBI has the names. So many people have testified with the names. Don't you have enough names?

Mr. Stripling: It is not for our sake, but for yours. It indicates that you have truly cut the ties and are willing to tell the truth.

Mrs. Foster: Why don't you ask me their plans? Their secret, terrible plans for taking over the country?

Mr. Stripling: We know those.

Mrs. Foster: Then why do you need to go on like this?

Mr. Stripling: We want you to tell the truth.

Mrs. Foster: Your truth. There is such fear of the effects of free speech in this chamber that men were forbidden to read statements and were cut off in mid-sentence lest they expose too much of what is going on here. Congress shall make no law — it says this in the Bill of Rights — about what people think or believe. Why is this Committee afraid to hear opinions of people they disagree with? Why do they insist that a criticism, everyone's right in a free society, is an attack? Why is this Committee asking people what they believe and then not letting them say fully what they believe? What is this Committee afraid of? Citizens thinking? Citizens trying to right the country and its injustices? People who tried to do that, no, they are the enemies of our country. People working for strong unions and for the Negro and those not given a fair chance and the migrant worker, for world peace, this is Communism. This, you say, is the work of enemies of our country, not of love of country. You say, those are all tricks to lure the stupid. You tell me I was duped to work with these people. I didn't care who these people were, they were working hard for things I believed in. You use this investigation as a cowardly cover-up to smear people who have no recourse. You spread a blanket of fear over the country.

Mr. (Chair): Order! Order! The witness will cease giving dramatic monologues.

Mrs. Foster: There you go, doing it all again.

Mr. Stripling: Mrs. Foster, you must cooperate.

Mrs. Foster: No one calls me Mrs. Foster. I am Miss Marrs.

Mr. Stripling: You were married to Mr. Foster.

Mrs. Foster: Mr. Foster was a rat. Gentlemen, this is my testimony. The Bill of Rights was not created to protect the status quo. Those who won national independence for the American people understood that the status quo, by virtue of its inherent strength, is always in the most protected position. The Bill of Rights was created for those who NEED it most. Those men accused of treason were writing about themselves.

Mr. Stripling: What men?

Mrs. Foster: Keep up with me, please. I mean our founders.

Mr. Nixon: They were writing for the future.

Mrs. Foster: Of course, but they were writing in a present in which their lives had been endangered because they had taken a position that would have had them hung for treason. They were not living in the snug, free country we have.

Mr. Stripling: Why are you giving us a history lesson?

Mrs. Foster: Because you have forgotten it.

"Listen to her," Dianna breathed.

Mr. Stripling: You are out of order.

Mrs. Foster: The Bill of Rights guarantees the persons with vision should have the dignity necessary to expand the American dream by pressing for its fullest realization. Regardless of the intricacies invented by the courts. So that is why I am here, precisely, because I believe in America's greatness and potential for greatness and because I have unlimited faith in my fellow citizens. And yet, despite that faith, my colleagues and fellow writers and I who have come here have been attacked as have those who have stood up for them. For what? For being actual citizens. For working for the elimination of poverty, slums, disease, for racial tolerance and preaching against all that bigotry that prevents people from living in peace and understanding. For some reason, this puts you under suspicion if you would even breathe some of this to the American people in a motion picture. That is not the American Dream, which is not about wealth or owning a house, but in freedom to live. The persecution of these people will naturally lead to the suppression of the ideas we represent, in movies such as *Crossfire, Pride of the Marines*, and yes, *The Best Years of Our Lives*. This Committee criticized these movies.

Mr. Stripling: The witness must come to order.

Mrs. Foster: This persecution of ideas and criticism from this body will lead to the extinction of artistic expression and the idolatry of conformity, exactly what the Communists are accused of doing.

Mr. Stripling: You have stated you were a member of the Communist party.

Mrs. Foster: For about ten years. I admit that I was not terribly active, especially after the war began.

Mr. Stripling: Now, according to *The Daily Worker* —

Mrs. Foster: Excuse me, but that is another thing that amuses me about this Committee. It criticizes *The Daily Worker* for being an untrustworthy, propaganda arm of the Communist Party, therefore full of lies, and yet that is where you get much of your information. That is funny. Well, Mr. Stripling, here is what I did as a Communist. I supported the New Deal. I know that Mr. Thomas and Mr. Rankin do not. I supported the anti-lynching bill. They did not. I also disagree, gentlemen, with you in my support of price controls and emergency veteran housing and fair employment practices. I passed petitions for these measures. I joined organizations that advocated them, including at one time, The Communist Party of the United States. Why should we not use them for *our* benefit? Your emphasis has been the other way round.

Who says we naïve little capitalist souls were influenced? I gave money to many organizations that supported these things. I spoke from public platforms. That is my right. As an American, I claim and insist on my right to think freely, to speak freely, to join the Prohibition Party, the Democratic Party, the Communist Party, or even the Republican Party."

Mr. Stripling: Mrs. Foster.

Mrs. Foster: As Mr. Jefferson said, if an idea is bad, the majority will knock it down after a while. Why don't you believe in the majority? Why don't you trust the people?

Mr. Stripling: We do the work of the people.

Mrs. Foster: I insist on my right and the right of all Americans who love this country to publish what I please, to fix my mind or change my mind, without any pressure from anyone especially Congressional committees, to offer any criticism I think fitting of any public official or policy, to join whatever organizations I please, no matter what you gentlemen think of them. If they propose to do crimes, our excellent justice system should take care of them. We cannot start imprisoning people before they do something, as if this were Lewis Carroll's *Through the Looking Glass*. I as an American challenge the right of this Committee to inquire into my or any citizen's political or religious beliefs, and I assert that not only the conduct of this Committee but its very existence are a subversion of the Bill of Rights.

Dianna looked at Bill. "Wow."

"Your grandmother was nobody's dupe."

Mr. Stripling: This is all irrelevant.

Mrs. Foster: I've noticed that everything is irrelevant to you if it regards people's rights and the Constitution. Interesting. The American people are going to have to choose between the Bill of Rights and this Committee. I believe in the people. They will rally to protect their birthright.

Mr. Stripling: You are in contempt, Mrs. Foster.

Mr. Nixon: Please answer our questions, Miss Marrs. I mean Mrs. Foster. Please.

Mrs. Foster: How can I when I hold you in contempt? You abuse the privilege of calling on me. This is an investigative committee with the intent of making laws, but you do not investigate what laws to pass. You are persecuting people for saying what they believe.

Mr. Nixon: That is Communist propaganda.

Mrs. Foster: There you go again. Criticize this committee, support organizations that criticize it, and automatically you consider that

Communist propaganda. You accept smears and innuendo but no proof and no truth. You do not allow the accused to face their accusers. You will be brought down by the very hate you nurture. Yes, my dear Dick Nixon, you too, who were once so promising. You want people to be in fear of something so you can get rid of anyone you think is an enemy, that is, the people who do not believe what you believe and who will not vote for you. Their fear will turn on you. Yes, I am in contempt of this un-American committee. Good day to you.

Chairman: The witness will remain. Will the bailiff please restrain the witness! Order! Stop the witness!

There was no more to read.

"She left?"

"They charged her with contempt," said Bill. "Apparently, no one stopped her. I'm thinking there was applause, but it doesn't say. The transcript usually reflects booing."

"Two days later, she was dead. Nana," Dianna murmured, fingering the sheets of paper.

"That's all I have."

All? This wonderful defiance, this determined ferocity and her frightening opinions. Why had her courage been kept a secret? Because she had been involved with Communists? She hadn't done it to overthrow the government. She'd done it out of concern for other people.

Then she had disappeared, and Anne Foster had done a political about face.

Why had her mother insisted on being quiet about politics and her father, too, on swimming along with the tide, on not passing this courage along when it was obvious that Alice Marrs and Anne Foster were women of guts and courage? Why was this story a secret? Just to protect the movie star status of the family? What if Alice had gone to prison like other writers?

Would she, Dianna Fletcher, have been happy if they had in fact gone full fury with guts and courage, probably denying her the career in movies that she loved because they too would have been blacklisted?

"You knew this when you were in Philadelphia?" she said, half accusingly.

"Yes. I'm sorry. But you were in no condition to hear it, and I wanted you to see the shorthand notes yourself."

She leaned back and addressed the ceiling. "Why did they let her be forgotten?"

"For some reason, this testimony was never made public. Maybe it was part of a deal. Probably it was too inflammatory. So no one remembers. Your mother does not speak of her. Alice Marrs taught dancing."

"I have to talk to them about this, but I can't do that on the phone, even in a letter. You should have shown this to me when Daddy was here."

"I thought you needed to think about it."

"You want me to turn against them. You want me to turn against my father. You called him a hypocrite. Is that your plan? To hurt them by hurting me?"

"Don't you want to know the truth?"

The truth that her parents had turned cowards?

Hadn't they lied to her about *Romeo and Juliet*? They had said there was a technical glitch, and she had believed the technical glitch was her own acting.

She should hate Bill for making her think these things.

"Nana was a dancer. She could tell stories in dance. And she wrote. She told them a thing or two, and she wasn't afraid. Now am I to wonder why is it she was killed two days later? A hit and run accident?"

"No one killed anyone who defied the committee. Some people died of the pressure." He stood up, looked out to sea. "Some people took their own lives."

"Why couldn't she be a dancer and a writer? Who would care?"

"This whole movement," said Bill, "of fear and suspicion — people just hid because they were afraid of anything remotely touching on what was perceived as Communism, which meant anything remotely having to do with helping people live in dignity, social justice issues. Movies focusing on those issues pretty much stopped being made a few years after the war. If your mother and grandmother were working with Mrs. Roosevelt and with suspected organizations, Mayer may have decided not to draw any attention to Alice Marrs. But some people must have known. If anyone spoke, it was in whispers."

"I'm going home."

"I'll walk with you."

"No." Her tone was fierce. "I want to think about all this. It's not just that my grandmother is almost brand new to me, but that my parents did not tell me the truth about her.."

She walked home slowly, watching the surf, trying to sort out confusion, wanting to believe her parents had tried to protect her and yet resenting that very care. And hating Bill for telling her.

Slowly, she climbed up the steps and stood on the patio, watching the sun set, the deep pink nestling inside the deep blue sweeping across the sky. She thought about the young people who had idolized her so much that they'd nearly killed her in Philadelphia. She represented something important to them, true or not, perhaps stability, perhaps a dream that was beyond them.

She was a princess in a lovely kingdom of magic, blessed by the gods. Well, that was what they thought.

She got busy again, so thinking about Frances Faulkner and Anne Foster happened in short drips. Personal appearances with the *Silver Sierra* cast increased. They rode in parades and appeared at rodeos. The guys left her alone, which hurt, but she understood. In the scenes they played, they displayed affection, and she leaned on that.

There were costume fittings for *Every Time*. Her bruises had almost mended, and her gowns didn't have to be taken out at all. Lily wasn't Millie. She wore strapless gowns, expensive frocks, and a sexy bathing suit. Mr. Sybuck called on her to discuss her part in depth, and she rehearsed some readings with him. It was invigorating work, and she loved that he listened to her ideas.

Bill never waved when he jogged on the beach in the morning when she ate her breakfast on the patio. He hadn't called about picking her up in the mornings, either, even though they would be working on the same movie, almost always together.

She couldn't bring herself to thank him for telling her these truths. She wasn't sure who she was at all now. She would at least have to be Lily. Just forget the rest.

35

Sybuck had up until now filmed the scenes with Carol Andrews, who played Bill's wife, the woman his character murdered. Bill's character, Jeff, changed his name to Mike, and it was as Mike, who moved to a new town and worked in a hardware store, that he met Lily, Dianna's character.

Sybuck had managed more to get more money for a color film, which had meant a hasty redesign of costumes.

In the first scene to be shot, Dianna was to enter wearing a white satin strapless gown of tulle and chat and flirt with an assortment of men while Bill's character, "Mike," who had come to deliver some equipment, stared at her as if having a vision.

When the AD called for her, Bill was not on the set. She and Sybuck quickly reviewed her blocking. She eased herself behind a door and concentrated on Lily as the scene began. On cue, she stepped through the door and started chattering. Sweeping her glance over the room, she saw BillasMike staring at her. She kept up a flirtatious chatter, took two young men's arms, and walked away with them to the door, tossing a line over her shoulder.

Fred Sybuck jumped up and down on her exit. "Wonderful! A revelation! No one has ever seen Dianna Fletcher like that!"

Well, so long as that was what the scene was about!

The coverage shots were tedious, though, standing and being beautiful.

"Just look, don't think," said Sybuck. "Like Garbo."

How could she not think? Once Balanchine had said the same thing to her. "Don't think, just do." When she'd asked him how that was possible, he said, "The body is smarter than we are."

She'd tried, but in this case, she was unsure. What had attracted her to the part suddenly became an obstacle.

"I don't want to be just a dream."

"I understand," said Sybuck. "But you see, the first part of this section will be our seeing you through his eyes and then seeing you for who you are, when you decide you must turn him in. It must be a shock."

That made sense. She'd trust him. Still, to do what Lily did…

"I don't know if I could do what Lily did."

Sybuck patted her cheek. "That is not what you should ask. But you will still love him. That is the tragedy."

As for Bill, she was annoyed. He went straight to his dressing room when they broke for lunch, and she left when she was done.

She had not seen him at all except as Lily.

The next day was harder because the scene involved just the two of them.

Sybuck explained, "The audience should worry about Lily but also have sympathy for Mike even as they know he killed his wife. That's tough. They should be torn about whether to root for this romance or not. Want what you want. I'll take care of the rest."

The scene required intense concentration to maintain the feeling of its master shot, which required several takes. At each break to adjust the lighting, Bill went back to his dressing room. She wrestled with her feelings as she wrestled with Lily, falling head over heels while she, Dianna, became suspicious and fearful — too early for Lily to have those feelings. She worried so much about Lily that she forgot to worry if she was any good.

The rest of the week involved a formal ball, she splendid in red tulle, he in a plain suit. They danced and danced, take after take, his arm holding her close, their faces almost touching. When she impulsively proclaimed her love looking into his eyes, his smile went from triumph to uncertainty. How did he do that? His total absorption of the character increased her need to get through to him, and was that Lily or Dianna feeling that?

Still, outside of acting as Jeff/Mike, Bill didn't even so much as say "good morning."

By the end of the week, her nerves and patience had had it.

The last shot of the week was a passionate kiss, not anything like the sweet little kiss they'd had on *Silver Sierra*. It all seemed mechanical. Her grasping of him was only to find someone else. Was this Mike? Jeff? Bill? Who was the man behind those eyes?

The first take was all wrong. "Give him about ten seconds," said Fred, "then give in to him."

"This may sound stupid," said Dianna, "but how do I show that?"

"Awwww," moaned the crew.

"I came to the right place to ask," said Dianna, flustered.

"It's okay," said Sybuck. "Just bend into him. Mike, you just – that's it," he said, as Bill grasped Dianna and bent over her. "You know what to do."

It was just good acting, his lips hungrily engaging hers as the camera pushed in a few inches away with Sybuck saying softly, "No tongue, Bill." Lily wanted Mike, so she slid her hands up his back as his intensity shocked her. Bill or Mike? Then it didn't matter because she wanted them both, her arms pulling her toward him, her lips hungry for his. Lily or Dianna?

Even in the just holding and talking part of the scene, she felt the same desperate violence in him. She couldn't put the two together either as Mike or Bill. Meanwhile, she had to be Lily and be fascinated. She wondered if her contradictory feelings would add or subtract from the effectiveness of her acting. But Sybuck seemed pleased.

It was a tough day, though, tougher with her confused emotions, tougher when Bill gave her a quick smile and a "good work today" and headed back to his dressing room. By the time she was done showering and changing, he was gone.

She could not work like this.

On Saturday afternoon, she checked to make sure Bill's car was in the driveway. She headed for the deck.

"Are you off to his place?" asked Lynne. Why don't you call your girlfriends?"

"I'll be back for supper," Dianna said. "Bye."

She hurried down the beach. Bill was coming out of the water, dripping, gorgeous, practically naked in his short, tight suit, and seeming larger physically than when he wore clothes. He did not look at all happy to see her. He kept walking toward his patio. She followed.

As she came up the sandy slope, he never cracked a smile as he toweled himself off.

"Going for a walk?" he said.

"Coming to see you," she said.

He wrapped another towel around his neck and stood there, waiting.

"Why are you so strange?" she asked. "Just a little while ago, you drove me to the studio, all talk. You came to Philadelphia from Massachusetts to keep me company. You were so nice. You showed me those transcripts. Now you don't want to say good morning. What's with you?"

He kicked up some sand, tossed on a light knee length robe.

"We've got to be more objective in this movie."

"You're an actor!"

"Right. Let's just act."

"Is it the thing with my father? Just tell me what it is. You shared all these other things with me about my mother and grandmother."

"I have work to do."

"I'm not leaving here until you tell me what I've done or what my father did or whatever is going on with you."

He looked up at the sky. He took a deep breath, his chest expanding, intimidating.

He walked up the steps to his deck.

People on the nearby beach watched them. She waved. They turned and rushed away.

"I'm following you," she said, running behind him. "I want an answer."

"I'm going to change. You want to watch?"

"I wish you would change!" she shouted. "I'm staying until you talk to me."

"Do whatever want," he called back and shut the door. She opened the little refrigerator.

"I'm taking a Coke!"

She sat down to wait. She heard the shower. She heard a drawer slam.

She sipped the Coke and watched the surf. And waited. She heard him coming through the house. He opened the door to the deck and stepped out wearing shorts, a tee shirt, and sandals, and carrying a beer. He turned a chair toward the water.

"Okay," he said. "I'm sorry."

"You have to tell me more than that."

He guzzled his drink. It took up several minutes. She waited.

"It's my Dad, right?"

He crushed the can. "Yeah, it came up to bite me in Philadelphia. I can't get rid of it. I try because I like you, kid, but I can't."

"What about my father?"

"I've been meaning to tell you. And changing my mind. Over and over. First to hurt you. Then because I thought you should know. Seeing your father in Philly, I felt myself not believing this thing I've known for so long. He was so polite and so good with you. You like him. So I'm thinking it's better if I keep my distance. I don't want to hurt you, either. You're a kid, after all. Even if you're his kid."

"Stop calling me that."

"You're a blooming little blossom. I have to kiss you and love you every day, and it's terrifying."

"That's the acting. I can do that, too." Well, she wasn't that sure about that, but it was better to say so. "Aren't we friends? Why do you ignore me?"

"Because, little girl, I am a mess," he said, leaning back. "Blow the siren. It's an alert."

For a while, all he did was drink his beer and look at the water. She waited before pouncing again.

"What did my father do to you?"

Bill fingered the beer can.

Finally, he said, "He killed my father."

36

"What are you talking about?" she flung back, after her first shock. "You never met my father until the Oscar dinner, and even before that you were angry at him. My father didn't know your name except from your movie."

"You asked a question, I'm telling you the answer."

"My father never killed anyone except Germans in the war."

"I saw my father pushed into a body bag and hauled away like garbage."

He looked so pained and desperate that she took pity.

"I'm sorry. I can't imagine what that's like. But how did my father have anything to do with that? Is there a warrant out for him?"

"It's not that kind of thing."

"I see. It's all in your head."

He leaped up and put his arms on the arms of her chair, his face into hers.

"I've been hauling this around for almost ten years. Don't call me a liar or a fool."

"Okay," she said, trying not to look afraid.

He backed off, but he didn't look at her.

"I'll tell you. Then you go away. My father was Ed Greene. Billed as Edward Greene."

"The name sounds familiar."

"You saw him in the John Garfield movie. The diner guy. He's in a lot of movies. He's the one you never see but the one who has to be there, a character actor, one of the best. He worked steadily in movies, television, regional theater, Broadway, New York, Hollywood."

"Why didn't you say he was your father?"

He waved his hand. "You saw him come on the screen and he wasn't acting, he *was* the character. They — he and my mother, she was an actress —moved here in '30 when people were lining the roads looking for food in garbage cans, on streets, anywhere. They weren't lazy. There just was no work. The bankers and Wall Street pulled the plug on the economy. My father believed that should never happen again. He joined organizations that wanted to fix things. He was involved in starting the Screen Actors Guild. He was in the Communist Party for a while."

She understood immediately.

"Your father was blacklisted."

"Yes. He felt the Communists had ideas about how to fix things. He left the party around 1940, but he worked in what could be called front organizations. He wanted to overthrow the bankers, not the government. The moguls, the bankers all consider themselves the government, so to them, such people like my father are threats to that idea of government. Theirs. The bankers and studio moguls fought these people using police departments who hosed them down when they gathered peacefully as is their right. Just like what they did in San Francisco."

"Are you a Communist?"

"No," said Bill, and he laughed. "Suspected me right away, didn't you? No, Lily, you can't turn me in. And my father wasn't one either."

"I don't see what this has to do with my father."

"My father was a capitalist, if you want to describe people with those inane terms, but he saw that capitalism, gone wild without protections for people, is exactly how a violent revolution could start in this country. Ironic, no? They accuse Communists of wanting to overthrow the country when it's really Wall Street doing that. I was thirteen or fourteen when things started to happen. Or not happen."

"So far, you haven't mentioned my father."

"Dad started to be turned down for parts. It's the business, right? Once he got a job in a television series. Right after he signed the contract, the television people said, sorry, we changed our minds. Here's ten thousand dollars, goodbye. Turns out he didn't get even that. More like a couple thousand. His name was in *Red Channels*, the list of people with suspected associations, even if untrue. Dad's name appeared with thirty or so organizations they claimed he'd been part of. Most were not true. It didn't matter. No one called. Guilty or innocent, he was controversial. Television dropped him. Movies caught the virus. He stopped getting jobs or calls to read. He had to —"

Bill stopped talking and stared at the restless water, the tide coming in stronger.

Dianna pressed, "He had to what?"

"Get a job as a waiter," Bill said. "And he was a lousy waiter. He and my mother had split up before that. When he was in New York, she was in Omaha. She didn't believe in Dad's political stuff, and that meant more fighting. I took Dad's side. I thought he had guts, standing for what he believed in no matter what. I quit school to help him out. I wanted to act. I started as an extra, got into some stunt work. Dad told me to change my name and get my own place. He knew what was up. I took Royce, which is my mother's maiden name and got a cheap hotel room. He was under surveillance. Those little noises on his phone. Agents knocking on his door with magazine subscriptions. Sitting in trees. Following him in dark cars. Then your dad called."

Dianna had to remind herself to breathe.

"It was '50 or '51. Dad had gotten a subpoena from HUAC. Your father called him up right after that was in the paper, the latest traitors, you know, so we knew he'd done this on purpose. Fletcher said, I'm getting a film going with Zanuck, and there's a part for you in it. It's a judge in a murder case that involves a few Negroes getting arrested and then lynched. Based on the Scottsboro case. It was a big part. Dad was floored. Your father was really going out on a limb for him. It took guts, even for your father, who's a powerful guy."

"There's no movie like that."

"Precisely. For a couple of weeks, it looked good. John Fletcher sent Dad a revised script. There were costume fittings. Someone mentioned he was cast in the press. No outcry. Preproduction work went on. My father was thrilled. He was an actor again with a great part. Then it all stopped. For three weeks, nothing happened. *Variety* said that the script was in revision. Your father would not take Dad's calls."

"Maybe he wasn't home."

"There was another revised script. The story had changed. It wasn't a falsely accused Negro anymore. The judge's part got very small. The lawyer had a little girl."

"*Larksong?*"

"That's the one. Your first starring role. The seven-year-old wonder."

Bill was pacing around the deck now, growing more agitated. "Dad was down to his last pack of ketchup. He was done. I was walking with him on the Boulevard, going to get him some food, and there's your father coming down and John Fletcher said neither hello nor goodbye nor how's the weather but walked right by us."

"Did he see you?"

"Of course he saw us. He was right there, two feet or less, and my father called out hello and waved, and your father walked right by us. He didn't know me, but he certainly knew Dad. It was worse than what most people did, cross the street to avoid us. It was a direct insult."

"He has this ability to concentrate that he can cross out everything around him and think about a part. That's who he is, that's how he's a great actor."

"No, sir. We were in his face. I could tell it just killed my dad. I went to a job. Dad got a room in a hotel. He took some pills, and he killed himself."

She could imagine that Bill, as old as she was now, coming upon a body bag, a life of promise abruptly ended. Of course he had to be angry at someone.

Bill kept looking at the darkening, restless water.

"I got a call. I went to the hotel, I kept saying it was a mistake. The police were there. There was a letter from John Fletcher on the table saying, I'm sorry, the script was changed, and there is no longer a part for you in it."

A letter was just a letter.

"Nobody gave a damn. I buried him alone. People sent notes, but I was the one at the funeral. Such as it was."

"No," said Dianna.

"My mother was in New York and married to a man who wouldn't let her walk a foot away from him. Attending the funeral of a blacklisted actor or writer can land you on the blacklist."

"Oh, Bill."

"Damn you, yes! It's happened! The FBI keeps tabs on anyone who shows an ounce of sympathy for these people. All of those actors whose union benefits Dad helped to make a reality stayed away. After the funeral, I checked his mail and there was a letter from the FBI saying he was cleared."

She took one of his arms and held it. Put her face against it. She felt his hand on her hair, but then he pulled away.

"So you see."

She stood up. "I am so sorry, Bill. But you can't blame my father. He did not give your father the pills."

"It was the last blow. Your father knew Dad was at his rope's end."

"It's natural you thought that and blamed my father, but he was not responsible."

He paced the deck. Round and round.

"John Fletcher knew the cost, but he turned coward. He changed the script and you became a little star. God's sakes, Dianna. And as if you can get over this stuff. I still think people are watching me. That feeling never goes away. No one, Dianna, who was blacklisted or close with anyone who was, forgets that feeling. I defy it. I'll write about them, talk about what they did. It's broken up marriages, ruined kids, sent talented people into exiles or jobs they're not suited for. And this from a government that says it doesn't want to interfere with our lives. People put up with it. But not the cowards who bent under the pressure!"

"You are calling my father a coward?"

"Yes."

"And you try to humiliate him by taking care of me when he's out of the country?"

He glared at her. "Yeah, that's the size of it. What kind of a father abandons his daughter to agents and servants?"

"Daddy will be back in a few weeks. Talk to him about it." It was all she could say.

"What the hell will that do?"

"My father will give you an honest answer."

"Honest? He'll just tell me I'm a fool."

"Maybe you are." She stopped his pacing by standing right in front of him and staring him down. "We became friends. Isn't that true? Even if you were thinking you were just taking care of me. There's something else in the way, and it's not just this, is it?"

"Go away, dammit."

"We've been close."

"It's the movies, our parts. Go away. It's not real."

"I think it is."

He didn't answer, just looked out at the sea.

"And I'm John Fletcher's daughter."

She felt for him, even if she disagreed with him.

"Yeah."

"And I got *Larksong.*"

"Yeah."

"Pick me up on Monday?"

"It's better I don't."

"Why?"

"You're just a kid."

"I can't work this way. You like me, you hate me. It's not just about *Larksong*. And I don't believe you really think my father killed your father."

"He was responsible!" Bill shouted. "More than all the others who dropped their eyes and crossed the street when they saw Dad. No, no, no. It could have been different if Dad had lived. If he'd done that part. My parents could have reconciled, he might have gone back on the stage."

"Is that my father's fault, too?"

"No! Yes! Dammit, why couldn't he have given Ed Greene a break? He could have changed it. He chose the cowardly way out, just like the rest. Why couldn't this country stand up for itself? John Fletcher is one of the most powerful men in the industry. But John Fletcher backed down. Soften up the damn story, make it less controversial, don't upset people. Don't look like a Commie. So he makes his daughter a star, and dammit, that's the only reason we know each other. Dammit."

She wasn't going to give him that.

"You just have a letter and your anger and your grief to go on. I don't think you believe what you say you believe. Because you were able to be friends with me."

"That was an act. I'm not hanging out with a sixteen-year-old. I've gotten in enough trouble."

She couldn't leave him hurting. She wanted to help him. Was this Lily? Millie? Betsy? Who in her loved this man, because she did.

"They'll be here after Labor Day for several weeks. You can find out the truth. Now what's the something else you don't want to tell me?"

"You think there's something else?"

"Yes."

"Go away."

"So go on the way you've been going on. Who gives a damn."

She hurried down the steps.

He threw a beer bottle down. It flew past her. She kept going.

"Dianna!" he called.

She kept going. Get off his beach.

"Dianna!"

He was running down the steps.

"Dianna!"

He caught up to her, grabbed her, hugged her hard.

"I'm sorry."

He still looked miserable, even scared.

"You'll have to tell me," she said.

"Such a kid," he said.

Now he walked away, toward the darkened surf and the rising moon.

"You keep saying the same damn line," she said. "Let's move to the next scene, already!" She ran to him. "Tell me."

He touched her chin, then her nose. "All right. I seem to have fallen for you. You're a kid. Like no kid I've ever come across. You don't let go."

A part of her was pleased, no thrilled. But this man was scary, and he was getting more so, and yet, she wanted to reach into him and pull him inside her and love him. And she wanted to run away.

"You're jail bait. Do you know I was arrested for soliciting a minor? I thought she was about twenty but she was sixteen and wanted a drink. Some years of therapy and Twentieth Century Fox got my record erased. So right, I'm going to keep you around. You're his daughter, too, damn. Do you know what you have? A warm heart in addition to being pretty and brilliant whatever else you do that stops me up. It didn't hit me until the end of Brother Luke. You do extraordinary things. You're not losing your talent, you're building one up. This movie is going to be damn rough working with you, trying not to be caught up with you. And, yes, I want to take care of you. Your father isn't doing that."

"He is."

"Leaving you alone with just the staff for months? I don't like that."

"Why not?"

He gave a short laugh and walked down to the edge of the surf.

She followed him.

"Why not?" She wanted him to tell her why because she hated that her family left her, too, but she wasn't going to say it, ever. It was business, after all.

He waved his hand at her, as if to ignore her words.

"This is why you've been cold to me."

"Dammit."

She took his hand. "No. You took care of me."

"That's what I want to do. But you're a kid. Jailbait."

"I'm sorry I'm a kid and that I'm sixteen and might not understand what you say. There's something more than I'm jail bait. Your womanizing is legendary. Picking up girls in bars."

He stared grimly at the ocean. "Is it, indeed." He turned, stared her down. "I once thought I'd try to seduce you to get back at your father."

She shocked herself, partly wishing he had.

"You're not telling me everything."

"No."

"Why not?"

"Come on, I'll take you home."

"You have to talk it out with Daddy."

"You are Pollyanna, aren't you? I don't see that happening."

"It's better to talk to him than keep this going inside you."

"I don't want to hurt you."

"I don't care!"

She lifted her face, gripped his shoulders, and kissed him. He grabbed her, and they sank into the sand, as the growing surf poured over them. His weight came crushing down on her while tiny shells and pebbles crunched into her back. She whimpered, but she held on as his lips pressed into hers with more hunger than Mike had. More tongue, certainly. She wanted his body to become hers, even if it killed her. She felt his loins pressing on her, and she rose up, like the surf, wanting him, finding him, sensing in him something dark and vicious that started to frighten her. Then he pulled her around with him so that he sank into the wet sand and she could be on top, just as a wave came surging over them. They sat up, sputtering, laughing, although she felt abandoned as they pulled apart. She responded with humor, breaking the intense mood. Relaxing him, maybe. Make it a joke.

"My parents did that," she said, laughing. "*From Here to Eternity*."

"They didn't mention the damn sand," said Bill, leaning back into the wet stuff. "Christ, it's all over us." He reached over and smoothed a tendril of her hair. "Christ," he said. "Why."

He helped her up and ran to the house to get towels. She went back up to his deck and waited for him there. He draped a towel over a chair so she could sit and then he knelt down and wiped the sand off her legs, efficiently and tenderly. She wanted to rub him down, feel his legs and become part of them, but he sat on the steps and did it himself as she watched and grew shy. The night came back. He was wonderful and he was hurting and he was angry and she wanted to help but didn't know how.

"We can do this movie and be friends. Honest."

"I don't think so. Go home, kid. Look what you make me do."

"Bill!" she shouted, frustrated.

She leaped off the deck and ran home fast.

They were acting, they weren't acting. They were dueling. They were playing games with the lines and the words, in character. She could not forget the sensation of his body pressing down on her and then, gently, lifting her around until she clung to him as the water poured over them, as they burrowed in the sand like the smallest essence of life that grew in the waters. She could still feel his arms grasping her, practically pulling her inside his body. And his hands, stroking her over her body. If she thought about it, she had to pause and close her eyes and try to think of her lines, her part.

But now, he kept his distance. If they were in love, they lived that love in a make believe world crowded with grips and flooded with light.

Lily had to make a decision. She had a great fainting scene. They had a passionate kiss even though she knew his truth. And then she walked into the District Attorney's office. The emotions of all that hit her hard, and she fled the sound stage without looking back.

After two weeks, she had time off while Bill's character went to jail and went through a trial. What she should have done was preparatory work for *West Side Story*. But she didn't. She had something to look into.

37

She spent as much time as she could at MGM's old writers' bungalow where the studio stored scripts and publicity information to search through scripts in which Frances Faulkner had a hand.

And once seeking, she found plenty. Frances Faulkner's scripts were all over the place: B movies, cops and robbers, detectives, melodramas, westerns, some that she wrote, co-wrote, wrote the story or treatment, or helped to doctor. Faulkner seemed to be able to handle any number of genres and styles.

She'd been Alice Marrs' own front.

Yet Alice Marrs, the dance coach (and choreographer) had been remembered, but not Frances Faulkner. Except maybe by those nasty men in Congress and perhaps some name droppers who tried even then to protect her. Otherwise, she'd been forgotten. Why? She'd been as prolific and talented as Dalton Trumbo.

Back to being Lily. On the back lot, she and BillasMike swam, rode, and enjoyed a picnic. BillasMike laid his head in Dianna's lap, and she played with his hair as he smiled up at her. But *Bill* didn't talk to *her*. They were only Mike and Lily. She hoped the hurt she felt wouldn't sneak through onto the screen. She was trying to figure out Lilly's inner workings and exactly when she decided to turn Mike in. In love and then to the gas chamber with you! Bill was, to tell the truth, making that choice easier.

As soon as she was free on the set, she biked back to the scripts.

Once a man in a gray suit and hat and a stocky build went to the desk and the librarian, Mr. Hessman, looked flustered. The man asked a few questions and left, but the elderly librarian pulled out a handkerchief and wiped his face.

Dianna went over to him. "Are you all right?"

"No, no," he said. "I remember things from Germany. Policemen coming and asking questions. He wanted to know if any students were looking at Russian movie scripts. I said, no, no. I do not lie. Today they are not."

"Was he a policeman?"

"Yes."

"Why would he care what students were looking at?"

"Russian movies — the Communists they ask, do they look at Russian movie scripts? Who? I do not tell. They come back. I want no more trouble with those people. I will put the Russian scripts away."

"Have you had trouble?"

He shook his head and walked away.

Why shouldn't students look at Russian movie scripts? Any scripts?

She turned to a stack of B westerns listing her grandmother as the sole author and opened up the first one and nearly stopped breathing.

In the story, a charismatic man came to town claiming he could work miraculous healings. He fell in love with a young girl and ultimately saved her life. *She* converted *him*. Dianna flipped back to the title page. The movie was called *When Brother Lord Came to Town*.

The *Silver Sierra* episode with Brother Luke was called, "Brother Luke Comes to Town." And several lines in this script, which apparently went unproduced, were an exact match to the *Sierra* script.

She thumbed through the next western. It was the same story they had worked on as the first episode of *Silver Sierra*. There was no mistaking it. The scripts were almost identical.

She hurried to the desk and persuaded Mr. Hessman to let her take the scripts out.

There was probably a simple explanation. Writers stole from each other all the time. Several *Silver Sierra* episodes were copies of movies, like the one where Chris was on a jury that was clearly *12 Angry Men*.

At home, she studied the scripts. All the good episodes for *Silver Sierra* featuring Betsy had been written by L.A. Franklin, who had also written the scripts for *Silver Sierra* that were so similar to these western scripts, and these western scripts had been written by Frances Faulkner, Alice Marrs' pen name.

Once home, Dianna sat on her bed, looking out at Los Angeles twinkling below. She looked at the picture of her grandmother, her mother, and herself. She still felt the hurt she always felt looking at that picture, but now it was mixed with an incredible thought.

On Friday afternoon, she had Reggie drop her at Mr. Goodman's office at Paramount where she finagled L.A. Franklin's address out of his secretary.

At eight Saturday morning, she was at Bill's door.

She had to ring several times. Finally, she heard someone moving about, yelling, "Who is it?"

"Me!" Dianna called.

She heard muttered cursing, a few minutes went by, and he opened the door, clad in bathrobe and probably not much else.

"Whatever you're selling I don't want any."

"May I please come in? It's important."

When he didn't move, she pushed through, glancing around to see if anyone else was there. There didn't seem to be. She was surprised and relieved.

"Are you doing anything today?"

"Yes. Nothing."

"Can you drive me to Santa Barbara?"

"That's a hundred miles. You have your own beach. It's right there. And you do have a chauffeur."

"I have to go to Santa Barbara, and I don't want Reggie to know."

"Are you robbing the bank?"

"You insisted I get into your car once. Now it's my turn to insist I get into your car."

"I'm taking a shower and when I come back, I'm going to kick your butt again."

"At least it will be with a clean foot."

She wandered into the kitchen while he went down the hall, and as the water turned on, she imagined him in the spray, all of him, and she thought, I can just open the door, take off my clothes, and go in with him. Unless he'd locked the door. Had he? Should she check? What a strange and yet compelling and weird idea this was. Instead, when he came out, she had thrown together an omelet and made the coffee.

"Since when do you cook?" he asked, appearing in trousers, tee shirt, and still glistening hair.

"I've got hidden talents." Was she flirting? Why should she? She had resolved to leave him behind her.

"Aren't you eating?" he asked.

"I'm on a diet."

Bill poured coffee. "That's all I've known. Cruel females."

"I made you breakfast. I would not do this if it wasn't important. What would have happened if my grandmother hadn't died?"

"You just changed the subject, right?" asked Bill, digging into the eggs.

"What would have happened to her?"

"If," he said, "your grandmother hadn't died, she probably would have gone to prison for contempt like the others. It is interesting to wonder what your father would have done."

"He stood by my mother."

"While she named *her* mother."

"That's not quite how it was."

"Families turning in their own. It happened all the time."

"What could she have done?"

"Refused! Not done it! She should have known that's what they were after."

"You don't know that. You don't know a damn thing."

"I do know how to drive."

"Okay. Think what you want."

"She would have gone to prison."

"Except she didn't."

"Because she died."

"She didn't *die*. She's alive!"

"Dianna," he said, without any humor.

"Listen!" She told him about all the scripts and their similarities.

Bill disagreed. "Television is always copying the movies. McQueen says he's done *Stagecoach* four times so far. Even *Rebecca*."

"Anyone can steal those. I'm talking about B movies. Unproduced scripts! Either someone has memorized the scripts or someone has the scripts or someone wrote the first scripts. I thought you'd be suspicious, so I brought this one."

Bill paged through the script.

'It is awfully close."

"See?"

He shook his head. "Forest Lawn wouldn't make a grave without a body in it."

She'd thought of that and the only solution she'd had was money.

"Either this person is stealing from Nana or *is* Nana."

"And you want to go to Santa Barbara and see which is which."

"Yes."

"And you're looking for Bill Royce's taxi service?"

"I promise, when I learn to drive, I'll drive you anywhere you want."

"You've been driving me many places already." But he smiled a short smile when he said it, although he didn't look at her.

"You want to go." She got up and started doing the dishes.

"Leave those. Peter and his mother are coming."

"Will you take me?"

He threw up his hands. "I was going to sleep this morning, and I can do that driving."

"Good. Can we go?"

"Santa Barbara's a pretty big place."

"I have an address. 3354 Cliff Road."

"Okay." He peered out at the sky. "Cloudy, but I think it'll be okay."

"If you don't want to go —"

"Boy, are you a woman. *Now* you give me the choice! No, I'll take you on this wild goose chase."

In the car, he went back to being Silent Bill. She rolled down her window and waved her hand at the orange trees and great palms. She remembered that she liked to watch him drive and looked over at his hands as one gripped the steering wheel and the other touched it lightly with his fingers. His right foot kept steady on the gas, at times lightly touching the brake.

"This might help you with your dissertation," she said, breaking the silence.

"Not the way UCLA wants to see it."

"What?"

"UCLA is under pressure to change its politics under threat of losing federal funds. That's as good as cutting the school's throat. We have these new hires in the political science and the theater departments who say that whatever our country does is right, whatever the Commies do is wrong, and if anyone criticizes the government, then they must be Commies because this is a time of war, you know. How convenient war is, right? But oh, we're free, not like the Commies, understand. Do they see the contradiction? They do not. But I go on."

"Are you going to stop working on it?"

"I am not having a peaceful bunch of days lately."

"I'm sorry."

"But my career. It's booming. Who knows, it could be a conspiracy, keeping me working and not doing my dissertation."

They were slowing down for traffic.

"Damn, this construction," said Bill.

"Can you go around it?"

"Only if my car has wings. They thought the freeways would bring people into Hollywood, but everyone's driving out. The town's going to die."

"What sort of movies *could* have been written?" Dianna asked, not caring about Hollywood's fate. "How do you figure that out?"

"Good, we're moving again," said Bill. "One way is to look at what was written right after the war until about 1952 or so. *Larksong* comes in right at that time, too. A drama with social concerns and criticism becomes sentimental and domestic."

"It was a good movie," she said, ready for his argument.

"You don't understand. A few years after the war, movies dealt with some heavy subjects like anti-Semitism, the justice system, fascism, how unjustly we treated the Indians, even world peace. Like *The Lawless*, which dealt with the migrant workers or *The Boy With Green Hair* or any number of titles lost to memory, like John Garfield's movies. *Larksong* took the easy way out. A little girl flings herself in front of her father and takes the bullet. That's quite a switch from the Scottsboro boys."

"Tastes change. One year musicals, next year not."

"No, it was a deliberate change."

She stared out the window, and there was a long silence.

"*Gentlemen's Agreement*," said Dianna, finally, "did not take the easy way out."

"Yes it did. Its moral was be careful about being anti-Semitic because the guy may turn out to be John Fletcher."

"Oh for heaven's sake. I'm sorry your father died, and my father wasn't responsible nor were the movies."

"It was smug and self-righteous, but it had its points. *Crossfire* was different."

"Never heard of it."

"A soldier beat up a Jew for no reason at all except that he was a Jew. In the novel, it was a homosexual, but movies can only go so far."

He was driving, so be nice, but she loved her father in *Gentlemen's Agreement*. He had been forceful and complex, struggling with his masquerade. It had not been a simple job.

"How is being anti-Semitic Communist?"

"Seriously, some people think that Jews are foreign agents. Some guy stood up in Congress and rattled off the real names of Danny Kaye and June Havoc and Melvyn Douglas. As if they'd changed their names as part of a conspiracy. Incidentally, many Jews tried to get into this country from Europe, maybe even the Frank family. This country wouldn't let them in. Prejudice."

"That can't be true."

"Then why have these movies about anti-Semitism?" he countered.

She had no answer.

"After the war, when the Soviet Union wasn't on our side anymore and swallowing up territory, all the things we'd fought *for* got lost. Instead we got fear, hiding in cellars, loyalty oaths. People turning in their coworkers, their fathers. Dalton Trumbo thought it was the beginning of American concentration camps."

"That's impossible." He was really off the deep end.

"No, ma'am," said Bill, and he pounded the wheel. "They were going to put suspected subversives into prisons. They'd started to set aside special places for them as part of a bill called the McCarren Act, the way they put the Japanese Americans away in camps during the war. They stripped American citizens of their property without due process and shipped them off to camps without decent facilities or even medical care. Whole families. That's what they were going to do to suspected subversives. Suspected! Writers like Michael Wilson and Carl Foreman believed they were going to be sent off. People were terrified."

"They did not do that to the Japanese."

"Yes, Dianna, they did. These people lost their homes, their businesses, everything. *They* weren't the enemy. We were."

She remembered something her mother had said, about losing the Japanese servants during the war, but she'd never said why.

"It was the lowest type of fear," said Bill. "It became fear of Commies, fear of spies, fear of anyone different or not white, fear of losing something, fear of Negroes, like the Scottsboro boys, fear all over. You'd think we'd lost the war. The McCarthyites pounded that fear home over everything else!"

"Who were the Scottsboro boys?"

"You don't know."

"No, I don't. I'm just stupid."

"It's not a pretty story. You won't hear it at Disneyland."

"You're a jerk."

"Yes, I am, and I'm driving this car. Anyway. It was in the 1930s. Nine Negro boys in Alabama were accused of assaulting a white woman. There was evidence clearing them, but frauds came forward to testify against them. For some reason, protesting against their treatment and fighting to get them a fair trial lumped you as a Communist. Because Communists are for equality, you see, everyone the same. No individuality. So people working for equal rights are labeled as Communists."

"That makes no sense. You can't be free without equal rights."

"Ah, there lies the great contradiction. The Communist party in this country worked for Negro rights for decades. If you were part of those organizations, they were listed with your name in *Red Channels*, and you were blacklisted. Dammit. Let's talk about something else."

"Okay, okay. You didn't want to come. You think I'm nuts."

"Frankly, yes, but I guess you have to find out."

"You don't want to have anything to do with me. You've been so distant."

He turned on the radio. So no more talking.

Finally, as they came close to Santa Barbara, Bill asked, "What's that address again?"

She reached into her purse for the crumpled paper. Her hand shook. Her stomach started to hurt.

"3354 Cliff Road. It must be on a cliff overlooking the water."

"I'll need more directions than that. It's a big ocean out there."

"Maybe this wasn't a good idea."

"We've come almost ninety miles, sweetie. Now is the time to think this is a *good* idea. Hey, look up there."

Directly above an Esso Gas Station, a huge billboard proclaimed that SILVER SIERRA, a full, hour-long, color, western series starring MARTIN

O'MILES, MIKE NORTH, CHRIS HILL, and starring DIANNA FLETCHER would be premiering on NBC Monday, September 19. There it was, a great big picture of all of them, but hers was set apart.

She groaned. "The guys will love that. They're already mad at me."

"I love that it's right over the gas station. Put on your dark glasses."

She ducked while he got out to ask directions and nearly burst out laughing when she heard the attendant say, "Hey, I know you! You won the Oscar for that movie with Paul Newman, right? How do you do? Where are you off to?"

Bill got off with an autograph and directions.

"So ends the life of Who's That Guy With You," Dianna said, as he pulled out of the station.

"I'm going to miss that guy," said Bill. "Quick before I forget. We get off the highway at the Garden Street exit, go *right* onto Shoreline Drive, take *another right* on Cabrillo, *left* on West Montecito, then *angle left* onto Cliff Drive. From there it's about four miles. There's our exit. Look out for the streets. Shoreline Drive."

"My stomach's a mess."

"Don't you get sick in my car."

"There's Shoreline!" She rattled off the turns as the streets came up. Cliff Drive, gorgeous with lush green parks, fruit trees, oaks, elms, palms, and the ocean below, came way too soon.

Bill said, "She's doing pretty well if she's up here."

"2500," she read.

The drives were long and she could tell they led to houses overlooking the beach on the various sides of a cliff. The view from the road was stunning, all blue above and below with sunlight creating brilliant creases, but she was looking at the mailboxes, her stomach tightening with each advancing number.

3300.

3330.

3354 was coming up.

"There," she cried out.

Bill turned onto a narrow road, with fields on both sides where fruit trees burst with apples, cherries, and pears. Dianna didn't think she could wait any longer for the end, but finally, there it was, a red ranch house, a little pond in front, wood slats shaping into a building below a grove of young pines.

A woman watering a flower bed.

The woman looked up as the car approached.

A woman with hair in a bun mostly covered with a hat watering a flower bed. Looking straight at them.

Dianna breathed out.

"Nana!"

Even before Bill stopped the car, she was opening the door.

"Hold on," he called, but she jumped out.

"Nana!"

The woman stood, water can in hand, as Dianna ran toward her.

"You're Dianna Fletcher," said the woman. She took off her hat.

She appeared to be in her mid-to-late thirties and she had a charming smile. Dianna stopped.

"Hello," she said. "I'm looking for Miss — Mrs. — Franklin."

Bill joined them.

The woman walked up to them, excited at this surprise. "Dianna Fletcher! I know you, too, sir. I just can't place your name."

"I'm Bill Royce," he said, offering his hand.

"Of course! I saw you at the Oscars. And in *Home From the Hill* and *The Sound and the Fury*. Did you like working with Yul Brynner? What are you two doing here?" She looked excited and curious. "I'm sorry. I'm Mrs. Milson. This is my place."

"Mrs. Franklin," Dianna managed to say.

"Oh, yes," said Mrs. Milson. "The Franklins left last week. I'm cleaning up after them, but they hardly left any mess. Paid up full, too."

"Mr. and Mrs. Franklin?" Dianna asked, wondering who Mr. Franklin was.

"Yes. Are you friends?" She was obviously curious.

Dianna could barely think, she was so disappointed.

Bill said, "Dianna and I worked together on a show and loved the script and wanted to meet the writer."

"That typewriter was going a lot," said Mrs. Milson. "You know what else? She tap danced. Tapping on the keys and on the floor. All that tapping! She converted the sun room into a real dance studio with mirrors. Kept her young, she said. I didn't mind. It made the room look bigger. And they were nice people."

Dianna nearly slid to the ground.

"Where did she go?"

"I didn't ask for a forwarding address, but they might have left one at the post office. I'm awfully sorry. Would you like to come in for a drink or something?"

It was a nice house, nothing special. A living room, dining room, and a kitchen on the first floor, and the sun room. Dianna walked the empty floors, her feet echoing. Here is where her grandmother had been.

"How long was she here?"

"Just for the summer," said Mrs. Milson.

The summer! If only she'd figured this out earlier, she could have met her grandmother. Who was alive! And yet, as elusive as if she'd left earth. She imagined the car pulling up and her grandmother there, and she running to hold her, a woman back from the dead who typed and tap danced.

Dianna lingered in the sun room as Mrs. Milson hurried into the kitchen. The floor was shiny wood; the mirrors circled the room. Dianna took a turn, an arabesque, and tapped out a time step. She tried not to cry.

"Just a few days, and I would have seen her."

"You know she's alive," said Bill. "You were right."

"I have to get out of here."

Bill called, "Sorry. We must be getting back. Thank you."

They hurried out. Mrs. Milson was right behind them, but they quickly got inside the car.

"The whole summer!" Dianna shouted, once in the car. "Oh, damn. Where did she go? And who's Mr. Franklin?"

For a while, they rode in silence. Finally, Dianna said, "They must have known. They lied to me. And to Nick and Chas."

"Maybe they would tell you when you got older."

"They didn't tell Nick. He would have told me. What other secrets are there?"

"I guess parents don't want their kids to worry about the past."

"Are you defending them?"

"Hard to believe, isn't it, sweetie?"

They stayed quiet, just listening to the music and the news. As they neared the city, Dianna said, "I don't want to go home yet."

"There's always the movies," Bill said, pointing to a drive-in featuring *Elmer Gantry*.

"They wouldn't let me go to the premiere, and I haven't had time. Have you seen it?"

"No time. Want to go?"

"I haven't been to a drive-in since *The Blob*." Should she go into the drive-in with Bill? "Maybe I should see them. Help me sort out my feelings."

During the Bugs Bunny opener, Bill went to get Cokes and popcorn. Dianna had never eaten popcorn while watching her parents in a movie.

John blasted onto the screen, full of energy and wickedness. Anne proved a spine of strength. The sexual charge between them was potent.

"He's not like that," Dianna said. "He's pretty quiet."

"Quite a part right after *Ben Hur*," Bill said. "I have to say I'm jealous. Brother Luke has nothing on him."

When the tabernacle went up in flames, Dianna turned her head away. "I can't watch her die."

"It's a movie."

"Still."

Bill dumped the popcorn and soda containers in a trash bucket, and when he came back, she cried, "Oh, Bill. Where did she go? We'd help her."

"It's okay," he said, taking her into his arms, and leaning down upon her, kissing her fiercely, holding her against him and against the car seat, grabbing her with increasing power, more than he'd done with Betsy, more than he'd done with Lily, pulling her in to him, his tongue opening her lips and making its way into her mouth, and one of his hands opening up her legs, feeling his way up her thigh.

It wasn't what he did so much as the excruciating hunger for him, a violence inside, that terrified her. She grasped his shoulders and murmured, "No, no, Bill." She pushed him enough that he came to his senses, sat up, and hunched over the steering wheel.

"I'm sorry," he said.

"It's okay," she said.

"No, kid, I'm sorry."

Kid.

Her feelings were so confused. He'd been harsh and she'd even sensed anger but also great need. She touched his arm. He shook it off.

"Don't. I'm really sorry. I'll take you home."

"It's all right," she said, even though she had no idea what her jumbled feelings meant. She did know that what he'd done had something to do with his own needs, with what he'd suffered, and she wanted to help him.

He pulled into her driveway.

"Good night," she said.

"Yeah," he said.

He backed out fast. Once again, his face held no emotion she could read. His acting was clearer.

38

When he had held her as if she were a floating bit of driftwood and he was drowning. When he had kissed her with a hunger that roused her own. When his hands had caressed her face like the gentle wings of a butterfly. When she had wanted to cry out to him except the lines she wanted to say were not in the script, and by habit and discipline, she said the words of the script as the camera three inches away recorded her exultant face, as the microphone picked up her memorized words written by a marvelous writer and carried them to the sound mixers, as the first and second assistant directors and wardrobe and makeup and script supervisor and cinematographer and who knows who else stood close to watch what was lit ever so cleverly by the DP and as Fred Sybuck kept having different ideas about how she should react, bouncing off her own acting, her own inner thoughts. And she wanted to yell, I know! Or was it Lily who knew?

In their last love scene, Bill gave her such a look of longing and desperation that it shook her. Was it real? Acting? Did she want to know?

It had been a tough week of neither talking to the other except as their characters of Mike and Lily. And then *Every Time* was done. So fast. Would they even remember this? The wrap party was held on the set, since there had never been much of a budget, and Bill just gave her a light peck on the cheek. They would never work together again.

At home, she found a letter.

"Dear Dianna, I hope you know that I would never write you unless I felt I had to. I hope you trust me. I lived with Bill for half a year, on and off, and I know that he is attractive to women, charming, often thoughtful, and seemingly wonderful. I saw you with Bill in his car a few days ago, and I felt I should write you.

I hope you are not involved with him. You are working in a movie together, and I know how that can be. And you're so young.

Bill is a wonderful guy but is impossible to live with. He experiences dark moments, times of pure rage, and while he never struck me, he did push me away a few times, and I mean push, so I was on the floor or hitting furniture. He was always apologetic. Sometimes, if I may say so, these dark moments extend to his love making. He lives in a dark world and will not let go its hold. I can sympathize with him, but to live with him is impossible. Please don't be angry with me for caring about you. I miss him, and I admire him, but it was good to leave him.

Sandi

What motivated Sandi to do that? Did she really care about her? Was she jealous? Bill suffered from dark moods, and he had a right to them, given what he'd been through.

She got on her bike and rode down to his house. She heard music. Several cars were parked in his driveway and on the road.

She caught a glimpse of him through the window, his arm around a girl, pretty, dark haired, not anyone she knew. Miss September?

Close the door on him, Fletcher.

But she couldn't.

The next afternoon, giving Miss Whomever time to go, Dianna walked down the beach. He was sitting on his deck, reading. She climbed up the steps.

"I want to talk to you."

"The movie's over."

"We've done more than the movie together."

"Go home."

"No."

He got up and went into the house. She was right behind him.

She'd experienced his moods. She had also experienced his intelligence, his brilliance, and his humor. She felt some deep connection with him. Didn't he feel one for her?

"Do I have to throw you out?"

"No." As Lily had done, she rested her head on his shoulder. His arms went around her. She sank against his hard chest and closed her eyes. He didn't push her away. She felt sweet pleasure, soft touches, caresses of her hair, light kisses, and she felt his anger dissipate.

"Now will you go home?" he asked, quietly. "Call Bruce or one of your boyfriends?"

"I want to be with you." She looked straight at him.

"No, kid. Lily got in my way there, but you're sixteen."

"Why don't you be sixteen, too? You never got to be."

He laughed.

"Holding hands, light kisses. What kids do."

His eyes misted, his voice choked, but his smile was the suave character. "I don't mind holding your hand and kissing you, but I think you have a strange idea of what kids do. I'll have to talk to Bruce."

"Do you love me?"

"Oh, for God's sake. Get over Lily."

"Do you? Are you Jeff? I had to turn you in. You said you cared for me."

"When you're eighteen. We stop here."

"Be sixteen."

"If the damn thing could be done over again," he muttered.

"Is the only way you can be a friend is to go to bed with a girl? Is that the only reason you liked Sandi? And Star? And Joy? Can you put the list in alphabetical order?"

He grabbed her by the arms and said, sternly, "Out of my business, kid."

He pushed her toward the door but it wasn't a hard push.

She pushed back. "I think you care about me."

He opened the front door. "Out."

She walked down the drive and took up her bike, not knowing what she could say now.

Then she cried out, "Oh, my gosh, look!"

She pointed up the hill, at her house. The gate was open and she could see two massive limousines.

"Mom and Daddy are home!" she cried. "They're early by over a week! And now, now, you big brave man, you can come and talk to Daddy about how he killed your father. We'll invite you to dinner. I'll let you know."

"Over dinner?"

"After dinner. He'll listen. Honest, they both will."

"I'll do it when I want."

"You've wanted to confront him forever. Are you afraid now the time has come?"

She ran down the drive and up the hill, leaving him with her dare.

Let him face his demons. If he hated her father, he should confront him.

She blew into the house and yelled, "Hi, everyone!"

John called out, "There's my baby!"

"Daddy!" she shrieked, running up to get a hug. "You're early!"

"Ha, you bet," he said, both hug and enthusiasm in *Elmer Gantry* style. "We could not wait to see you. And hug you like I could not before."

"Is that our baby?" called Anne.

She wore an ancient terrycloth bathrobe, its threads all over the air, but to Dianna she was beautiful, and she ran to hug her.

"When did you get back?" Dianna squealed.

"Barely half an hour ago," said Anne. "My God, I forgot how much I loved this house. I love seeing you in it!"

"I love this house and I love seeing *you* in it," Dianna echoed, playing the part of the happy child.

"I'm out on the patio," said Anne, pulling Dianna after her. "Look at that ocean! Damn, I missed this. And I am so tired. Just working."

"Yeah," said Dianna.

"You look lovely! Everyone says you look like me! Sit down. I'm just trying to relax. Lynne, get Dianna a Coke."

"Ginger ale," said Dianna. "I am so glad you're back. Those phone calls were awful. Three minutes and you were gone."

"We could hardly hear you, and I know, it was criminal that I hardly wrote, but neither did you."

Her father joined them. He was in a bathrobe too, but he always looked elegant. He ruffled Dianna's hair and gave her another hug and sat on the other side of her.

"We missed you," he said, pulling out his cigarettes. "Too long apart."

"How is *Lawrence of Arabia*?" Dianna felt she had to ask. She was trembling, even if they seemed filled with the usual joi de vivre – but did it seem too much?

"Too damn solemn," John said. "I tried to inject some humor into it. Even the desert is solemn. I am just glad not to be the star of this epic. Wait until you see your mother as Anna Karenina. Stunning. Why didn't they think of you for Cleopatra?"

Anne groaned. "That thing. Poor Boyd and Finch."

Dianna sipped her ginger ale. Couldn't they tell she had changed? How could she begin about Nana? About the secret they'd kept hidden?

"Where's Nick?"

She didn't want to lose them. Would she if she said something about the truth?

"That's news," said Anne. "He's in New York."

"*Hamlet*," said John.

"Of Denmark?"

"Of Broadway. He wants to be irreverent and shocking and I cannot wait."

"He's in New York?"

This was bad news. She'd needed to talk to him.

"We left him there," said Anne. "We're going to have to get you out of that series, aren't we? I knew it. How awful you had to go back and forth."

"Mary Everett is coming on to play the mother," said Dianna. "My part is pretty small now."

"Then you can come off," said Anne, sipping her gin. "Everyone wants you now. I have a stack of offers myself, dear. It was just a hiccup. We are *wanted*."

"What's up next for you?"

"After that wretched *Children's Hour*, which I'd gladly give up to Audrey, what's up next is *A Doll's House* on Broadway. We lost a theater, but then one opened up and they pounced on us. And I might pitch in on *Gypsy* – and there's talk of me doing the movie. All right, I can play a mother."

"What about *Lawrence*?" Dianna asked, stymied. Were they going to leave again?

"They will not need me again until sometime after the New Year," said John.

"You'll be leaving again," said Dianna.

"*Doll's House* is just a few months," said Anne. "Then I'll be coming back to do some sort of haunted house picture, and in between *Gypsy* in New York, and then we are going to do *Night of the Iguana.*" She growled affectionately at John.

"I finally saw *Elmer Gantry*," said Dianna. "You were brilliant."

"Wise child," said John.

"Where's Chas?"

"In his room," said Anne. "Didn't sleep much at all last night."

"How was that school?"

"We'll find him a better place here," said John. "Now tell me, how about you and your acting? You were unhappy during *Picnic*. What happened?"

"Things are better. *Silver Sierra* premieres in two weeks. Betsy has been fun. Not much of a challenge, though. Except all that memorizing."

Why didn't she tell them she knew that Nana was alive and writing for *Silver Sierra*?

"Betsy is the one ...?"

"*Silver Sierra*," said Dianna. Didn't they remember her character's name? "Will you be here in two weeks?"

"Yes, yes," said John. "We need a rest, and we do have to make appearances here and there. *Spartacus* is opening in early October, so we will have our big party for the premiere."

"*Romeo and Juliet* is opening, too," said Dianna, carefully light. "In December."

"I did not think I would see the day," said John.

"I did," said Anne. "Darling, we didn't want to worry you."

"The thing is," said Dianna, deciding to be honest, "I thought I was the glitch. I thought I couldn't act anymore and that I was awful."

John and Anne exchanged glances.

Okay, what did that mean.

"Everyone has doubts," said John. "They keep one humble, but they should not stop you."

"Every time I get an award," said Anne, "I plummet."

"Oh, we went to see it at Oxford. They ran it again. And again." John pointed at her. "The audience reaction is thrilling."

"What did you think?"

"You are absolutely luminous," said Anne. "Audiences stand and cheer after they get through weeping. And just look how you've grown, you were still really a baby then. You take after me."

"With breasts out to here," said John. "Otherwise, you take after me."

Why didn't she say, Nana is alive? Yet how did she know for sure? Someone named Franklin who had written a script almost matching the script her grandmother had written? What if it weren't true? It didn't seem true now. Things seemed normal now. The way they'd been before. Except she felt impatient and some anger at them, but she didn't want to feel that way.

Her parents were home, and she wanted to be happy.

"You were very clever bringing all that attention to it," said Anne. "But you're not going to talk about Communism with the publicity, are you?"

"They asked me not to."

"Good," said Anne. "Nothing makes a story more romantic than a dose of Marxism. Marks. Marx. No one's done that yet, thank goodness."

"I haven't heard anything about Marks and Grey," said Dianna. "Do they know about all this?"

"I believe they're trying to avoid any press," said John. "The last thing I heard is that they had left England and no one knows where to. Took their families with them. But if it's a hit – who knows. I hope they're coming back, at least for the movie. But no one seems to know."

"I thought this would help them."

"You thought it would help you," said John.

Did she have to feel guilty?

"If it's a success here, money forgives all. Won't that help them?"

"Dianna, you wanted *Romeo and Juliet* out for your own reasons."

"But the blacklisting was wrong!"

Anne helped change the subject. "We're not the judge and jury here. Let's talk about what we know. You finished a movie with this Bill Royce. Is this a romance?"

"I like him very much. But I'm sixteen and it makes him nervous. No romance. He has other girls."

"I should talk to him," said John. "Make him more nervous."

"He wants to talk to you," said Dianna.

"Does he?" asked Anne.

"Not about me. Something serious."

"Mmmm," said Anne. "He's handsome, he's talented, he's nice. I hope he's patient."

"He's got a reputation," said John.

"Daddy."

"Do not worry," said John. "I will be gentle. You have a ton of work coming up, daughter. *Cinderella* and *West Side Story* and *Forever Is Now*. Or is it *Now Is Forever*? We'll get you out of the series, don't worry."

"I enjoy it, but it's a ton of work, and everything is done so fast. Do I have to do another season? I'm doing all these extra episodes, but Mr. Goodman seems to think I'll be there forever."

"We will get you out of it, princess," said John.

Maybe if she told the truth, she would destroy the normalcy she so much craved. It was best not to tell anything, and to wait until she found out more.

"Walt wants to do *Meet Me in St. Louis* with you," said John. "Live on television."

Dianna groaned.

"I don't know about that," said Anne. "Dianna should be doing more sophisticated work than another turn of the century gal. Honey, there's talk — just talk — about you doing *Gypsy* as a film with me. Wouldn't that be fabulous?"

"Gypsy Rose Lee? Me?"

She strutted. Her parents laughed.

Forget the ominous undertones. She needed this. Her family.

"And there's that inauguration thing," said John.

"What's that?" asked Dianna.

"If Nixon wins," said Anne. "He wants us all to perform for the benefit the night before he's sworn in. Do you think you could be bipartisan?"

"He's not going to win," said Dianna. "Kennedy's invited us to do his gala."

"Kennedy is too inexperienced," said John.

"I want to go swimming," said Anne, pulling off her robe. She was naked. John, also naked, dove in beside her.

Dianna ran upstairs to Chas's room. She knocked, opened the door.

"There you are!" she called, and she stopped, amazed. There he certainly was, also naked, and dancing around a pile of books as if he were an Indian and the books were a fire. He saw her and his face crinkled into one of deep joy and he ran to her, wrapped his arms around her, and cried out, "Dianna! Dianna!" so desperately, that it wrung her heart.

Lynne appeared and gently disengaged Chas's arms from Dianna. "Put your pajamas on," she said.

Chas looked at her as if she were crazy.

"I have to do this," he said, and he went on dancing.

Lynne pulled Dianna out the door and closed it.

Dianna flew down the stairs and waited for Anne to climb out, dry off, and put on her robe. John was still doing laps.

"What's wrong with Chas?"

Anne sank down on a chaise lounge, closed her eyes, and was quiet for several moments. Dianna waited, watching the lines forming on her mother's face.

"He just got worse and worse," Anne said, and she opened her eyes. "They threw him out of school for beating up boys, and he killed two of your grandmother's cats." Her voice choked.

"Chas?"

"We couldn't figure out what was wrong. He'd be reciting lines from *Pigskin Pete* movies, from that serial he did for *The Mickey Mouse Club*, from *Pollyanna*. The doctors all called it a nervous breakdown. Said he'd get better. We are going to look at a school next week, and we have to keep it quiet, of course, for his sake, but he's just falling apart, and I don't know why and what will happen."

Dianna was not sure what you did with a crying mother.

"I'm sorry, baby, it's why we hardly talked to you. You were doing fine, so was Nick, and we had our work, and then this. My baby. I love that boy. He came, Nana died."

Dianna tried to find words. She knew that Nana had not died. Didn't her mother know?

"We have to put him in a home, and I can't stand it. We have to hope for the best. Of course, he'll get better. Now, you and your Mr. Royce." Anne wiped her eyes and smoothed her daughter's hair. "Invite him to dinner on Saturday. Chas will be gone by then. We'll be more settled. It is a romance?"

"No," said Dianna, her voice shaking. "He's been a good friend."

"We want to know him. He's a rising star." Anne seemed brighter, snappier. "Nothing much. Just grilling on the deck. Steaks," she added, "not Mr. Royce."

Dianna said, slowly, "Do you remember that talk we had before you went away? You suggested I could get an IUD."

"Do you want one?" Anne was instantly a suspicious mother.

Dianna, traced the rosy pattern of her chair arm. "I think it would be a good idea."

"You and this Royce?" Anne demanded.

"I have plenty of boyfriends," Dianna retorted, and then realized that was probably not the best thing to say.

Anne laughed. "I was sixteen when I fell for your father. We Foster women find men early and we don't let go. So I am worried about this Royce."

"Nothing's serious," said Dianna.

"Nevertheless," said Anne, "it is a good idea. There's a pill out, but I'm not sure I trust it. It's only for married women, anyway. Look, Dianna, it's your body. If you don't want someone inside it, you don't take him. Understood? God gave us feelings that make all this pleasurable, but sometimes men don't understand that pleasure goes two ways. God gave us feelings and brains, so you deal with your brains and protect yourself. This can be a lousy business for women. A hundred years ago, actresses were thought to be prostitutes, and some of that stuck because, well, men want it. So yes, now that you've asked for it. Okay."

"Yes, Mom," said Dianna, dutifully.

"Some might call this bad parenting, but this business isn't high school filled with shy little boys. Some high powered producer snagged me a long time ago when I was just a chorus girl and didn't know I had the choice."

Dianna knew the story, and she hated to hear it. As for the shy little boys, she knew all about them.

"I don't want anyone pushing you into making desperate moves. It's you they want, so you're in charge. That goes with cheesecake photos and all that business. That's what it is. You become a product to them, but you can't confuse yourself with that. I need to speak to Uncle George. There's been enough of that where you're concerned."

"Okay."

"Just remember, you're in charge of the product. And John and I have a little clout. I'll arrange for your IUD. Just don't lose yourself. I was damn lucky to find your father. He protected me from a lot. Our marriage is for keeps."

John came roaring up from the pool, and Manny brought out drinks. Dianna left them and called Bill.

"I couldn't say a thing about Nana. We were so happy. I haven't had them home."

"Sure." She thought he detected impatience.

"They're upset about something." Dianna couldn't bring herself to say what.

"Sure."

"You're invited to dinner next Saturday."

"Putting me on the grill?"

That joke again.

"They want to meet you."

After a long silence, he said, "I'll talk to him."

He would confront her father, and that would be it. He'd be off to New York for his pool player movie, and she'd never see him again.

39

Every night that week, her parents dressed up and went out to remind Hollywood they existed. They went to premieres, nightclubs, enjoyed a romantic dinner at Romanoff's, and dined and danced at the Grove with the Stewarts. They made public appearances at theaters where *Elmer Gantry* was showing.

Dianna stayed at home and worked on her songs. She hadn't seen anything, she'd been so occupied, but she was glad when her parents were able to screen movies she'd wanted to see: *The Apartment*, *From the Terrace*, *Ocean's 11*, and *Let's Make Love*. The films left her only with an anxiety about how she would make the leap to being an adult in the movies. And also the tremendous responsibility now to make money. There was enough in the press about *West Side Story* being an artistic picture, expected to break even if that. With that and *Every Time*, she probably was going to lose her gamble. Neither would be blockbusters.

The day came when she had to walk into the recording studio for her first attempt at playing Maria. It was just her in that little sound booth, singing to the mike. She remembered Esperanza in *Salt of the Earth*, and tried to have that character in mind to sing with her. Even with *I Feel Pretty*. Certainly, with *Tonight*, with Rusty Tamblyn in the next booth.

She had coached with Roger Edens, who had worked with Garland, Grayson, her mother, and shared the same birthday with Kay Thompson. With Johnny Greene's orchestra coming right through her earphones, she gave as much heart she could give, investing Maria with strength and passion. With all this work, and being in another world, she only realized Chas was gone on Saturday morning when Anne told her.

"Why didn't you let me say goodbye? He'll think I didn't care! Why do you keep so many damn secrets?"

"What secrets? It's just that he would have been upset to say goodbye to you. It's for his sake we keep it a secret. His career, he could start it again."

Did her mother really believe that?

"I kept asking you how he was! You never answered! What aren't you telling me?

"Nothing, baby," said Anne, hugging her. "He just needs to have some special care for a while. He will be all right. Please understand."

"Can we visit him?"

"It's a private school in Bel Air. We'll all go."

Dianna couldn't think about this. She had to think about Maria. She was responsible to the whole production. She sang Maria, closing her eyes, picturing what was happening in that one joyful, then tragic, twenty-four hours. That was all that mattered. The recording was tedious, repeating songs over and over. Robert Wise came to listen and said little. Robbins, however, handed her several notes, which Dianna leaped at. She wanted, above all, to please Robbins. He also listened to her ideas. They seemed to be in full agreement about the character. So even if the work was tedious and exacting, she was filled with purpose and the work consumed her.

Until Sunday.

Bill arrived promptly, dressed with a deliberate casualness in trousers and a cotton shirt, blue, of course. Her parents were on the beachside deck, Anne in a yellow sundress with a halter and John in shorts and Hawaiian shirt. Dianna wore a blue sundress.

They were all so pretty.

Anne welcomed him with her ebullient charm. "Come and have some shrimp and crabmeat. We've got great steaks, too."

"What can we get you to drink, my dear boy?" John asked.

John asked Bill about his background. Bill tersely described his life, not mentioning his parents.

"I hear only good things about you," John said, "your acting, your discipline on the set, and your talent."

They talked about plays. John asked about *Bus Stop*. Then television. Bill had played Juror #5 for a television production of *Twelve Angry Men*, and John played off some dialog with him. Bill also admitted to playing Heathcliff in *Wuthering Heights* on television, so Anne, who had played Isabella in the movie, flung herself at his feet. Soon they were merrily criticizing movies, talking about Italian films, and arguing over whether movies should tell a story or be visually compelling. Dianna barely said a word, tense over Bill's presence. She wondered if it had been a mistake to insist he confront her father. Maybe it would have been better to just be friends all round first.

It might have happened that way, if not for Anne.

She asked, "What sort of actors were your parents?"

Bill glanced at Dianna.

She couldn't signal either way.

"Something wrong?" John asked.

"I've been eating your food, enjoying your company," Bill said, as if to himself.

"Beg pardon?"

"Bill's needed to talk to you, Daddy,' said Dianna.

"I don't think I can do this here after all," said Bill. "I've enjoyed being with you."

He stood up.

John stood up, too.

"I do not know what's bothering you, son, but do speak your piece if you need to."

"Not if it makes you sad," said Anne, "You're our guest."

Bill kept standing. So did John.

Bill said, "My dad was," and he paused in the second before he removed his mask, "Edward Greene. And my mother —"

"Oh, my God," Anne whispered.

John cast Anne a strange look. Fear? A warning?

"Your mother was Polly Royce," Anne said. Now she stood. Smiling too hard. As if to change the subject but not really. "A fine, fine actress."

"I knew your father," said John. His voice was quite soft, but his words were deliberate and slow. "I do not think there lived a better character actor."

Bill said, "No."

"You changed your name," said John.

"My father wanted me to. I was young when I started acting, as an extra and a stuntman. He said, don't be my son. Do you hear that? Don't be my son! He couldn't get jobs except as a waiter or a salesman, and he kept getting fired from those. I changed my name, although Greene is pretty innocuous."

"A terrible thing what happened," said Anne.

"We kept thinking all that political mess would end soon," said John.

"Dianna wanted me to talk to you," said Bill. "She has great faith in you."

"Faith about what?" asked John.

"The thing is," said Bill, who was trying to keep his composure and his voice light, "You're responsible for his death, Mr. Fletcher."

Anne's face grew a ghastly pale color. John, however, merely said, "People get all sorts of ideas in their heads. How did this get in yours?"

Anne sank back on the chaise lounge, but she spoke harshly. "Your father took his own life."

Bill said, "I was on a set when a messenger came with a note that I had to go to see my father in a rundown hotel. The police were there, and so was my father. I had to identify him. Had to pay his bill, too."

John looked at Bill for a long time.

No one said anything.

The surf grew louder, the tide coming in.

"How do you figure I am in on this?" John finally asked.

"Because, Mr. Fletcher," and Bill's voice slowed and grew in vowels and volume, well-rehearsed. Dianna sensed this was a bad idea, but she couldn't stop him. "Right on the table next to him was a letter you'd written him. This was not his home. He'd brought this letter, dated just a few days before. It was the last thing he read before he died, and he must have read it several times over. So did I. It's been in my head all this time. 'There is absolutely no chance of your playing the judge in *Larksong*. I trust that you understand the reasons for this. Very truly yours, John F.' On *your* letterhead."

John's face was impassive, but Anne said, "That could have meant anything, nothing. And you blamed John?"

"My father could not get work. For years. Despite the fact that his union work still stands today to the benefit of thousands, along with his defense of equal rights, freedom of speech and belief, his defense of Roosevelt's help in providing jobs and help to those who had been devastated by the Depression, his support of Henry Wallace, his right as an American to support his elective choices. That's what Dad died for."

John shook his head at Anne, as if to say, don't say anything. I have this.

"I do not see how I am guilty."

"You were the one who appeared with hope. You told him you had a script in development based on the Scottsboro case, that you wanted him to play the judge, an important part. You approached him, knowing he was blacklisted."

"Yes," said John. "I thought he would be the ideal person for that part."

"You pulled it away. You changed the script. The judge got whittled down to a few lines in a few scenes, and even that you took away from him. That part had been his only hope. He thought this would be a new beginning with none other than John Fletcher supporting him! How do you think he'd react?"

Dianna, the only one sitting, looked at three people she loved, and she could not speak.

"You don't know anything," said Anne.

"Let us not borrow from bad plays, Anne," said John.

"This whole thing is a bad play!" Anne shouted. "I'm not doing this thing again!"

"What thing?" Dianna shouted, and now she stood. "What can't you do again?"

"This whole business will not live in this house anymore."

"Bill, I can understand how you would feel the way you do," said John.

"It's the truth," said Bill.

"It is *your* truth," said John, with an edge of acrimony. "I understand that does not make it less real. Here you are, eating my food and being quite friendly with my sixteen-year-old daughter. Didn't that present any problems to you?"

Dianna thought, when am I ever going to be seventeen.

"Yes," said Bill.

"You used her to get to me, is that it?"

"Of course," said Anne.

"Daddy!"

"The truth?" said Bill. "It crossed my mind at first. But, here's the irony. I like Dianna. Pity, right? I told her about this, and she wanted me to talk to you and clear the air. She trusted that you'd listen to me and that you had an answer. I wasn't as sure. I guess I was right."

"Dammit, dammit," said Anne. "I won't do this again."

"Do what again?" cried Dianna.

John reached for his pipe. "Everyone calm down."

He sat down. The others followed his lead except for Bill, who remained standing. Dianna stood up again. She tried to take his arm, but he pulled away.

John lit the pipe, shook his head at his wife. "Let me tell you about *Larksong.* It became a lovely movie, and it brought Dianna to everyone's attention, deservedly so." He leaned back, concentrating on Bill, and spoke calmly, his British accent heightening the supposed reasonableness of his story, which Dianna could tell further irritated Bill.

"As you may know, *Larksong* began as *Larkspur.* I forget why we called it that, but it was originally to be a film about the Scottsboro boys. Yes, we were hot and heavy into social justice and issues we thought were of national concern. I had a script written and brought it in to Zanuck, but he wanted it tamed down. How do you tame down that story? All this was before your father was blacklisted. I suggested him to Zanuck, and Daryl said, perfect choice. Fox's fortunes have always been a little on the volatile side, and the rewrites were received with less and less enthusiasm. The climate in the country grew more intense, and studios grew increasingly cautious. Your father's name appeared in *Red Channels.*"

Bill had been looking down at his hands.

"Bill, I want you to hear me. Ed and I were friends, and we had a disagreement. I don't remember what it was about. Zanuck pressured me to have the script changed even more, and it ultimately became about a lawyer and his little boy, but then the boy changed into a little girl, and we had *Larksong.* Your father was understandably upset about his part being cut. As my memory serves, though, this was not our disagreement. I understood his frustration, and I tried to beef up his part, but it did not work. This happens all the time, Bill. You must know that."

"Sure, but I was with him," said Bill, "when we were walking down the Boulevard, and you crossed the street without saying one word, and we knew you'd seen us. A lot of people did that, but you came right in his face."

Anne said, "Let's stop this."

Bill said, "He can't answer me."

"He doesn't have to. John, tell him."

John said, "As I said, we had had a disagreement."

Anne made a frustrated sound.

Bill looked frustrated, too, as if he couldn't find the target he was aiming at.

"No one knows why a man kills himself," said John. "I accept your loss and your grief. You were just a boy. I do not think I was at fault here. How about another drink?"

Bill was quiet for a few moments. Then he said, "Thank you. I'll be going now."

"About time," said Anne.

"Mom!" Dianna shouted.

"I'm not doing this again," said Anne. "All that stuff just brings trouble. We have gone all this time without any trouble. I don't want it interfering with us anymore and certainly not hurting you, Dianna."

"It's all right, Anne," said John. "Bill had to say what he had to say. But he should go."

Bill nodded abruptly to Anne and headed around the deck to the front of the house.

Dianna jumped up and caught up with him in the street.

"What are you doing?"

"You believed him?"

"He's my father."

"Ed Greene was mine. Sweetie, I'm a bastard and so's your dad. Let's call an end to it."

"Are you saying you'll just give up our friendship?"

"It was stupid of me to think it could work. And we should never work together again."

"Your father never accused my father. Your father swallowed those pills himself. No one knows why he did. You just fixated on *my* father. You won't give it up either because you feed off it."

"See you at the movies," he said, walking away.

"Damn you!" She rushed after him, grabbed his arm.

"Go away!" he shouted, shoving her.

John was waiting for her by the front of the house. He took her into his arms. "Please do not blame him."

"It's stupid, and I will blame him."

"You acted together. That does not last forever."

She marched back of the house to where her mother was pacing.

"How could he say that in our home?" Anne shouted. "How could you let him believe all that?"

"I thought he should have his say." Even as she said it, she realized she'd been a fool.

"Give him time," said John.

"I don't want time," said Dianna. "He's my friend, and you and your damn blacklist. Why couldn't his father be in that movie?"

"What do you know?" cried Anne. "About anything? Just what he's told you? Damn, I will not do this again!"

"The things you don't say," said Dianna. "I know you," and she pointed to her mother, "you worked with Eleanor Roosevelt, and Nana wrote speeches for her. You attended Communist party meetings with her. I know. Bill has testimony. He's been doing research."

"My God!" cried Anne. "He's doing what? Why?"

"You went before that committee," said Dianna. She stopped herself. She couldn't say she'd read the testimony. "What's happened to both of you?"

"Stop that," said John.

"You can't possibly understand," said Anne. "It's not so simple."

Dianna ran to her room to slam the door. She heard, as she leaned against it, her father say, "She will be all right. She will be busy. She will forget."

"We should tell her something."

"Let it go. She would not understand."

She didn't want to. She wanted to forget Bill and the blacklist and get her life back to where it should be. She was busy, and she was about to get more so. *West Side Story* crammed into her life, as filming began at Goldwyn, but she felt more able to play Riff than Maria.

She would concentrate on her work.

Jerry Robbins was tough, after all.

She was rehearsing the bridal shop scenes, the "I Feel Pretty" and the "One Hand, One Heart" scenes, and Jerry kept stopping her.

No, no, like this, he'd yell, and she'd try something and he'd yell no no like this, and she'd try it again, and he'd shake his head, yelling louder, no no like this, and she would barely move a muscle, and he'd say, "That's right! Good!"

For all his toughness, Robbins understood she was trying to bring strength to Maria. When she said, "The strength of her faith, the strength of her love, the strength she discovers in herself," Robbins understood her instantly, but he kept wanting more from her. Wise would listen quietly and hold a long conversation with Jerry.

She wondered if she were fooling herself. She wasn't strong. And she only thought she'd found strength in love. Actually, it was just emptiness, but she tried to push that thought aside. Maria, help me. Maria would be strong.

She worked all day in the cavern of the studio, went home and worked on her lines and her part. Chas's empty room haunted her, however. So when she came home early one day, she called for a cab. Reggie gave her the address on condition she wouldn't tell her parents. Dianna sensed a whiff of disapproval.

The building was a small brick, three-story building in Bel Air, surrounded by pine trees. And a tall fence.

She asked to see Chas. Instead, she saw a nurse, Mrs. Inninger, small, gray-haired, tough.

"How lovely that you came to visit, but he can't have visitors now."

Dianna pretended to leave but instead went around the house where she heard children playing. A bunch of them were running races, but there he was, alone, running in circles all by himself. She opened the gate.

He ran to her immediately. "Dianna! Dianna! Did you come to take me home?"

"No," she said, and his tears started falling down his cheeks. She felt them as she held him tightly.

"Take me home."

"It looks nice here," she said.

"It's lonely. I want to go home. I want to talk to Mom and Dad, but they say I can't. Please take me home."

"I think you have to stay here a while. Why not play with the others?"

"I'm organizing a baseball team for Jefferson Park. We're not letting girls in."

"Don't be funny." Jefferson Park was the town in the *Pigskin Pete* series.

"We don't want girls!"

A hand took Dianna's.

"That's all right," said Mrs. Inninger. "She won't play. Come on, Dianna."

Dianna walked back to the cab with the nurse. "He seemed fine. But then he started to be Pete."

"He is getting better," said Mrs. Inninger. "We are working with him carefully, so you must tell us in advance you are coming. Give us time."

Once home, Dianna wanted to tell her mother what she'd done, but Anne was laughing it up with Deborah Kerr, Cyd Charisse, and Donna Reed, and it was good to see her laugh, so Dianna didn't have the heart.

Still, Chas's sad face stayed with her and with it, the fears of what had happened to her grandmother, still out there, alive. Somewhere.

That Saturday afternoon, she sang at Disneyland, barely able to sing all those peppy Davey songs that were still in the top ten. After, she raced to the parking lot wearing her sunglasses and scarf and took a cab on a long ride to Paramount to see Mr. Goodman who always worked on Saturdays.

"We're going to need to see you in more episodes," he said.

"I don't know where you'll find the time in my schedule!" She didn't want to fight. "I want to write to Mr. Franklin. Can't he write more episodes? I love his. Something about suffrage! Betsy should be working for the vote."

Goodman just chuckled. "Franklin went to Europe. He's not able to write for a while."

"I just want to thank him."

"I'll give you the address I have. Care of the American Express company."

She wrote notes and tore them up. She couldn't decide whether to address it to Mr. Franklin or to her grandmother. In the end, she couldn't bear not to reach out.

> Dearest Nana, because I think that is who you are. I have missed you all my life, and I think you are alive. I think I know why you are not in my life. Nana, please come home. We need you. Something is wrong with Mom, something is wrong with Chas, something is wrong everywhere. I don't want you to be hurt, but please come home. Love, Dianna.

She had done what she could. She had to think about Maria and not about anyone else. She was the star. She was responsible. She had to carry the show.

40

The day came when *Picnic* was broadcast.

Too ashamed to watch with her parents, Dianna watched it in her room. To her surprise, before the broadcast began, a magnificent peacock, spreading its brilliant multi-colored tail feathers, appeared on the screen. "The following program," solemnly intoned an announcer, "is brought to you in living color on NBC."

The theme music began, the credits shown against a train moving through pretty country and some of the people working and playing in it. When the train stopped, a man jumped out. Bill. She winced on seeing him so cocky, his hands in his pockets, his walk slow, almost sensual, his first scenes texturing that cockiness and sensuality with uncertainty. How did he do that?

Millie looked mad throughout the whole piece, and was tiresome, as was her overacting. Occasionally, glimmers of an independent spirit burst into the story, and her rapport with Bill came off surprisingly well, but it all felt lopsided. The camera never favored her, never paused over her face to see the hurt or ferocity that she'd thought she'd given Millie. Her dance with Bill was embarrassing. His dance with Star – she could practically see the flames on the screen, and she decided that they'd gone to bed together during *Picnic*, and probably before, even when Sandi was furnishing Bill's house. As for the famous jackknife that had made it into national magazines, it lasted a few seconds, the camera lingering on Hal's reaction and his bare chest.

When she went downstairs, her parents stopped talking. She must have really been awful. But they were polite. "You have presence," John said. He might as well have punched her. "But it was as if you were in a different play."

"Not everything works," said Anne. "You find things out."

"No," said Dianna. But her faith in her work was again shaken.

The critics praised Bill to the skies. They said she overacted like a silly teenager. The kind ones said she was miscast although there were flashes of brilliance that made them want to know more about Millie. Angelini's mistreatment of her appeared in almost every review, and it did not help him. Lucille Ball, along with Bill and Star, won the critics' favor.

And there were pictures of Bill in the news, too, out to dinner at Romanoff's, with a girl she'd not seen before. It was like looking at a stranger's picture.

Her parents had not spoken about the blacklist or any of those other things since the day Bill had come. Dianna again raised the topic of the speeches

Alice reportedly had written, but Anne said, "I told you. It was nothing. Mrs. Roosevelt was just being polite."

Dianna didn't believe her mother. The tension between them was such that Lynne accompanied her to the doctor's for the IUD. The doctor, a woman, said nothing about her being sixteen. Dianna hated the procedure and wondered why she had troubled herself to get it. Bruce certainly wouldn't be a factor, and there wasn't anyone else.

She thought about Bruce, though. She needed to understand more about what her grandmother had stood for. And maybe her mother. Bruce was surprised when she called him.

"Your group sings for the migrant workers. Can I come?"

"Wow, yeah. You can sing 'If I Had a Hammer,' right? And 'Michael Row Your Boat Ashore'?"

She had expected little cottages and people working in the fields. She had not expected whole families living in what looked like lean-tos made of canvas without any evidence of plumbing. She also had not expected to see small children, barely five years old, picking tomatoes in the sun and dragging heavy baskets. It looked like *The Grapes of Wrath*.

The back of a truck served as a stage.

"We can rehearse," said Bruce. "In half an hour they'll have a break. They'll eat while we sing."

The women's eyes were set deep, like old people's, and their hair was half gray, and yet they herded young children with energy, laughing. Some of them walked toward the singers and poured warm water and handed out biscuits on a ratty tin plate.

Many of the women and little girls surrounded Dianna, calling her name. How could they know her? She sat down and signed autographs on rust stained papers, and for the children, she told the story of Cinderella, singing all the cartoon's songs with a wicked glee. The children ate it up, especially when she imitated the mice.

A car came down the dusty road. It parked. No one got out.

Dianna joined the others to sing a few songs. They sang "Hard Times Come No More," which Dianna did not know, so she took the tambourine and danced with it.

The car door opened. A man in overalls got out and started walking across the field.

"One last song, from our movie star, Dianna Fletcher," Bruce called out.

"What song?"

"The Disney song," said Bruce.

Was he crazy?

They plucked a few chords with their guitar, banjo, and bass, and Dianna plunged in. "When you wish upon a star," she sang, and to her amazement, mothers, fathers, and children sang, holding hands, smiling.

The man across the field stopped walking. He bowed his head as if in prayer. When she was done, he started walking toward them.

"Thank you, folks!" Bruce called. "We hope to see you soon!"

"I see you're back," the farmer said, "bringing your music to stir them all up."

"Dianna Fletcher was singing Disney's song," said Bruce. "From *Pinocchio*."

"Dreams for them mean they stop picking my tomatoes."

"I'm sorry," said Dianna. She wanted to punch his gut. "Why don't you treat them better?"

"I didn't think you were one of them," said the farmer.

"Them?" Dianna asked.

"These kids are Commies. You're not one of them."

"I think children should grow up decently, with food, clothes, and shelter," she said. She thought of Nana, and she had to say what she felt.

"That's the parents' job. It ain't mine. I want you off my land."

"We're going," said Bruce.

They were packing up the car when the farmer came over, a notebook in his hand.

"My wife won't believe it," he said, thrusting the notebook at her. "Sign it for me?"

She smiled. "Certainly."

Unable to resist the temptation, she added to her name, "for my mother, Anne Foster, her mother Alice Marrs, and their friend Eleanor Roosevelt."

He barely looked at it but put it in his pocket.

"Thank you for your hospitality," said Bruce.

Dianna hopped into the car.

As he turned the car back on the road out, Bruce said, "There was a time about ten, fifteen years ago when there seemed to have been some changes, but after the war, it all ended. They're back to almost nothing."

"I read that everyone in this country is practically all middle class," said Dianna.

"Everyone you can see," said Pam. "There are thousands of people you can't see. Factories shut down, farms don't produce, people can't get jobs."

"Is anyone doing something?"

"No one seems to know what to do."

She thought of Kennedy's speech. Maybe he knew.

She went with them to see *The Boy With Green Hair*. She remembered that Bill had mentioned it. The film concerned little boy whose hair turned green, the color of hope. A war orphan, he went around telling people that there didn't have to be any war. That message frightened almost everyone, and his green hair scared them, too. So they forced him to have his hair cut. Hope cut, war won. But the boy thought he would be able to persuade them again.

The people who created that movie had been blacklisted.

Bruce took her home, and it wasn't until he was helping her out of the car that he said something, which was, "You and Bill are a thing, aren't you?"

"No."

"Okay." He leaned over and kissed her.

He was getting better.

When she suggested that her mother could go to the fields, Anne looked incredulous.

"The poor will always be with us, said Jesus."

"He also said sell everything and give it to the poor."

"They want the work. They come here. They take the money."

"But Mom, this is the United States. There isn't supposed to be anyone here who's hungry."

"And who told you that?"

The conversation wasn't going anywhere. She tried another question that would also probably be fruitless. "What's really happening with Chas?"

Anne gave her daughter a long stare.

"I went to see him."

Anne got up and walked around the room as if trying to figure out what to say and how much. Finally, she sat next to Dianna, taking her hand and looking at her straight.

"All right, I'll tell you. If you want the burden, all right then, I'll share. I don't know what's happening with him. The last movie, they had to start feeding him the lines, sentence by sentence. Even word by word. God knows how they put it together. He'd go off into the woods back there, pretending to be a car, shifting gears. He'd tape his voice, and I'd find that he's Pete, and he's reciting lines from all the movies. It got worse. The closest anyone knows is that it's a breakdown, but this killing of animals and violence with other boys, picking fights, carrying knives, Dianna, it scares me."

As Anne's voice grew increasingly shaky, Dianna realized she shouldn't bother her mother about anything else.

"Your father insists Chas will get better. That he needs a better part. Acting! It's all that man can think of."

"Maybe if Chas did get a better part," said Dianna.

Anne sank deep into a thickly cushioned chair, curled up, leaned back, eyes closed.

"I was pregnant with him when all that business came up with the House Committee. They could have called both of us, but they called me. I was scared. Daddy could have been thrown out of the country. He was shooting down Germans before any American climbed into a plane. But a equals z to these people, and you have no defense. They want to show their voters they're after the Commies, no matter who they call upon. And they loved to go after movie stars. I was so scared, Dianna. They could hound people to death for no reason at all. I know that. Kill careers. I drank, I took pills, I smoked all the time. I shouldn't have, I never did with you and Nick. If I hurt him, if it's all my fault."

"Lots of women drink and smoke when they're pregnant." Actually, Dianna didn't have the faintest idea. "They didn't call Daddy to testify?"

"He went later, when the plague hit. By then, we'd gotten wise, stopped doing all those causes that could be fronts. We gave our money to hospitals. Danny's Saint Jude hospital fund. Walt Disney took Nick in. Then all of you. Yes, I knew that would be good for us, working with Walt. He is a genius, and he is above reproach. That would silence the questions. Still Congress called for Daddy. They grilled him over and over."

"Why?"

"Because —" And it seemed as if she was about to say more, but she stopped herself and took Dianna's hands. "Who knows? Everyone was scared and people would toss names out. A grudge, envy, who knows? Daddy never did anything political except fight in the war. He is an actor. It's his life. They called him and called him. They were private meetings. That was good, but there were no witnesses. He'd come back exhausted. He's not made for this sort of thing. Imagine fighting for freedom and coming back to this. He spoke the truth, again and again, but they kept after him. I was pregnant then, too. I lost the baby."

"What? Mom!"

"It's okay. No one knew but Daddy. I couldn't have any more children. I love your father so much. He walks around in a cloud half the time, but he's a loving, creative artist. I want him left in peace so he can do what he must with his talent. My God, after the war." She paused. "After the war. Dianna, you can't imagine what it was like."

Dianna waited.

"Whatever he saw, it broke his heart. I almost lost him. Not to Nazis shooting him down in a plane or on the ground. I almost lost him on our patio."

Dianna waited.

"He went back, you know, with George Stevens' film unit. They went to concentration camps and filmed the liberations. And when he came back, he couldn't talk. He couldn't eat. He had nightmares when he'd wake up screaming. Jimmy Stewart and Hank Fonda would come visit, and they'd sit out on the patio, not saying a word. Your father would have fits of rage, fits of crying, nightmares. He refused to have anything to do with movies. Eventually, it came out all right. John Barrymore came by, told John to sit up straight, that shooting movies was a good sight better than shooting people. Your dad and I played in *The Best Years of Our Lives*, and Jimmy and I did *It's a Wonderful Life*. I got my husband back. When he did talk about it, he would say, the shock of seeing what humans could do to other humans, including children, had left a great scar even greater than the shock of being able to kill other humans without thinking. Later, he would talk about how easy it was for leaders of countries to encourage hate that merely served their own purposes. He resolved to do something to erase this horrible thing from the human soul. That was the dream, anyway. Oh, but to get there."

Dianna wrapped her arms around her mother.

Anne wiped away tears. "Yes, my mother. And Eleanor Roosevelt. We traipsed across the country and brought dance and music to people. Oh, damn. Why bother doing what you love when you get killed for it."

"Joan of Arc knew," said Dianna, referring to one of Anne's movies if only to help her smile.

"Joan of Arc was in over her head," said Anne. She took Dianna's hand. "It felt good to tell you."

Dianna almost said something about Nana, but Hilda arrived with the news that the Stewarts had arrived for dinner.

Dianna tried staying close to Anne when they were both home, but Anne and John were involved in their work, and so was Dianna, battling the pressures of dealing with dueling directors.

"The boys like that will give us trouble," Rita Moreno joked, riffing off a line from her song. The boys, Jerry and Bob, took time to discuss every angle and every interpretation at length. The shooting schedule, already late, went way off. The producers, the Mirisch brothers, came to the set many times to apologize to the actors and crew. Dianna knew that she would ultimately be blamed, and she worked like mad to give Maria life, thinking about her, learning some Spanish like the Catholic prayers, pacing through Maria's life and why she'd fall for Tony so fast.

She worked hard, on the set and at home, to bring Maria alive. Bruce called a few times, and she turned him down, but once, when he invited her to a concert, Pam called to insist she come. "You can't treat Bruce like a dog on a leash," she scolded.

"I'm busy."

"Doing work you love and so's he. He gets it, but you say no too fast."

Dianna resented this folk singer's interference. What could she know?

"We're in the concert. It's a big deal. Pete Seeger."

Dianna didn't know the name. But Pam had aimed her dart straight at the prickly guilt she felt about Bruce, so she agreed to go to this concert at UCLA, even if she wasn't going to sit with anyone but by herself in the bleachers with total strangers who would ask for her autograph throughout the concert.

Except they didn't. When she climbed up to her seat with Bruce's help, the students called out to him, and a few said, "Hi, Dianna!" but otherwise left her alone. And she felt alone.

Pete Seeger's America wasn't jazz. It wasn't musical theater. It wasn't pop. It certainly wasn't classical. It wasn't like any singing she'd encountered ever. And he wanted you to sing along.

There was no doubt that he was a brilliant musician, although nothing about him said that. He simply talked about the songs he was going to sing, as if he were in your living room. And he culled those songs from all over the world, catching the choruses, inviting their participation. She recognized a few songs, like "Water is Wide," which he sang with a mournful sympathy, and certainly, "Good Night, Irene." That she recognized with a shock. That had been a hit a few years before. But he introduced it while talking about the American Indians and how they would sing to remember people not there. He sang it for someone named Huddie Lead Belly, and everyone joined in. Dianna decided to sing along, cautiously. The girl next to her put her arm around her shoulders, and they exchanged the briefest if small, shy smiles. He encouraged harmony, and Dianna found some.

This tall, skinny guy with the guitar and the banjo both scared and fascinated her. Bruce, Pam, Andy, and Phil, played along with him with guitars and bass while Pam kept the tambourine going and while Seeger soared above them with a glorious falsetto.

One thing he said during the song, "Huddie used to say that Irene was a real person and she was sixteen years old and had the misfortune to meet up with a rambler and a gambler. You caused me to weep, you caused me to moan, you caused me to leave my home, but the very last words I heard her say was 'please sing me one more song.'"

If I Had a Hammer. Danger. Warning. Love between my brothers and my sisters. A bell. A song. She'd known it, but now it seemed a warning. Everyone around her sang as if it were the most important song in the world. *Wimoweh*.

He coached the low voices. And Dianna joined in with "Wimoweh" – which she vaguely remembered. Seeger took this weird falsetto that fascinated her. That was when she realized that he was a genius, and she started to cry and had to stop singing. She could not join the enthusiastic applause. She was too overwhelmed.

In between the songs, Seeger talked. What he said, she resisted. Her America was about individual work and achievement, not about blaming others for your failure. But was he doing that? And then there was his next song.

I've traveled round this country from shore to shining shore. It really made me wonder, the things I heard and saw. I saw the weary farmer a-plowing sod and loam. I heard the auction hammer just a-knocking down his home.

But the banks are made of marble with a guard at every door, and the vaults are stuffed with silver that the farmer sweated for.

I've seen the seamen standing idly by the shore, and I heard their bosses saying, got no work for you no more.

But the banks are made of marble with a guard at every door. And the vaults are stuffed with silver that the seaman sweated for.

I've seen the weary miner scrubbing coal dust from his back. And I've heard his children crying, got no coal to heat the shack.

But the banks are made of marble, with a guard at every door. And the vaults are stuffed with silver that the miners sweated for.

I've seen my brothers working throughout this mighty land. I've prayed we'd get together and together make a stand. And might ope those banks of marble with a guard at every door and we would share those vaults of silver that we had sweated for.

It was like sanctioning bank robbery.

Yet when people sang with him, he beamed like the sun and howled a harmony.

"These old songs," he said, "are never going to die out. These songs are the whole human race. Everybody's history. Cross the ocean, we thought we solved all those problems. Get that job, get that home, cross that river and find you get shackles on your feet. And who's that judge? No matter what mistakes we ever made, we still got a last verse that holds out hope."

He sang about a coal miners' strike in Kentucky, when the churches weren't always on the side of the strikers of the union. *You know, in the sweet*

by and by. You will eat by and by in that glorious life above the sky. You'll get
by in the sky when you die.

But, said, "We rediscovered our own humanity by learning the songs of
black people. The slave master brought the Bible, obey your master. That was
what they should learn. Ah, but they turned the page and found that Moses
freed the slaves. In the 1930s, it was the Negro people who changed the words
a little more, not Jesus is my captain, I shall not be moved. Now it was we
shall not be moved."

And he sang it. She'd heard that song before, when? She remembered. On
television at the San Francisco demonstration. We shall overcome. We shall
overcome some day.

"Sing with me!" he cried, exultantly. "These old folk songs have different
ways to sing, this is one of my favorites. We are climbing Jacob's ladder," he
sang, his face shining.

The simplicity and honesty of what she heard encouraged resistance in
her that she couldn't counter.

"Michael row the boat ashore." Dianna had learned that song when she
was still going to school. The girl next to her started swaying. The boy who
was on her other side put his arm around her shoulders and swayed. It wasn't
anything but friendship, and he would have done it to anyone. She swayed
and sang. It felt powerful. But it scared her. She couldn't quite say why she
felt threatened.

The applause went on for a long time. Seeger disappeared behind the
curtain. Bruce came out and beckoned to her to come down. People called out
her name and applauded her. She smiled and waved.

She was introduced to Seeger, whose eyes crinkled.

"Anne Frank," he said, and he hugged her hard. "You made me cry," he
said. "I watched you at the Oscars."

It didn't seem to be the kind of show he would watch.

"Your little speech," he said, "moved me so very much."

He put his hand on his heart.

Dianna said, "I'm sorry, I never heard anything like this before."

"Good," he said. "You walked through a new door tonight."

And hit my head, she thought. His smile made her think of one word,
golden. He seemed so calm, so sweet.

Bruce said, "I can't believe you never heard of these songs."

"I know a ton of songs," she said. "I just didn't travel down his path."

"These are the songs that are important today," Bruce said. He was
probably still mad at her for turning him down, and he was criticizing her top
ten tunes.

"All songs are important," said Seeger. To Dianna he said, "You have a great talent. You can bring people together."

He turned away to talk to other people.

"You just hurt my feelings on purpose," she said to Bruce.

"I voiced an opinion. These are great songs. You should sing them. He was blacklisted, you know. They hit number one on the charts and someone whispered 'Communist' and he couldn't get on television."

"I can see why. And you telling me my music isn't worth much." She headed for the door.

Out on the street, she waved down a cab.

Bruce pulled out his wallet. "Look, I'm sorry."

"Don't bother. I have money from those terrible songs."

She pulled the door closed.

Not a spark of romance about this guy.

Back to work.

They made up. Well, he did. They went to movies and argued about them.

Despite going out to hamburger hangouts with her old Disney pals or going to movies with Bruce in her rare free time, and whenever Rusty Tamblyn touched her to kiss her or proclaim his love for her, she missed Bill. It didn't help that his name was suddenly everywhere, in the press and on people's lips. *Picnic* brought him prominence. His casting in *Breakfast at Tiffany's* had been a surprise, a late choice caused by a disagreement between Audrey Hepburn and George Peppard, and that only won him extra points. Hepburn praised him and called Bill a gentleman and "delightful to work with." An article in *Time* called him "the most exciting actor of the new generation." Not a Method weakling, mumbling his words, but a powerful, virile presence who could still express his emotions. It was so much press pablum, but that powerful, virile sentiment was everywhere.

She was envious. Missing him made her angrier. She turned on the first presidential debate, hoping to criticize Bill by criticizing Kennedy's speaking.

She didn't get the satisfaction. Jack Kennedy had clearly benefited from Bill's coaching. Dianna pitied Nixon, who looked haggard and pale, agreed with Kennedy many times, and seemed so weak.

During a long exchange between the candidates about two islands Dianna had never heard of, Anne, who had joined Dianna, said, "They always talk about things that don't matter. Dick is a smart man, but you don't see any of that intelligence here. Look at Kennedy. They're about the same age, but so different."

Dianna almost asked Anne about Richard Nixon playing the piano in the Whittier dancing studio, but she knew that would lead to more questions. She did notice, however, that Anne watched Nixon with what seemed like intense unhappiness.

"I hope," said Anne, "that Nixon loses." She looked over at her startled daughter. "Even though, yes, I will vote for him. But look at Kennedy. Damn, he's good."

Kennedy's speech patterns, much improved, and his energetic demeanor, spoke hope, even though he spoke about problems. He seemed ready to solve them if someone would only say, "Go." Bill had really helped him. Dianna realized she felt proud of him. Damn it. She reached for her mother's hand.

"I miss him," she said.

"You'll get over it," said Anne.

41

If you were anyone in the film industry, you were at the Annual Fletcher Autumn ball.

The evening began with a movie premiere – last year, it was *The Big Country*. This year, it was *Spartacus*: Kirk Douglas's sprawling epic with an international cast and the appearance of blacklisted Dalton Trumbo's name on the screen for the first time in ten years. After the premiere, the lucky guests would head to the Fletcher mansion, wander through the main rooms, across the courtyard, and into the great mirrored ballroom adjoining the massive formal dining room, sit and eat at one of the four long tables piled high with food, or nibble and sip the food and champagne circulating on trays carried by fleet-footed waiters in red coats. They could eat near the pool or the marble fountain spouting multi-colored champagne or under a huge tent in the garden, dance in the ballroom, and gossip in the parlors. The feasting and fun would last until after dawn.

This was the first year Dianna was allowed to attend the entire event.

She asked Bruce to be her escort. She knew he'd be thrilled, and he was.

Nick couldn't come; he was about to open on Broadway. On the phone with him, she spilled out all that had happened about Chas.

"That place is probably good for him," said Nick. "He can be dangerous."

He didn't seem to care. He was absorbed in *Hamlet*. He was learning it backwards.

"Why?"

"Because everyone knows it forwards," he said, as if that explained everything.

Bruce could barely say hello when John greeted him, and he descended into mute wonder when Dianna rustled in wearing a pale pink taffeta trimmed in black, with miles of skirt and tulle except on the strapless bodice, her hair tied back in a cluster of curls. Anne appeared in a comparatively straight gown, the bodice cut across her shoulders in dark blue, the skirt pale blue, her dark hair swept up over her head. She kissed Bruce on his cheek, and Dianna thought he'd faint.

What was the line in *The Band Wagon*? Everyone is here, simply everyone! And everyone did seem to be at the premiere from producers to writers to second assistant directors, all of them stopping to talk to the Fletchers. Dianna kept introducing Bruce, but Bruce couldn't talk.

As soon as North's martial music began, with its highly optimistic theme of forward movement, Dianna knew *Spartacus* was going to be good. When Trumbo's name appeared, the audience cheered. Could the writers come back from the wings and write with their own names again? She was surprised she was so moved, so hopeful.

Spartacus proved a dynamic picture, with plenty of chances for Douglas to show off his physique and his physical abilities. He was not the most subtle actor, but Spartacus wasn't subtle: His emotions and thoughts were larger than life. As for her father, his underplaying, his crisp British accent, and his cold eyes all perfectly described his character. What a contrast from Elmer Gantry!

His seduction of Anne was simply you are mine and that's all there is to it. Anne, sexually giving to Douglas, was filmed lusciously nude in two scenes (who could say she was aging?), but turned another eye at his enemy. She knew what Crassus wanted, hated him, and yet did not put him off. Their byplay riveted.

How brilliant her parents were! Could she ever be like that — charging into parts and carving out people who were alive and vibrant?

The last scene, with Spartacus hanging on the cross, could have been maudlin but Anne was fierce. "Die, why don't you die?" she insisted, almost cruelly, as she showed the man his son. The cost of freedom. A grieving woman and her baby barely getting away with their lives. The music, optimistic as they rode away, with the same martial uprising as at the beginning, provided a clue. Here was victory in what appeared to be defeat.

The audience rewarded Douglas with a standing ovation. Bruce kept yelling, "Hoorah!" and that was silly except she started doing it, too. She hugged Bruce, hopping up and down. He grinned at her.

Kirk Douglas broke down while giving his small speech. He called out the cast for plaudits, and then he added, "By the way, the American Legion has some picketers out there. The security guards have them contained, so don't worry, just know they're there."

"What are they picketing about?" Dianna asked her parents.

"*Spartacus* is a popular Communist theme," said Anne.

"Sounded pretty American to me," said Dianna. "Freedom and all."

"And then there's Dalton Trumbo," said Anne.

"Well, too bad," said Dianna. "He wrote it. They didn't protest when he wrote things and another person's name showed."

Anne looked at her daughter intently, then said, "No."

As they left the theater in a hubbub of congratulations, Dianna saw, to the side, a large crowd with people waving signs and yelling, "Communists! This film was written by a Communist about Communists!"

"You dupes! Dopes!"

"Traitors! Hang them for treason!"

"Aid and comfort to the enemy!"

Flimsy wooden barricades set them off from the theater goers. Remembering the mob after *Bandstand*, Dianna gripped Bruce's arm.

He said, "Don't worry. See all those police? And the press is all over the place."

"The press will save us?"

"God Bless America!" people shouted.

"Go to Russia if you love them!" others yelled.

"Death to traitors!" screeched a man, standing on a box. "Get the Commies out of our movies!"

"Corrupting our youth!"

Dianna smiled and waved at fans, cordoned off on the other side, and someone stopped her to ask about the movie and someone asked her about how *West Side Story* was going and someone asked her who Bruce was and someone broke through the wooden barricades and past all the police and all the press and ran up to her, pushing a picket sign in her face.

"Dupe!" he yelled. "Get wise! Your parents are Commies!"

"Hey!" Bruce yelled.

Dianna felt someone grip her waist, pick her up, and put her down several feet away.

She knew those hands.

Bill Royce grabbed the picketer's arm, wrested the sign from his hand, and gave him a punch that landed him a few feet away in the other direction. The fans cheered. Photographers popped. The police grabbed the screaming protester and hauled him away. All of a sudden, more security guards appeared, and about a dozen more policemen showed up to arrest the picketers.

The fans and the people coming out of the theater cheered Bill, who turned to Dianna and said, "Are you all right?"

"I'm not the one you punched," said Dianna, but her voice shook. Out of nerves or out of having seen him just come in from nowhere and felt those hands of his? Yes.

Bill said, "Hey, Bruce, if there's a lady in your charge, you take care of her."

"The police were here," said Bruce.

"I thought you were in New York," said Dianna, trying to figure out how she felt about this man who had, the last she heard, wanted her out of his life.

He spoke naturally, smiling. "I've got a few days off before we pick up here. I thought I'd come to the opening. Good movie."

Her parents had pushed through the crowd.

Anne grabbed Dianna and held her tightly. More photographers rushed forward. The fans cheered. Many called, "Dianna! Dianna!" in a chant, which scared her more than that picketer had.

John shook Bill's hand. "Thank you. Are you coming to the party?"

Bill didn't answer but looked as if he wanted to if he only knew the answer.

John held on to his hand and said, "You are welcome to come, Bill."

Anne gasped, started to say, "John," and then shut up.

For a moment, Dianna thought Bill would say, "No, thanks," but he said, "Sure. I'll come."

"Good, we shall talk there."

Bill seemed somber, chastened.

John, however, was ebullient.

"Bruce, how did you like the movie?"

"You were great, sir!"

"Excellent response," said John. "Let's go, kids."

Bruce gripped Dianna's arm.

Dianna turned to Bill. "So you're Dr. Jekyll tonight? Where's your date?"

She didn't wait to hear his answer, even though a pained look crossed his face. Tempted to soften her behavior, she resisted and took Bruce's hand and walked toward their car.

A police escort wailed away in front of them, leading to the early edition stories that Dianna Fletcher had been hurt. That story had played well before.

At the house, Dianna showed Bruce the ballroom, with its balcony encircling it, the mirrors on the walls, the doors flung open to the gardens and fountains. The orchestra swung into dances based on movie themes. Bruce could only say over and over, "It's like a movie."

The hired staff were in place, the crab, shrimp, and caviar were out, and the bars were ready. The parlors began to fill with people running across the rooms to kiss and hug and praise the movie and talk about themselves. Finally, trumpets blared, meaning that it was time for the grand march. Across the lawn and into the ballroom they went, laughing and prancing. Dianna waltzed with Tony Curtis, cha cha'd with David Niven, twisted with Jimmy Stewart, and rumba'd with George Stevens.

She didn't see Bruce. She had seen Bill briefly, with a curvy blonde.

She ended up eating at a table in the garden with the Douglases, who arrived late after stopping in at the official premiere party. The fountain was whooshing, a gentle breeze blew, and a silver moon shone — all quite perfect, as if God worked for the industry, someone said. If only He would pay for it, someone else said.

Douglas was preaching. "Was Dalton Trumbo our enemy? No. Nor were his children or his wife. The whole thing is a travesty. No one would admit there was a blacklist because that's illegal. But it was sure real. If they can do this, then who's to say what else they can do? Blacklist a minister? A teacher? A whole people? Or you for saying what you think?"

"Not even saying out loud," said his wife. "Their silence sent them to jail."

"Like Thomas More," said Dianna.

Douglas leaned his face into hers.

"Do you know, Dianna, Howard Fast, who wrote the novel *Spartacus*, can't speak at college campuses. They have him under surveillance. In the United States of America! Pretty soon they'll be soldiers in train stations and airports, ready to shoot anyone they think is an enemy. Unless we the people care. Indifference has become a substitute for integrity."

"Maybe you're Spartacus' son," said Dianna.

"Douglas grinned. "Oh, what a lovely thing to say, Dianna. Honey, do me a favor. Marry *my* son." He squeezed her waist.

She smiled back. "Time for me to mingle."

She crossed the courtyard.

A man sitting by the fountain stood up as she approached. As she came into the lights around the fountain, she recognized Bill.

"Aren't you eating?"

"Came out to think."

"You disappeared," she said, with all the sharpness she could muster. "Again. Where's your date?"

"Couldn't get one on short notice. I was talking to your father. It was tough."

"Tell me."

"I was a rat these last weeks with you, and it wasn't your fault."

"Tell me something new."

He looked impatient, as if she should forgive him now that he'd apologized. Someone whispered her name.

Bill looked around. She heard the whispering again. Chas stepped through the hydrangea bushes. For a moment, she had the weird feeling that he'd just run down the stairs to peek in at the crowd, as they'd used to do in other years. Then she realized he must have escaped from that home. He hurled himself at her in a great hug. In his sandals, undershorts, and tee shirt, he looked thin, small, and scared.

"How did you get here?" she asked.

But he only said, "Dianna," and burrowed his head into her chest. She wrapped her arms around him and turned so that no one would see him, although most of the diners had gone back into the ballroom.

"I have to go upstairs," she said to the puzzled Bill. She wasn't going to explain. She didn't know what she could say, anyway. Let him guess.

"We're going to eat and watch TV," said Chas.

"Come on." She drew him to the door and dialed the security code. She hurried him up the stairs, but he kept turning and saying, "I wanted the food, like we always do. And we'll watch old movies."

His room was just the way it always was, with the map of the United States, pictures of sports stars, and all those pictures of him being honored by Chambers of Commerce, sports heroes, and President Eisenhower.

"How did you get here?" she asked.

"I snuck into the laundry truck."

"Are you okay?"

"I want to be here."

"I missed you."

"Don't let them send me back. I'm not crazy. I just like to be by myself and play. Let's get some food and watch some television."

"I'm at the party, Chas."

"I want to watch television with you," he said, his face getting red. "I came all this way. Why don't you want to watch with me?"

"Because I want to dance," she said, getting nervous. She needed to get to their parents. His plaints seemed off somehow, not just little brotherly nagging but containing a deeper desperation. "You understand, don't you?"

"Where's Nick?"

"Nick's in New York."

"I want to eat and watch television with you. Like always. Why don't you? I don't want to be by myself." He started hitting and kicking her and crying, "Watch television with me!"

She shoved him back and ran for the door, but he ran faster and grabbed her arm. She pushed him into the room.

He pulled out a knife. He put it up to her face.

"I'll cut you up. You won't be in movies again. You'll have to stay with me."

Crazily, she thought of *Psycho*.

"Chas," she cried. "Why?"

"I have to. I'm sorry."

And he waved the knife.

42

S he had the crazy thought, use it for Maria.

"Why are you so angry?" she managed to say, her voice eerily steady.

"You don't want to watch television with me."

"But you want food. I have to go get it."

His face cleared. "Oh, you were just teasing. All those people at that place don't know how to tease." He dropped the knife and sank to the floor, but his lovely wide eyes in his cute round face looked up at her. "I want to come home."

"I'll come back with shrimp and stuff," she said, feeling awful because she was lying.

She opened the door, backed out of it, shut it. Someone had changed the lock from the inside to the outside. She leaned her head against the door as she twisted the lock, realizing that her parents had been afraid of him for a long time.

"Dianna! Come back!"

It was a plaintive wail, cutting into her fears and letting loose memories of past laughter and innocent wishes.

"No, Chas, you come back," she whispered through the door.

She hurried down the hall.

"Dianna!" Chas screamed.

She remembered that Reggie was tending the front door and hurried downstairs.

"Chas is here," she said. What did Reggie know, she wondered.

Enough for him to look serious.

"I'll get your parents. Are you all right?"

She sank into a chair. "He pulled a knife on me."

Her parents were there in a few minutes, Anne grabbing her and holding her, her tears mixing with Dianna's own.

"I locked him in," said Dianna. "It hurts, Mom."

"I know."

"I will call the home," said John, quietly. "Reggie, stand by his door until I go up. Anne, stay with Dianna."

"I want to see him," Anne said.

"No," said John. "We don't know when he'll turn. Reggie, make sure the guests stay out of the house for a while."

"Oh, my baby," Anne murmured. "What are we going to do?" She clung to her daughter, murmuring, "What are we going to do?" over and over.

It took only half an hour for the car to arrive. Mrs. Inninger came in with two men, who hurried upstairs with Reggie.

Mrs. Inninger spoke soothingly to the Fletchers. "He wants to be all right, but he also is still lured to the other things. We are making progress, and that must be why he remembered that he wanted to come here today."

Lured to the other things? Dianna started shaking.

"He pulled a knife on Dianna," said Anne. "I'm not losing her, too."

"He would not have done anything to hurt her. He's said over and over that he loves her."

"He punched me," said Dianna. "I don't know who he is."

"He will get better soon," said Mrs. Inninger. "He did not take his medicine this afternoon. I am investigating why."

One of the men came down carrying a struggling Chas. His lips were bound with tape. Anne stood up and tried to embrace him, but he kicked at her.

"He doesn't know what he's doing," said one of the men.

"Don't bind him like that," Anne cried, clinging to Dianna. Her whole body was shaking. "Let me hold him."

Mrs. Inninger said, "Let him go for now. In a few months, he won't remember any of this, and you'll have him back."

Anne moaned. "Please take care of him. Take that thing off his mouth."

"We didn't want him to yell and disturb your guests," said Mrs. Inninger. "We'll take it off in the car."

"Damn the guests! It'll hurt," said Anne. "I want to see you do it so it doesn't hurt."

She ran out after them. Dianna followed, not sure who she was protecting.

Chas was still kicking and struggling.

"Take the tape off his mouth," Anne screamed.

One of the men in the car started to remove the tape, slowly.

Chas gave him a kick, and the tape was ripped off.

Chas yelled.

"You hurt him! Stop that!" Anne yelled.

"Mom!" Chas called, in a voice filled with entreaty, tears pouring down his cheeks. "Dad!"

"Wait!" called Anne.

"Wait!" called John, now at the car and banging on its roof.

"It's all right," said Mrs. Inninger. "You can come visit him tomorrow."

The car zipped away, with Chas yelling "Mom! Mom! Dad!"

Dianna started to cry and fell to her knees on the sidewalk.

"Oh, my God," said Anne, sinking into her husband's arms. "He's worse than ever."

"He is not like that when we see him," said John. "Do they drug him?"

"We have to find another place," Anne said vehemently.

"He wanted to be here," said Dianna. She screamed at her parents. "What are you doing to him?"

"No, no," said Anne. "He gets violent spells. We can't have him here."

"We have to go," said John. "We have guests."

"Are you crazy? I can't go back there," cried Anne.

"We cannot do anything now," said John. "We will see him tomorrow. Today, we cannot betray him."

"We are going to do something," said Anne. "We have to find another place for him."

"Yes," said John. He took her in his arms and held her tightly. "We shall find another place. We shall get him well."

"Please," said Anne softly. "Please."

"We have to get back," said John.

"Dammit," said Anne. "I'm a sight. You go first."

"We go together," said John.

"She'll be right down," said Dianna. She pulled Anne upstairs into her sitting room and helped her comb and spray her hair, trying to suppress her own tears. Lynne came, saying nothing, but mending Dianna's gown that had ripped when she'd fallen to her knees.

"He wouldn't be like this," Anne muttered, "if I hadn't done all that drinking and those pills. If I hadn't been so afraid. It's my fault, poor Chas."

"No, Mom."

"I tried, dammit. I had to save my family. I kept you safe. And your father is all dreams and acting. It's his religion. He is beyond politics. I had to fight. I *had* to fight. Do you understand? They would destroy him, all of us, just to win."

"It's going to be all right."

"They say mental illness is punishment for some awful sin."

"Mom, no."

"It was a terrible time. This is turning into a terrible country. Have to be careful. Can't fight."

"What are you talking about?"

"Your friend Bill. He wants to fight it, but it's so big, Dianna. It's too big. He doesn't know. We created a monster. It's better to hate people here, and they'll tell us who to hate, make up enemies out of thin air —"

"Bill's strong," said Dianna.

"It's too big. We were born to be creative people." Anne spoke the last sentence with the sudden, practical Anne Foster delivery and looked at herself in the mirror. "I wish Kath had come, but she wouldn't come near this dance. Shit, I could do *Long Day's Journey* now, easy."

When they went back to the party, arm in arm, Dianna and Anne looked splendid and earned a ballroom full of applause.

Anne joined John, the Nivens, and the Stevenses. Dianna crossed the yard. Was Bill still there? There was the fountain, and above it, clouds rushing past the moon. Chas, fleeing from her sight.

"Is everything all right?"

She didn't turn around. She could feel him beside her. She felt his jacket covering her shoulders and took a deep breath. If only some place could be safe. Somewhere. Uncanny how her thoughts turned to the *West Side Story* song. Silly.

"What's wrong?"

Brother Luke, Mike, Hal, whoever he was.

"Everyone goes. They come, they go. You too," she said. "Everyone. Everything."

"Bad stuff?"

"Bad stuff."

He wrapped his arm around her. Oh, Dr. Jekyll. She could easily run away with him this very night. All he had to do was ask. But perhaps she should run from him.

"What did my father say to you?" she asked, almost without emotion.

"It was hard to hear. He said, I understand how you feel. I'd feel the same way. If you can accept my hospitality, you are welcome to it."

"That's Daddy." She hid her head in her hands.

He leaned against the fountain, still holding onto her.

"I still think his letter was my father's last straw. Maybe he does, too. I don't know. It's hard to let go of the anger, and he accepted that. Damn fool."

"You don't want me around. You don't fool me."

"I thought you didn't want me around."

"I didn't."

"I fool me. I went to New York on location for *Tiffany's*. Playing Paul with the great Audrey Hepburn's Holly Golightly. Know what I realized? Holly is me. I've been playing jazzy games and running from this thing that I can't shake. That my father shouldn't have died. Women don't understand me. They want me to be hearts and flowers and don't want to know anything else. You want to know. You're the one I can talk to about it, you kid."

"I don't know what to say."

"I went to Disneyland to see you."

The Magic Kingdom. A dream is a wish your heart makes.

"Why?"

"I am trying to figure you out. What a place. I felt the normalcy that I always longed for as a kid. And there you are, smack in the middle of those feelings."

Normal? Her dead grandmother wasn't dead, her older brother was reciting Hamlet backwards in New York, her younger brother was half crazy, and people around the world envied them.

Dianna spoke slowly, afraid to give away too much. "You're a great actor, you're smart and funny, you're nice, usually, you're nice to look at, and I feel safe around you, except when I don't. There's a lot I don't understand. It does seem as if the whole world is falling apart. I feel as if nothing and no one will be around tomorrow. Who needs the bomb? We have us."

"Friends, at least?"

"Just don't throw me away again. Then it's over."

"I'm not entirely forgiving of your father. His letter was the last straw for Dad. My father stood up for what he believed. So many men and women had courage. The cowards betrayed them, named names, refused to see them. I don't know if I could. I wanted to live up to him. That meant showing up John Fletcher."

"Maybe," she said, "we should talk about something else." It was getting a little too heavy for her, and she needed to lean on him tonight. Of all the people in the world, she felt safe with him. Even when he was mad. Still, she had to say, "Just remember. You push me away again, and it's over."

"I don't want to."

He was so docile, it was unreal. What had happened with her father? "Are you here for a while?"

"We're shooting at Paramount now. We may go back to New York later for a few days."

"How is Audrey?"

"She is one lousy actress. A lovely person, so you barely notice. The charming thing is that she knows it. Every girl who watches it will want to be a call girl. She's insecure, so everyone works to make her feel secure and everyone ignores me. How are you doing?"

"No one ignores me." Talking about work helped. "Mr. Robbins is mean and brilliant. Mr. Wise is lovely and patient. It's a very different set from what I'm used to. A lot of wrangling and discussion over just about every shot."

"You're still trembling. Why?"

"I can't tell you. Just don't let go."

He didn't. Instead, he kissed her. Not hard, but it felt good. She could sink in his arms and forget everything. Sink into Bill.

"Let's dance," he said.

First, they both gulped champagne and waited until the orchestra started a new dance, a waltz. She could blur everything out and just sail away in his arms. He dropped one arm, put his hand behind his back, and slid his other arm to the small of her back, guiding her round and round.

"What are you doing?"

"I was a dress extra, remember?" he said, calmly. "I had to learn this stuff. Now let go."

If only. "Of what?"

"Of me. Let go. It's okay."

She flung her arms out and for just a fraction of a second, he pulled his supporting arm away, and she felt both free and falling. Then he slid his other hand behind her back, catching her.

"I'll never let you fall," he said, as people around them applauded.

Was he really this serious about her? Could she deal with that?

"Where's Bruce?" Bill asked as the waltz ended.

"I bet he's holding a film symposium," said Dianna.

He was doing just that in one of the small parlors, engaged in an earnest discussion with Ernest Lehman about *West Side Story* and how the movie had to differ from the play.

Dianna said, "I can't stand it. Let's go out again."

"Can we go on dates?" Bill asked, once they were back at the fountain. "Just dates. I pick you up, I bring you home. Be sixteen, like you said."

Did Bill "just date" anyone?

"When? We're both so damn busy. As soon as I finish *West Side Story*, I have *Cinderella*. Then I have this teenage angst movie. MaryAnn got it for me. But by the time I can find a minute to go out with you or anyone, I'll be ninety."

"You have to relax sometime. We can meet for dinner. The Velvet Room, that new place. All the room draped in different colors."

"Can it ever again be normal."

She should have said goodbye to him long ago, and now it seemed too late, and she didn't want to.

When she came down the next day, the house was sparkling clean, and her parents were in the den phoning down new places for Chas. Dianna went to the gym, which showed no evidence of a ball. She rehearsed with the mirror. She sang with the playback recording. And danced. Whatever she was doing, she'd better be more than just good. She had to be great. Her name led the cast.

It felt good to concentrate. Yet, as she danced, she could feel his arms around her and then, for a mere second, the freedom of flight knowing she would not be alone.

But it could be an illusion. She could fall. They all could. Just one more thing, and what supported them would fall away.

43

After Bob Wise and Jerry Robbins watched her dance to "I Feel Pretty," they went off to a corner to "discuss." Dianna sank into her chair to catch her breath.

It didn't look good. Their discussion looked intense, and Robbins raised his voice more than once.

She said to Fapp, the cinematographer, "You can please one of the directors some of the time, but you can't please all of them all of the time."

"It's rough on you, isn't it," said Fapp.

"Oh, no, I thrive," she said, pretending to faint.

"You're doing fine," he said.

Fine. Great.

Russ arrived to do his part of the scene, and they performed the song "One Hand, One Heart" in the midst of a battle between Jerry and Bob who were, Rusty muttered, obviously not ready to get married yet.

Rusty gave Tony a toughness and an awkwardness believable for an ex-gang member now in love. He fought that interpretation out with Wise, who favored a more traditional musical leading man, feeling that people wouldn't like a tough romantic lead. Everybody fought about it, and Russ always landed in the middle.

"He thinks it's *Oklahoma*," he complained to Dianna. To break up the tension, when Wise called, "Action," they sang "People Will Say We're in Love," and Robbins, getting the joke, yelled, "Keep it in!" Wise just smiled and called for another take.

Much as Dianna loved Jerry Robbins, and believed in his concept of the musical, it became obvious that he could not adjust to the realities of working with film that demanded so much collaboration. She had a dreadful feeling that all her sweat was going down the drain. The movie would disappear quickly, a disappointment and a terrible shame given Jerry's creation and gutsy approach. And although everyone seemed happy with her performance, she chafed that she was coming across as a sweet young thing when she wanted to match Rita Moreno's brilliant fire.

She was able to escape on Saturday.

"You're going with Bill?" Anne was astonished.

"We are in Act Two," said John. "It is not so simple as that, but he is no longer accusing me of murder."

"How nice. Dianna, he's too old," said Anne. "And his reputation. Be friends."

"We're just going to dinner."

"What's on the menu?"

"We're going to talk, Mom, okay?"

"He hates your father."

"No," said John. "But he had reason to. My letter was the last thing Ed saw."

"God, you two! Stop being so goddamn kind and seeing other people's points of view. Stop being such a damn nice guy, John."

"Bill is Ed's son. How would you feel?"

"I'd want to know the truth. So why not tell him the truth?"

"What truth?" asked Dianna.

"That Bill loves his father," said John.

"Oh, you," said Anne.

"Daddy, if you knew he was blacklisted, if you knew the part was so important to him, why didn't you tell Mr. Greene in person?"

"Oh, good God," Anne muttered.

"What?"

"I was out of town," said John, turning away. He reached for a book on a table and sat down with it.

Anne stalked out of the room.

Dianna didn't believe her father, but she couldn't say he was a liar. Instead, she muttered, "You always are."

Her parents knew something else about Ed Greene, but they weren't going to say it. Perhaps her father had wanted the movie all to himself. There was more to the story, and they weren't going to tell her.

Anne returned to ask, "Are you sleeping with him?"

"No, Mom. I like him. We are just going to dinner."

"I don't like this."

"I do not think we can stop it," said John, coming back to the conversation. "She is your daughter."

"I am in Hell," said Anne. "Do whatever the fuck you like."

"Mom, it's just dinner."

Being back in Bill's car was like going home, the home that used to be. She relaxed, watching him steer, enjoying his hands. Her first cocktail dress, deep blue satin, pleased her too, not that she could drink cocktails.

Bill had ordered a table outside on the terrace by the pool, away from the gossip columnists who frequented this and other popular places. They were there, perhaps tipped off by the restaurant as to who had made reservations — Mike Connolly and Sheilah Graham, and later on, Hedda Hopper toddled in. No one missed Bill and Dianna walking through to their table. Indeed, someone had leaked they had a reservation to the press.

Bill handed the maître d' a fifty dollar bill.

"No reporters," he said, amiably. "Or that's all you get tonight."

"You've been here before," said Dianna, as she settled in her chair.

"I never spent that much money before ordering. You really are an expensive date."

They danced to Lester Lanin's band. Bill's hands were firm, his arms held her tightly, his shoulder was strong, and he could dance like no one else. In movie terminology, this was a Happy Interlude, and she was going to enjoy it. People stared at them, a few men tried in vain to cut in, but after a few moments, they didn't exist.

They talked about acting — not the business, not gossip, but acting. Bill talked about the difficulties of playing what was essentially a passive role on *Tiffany's*. "How do you make that interesting?" How did he solve it? By finding some layer in the man who resisted his own placid nature, "a little god of war buried in me. Playing against what you're given can be good. Like your Anne Frank." Dianna confessed to the same struggle with sweet Maria who had to suddenly come up and be strong. "It seems so sudden, but I've been trying to show it in increments. Hard, isn't it, when you get two minutes to shine before they yell cut. I make good script notes. And Jerry's over here and Bob is over there."

"How do you find the character?"

"I just think the character comes and fills me up and I feel the way she does."

"You have got to be kidding."

"It's not the Method. You do that, right? Hole up in your dressing room thinking of all the things in your life feeding those emotions. It's not about you. It's about the character. They are completely different people from me."

"It's not me at all. But sure, I get there through my life. It's all I have to work with. Not always pretty."

She replied with some ruefulness. "I've had a pretty life, pretty much. But I can imagine. Daddy says that imagination is the gift of the gods."

She was afraid that her technique, not that she had one, would not be enough for the parts she wanted, and although she resisted a "method," she listened when Bill talked about his work.

She told him about some of the difficulties on the set, although *West Side Story*'s difficulties were now being reported in the press. Some in the production had gone to reporters to protect their reputations in case the movie flopped.

Bill gave her a wry smile when he said, "Jerry Robbins named names, you know? Saved his career."

"You think that's cowardly."

"Yes."

"But he's brilliant. There wouldn't be *West Side Story* if they'd put him in jail or exiled him from his work."

"No, there wouldn't." He changed the subject but they still talked about movies and plans and danced again.

Eventually, they talked about actors, mostly disagreeing. Dianna said, "Everyone thinks Henry Fonda is a great actor, but he has the same rhythm, the same voice for every character. I just don't see it. Daddy is a different person with a different voice each time. And he's won some Oscars."

Mel Ferrer and Audrey Hepburn walked through the restaurant. Dianna could feel the ripples of excitement before the couple reached their table. Bill leaped to his feet. Dianna reached out a hand to Hepburn, who shook it and said, "We have never met, but I just had to say you were so marvelous. I am so glad you won the Oscar playing Anne Frank."

Ferrer kissed Dianna. Bill said, "Hi, Holly," and kissed Audrey.

"Hi, Fred," said Hepburn, and then, slyly, "What a sweet couple you make."

Bill just smiled.

"Great lady," he said to Dianna, when he sat down. "He doesn't deserve her."

He slipped some champagne into her water glass, and they toasted each other. He kissed her hand, holding it in both his. (That was the picture that appeared the *The Los Angeles Times* and then in newspapers across the nation, generating wild discussion. Dianna's fan clubs held emergency meetings with heated discussions, and her fan mail grew heavier. Not that she read any of it.)

In the parking lot, as stars glittered over them and they looked over the glittering cities, they kissed unnoticed, holding onto each other because they had to. Dianna loved the feeling of his body against hers, and she didn't want him to let go, but he did, too soon. He peered outside perhaps in case a policeman wondered what he was doing with a sixteen-year-old, but the Velvet Room had probably taken care of that sort of thing in advance.

What were they doing? Dianna didn't know, but she wanted to keep doing it with him, even knowing she was probably heading for disaster. But weren't they all, so why the hell not?

44

On Monday, Dianna arrived on the set in a white dress and a better frame of mind, ready to meet Tony. Two adjoining soundstages had been joined together to represent the gym.

Rita, in tears, grabbed her.

"They fired Jerry."

Not one dancer was stretching or working out. They were sitting glumly or talking angrily.

The disaster had arrived, and she was in the thick of it.

Larry hurried over to her.

"The Mirisches did it. Jerry took so long in New York, and they're weeks behind, and they both can't agree on this thing. Bob has the film record, and he's a producer. We're gonna lose our grit and be just this pretty musical. Bob has no idea what Jerry's about. Why do they think we all wanted to work on this picture?"

Bob stood in a corner with Fapp and what seemed like a dozen assistant directors, all talking among themselves. For their part, the dancers were all arguing. Dianna could sense the threats and the "we'll quit or else" talk. Not that she blamed them. She was ready to pack it all in as well. Without Jerry, how would this movie have any bite?

She was the star of the picture and had to be responsible. She couldn't let it fall apart or she'd never work again. She went over to Bob.

"When are we going to start work?"

Bob smiled at her tightly. "I'll give them some time. It's been a shock. I understand."

"If Jerry's gone because he slowed things down, shouldn't we get to work?"

She grabbed the megaphone and called everyone into position. No one moved. Dianna walked to her place in the gym, grabbing George Chakiris' hand.

"We have a movie to do!" she called.

Everyone followed, although reluctantly. It was a tough scene. They had to be loose and joyful when they were completely the opposite. But they were all professionals and knew they had to work. Jerry's assistants started giving directions to the dancers.

"We have to finish it for Jerry," Dianna muttered to Larry, who spread the word around.

"Is Rusty ready?" Bob called.

Rusty was, although he looked angry and not quite like a boy about to fall in love.

But they were actors. Disciplined as they were, they could leap into other worlds in a moment. The lights shone on them, and their eyes met, and they were in love. She walked toward Tony with great joy to begin the most tragic hours of Maria's life. She walked on a tightrope wire that felt more secure than the danger around it.

The production moved on, and *West Side Story* stayed alive.

The story of Robbins' firing zoomed around Hollywood, and the "picture in trouble" gossip grew more intense. Dianna knew she would be included in any blaming. Already some reporters repeated the "she can be difficult" story that started with *Diary*. This meant she could not dare lose her temper over anything on the set. Robert Wise vehemently denied that, but who would believe him?

John helped with a comment to the *Reporter*, "Two directors. Whose idea was that?" Dianna wished he wouldn't defend her.

The press was also after her about the date with Bill, and George's office, used to handling publicity, put out the "just friends" story. It didn't play well. Connolly and Graham ran critical pieces on Bill and his women.

"The guy's a wolf," wrote Connolly, "and now he wants to bite into the sweetest fruit Hollywood has to offer."

On their next date, at the advice of Bill's agent, Dianna and Bill doubled up with the Coburns to go see *The Magnificent Seven*. It was also Bill's birthday celebration. Coburn handed Bill a set of vampire teeth. "For biting into sweet fruit."

The movie was rather a letdown. The film hadn't had an opening, it was simply released everywhere, rather than slowly to a few city theaters for roadshow engagements, which was how the major pictures were released — building up word of mouth and anticipation. Obviously, then, the studio didn't have much faith in *The Magnificent Seven*. It would be another B western.

Elmer Bernstein's music was a rouser, but Dianna found the story odd and something of an excuse to let boys play shoot the bad guys. Eli Wallach chewed up the scenery, and Bill had great scenes, and when he got killed, she shrieked.

"You should have lived after all that."

"You didn't mind when I died," Coburn whispered.

"Who would?" Bill whispered back.

She made some peace with the movie when Brynner said to McQueen, "The farmers won." It seemed to be a lot of work and blood spilled just to get that line, though.

Reporters found them out and were waiting outside the theater with their photographer pals. Dianna smiled and waved. Bill muttered obscenities.

They ended up at the Brown Derby, hiding among other celebrities.

"This wasn't a good idea, was it," said Bill as he pulled up to Dianna's house after leading some reporters on a mad chase through Los Angeles.

"They'll find something else," said Dianna. "We're not doing anything wrong. You're getting to be a star, and they'd be following you anyway."

She handed him his present, bright ruby cufflinks. He thanked her, but something was off.

"I'll be going to Dublin to make that picture Burton turned down," he said. "I'll be leaving in early December."

That meant he wouldn't be around for Christmas. She had thought she might stay in town to be with him even though the family would be in New York. Broadway's *A Doll's House* starring John Fletcher and Anne Foster would not close their theater for the holidays.

And that meant that he'd have four starring parts in a row. He wanted to ram his career down everyone's throat! Plus, he was still helping Kennedy, who called at odd times to review speech patterns.

But now, Bill pulled her over for a good, long kiss.

"I'm sorry I'm so gloomy," he said, caressing her with the hands she loved. She could almost forgive him for abandoning her.

"I'm sorry the reporters are bothering you," she said, smoothing her fingers across his face.

At her door, she waved him off and went into the house. She longed for his hands to keep touching her.

Her parents were leaving for New York. Goodbye, everyone.

To her queries about Chas, Anne said, "No visitors. His new doctor says he will be out by Christmas and will be fine."

"He'll think we abandoned him!"

John shook his head. She mustn't upset her mother.

"You'll fly to New York for Christmas," was the unhappy answer. "We'll all be together."

"Chas, too?"

"We hope so," said John.

Dianna had not said anything about Nana being alive. If she was. She had not received any response to her letter, and so she sent another one, this time saying that Chas was not well.

She moved back to Malibu. She worked on Maria, all day, all night. She didn't see Bill. He was busy, too, and he didn't call.

On Election Day, the cast was still in the gymnasium set, where there was very little for her to do. Although the lengthy discussions between Robbins and Wise had ended, the set still seemed grim and tense. She worked hard, finding some strong places even though the script painted Maria as sweet and sappy. To her surprise, Bob Wise liked what she was doing.

Bill finally called that night just as she finished supper. "Come on over. We'll watch the returns. There are some people here already."

She hurried over and found his fireplace roaring, the television on, and a lot of people she didn't know. And why was Sandi here? The law student and fashion model, looking quite unglamorous in jeans and a sweat shirt, certainly saw her come in but didn't bother saying hello. She did seem busy and used the phone a lot.

Bill was not shy about his feelings toward Dianna. He indicated the place next to him on the sofa, and he put his arm around her. Was he trying to hurt Sandi?

Well, Sandi had tried to hurt her.

Huntley and Brinkley were reporting election results based on a computer's projections, which swayed back and forth between Kennedy and Nixon. Dianna, so distant from the whole campaign, living as she did in dark studio caverns, began to be caught up as if it were an exciting game, but even the future of the nation couldn't sustain her interest. She dozed off and woke up with Bill's arm still firmly around her shoulders and Kennedy ahead in electoral votes and two million ahead in the popular vote. The computer's projections looked good for Kennedy.

Sandi had left.

Dianna fell asleep again, and when she woke up, people on television were singing, "We want Nixon," and Nixon and his wife were standing on a platform.

"Oh, God," said Dianna, amidst the cheers, wiping her eyes. "Did he win?"

"It's been damn close," said Bill. Wasn't his arm tired?

"If the trend continues," Nixon was saying, "Senator Kennedy will be the next president of the United States."

"Is he conceding?" someone shouted. Over at the Ambassador, people were chanting.

"We want Nixon! We want Nixon!"

Nixon continued. "And I want to say that one of the great features of America is that we have political contests, that they are very hard fought... and once the decision is made, we unite behind the man who is elected. I want all of you to know, and Senator Kennedy to know, that certainly if this trend does continue and he does become our next president that he will have my wholehearted support ....I'm now going to bed and I hope you do, too."

Huntley and Brinkley couldn't decide if Nixon had just delivered a concession speech.

Kennedy, they said, was leading by one million votes.

"It's the electoral votes that matter," said Bill.

"Why is that?" she asked. "Why not the man with the most votes?"

"Because we're the *united states*," he said. "Each state is a vote, so to speak, with electors based on population. Otherwise, a lot of densely populated states could swing the election by themselves. So it's the most electoral votes by state."

"But then fewer people can elect the president. Aren't we one country?"

Bill grinned at her. "It's only a good idea if the guy you like wins both."

Hours went by.

The popular vote grew agonizingly close enough to be a tie, 50.0 versus 49.1.

She'd been up all night except for her naps, and she hated to leave, but she had to shower and go to work. As soon as she got to the studio, she learned that Nixon had conceded for real. Kennedy's electoral college win had not been so close.

She so much wanted to talk to Bill, to see how he felt, to be happy for the victory he had helped win in California. And he was happy, but once again, it was stop and start: in a few days, he was heading to Hyannis Port to further coach the new President-Elect.

At least, the gym scene was finally coming to an end, but a big one was coming up right behind it. This was when Maria, departing from Juliet, decided *not* to take her life.

She worked privately in one of the rehearsal studios, trying to feel what Maria felt. She felt empty.

As she walked slowly back to the soundstage, a page raced up on his bike.

"Phone call for you. Urgent! In the office."

Something must have happened to her parents. Or Aunt Dot had suffered a relapse.

Neither.

It was the nurse at Chas's "home."

"Your brother has run away. Do you know where he could be?"

"The Manse," said Dianna, quickly. "He'd get there somehow. I've got to get home," she said to the secretary. "It's an emergency. I'm sorry."

She called the Malibu house. Thank God, Lynne answered.

"I need Reggie," Dianna said. "I need him to meet me at the Manse."

The guard called a cab for her, and she soon arrived at the front door.

"Wait here. Keep the meter going. Someone will pay you," she said, as she took out the key. The door was open. Did Chas still have his key? That he might have kept it moved her, tears filling her eyes.

Inside, the house was dark, with the dim light from closed off windows casting nerve wracking shadows. She pressed on a light. Nothing happened. The electricity had been shut off.

"Chas? Are you here?"

The higher she climbed, the darker the house grew. She kept calling out his name as she went up. There was no answer. There was nothing except her memory of Chas sliding down the bannister and shouting, "Whee!" The memory scared her for some reason. He wouldn't hurt her, would he?

"Chas? Please be here!"

Why hadn't she looked for his "school"? Found out where he was? Demanded to know where her parents had put him? She hadn't made time.

Thoughts of him with the knife. Coming at her. That was her excuse.

Could he be up there, waiting for her?

She heard a car pulling up, stopping. Reggie. Thank goodness.

"Chas?"

His door was closed. Her door wasn't. Had he gone in there? Her heart was pounding, her body too tense. This was silly. She stopped at her threshold.

"Chas?"

No answer.

She backed away, went to his door, tapped on it lightly.

"Chas?"

She opened the door. There was more light here, softening the pictures of the United States and those sports heroes.

"Chas?"

"Dianna?" called Reggie.

"Up here!"

She could see, dimly, the colors of the different states in the map and the glimmering frames of sports pictures and pictures of Chas as Pigskin Pete.

"Chas! Come on! Stop playing!"

Still no answer.

"Chas?"

She pushed open the bathroom door.

Light came through the large window looking out over their magnificent yard, where they had played softball and knight and relay races.

She heard running steps.

"Dianna?" called Reggie. He was in the doorway, shining a flashlight.

The beam rested on Chas, in a bath of blood and water, his eyes open, tears on his cheeks.

Reggie yelled. She never remembered if she did, but she remembered reaching into the bath, holding him in her arms, and leaning her head against his heart.

45

Chas (Pigskin Pete) Fletcher Dead in Bicycle Accident
Young Fletcher Killed Instantly
Fall Witnessed by His Sister, Dianna Fletcher

Little Pigskin Pete had been loved all throughout the United States, Europe, the entire western hemisphere, and the entire free world. His fan clubs held candlelit ceremonies. Condolence telegrams flooded the Disney Studios.

Sheilah Graham reported that John and Anne were looking after Dianna, who could not get over the sight of her brother hurtling over his handlebars and his head cracking down on a rock. Their scenes from *Pollyanna* and his as Pigskin Pete ran endlessly on news programs as were clips showing the Fletcher kids at the opening of Disneyland, waving to crowds as they flew to Switzerland for Christmas, playing baseball outside the Fletcher Manse, riding on Walt Disney's train, and running relay races on the Disney lot between takes.

Disney took a full day to make a statement and even then he could barely speak. "He was the epitome of every American boy's dream. We all want to be like Pigskin Pete, but only one boy was. That was Chas Fletcher."

Friends packed the Church of the Good Shepherd while massive crowds waited outside. Anne, in black, wore a veil. Dianna, also in black, carried white flowers, which she had laid on the closed casket during the service. Nick followed his parents and sister. He alone acknowledged the assembled crowd with a nod.

As the casket was lifted into the hearse, Anne clung to it. At Forest Lawn, near the Alice Marrs plaque, she stood ramrod straight while prayers were said. George and his wife Gladys, rarely seen together, stood behind them. Dianna knelt by the coffin and placed more colorful flowers to mix with the white. Nick helped her up, and she clung to him in a way that brought a wave of emotion onto the quiet crowd. As the Fletchers walked away, a ray of sunshine burst from behind the clouds and struck the casket, as if God were blessing the boy and taking him up to heaven.

The famous slipped away in cars, following the Fletchers to their home for a private memorial, where the large double parlors in the Manse were filled with flowers, two bouquets from the Vatican, and pictures of Chas from his various movies and television shows.

Always the sweet smile and the wide eyes.

Seats were set up for fifty people, but John kept inviting more, and a hundred folding chairs had to be crammed into the parlors. Even more people came than there were seats so they stood around the room. Richard and Pat Nixon walked in slowly, and two empty seats materialized.

"I want to say something," Nick said to George.

"All right," said George, and he looked at Dianna.

"No," she said. "I can't."

"For Chas," said Nick. "Stand with me. All this grief is sick."

Fine. She'd been following orders for days. When she thought about Bill, she was mad. He was with Kennedy. He should be here.

The director of *Pigskin Pete* movies spoke with some humor about Chas. Jimmy Stewart barely made it through the traditional complaint, a myth so often repeated over the years that it had taken on the mask of truth, about the Fletcher kids hitting baseballs through his kitchen window. Lucille Ball tearfully described Chas running down the street pretending to be chasing bad guys. Walt Disney spoke in a broken, choked voice of his affection for Pete, and he read a few telegrams from fans from other countries, in their languages.

Dianna stood beside Nick while he told stories about dealing with his little brother, and about the day Chas came home, bloodied and dirtied, after fighting with some boys because they had been taunting then eight-year-old Dianna that she still believed in Santa Claus.

Dianna felt she had to speak.

"My brother would not like us crying," she said in a monotone. "He was the darling of the whole world — " She stopped and looked at them. How dare they sit there and listen to lies?

"I won't!" she cried, and she ran from the room.

Nick started to follow her, but Anne held onto him. If only to cry out loud.

Dianna ran up into her suite and threw herself onto her bed, beneath her grandmother's picture, unable to control her sobs.

Chas had killed himself perhaps over the very lies they were telling, as if nothing had been wrong with him when he had been trying to tell them all along that something was terribly and terrifyingly wrong. The worst was that they had shut him out.

She was crying so loudly that she did not hear the door open. She did feel the hand smoothing her hair, and she turned round, and it was indeed Bill, and he was saying, softly, "I'm so sorry, I'm so sorry." He wrapped his arms around her, pulling her to him. "I'm so sorry, Dianna, that you had to see him die."

She pushed away, looking at him with horror.

"But it's not true," she said. "That story they tell. It's all a lie."

She paced the room.

"It's all a lie. To make THEM feel good," and she pointed at the window. "All of THEM. It's a lie. He didn't fall off his bike. There aren't any rocks on those trails, unless they put one there to prop up their story."

She circled the room.

"But I did see. I did see."

"What did you see?"

"He got out of the home he was in that was awful and put into another home. That was the night of the ball. The press calls it a private school. They didn't even ask the name, just wrote down what they were told. Private school. You saw what he was like."

"He got out again."

"They called me at the studio. I knew he'd come back to this house. My little brother." Her voice broke. "I should have taken care of him."

"Tell me."

She told him about coming into the house and finding him. "He couldn't have been gone for long. He had tears in his eyes, down his cheeks. He'd been crying. He was so alone. He was my little brother! Oh, God, he was so alone and no one understood anything that he was going through, and now he's gone, and I couldn't help him. Not that I knew how."

Bill reached for her, held her.

"It wasn't you. No one knows why."

He knew that. Now he was saying it to her. No one knows why. John Fletcher, Ed Greene, Nana, the House Un-American Committee, the despair, the American people. Who is to blame? Who knows?

"Stupid television," she said. "If it hadn't driven out movies from the studios, my parents would be home more."

"Life. We all have to put up with it."

"That's a stupid thing to say!"

"Yeah."

That brought a wisp of a smile from her.

"I'm glad you're here."

"I'm always going to be here."

She rattled on. "Chas was loved all over the world, but could that help him? We got a wire from Khrushchev and Eisenhower. Nixon's here! We could solve the cold war right now if we had our heads on straight. Pigskin Pete brings world peace. Mom drank a lot when she was carrying Chas and took pills when Nana was having that trouble. She blames herself for that and that she wasn't here and that she trusted those people at that home. They all said he was getting better. Oh, poor Chas, so alone! He scared me. He came at me with a knife. Nobody could reach him. Nobody."

"What about before?" Bill asked, stroking her fingers.

"Before?" It was as if a time before hadn't existed, but now she remembered. "Yeah, he was cute. He was a lot like Pigskin Pete except I was a better pitcher."

"Tell them that. Talk about him like a sister talks about her little brother. You started to. Keep going. You'll wish you had later for his sake. I always wished I could have done that for my father. He was more than a suicide. He was a force of energy, and I denied him that. Even though no one was there to listen."

"It hurts."

"I know."

"I guess you do."

"There wasn't all that much press coverage when Dad died. I was spared the telegrams from world leaders. Did Jack send one?"

"Mrs. Kennedy did. All right. I will try again."

"I'm going downstairs. Can I trust you to come without me?"

"No." She went into the bathroom and washed her face. She combed her hair.

"I'm going to wear white."

She stepped into her closet and came out a few minutes later in white lace over satin. She pinned a black bow in her hair.

No one was near the stairs as they came down.

One of the *Pigskin* writers was speaking. When he was through, Dianna went to the podium.

"I'm sorry I ran off," she said, and then she spoke about Chas, her little brother, annoying, funny, a practical joker, a ham beyond hams, cartwheeling around the house, planting frogs in the vases, putting worms in the refrigerator in the same wrapping as the hamburger meat.

Walt Disney's face was awash, but he smiled at her and when she was done, her voice breaking finally, he was the first to stand up to reach out to her. His sobs drenched her Plunkett bow.

A veiled woman in black walked into the room and stood over Richard Nixon's chair. The Vice President turned round, and said, "Please," and the woman sat next to Pat Nixon. The Vice President stood stoically in the back of the room, hunching his back up straight as if he were proud to be there.

As they left, the guests held on to Anne, embraced John, and gripped Dianna tightly.

Nixon said to Anne, "Pat and I are deeply sorry. Let us know if there is anything we can do."

John shook Nixon's hand, and the soon to be former Vice President walked slowly toward the door, past the veiled woman, who said, softly, "Mr. Nixon." Nixon looked at her, then looked down at his feet and moved on. But he turned and looked back at the room before his wife tapped his arm gently and they left.

Bob Wise wrapped his arms around Dianna.

"Take the time you need," he said. "Don't worry."

The close friends stayed behind. The Nivens, the Stewarts, the Fondas, the Douglases, Sinatra, the Masons, Burl Ives, the Kellys, Astaire, Eve Arden, Ginger Rogers, fragile Judy Garland, who had flown in from London, and Aunt Kathy, who'd come straight from Connecticut. Jane Fonda hugged Dianna and wouldn't let go for several minutes.

The woman in the veil had taken a seat in the corner and extended her arm to Dianna, who went over.

"May I help you?"

The woman raised her veil. "My dear Dianna."

There were lines in her face and in her hands, but Dianna recognized her and flung herself at the woman who gripped her.

"My dear Dianna," the woman murmured. "I just received your letter when I heard. My dear Dianna."

Anne cried out. Conversation stopped.

Alice Marrs stood up, held out her arms. Her daughter raced into them.

"Mama!" cried Anne. "Oh, how could you come, how could you!"

The guests were so startled and so embarrassed at being at what was an intimate moment that they did not understand, and they quickly found a way out. Except for Gene Kelly and Fred Astaire, who looked stunned. Katharine Hepburn stood for some moments looking at Alice Marrs before she left.

John, pale in his surprise, whispered, "Alice?"

"Hello, John."

John clutched his mother-in-law.

"Is that Nana?" Nick asked, incredulous.

"Yes," said Dianna.

"She's alive?"

"It's not a resurrection."

"Fuck this family," he fumed. "Fuck it and all its lies. Is Chas dead?"

"I saw him. You don't know what's going on."

"It's over. I'm done with them. They killed Chas."

She now understood the meaning of the phrase "to see red." It was exactly as if flames erupted in front of her eyes.

"They were a continent away."

"They killed him with having him do that stupid character."

"He was good at playing Pete. He loved it."

"But nothing else!"

"He played *Circus Boy*. He was in *Spin and Marty* and *The Last Hound Dog.*"

"They went to New York when they knew he was sick. They put him in a home here! Not even near them! Maybe they thought the press would follow them and find out."

"They did their best. Would you keep them from doing the work they love?"

"Why the hell are you defending them?"

"Maybe they made a mistake, but who knows what happened to Chas? He was sick! Who knows what it was?"

"They killed him. They'll kill you, too. You and your Disney princesses."

"You really are stupid. Go bury yourself in your ego at how right and perfect you are."

"It's all coming down on their heads. You wait."

"Hasn't it already?"

Why did she defend her parents? Because she had to. She couldn't bear to hurt them or lose them. Nick was a fool. He blamed them for everything.

She found Alice and Anne sitting side by side, their arms around each other.

She heard Astaire say, "We won't say a thing unless you do."

John said nothing in response. He kept looking at Anne and Alice.

Alice said, "Tell me about Chas," and Anne was ready.

"He did as he was told, every word, and he had the most angelic smile."

"Never did get rid of that baby fat," said John, but his voice sounded stiff.

Dianna went over to Bill who looked as stunned as anyone.

Anne said, "He had the sunniest disposition. Dianna threw her dolls around, and Nick banged his fist on the walls, but Chas, nothing, just a smile. Oh, why was he so sad? We were helping him. He had to know we loved him."

John said, "Alice, is it safe for you to be here?"

"I wanted to go up to Dick Nixon and say howdy," said Alice. "No, John. If they knew I was back, they'd charge me in a second before a new President took over. I've never been blacklisted, which is funny, but I can't put my name on anything. I wouldn't be here, except Dianna hunted me down, and I knew I had to come."

"What?" cried Anne.

"She wrote scripts for *Silver Sierra*," Dianna said, her voice hoarse. "Good ones."

"For you," said Alice.

"You knew about Nana?" cried Anne.

It was a relief to tell some truth. "I found out she wrote movies for one thing."

"How?" cried Anne.

Bill, his arm around Dianna, said, "From me. I'm studying the blacklist. I'd never heard of you, but I went with Dianna to Forest Lawn, where you are supposedly buried. I found a transcription of your testimony. And yours, too," he said to Anne. "All these secrets."

"We can't bury anything," said Anne, bitterly. "Only my baby."

"Studying the blacklist," said Alice. "Why in God's name?"

"His father was Ed Greene," said John.

Alice studied Bill for a few moments. "You look like your mother. I knew Eddie. He loved justice and wouldn't stop. Dianna, how did you figure it was me?"

"You used the name Frances Faulkner for your movies. I learned that from the transcript Bill had. I found scripts that were exactly like *Silver Sierra* scripts under her name. You were L.A. Franklin! Bill and I went to find you in Santa Barbara in September, but you were gone."

"You could have said something," said John.

"I didn't know if it really had been her. Besides, when would I have told you?"

"That's not fair," said Anne.

Alice said, "I moved around a lot, but I moved to California because I wanted to write for you, darling girl. Now I can't stay long. I wanted to see you all, and my poor Anne."

"Can't you stay the night?" asked Anne.

"If they find me, it's the crapper for sure," Alice joked.

"Not knowing where you are, not knowing!" Anne said. "It's been hell."

"Not knowing was hell," said John.

Anne shook her head. "I cannot deal with that now."

Dianna realized then that her mother had known Alice was alive and had probably helped her. And she also realized that her father had not known Alice was alive all this time.

"I'm going upstairs," she said. "Please be here in the morning, Nana."

"If I am here, so will the FBI be," said Nana.

"No one will tell."

"They have ways," said Alice. "A car is picking me up at ten o'clock tonight. On Roxbury, not here."

Dianna flung her arms around her grandmother. "Please don't go!"

"Of course, if I'm in jail, we can visit more."

"We need to talk," said Anne.

"Yes," said John.

"Mama," said Anne, "let's go upstairs."

"I don't have much time," said Alice.

Dianna hugged her grandmother. Her parents seemed frozen, as if neither could think of their next line.

Bill followed her into the hallway.

"Are you all right?"

"I have no idea."

"I'll stay, if you want."

He held her as she shook, but she said, "Come early tomorrow," before fleeing upstairs.

In her room, she broke down again. Chas, come back. We meant well. We love you. Come back. Nana's here. We'll fix you up. Come back.

She got down on her knees.

Please, God, where you are, please hold Chas in your arms. Please make him smile and stop his tears. Please tell him we will miss him forever but not to be unhappy. Please be there. Please be God. Please be real. Please hold Chas. Because I can't.

46

A lice Marrs found her granddaughter on her knees, her face pressed against the mattress. "I thought I'd better spend some time with you, my darling, brilliant girl," she said, settling on the bed. "I've seen all your movies and cried through even the funny ones. You are my kid. I took care of you until I walked into that hearing room. I sang to you and read you stories, just as I had done with your mother. And you found my testimony."

"Bill did. You were wonderful."

"And dramatic."

"Why did you make us think you died?"

"I wasn't going to go to prison. It would have killed me, and I knew that was where the whole thing was headed, even though settling the court cases took years. I just wanted to write. I thought they might put me in that camp they were starting. It felt so cloak and dagger! Who knew it would last so long? Anne helped me, and I pledged her to silence. The more who know, you know. Richard Nixon, that dear boy who could play the piano, he helped, too, oh yes. He never talked, either, and he had the most reason to. My life hung on his coattails, but for this, I trusted him. He always had a crush on me, and in some things, he's got a conscience. Your mother has been playing Republican ever since. I think she was afraid he might betray me if she didn't. She wouldn't do the old causes we used to do. It makes me sad, but she didn't want to call attention and hurt you. And she was grateful to Nixon. So am I. And what the hell."

"Are you a Communist?"

"That's a bad thing in your book, isn't it?"

"No," Dianna fumbled. "I mean, I understand that during the Depression, it made sense. But it's not about freedom, and the Communists want to destroy us."

"Dianna, are you free? I will tell you. I am a Marxist and a Socialist and a pacifist and a writer and a dancer. I believe in the United States Constitution, but capitalism without restrictions is a killer. Why can't the richest nation on earth help its people? Because the rich people are few, and *they* are the richest nation. And capitalism isn't in the Constitution. But I tell you, the Soviet Union has the government running everything. We have big business running everything. I believe that we should be helping each other and not fighting wars. In some people's books, all that is just as bad as being a Communist if not the same thing. People think, I've got mine, too bad about you. All that is fear and guilt, but who wants to hear that? No world on earth wants me."

"Is it wrong to be wealthy?"

"No. It's wrong to be so poor you can't live a decent life and give your children one."

"I never knew people could starve here. I went to a migrant camp, and I saw they can. I've seen pictures of a part of the country called Appalachia. How can you help if you're in hiding?"

"How can I help if I'm in jail?"

"It'll be better now."

"Who is this Bill to you?"

"He's brilliant." Dianna smiled at the sudden change of topic. "You should see him in your Brother Luke story. But he has dark times because of his father. Please, can't we find a way for you to stay? Mom is so broken up by Chas."

"The only thing that will help me is a presidential pardon," said Alice. "But I'd just get into trouble again."

"Can't Nixon get it for you?"

"I wouldn't chance it. He still wants to be president, so there is a chance he'd want to throw me in jail to prove he's still got his anti-Communist chops. I know that. He knows that. The poor man doesn't know how to be human, and he tries so hard. What a shame. He played the piano beautifully. Something killed his soul."

"I'll ask Senator Kennedy. He'll be president. He likes me."

"So I've heard. Pardon a Communist first thing? That won't happen, my dearest. I've been hiding out here and in Europe and Mexico. There are many of us, and we help each other. We get assignments from Dalton Trumbo."

"We?"

"Jim! I can still have a boyfriend. He writes crime dramas. He swears he will never set foot in this country again." She then released a torrent. "Anne and I both got subpoenas. We felt trapped. I saw nothing good coming out of Congress. They exploited fear to manipulate voters and grab power from the Democrats and undo everything done in the New Deal. The Hollywood Ten — I'm invisible even in that, they — we — were not out to take over the country or bring in Moscow. We were like any political party. We could never agree on anything! What depressed me was that the public did not fight back. It breaks my heart," and here she banged the mattress, "but the American people are stupid. They think the American dream is a house in the suburbs with a garage and a patio and a television. My God, have they forgotten it's the dream of the founders, that all are created equal? No, they are so afraid, so as long as they have theirs, who cares. The least problem will set them all against each other. What will wake them up, Dianna, is to lose all that stuff. If the middle class is happy, the government is secure. But if they lose their stuff, the government will fall." She laughed. "We won't bring about the revolution. Wall Street and the bankers will by grabbing everything."

"I don't think the people are stupid," said Dianna. "I'm sure they care."

Alice sighed and put her arm around Dianna, who got as close to her grandmother as she could. No matter what she was saying, she'd stay close.

"I'd had such optimism after the war," said Alice, "but then it fell apart. This country let the Communist enemy, Soviet Russia, rule us from afar because Russia's imagined reaction dictated everything. They surrendered our rights and let the enemy win. We love freedom! They shout that while they give it up."

"I don't think so," said Dianna.

"Darling, it's the way things are. People need to make money, so of course they want to make a lot of it. No, the public doesn't give a damn. They don't want to be poor, and who can blame them? Money is power. So you make a lot of it, Dianna. But the way things are now. Men making their own companies and making movies based on their own fantasies. It's dangerous. Sex will sell. And why? Because men will pick the movies and the women will go along. Sex and violence always sold, but they had to keep a lid on it. Please watch yourself. Don't let anyone use you, turn you into some unthinking object. I wrote Betsy as a young woman with many dimensions. You won't always have a character like that, and your parents won't always be able to protect you. Don't confuse stupidity or giving in with freedom. Oh, what am I saying? I do run on." She gave Dianna a squeeze and a kiss. "It's true. This wonderful idea from Russia was pulled apart by hate and worse in the Soviet Union. But Dianna, the warning signs of that hate are right here. So are you here, my darling, and many good people. I have got to go or the FBI will grab me and put me in one of those concentration camps they got ready for us. Stay well, get through the storms, put one foot in front of the other."

"Please find a way to come back!"

"I don't think I could live here again. I wish I could, for you. I wish I could be free. Someday. Goodbye, my darling."

It felt like a dream. Dianna fell into one and woke up hours later.

Bill was in the kitchen, finishing a second breakfast courtesy of a weeping Joanne.

"Okay?" he asked, as Manny put orange juice in front of her.

"I don't know what I'll do until tomorrow."

"Are you going to work?"

"Have to."

"I heard Bob Wise say over and over that they'd shoot around you."

"They can't shoot around me for the death scene. I'm the one who lives. You have to go, don't you?"

"I'm on location tomorrow, but the weather looks good, so I should be home by six. I have class later."

He took her hand, and they walked out to his car where he kissed her for a long time, but she didn't feel a thing, and that scared her.

She found her parents in the kitchen and sat down with them.

"You should have told us," said Anne.

"You didn't tell us anything."

"I'm sure you were surprised," said Anne.

"That you worked with Communists? And that my grandmother is alive?"

"She was my mother! The fewer who knew the better."

John exploded. "We are husband and wife! That is the commitment. Who helped you with this stunt?"

"Daddy!" Dianna, so used to her father being calm, felt the world ripping apart as he cried out his suppressed rage.

"I lost track of her," said Anne. "She stopped writing. I didn't know where she was. I don't know where she's gone."

"I want to know why you kept it a secret from me."

"I would think that it was obvious."

"Leave us," said John, dramatically, as if it were the end of the second act. Dianna ran out. She heard her father yell, "What sort of marriage is this?" and "Nixon? Was it Nixon? Have you sold your soul to that? Is that what happened to you? Making me think it was a joke?"

Dianna ran back into the hall. Anne was coming up the stairs.

"Don't bother. He's crazy."

"How dare you say that?" John shouted, but his voice broke. "You went to Nixon for help! I am your husband!"

Dianna pushed her mother into her bedroom and shut the door.

"She would have gone to prison," said Anne. "We saw the writing on the wall. No, I didn't tell your father. He was grief stricken when she died, and I felt like hell, but if John knew that Nixon helped — He so hates the man. He was not happy when he showed up at the service. But I could not say no. I had to carry this. I had to go to the devil to help my mother."

"You turned away from things you believed in."

"We all change our minds."

"That's not what happened!"

"All right! I had to. I had to protect you."

"You put us in movies so we would be this cute family."

"Would you have preferred a normal childhood? You were kicking to get started. It's in our blood. I couldn't tell you the truth. You can see that."

John appeared in the doorway.

"You should have told me."

"Give it up."

"It was a tremendous burden and you would not share it."

"You don't give half a cock about politics," said Anne, digging her nails into Dianna's chair.

"I care about my family. Alice was my family, too."

"It had to be this way."

"Daddy, don't," said Dianna.

He walked away.

"He carries a lot," said Anne. "Chas, Nick not wanting our help for anything, and this. This is why I wouldn't tell him. I need him. I need you, too. Am I going to lose you both? You're so strong, Dianna. You're like my mother."

Dianna caught up with her father the next morning as he was assembling papers on his desk.

"I'm supposed to protect her. And you," said John. "That's the deal."

"Daddy, it was her mother."

"And now, we have to work together." He took Dianna into his arms. "I am sorry, my darling, but remember, we both love you."

And then he wept on her shoulder. "She didn't have faith in me. She didn't have faith in me."

So did Anne weep. "I hid who I was. From you, from myself. I couldn't fool John. But they were after liberals. Commies in training, they said. They accosted our movies. Anything criticizing this country was treason. I wasn't going to go to jail. I wasn't going to let John go to jail. Or be blacklisted. I needed to protect you and Nick and Chas. And John. The public had to think of us as all-American. So we became the perfect family."

"You turned away from what you believed in. You didn't have to do that."

"I grew up. I saw reality. Dianna, all of me is chopped up in pieces. I pull 'em out for show, but I put them away and I can't put them together the way they should be. And for this, I get Oscars. I don't know who I am or what I think anymore. But it sure helped my acting. It is when I act that I feel most real."

"Aren't you real for me?"

But Anne didn't answer.

Her parents left for New York that night, two numb people not speaking to each other who somehow had to work together for the next six months. And on such a play. John muttered in her ear, "I could play Nora."

She was glad to see them gone, glad to get back to Malibu and the breath of the sea.

The news of Clark Gable's death hardly affected her numbness, although the entire town was talking about it, that and Monroe and Miller's impending divorce. A dark shroud hung over brilliant Hollywood.

It deserved it.

It was time to go back to work. Maria. Where was she? Dianna couldn't find her, even when she sent searchlights through her soul. Maria didn't want to face what was out there.

47

The cast and crew had piled stuffed animals and flowers into her dressing room. Bill sent roses. She felt numb going through makeup and putting on her red dress — Maria finally got to wear a red dress, to symbolize her womanhood after having spent the night with Tony.

All Dianna could think of was blood.

The set had been designed to look like the playground at night, elevated two feet off the floor so that the camera could pan up, with some bright lights casting eerie shadows that made her shiver.

Death in the darkness. Tears as the light shone on him.

Bob Wise took her hand as they walked through the scene. They had shot around her for the terrible finale, but now they had to fill in her part. They were running very late. She was the star. She was responsible.

Rusty gave her a kiss and a hug, then took his place at the far end of the shot as the camera, high up near the ceiling, focused on Dianna emerging from the shadows. The wardrobe mistress draped a shawl around her.

"Run," someone said.

She ran.

"Bang," someone said.

Rusty fell into her. Dianna sank with him to the floor of the playground.

She took Tony's hand as the camera moved in.

He said, "I didn't believe hard enough."

Her acting brain knew her line, but she took a long time to respond.

"Loving is enough," she said, flatly.

Who could believe that nonsense?

Bob cut. "Let's try it again."

Again. And again. And again.

They relit for close-ups. Fruitless. Empty. Nothing. She despised her line. Loving is not enough to save the world or a poor little romance or a little boy. They were going to blow everything up, and so what. Hate would triumph. The gangs were going to win.

Wise switched to her scene holding the gun, but when it came time for Maria to break down, she could not. She had better not.

Wise tried a few more takes, but it was obvious to everyone there was a problem.

Finally, he went over to her and said, "We'll try again tomorrow."

They couldn't shut down. It would be her fault.

"No, let's do it again. I can do it."

"You go home."

They'd have to pay everyone for what was less than half a day's work. This would be all her fault.

"I can do this."

"We'll try again tomorrow. Don't worry."

She was sent home in a studio car, the worst sort of reprimand.

It was raining, so she knew Bill would be home. His line was busy, so she left a message with his service and fell onto her couch.

The phone rang. It was Bill.

"What are you doing home?"

"I was awful," she said, her voice softer than she'd intended, as if she had lost all air. "They shut down because of me. Can you come over?"

"I'm getting a scene ready for class. Why are you home?"

"You don't need a class."

"I damn do. Come to class. Jeff can help you."

"Oh, God, that's the worst thing! I'll be all right. I'll get some sleep."

"I'll pick you up at six."

"Bill!" she yelled. "You know I hate that stuff. I can't do it now."

"See you later."

When he pulled up, she came right out, wearing a babyish sailor suit, her hair in a ponytail. Let them try to hurt her. She was just a kid.

"You'll like the class," Bill said. "Interesting people in it. Jeff will ask you to do the scene."

"What? You told him?"

"It isn't that. He won't take auditors. He puts people right to work."

"I won't do it!"

"I'll push you. They sent you home, you said."

They rode in silence the rest of the way while she simmered.

Jeff Corey held his class in what must have been a garage next to his modest house in the hills. He was tall, rugged, and gray, with a voice that could boom through a stadium.

"Thank you for coming," was all he said. Bill jammed some bills into a cash box monitored by a young girl who smiled shyly at him.

Dianna gazed round and recognized some of them: Leonard Nimoy, who'd played a bad guy on *Silver Sierra* and, surprise, Star Worthington. A small suspicion crept into her thoughts.

Corey called on Bill first, along with two others, to do a scene from Bill's next movie. The two other actors played his landlords. Bill's character was beginning to realize that his life was crashing down on his head. He had just been exposed by a newspaper as someone who had been jailed for intent to molest a little girl, and now he had to face this couple.

Dianna felt a glimmer of concern. Bill was hurting. His speech was halting, and he seemed confused.

Corey pushed for more. He gave the actors a scene to improvise.

If he told *her* to improvise, she'd tell *him* something else.

Bill and the other actor delivered a compelling scene while not saying anything important. When they repeated the real scene, that dynamic carried over. Dianna still thought improvising was stupid.

As Bill sat back down next to her, Corey called, "Miss Fletcher? You're working on *West Side Story*? What scene?"

"The last," she said, without thinking.

"Can you show us?"

"Well," she said, "it needs a lot of people."

"No, no, we'll just get a Tony. Come and show us."

She felt Bill's hand under her elbow. She shoved it away. All right. She'd show him. And Star. And the rest. She'd be lousy. She would get it out of the way and then go home. She hated their invading her acting, being conspirators to her downfall.

She walked down to the performing space, aware they all stared at her, this Oscar winning Disney actress whose grief they thought they shared. She wasn't going to show anything. Her feelings were hers and none of anyone's business. She looked at the floor.

"Jack, you be Tony," said Corey.

"I don't know the scene," said a scruffy young man, getting to his feet.

"You tried out for Tony and you didn't read the play?"

"Yeah, but I don't remember the scene."

"You just have a few lines and a song, but we can skip the song for your part," said Corey. "I don't want to scare the others."

That brought titters.

"Miss Fletcher, could you describe the scene?" asked Corey.

She looked up from her hands. Bill was leaning forward, elbows on his knees, looking at her intently.

Damn him.

Okay, she'd describe the scene.

"Tony thinks I'm dead, that Chino killed me, and he runs into the street, yelling for Chino to kill him, too."

"That's before. Tony sees you. You're alive, not dead."

Those words hurt.

"He runs to me," said Dianna, finding it odd she had to struggle to remember. "There's a shot. Chino shoots him, and he falls, and I hold him."

"All right," said Corey. "Jack, what lines you don't know, just mumble. But mostly, you're lying there dying. I'll do the shot. Jack, run toward Maria."

This strange man who was supposed to be Tony ran toward her. She heard a loud bang, and he fell into her arms, looking wildly surprised. She sank down under his weight as he dropped to the floor and heard herself say, "Loving is enough." She could barely get through that line before breaking down, way before Maria was supposed to, and it was all anger and gasps of fury. She ran for the other wall.

"I think that's too soon, Maria," said a voice from somewhere.

She said, "I know," surprised by the steadiness in her voice.

As she turned back to the others, she saw Corey talking to Bill and Bill nodding. She heard him say, "Yes, she did."

Corey said, "Start again, Dianna."

Years of taking direction kept her from running away.

Jack pushed himself off the floor.

"Did I run into you too hard?"

"It was fine."

This time, she tried to think he was Tony. So happy, then so sad, but some of the happiness was still there for he was alive yet. She had not thought of that. If only he'd still been alive when she found him. She spoke her lines as this poor Jack fellow mumbled.

She sang a little of "Somewhere," and her voice broke.

"I'm Chino," Corey said.

She walked over to him and held out her hand for the gun. Corey handed her a prop gun, or maybe it wasn't. Her hands trembled as she held it.

She said the line about the gun with a wavering voice, spoke the lines waving the gun at the class, and then broke down in tears. No, she wailed, again, much too soon. She fell to her knees on the rough carpet over the cement floor. She was almost screaming as she bent over. It was not something she could control. Chas, her grandmother, her parents.

"We'll try that again," said Corey.

The class stirred with uneasiness. Someone — was it Bill? — said, "Jeff, don't you think —"

"Please do it again," said Corey.

She was too tired to protest. Maybe she was stuck in this scene for the rest of her life. She handed him the gun and dragged her feet back.

She played the scene again. More tentatively in some spots, more frantically in others, but in her mind, something was gelling, even as it hurt. Chas, she thought, I'm acting. I'm taking away from this thing you did and turning it into Maria. I'm sorry. She held back, but she didn't want to. It ended up a struggling hodgepodge.

"Try it again," said Corey.

She had to get through this scene or else it would never end. Maria was going to go on. Chas, I'm alive, and I'm letting Maria in. You'll be proud. You'll be sorry you left.

She shouldn't think that way.

She was beginning to think Maria was close by, to understand her strength and wish she had some of it. When she asked for the gun, she was angry. She yelled at the class, whirling with the gun, hate in her soul. She broke down, feeling fake as she did. Yet she gave a wail of anguish as she had never howled before. Her own emotions of loss and anger swirled around her. Somewhere in there, she recognized Maria.

Maria had come back.

Dianna stopped, lowered her arm with the gun.

"I'd like to start from the beginning."

"Go ahead," said Corey.

This time, she could feel her love for Tony. This time, she could feel Maria's anger and despair and power as she took the gun from Chino (why would he give it to her? Because her power demanded it) and then she whirled with hate about their hate, and when she broke down and screamed out, a primal and conflicted scream, it was about what had happened and why and Tony and Chas and Bernardo and it was all one, and the conflict between her happiness and her anger and her grief, and the world was so complicated and awful and bitter and they had loved each other and were going to go somewhere, and now it was all over, they'd killed it, they'd killed him with hate, and she fell to her knees and cried and cried, then, at the imaginary cop stepping forward, she ran to protect Tony's body. As she yelled, "Don't you touch him!" she looked desperately at the students, begging them to change the past, as she stood slowly, looking at them with burning eyes.

"Yes," said Corey. "Thank you."

She leaned against the wall as the class wiped its eyes, applauded, and stamped for her.

"An artist takes life and then gives, empties out," said Corey. "It ain't easy, and all it takes is courage. Thank you. Would someone please get Dianna a glass of water?"

The young man who'd played Tony reached out to shake her hand.

"What is your name?" she asked, barely whispering. "Jack?"

"Nicholson," he said. "It's been an honor."

"Thank you," she said.

She went back to sit with Bill, who put his arm around her. She tried to follow the last scene presented, which had some long explanations from Corey, but she was pretty drained when Bill took her arm to go.

"Thank you for putting up with me," she said to Corey.

He put a hand on her arm. "Come back again," and to Bill, he said, "Good luck in Dublin."

They walked quietly to the car. Just as they reached it, Dianna said, "I'll put off killing you until you get back."

"Damn, I almost dragged you out," he said. "I couldn't believe what Corey was doing. It was so terrifyingly exposed. But Corey pulled the craft out of you. You pulled the craft out of you."

"How about that?"

"He was blacklisted, you know."

"Of course. You could start telling me who isn't. It will be easier. The whole world unable to do what they love."

"The studios respect him. They won't hire him as an actor, but they'll send actors to him."

"The world is crazy." Then she had a suspicion. "Did Bob Wise talk to you?"

"Would it matter?"

"Thank you."

The next day was different. There were other actors, a real Tony, and she reacted off every one. She took the gun and she was strong. The actors pulled back as she waved it around, and then, when she broke down, all she was thinking of was Tony, but it could have been Chas, too, and her grandmother, and her parents, and her brother Nick. Her cry echoed through the studio. Her "Don't you touch him!" came out as a primitive roar. When she looked up at them all, her face was torn, drawn, pleading, yet defiant. The set, certainly quiet, felt even more so.

Bob Wise needed only one take of the master, although he took two. Dianna preserved the same mood, although some of her feelings were different, and the quiet held as the crew spoke only in hushed whispers. After calling "Cut and print," the second time, Wise crossed himself. He embraced Dianna. "Thank you."

"I'm sorry about yesterday," she said.

"I think you made up for it." The cast and crew applauded her as she ran to her dressing room.

It wasn't just acting. It wasn't just giving a good performance. It was taking life and giving, just as Corey had said. It was truth dragged through experience to the other life. It hurt like hell, but it was like Greek theater. It told the truth. She got in her shower and wept.

Acting was damn real, and it hurt. Why would people do such a thing? Who had the nerve? Well, she'd found out that she had the nerve, and that was damn scary. This was, she realized, how Bill pulled a character out of himself. She wondered if her parents were this gutsy, and they were, so how they could be driven apart now, for acting had kept them together for years. She felt a great love for them, a love stronger than she'd ever felt, despite the pain they'd caused her. She also felt an intense love for her craft even as it frightened her.

Her father was right. Their craft was more powerful than any bomb, and it could bring life.

The whole damn world should be grateful to actors.

48

D ianna froze in the limo as applause and screams filled the air. The screams stopped as their limos pulled up to the Pantages Theater for the opening of *Every Time We Say Goodbye*, a charity benefit for the Muscular Dystrophy Association of which she was the honorary chairman, so she felt she had to go. As Bill helped her out, the crowd stood up from the bleachers and offered what could be called respectful applause, no screaming, not even cries for autographs.

The filming and postproduction had been so short that she'd never thought how the finished piece would look except that it would show in a few theaters and fade away. When she'd suggested the picture for the MDA, she was surprised they had accepted. She was also surprised at how some actors, including Paul Newman, had mentioned the film in some publicity and spoke highly of Sybuck. Dianna had been too involved with her pain and her work to hear the current of talk around town that "Sybuck was back."

She was therefore astonished at what she saw. The movie done on a few dimes in a few weeks proved luminous. Sybuck had created a magic kingdom of his own, one that found her fighting back tears at the final scene.

Watching Bill in turns suave, guilt-ridden, humorous, desperate, and wildly in love with her character startled her. And she no perky imp but a stunning, glamorous, passionate girl in her first experience of love, took her own breath away. The part had not required great acting but it would seem that she and Bill had turned up the temperature of the picture.

Afterwards, when people hugged Dianna, she saw a respect in their eyes she had not seen before. The word floating around on the air was "masterpiece" — for this cheap little movie! Actors she respected congratulated her: David Niven, Tony Curtis, Karl Malden, Agnes Moorehead, Deborah Kerr, Yul Brynner, Barbara Stanwyck, Jimmy Stewart all praised her highly. George Stevens hugged her for a long time. Robert Wise took her hand and said, "You have a gift." Bill too found himself surrounded with accolades, his friends slapping him on the back and shaking his hand.

Dianna and Bill skipped the reception and went to her house and a supper of shrimp and steak. Saying good night, Bill said, "Who would have thought it?" and then he kissed her seriously, that's what it was, one serious kiss. It started with his lips softly brushing over hers, playfully, wonderingly, then wanting more and more. She didn't want him to stop. What affected them? The movie? Or the lives that entangled their own reality? Within these questions, she felt a longing to care for him, to bring him out of his past, to love his present success.

To the surprise of everyone from Paramount's stockholders on down, *Every Time We Say Goodbye* turned out to be a critical success that brought in good money. Kids loved it. Adults loved it. It would stay in theaters for years. Sybuck had proven his genius on his return from exile, standing in for the forgotten artists, according to reviews that celebrated his style. Bill was praised for a "practically flawless performance that pulls you in to guilt, defensiveness, and passion." Dianna was praised for her "delicate evoking of love and passion with a skill we had not expected. She has grown into a lovely, mature actress."

"What is meant by practically flawless?" Bill asked, when they met again on his beach just after sunset.

"How did I delicately evoke passion?" she responded.

He was going away again.

And he was quiet. She asked him what was wrong. "Is it the part?"

"Yeah. Too close to home."

"What?"

"No," he said, tossing a cigarette into the sea.

"Jeff Corey," she said. "Do you want me to push you?"

"I don't think I'd take it as well."

"You know I care. Don't think I'm just a kid."

"I don't think you're just a kid. But that's what I tell myself to protect myself."

"Don't."

"I could so easily scare you away."

"You're not going to scare me away."

She thought of Sandi. *She'd* been scared away. How many others?

His face seemed filled with stories she could barely imagine. She touched his cheek. He grabbed her hand and kissed it.

"I want to love you, but that's a world I can have only when the camera rolls. Dianna!"

Was he crying? For a few moments, all she heard was the surf rolling in and out and his deep breaths. The sky above had grown purple and dark blue. She waited. He didn't say anything.

"Why not?"

"I care for you a good deal. And you're a kid. Even if you weren't —"

He looked out at the dark sky.

"Tell me," she said.

He tossed another cigarette into the sand.

"And then you'll run away."

"No."

"We'll see." He looked out to the sea, not at her. "When I was ten, my parents split up. I went with Mom. She went to New York to be in a play and married one of the actors. It nearly killed Dad. The play didn't do well. My mother got a television job, my stepfather didn't get anything. He started drinking and beating her."

Dianna had never heard of such a thing except in bad movies.

"I started beating him up. I won when he was drunk."

She tried to imagine him as a boy punching a strong man while his mother watched and tried to stop them both. For an odd instant, the boy she imagined was Chas. She shook that off.

"Times got tough so he brought in his sister, or so he called her, to share the rent. She called herself an actress. We didn't have another room. Just their room, a little kitchen, and a living room, which is where I slept on a pullout couch."

She was scared because what she was beginning to imagine couldn't possibly be true.

"Anyway," he said, looking out at the blackening water and not speaking for a while.

"I'm here."

"It gets tough."

"I'm here."

The moon disappeared behind the clouds, leaving a black sky.

There was nothing left. Just them. Bill's face, in profile, was dimly lit, an outline with only some light.

"Her first night, she climbed right in and went to work on me. I was twelve."

She wanted to blot out whatever he saw. A woman of that age "going to work on" a boy of twelve? She remembered the kids who had pulled her into the locker room and felt queasy and then angry for him.

"I was a kid. I wasn't clear about what was going on. A part of me resented her, a part of me was curious and excited about being treated like an adult, but I was thinking, I'm the man, I'm supposed to be in charge, and I wasn't. I didn't know how, but oh, she knew."

She reached out a hand but he ignored it. "This is hard for me to understand. Did I want this? Was I scared not to do this? Where was my mother? Where was my father? Who was taking care of me? But I was the man, and I wanted to be a man. I was mad that she wouldn't let me. I hated her, but she was bringing me into a world that I was curious about, a world men knew, and for night after night and month after month, she was there."

Bill kept watching the waters while the moon stayed hidden.

"A part of me knew it was wrong and that I didn't have a choice. A part of me wanted to go along with her. I was really confused."

Dianna leaned her head against his arm.

"I'm so sorry."

"My mother finally got up the nerve, and enough money, to leave this guy and come back to California with me. She never spoke of what happened, but she knew. I thought I had done something to break up their marriage. I turned into a wild kid, the kind you wouldn't want to know. Hanging out with older guys and even going down to the Strip and trying to impress prostitutes and get revenge with them."

Dianna gripped his arm.

"I'd talk to them and pretend to reject them. I went to school, skipped two grades. Dropped out. I got picked up by the police on the Strip. Dad grabbed hold of me and threw me into the business, made me get a high school degree. I started out as an extra and a learned to be a stunt guy, and I took the name Royce. The blacklist was on, and Dad wanted me to change my name, to not stick around him. We fought about that, but I did what he wanted. I helped him with my money. Mom had disappeared. And then Dad killed himself."

She moved her chair, put her arms around him. He took her hands, covered them with his own as the darkness descended on them.

"Talk about hitting bottom. Finally people stepped forward, mostly actors who helped me bury my father even if they didn't show up. They were that scared that someone would see them there and report them and they'd be blacklisted. One of Dad's friends sent money and said, whenever you're in trouble, call on me. He helped me get back on track, I spent some years talking to a psychiatrist who was also a religious brother, and I thought, what does he know about women and grief and it turns out he'd lost his wife and kids in a car crash. Still he loves God. Tough customer. I got into UCLA with the help of those two men. I never forgave that guy for not coming to pay respects to Dad. I understood why he didn't, he wasn't too powerful. His money's gone, my money's mine and earned, and I never want to work with or see him again. I despise cowards. Men stand up for what they believe in."

She didn't ask who it was

"My mother did not come to the funeral, but she visited the cemetery and I met her there. Parts were getting hard to come by. She got a job managing an apartment building Loretta Young owned. I didn't have much to do with her until she got sick."

The surf grew louder.

"I know I took it out on women. I'm the man. I was rough, and some of them liked it, some of them didn't. And I got good work. I was realizing I was a good actor, that I had talent, that I wanted to study the monster that killed my father. Things got better. I have been seeing women, and I try to stay with them. That's been getting easier, but nothing's worked out. Then you come along. You sixteen-year-old daughter of John Fletcher. Beautiful, brilliant fruit on the tree."

She kept her arms wrapped around him.

He smoothed her hair. "My mother got cancer, so I took time off to help her. She was living with so many regrets. My father. Me. I couldn't let her die like that. We read plays, talked about old times. She asked me to forgive her. No one wants their parents to die feeling like failures. My father had. I couldn't let her die feeling she'd failed me."

"Yes," she said.

The moon slowly emerged from the blackness, then hid behind a thin veil of cloud.

"I got myself checked out to a clean bill of health. Kept trying to be responsible to women. I met you. A part of me thought I could be sixteen again, starting over, no stepfather, no awful stuff dragging me down. It's impossible."

"Why?"

"Down in Mexico, when we were filming *Magnificent Seven*, we all went to some brothel, and I found I can still be rough, not caring for what the woman thinks. Scared the hell out of me. It's still there, not with women I like, but that anger is still there. And the last person on earth I want to hurt is you. So I try to stay away, but I can't. It almost helps that you're a minor. Like a wall around you. I got seduced by one. You know that. So go away."

Dianna held him tighter. A sexual innocent, she knew she didn't fully understand except that he was in pain and that she hurt for him and that she loved him and wanted to help.

How sinister that blacklist was, banishing her grandmother from her family, terrifying her mother to believe something she did not, indirectly causing the death of her brother, killing Bill's father, destroying his family, and trying to take his soul.

How criminal to wrest away independent thought and the protection of rights and how awful the exploitation of fear, affecting the most innocent and personal crevices of the heart.

"Because of this," she said, "you can't be friends with me?"

"I thought, hey, I can be your big brother and take care of you because your parents weren't around. But then came Brother Luke, and Lily exploded in my face. You've jumped from cute kid to teen to dream and brilliant —

Anne Frank and your singing at that fundraiser and your acting and your struggle to get better — I thought I can't love this girl, but I do. You're so lovely and brave and the art you have in you is mind blowing."

"I love you, Bill."

"Thank you." He took a deep breath. "I love you, Dianna. And damned if I do."

The moon never came out again that night, but there was still some light in the deepest places as they held onto each other.

49

"Looks a little long," said Dianna, glancing at the music. She'd been called to a rehearsal hall to work on Maria's rooftop dance. She'd already rehearsed it with Tony, the dance captain, but then she was called to another rehearsal.

"I don't need this," she said to Tony. "I have it down."

"Lenny did a revise," said a voice from the door. Jerry Robbins came in, sweatshirt, sweat pants, sneakers. She ran to hug him, then pulled away, confused.

"Aren't you off this movie?"

"Special assignment. They want to do a longer rooftop dance, and Bob asked if I'd jump in. Hi, Tony."

This was confusing, but Dianna said, "Let's go to work."

The dance started small with Maria wandering on the rooftop, looking at the night stars. Jerry demanded that she leap around the circumference of the roof.

She had not danced like this in a long time, and she found it invigorating. She had kept in shape as part of her routine, but she hadn't performed much as a dancer except at Disneyland.

Starting sweet, gaining power.

Jerry had her leap, snap her fingers, and extend her leg as the Sharks did. He had her run, snap her fingers, and leap as the Jets did. She understood. She was answering the Sharks and Jets and bringing them together, just as Maria and Tony were hoping to do that night. Her moves were powerful, yet graceful. Jerry yelled. Reach more. More. More. Her muscles ached with the repetitions. He had her do a combination she loved, leaping off the floor, turning, and landing as she moved into arabesque. He wanted it higher, her leg stretched further. More. Better. Her body felt soaked and hot with sweat and floppy like a rag doll, and he kept yelling for more and better while the skinny pianist kept playing. How long was this dance going to be? It finally ended with a quiet section where she danced lightly, feeling her arms, seeming to love her body, playing with her skirt, delighting in her feet, and at the close, she stood absolutely still, looking at the stars, just standing there.

He made her repeat it all.

"Reach," Jerry shouted. "Come on. You've got great long legs. Get those arms out. Eat up the space. You own it. You own the world!"

He drove her to sweating buckets, threatened her, praised her, and when the four hours were up, there was a completely different rooftop dance, and a different Maria.

"She goes from sweet to powerful. I love you, Jerry."

She knew this was brilliant. It was also way too long.

"Yes," he said. "The camera is going to pull away and up while you're standing there. It'll go to that other, violent world. We felt Maria needed to make her statement, and besides, you can dance, and you should have a go at it, the way everyone else gets to do."

"But it's hours long, Jerry. They'll cut it."

"It's four minutes."

"They won't do it."

"Yes, they will." He kissed her. "I have to catch a plane. I'm making a ballet without any music. That'll keep audiences quiet."

She felt sad as she walked into the soundstage. This dance would be the end of her playing Maria. After a week, she would go straight into rehearsal for *Cinderella*, scheduled to be broadcast live in January. She did not mind keeping busy.

She felt alone. Bill was in Dublin. MJ was married, a secret ceremony by a justice of the peace, and she didn't call any more. Sandra Dee and Bobby Darin were married. Lana Turner and Fred May were married. Maria and Tony would have gotten married. Everyone should get married, the culture screamed. All the teen magazines assumed their readers would get married after high school. Jewelers gave small hope chests to girls graduating. Two by two into the ark. If you weren't going to get married at eighteen or nineteen, the experts told girls, you'd become a lonely career woman. She was beginning to think that was where she was headed, but why did career women have to be lonely? The only man she cared about was Bill, not Bruce, not Larry, not anyone else. And Bill was so dark.

The columnists crowed, The wolf is at the door! And they lit into Bill.

It was too much to think about.

Back on the set, she marked her dance moves with the ADs, Bob Wise watching carefully along with Fapp, and a few other crewmen.

"Can I have the playback?" Wise called, and an extraordinary orchestral arrangement filled the studio.

"Where'd that come from?" Dianna asked.

"Lenny sent it to us," said Wise.

So Bernstein was in on it, too.

She was overwhelmed by the generosity.

They blocked the dance to check the lighting, Dianna still marking it, although it was hard to mark leaps and stretches. She tested the leap around the set, which, raised up two feet, held a bit of rooftop danger.

"Let's go through it," said Wise.

She did the dance full out to the playback, Bernstein's lush reminders of "Somewhere," "Maria," "America," and a mambo along with "Tonight." At the end, she was panting, and her muscles were sore, her feet were aching, and she could barely walk. Her whole body was damp.

"Good," said Bob. "That works. Let's take ten minutes. Ladies, can you change her now?"

She was surrounded by wardrobe women with towels, water, and a second slip and dress.

"Hey, I have a dressing room right over there," she said, as her clothes were lifted from her. She looked up to check if there was anyone up on the catwalks looking down.

Maybe they just did not want her to sit down. Which her muscles were screaming to do.

"This is a take," said Wise, and people yelled for quiet all over with bells ringing. Dianna closed her eyes. She stretched. Maria. Come on, Maria. One more time.

The playback started. She counted six. She started lightly, she danced like a happy girl, and then her leaps and complex steps began. She flew around the soundstage, Maria growing stronger. She flung herself across the space and leaped into an arabesque. Then she stood very still as the camera pulled up on the crane above her, making Maria diminish, growing smaller against the threat in the night as the last notes of "Somewhere" drifted into the fake sky.

"Cut, that's a print, thank you," said Bob Wise.

The crew called out bravos, stamping and clapping. But there were more people than just the crew.

George Chakiris grabbed her and brought her down to the floor. The cast surrounded her, applauding, hugging her.

"That's my little sister," George said, kissing her.

Rusty knelt at her feet and presented her with flowers.

"It's too long," she muttered to Bob.

"If they can't sit for a few more minutes," said Bob, "I'm out of this business."

"Thank you," she said, and she started shaking hands with the crew.

"Won't this stop the movie? Right after the rumble?"

"We'll put it in before," said Wise.

"Before is the 'Tonight' quintet."

"You've read the script!" joked Wise. He grew serious. "This part was made for an actress who could sing. We decided to put in that this actress who sings is a strong dancer. Besides, it summarized better the character you've defined so well."

"Wow," said Dianna. "Thank you."

"Let's work together again," said Wise. "See you at the party."

The Sharks and Jets were gathering. It was time to go.

Inside her dressing room, she found Mira.

"I've come to say goodbye," the social worker said. "I'm going to be working in a law office."

Oddly, Dianna felt her loss when she hardly knew the woman.

"Good luck, and thank you." She felt like crying at this leave taking.

Mira did not move. "I didn't think you should do this part. You're playing a Puerto Rican, but you are wonderful and a fighter, and I have learned a lot from you. I hope you learned that skin matters and doesn't."

"Good luck, Mira. Let me know where you are."

All the time she had longed to play Maria, and now it was all over but for the looping.

She went to the party but felt numb through her smiles.

Casting off Maria was not easy to do.

She went with Bruce to see *Exodus*. Newman was dull, Anne listless, the picture pompous and self-important, and Sal Mineo stole the movie.

A few days after they'd wrapped, the *West Side Story* cast was scheduled to appear at the Hollywood Bowl with a special sneak preview. Because of prior commitments for much of the cast, this translated into the Jets singing "Cool" and Dianna singing "Somewhere."

She wasn't thinking about anything in particular except getting through the words. She found the microphone and looked up at the rays of blue light. She couldn't even see the audience, although she knew it stretched far above her, every seat filled for the benefit performance. They'd just roared their approval for Larry and the boys and "Cool." She started to sing "Somewhere." It was all going well, but she started to shake. About halfway through the song, she choked with tears and had to stop. She held up her hand, muttered, "I'm so sorry," and hurried off stage. Debbie Reynolds, waiting to go on, ran after her but Dianna shook her off and kept running.

The strange thing, as she later pondered it, was that no one called her about it, even though the story appeared in the newspaper. A week later, she received two wires, one from Nick, who said, "Sorry. You'll be okay." And Bill cabled, "I'll hold you in DC."

Did her parents not know what had happened? Were they that busy?

She dreaded going to New York.

Not going was unimaginable.

She flew this time and hated it.

Nick grudgingly came to the Plaza, bringing his girlfriend, a folk singer named Silver – or Sylvia – dressed all in black.

John and Anne barely spoke to each other.

But families pretend to get together for Christmas.

Dianna received a fur lined muff from Bill. A pair of Irish linen gloves were tucked inside and inside the gloves, an emerald necklace and earrings. Her parents gave her the deed to the Malibu house and a large line of credit at Bonwit Teller's. It felt so cold. She saw herself alone in the Malibu house.

It was, however, almost like old times when they rehearsed their long medley for the Inaugural Gala, hams all. When they stopped singing, the quiet returned, and they all went to their rooms. Anne slept in Chas's old bedroom, John in one down the hall. Dianna tried to stay with her mother, but Anne didn't want company.

Her family was breaking apart, and she couldn't stop it.

A Doll's House was a hit. Dianna could feel Anne trying to bust out of her cage while at the same time wanting to stay in it. As for Nick's Hamlet, critics said he was either brilliant or insane. Dianna began to wonder if she were the least talented member of the family.

For New Year's, they went to a party upstate thrown by Bennett Cerf. Dianna sat quietly throughout the evening of witty ripostes on this, her seventeenth birthday.

Finally, finally, *Romeo and Juliet* opened, a late opening, eleven at night, so that her parents and Nick could attend. The colors burst off the screen, and although she felt she overacted, the critics said she behaved just like a fourteen-year-old. Critics compared her to both her parents. Everyone was agog. The names of Marks and Grey on the screen brought cheers. But the director and the writer did not appear. She had sent telegrams to them, but she'd not heard one word back.

John praised her performance to Ed Sullivan. Anne praised her to Hedda Hopper.

Back in Los Angeles, Dianna found that, for the first time, her measurements were published. The press regularly published women's measurements. 35 22 37 — those were Anne's, and now hers were public knowledge: 32 20 32 ("And she's still growing!"). Crewmembers yelled the numbers at her at Paramount. She pretended to enjoy it.

She was becoming a major star, although she wasn't sure about that. She didn't feel the need of the country to load their love on her, to wish for her a happy ending.

She rehearsed *Cinderella*. Her co-star was a handsome man whose wife was his agent, and he thought he was the star. She didn't fight him, but she didn't have to. She held the title role, and it was easy, right in her range, and she could toss in some of her old perkiness. But it wasn't *Every Time* or *Romeo and Juliet*, and she began to wonder if she should have done *West Side Story*, which would probably fade away as a musical that couldn't make it as a movie.

She snagged her license in a driving test on the lot. Chevrolet immediately filmed a three-minute television commercial with her driving a couple of girls and boys, all of them singing one of her pop numbers.

Doing commercials wasn't what movie stars did, but nobody seemed to care. Dianna's stardom was blooming, taking on new dimensions. It was extraordinary how well received *Every Time* had been and how many magazines featured pictures from the film of she and Bill together in romantic clinches. Uncle George's office churned out articles about Bill's good qualities – taking care of his mother, being on his own since he was sixteen, never having a chance to be a kid, and how Dianna attracted what was his native goodness. She was beginning to feel trapped in a way she didn't like.

Silver Sierra turned into a hit. Her fan mail multiplied. There was a demand for her to appear at more rodeos, and for solitary public appearances on behalf of the show and NBC. She had to turn them all down. But with *Every Time* and *Romeo and Juliet* out, *Silver Sierra* was not a lowly television show, but a weekly feast for her fans. Even though the episodes were fairly split among the cast, Dianna received the most press coverage, annoying her cast mates. Again.

"Brother Luke" was broadcast the second week of January. Nearly one hundred million people watched the well-advertised episode featuring the stars of *Every Time We Say Goodbye*. Bill's performance soared, stole the show. She felt jealous and wanted to work with him again. And didn't.

Anne called, talked about the play, so did John, saying the exact same things Anne had said. She knew they weren't together. They weren't even in the same hotel anymore. Anne had moved to the Sherry Netherland.

On another phone call, Anne said, "As I think back, our lives were dictated by the blacklist. Protecting you, Nana, John. And John hates me for that. But he is not political. He is a genius."

"Mom, he wanted to share that."

"No, no, it had to be just me. Just one person."

John said, "She does not know me. She thinks so little of me."

"No, Daddy, she loves you."

"You don't understand, Dianna."

They were all riding on empty. The only quirk of happiness Dianna could feel was the upcoming trip to Washington, DC, and the hope that the magic of the inauguration would somehow bring her family back to life.

They were trying to be together at least. That was important.

Magic City

50

W hen her car passed the White House, the driver assured her that President Eisenhower did live there. "But not for long."

He drove up the curved drive to the Statler Hilton where several red and gold uniformed attendants surrounded the limo to help her out. A crowd gathered, people called out to her, and they clapped as she smiled and waved and went inside.

The concierge strode over to greet her, signal a bellboy, and assure her he would attend to her registration. Bellboy and luggage following, he escorted her to the elevator as people in the crowded lobby stared and pointed. Thankfully, no one asked for her autograph.

"Are my parents here?" Dianna asked, as the bellboy opened the door to a corner suite marked "Royal."

"I don't know, Miss Fletcher."

He gestured to a door across the hall. "Mr. Sinatra reserved the Imperial suite for the performers. There's going to be a party there every night."

"Oh, boy," said Dianna, stepping inside the Royal. It looked like a hotel suite. The parlor was stuffed with furniture and bottomed out with a thick rug of red and gold.

The bellboy picked up an envelope addressed to her and went through the rooms, opening doors, pointing out the small kitchen and the stock of food in the refrigerator, the small safe in the small den. Down the hallway, he pointed out the three bedrooms, each with its own bath, all in various shades of blue and gold. She tipped him with her last ten dollars and took the envelope, probably a note telling her when her parents would arrive. The bellboy asked for her autograph on the ten dollar bill.

A plump older woman tapped on the door and came in, introducing herself Dianna's and Anne's maid, whereas John and Nick would have a personal valet. While Peggy hung up her gowns in the second largest bedroom, Dianna kicked off her shoes. She hoped that the time with her family would be a good one; they had been almost like their old selves when they'd rehearsed for the program. She opened the note that had been under the door.

> Sorry, darling, I've sprained my ankle in the dance the other night, and I have to keep off it as much as possible. The real problem is that we're doing so well Shu won't let us out, and he won't sell out the house to Sinatra because the house already sold out for the whole month. Nick has the same problem. His theater is mobbed with

standees. DC is due for a blizzard, and I am not up for that. Not sure I'm up for the whole thing, anyway. Daddy sends his love. Come by as soon as you can. My love to Frank. I've already told him. Love, Mom

Couldn't they have gotten other actors to replace them? Sprained ankle! They just didn't want to be together.

They didn't care if she was alone, either.

Well, so much the better. She was in Washington, DC all by herself and now with no work to do! With a blizzard to top it all off! Resentment fueled pleasure. Maybe she would be snowed in for weeks! Finding a stack of telegrams and messages in the living room, she read through them quickly. All invitations to parties! The thrill of pleasure, long denied, burst through her, reveling in freedom. Bill would be here, too.

Snowed in with Bill. To hell with her family.

New President. New Life. So there. Why feel sad?

She would not!

The phone rang.

"Darling," crowed Frank Sinatra. "I told them to tell me when you were in. Nice flight? You heard that your family isn't coming?"

"I'm so sorry, Uncle Frank. Is it a lot of trouble to reorganize the show without us?"

"What's to reorganize? You're going on."

She was silly to think she'd have gotten out of it all.

"My two songs. Sure."

"No, no. You're getting the full time your family had. Twelve minutes."

"Wait a minute," she stammered, the delicious sense of freedom backing out as if it realized it had accidentally come to the wrong place. "I can't do twelve minutes. You won't have two minutes to live when everyone else hears that."

"I've got protection. Baby, you have to represent your family."

"I do not!"

"By special request of the President-Elect and his wife," said Sinatra, throwing down his winning card.

"Huh?"

"I told Jack first thing, and he said, Dianna can sure hold a stage, and Jackie, Mrs. Kennedy, she didn't get to see you at the fundraiser and loved you at the convention, she said to me, and mind you, she hates me and will only talk to me when necessary, she said would you please ask her if she could sing for that time? She will be a symbol of youth. That's what she said. It's a royal request."

"We don't have royalty!"

"He's your commander in chief."

"He is only commander in chief of the armed forces. He works for me. Make him sing!"

"The man's been elected President. He loves Broadway musicals, and he wants the whole medley. You'll close the first part because Mrs. Kennedy might not stay for the whole thing, just having had a baby. And we have a big close."

"We could have people join in with me."

"He and Mrs. Kennedy want you. Dianna Fletcher."

"The whole thing by myself? The keys are different, I'd have to learn the words —"

"Baby, don't worry. Kay Thompson is here. We'll give you all the help you need. Nelson's redoing the charts right now. Lenny's going to conduct. It's a thrust stage, you know, and his orchestra will be raised in back. We'll work on it tomorrow for a couple of hours."

Kay Thompson for a couple of hours meant no fun.

"There's a party at the Smiths' tonight. I'll take you. We'll get the charts to you before that, and I've sent up the lyrics for all the songs in their order."

"Uncle Frank!"

"It's Frank, baby. You're seventeen now."

"I haven't sung in public since the Bowl, *Frank*."

"Aw, that was a month ago. You'll be fine. I gotta run. See you tonight."

There was a knock at the door. Peggy came in with a manila envelope and an excited look. "Urgent from Frank Sinatra."

Dianna sank back in a chair. "I was going to have fun here all by myself."

"Isn't your family coming?"

"They can't get out of the theater. The producer's a Republican. And my brother's an ass."

"Should I move your things to the master bedroom?" Peggy took this earth shaking news calmly. "The view is better. You can see the White House."

Dianna gazed out at the city. She wouldn't see much of it.

She could say no. But after her fiasco at the Bowl, a part of her didn't want to quit. She had to get back up on that horse.

The phone rang.

"Darling, your parents aren't coming?"

It was Janet Leigh.

"No," said Dianna. "News travels fast."

"What about your spot? That's about ten minutes left hanging."

"Yeah, that's right."

"Tony and I could make a longer skit for the three of us. We have some ideas."

That might be fun. But she couldn't accept.

"Thank you! But you'd have to speak to Frank. He's in charge of the show, and I can't make a move without him. I wish I could."

"Sure, honey. We're heading to the Smiths at seven. Why don't you come with us? Are you okay to do parties?"

"Thank you," said Dianna. "I'd like to come. I'm dateless. Frank said he'd pick me up, but I'd rather go with you." And Tony.

"We're at 1204, east side. Come when you're ready. We have a great skit where you'll play my little sister. Frank will love the idea."

That was doubtful, since the Kennedys had given the order.

Dianna thought of wiring Khrushchev. World War Three could possibly get her out of this.

Instead, she called the desk and asked them to take messages and would they please leave one for Sinatra saying she was riding with the Curtises. She hadn't liked the idea of getting in a car with Sinatra.

She opened the envelope and stared at the lyrics. Another knock brought charts and a note from Riddle: Rehearsal at nine until noon the next day in one of the basement conference rooms.

Every nerve in her soul screamed. It wasn't fair that she had to work.

Jean Smith, the President-Elect's sister, broke the phone barrier. "I want to make sure you're coming tonight, honey."

"Is there food?"

Jean Smith laughed. "We'll make sure you have a good time and lots of food."

Dianna tossed the charts on the bed and called Peggy to help her dress.

In a few hours, she was standing in the Smiths' doorway in a pink satin gown. A band played somewhere.

"Is there dancing?" she asked the Smiths who came to greet her and the Curtises, who had fought in the car but now were all smiles.

"We've got records going downstairs," said Jean, a husky looking woman. "The food's up here. The drinks are everywhere. We won't ask how old you are."

As soon as she walked in, Laurence Olivier embraced her and led her over to the table with people she didn't know, pulled a chair up for her, and introduced her to his soon-to-be wife, Joan Plowright.

"Where are your dear parents?" Olivier asked.

Dianna looked gratefully at plates coming at her with cold turkey, stuffed mushrooms, and shrimp.

"Could I have some ginger ale?"

"Have some of this wine," said Olivier. "It's just between us. Did you hear that Mamoulian is off *Cleopatra*? I cannot wait to see how it all ends."

"I think she dies," said Dianna. Joan laughed.

She sat through a discussion of the United States' power and how it must be used for peace, but she kept tapping her toe to the music.

Someone stepped right up to the plate. He looked like a Kennedy, and he sounded like one. "Would you like to dance?"

Unfortunately, the youngest Kennedy son proved a clumsy dancer, but it didn't matter because men constantly cut in. Although the party was supposedly for the entertainers, Dianna didn't see many. Her partners were all politicians or journalists interested in staring down her dress, pulling her too close, and pretending they were authorities on movies. She wasn't sure if she could slap them without causing some crisis.

A burst of applause from upstairs made her wonder if Sinatra had arrived. As she waltzed with a one two-timing Senator from Illinois to Rodgers' and Hart's "Lover," she heard a stirring of murmurs. Turning, she saw Bill coming down the stairs, looking like the movie star he'd become, and no sooner had she called out his name, then he'd swept her into the waltz without even asking permission of her partner. People applauded the stars of *Every Time* and gave them the floor while photographers went crazy.

They ignored all that. Dancing with Bill was too much fun to think of anything else.

"I left your Christmas present home," she said.

"No, you didn't." Bill held her closer. Did she mind? No! It was good to feel his arms around her again.

"I've missed you, sweetie."

"When did you get back?"

"Last week. Had to meet up with Jack right away. I mean the President-Elect. It's been crazy."

"Is he here?"

"He came to see Truman."

"President Truman is here?"

"Want to meet him?"

"I really want to go home, I mean to the hotel."

"I'll take you. The Statler, right?"

A hotel with Bill in it and no parents. They didn't mind leaving her alone? Fine then.

They finished the dance. Bill waved people onto the floor, so they had more company, even as the music slowed and his lips brushed her cheeks.

She was glad her parents weren't here.

Upstairs, John Fitzgerald Kennedy was talking to the poet Robert Frost and former President Truman, who kissed her hand.

Kennedy said, "Good to see you again." He winked. She winked back.

"Exciting time," was all she could think of to say.

"Come and sit with us," Kennedy said. "We'll get chairs."

Bill said, "Dianna wants to get back to the hotel."

"I have to rehearse early tomorrow," she explained. "Or I'll fall flat on my face in front of the President-Elect."

Kennedy grinned. "Can't have that. You're taking her, Bill?"

Bill smiled.

Kennedy pulled out a pen, grabbed a napkin, and scribbled on it. He folded it and handed it to Bill.

"I got that from Bobby. The future attorney general."

Bill unfolded the napkin, looked at it, looked at Kennedy.

"Right," he said.

Kennedy saluted him. "I'll call you tomorrow."

Mr. Smith corralled one of the cars for them. Once inside, Dianna asked, "What was that he gave you?"

"Something for the speech."

"Look at you. On the precipice of power." She was really impressed, and she felt much closer to the historic events of the next few days.

He laughed. "If it's great, they'll forget I helped. If it's lousy, they'll blame me."

He took her hand and held it. The car radio played, "Unchained Melody." *Oh, my love, my darling, I hunger for your love.*

They didn't talk until they got to the elevator.

She rummaged in her purse for the key.

"What floor?" asked the elevator attendant.

"Twelve," she said.

"Are your parents here?" Bill asked.

"No."

"Not yet?" he asked, as they stepped into the hall.

"Not ever. They couldn't get out of their shows."

Bill paused at the door she indicated.

"Are you here by yourself?"

"I found out when I got here." She wondered what he thought.

He took her key.

"Why do women hand men their keys?" she wondered. "It's not hard to open a door."

"Sometimes it is. And the guy looks like the fool. Here you go. Wow."

"Big suite all to myself. Thank you. What floor are you on?"

"Ten. Are you going to be all right?"

"Yes." What was he thinking? "Your President-Elect and his wife want me to sing the full set we were all going to do. So I'm stuck with all this rehearsing. Everyone's going to hate me, and I'm going to have a lousy time."

"Not if I can help it. How about breakfast?"

"About eight?"

Wasn't he going to ask to come in? Should she ask him in? Was he going to make a move? If he did, should she get mad?

Instead she asked, "In that garden place where the plants are?"

"Sure." Bill peered into the suite again. "Call me if you get worried."

"Okay." She closed the door, but he pushed back, gave her a good hug and a nice long kiss.

"I waited a long time to do that," he said. "I missed you and worried about you."

"I'm okay."

Why didn't he ask to stay?

She closed the door.

There came a knock. She opened it fast.

"I want to hear the lock," he said. "And put the chain on. Don't open the door if you don't know who it is."

"Yes, Dad. Good night."

She closed the door, slid the bolt, put on the chain.

Another knock.

She undid the chain, slid the bolt back, and opened the door.

"Don't call me Dad. And check before you undo the chain."

"Good night."

Frank Sinatra was walking past with a few blonde ladies.

"In or out, make up your mind," he called.

"Good night," said Dianna.

She shut the door, slid the bolt, and put on the chain.

"Good girl!" Frank called.

She headed into the master bedroom, undid her pearls, and sank onto the bed, wishing she'd invited Bill in. But she had to think of work.

The buzzer sounded at the door.

It was Sinatra, minus the blondes.

"Come on over, honey. We're all here."

"I have to work, dear Frank."

"Want any help? I can sing pretty good."

"Good night." She shut the door.

"I'm great at phrasing," he called through the door.

"And other things!"

That was a mistake. He buzzed again. She ignored him. She thought of calling Bill, but the buzzing stopped after a few minutes.

"Aw, baby!" he called. "I'm gonna make sure you have some fun."

He hadn't helped much so far. It was work work work she was thinking as Peggy came in with a three-ring binder of all the re-charted music and lyrics. And some coffee. She got to work and shuffled the songs back in the order they'd sung them in New York. Bernstein would just have to re-do the segues.

51

Bill was in the restaurant the next morning. As he kissed her cheek, a camera flashed. Bill stepped toward the photographer who dashed away.

"I can't eat," she said. "My stomach's a wreck."

"Fruit cocktail," Bill said to the waiter. "Are you drinking coffee yet?"

"Oh, yeah."

Gene Kelly pounced.

"Dianna, I heard that your parents and Nick aren't here."

"No."

"That leaves you with all that time, doesn't it?"

"Not exactly."

"I'd say ten more minutes. Are you singing?"

"Yes."

"Good," said Gene. "We can fill up that time. Nothing crazy, something with time steps and waltz clogs. It won't be anything to learn." He glided through a few steps to the delight of people eating nearby. "They'll love it."

She liked Gene Kelly, but right now, she wanted to punch him in the face.

"I've been instructed to tell you that you will have to make any requests about the show to Mr. Sinatra."

"Yeah, honey, but if you and I go in to him together..." His grin was engaging, disarming, and deadly.

Her fruit cocktail came. The knots in her stomach grew tighter.

"I'm supposed to sing the whole twelve minutes."

He looked incredulous. "Are you joking? You get twelve minutes? I get barely five?"

"Talk to Frank."

"What a lousy thing to do to you. You couldn't do three minutes at the Bowl."

That was dirty pool.

"Why don't you let her eat her breakfast?" Bill said.

"Yeah," said Kelly. "I'll take care of this, honey. I'll go tell Frank he's nuts. It's terrible to put you through that."

"You okay?" Bill asked as Kelly went off on his good will mission.

"He should get more time than me. He's Gene Kelly, for God's sake."

"What are you doing after this rehearsal?"

"Study. What are you doing?"

"I'm off duty. The soon-to-be President is going to New York, and so I might just take a walk. I was wondering if you'd like to break away from this mob and —"

"Darling!"

Bette Davis graciously sat herself down, cigarette in hand. Dianna waved the smoke away.

"You're all alone here?" Davis said. "That's terrible. Has Frank assigned the extra time? I was thinking we could do a nice duet. Young girl, and not so young girl. Very easy to learn. Very sweet."

At least Sinatra had saved her from this.

"Check with Frank," said Dianna. "That's what I'm supposed to tell everyone."

"What a tyrant he is," said Davis. "Mr. Royce, you were nothing short of glorious in *Every Time We Say Goodbye*. We must work together sometime."

And then she was gone.

Dianna's hand shook as she picked up her spoon.

"We could do dinner and dancing," said Bill.

"I have to work. I can't forget my words or anything."

"You have to relax. I insist."

"Oh, Bill," she began, but Harry Belafonte pulled up a chair.

"Dianna, why don't we do something together?"

"Excuse me," she said. "I have to go. I'm sorry."

"Have some coffee with me," said Bill. "I'm writing about the blacklist for a dissertation."

Belafonte sat down. "Damn! How'd you do that? I hear the universities are getting pressure."

Grateful to Bill, Dianna hurried out of the restaurant.

Leonard Bernstein greeted her with ebullient excitement, and Kay Thompson pounced in, scary as usual. The rehearsal would have been unbearable if not for Bernstein's enthusiasm. Kay kept saying, Be young! Be breathtaking! Be exciting! Hard to do when every move and note were being analyzed.

Sinatra came in to watch and make a few comments. Dianna resented his interference except he was always right.

After two run-throughs, everyone seemed satisfied except Dianna, but she was too nervous to say so. The set involved her dancing from microphone to microphone on a stage she'd never seen. With a long skirt and pumps, she was going to fall flat on her face as she'd predicted.

Back in the suite, she ate a sandwich and took Bill's message: dinner at six. With dancing.

She let him talk through dinner because she wanted to listen and because her voice needed a rest. He talked about how hard his movie was, hardly cheery stuff. "I was in every scene. And I may die on my sword because of it. Wilson's blacklisted, although thanks to *Spartacus*, it looks as if we won't have your *Romeo and Juliet* trouble. It probably will only play in cities, though."

When they danced, he wouldn't let anyone cut in, and she leaned on him. His body satisfied her and she wanted what her mother had once said, that real pleasure came when you knew each other's bodies.

And he was good, getting her back to the hotel at ten.

Up in the hall, a great deal of loud piano music, singing, and talking came from Sinatra's suite.

"Maybe we'd better go in," she said.

"He's after you," said Bill.

"Too bad."

Sinatra greeted her with a wet kiss. She raced for dear Jimmy Durante singing his famous *Inka Dinka Doo*. "Ah, there's Dianna," he crooned.

Olivier shared a sofa with Anthony Quinn, his *Becket* co-star. They moved over so she could fit in the middle, and she felt panicky when Bill headed deeper into the room. Beautiful women instantly surrounded him, and he was laughing in seconds.

"He's some magnet," said Janet Leigh. "Say, Frank said you're doing the whole time. Is he crazy?"

"Yes."

"He gives you twelve minutes? What does that say about the rest of us?"

Seeing other performers huddled in a corner, Dianna thought they might be complaining about her. She hurried over.

"We might not go on," said Belafonte.

"Why not?" Dianna asked, ready to fight.

"Sinatra told Sammy to stay home."

"Kennedy asked him, but I'm sure that came from Joe," said Kelly.

"I don't understand," said Dianna.

"Sammy married a white woman," said Belafonte.

"We don't know that's why," said Curtis.

"Sure we do. That's Joe Kennedy," said Nat King Cole.

"But of course," Bette Davis said, "no matter what, Dianna will go on."

The way she said it, and the way people looked at her, made Dianna realize they were mad at her.

"Yes," she said. "I am representing my family at the President-Elect's request, so shove it."

She headed for the door. Bill followed her, but she didn't wait. She was near to tears by the time they reached her door.

"These damn people want me to fail."

"No, they don't, and you won't fail."

"And you, with those women."

"Clucking chickens."

He unlocked her door.

She put a hand on his arm. "Don't go."

He looked pained. "I think I'd better."

"Come in."

"Dianna–"

But he came in, and she closed the door. Now or never. But she found her nerve failing her fast.

"Could you stay in one of the rooms? I'm nervous with this party down the hall and — Sinatra kept buzzing — I didn't sleep much last night, and I'd feel better if you were —"

He looked down at her, grinning. "If you want me to stay, I will. But I'm not going to sleep down the hall."

"I can't think about anything like that tonight." She looked and felt confused. Should she be angry? Delighted? Indignant?

A knock at the door. Sinatra's voice, saying, "Dianna, are you all right tonight?"

Bill reached for the doorknob.

She put her hand over his. "Yes, Frank. Uncle Frank. Good night."

"God knows what he wants. What were you saying?"

Bill held onto her hand, and he put his arm around her waist.

"Oh, damn," she said.

"What I mean is, sweetie, I'm not sleeping in the next room. If you want me to stay, I'm sleeping with you. I understand you don't want to do anything other than sleep, and that's fine."

What a wonderful thing for him to say. Should she slap him?

"If anyone finds you with me, you'll be arrested."

He pulled the paper Kennedy had given him out of his pocket. "I have it on the assurance of the next president and his attorney general that the age of consent in the District of Columbia is sixteen."

"Huh?"

He grinned. Damn he was charming.

"No one's going to arrest me. I'm not breaking the law if I sleep with you tonight. I'll be good. I promise. The next time, I don't promise."

"Are you sure you can do that?" she asked, thrilled and embarrassed and anxious and horrified and excited all together.

He laughed, but quietly. "No. But I missed you and I promised myself —" He didn't finish the sentence as he put his hand back on the doorknob. "That doesn't mean I won't touch you. You are," he said, stroking her face gently, "going to have to trust me. And I'm going to have to trust me. I'll go get my stuff."

A voice in her head said fool, fool, fool.

"Don't come back with ugly striped pajamas."

She took a quick bath, sprayed the room and herself with Chanel, and wondered why she'd bought a flannel nightgown. At the time, it had seemed like a fun idea — cold, winter nights and all. She hadn't expected to be sharing her bed with Bill. When had she gotten that idea?

Good God, what was she doing?

Hearing a knock from somewhere, she put on her robe and hurried in its direction, and she heard, "Hello?" from behind the service door in the kitchen. There was Bill, complete with bag, a grin on his face.

While he took possession of another bathroom, she went into the bedroom, the big bed's blankets all turned down.

He popped his head in. He looked downright gleeful. Damn him.

"Ready?"

She stared at him from under the covers. Ready for what?

He was not wearing striped pajamas but a simple tee shirt and what looked like silky smooth black pajama bottoms. She felt like a little girl from the country in her flannel nightgown.

"Are you okay?" he asked.

"Sure."

Of course she was.

He turned off the main light switch. "Hey," he said, "that's the White House. Want to go there?"

"Now?"

"Day after the inauguration. I'm invited to a reception."

"Are you going to be in the Cabinet?"

"All the good spots are taken."

He pulled back the covers and climbed in with her.

No cameras, no lights, no people. Just them.

She leaned back to turn off the table lamp.

"Wait," he said. "I'm savoring the moment."

That made her giggle.

She was the one to reach out as strong feelings overcame her fatigue. Bill who had so much to put behind him, Bill who had become a great artist in spite of it all, Bill who struggled daily to put bitterness behind him. He'd tried so hard to avoid her, too, and now, here he was.

Now he took her hand, kissed it, put it back on her stomach, and began caressing her, his hand smoothing over her hips.

"Sweeter than all," he said, as they kissed.

She was wrought up with emotion. "I love you, Bill. Did I tell you?"

He smoothed her hair, kissed her, and continued to feel her body through her funny flannel nightgown.

"Thank you," he said. "Did I tell you, I love you, too? But not," he added, "like a boy of sixteen."

She loved the feel of his body, with her, holding her, shielding her. They kissed, longer and deeper. Their touching grew more intense. When he said, "Sweetie, we'd better stop. You need to sleep," she was ready to disagree.

She wondered if she could sleep with his arm around her, his breath on her hair, his smooth caresses easy and lulling. The street sounds were gone, the occasional laughter from Sinatra's suite faded, even the White House disappeared as she closed her eyes. Bill, the famous womanizer was with her, his arm firmly around her, and she felt safer than she'd felt in a long time.

She was going to keep him.

When she woke up, he was not there. The clock read nine thirty. She scrambled into her robe and slippers and got as far as the bedroom dresser, where he'd left a note. "Off to Georgetown to listen to Himself one more time. Sorry, B."

He'd taken all evidence out that he'd been there, probably wise given the gossip of a hotel, but it made her feel uncertain that he'd come again.

She arrived at the Armory across town after an irritating long cab ride. It was cold outside, and it was cold inside that vast, barren barn of an Armory. None of the other performers had gotten there yet.

Throughout the rehearsal – singing with the orchestra and blocking her movements – her brain rattled around. The enormity of the hall, the enormity of the evening, and the enormity of what she had to do fell on her. As she sang through the medley, she felt homesick for her father's sly subtlety, her mother's punching up words, and her brother's shrugging way of moving through a lyric. The audience wasn't going to see any of that.

Once outside again, though, her dour mood altered.

It was snowing.

"It's lovely," she cried to the driver who met her.

"Nope," he said. "Traffic's gonna stop."

"They'll keep the streets plowed. They do that in New York."

"Honey, this ain't New York. This many politicians in town, nothin' works."

She loved watching the snow coming down as slow, gentle flakes, but by the time the cab pulled up to the hotel, the snow was coming down harder, hitting her in the face when she got out.

She checked the desk for messages and found several from reporters, which she tossed. Bill had called, too.

"Scrabble?" was all the message said.

Bill, PhD aspirant, came up with words she had never heard of. After an hour of this torture, a gleeful Bill looked up and said, "Whoa. Look at that."

"That" was a vista of dark sky and pelting snow. Dianna hurried to the window, stood on a chair to look down at the street and was delighted at the unplowed streets, cars stuck every which way and the car horns blowing.

Bill turned on the radio. The announcers were announcing with horror comparable to the end of the world that the snow was expected to keep on coming down and probably would amount to more than a foot.

"They wouldn't cancel the gala, would they?" Bill asked.

"They wouldn't dare," said Dianna, although she hoped they would. "Frank wouldn't have it. The show must go on stuff."

The phone rang. There he was, on cue.

"Baby, I'm trying to get everyone together and get back to the Armory. The hotel will help you get a car."

Bill called the concierge while she gathered her wits, clothes, and makeup and tossed her music book in the case. The bellboy collected her bags while she wrapped herself in her coat and scarf and pulled on the boots the hotel had sent up. In the lobby, the doorman had somehow obtained one cab.

"It's tough going out there," the doorman said.

Bill slid him a twenty.

Bernstein ran up. "Can I hock a ride with you two?"

"Can't get along without you," said Dianna.

The bellboy loaded the trunk. Dianna ended up sitting in between the two men, her feet perched high on the hump.

"Can you take one more?" the doorman asked.

Dianna peered out. "Oh God, it's Davis."

"I'll get in front," said Bill.

"Wait, there are two of my musicians," said Bernstein, as Bette Davis took Bill's seat.

"Isn't this dreadful?" she declaimed.

Her fur coat nearly smothered Dianna's face.

The two musicians handed their violins to Bill and rode the running boards on each side.

"Is that safe?" Dianna called.

"At the speed we're going?" Bill called back.

When their cab didn't crawl, it stopped. The snow pummeled the windshields, slowing everyone down to a frustrating halt.

"Where are the plows?" asked Dianna.

"I for one want my tax money back," said Bette, opening her purse, and to Dianna's horror, taking out a cigarette case.

"Are you going to smoke?"

Bette lit up.

"Bette, have a heart. Dianna's singing tonight," said Bernstein.

"Not for a long while," Bette puffed away. "And she's young."

Bill turned to glare at the star. The car inched forward through the cold, uncaring that warfare could break out inside.

"What happened to the heat?" Dianna complained.

"Sorry, miss," said the driver. "It's done all it can."

Dianna burrowed against Bernstein and covered her mouth as Bette puffed on. Thirty minutes later, frustrated in her cramped position, with Davis on the tenth cigarette not yielding on simple threats, and Bernstein roiling with long, heavy coughs, Dianna grabbed the cigarette out of Davis' mouth, reached over Bernstein, rolled down the window, and tossed the smoldering barb out.

"You little bitch," Davis said. Dianna grabbed the woman's cigarette case and tossed that out, too.

"Just be glad I didn't toss you out!"

"You obnoxious little tart," said Bette. "Who made you better than anyone?"

Bill said, "If I were you, Miss Davis, I'd shut your mouth."

Handsome men had an effect on her. She looked out the window and sulked.

"What time is it?" asked Dianna as Bernstein leaned forward and kissed Bill's cheek.

"Almost five," said Bill. They had reached an intersection. A police car sat there, unhelpfully, its red light flashing.

"I don't think," Dianna said, "that I can sit like this any longer without screaming."

"Don't go anywhere," Bill told the driver.

"Like I have a choice?" the driver called, as Bill jumped out of the car, upsetting the first violinist, and ran over to the police.

When he got back, he said to the driver, "When you get to the intersection, pull onto the sidewalk."

"What?" everybody shouted.

"The police are going to go ahead and blow the siren. Follow them."

"Why are they so helpful?" asked the driver.

"They had a picture of you in your bathing suit on the dashboard, Dianna."

"I'm glad I come in handy," she muttered. The idea appalled her.

It was exciting as the siren blared and they progressed slowly but they kept moving – on the *sidewalk*. Naturally, other cars pulled behind them, and there was honking galore back there.

It was five twenty when the driver made it to the Armory's great doors.

"Thank you," Bill said, tossing some money into the car. Bernstein threw some in, too. Dianna thought she couldn't move, but Bill helped her out, practically pitching Davis on the sidewalk.

"Who knew that a circle of hell could be so cold," Bernstein muttered.

It was barely any warmer in the Armory. A few musicians played in the pit and some vendors were heating up what smelled like hot dogs.

Sirens shrieked all over the city. It sounded like a nuclear attack. Dianna hoped they'd stop before the music started.

Bernstein shook off his frozen funk and strode toward the orchestra, although it was at the moment more like a quintet.

Sinatra was on stage, arguing with a few of the tech people.

"Show's on, sure," he was calling. Seeing her he gave her a big kiss, ignoring Bill. "Dianna, your dressing room is downstairs. You have to come up from the doors in the audience."

"Is there someone to help me?"

"You need help, I'll give it."

"And where is my dressing room?" asked Bette.

Another tech waved at her to follow him. After shooting Dianna a look that should have blinded her, Davis disappeared.

"Need help?" Bill asked.

"Guard the door?"

"Sure."

"You're being awfully nice."

"I'm looking forward to being warm and cozy later."

As if she wasn't nervous enough. They went downstairs and a stage manager pointed to a tiny room that didn't even have a mirror. Well, she had her makeup mirror, framed in light bulbs. She plugged it in and closed the door on Bill. She curled her hair. She dressed in her off-the-shoulder golden satin gown. She calmed down. She heard voices. She heard voices in the *audience*.

When she opened the door, Bill had moved down the hall and was talking earnestly to Harry Belafonte and Sinatra.

"It was definitely targeted to liberals," said Sinatra. "The Republicans started it."

"In Congress," said Bill.

"And racists," said Belafonte. "Anyone who pushed for equal rights for all races. But Frank, a lot of Democrats went right along. They are too scared to stand up for this country and its citizens. Kennedy's one of them. You know that."

Sinatra shook his head. "No, no, that's not true." And as if looking for a way out, he looked up and saw Dianna.

"And you can never tell. Ed Sullivan, of all people, cleared me," said Belafonte.

"Oh, baby," yelped Sinatra.

"Can someone zip me up?" asked Dianna.

Bill tossed his cigarette and strode over.

"Does he have zipping up privileges?" Sinatra demanded.

"Yes," said Dianna.

"How'd he get them? I'm like your uncle."

"Like you should remember that, Uncle."

"I passed the essay test," said Bill.

Belafonte grinned. "Good job, both of you!"

"Lobby doors are closed!" called a voice through a microphone.

Everyone headed up the stairs, but Dianna, Bill, and a stage tech waited by a door leading into the audience.

The orchestra shifted into "Hail to the Chief," meaning that the President-Elect had arrived in his box.

The show was definitely going on.

Dianna took a deep breath. Bill took her hand and kissed her on the neck.

Bernstein launched the orchestra into *Stars and Stripes Forever.*

The rest of the cast then marched in from the end of the auditorium, singing an obnoxious "marching down to Washington" song. Having seen the tune ahead of time, Dianna had begged off anything more than her medley. But once she'd done that, she'd been forced into a complex entry.

The stage cleared. Dianna leaned against a wall. Bill stood with her.

"I don't want to wrinkle my dress," she said.

"Me neither."

The tech quietly opened the door. A ramp led down the aisle to the stage. Dianna closed her eyes tight for a few moments, then opened them again, a trick she'd learned from her mother about how to see in the dark.

On stage, Bette Davis delivered some strange remarks about the fourth or fifth or sixth estate. Anthony Quinn smoked a cigar while not selling a song that spelled out John Fitzgerald Kennedy. Olivier spoke beautifully but incomprehensibly.

Dianna's cramps returned as she listened to Ella Fitzgerald sing "But Not for Me."

The great Ella should have gotten Dianna's extra minutes! How could any singer follow Ella? Gene Kelly did, energetic and engaging in an Irish salute. Other performers came, sang for a few minutes, then departed, followed by Joey Bishop, who got everyone laughing but her. Her legs felt stiff.

Frank sang "You Make Me Feel So Young." She stood up straight.

Bill took her hand as the tech set up the microphone.

She circled, making sure her skirt did.

Bill kissed her hand and headed up to the aisle seat being held for him.

Frank announced her, explaining about her family. "Representing her extraordinarily talented family, the extraordinarily talented Miss Dianna Fletcher. Dianna, where are you?"

He disappeared, where, she couldn't guess and didn't care.

She stood at the microphone and looked over at the tech, who nodded. She lifted the mic into her hand as the orchestra played a strain from "Do I Hear a Waltz" and Dianna, her cue and her note resonating in air," hearing only her family's voices in her head, began to sing alone.

52

She stretched out the words "Do I Hear a Waltz," and her disembodied voice had everyone looking around. A light shone on the aisle. As planned, she ran into the light while Lenny kept the strings going. As the applause started with people realizing who was singing and where she was, she sang another line in the aisle, handed the mic to the tech in the shadows and hurried down the aisle, up the steps, to the standing mic, and sang another phrase. "I do hear a waltz!" She hadn't tripped, thank God.

She whirled around the stage, eyeing the microphone that the light hit next, and launched into "It's a Grand Night for Singing!" She looked around at the applauding audience as she sang, "I think I am falling in love" before waltzing around the stage and ending up at another mic. She looked up at the boxes. There they were. President-Elect and Mrs. Kennedy. Kennedy waved at her. Dianna waved back. Mrs. Kennedy leaned forward, smiling. She was elegantly dressed, all in white and diamonds, or it seemed so.

What a place she was in! Singing to the next President! And, as Dianna sang "I'm in Love With a Wonderful Guy," she realized she was in love. Well, wasn't she? She stood at the center mic, staunch and firm, realizing she had the audience with her. Each time Lenny brought the orchestra to a waltz line, she danced to another mic, except once when she launched, on the spur of the moment, into a cartwheel that thank goodness worked and brought cheers and laughter. Did she do it for Chas? Who knew? "I'm in love I'm in love I'm in love with a wonderful guy!" she cried. If she hadn't thought so before, the song convinced her.

Then she said, catching her breath, "My mother was going to sing this." She sang a soft ballad, "Out of My Dreams and Into Your Arms I Long to Fly," taking quiet gulps as she breathed, listening to her mother singing it in her head. The lights darkened around her. Her voice growled a bit, thanks to Bette, but she could adjust for it, and the growling left as she soared into the life of the material.

She finally took a good look at the audience, which was full on the floor level, bless their stalwart hearts. but the seats above the boxes looked empty.

"Nick would have sung this," she said, starting slow into "Oh, What a Beautiful Morning." She caught sight of Kennedy's head bobbing along in rhythm. She sang another of Nick's songs, "This Nearly Was Mine." Nick had almost talked it in their rehearsal, and she adopted that. She was thinking she had lost her family, her father, her mother, and then, what if she lost Bill.

She kept her face close to the mic, soft, regretful, sad, and the audience in the arena too, kept completely quiet.

When the music sped up, she sang the theme from *Paint Your Wagon*, "Got a dream boy?" raising her arm to indicate the President-Elect, causing laughter.

The music slowed again, and she moved to center stage, to another mic.

"My dad was going to sing this," she said, and quietly began "How to Handle a Woman" from *Camelot*, which brought some titters. But she sang it sincerely, "Love her, simply love her, merely love her…" And she almost cried. There was too much there. Daddy, she thought, please. As she segued into "I've Grown Accustomed to Her Face," she heard her father's voice and tried to sing with him. Oh, how she missed her family and the old easy camaraderie. Why had she been glad they hadn't come? She moved forward to the front mic and sang, her voice quivering, the theme from *Camelot*. And though she was singing about the Arthurian tales, she was singing of her family, breaking apart into their little wars. Her voice caught, but she kept going, and, glad for the change in tempo, she ran to another mic to sing "Show Me" and "I Could Have Danced All Night." Dancing again.

For the first time, she saw people standing back in the lobby area. "I never know what made it so exciting" she sang, remembering dancing with Bill – where was he sitting, anyway? – and the orchestra slowed, was this the end?

She stretched out her arms and the "all night" as the audience applauded and people started to stand, and then everyone was standing and applauding her. She bowed, bowed to Kennedy and his wife, hopped off the stage, and came back for a formal bow. The audience kept standing, and there were the people from the back streaming into the aisle. They were most of the performers standing in the aisle and applauding and cheering her.

Dianna heard Lenny beat his baton on his podium, signaling for the first encore. She wasn't sure she could get through it, but it seemed like a good thing. She sang "The Sound of Music" from that show, the meaning being "I'll sing once more," at the end, a cry of triumph that she had made it through after that disastrous Hollywood Bowl performance.

Still they wouldn't let her go. Sinatra, standing at the head of the performers, blew kisses and wiped his eyes. Gene Kelly saluted.

She took a breath, looked for Bill, didn't see him, then nodded to Lenny. The orchestra softened, the audience sat, and she sang Chas's song from *Pigskin Pete*, the one he'd sung at the Oscars.

Look at the stars, far away shining, they are but us by and by, remember, and always see.

Look to the stars. Do not be afraid, they give light to you and to me.
Light for the darkest times,
light for our joys,
hope for all days.
Look to the stars, far away shining, let them come close, and always see
They are always there.

He needed to be heard, too. The song was so famous, that everyone knew what it was, a song of hope, of refusing to give up, but also intertwined with the loss of that little boy. Her eyes filled with tears, and she could barely see, but her voice held steady as she sang to her little brother. Chas was singing along, right there with all of them, helping her keep going, and now her family was together once again as she sailed into the long final note with the violin.

And that was that. The cheers that filled the arena, the performers running onto the stage to embrace her, Lenny running to hug her tightly, tears pouring down his cheeks. She bowed to Kennedy and his wife, and she disappeared down the stairs and down the aisle, through the congratulating performers, most of them weeping, and then Bill grabbed her into a kiss.

"Brilliant," he murmured into her ear. "How did you do that?"

"I'm all sweaty," she said, not knowing what else to say.

Ella hugged her.

Bette Davis stood right there.

"You gave me what for," she said sternly, like a schoolteacher. Her smile looked like diamonds radiating great beams of light. "You were right. You stood up for yourself, like a star. You've got more gumption than I thought. And kid, you are great." Before Dianna could respond, she walked away.

Gene Kelly hugged her and said, "Next time I try and steal time from you, slug me."

"You bet."

"Okay," he said. "I've been told." And then he waltzed her around in a circle.

Jimmy Durante, Helen Traubel, Joey Bishop, Tony Curtis, Olivier, Quinn, Belafonte, Cole, and then Ethel Merman surrounded her, shook her hand, kissed her. Sinatra pushed through and said, "You are the greatest, baby, and I say that before you all."

She knew that wasn't true. These people were the real stars. She'd been good, but in a way, she'd done it with her family. Still, she had loved every moment of it.

Holding onto Bill's hand, she hurried down the ramp. She had to change.

Bill kissed her hard, whispering, "Damn, but you're brave."

Sinatra said, "Do you have kissing privileges?"

"Shut up, Frank," said Dianna.

"That," said Bill, "was the multiple choice test."

"Don't kiss me," she said. "I'm all sweaty."

"Best time," Frank called after them.

"Who's going to follow that?" she heard Janet Leigh ask. Sinatra called, "Ethel!"

Dianna was hungry. She had no more than said so when someone handed her two hot dogs. The stage manager handed her a note. "Thank you for your wonderful singing. God bless you and your family. – Jacqueline Kennedy"

"She left," said the stage manager. "She wanted to hear you."

Dianna changed into her duplicate dress, and Bill escorted her down to the audience to seats up front in the second row. She smiled at the applause that greeted her, made a little curtsey, and sat feeling pounds lighter as the second part of the program bellowed out with Ethel Merman, Republican, wearing the same cloth coat she'd worn all day, singing out, "You'll Be Swell! You'll Be Great!"

The rest of the show flew by until Sinatra stepped forward, looking emotional, put on glasses, and read about Lincoln. Dianna hurried up to join the cast as Sinatra announced, "The President-Elect of the United States, Mr. John Fitzgerald Kennedy."

Ella Fitzgerald grabbed Dianna's hand.

Kennedy spoke from his box. He went a little over the top congratulating people for coming through the winter of adversity in the worst snowstorm of the year. Even so, Dianna's eyes filled with tears of love of her country and terrible regret that her family, including Nana, could not be here.

"Do you want to go to Joe Kennedy's party?" Bill asked her when it was all over.

"I want to sleep for a million years."

"It's going to be a mess to get back."

But Ella Fitzgerald was not going to Joe Kennedy's party, and neither were Harry Belafonte and Nat King Cole. Cole had paid a driver to meet him, so they all jammed into the waiting car.

Dianna, sitting on Bill's lap, enjoying his arms around her and his thighs beneath her, said, "I wish Sammy had been here."

"Say what you will about Kennedy, this isn't good," said Belafonte.

"He'll need some pushing," said Bill.

"A damn sight more than a push," said Belafonte. "You keep thinking, things will change, and they never do. I sure pray his dad stays out of things."

The snow was still falling, but the main streets were plowed, and even some of the sidewalks were shoveled.

At the Statler, Bill collected her things from the trunk. Dianna picked up some snow and flung it at him.

"Is that fair?" he retorted. He put her things down on a cleared-off bench, scooped up some snow, and got her right back while the crowd laughed and applauded and begged for autographs.

After that hubbub, they were quiet in the elevator. Bill opened her door and brought her things in to the master bedroom, putting them down on a chair.

He was looking at his shoes. That couldn't be good.

"I shouldn't have said that last night. I shouldn't have made conditions."

Had she snored?

"I didn't mind your sleeping with me last night."

"I shouldn't have made a condition about tonight. For one thing, you must be exhausted."

Was that an excuse?

"I agreed to it."

"I forced you to."

"No, you didn't. And I'm not tired. I could dance all night."

He smiled at her allusion, but then he started pacing.

"The last few months, when I was away, all I could think about was you. There I am in Dublin, and everyone's trying to get me a date."

She thought he'd been too busy!

"They were all beautiful and smart women. And you know what? I drove them home. They made me miss you more. And it's driving me mad."

Who was this man now in her suite of rooms? Neither Jekyll nor Hyde.

"I have no right to ask you to grow up any faster because I need you to. What are the fan magazines saying? That Dianna Fletcher stopped me and my womanizing ways in my tracks." He extended his arms in a dramatic gesture. "They're right!"

She pulled a gesture out of her repertory, one she'd had when she was five years old on *Show Boat*. She placed her palm on his cheek. "I feel safe when you're around."

"Maybe," he said, "you shouldn't."

And at the back of her mind, she thought, my family is crumbling, and I am here and seventeen as my mother was seventeen, and we will do this again. She pushed that thought back. She was not going to think about her crumbling family.

She put her arms around him. "It's four in the morning. What are we going to do?"

"I should go. Unhand me, girl."

"Do you want to go?"

Was she flirting or did she mean it?

"Maybe this is not a good idea."

"Bill," she said, "I love you. I'm not a kid. I care for you."

"You don't know," he said.

"I do know. Foster women know. My grandmother, my mother, me. We know."

Now he placed his head on her shoulder and clutched her to him. She thought he was sobbing, yet when she pulled away, his eyes were clear, but intent on her.

She wanted him near her. She remembered that time on the beach when they'd clung to each other as if it were the most natural thing. The feel of his body, the power of his arms, the need in his soul. She thought of the hurts he'd been through and the ones he'd helped her through. He wasn't perfect, his dark periods puzzled and worried her. Nevertheless, he was a brave and wonderful person. What he was, not what he had been.

She said, "Please stay, Bill."

She kissed him, maybe it was Maria or Lily or Juliet or her own dreams, but she kissed him and held onto him until he seemed to come back to the moment, and they fell back together on the bed, and then they started laughing.

He smoothed his hand along her body, pressing her skirt close to her, his hand moving up slowly. Even over her clothes it felt delicious. His face was over hers, and she reached around him and said, into his ear, "Don't go. It will be fine." She was assuring him!

They kissed for a while. He started removing her clothes, so she started removing his, turning it into follow the leader. Some improvisation was often necessary.

Suddenly, he was going through his pants pockets.

"Your father will be killing my father's son if I get you pregnant."

"I have an IUD."

That stopped him.

"Why?" he stammered.

"Mom made me in case some mad producer grabbed me. One almost did."

"What producer?"

"I'd best not say."

"And Angelini," he said. "I'm a boor."

Juliet, reaching out.

"No one's tested it before."

He laughed, and there he was, Bill, tossing off his past, his angers, his guilt, tossing off the women he regretted using, tossing off that awful bitch who'd started it all, returning to his youth, returning to hers. Powerful feelings indeed, for both, as he once again held her in his arms and as she pulled him earnestly and tenderly toward her.

"I'll try to make it easy," he said.

"Why?"

She'd been in bed before — with Romeo, with Tony — and while those had been staged scenes, she'd imagined what went on with them when the cameras were not prying. She had imagined Juliet reaching out eagerly, Maria reaching out tenderly. Maria's faith, Juliet's impulsive passion. Eagerly because she felt eager. Tenderly because she loved him.

Outside, the wind started gusting around the corner, and the snow pelted against the windows.

"Come," she said, his muscular body thrilling her. She wasn't sure what to do, but she kept reaching out, whispering his name. What made it adventurous was that he allowed her his body and she allowed him hers. Had Lily done this before turning him in? Would Betsy have let Brother Luke in? She felt both afraid and safe. The wind rattled the windows, and far below were the cars, the plows, the excitement of a city on the verge of dramatic change and loving the energy that belongs to the young, who had taken over.

Somewhere, in the depths of the night, Dianna awoke to find he was touching her hand gently, and she could see with the one light that was on, tears in his eyes and on his cheeks. He smiled at her and whispered, slipping his arm around her, "I need you. Don't leave me."

"Okay." She moved closer. They fell asleep.

The phone rang, jolting Dianna, jolting Bill. She peered at the clock. It was eight. She reached out for the phone. The room was cold.

"Hello?" she asked, and her voice croaked.

The voice at the other end was unmistakable.

"Good morning, Dianna!" he called into her ear. "I'm looking for Bill Royce."

"Aren't you going to be President today or something?"

"I want to go over my speech. Is Bill there? I'm sorry to ask, darling, but he's not in his room."

She looked over at Bill, who was lifting himself up, and she loved his chest, and why did John Kennedy think Bill was here?

She disappeared with the phone under the sheet.

"I'm sorry, I don't see him now." (Actually, she did.)

"Are you lonely?"

"I'll leave him a message. Maybe he'll get back to me, Mr. Almost President."

"I'll wait ten minutes and then call," Bill said, after she hung up. "I don't think we're fooling them."

He reached over, pulled her toward him.

"Are you all right?"

Hal had said that to Madge.

She smiled up at the ceiling. "Are you all right?"

"I don't know."

"Why?"

"I should not have stayed, but I did."

"I love you."

"How can you?"

"Because you're Bill."

"Fancy that."

She studied his body when he got up, reaching for his robe, and she wondered at how it could be hers now. Was it? Now, suddenly, Bill the Womanizer entered her mind and with it, for the first time, fear that this would never happen again. She was afraid when he left that he would not return.

She was having toast and juice and wrapped in a terry cloth robe when he did come back, full of energy and gossip.

"Peter Lawford has a hangover. Eleanor Roosevelt doesn't want to sit near Joe Kennedy or Nixon. That leaves two empty seats. At Mrs. Kennedy's request, the family shuffled around, and you and I are sitting three rows behind Mrs. Kennedy. The tickets were already under your door. All we need is you and me dressed for the occasion, and we have to be at the Capitol by eleven."

"We're sitting behind the President? When he's sworn in?"

"And very visual on television."

"They won't be looking at me."

"Are you kidding?"

She ran to the window. "It's beautiful out!"

The sun had turned the foot-high snow into glistening diamonds.

In an hour they were heading out. Bill wore a morning coat and carried a top hat — Kennedy had ordered the men to wear one — at a distance as if it were a python. Dianna's blue dress brought out her eyes and hugged her curves. She wore pearls and a simple oval blue hat trimmed with fur at an angle, white linen gloves, black pumps lined with fur, and a wraparound cape, also lined with fur. She carried the muff Bill had given her for Christmas.

"Every woman is going to be buried in mink and looking as fat as Orson Welles," Bill said. "You are going to bring freshness and youth."

Awed by the great rotunda in the Capitol, Dianna tried to keep calm and not run up to the Supreme Court justices for autographs. Mrs. Kennedy entered, elegant in pink. She wasn't wearing a fur coat, either. She took Dianna's hand and said a soft, excited good morning.

Mrs. Eisenhower asked for their autographs.

President Eisenhower and Jack Kennedy stepped into the rotunda.

Dianna realized where she was. And wasn't sure she believed it.

An usher in military garb complete with gold braid led them to their seats outside.

Dianna huddled next to Bill, her hands deep into her muff, eyeing the TV cameras high up on a platform across from the podium. She realized that Bill was too nervous to talk, so she looked out at the thousands of people mobbing around the Capitol, the crowd stretching all the way down the National Mall, waiting beneath a crisp blue sky.

Two ushers led Robert Frost and Marian Anderson down the steps.

The Nixons. Mrs. Kennedy. Lyndon Johnson. Then John Kennedy.

There were prayers and songs and prayers and songs.

The Vice Presidential oath was long.

Her feet got cold.

Another prayer. Could someone pray for heat?

Yet the sun was so strong. Robert Frost stumbled in the brilliant light, unable to read a new poem. So he recited an old poem from memory. He shook, he was frail, he was old, he was theirs.

As the Supreme Justice, Earl Warren administered the oath of office, Dianna felt that the sky burst into a new and gorgeous blue and that the world had changed. She slipped her arm through Bill's and leaned against him, loving the body she had begun to know.

Kennedy stood at the podium without coat or hat and opened the cover of his speech.

Everyone else sat down. Except the millions of people on the Mall.

The new President's words took flight as frost into the air, his right hand coming up and down, and his phrases rhythmic as he looked down at his text and then up at the people before him. As Bill had directed.

"For man holds in his mortal hands the power to abolish all forms of human poverty and all forms of human life...the belief that the rights of man come not from the generosity of the state but from the hand of God...

Dianna looked up at Bill, who was watching intently, and she had to smile, for he was shaping the words as Kennedy spoke them.

Her toes ached with cold. A gust rattled Kennedy's pages, tossed Bill's un-top-hatted hair, bit into her face. What fool had moved the inauguration from March to January and insisted people do it outside? But the people had to see.

...If a free society cannot help the many who are poor, it cannot help save the few who are rich.

He kept speaking, the blue sky seducing optimism, his clear voice ringing out above the Mall, the flags flying, the total silence as the Nation listened. He spoke of the threat of Communism with power and faith. Then he said:

...Let both sides seek to invoke the wonders of science instead of its terrors. Let us explore the stars...eradicate disease...and encourage the arts and commerce...let both sides join in creating a new endeavor, not a new balance of power but a new world of law where the strong are just and the weak secure...All this will not be finished in the first one hundred days nor in the first one thousand days of this administration nor even in our lifetime on this planet. But let us begin."

But let us begin.

The words resonated within her. Bill could take his place among the great new actors. Her parents could find forgiveness for whatever they were angry about. Nana, her parents — they could all begin again in truth.

All of this seemed possible.

...And so, my fellow Americans, ask not what your country can do for you, ask what you can for your country...Let us go forth to lead the land we love, asking His blessing and His help but knowing that here on earth God's work must truly be our own.

53

*B*ut let us begin.

The new President, surrounded, shook hands, nodded to people he couldn't reach, and slowly made his way up the steps. When he stopped by their row, he reached way over and called out, "Bill." The two shook hands. The President tapped Dianna's cheek with his finger and winked at her before turning away.

When Nixon passed, he took her hand. "We'll have to get you back in the party." He laughed, a hollow, nervous laugh. "Give my best to your mother."

"That was an exciting moment," said Bill once Nixon had passed. "He can always run again and exile you to Alaska."

"The country wouldn't elect him."

"It almost did."

It took a while for them to move. People stopped them, wanting to shake hands or have their program signed. Dianna didn't mind; they were full of compliments, the air was crisp, and Bill was signing right next to her.

Once they were out of the Capitol, Bill tried in vain to get a cab. They walked down the Mall, and Dianna's feet were about frozen when a limousine stopped, the door opened, and it was no one they knew inside, but the old woman was friendly, and she loved *Every Time*.

Back at the hotel, Dianna tossed off her shoes, wrapped her feet in a blanket, and fell on the bed.

"I want to sleep for hours."

"Mind if I turn the television on?" Bill asked.

She didn't mind. She changed to her nightgown and burrowed into bed. Bill turned on the inaugural parade, took off his shirt, and climbed in beside her. She drifted in and out of the television coverage before falling asleep. When she woke up, he wasn't there. Peggy was. It was time to get ready. When Bill came back, suited up, so was Dianna in a striking red gown with blue flowers and white tracing.

They decided not to go back to the Armory, which, Bill heard, would be mobbed. They stayed right at the Statler. Dianna and Bill danced and danced, Bill ignoring men who wanted to cut in, except for the President, who arrived without his wife. He wasn't a dynamic dancer, sort of a one, two guy, but they didn't elect him for dancing. As Dianna taught him to rhumba, the photographers got their fill.

"You could swivel your hips more, Mr. President," she said.

"After the next election," he said, but he did twirl her.

"You come see me anytime," he said to her when the music ended. "And teach me to dance."

When Bill came back, photographers kept snapping as Kennedy shook Bill's hand. "We appreciate your help. You two are our favorite movie stars right now."

"Right now," Bill echoed, grinning.

He and Dianna did their version of a rhumba, which everyone in the ballroom watched. It earned applause and Kennedy shook Bill's hand.

Reporter Dorothy Kilgallen pushed her way through the crowd to say, "Dianna, what do your parents think?"

"About what?"

"About your being with Bill."

"Ask them," said Dianna.

After more dancing, Bill led her off the floor and retrieved their coats.

"Where are we going?" she asked.

"Don't you want to sample some more eastern winter?"

It was freezing cold in the courtyard and empty, all humans sensibly inside except for the two of them. But it was beautiful with its frosted young pines and frozen fountain, like a fairyland.

And there, Bill Royce plunged into a speech, completely disobeying his own advice to the President of the United States. He talked fast.

"I have a lousy history, one you should run from. I know you're a kid, but I have to say I have never felt this way before about anyone. You're the best friend I've ever had. You don't scare easy, and you're just brilliant, and yes, I love you, I admit it. I want to take care of you and keep you near me. Will you please marry me?"

He took a box out, opened it to show a diamond ring with sapphires.

"I bought this in Dublin. I knew then what I wanted to ask you, even if I didn't have the nerve to believe it."

Something told her, don't do it. Something else told her, you've slept with him, and you wanted to sleep only with him, so you'd better. This is your destiny. On the one hand, she felt as sure as anything about him; on the other, she didn't have a clue. And then there was all that stuff with marriage — that even though Anne had kept her career alive, most women didn't.

"The ring comes with you, right?"

"That's the deal."

He really meant that he loved her. She knew that. She thought of all he had gone through in his life and how magnificently he'd conquered all that.

"You're my best friend," she said, realizing that was true as she said it, even if she wasn't sure what she was getting into if she said yes.

Bill grabbed her and kissed her. Damn.

She wanted to live with him. She wanted to move in with him right now. But what about Dr. Jekyll and Mr. Hyde?

He said, "I know we should wait to be together until we're married, and I'm half sorry I didn't. But I couldn't."

"I would love to marry you, but Bill, I'm not sure I'm ready for settling down and children and all of that."

He shrugged. "Why would you have to? You're a brilliant actress. We'll have kids when we want them, and I'm not sure I'm ready, either. I just want you around all the time. Anyway, we shouldn't get married before you're eighteen. I'm sure your parents would prefer that. They might not prefer me."

"Will you come to New York and tell them with me?"

Had he really called her a brilliant actress? How could he say that? She wanted to believe that.

"I need to get back to Dublin."

"You'd go out of your way for the President but not me?"

"Trapped!"

They laughed.

"Sure. Of course. Dianna, did you just say yes?"

He had her there. She felt a thousand hands pushing her to say yes, but she also felt she could sense whispering protests in the back of her mind: her work, her sense of independence, her family, her topsy turvy emotions of late. Her grandmother liked him, well, what little she had known she'd liked. Katharine Hepburn liked him. Her father liked him. And she? She loved him.

He was peering at her, looking nervous.

She smiled. "Yes, I'd love to marry you."

This was a magic time, one filled with promise and hope and love. One needed to seize such times and believe in them. Otherwise, what was life?

They spent the night together again. Dianna felt more nervous and so, it seemed, did he. The night before, he had been careful, curious, even worshipful and at the same time, fun. Tonight, he was powerful, dominating, victorious, and not at all curious but forceful. When she pulled away, complaining, he apologized, almost in tears. Her inexperience and her independence saved her, the inexperience egging on the independence, for while she felt a new strength in herself and her art, she also wanted so much to love and be loved. And the only person she felt that way about was Bill. She reached out, and it all ended better than it had begun, although it was not the epic journey they'd taken the night before. Perhaps it was better, because they had to figure things out together, for good or ill, and they clung to each other.

She remembered what Anne had once said, about how wonderful it was to know one another's bodies, which came with years. Anne had been talking about her love for John, and Dianna believed her parents still loved each other. She had to believe that.

They both slept late, so they missed the papers and arrived at the White House, garnering considerable attention and finger pointing. Dianna wondered if they knew as she touched the ring under her glove.

They joined the reception line, shaking hands with strangers. Lyndon Johnson kissed her hard. His wife took Dianna's hands and said, "Thank you for that lovely performance."

Mrs. Kennedy kissed Dianna on the cheek and said, "What a wonderful gift you have. We will invite you to the White House soon to entertain us."

Greeting President Kennedy, Dianna grabbed her nerves.

"Mr. President, I have a favor to ask. Should I write you?"

The President grinned. "Why don't you meet with me in the Oval Office after this luncheon is over? I'll have someone bring you over."

Bill said, "Thank you. We'll be happy to come."

Kennedy punched his arm. "I'm sure you will."

Done with the line, they moved into the room, slightly adrift among the politicians.

After a dull luncheon, a military aide escorted them to the Oval Office. Kennedy proudly showed them his desk, and when Dianna asked about a pineapple propped up on it, he told them about how the Japanese had sunk his boat and how he had swum looking for help and then handed some natives a pineapple with a carved message. And they'd gotten help! The slimmest of chances had brought him and his men home alive.

"They'd never believe that in a movie," said Bill.

The President laughed, and once seated, he reached to his side for a box and handed it to Bill. The box held two books, one a copy of *Profiles in Courage* and the other, a book, or rather, a set of galleys. Dianna could make out the title: *PT-109: John F. Kennedy in World War II.*

"It's coming out soon," said Kennedy. "Why don't you read it? It's going to be a movie, and I'm recommending you to play me."

Bill looked completely flummoxed.

She felt for him. The movie would have to be ultra-polite and one-dimensional.

"You wanted to ask me something," Kennedy said to her.

"Yes, sir, for a pardon."

She could hear Anne pleading, "Don't tell the truth."

"I don't think you two need my pardon."

Did he mean what she thought he meant? She thrust that idea back and plunged into Alice's story.

Kennedy was enthralled and intrigued.

"Where is she?"

"I don't know. Mr. President, she didn't do anything. Could you pardon her?"

She was disappointed by his answer.

"I will look into it. It may take a while."

"Everyone should be pardoned," said Dianna. "The whole thing was a farce."

"Not the whole thing, Dianna. Many people believed we were protecting the country. A free country can be a dangerous country. But I promise I will look into it."

"She worked with Mrs. Roosevelt. That might give you two something to talk about. You crossed the picket lines to see *Spartacus* and said you liked it. Mr. President, this business must stop."

He pushed out of his chair. "*Spartacus* was a fine movie. Tell your parents."

"Thank you, Mr. President," said Bill, taking Dianna's hand.

"Do you think I should have told him?" she asked as a car pulled up for them outside the White House.

"I don't think he can go right up and say I pardon this Communist who faked her death and showed contempt to Congress. The Republicans would use something like that to pound him with."

"I had to ask. Anyway, he's the President."

"I would have asked, too. But he needs to work with this Congress."

They visited Arlington Cemetery and the Lincoln Memorial, stood quietly inside the Jefferson Memorial, and once back in their room — or, rather, her room — they finally saw the newspapers.

"Christ almighty," Bill said.

Pictures of them, dancing close, at the Inaugural, in the lobby of the Statler.

"Except in bed, thank God," Bill said. "Front page! Stars William Royce and Dianna Fletcher Keep Each Other Warm During Freezing Inaugural."

"Did anything else happen this week?" Dianna asked.

"Look at this stuff! How I used to prowl around the Sunset Strip for girls with my pal Steve McQueen. Well, that'll be nice for him to read. And Neile."

"Have they said anything that isn't true?"

"That's the trouble!"

The phone rang. Dianna picked it up, half suspecting and fully right.

"Yes, Mom. We're coming tomorrow. Both of us. We're taking Frank's plane. Yes, I call him Frank now. He asked me to. How is the play? No, I don't have to be back until Monday for *Silver Sierra*, and there's less and less for me to do, and what there is is awful. I'll see you tomorrow. Bye."

Bill was nervous during the whole flight and more so as they came into Manhattan, their cab inching through the Holland Tunnel, slowly moving up Eighth Avenue, then turning onto Forty-Second Street and up to Times Square beneath the smoking billboard.

"Aren't you the least bit nervous?" Bill demanded. "Like me?"

"What can they do? Disown me?"

"At least be nervous for me? I don't want to end up in a cheap Hercules picture."

"Don't be silly. Everything will be fine," she said as they pulled up to the Plaza.

It wasn't.

Once everyone was sitting down, John said, "Did you have to be so public about it? I would have thought you would have better sense. The papers are filled with this stuff about everything you two did. "

"Not everything," said Dianna.

"Did you two go to bed?" asked Anne.

"Mom, you told me when it was time, it was my choice."

"You gave her carte blanche?" John yelled.

"I had her get an IUD."

"Good Lord," said John.

"Men can't control themselves, so she needs a defense."

"I didn't run out and go to bed with everyone," said Dianna. "What are you crabbing about, Mom? You were sixteen. I'm a year older."

Anne threw up her hands. "Pigeons are roosting all over."

"Lots of girls get married at seventeen and eighteen," Dianna said firmly. "It's the way things are."

"Married?" John shouted.

Dianna took off her glove.

"Oh, my God," said Anne.

"I love your daughter," said Bill.

"I love him," said Dianna.

John sank back in a chair. He started to laugh.

"We're not getting married this instant," said Bill.

"When you're starting to have such success?" asked Anne.

"I'm not stopping acting," said Dianna. "You didn't. I don't understand why you're mad."

"You're much too young to know your mind."

"You knew yours." Dianna kissed Anne. "None of this is playing, Mother. You once said Foster women know right away."

"Maybe we had better talk," said John, gesturing to Bill.

Anne laughed with some hysteria. "No, no. John, we must get off this script. Nick married, now you. To Ed Greene's son! What the fuck, I don't care."

"Nick?" cried Dianna.

"Nick's getting married tomorrow. He was waiting for you. All my babies leaving me."

"Nick?" Dianna shrieked. "All the news hounds are on *my* case, but not one word about *him*?"

"*He* has been discreet," said John. "Dating anyone who walks." When Dianna made a face, he said, "It is different for a boy. What gossip columnist goes to see Shakespeare? The inauguration was the news. Nick's wedding is some sort of beatnik thing in the Village. Tomorrow afternoon."

"Who's the girl?"

"That folk singer, Sylvia. They have been together a month, which for Nick is pretty good."

"How is *Hamlet*?"

"It is brilliant," said John, as if that was the most important thing after all. "He has done something that is blazing fun. When are you going on the stage, Miss? You have some electricity, apparently, judging from you upstaging Olivier and Gene Kelly."

"That was enough for me," said Dianna.

"Hell," said Anne. "Dianna, listen. When you get married, you are technically your husband's property. You become an extension of him legally. Fame helps. You'll keep your real name."

"Is that a blessing, Mom?"

"Dianna's her own person. We are turning what was sour into what is good," said Bill, a bit pompously, Dianna thought.

"George will hit the roof," said John.

"So what?" said Dianna. "Perky is past."

"So this is a career move?"

"Mom!"

Would Bill think that? He was smiling, but what did he think?

"Please can we hold off on an announcement until, say, May?" asked Anne. "When you've had a chance to think it over?"

"Why?" asked Dianna. "We won't get married for a year. You don't want to announce our engagement?"

"If we announce it now, maybe they'll think it's a shotgun wedding."

"Is it?" asked Anne.

"Mom. Remember?"

"I didn't think you'd do it!"

"I'm seventeen. You loved Daddy. I love Bill."

"Is it our business, John, or theirs? I forget. When do we stop owning them? Do we have children anymore?"

"We have three children," said John. "All of them in different places."

"I just wish it were later and with someone else."

Bill said, "Someone other than Ed Greene's son?"

"You hate my husband."

"No."

"You're doing this to get back at him. I should tell you some things."

"Anne, enough," said John.

"When do we get back at Ed Greene, that's what I want to know."

"What for?" asked Bill.

"Stop it," said John.

"Blaming his death on you. Are you still doing that blacklist crap?"

"Yes," said Bill.

"I see no point in that."

"The truth is important."

"Like hell. You don't know the truth. You aren't the truth judge."

Dianna, uncertain about what was going on, changed the subject. "Have you heard from Nana?"

"I wouldn't tell you if I had," said Anne.

"Why?"

"I need to protect her. I don't know what world you two are living in, but you'll find out eventually."

"I know what world I'm living in," said Dianna, taking Bill's arm. "Please be happy for us."

"Fuck," said Anne.

"Anne," said John. "Let them lead their lives. It's their world."

"Fuck you," said Anne. "Truth will be my best revenge."

Her mother was drunk. Dianna grabbed Bill's hand and pulled him out of the suite and down the hall.

"I'm sorry."

"It's okay," said Bill, but he looked not okay.

To help his mood, she pulled him into the elevator and down to the Oak Bar, where they got a table in the back of the glittering, golden room and toasted each other with champagne.

Nick's wedding at the White Horse Tavern in Greenwich Village was a hootenanny, complete with guitars and calls to sing along. Almost everyone was dressed in black except for the bride, who wore green, for, as she said, "I want this marriage to be fruitful." Nick wore jeans and a black shirt. John and Anne left after the vows.

"Thank God, you finally found a boyfriend," Nick said to Dianna. "And thank God, it wasn't a choir boy. That should keep your career going."

"As if that's why," she said, punching his arm. "Are you happy?"

"She loves me, she's going to take care of me. That's what I need." Nick savored a beer. "It's a great life. New York in the Village has busted wide open. It's not about stardom, little sister, or even the number of people you fuck. I'm not going to get caught up in that Hollywood shit. It killed Chas."

"We don't know what killed Chas," said Dianna. She wasn't going to fight that fight anymore.

"Suit yourself. I will."

Bill and Dianna saw *Becket* and Olivier that night and spent one more day in New York, seeing *Hamlet*. Dianna could tell that Bill was impressed because he raved about the play to Nick, not giving her much chance to talk, and at Sardi's, he and Nick talked about acting while people pointed and waiters hovered.

"We're still engaged?" she asked when he left for the airport. They had decided to say their goodbyes in his room at the hotel.

He kissed her and eventually came up for air, but she held on.

"It'll be better when it calms down," he said. "I'll be back in a few weeks."

She thought she'd never see him again.

When Bill was gone, Anne and John confronted.

"I know you think it's romantic and all, but it's not going to work," said Anne. "He's dark, he's a playboy, he's dangerous."

"That's not why you don't want me to marry him. It's the blacklist thing."

"It's dangerous," said Anne. "He has a dangerous mind."

"I'm sorry you're not happy for me. What is wrong with you? I don't want my family to die."

"We're trying to save you!"

"You don't want to see me as I am. I love you. I know how much you give yourselves to your art, but I have to tell you. When have you been there for me? He has. All the time. Maybe that is why you don't like him. Enjoy your doll's house."

She got her things together and headed for the train station with not one kiss for them, even if it hurt so much not to show them her love. They were just so hard to understand.

Thank God for Bill. Now her life would begin. Still, she wondered if he would still want to marry her when he came back home. Of course she would.

54

A home, a call sheet from *Silver Sierra* greeted her.
"I don't understand," she shouted into the phone to Goodman. "I'm way over my quota of eight, even ten featured roles." As much as she loved Betsy, they were ruining her character, turning her into a screaming or silly girl, constantly being kidnapped, and she wanted out of it.

"Your father wants you off the show after this season. We have a contract for two seasons, which means sixteen episodes featuring you and eight others. I'm going to get them in. That's our deal."

Her father had agreed to that?

"The guys are mad at me."

"Don't worry about the guys."

MaryAnn said, "I'm working on it. Don't worry."

"I cannot go back there! It's done!"

"You made an agreement."

"I made an agreement for one year. Everybody else agreed to whatever else."

She was in a rage. Someone sent her an unpublished piece, from the scandal tabloid *Confidential*, dated September 1958, all about Bill's earlier dalliances with prostitutes on the Sunset Strip. She tore it up. She wished she hadn't. She wanted to keep being angry.

It wasn't fair. Bill had worked hard to work his way out of the darkness.

She flung herself into *Cinderella*. She had to be more than just good. People expected something. She fixated on tempi, fussed over costumes, insisted on rehearsing over and over so there would be no mistake. Her Prince Charming, who had theater experience, trembled in the face of her fury during the live broadcast at eight o'clock Eastern Time for the Eastern, Central, and Mountain Time zones. Californians were able to see it live as well, but it would be rebroadcast at eight o'clock, Pacific Time.

The broadcast won the ratings race. The reviews glowed. Walt Disney called to congratulate her. "Maybe we'll do *Meet Me in St. Louis* live," he said, to her horror. The one good thing was that she had fulfilled all her obligations to the park. If Disney wanted her for something else, he'd have to negotiate another contract.

He also said, "Go carefully with that young man."

"Daddy likes him."

Kilgallen was still on her case, blasting John and Anne for letting Dianna see Bill. "She's too young! She's too sweet! They are letting her grow up too fast!" She implored John and Anne, whom she loved, to step in and save their daughter.

Fortunately, Dianna could lose herself in another movie. The first scenes to be shot for *Forever Is Now* would be in the wilderness of Oregon.

The director, Mike Beck, took her out to dinner to discuss her character, Linda, and slid his hand everywhere he could under the table while telling her she was brilliant. She took his water goblet and poured its contents onto his pants. He laughed it off, and after that, he wasn't a problem. In fact, he was an engaging director, eager to listen to her ideas, to experiment. "Show me," he said to her, when she had an idea. She thought of Angelini, who had said the same thing. Now she didn't feel threatened at all. Had she been wrong about Angelini? That was a tough idea. She studied her script more scrupulously now, focusing on feelings, relating them to her life. This girl, so confident, so heading into heartbreak and anxiety. She worked against the character, not simply depending on the lines. She developed subtext.

Her character, Linda, had won a science scholarship to college but was hounded almost to suicide because of boys' attention to her body. Dianna fought any sense that Linda enjoyed what was happening, even if her lines and her smile made people think she did. Linda's boyfriend, played by Steve Skinner, was sweet off camera and listened to her every word. She guessed he was falling in love with her, and she liked the sense of power, but she kept her distance off the set.

Bill was still in Ireland, but one night, Neile McQueen called.

"We bought a house in Malibu. Seeing as you're a neighbor, we'd like to invite you to our house warming next Sunday afternoon until whenever it ends. Can you come?"

Katharine Hepburn called. "I've been terribly negligent not calling you. I'm working on this O'Neill play, and I could use some help. Can you drop by Sunday night for supper?"

That would give her an excuse to leave the McQueen party before it got too late and perhaps too wild.

To her surprise, she had a good time. She scored well in beach volleyball and was put in charge of grilling the hot dogs. Steve said, "Bill said to give you a big hug," and he did, and then he said, "I'm sure if he were here he'd say hug her again, Steve," and he did, while she laughed but wished he would stop.

"Bill wouldn't say that."

"Hey, he's not here."

Neile took her aside in the kitchen. "We've known Bill for years. Steve knows him longer. He and Steve should be rivals, but they're having too much fun being friends. There was this time Steve was out of work for months. Wouldn't tell anybody, but Bill figured it out and got him jobs in television shows until he was a little steadier. Bill's been through bad stuff, but he's a good guy. When it comes to who comes home, you want a good guy." She looked thoughtful as she whacked the counter with a cloth.

Feeling able to ward off criticism, Dianna drove to Hepburn's house at George Cukor's estate.

"Why didn't you tell me you're engaged?" was the first thing she heard.

"Not officially yet. Do you like him?"

"Do YOU like him?"

Dianna sank onto the floor at her alternate godmother's feet. "Yeah."

"Other than the fact that he's drop dead gorgeous and talented and smart as hell, why?"

Hepburn dropped onto the floor next to her, and they leaned against the sofa, munching on sliced apples and cheese.

"I hated him at first. He thought I was Pollyanna."

"You made him change his mind."

"I didn't set out to."

"I'm sure you did."

"We fell into something together. Can I tell you?"

Hepburn hesitated, studying Dianna's face.

"Bed?"

Dianna giggled.

"Well, there you go. It makes a difference."

"I can't tell many people."

"You can tell me and your mother. So long as you and he are careful not to get caught unless you want to, not getting pregnant and all that nonsense. Your mother told you about birth control."

Dianna hoped she wasn't going to get a lecture on contraception.

Instead, Hepburn said, "When you look back, you don't regret loving at fever pitch. Even if it doesn't work out in the long run. I'm not saying it won't. Passion — living life at fever pitch — loving through it — having fun through it — if you don't have much of that, I don't think life's worth living."

She ran her hand through Dianna's hair.

"Where is Alice?"

"Don't know." Dianna laid out the whole story. About Bill's dissertation, about the testimonies she had read, about her mother's change of politics.

"I know all about how your mother changed. Had to. Don't blame her. It took guts, and she lost friends over it."

"Why?"

Hepburn shrugged. "John was suspected. So was she. She fixed things for her family. That may not seem much, and we may not agree, but she held on."

Dianna talked about Bill's father. Hepburn listened, her face both impassive yet showing flashes of interest and of compassion.

"I never worked with Ed Greene, but I knew him. People respected him. He was a big man, like Bill, tall, muscular, powerful, with a face like poached eggs. Good organizer. Bill looks like his mother, Polly. Beautiful woman. A little affected. Ambitious, too, but who am I to criticize that? A good actress in her niche, silly, comic. Killed by the blacklist. She was married to one, you see. She must have been scared. The blacklist scared everyone. It scared the studios silly. I could have been on that list, so could have many others."

"You?"

"One day, I got up on a stage — wearing red, mind you! — and supported a Communist for President of the United States."

"That's a joke." Dianna had felt her godmother was apolitical, or at the most a conservative New England type, except for her abandonment of marriage.

"Henry Wallace. I got up and gave a speech supporting him. J. Parnell Thomas, you know the one, head of that committee, he told the country that movies were infiltrated by Reds. Reds Reds everywhere. Trumbo wrote a great speech. Well," she smiled and added coyly, "I helped." She declaimed the next sentence, "I speak because I am an American and as an American I shall always resist any attempt at the abridgement of freedom."

"But that's right."

"I thought so. Said so. Right out there at Gilmore Stadium. I felt that if enough people cared and did something about it, the petty Thomases would disappear. Eddie Robinson was going to make that speech, but he's Jewish and left left left, and my people were on the Mayflower, so I stepped in, silly us. We fed the fodder of fear from Hollywood to the country. Fell right into the trap. And I went out there with a red dress."

"I wish I'd been there."

"I was something. And I could have been fired. LB thought we liberals were going to destroy the country. But he liked me, and I liked him, even if he wasn't on my side of the fence. He loved movies. Everything else was secondary. I stayed out of trouble. So did your mother. As far as I'm concerned, she put the best part of herself away, but then again, maybe I did, too. Maybe I got it with my acting, maybe it shows in my acting. I denied my own freedom of expression, though I can make it sound as if I didn't."

"You don't give fiery speeches anymore."

"We thought the public would care. The public cowered in fear. They live off us. We don't inspire them except to want to become movie stars. They're safe in the dark with us, see. That's what we found out. Don't be hard on your parents, Dianna. They're good people, and they made it through the fire. They're great actors and the parents of great actors. We've been through a time when there wasn't any way out. For anyone. But we are getting through."

"I think people will fight for their country," said Dianna.

"I wish you were right."

Dianna went to bed as soon as she got home and fell into dreams. Dancing on a rooftop, as Maria, when the rooftop disappeared, so that she was dancing in the sky, then lying down, the wind fingering her hair and caressing her, saying her name softly.

She opened her eyes. That was no wind. Someone was in bed with her.

She sat up, ready to yell.

"It's me," said a soft voice.

This was no dream. This was Bill.

He tapped her lips lightly. "Miss Fletcher, you should lock your balcony. Anyone could get in here."

"There's a gate," she murmured.

"I've watched you dial that code several times."

He pulled her toward him.

"God, how I've missed you."

"Welcome back to America, Mr. Royce."

"I was in almost every scene, so I was there almost every day, ten, twelve hours playing that poor guy. The sets are cold. The people are cold. Schell was cold."

"You're home now." She kissed him, and he pulled away just as things grew intense.

"No," he whispered. "I don't want to bring on your people. They're here, aren't they?"

"A few."

He gave her one more kiss. "Come over at noon. I headed here as soon as I got home. I'm beat. Too much flying. We need to talk about something."

What did he mean by that? But when a knock sounded at her door, he slipped out quietly.

Joanne popped her head in. "I heard voices."

"I had the TV on," said Dianna.

Joanne turned on the light, looked, saw just Dianna and no one hiding. She peered into the bathroom. She felt the TV.

"Joanne!"

"I heard a man's voice."

"You were dreaming."

Joanne looked out over the beach.

"I'm nervous about you and that man."

"His name is Bill. He's in Ireland."

"He's back."

"Bye, Joanne."

Joanne turned off the lights and left.

She'd have to get rid of Joanne. She was the cook, not her mother.

She ran over to Bill's just before noon, a coat over her head to protect her from a chill rain. She ran up the stairs to the deck and peered inside. He was standing in the living room, facing the door, on the phone. He looked splendid in a tee shirt and jeans. His hair was not brushed. She pushed open the door, pleased with herself that they were engaged and hoped he hadn't changed his mind.

He was saying, "That script is perfect."

He reached out his hand for hers and kissed it.

He said, "I'll ask her. She's here. We're neighbors, Bernie. She came over to borrow a cup of flour. Dianna, have you seen a script for *Love in the Afternoon* yet?"

She settled into his sofa. "No."

He leaned over to the coffee table and pointed to a script. She opened the page, skimmed the first page, and shook her head.

"She hasn't seen it. He didn't tell her. Tell them it's a mistake, that they're sure she wants to do it."

Dianna made a face.

"I'll call you back. I told you. She's borrowing sugar. I mean flour. What? I don't know. What? Kilgallen? Oh, damn. Goodbye, Bernie." He hung up. "The man thinks he's my mother."

She was scanning the script's pages.

"Who's the love detective? I'm the cute daughter and you're the seducer?"

"Type casting." He picked her up and she dropped the script.

"Did you miss me?" she asked, when she came up for air.

"The script is over there."

"It fell on the floor. I forget why."

They were back on the couch. She didn't care. There were so many serious issues, but he was back.

"It's a Billy Wilder, a light romantic comedy, set in Paris, lots of fun," he said. "It's been hopping around since Gary Cooper turned it down, said he was too old for this stuff, and they were pairing him with Audrey Hepburn."

"Her again!"

"Then they wanted to put him with Grace Kelly and he turned that down. Prince Rainer doesn't want her working ever again. Yul turned it down. Cary Grant doesn't like Billy Wilder. Etc etc. Eventually, they got to the R's, and I said yes. After all the psychologically scary parts I've had, this is a delight. It means location shooting in Paris, and I want you to be the girl, and Wilder's dying to get you. She's charming, young, absolutely lovely. Typecasting, I'm afraid. The thing is, they're set to do it almost immediately."

"I'd love to do something like that. After all those nervous breakdowns and gang wars and sending you off to the chair."

"Bernie told Wilder, Wilder said great, Wilder called your uncle, and your uncle said no."

Dianna struggled out of Bill's arms and put her feet on the floor. She picked up the phone.

"What's Bernie's number?"

"It's right on the table."

"Are you Bernie?" she asked when someone answered the phone. "I'm Dianna Fletcher."

"What can I do for you, darling?" He had a gravelly voice, and even over the phone, she could smell his cigars.

"Bill told me about that script and I took a look at it, and I'd love to do it. Uncle George did not bring it up with me."

"He thought you were too young."

Dianna let out a low scream. "I wanted to do *The Diary of Anne Frank* and everyone said no, and I did it and won an Oscar. I wanted to do Maria in *West Side Story*, and they said no, and then they came back to me after testing over one hundred girls. Can we make this less painful?"

He laughed. "One more year and you're not a minor, but Allied Artists can't sign you. I can tell Wilder you want to do it. Just get George to say yes."

"I'm firing him. You can be my agent."

"Your father has to fire him, and when he does, it'll be front page news. Get George to say yes."

She pressed the hook to get a dial tone. She dialed the Operator and asked for Western Union. Bill watched her from the sofa, grinning.

"Yes, collect. Dianna Fletcher. To George Bennett, care of the Plaza Hotel, New York City. Thank you. Bernie Bosco to call stop I am doing Love in the Afternoon stop I am not doing Silver Sierra again You are fired stop. Love Dianna stop."

Bill laughed.

Dianna hung up.

"You can't fire him," said Bill.

She shrugged. "When is it filming?"

"Late April, May, June," said Bill. "April in Paris. You free?"

"I'll get free. What are we doing today? I need to have fun, please."

"Wait," said Bill. "Killgallen's onto us. She heard from someone on the hotel staff that I was spending my nights with you."

Dianna shrugged. "My faithful maid Peggy. Can we think about it later? Let's go to POP and ride the roller coaster and stuff. The sun's coming out."

"The fans," he offered.

"Hang them. I want to ride a real roller coaster and not a metaphysical one."

He laughed. "Yes, ma'am."

Dianna had not been to POP since before *Ben Hur*. She had forgotten how exhilarating the mammoth amusement park over the Pacific was. Although the people called out, "Dianna Fletcher!" and everyone recognized Bill, it was pleasant. They waited in line for all the rides, signed autographs, and listened to compliments for *Every Time*, even *Picnic* and *The Magnificent Seven* as well as for *Silver Sierra*. Several said they couldn't wait to see *Romeo and Juliet*.

Bill seemed so young, finally, and she thought as they soared on the magic carpet ride, this is what life will be like. He's going to be all right now. We both will be.

55

Bill showed up for breakfast the next day.

Joanne didn't appear, so Dianna burned some pancakes.

Bill glanced toward the clock. "Turn the radio on."

"Why?"

"Oscar nominations."

"My God," she shrieked, dropping a pancake on the floor. "I forgot all about them. No dinner?"

"They chucked that. Got too weird. Who do you invite?" He switched the radio on.

How different things were this year! Chas was gone. Her grandmother was alive somewhere, a fugitive. And here she was with Bill. Just Bill, no family, no dinner, just the two of them, a radio, and a newscaster reading off the nominations.

After the foreign language, documentaries, and short subjects (with Disney getting a few nominations), costume, art, set design, and cinematography had been announced, on came the major awards. By then, to their surprise, their little film *Every Time We Say Goodbye* had been nominated for art, set decoration, and cinematography. *Romeo and Juliet* was doing well, too. It had been nominated for the best score.

"For Writing, original story and screenplay: Richard Gregson and Michael Craig, story and Bryan Forbes, screenplay for *The Angry Silence*; Billy Wilder and I.A.L. Diamond for *The Apartment*; Peter North and Frank Michaels for *Every Time We Say Goodbye*; Marguerite Duras for *Hiroshima Mon Amour*; and Jules Dassin for *Never on Sunday*."

"Our little movie!"

"They're welcoming Fred back. And it's not a bad movie."

Fred Sybuck was nominated for best director along with Jules Dassin, Alfred Hitchcock (for *Psycho*, making Dianna groan), Billy Wilder (*The Apartment*), and Fred Zinnemann (*The Sundowners*).

"We made the big time," said Bill.

"It made money," said Dianna.

Then came the Best Actress nominations, and Dianna's was first off , for *Romeo and Juliet*, followed by Greer Garson (*Sunrise at Campobello*), Deborah Kerr (*The Sundowners*), Shirley MacLaine (*The Apartment*), and Elizabeth Taylor (*Butterfield 8*).

"You've got to be kidding!" Dianna shrieked.

"That's quite a list," said Bill. "With you on it! And Kerr and Garson!"

And Taylor.

And not Foster.

"You'd better get a nomination," she said.

He did. Along with her father for *Elmer Gantry*, Trevor Howard for *Sons and Lovers*, Jack Lemmon for *The Apartment*, and Fredric March for *Inherit the Wind*.

She and Bill danced around, as the next announcement came.

"For Best Picture: *The Alamo*, United Artists, John Wayne; *The Apartment*, Mirisch, United Artists, Billy Wilder; *Elmer Gantry*, Brooks, United Artists, Bertrand Smith; *Every Time We Say Goodbye*, Mantiss Productions, 20th Century Fox; and *The Sundowners*, Warner Bros, Fred Zinnemann. That's it. The awards will be presented April 17 at the Santa Monica Civic Auditorium, with Bob Hope as the host. Have a lovely day."

"Santa Monica? Why out there?"

"To hell with where," said Bill. "Here's to us."

They clinked orange juice glasses.

"A little movie made on the cheap in just a few weeks and it sails out of the ballpark!" said Bill. "Let's call Fred."

Dianna settled back in her chair. "Mom didn't get nominated. It was a lousy part, I guess. And no Nick. But look at you! You sailed right up there, all on brilliant talent."

"So did you, my dear. But I think your dad's going to win."

"I won't win. But! Right now, we're all winners."

As if to prove that, the phones started ringing all over the house.

They went for a walk to escape, but it started to pour, so they went back to Dianna's where she proceeded to lose game after game of Scrabble.

The phone rang.

Dianna picked it up.

"Dianna," she heard her father say.

"Daddy! Congratulations!"

"Alice," he began. "Dalton Trumbo heard that she is in a Mexican jail."

The Oscars were forgotten. "What for?"

"From what we can gather, Alice is in prison awaiting extradition to this country. Somehow the FBI is in on it. We think Nixon recognized her at the funeral, and he notified the FBI. Or," he added, "we are paranoid. The story's going to break soon. Then it will be all that business all over again, plus stories of us plotting to deceive the government. We are not sure what to do because we do not know who is behind this. It will definitely hit us, and we would like to keep you kids out of it, but I am not sure that is possible. We have said she was dead, and she is not dead. There's a fake grave at Forest Lawn."

"What could they —" Who *was* they? — "charge Nana with? Walking out on Congress?"

"She deceived Congress with our help."

Anne came on, "My help. Oh, my baby!"

Anne's voice sounded like the helpless, trapped bird of Ibsen's early Nora's.

"I can't stand it, that she's in jail down there. Not a pot to piss in. The truth, dammit. It's coming out."

"I'll come to New York," said Dianna, worried at her mother's tone.

"No. We'll get through this, but you don't comment on it. Leave it to us."

"Could Trumbo be wrong?"

"He has too many good connections. He said she was at Puerto Nuevo, but when he went to see her, they said she'd been moved, but where? I can't stand it. To get her out, we'll have to tell her story."

"Okay, Mom. We'll figure it out."

Dianna summarized the story to Bill. "I think they'll want to get private investigators. They're sure someone is going to put this story out, and that we'll be banned from these shores for obstructing justice and for fraud. I'm to say nothing. They don't want to call anyone in Washington."

"There has to be someone who can help. Want to come over and spend the night, and we'll work on it?"

She would. Lynne said, "You're not married yet. Pack your own bag."

This hurt, but it occurred to her that Lynne was hurting, too. She tried to talk to the maid, but Lynne would not respond. But Dianna heard her mutter, "I don't know what's right and what's left anymore. It's all crazy."

At Bill's, they watched a *Perry Mason* episode. Old movies came on, and they kept watching. When they went to bed, she felt she was the aggressive one, although he said, several times, "I need you." Nothing else mattered to her except that.

The phone rang at four in the morning. Bill answered. "It's George. Lynne told him you were here."

George said, "Anne broke down in the play last night in the last act, when she was telling Torvald she was leaving. Cried, fell to the floor, grabbed the sofa, just wept. They rang the curtain down. They'll be in LA in another hour and join you at Malibu."

"I'm going to try to get through to Bobby," said Bill, after she hung up, meaning Kennedy. "He'll be able to dig up information."

"I have been thinking that Kennedy did this. Maybe he thought it would make him look super anti-Communist or something."

"Putting your grandmother in prison? He's after bigger bait like Castro. I won't call if you don't want me to, but your grandmother will be in legal hot water and your family in publicity hot water if she does make it out of jail."

"We can keep it under wraps."

"Under wraps? She defied Congress, didn't really die in a traffic accident, wasn't just a dance coach, and worked with organizations considered Communist fronts. Your parents were called before HUAC in sessions that were buried at the bottom of the nation's trunk, and Congress learned that your mother attended Communist meetings with her mother. Keep all that under wraps? Lots of people alive will still know her."

"My parents aren't traitors! Neither is Nana!"

"The way it comes out could bring a lot of questions and confusion to your family, identified with wholesome Americanism."

"We are wholesome Americanism."

"Not if you suddenly become a front for Communists."

"Bill! That's crazy!"

"I'm telling you what it could look like, not what it is. What it looks like is what people will understand. And the first family of Hollywood tumbles down. It's a great story, true or not, and everyone loves a good take down the important people story. I want to call Bobby to find out if he knows anything about this. Just to clear your mind that the President might have done something to tip off the FBI, either accidentally or on purpose."

"You're trying to help my family. Fancy that."

He stared at her for a moment. "Yeah. Fancy that."

He called Robert Kennedy as soon as noon hit.

"Jack hasn't done anything. So anything you said to him didn't bring this on. There are other possibilities. The FBI may have been on her track for a while. Someone may have blown the whistle on her. Or Nixon recognized her. They may have just grabbed her now for no other reason than they grabbed her."

Dianna gestured to the window. "My parents are home. Let's go."

Despite the long trip, Anne was wound up.

"I think what we have to do now is tell the truth."

"Mom," said Dianna. "Bill has a plan."

"Does he now? Do you, Bill?"

"I've contacted the Attorney General."

"That's very good of you," said Anne. "My son is dead because of you."

"Mom!" Dianna shrieked.

Her mother was losing it. Chas, she thought.

"Mom is tired," said John.

"I am fine," said Anne. "We're going to break the story. That's the only way we can own it. Tell the truth. Tell it loud."

"The whole business will come out," said John. "It will ruin you."

"What do we have to fear?" asked Anne. "Let's break the story. We're the Fletchers, damn it."

"What story are we telling?" asked John.

"She's in jail."

"She's also alive," said John.

"And that makes you so mad," said Anne.

"No, it makes me mad that you kept it from me. Me! Imagine how others will feel."

"If you didn't know, you couldn't lie. I was right, because they hauled you in seven times to check on you. God, what hell that was!" She laughed. "And all because of that man's father."

"Anne!" John shouted.

The phone rang. Dianna jumped. Anne picked it up. "Yes, come right over." She hung up. "I knew Kilgallen was in town, and I am going to tell her the story."

"Kilgallen!" John rarely shouted, and now he'd done it twice in a row. "She is Hearst! Anti-Commie to the core! She has been on our case for months. And Dianna's."

"I like Dorothy. I trust her. I was saving my mother. The news will be that we lied. I lied. It will swallow us up unless we ask her help."

"This makes no sense. All your life," said John, "you have been holding onto all these secrets, and now you want to blab them to the very reporter who has been blasting at us for months?"

"Truth, John," said Anne. "I'm sick of lying. What's it gotten us?"

"Wait for George, please. He will know what to do."

"No, he won't," said Anne.

"Would you explain what you just said about my father?" asked Bill.

"No," said John. "Anne, shut up."

Dianna felt the room was shaking and went to stand by Bill.

"What did you mean?" asked Bill.

"All this time," said Anne, "you've been accusing my husband of killing your father."

"I don't hold him responsible now," said Bill.

"That's very nice," said Anne.

"Do not do this," said John.

"Do what?" Bill asked.

Anne strutted. "Why not tell our future son-in-law the truth? You haven't come across it yet in that lovely box of shorthand notes. The reason John was called by the House Committee was because your father named him as a Communist."

Dianna thought, her mother had gone over the edge.

"That's crazy," said Bill.

"In sole and petty revenge for his part being cut to just a few lines," said Anne.

"Annie, stop it."

Dianna held onto Bill's hand, but as Anne continued, becoming less fragile and more powerful, rising up before them, he pulled it away.

"I kept my mouth shut, Dianna, for you, for all of us, but no, truth is best, right? John, Ed could simply have hated you for life without turning your name in to the Committee. Act of desperation, I understand, but he went in and he named Henry Fonda, and Gregory Peck, and John Fletcher. And because John had spent one week in Russia during the war and was secretly working for Roosevelt, HUAC went after him. They called him back and back, and it nearly killed him and nearly killed me, and it killed the baby I was carrying. So imagine my surprise when Dianna brings you home, and *you* accuse John of killing *your* finking father."

Dianna grabbed for Bill's hand, but he moved away.

"You'll excuse me," he said.

"Daddy!" cried Dianna.

John looked so tired. "Your father gave in. He wanted his life back. I guess he could not live with what he had done. Neither could I. I could not look at him without wanting to kill him. He talked to me at length before it went sour. He felt guilty and ashamed that he had abandoned you for some pretty bad years. He wanted to make it right. Maybe that and going to HUAC was too much."

"Stop it," said Bill.

"He had so much guilt. It must have been unbearable."

"He should at least have felt guilty for turning you in," said Anne.

"Of course he did. They could not find anything on me. They did keep it private. They did not do to me what they did to Lee Cobb, though we did not know it at the time. In the end, it was okay."

"I lost a baby. I couldn't have any more."

"And you lied to me," said John.

Anne sank back, stared at him. "Back to that again."

Bill said, "Goodbye."

Dianna ran after him.

"Your father must have been desperate," said Dianna. "Bill, it wasn't who chose what. It was who made them choose what was evil."

"If it's true. I have to think about this. Check it."

"I don't care if it's true or not! Was your father supposed to be perfect all the time?"

"Dammit, Dianna, this will never be over. I accused your father of murder, and he knew it wasn't true but let me keep believing in my father. What is true, damnation? Because this makes sense, too. This is why your father passed mine on the street. This was why your father was called several times before HUAC and why your mother lost a baby. All because Ed Greene got scared and desperate. And why had he become scared and desperate? Because he had fought for his union, joined the Anti-Nazi League, worked to send relief during the Spanish Civil War, and supported the Scottsboro Boys and spoke against racism in the movies. And that made my mother mad, and she left for a rotten man, and my father blamed himself for that, too. Because he'd worked with Communists about those issues. Because fear spread over the land, and we could not be the truth of what we were. It will never stop."

"Don't blame him."

"He could have had some courage! Dianna, I shaped my whole life around him, this thesis, my political work, my acting, my anger, and my anger shaped my acting, everything. Even with you — how we started —"

"Do you love me?"

"My father hurt you, your parents."

"You do not have to pay for his sins. You don't know why he did it."

"For headlines? To get back in the business? Guilt? All of that? He wanted to marry my mother again. Was this how he was going about it?"

"Give it a few days. Bill, he obviously regretted it."

He took a deep breath. "He could have made amends. The hurt he caused you."

His voice broke.

"This is silly!"

"How could you feel anything for me when we tried to destroy you and your family?"

"You could love me even though you thought Dad killed your father."

"Your father is a loving man. His loving is part of his genius. I cannot possibly find that in me right now."

He started walking to his house. She ran after him.

"I'll stay with you."

"No. That's it."

"That's it?"

"I have to get away from you."

"Coward!" she cried, her anger and impatience seething out. "All your noise meant nothing!"

"I mean what I say."

"You're a coward because you can't face the truth. My mother was right. So stay away from me, and damn you to hell."

She fled home.

And they were going to star together in a romantic comedy! Well, that was months away. Maybe she could get out of it. If only she didn't have time on her hands and a few months with nothing to do where she'd go crazy. Imagine, she'd been dying for nothing to do.

She heard voices on the deck. Dorothy Kilgallen was there. Anne was about to finally, after all her protests, tell the truth. Wasn't that funny.

56

John insisted they get to England before Kilgallen's story came out, John and Anne to make some picture deals and Dianna to star in a little play off the West End, a revival of *Gigi*.

"It will be good for you," said John, but Dianna felt they were fleeing the country. She wanted to keep trying to get through to Bill, but he wasn't answering the phone or the door. It scared her, so she asked the McQueens and Coburns to check on him. She hated to go, but she couldn't leave her parents. Still, she felt as if she were walking on a lonely beach.

The stage proved to be a different planet. It wasn't like singing, and there were no microphones. She had to learn to project her lines and her movements. She couldn't depend on the intimacy of the camera. She couldn't stop to correct what she did. She had to keep going from beginning to end and pace her energy. And there were the "theater snobs," including her co-stars, smiling when she did poorly. And she hated Gigi.

"It's a poor man's *My Fair Lady*," she grumbled.

John said, "It is a charming part. You are looking at it from the outside."

She was on the outside. Again. The critics loved her singing and hated the rest. They were vicious in the "who does she think she is" mode.

After the reviews were out, Dianna would not go down to dinner. Her parents brought dinner to her, along with her grandmother, Anne Fletcher, one of the finest actresses on the London stage, and Dianna's namesake along with her mother (Di for two Annes). Anna, as she was called, sat with her, talking about her own errors at the beginning of her career. "I didn't have the world press corps eyeing my every move. You should study your craft, get away from the microscope."

"Movies are my craft," said Dianna. "I love them."

"The stage," said Anna, "is beautiful. You and the audience. When it works, it is heaven."

"Singing is like that."

"Then sing your parts, why not? Now, Dianna, I could never act in films. You do the hardest acting of all. You can convince people you are your character in a close-up, with nothing else but your face and your eyes. That is the mountain top. What you can try, with the right part, is to bring that same quality, somehow, to the stage. You must work."

Dianna tried different things, and some critics noted how much better she became at the end than at the beginning. Still, Dianna knew she had much to learn. Bill had once said that the best actors on screen, larger-than-life people, had all excelled on the stage.

It was sad seeing Aunt Dot half paralyzed. The woman would simply take her hand, which Dianna held for hours in the afternoon. She attended few parties, except one that was given for her after *Gigi* opened, but stayed with her grandparents, reading plays with them while her parents went out.

But there was mercy. To the Fletchers' surprise, Kilgallen did not directly state that Anne was responsible for any of Alice's "death or resurrection." Her story about a Communist in a family of patriots did not explode the way it might have, either. People were fascinated, but an uproar of universal condemnation did not follow.

Because Kilgallen's article contained a surprise paragraph.

Former Vice President Richard Nixon said, "Alice Marrs is a wonderful human being. She worked hard to bring dance to the west, to towns too poor to engage in such a luxury as dance lessons. She was a strong determined woman who had great compassion. That's probably why she joined the Communist Party. She thought it was different. I can believe she got out when she found out it wasn't. I wish she hadn't felt she had no escape. President Kennedy should find her and pardon her. I think it is true that in its zealousness, the Committee went overboard sometimes. Not all the time. Our free society must be protected. But Alice Marrs – she is a good person. I am glad to hear she is alive, and I encourage President Kennedy to pardon her. I would have."

"Nixon said that?" John yelled when he read the story in the *London Times*.

Anne said, "He truly loved her. I'm sure that wasn't easy for him to say. He does have a goodness inside him, John, buried deep."

"He is baiting Kennedy," said John. "Imagine him forgiving a Communist."

"He reads the public. He'll do what they want. I think he's reading that people are tiring of the accusations. He is saying, let's focus on the Soviet Union. Let's stop hunting each other down."

"I cannot believe Nixon would think that. And it will not work. Too many people make a living off hate."

Dianna wondered where her father's faith had gone.

Many letters to the editor throughout the country implored President Kennedy to free Alice Marrs. Gene Kelly wrote that the situation with the Fletchers only showed how deeply the blacklist had hurt all citizens.

There were, indeed, other voices who insisted on a full investigation of the family: "Did Communists infiltrate the leading stars of Hollywood? We must be certain they have not. Are the Fletchers carriers?"

These people picketed at the Fletchers' gate and marched around the White House with signs: "Alice Marrs is a Communist!" "Alice Marrs Is Innocent!" "The Fletchers are Commies!" "Pardon the Hollywood Ten!" and "God Bless the Fletchers!"

There were a lot of these crackpots who refused to understand the human soul and could only sing the song of hate and judgment. Some went to *Spartacus* and stoned the screen.

Meanwhile, Alice was still in jail somewhere.

Walt Disney was disturbed by all this, but he listened to Dianna in a phone call across the Atlantic.

"Mr. Disney, without Alice Marrs, there would have been no voice of Snow White. Remember that, please."

Disney's voice was shaking. "I remember," he said. "You are all dear to me. But I learned a hard lesson. The Communists sneak in and destroy all we hold dear."

"Do you know, I went to sing for some migrant workers. I sang "When You Wish Upon a Star," and they all sang with hope and light in their eyes."

"They did?" he asked, his voice choking.

"Give it to them."

"You come and sing for us anytime. We must move on."

He was right. It took but a few weeks for the news to die down. Letters to the Editor of most newspapers howled either for or against the Fletchers, against Hollywood and all those Commies. Many people found explanations in their hearts, but the fools, the haters, the monotonous of the heart stayed alert and protested. The Fletchers would not be universally beloved ever again or thought of as representing America. That was clear.

Abruptly, however, the attention of the nation shifted. Another story jumped right on top of the Alice Marrs story and ate it up.

Elizabeth Taylor lay near death. Reports varied. She was dying. She'd had a tracheotomy. She hadn't had a tracheotomy. She'd had a toothache. It was fatal. She might pull through. She might not. She'd stopped breathing. She was breathing again. No, she was gone. The childhood actress who could not find love, who stole Debbie Reynolds' dear Eddie, was about to go out in a blaze of tragedy.

"Liz can blow a whole story about betrayal and patriotism off the cover of *Life*," said Anne. "What a fucking lovely thing she is to fall down and die."

Most of the Hollywood news portended death along with Taylor. *Cleopatra* was stalled, *Mutiny on the Bounty* had lost so much money that MGM pulled its cast from Tahiti to MGM soundstages and fired the director.

Dianna hurt for Bill. She sent him a wire to say that she was finally appearing on the stage. He did not answer.

Finally they went home to Malibu.

Nick and Sylvia joined them. He'd handed Hamlet over to Anthony Perkins for a while.

They were all together again, at breakfast at Malibu, overlooking the ocean, but they spoke like strangers.

Nick tried.

"What about your company, Dad?"

"We are going to do it," said John, with a not convincing grin. "We are going to center it in London, although there will be American topics."

"We're selling Nana's dance studio," said Anne, abruptly. "And the Manse."

"Why?" asked Dianna, shocked to hear this.

"I'm not going to live in it again."

Too many holes in the heart, thought Dianna. Breakfast uneaten, she went walking on the beach. Bill's car was not in the driveway, and his house was dark.

Nothing was settled. The country was confused, Bill was lost out there, movies were unsure where they was stepping, and Alice was still in jail.

57

That evening, Dianna drove to West Hollywood. Putting on her scarf and dark glasses, she walked toward the Alice Marrs Dance Studio. A light shone in the office. From her childhood, she remembered hectic Saturday afternoons, the trampling of feet, the endless counting, the taps, the "and 1,2,3,4's." She hurried up the steps and rang the bell.

As she waited, she looked toward the corner where Alice Marrs had supposedly lost her life. It was just a street corner, cars coming through, stopping on red.

Dianna recognized the bookkeeper who opened the door.

She removed her sunglasses. "I thought I'd give the floor one last try."

The elderly woman's red head bobbed up and down. "Dianna! How is your mother?"

"Better, Mrs. Gaumer," said Dianna.

"I pray for her," said the bookkeeper. "Studio A? I'll leave a key on the desk. I wish I could stay, but I'm late getting home." She hesitated, then asked, "Are you selling the studio?"

"I don't want to, but yes. Tap's out, musicals are out. So goes the world."

"Where is Alice?"

"I don't know. None of us knows."

"She's alive here," said Mrs. Gaumer. "Always was."

Dianna worried. What if the government really was running those camps for subversives? What if they'd grabbed her grandmother and put her there, and no one would ever know?

"We had some picketers for a few days," said Mrs. Gaumer. "I called the police. It all stopped. Just crazy people who have to hate something to feel alive. A few policemen may still come and stand here. Just in case you see them. Otherwise, we had an uptick in enrollment, and lots of people want to know more about Alice. Please don't sell."

Dianna hadn't been in this building for some years. When she was younger, she had come to dance at least once a week. Ballet. Tap. Social. She went down the few steps to Studio A and flicked on the lights.

It looked just the same. Mirrors from floor to ceiling on all four walls. Folding chairs along the sides. A dressing alcove. A barre. Changing to her tap shoes, she saw the teen magazine *Ingenue* on one of the chairs. There she was, favorite actress next to Fabian, favorite actor. Underneath that, *Movie and TV Star News*, with Dianna and Bill on the cover. Bill. She took the magazine and flung it across the floor.

Neile McQueen had called. "He's with us. He was drinking for days, and he stopped. He just holes up and reads. Steve got him a job in a war movie with Coburn. The buddies are looking out for him."

She knew he'd reject her if she sought him out. And she had some ill feeling, too, about his father who had tried to hurt her father. Which was unfair, but now the shoe was on her foot. It was such a mess. Damn the blacklist.

Standing up, walking to the shelf, her shoes tapped and echoed. She tried not to let the sounds spook her.

This was where her whole family had begun, in the determination of Alice Marrs, in the talent of her mother and grandmother. The quiet that took in her tapping echoed her loneliness. She had, she realized, no close friends. MJ hadn't returned her calls. Neither had Larry. No one gave a damn. She had heard her mother say that the timing of Fletcher pictures might be under reconsideration. Dianna was afraid to ask anyone about *West Side Story*.

Hunting through the shelf, she found some Jimmy Dorsey records and put on "So Goes the Time." She knew the dance her mother had done with Fred Astaire in *Her Leading Men*, Anne's first big musical back in 1941. The dance had been coached by Alice Marrs. Dianna, who had learned it from her mother, hadn't danced it in over a year. She would do it one more time.

Her feet remembered most of it, but she had to refigure the rhythm for the Dorsey recording. She watched her reflection intently, critically. She listened hard to her tapping, and her feet were saying, hey, wait a minute. She circled, her skirt flaring out. She charged into the break, then stopped when she forgot what happened next.

"That stunk," called a voice from the door.

Dianna looked up, panting. Anne leaned against the doorjamb, slipping a key into her purse.

"Two souls with but a single thought," said Anne. "Wanted to give the old floor a last try?"

"Yeah," said Dianna, wiping her face.

"Me too," said Anne. "Okay, you be me, and I'll be Fred."

"Which part are we doing?"

"Second part. Tuck in that tummy."

They danced it, swinging, swaying, kicking.

"My feet are dying," said Dianna, as she fell onto a chair.

"Mine too," said Anne. "Nora did not tap dance."

"Not until she left Torvald," said Dianna, her face in a towel. "Hi, Mom."

"Hi, yourself," said Anne. "Dianna," and there followed a silence. "I shouldn't have said anything."

"Oh, Mom."

"No, you were happy. I shouldn't have said anything."

"You kept too much to yourself."

"And now I've lost my son and my husband. Please don't say I've lost you."

Dianna took her mother's hand. "I'm here." Why wasn't she angry? Her mother had ruined her life with Bill. No, Bill had done that. If she thought too much about it, she would never stop thinking about it.

Anne said, "I wish I could remember more of what Fred did. Let's try that break again."

That break, where the music stopped and they danced through the silence, consisted mostly of time steps and variations. Neither one was getting them right.

"We can't leave here until we can do this," Anne said, as they sank down onto the chairs and guzzled some water, both gasping.

Dianna put the phonograph needle back where it belonged.

They danced. And started to laugh at how bad they were.

"Shit," Anne kept saying.

"You're telling me," said a voice from the dressing alcove.

Anne slid to the floor. "Oh, God."

The woman, wearing a bright red skirt over black leotards and tights, stepped forward.

"You both are pretty awful," said Alice. "Thank God I'm here to help you out."

Dianna helped Anne to her feet.

"What are you doing here?" Anne whispered.

"They opened the door and let me out." Alice looked hale and hearty for a sixty-one-year-old woman who had just been in prison. "I was pardoned. Kennedy stuck his neck out, but we should keep it quiet. Do you know that all I did was steal some paper from a bodega? It blew up to this mess. A car brought me to Los Angeles, and I wanted to come here first before I knocked on your door. Turns out we all came home."

"Mama," cried Anne, as if finally realizing the truth, and she ran into her mother's arms.

"Then it's over?" asked Dianna.

"It won't be over. Ever," said Alice. "This was not about me. I am going to make sure it's not just about me. But first, I need to be with my family, oh, Dianna!"

Dianna ran to her grandmother, and the three held on to each other for a long time, breathing in lost years and holding onto each other no matter what.

"I was here last night," said Alice. "Came in when a class was in session and snuck downstairs. I heard you're selling the place."

"Yes," said Anne. "Do you mind?"

"I do," said Alice. "I want to get right back into business. The first thing I want to do is…get you to do this dance right."

She drilled them for the next hour and a half.

"I danced all those years," she said. "Helped keep my sanity. That and writing scripts and episodes for you, Dianna."

"I'm sorry you couldn't write more. *Silver Sierra* stinks without you."

"I wrote a lot. Trumbo gave me work he couldn't do, and John sent scripts over."

"My John?" cried Anne.

"He sent scripts or books to be adapted over to Trumbo, who passed them out to other writers in our Mexican exile. He paid the standard rates, too. John helped keep our whole group going. Didn't you know?"

"That damn fool didn't say a thing. That's where the production company money went! And he talks to me about secrets! What can you do with a man like that?"

"I know what I'd do," said Alice, smiling. "Jim was pardoned, too. He'll be along after he sees his family. I think Mr. Nixon persuaded Kennedy, but I'm not sure. The words in a note said that our old friend had persuaded him. No one will admit anything. Heaven forbid it be found out that two rivals worked together for something so small as me."

"Maybe it should be found out," said Dianna.

It was a most exhilarating hour and a half. When it was over, they sank to the floor and wept, holding each other.

"Okay," said Anne. "I won't sell."

"I have an idea," said Dianna.

"It's gutsy," said Alice, after Dianna explained.

"Shall we?" asked Anne.

"Absolutely," said Alice.

"You know," said Anne. "We'll have to fight about a few things some day."

"I look forward to it," said Alice. "By the way, your daughter is lovely and brilliant."

"Yes," said Dianna.

"Takes after me," said Alice.

"Now there's a curse," said Anne.

The Thirty-Third Academy Awards

58

The Thirty-third Annual Academy Awards Show was broadcast live over ABC television on April 17, 1961. It would prove to be quite different from the show aired the previous year when the awards had been dominated by *Ben Hur* and the Fletchers. People were still talking about the Fletchers and how they'd fooled the public and foiled Congress about Alice Marrs, but that dust had settled somewhat. People were talking about how awful the blacklist had been and how it had affected families.

Not everybody, of course. Dianna read some editorials criticizing the free pass Alice Marrs was getting. After all, she'd been a Communist! Now, however, most people were saying that the story would make a great movie.

Spartacus was a hit, and the stone throwing stopped. By now, the sense was that Alice Marrs' story was about "old" Hollywood. The blacklist itself was old news. People wanted to get over it all; arguments turned stale. But Elizabeth Taylor was new news. The press had been building her story for weeks, and it had grown tall and fat and strong.

Forgiveness was in the air, if only people knew how to proceed. For Alice Marrs and for Elizabeth Taylor. For Dalton Trumbo, too. But not for everyone.

Bill sent Dianna a note that he was taking Sue Weitz to the ceremony.

He knew how to hurt, even if he hadn't wanted to.

Dianna had been asked to perform (actually, she'd called to ask if she could) and had rehearsed the day before, mostly to direct the lights ("everything bright on stage!") and to set the tempo with André Previn, who was puzzled by her choice of music. He'd assumed she would sing the theme from *Romeo and Juliet*. She was also presenting the Best Actor award and wondered how she would feel if Bill won. He was a front runner in the press. She wasn't, but she didn't expect to be.

So once again, she was with her family in the limousine, pulling up to the Oscar door.

Helen Rose designed her gown, a dark red dress with a graceful flowing skirt that was not too full, and for the first time, Dianna wore her hair up in a simple bun, decorated with pearls. Anne wore soft gray with black trim. Alice wore sleek olive green, elegantly corresponding to her silver hair, which was pulled back. She looked stunning and happy, for Jim was with her, a very tall, quiet man with an impressive dignity.

John wore white tie.

Nick and Sylvie wore black.

The crowd cheered them, but the family did not stop to be interviewed, although someone shouted a question to Dianna. "Was that Bill Royce's mother with him?" Dianna just smiled and waved.

They got into their seats just as the lights went down. André Previn started up an old-fashioned medley, leading off with "You Are My Lucky Star," from *Singin' in the Rain* and all the *Broadway Melody* pictures going way back to the emergence of sound. Alice hummed along and grabbed Dianna's hand. Dianna thought of Chas.

Bob Hope emerged with jokes Dianna couldn't laugh at, directed at just about everyone.

"It's his timing," Alice murmured. "Without it, Hope's nothing."

Janet Leigh and Tony Curtis presented the first awards for documentaries. Walt Disney nabbed one. Polly Bergen and Richard Widmark presented the special effects award to *The Time Machine*. Robert Stack and Barbara Rush presented best costume awards, and *Spartacus* won its first of the night. Eva Marie Saint presented Peter Ustinov with the award for Best Supporting Actor, another *Spartacus* win.

Dianna glanced over at her father. He wasn't keeping score. He didn't seem to be paying attention. He chuckled when a couple starring in *Where the Boys Are* presented a sound award to *The Alamo*.

"I will bet that is all they get," said John.

Danny Kaye jogged onstage to talk about Laurel and Hardy and to accept an award for Stan Laurel, who was ill. Eric Johnston presented foreign language awards, and the best picture in that category was Ingmar Bergman's *The Virgin Spring* from Sweden. *The Apartment* won its first award, for editing, presented by Adolph Green and Betty Comden.

Bill received strong applause when he walked on stage to present the award for Best Supporting Actress. He looked dashing and dignified, with that slight smile into the camera that could make any woman swoon.

He read off the names of the nominees with a light touch: Glynis Johns for *The Sundowners*, Shirley Jones for *Elmer Gantry*, Shirley Knight for *The Dark at the Top of the Stairs*, Janet Leigh in *Psycho*, and Mary Ure in *Sons and Lovers*. Shirley Jones won, making it the first win for *Elmer Gantry*, and she headed to the stage dwarfed by her huge gown.

As Tony Randall awarded art and set decoration awards, Dianna was waiting out in the wings for her number to start. She was nervous and excited. How would the public take what was about to happen?

Hope was back on stage. "Last year, a lovely young lady won the award for Best Actress. Before we get to the music of the evening, here's a blast from the past danced by this gorgeous babe of the future, a dance routine from

Her Leading Men, a picture from 1941 that starred Fred Astaire and Anne Foster. Here is Anne Foster's daughter, nominated for Best Actress for *Romeo and Juliet*, star of *Every Time We Say Goodbye*, and soon to be seen starring in the film version of *West Side Story*, Miss Dianna Fletcher, dancing to 'So Goes the Time.'"

Dianna walked out to warm applause and sang a jazzy rendition of the standard, stretching out her arms at the end of the verse. She started to dance, her mother's dance, slight taps, time steps, shuffles, some kicks, a leap. The audience clapped and hooted. She whirled, her skirt swirled, she smiled, and the audience threw energy at her. She called out, "Come on out, Mom!"

The audience roared its approval as Anne appeared in the identical red outfit. Dianna and Anne had been dancing together at home for years, but now the world was seeing it. Mother and daughter grinned at each other and challenged each other, shuffling along, doing time steps, quickening their rhythm to what seemed too fast but wasn't, and then, as the music stopped, they headed into the break.

"Help us out, Mom!" Anne yelled.

Alice whirled out. Dianna's happy face and welcoming arm gave them all the clue they needed. The audience rose to its feet and cheered and applauded. Men's feet stomped the floor. Three generations of women, born to entertain, to feel deeply, to want to make people happy, they kicked their legs out, tapped together in well-rehearsed unanimity, whirled, tapped with powerful feet, and danced even faster as the astonished Previn picked up the melody. At the end, they stopped on a dime.

It was just like a movie.

The applause kept storming the auditorium, threatening to bring the new theater down. The three women bowed, blew kisses, their faces shining with sweat and joy.

Something in the air was changing.

Something that said, we're all home in the land we love. Isn't that all that matters?

Could that something last? A dance couldn't seal the deal, but it could bring hope to the fore.

Alice and Anne broke down in the wings. Dianna clung to them. Stagehands and stars embraced them.

Bob Hope, unsmiling, said, "It was just supposed to be you."

"Surprise," said Dianna, sweetly. She kissed him. "Invite me along next time you go somewhere for the troops."

His smile softened into a real one. "That'd be a blast. Your boyfriend coming?"

She didn't answer but hurried to the dressing room to shower off the dance sweat and change for her dreaded presentation.

As she listened to the ceremony over loudspeakers, she felt sorry for *The Magnificent Seven*; Elmer Bernstein's score had been its only nomination, and it hadn't won. (*Exodus* had.)The western had come and gone and not made much fuss. Europeans loved it, though.

Jayne Meadows and Steve Allen presented the Oscar for best song to *Never on Sunday.*

Gina Lollabrigida ("Italy's loveliest export," cracked Hope) gave the award for best director to Billy Wilder for *The Apartment.*

"You're lovely, discerning people," Wilder told the audience. When he came backstage, he kissed her and said, "Next year, us."

When her turn came, Dianna walked on out, feeling quite alone, and read off the nominees for best actor. "John Fletcher for *Elmer Gantry*, Jack Lemmon for *The Apartment*, Laurence Olivier for *The Entertainer*, William Royce for *Every Time We Say Goodbye*, and Spencer Tracy for *Inherit the Wind.*"

She opened the envelope and tried hard to smile. "The winner is William Royce."

Bill strode onto the stage. He gave her a quick peck on the cheek, a quick half of a hug. She handed him the statue and stepped back, fighting tears, trying to smile.

Bill looked at his Oscar for a long time. Dianna felt the audience grow restless.

Finally, he spoke. But he still looked at the award in his hands. "Last year, I wanted to dedicate my award to my parents and tell you about them, but I got nervous. I said thanks and left the stage. Now, with all that is happening, I must say something."

Dianna felt her stomach cave in. She heard Hope say, "Oh, sweet Mother."

Bill continued. "My mother, Polly Royce, was an exuberant, funny, gifted actress. My father appeared in countless movies and plays as a supporting actor. He also supported workers' rights to dignity, all people's rights to dignity, and for this he was blacklisted. My father is Edward Greene."

Bill paused. Dianna thought she could hear the audience's quick intake of breath and the sudden silence that followed. Was he going to accuse his father of naming names?

"This thing we did," he said, "this thing we couldn't even admit to, the silence that shrouded this thing. Oh, this quiet thing, it touched every single one of us here in this country. This silent thing was wrong. We all know that. We should say it. It was wrong. It hurt many people. It hurt us. We should say that. People who worked here and loved their work should be seen and remembered, not banished from memory. We have lost so many, not only their names, but their talent who were accused of crimes they never committed except in the minds of people who can only hate and who lack understanding and compassion. We can't look at each other with suspicion and give in to unreasonable fear. That is not the joy and courage behind the founding of our country. Fear killed my father because he wanted to do the thing he loved and make it better for all, and he was unjustly treated. And," said Bill slowly, "he treated others unjustly because of fear. Fear destroyed my mother. Fear destroyed my family. Many families. Fear perhaps destroyed our trust in our government, in our goodness, and in our sense of fairness. My father believed in many good things and that we were good, and people suspected him and were afraid of him. Fear is contagious. Fear makes us angry at what we don't understand, and we all give in to it, don't we. We have to stop. We who are actors particularly! The best parts we play are about human weakness, portraying that well is what gets us awards and acclaim, and yet human weakness is the thing we find most difficult to understand and forgive."

She wanted to rush over and hold him.

He continued. "I would like to dedicate this award to my parents, Edward Greene and Polly Royce Greene, and to all who suffered because we forgot who we are. You should know that in honoring me, you honor them. Let us hope for the future. Thank you."

He walked right past her and she tried to catch up. Silence followed them off the stage until the applause began. Dianna heard strong bravos and a few boos.

He rushed past her, even as she reached out to him. She barely grazed his hand. The press swallowed him up.

Bob Hope stopped her. He looked grim. "Best Actress award is next."

Did she care? She wasn't going to win.

"Did you hear what he said? What those boys of yours fight for."

But she stayed.

Yul Brynner read off the nominations, and the roar of applause told her what everyone knew, that she'd lost to a tracheotomy. Elizabeth Taylor walked slowly down the aisle, led by her spotlight hogging husband, Eddie Fisher.

As soon as she heard the first syllable of Elizabeth's name, Dianna ran out to the press tent and was surrounded with questions about Bill, her losing, her grandmother. She barely registered that *The Apartment* won for Best Picture.

She didn't see Bill. He had left without her.

She fled to the ladies' room and closed herself into a stall. Leaning against the door, she sobbed quietly while women argued about the blacklist and how people should have fought harder against it. Dianna wished they'd shut up and leave, and they finally did.

She came out of the stall to wipe her eyes and there was Elizabeth Taylor, with her Oscar. She was sitting, and her head was down.

Dianna said, "Congratulations. Are you all right?"

"I didn't deserve it," Taylor pulled a cigarette case out of her purse. "One smoke, I'll be fine. What did your mother say when I was nominated?"

"Damn that bitch," said Dianna, smiling.

"Seeing you three together — I don't understand it all, but I don't care. Seeing you together was truth enough."

Out of the mouths of damn bitches.

Taylor patted the statue where the genitals would be.

"Can't even depend on Oscar."

Dianna pushed her way out to the theater entrance, where an energetic gentleman with fading blond hair stopped her.

"Bud Yorkin. I'm with NBC."

She remembered him from the dinner in New York. She couldn't remember if he'd been one of the pinchers and patters.

"We want you to do a musical special next season," he said. "Really classy stuff but still aimed at young people."

"Still?" she asked, impatiently.

"We're sending stuff on to George."

"Can I name my guest stars?"

"Sure, of course."

Which meant maybe.

"I'd like to have Larry Rounseville, Riff on *West Side Story*, and Teresa Paganos, a beautiful singer and dancer."

"Paganos," he said. He shrugged.

"Paganos," she said. "And maybe Hilda Johnson. She sings jazz."

"Never heard of her. But your name is good enough. People think you're not your parents, you know?"

What the hell did that mean?

"There you are," said John. "We have to go."

Anne joined them, took John's arm, and leaned her cheek against it. They were sleeping together again, and Dianna could feel the healing.

It would have been a long, quiet ride to the Beverly Hilton, except that Alice kept chattering about people she hadn't seen in years. She looked fabulous — radiant, hopeful, younger. Every so often, Jim leaned over and kissed her. Dianna felt jealous.

At the hotel, the orchestra played the theme from *The Apartment* and Alice, Anne, and Dianna danced to happy applause.

Astaire asked Alice to dance. John and Anne danced. Jack Lemmon asked Dianna to dance.

Back at the table, Nick and Sylvie were drumming with knives. John and Anne talked to Bob Hope about England.

"The place of my greatest performance," said Hope. "I was born there."

"Where's Mama?" asked Anne.

"Can't get her off the dance floor," said Hope. "You know, I just talked to Nixon. He thought she was ill used. I'm glad she's out and free. That dance was wonderful."

When had he talked to Nixon? Apparently, it made a difference.

"Come on, Di," said Nick. "Let's tour the floor."

"May I dance with your lovely wife?" asked Hope.

"No," said John. "We are dancing together. But keep Hope alive."

The whole family was dancing (Sylvie had snagged Peter Ustinov), and Alice was dancing with Billy Wilder.

Onto the dance floor, a parade of men in dark suits lined up, and someone stepped through the crowd with short, awkward steps and a nervous smile.

It was Richard Nixon.

The Fletchers immediately moved protectively toward Alice, as Nixon, oblivious to the chatter and surprise he caused, asked of Wilder, "May I cut in?"

Wilder was unable to deliver a snappy reply.

Nixon danced awkwardly, straight and narrow, with occasional graceful sweeps that seemed out of place. He stopped at the edge of the dance floor, and the Fletchers followed him to the end.

"I brought you," he said, "a passport." He took the booklet out of his inside pocket.

"Thank you," said Alice, pausing to slip it into the drawstring bag that dangled from her arm. "Do you think I should leave the country?"

He smiled stiffly. "It is good to see you. As soon as you can. For a while. Please."

They danced a little more, Nixon obviously uncomfortable. He didn't let anyone cut in. Both John and Nick tried.

"It is good to see you, Richard," said Alice.

"You are always beautiful. I remembered."

"You lost your music. You used to dance better, too."

He laughed in that not convincing way he had. "I did." He looked away. "Yes, I did. You have not lost your music or your beauty."

"Goodbye, Richard," said Alice. "Thank you. May you still have a little music in the years to come."

He bowed, turned to Anne.

"It would give me great pleasure to dance with you," he said.

"No, thank you, Mr. Nixon," said Anne.

He nodded slowly, head down, head up, eyes straight at her. "Thank you, Mrs. Fletcher."

He stepped away, bowed awkwardly, gave them his foolish grin, and walked off the dance floor with the men in dark suits.

"Like hell I'm leaving," Alice muttered.

Dianna hurried off the floor. She had to find Bill.

He was standing outside the hotel, watching Nixon's limousine leaving the drive, pacing on a small plot of grass, smoking a cigarette, his Oscar on a small brick wall.

"There you are." Her voice shook.

"I'm sorry," he said as she came closer.

She was about to fling her arms around him when she realized he meant he was sorry that she'd lost the Oscar.

"You should join us," she said. "Congratulations, by the way. Where's Susan?"

"She wanted to go home. She fell asleep out of boredom."

"Join us."

"No."

Her nerves got the best of her. "Who's the kid here?"

"Don't start," he said, lashing back. Then he calmed down. "You ladies were great. And watching it — damn — as if this curtain of forgiveness was just coming down over everyone. Except me. I'm just not there."

She touched his arm. "That was a lovely acceptance speech."

"Hurt like hell. I'm as bad as anyone. I've lived off hate, for the wrong reasons." He released his cigarette and stamped on it. "I found the transcript. He poured out names you wouldn't believe."

"They were only human beings."

"It won't work. I despise that cowardice."

"You're scared to face it."

"Hell, yeah. It's all mixed up with revenge and hate, and all for the wrong reasons. I was so self-righteous. I could be just as cowardly. Do you know, when I saw Jim, I thought, why couldn't that be my father? And then I could sock him one."

"You could forgive my father before you knew the truth. Forgive *your* father. You don't know what was going on with him."

"How can I? He could have hurt your father, your family, you. Is that in me, too? Would I spill innocent names?" He looked at her with such an anguished face that she wanted to smooth and kiss. "You're like a brilliant star. I know, it's corny, but you make me see a way out, and then I can't. How can the world be made safe for us and our children? Sue said I should go back to you. Damn. I don't see how it's going to work. Us."

"This is a bit much. Please calm down."

"Who am I?"

"You're Bill," she said. "I love you. Perhaps your father has been reaching down to help us."

"To torment me?"

Good, she thought, he was trying to joke, and she touched his hand. She loved his hands.

"To help you. He loved you. I'm sure he was sorry. Someone said to me," and she tried to remember, "that you never regret loving at fever pitch. Passion — loving through it — having fun — if you don't have much of that, life's not worth living. Oh, Bill!"

"There's so much to unravel." He sank against a tree, yet he tightened his hold on her hand. "I don't know where to go next. There's so much to do and work through. And you're just a kid."

"I'm Dianna."

He shook his head, closed his eyes.

"But let us begin," she said.

He opened his eyes, gazed at her, and then he smiled slowly, catching the reference.

"Call me back," she said, and she walked away.

For too many steps, he didn't say anything. Well, perhaps three or four, and still, he didn't say anything, but she heard something, his footsteps, and now he was behind her, and taking her up in his arms and saying, softly, "Dianna, come back."

And he kissed her and held her, both oblivious to shrieks of delight from fans far away behind a fence.

"Damn," he said, his tears on her cheeks. "I love you, brave kid. How'd that happen?"

"I got in a car with you," she said softly, oblivious to the people gathering. "I got in a bed with you."

She opened her purse and took out the ring he'd given her. He slipped it on her finger.

"Okay, sweetie," he said. "I'll stay in the car and anyplace else you are."

They kissed again. It was a good kiss, Bill leaning over and holding her so firmly, she didn't want him to stop. Photographers were jumping out of bushes and snapping their picture. And there was plenty of time to get a good picture.

"You don't look like a loser, Dianna!" one of them shouted.

"Don't forget your Oscar!" yelled another, handing Bill his award.

Dianna and Bill went into the Beverly Hilton and danced. Caught up in the whirl, John announced their engagement, and everyone in the ballroom cheered their heads off.

As the evening moved toward dawn, and as they came out of the hotel, hundreds of people yelled at the Fletchers from the sidelines. Some yelled, "God bless you!" and "Dissent is American!" but some yelled, "Commies! Traitors!" Others yelled, "We love you!" or "He's no good for you!" They got louder, and then they all started to fight each other. Security guards moved in.

Bill and Dianna looked out at the crowd. They smiled. They waved.

The people were still fighting as the members of this beloved American family — well, many still thought so, but perhaps now some didn't — were escorted into cars that disappeared into the darkness.

But if you look away from the fighting, which admittedly is exciting, you will see that the headlights never quite disappeared, and if you remember to look, those lights are still there.

THE END

Acknowledgments

No writer is an island, although we often like to think we are.

My editor, Pat Dobie, read the original manuscript, then scored over it several times, offering valuable assistance in its structure, weaknesses, and strengths. Plus she cried at the end. The endlessly patient Debra Rhoades eyed the script with her copy editing skills. My good friend Elizabeth Rake proved both honest and helpful with comments. Merritt Lori McKeon, whom I met at a writer's convention, took the Paramount tour with me and had several stories to offer about the effect of the blacklist on people she had known. Jessica Valiente provided information about *West Side Story* from her personal research.

Alone: Music by Nacio Herb Brown and Arthur Freed. Lyrics by Johnny Hartman. © Sony/ATV Music Publishing LLC. *State of the Union* (1948). Screenplay by Myles Connelly and Anthony Veiller from the Russel Crouse, Howard Lindsay play of the same name. Directed by Frank Capra. Produced by Frank Capra and Anthony Veiller. Liberty Films. *Mr. Smith Goes to Washington* (1939). Screenplay by Sidney Buchman and Myles Connelly. Produced and Directed by Frank Capra. Columbia Pictures.

Restorations

No real amends can be made to most people who lost jobs because of the blacklist, but the Writer's Guild of America West has been trying to set things right in the last decades. "It is not in our power to erase the mistakes or the suffering of the past," former WGAW President Chris Keyser stated. "But we can make amends, we can pledge not to fall prey again to the dangerous power of fear or to the impulse to censor, even if that pledge is really only a hope. And, in the end, we can give credit where credit is due." In another statement (2000), the Writer's Guild stated, "The Hollywood blacklist destroyed the careers and lives of numerous Americans — not only artists but also those in government, in academia and the unions...Because of the unchecked zealousness of HUAC, the list also managed to include non-Communist liberals and even victims of mistaken identity."

Some Restored Credits:

Adventures of Robinson Crusoe (1952): Screenplay by Hugo Butler and Luis Bunuel. *An Affair to Remember* (1957): Screenplay by Delmer Daves and

Donald Ogden Stewart and Leo McCarey; Story by Leo McCarey and Mildred Dram. *Autumn Leaves* (1955): Written by Jean Rouverol & Hugo Butler and Lewis Meltzer and Robert Blees. *The Big Night* (1951): Screenplay by Joseph Losey and Stanley Ellin and Hugo Butler and Ring Lardner, Jr. *Born Free* (1966): Screenplay by Lester Cole. *Born for Trouble* (1942): Written by Doreen Montgomery and Derek Frye. *The Brave One* (1956): Screenplay by Dalton Trumbo and Harry S. Franklin and Merrill G. White. Based on an Original Story by Dalton Trumbo. *The Bridge on the River Kwai* (1957): Screenplay by Carl Foreman and Michael Wilson. Based on the Novel by Pierre Boulle. *Broken Arrow*: Screenplay by Albert Maltz; Based on the Novel 'Blood Brother' by Elliott Arnold. Captain Sinbad (1963): Written by Ian McLellen Hunter and Guy Endore. *Cry, the Beloved Country* (1952): Screenplay by Alan Paton and John Howard Lawson. Based on the Novel by Alan Paton. *The Day of the Triffids* (1963): Screenplay by Bernard Gordon. Based on the Novel by John Wyndham. *The Defiant Ones* (1958): Written by Nedrick Young and Harold Jacob Smith. *El Cid* (1961): Screenplay by Philip Yordan and Frederic M. Frank and Ben Barzman. Story by Frederic M. Frank. *Friendly Persuasion* (1956): Screenplay by Michael Wilson. Based on the Novel by Jessamyn West. [On its release, because no credit could be negotiated, the movie had no writing credit. The actors were just good ad libbers.] *The Girl Most Likely* (1957): Screenplay by Paul Jarrico and Devery Freeman. Story by Paul Jarrico. *Inherit the Wind* (1960): Screenplay by Nedrick Young and Harold Jacob Smith. Based on the play by Jerome Lawrence and Robert E. Lee. *Ivanhoe* (1952): Screenplay by Marguerite Roberts and Noel Langley. Adaptation by Aeneas MacKenzie. Based on the Novel by Sir Walter Scott. *Lawrence of Arabia* (1962): Screenplay by Robert Bolt and Michael Wilson. Based on the Life and Writings of Col. T.E. Lawrence. *The Magnificent Rebel* (1960): Written by Joan Scott (who used the name Joanne Court, to conceal her relationship with Adrian Scott, when she wrote the script for Disney). *The Misadventures of Merlin Jones* (1964): Screenplay by Alfred Lewis Levitt & Helen Levitt. Screen Story by Bill Walsh. *The Monkey's Uncle* (1965): Written by Alfred Lewis Levitt & Helen Levitt. *The Prisoner of Zenda* (1952): Screenplay by John L. Balderston and Noel Langley. Adaptation by Wells Root from the Novel by Anthony Hope and the dramatization by Edward Rose. Additional dialogue by Donald Ogden Stewart. *The Robe* (1953): Screenplay by Albert Maltz and Philip Dunne. Adaptation by Gina Kaus. Based on the novel by Lloyd C. Douglas. *Roman Holiday* (1951): Screenplay by Dalton Trumbo and Ian McLellan Hunter; Story by Dalton Trumbo.

For more information, go to
https://www.wga.org/the-guild/about-us/corrected-blacklist-credits

Several fictional people or names used as fronts were nominated for Academy Awards because the actual winners were blacklisted at the time. There are always discussions of "who deserved to win" after an Oscar ceremony, but these people really didn't deserve it: Pierre Boulle (1957): Best Writing Adapted Screenplay for *Bridge on the River Kwai*. Who did deserve the Oscar? Carl Foreman and Michael Wilson. Nathan E. Douglas (1958): Best Writing, Story and Screenplay – Written Directly for the Screen for *The Defiant Ones*. Who did deserve the Oscar? Nedrick Young and Harold Jacob Smith (Director Stanley Kramer slyly cast Young and Smith in bit parts and they received screen credit for those gigs). Ian McLellan Hunter (1953): Best Story for *Roman Holiday*. Who did deserve the Oscar? Dalton Trumbo (although Hunter's son refused to give up the award to Trumbo, so a second Oscar was presented). Robert Rich (1956): Best Story for *The Brave One*. It was a rare moment at the Oscars when NO ONE stepped up to claim the Oscar! Most people ultimately suspected Robert Rich was one of Dalton Trumbo's cover names. They were right.